Kirinski's Life & Times

a novel

D AVID B ACHNER

W OODLAND A RTS E DITIONS

Oneonta, New York

Cover photograph: "Man Walking Alone on a Beach" by Stuart Aylmer/Alamy Stock Photo.

Cover design by Robert Bensen.

Trillium flower (beadwork) by Michele Dean Stock (Ga-wen-noin-des, Seneca), 2000.

Library of Congress Control Number: 2021904257

ISBN: 978-1-7353161-5-4 (paperback)

ISBN: 978-1-7353161-6-1 (eBook-EPUB)

ISBN: 978-1-7353161-7-8 (eBook-Mobipocket)

Woodland Arts Editions
14 Harrison Avenue
Oneonta, New York 13820

First Edition

In Memory of Helen, Jerry, and Liz

There is no way I can tell you everything, though I'd like to. One of the problems with all stories is they have borders. Then you extrapolate, like in algebra. You use the things you know to guess at what is left outside the border.

Frederick Reiken, *The Lost Legends of New Jersey*

Contents

Prologue: 1946 1

Part One: The Kirinski Family of Belmar, New Jersey in the
       Summer of 1980 3
   1. Royal Flush 4
   2. Carousel 23
   3. Solace 41
   4. Child's Talk 46
   5. Writing..50

Part Two: *The Inner Lives of Boys*, Nathan Kirinski's Memoir,
       1946-1962 51
   1. Provenance..52
   2. Adventures in Communion and Solitude....................................65
   3. Louie's Charm...64
   4. Tommy..66
   5. Roy and Dale Will Adopt Me...70
   6. Miami Beach 76
   7. The Skylight..79
   8. Denny 84
   9. American Pogrom.. 87
   10. The School Bus 93
   11. Interlude 96
   12. Greenbaum and Rosenzweig... 97
   13. Intimations of Something More..101

Part Three: *The Excruciating Confusions of Youth*,
       Nathan's Memoir, 1962-1980 104
   1. Liberal Learning..105
   2. Holly...110
   3. Halls of Tangled Ivy 114
   4. West Virginia..126
   5. Almost Heaven: A Diary..132
   6. Fathers without Children 163
   7. Sunshine...164
   8. Jerusalem the Golden 173
   9. Hawaii..191
   10. Anchorage 200
   11. Deborah.. 213
   12. Morton and Fay... 219

Part Four: *Householder Again*, Nathan's Memoir, 1980-1990 220
   1. Helpmates... 221
   2. Visits 231
   3. Days of Awe..235
   4. Useful Ideas..245

Part Five: *Leaving, Returning, Leaving*, Nathan's Memoir,
          1990-2012 263
   1. Ellen... 264
   2. Korea, 1995 269
   3. Return.. 274
   4. Reunions.. 281
   5. On Disappearing: A Farewell 288

Part Six: Hurricane Sandy, 2012 292

Part Seven: Which Way Now? 2012 – 2016 308

Part Eight: This Way Now, 2017 331

Appendices:
I. Nathan Kirinski's Summary of His Books 339
    – *The Language of Art, the Language of Science,*
       and the Epistemology of Portrayal 340
    – *Useful Fictions and Fictions as Truths* 342
    – *Is Change Possible?* 342

II. Nathan Kirinski's Overview of the Gurdjieff Work 344
III. Arnold Kirinski's Efforts at a Different Kind of Writing..................... 351
IV. Arnold Kirinski's Interest in Meditation 360
V. Arnold Kirinski's Typology of Death And Dying Theories 363

Acknowledgments... 372
Works Cited 373
About the Author... 380

Prologue
1946

NATHAN KIRINSKI, AGE TWO, toddles south along the boardwalk in Belmar, New Jersey. Behind him, his mother pushes a stroller holding Nathan's brother, Arnold, who has not yet learned to walk. Nathan's birth preceded Arnold's by four minutes and eight seconds, a fairly good head start in proportional, immediate post-natal terms but hardly enough to account for the many differences already apparent between them.

"Nathan. Stop," their mother yells, worried that he is getting too far ahead. "I mean it, Nathan. Right now." Nathan only goes faster.

This is Arnold's first and longest-abiding memory: Nathan in the lead, Arnold coming along behind, following this person destined to inspire and trouble him the most. This person he will always love the most.

Part One

The Kirinski Family of Belmar, New Jersey

Summer 1980

1

Royal Flush

NATHAN DREAMS DREAMS THAT are lavish with lights and sirens. They are machine dreams, crowded with screws and electromagnets and buzzers and flashers. They are his happiness in the night, and it is a curse of wakefulness that he must let them go.

One buzzer sounds now for an inordinately long time. Monotonous and insistent, it pulls him from the rhythm of his dreaming. The lights and sirens fade. Furious, he bellows himself awake and smashes the offending alarm clock against the headboard. Baby Ben falls to the floor and ticks its last at 1:30 p.m. on Friday, the 20th of June 1980.

Nathan is jubilant at the destruction, at having struck an instinctive and telling blow against intrusion. His action stimulates him. He feels courageous, a man with ambition and plans. Still lying in bed, he formulates a schedule for the day. First he'll eat. Then he'll go to the arcades. Then...Shit. It's Friday. He has to go to his parents' house for the Sabbath, where the food will be good but the arguments and criticisms of him tiring. Yet going there is unavoidable.

So, redo the schedule. First, eat. Then, the arcades. Then, back here to rest and clean up before going to his parents'. From there, back to the arcades until bedtime. Kirinski likes this plan; it accommodates both his needs and his obligations.

Nathan rolls from his back to his side preparatory to putting his feet on the floor. Four inches from his face he sees a hair. He picks it up, brings it to his mouth, bites down, and pulls the tight curl of it through his teeth. His groin tingles as he envisions the source of the hair. Abruptly, he puts on his glasses and lumbers to the floor, kicking his way through deposits of paper and clothing until his foot finds the telephone. He dials. The phone rings a long time before he hangs up. Disconsolate, he resumes chewing the small hair plucked the night before from the pudendum of Esther O'Connell. Without a time for Esther, today's schedule is imperfect after all.

Twenty minutes and two glazed donuts later, disconsolate still but reviving, he leaves his Ocean Grove garret and heads south along the boardwalk into Bradley Beach.

"New Jersey," Nathan once wrote as part of an article about his life for *The Harvard Crimson*, "is among the most maligned places in the United States. Images of the state are indeed harsh. For the outsider, the very name New Jersey is enough to conjure up some horrific vision of 'The Turnpike,' replete with the odor of Secaucus pig tanneries, diesel trucks that swallow up care-less Volkswagens and Toyotas, sunsets refracted through multiple layers of chemical pollutants, and people with ugly accents living in proximate, dense colonies, much in the manner of insects. Strange fears accompany these visions—fears, for example, of getting a flat tire and having to brave the certainty of foul air and the likelihood of assault by hooligans who hide like trolls in the 'Pike's noxious culverts. People must believe that pride of place is totally absent in New Jersey, unlike, say, in Oregon, New Mexico, California, New England—even in New York or Ohio. People must believe, too, that one resides in New Jersey only because fate conspired to see one there at birth, or because one's company is located there, or because some other sad event beyond one's control left one gulping killer fumes in the ironically nicknamed Garden State.

"So much of this prattle is unfair, more a consequence of stereotype than fact. There are enclaves in the state that are fascinating for their history, scenery, and local color. One such area, known to detractors and supporters alike as the Shore, is the line of communities that stretches along the Atlantic from Sandy Hook in the north to Cape May in the South. Within a six-mile section of this line lies the heart of the Shore, which incorporates the towns of Asbury Park, Ocean Grove, Bradley Beach, Avon-By-The-Sea, Belmar, and Spring Lake. The towns are contiguous, and for the outsider it is difficult to tell where one ends and another begins. When one becomes familiar with the towns, however, they are as different as six countries. They are unique, like pearls in a necklace, each with its precious irregularity: the decaying Coney Island atmosphere of Asbury Park; the evangelical influence of Ocean Grove; the multicultural mix of Bradley Beach; the stable affluence of Spring Lake and Avon; and the fishing-fleet, summer-rental economy of Belmar. These are varied places, memorable places, exciting and inspiring places. For those of you who may have been laboring under misconceptions about the state, I commend these attractions. As for those of us who were fortunate enough to have grown up at the Shore, I cannot do other than predict that we shall at one time or another be drawn back. It is a place for returning and settling in...."

True to his prediction, he's back. Nathan Kirinski: Belmar Grammar School; Asbury Park High School; Exeter Academy; bachelor's, master's, and Ph.D. in philosophy from Harvard; fast-rising professorial star at his Ivy League alma mater—legendary teacher, popular speaker, and lauded author.

But his impressive trajectory took a dramatic nose-dive in 1978 when he was denied tenure. His confidence shattered, outraged but helpless against Harvard's opaque promotion process, he resigned his position, soured forever at age 34 by the very idea of academia. After a year on a commune, a failed marriage, a 5,000-mile separation from his daughter, and only temporarily recuperative sojourns in Israel and Hawaii, he re-thought his options and settled on two: returning to the Jersey Shore and devoting himself to Gottlieb's Royal Flush, a pinball machine.

Nathan sits at the counter of Morton's Carousel Diner, ladling over-easy eggs into his mouth with a spoon. His brother Arnold works behind the counter, taking orders from other customers, working the cash register, bussing tables and cleaning up. *My amazing brother Arnold*, he thinks. *While I wallow in self-pitying inaction, he manages to help out at the diner nearly every week-end, even as he labors at his doctoral dissertation in New York City during the week. I marvel at his humility and work ethic, his ability to balance the menial with the heady.*

"Arnold, Arnold," Nathan says between draughts of yoke, "you're so good to me. I shudder to think what would become of me without you, Ar-nie. You're my savior."

Arnold reddens at the hyperbole. "I'm your brother, Nate. So I take care of you." Arnold was never good at feelings.

"You're my brother, sure," Nate acknowledges. "My fraternal twin. We may not look or act alike, but we have the same blood—a little of Morton's, a little of Fay's." They laugh a brotherly laugh. "But seriously, Arnold, you're a lot more. You're my savior. Yes! I'll accept no argument. You help house me, you help feed me. You help out here at the restaurant during breaks from school. You handle our crazy family. You continue to contribute to my ex-penses even when I spend what you give me on pinball. You're an admirable man, Arnold Kirinski. You gave me regard when I was considered a genius, and you still give me regard now that they call me a fool. I love you and I respect you and I appreciate you, Arnold."

Moved by affection, Nathan rolls off his stool and walks around to the back of the counter, where he embraces his brother and kisses him tenderly on the forehead.

"Come on, Nate, quit it," protests Arnold, a slight man 90 pounds light-er than Nate. Arnold glances out the window facing Lake Avenue and pulls away, worried that passersby might see them. But he's smiling. "People will think we're strange. I love and respect you, too, okay?"

Nathan stares at his brother, mustering a semblance of sternness. "Sure, love and respect," he pouts. "But what about appreciation? I said I love and respect *and appreciate* you."

Arnold is laughing now. "Yes, Nate, I appreciate you, too. Very much. Here, have some more coffee. Go on. Go sit down. Have the coffee."

Nathan reseats himself and considers his brother, who has begun oiling some saucepans. *Arnold is a mensch, a quiet and upright man who idolizes me for being neither quiet nor upright. It is one of God's mysteries that we are twins, however un-identical. Another that this brother cares for me. So who am I to show ingratitude by questioning miracles?*

He finishes eating and stands up. "Look, Arnie, I've got to get going."

"Will I see you at Fay and Morton's tonight?"

"Of course," Nathan shrugs. "Far be it from me to stand up Queen Sabbath on a Friday night date. Speaking of which. If Esther drops by, would you please ask her to meet me at my place tonight, maybe around nine? Okay? Thanks, my brother, my savior. See you tonight."

He turns at the door. "And don't worry, Arnold. I'll make nice with the folks."

Arnold nods. "Good, Nate. Put some scores on Flush for me, okay?"

There seem to be no limits to my brother's acceptance, Nate marvels, *or to his empathy. Were he in a state of despair, unlike me Arnie would continue to work. Constructive perseverance would be his solace, for there is nothing frivolous or self-indulgent in his nature. Yet somehow he not only understands my despair, but also my odd way of easing it.*

The brothers trade looks full of fondness. Then Arnold returns to the saucepans as Nathan heads east down Lake Avenue, past the historic merry-go-round at Palace Amusements that gave their family's restaurant, The Carousel Diner, its name.

Nathan moves with surprising gracefulness for a 250-pound man. He feels that grace now, walking smoothly, head up and arms balanced, a contrapuntal study in obesity and economy. He is proud of his motion and likens himself to some powerful running back—a Jim Brown, a Franco Harris, a Pete Johnson. When he is in motion, his grace transforms his corpulence into charisma. When still, he appears merely fat.

He is purely fluid now as he moves along the boardwalk, an imposing and attractive man. He draws glances from schoolgirls on vacation, much as he did from an earlier generation of schoolgirls in Harvard Yard. Then, he reveled in the glances and tried to parlay the more lingering among them into liaisons. These days he is barely aware of the faces or the bodies or the possibilities. He is distracted by this place—by the ocean, the playgrounds, the miniature golf courses, the hotdog stands, the ramshackle beach buildings. He is taken up with his daily rediscoveries of the Shore, happy that his wanderings are over, content to be home.

He crosses the drawbridge on Ocean Avenue that spans the inlet between Avon and Belmar. From the top of the bridge, standing next to the bridge keeper's kiosk, he can see north as far as Convention Hall in Asbury Park and south nearly to the divide between Spring Lake and Sea Girt. Looking west he can follow the wide path of the inlet as it slides under Belmar's other two drawbridges, the first on Main Street and the second on Route 35, to harbor itself, at last, in Shark River. For many years, this has been the home of Belmar's fishing fleet. In one particularly momentous year, Shark River was also the site where, as an 11-year-old Tenderfoot Scout in Troop 40, he was introduced to masturbation, the only craft in which he might ever have qualified for a merit badge. Looking east past the twin jetties that guide the boats in and out of the inlet, he tries to envision the coast and mountains of Spain, which he and Arnie once calculated to be directly opposite the coast of New Jersey. He waves now, resigned that his greeting will go unrequited, to the pilgrims he imagines making their fervent way to Santiago de Compostela.

A bell clangs and the bridge men set up gates to stop traffic. The bridge goes up and charter boats sail to and from the sea. A man waves from the deck of one and holds up a string of sizable Blues. Enthusiastic with bonhomie, Nathan gives the man a thumbs-up. The aquatic parade continues to pass, the marchers mostly vessels that were antiquarian even when he and Arnie were boys: the Gertrude H., the Lennie, the Optimist II. These old ones are a pleasure and comfort to him. He salutes each of them with seriousness and genuine regard as they float beneath the bridge.

The fleet passes, the bridge closes, and Nathan descends its southern slope into Belmar. This is his true home, the town of his upbringing, the incubus of his memories and personality since he was two, when the Kirinski family moved from the Bronx. Once, he thought he would live here forever, content to carry trash, paint benches, and clean beaches for the municipality's department of public works, where he was employed during high school summers. But his ability to score well on multiple-choice aptitude tests and an IQ assessed by educators as "off the charts" conspired against his opportunity to remain a colorless small-town boy aspiring to nothing of note. In 1960, his sophomore year at Asbury Park High School, his parents and teachers arranged for him to enter the 200-year-old Phillips Exeter Academy in New Hampshire on full scholarship. At 15, prep school for him was foreign. He did better than well academically, but he was unhappy in the elite institution's social bubble, surrounded by classmates he considered schmucks and putzes, obnoxious jerks obsessed with success and popularity and the bi-annual purchase of white buck shoes with argyle laces. Disappointed by the end of a windfall but nevertheless sensitive to their son's misery, his parents brought him home for his last two years at Asbury High.

Despite this descent back into public school, he became a scholar. Where he had been satisfied to be ordinary, he was thrown into settings that only highlighted his abilities. And soon he grew to enjoy the success and popularity that he had so despised in the motivations of his former Exeter peers, although he never did take to wearing white bucks. He became a bigshot professor, an accomplished academic. No doubt, judging from the fact that at least four former students had published reminiscences of him, he was also an outstanding teacher. To metaphorize in the old Asbury High manner, he had the world by the balls and could pinch or fondle them as he pleased.

At age 29, he embarked on his third book, a study that took three years of Promethean effort. It alternately invigorated and wore him down, with the periods of invigoration gradually becoming more and more difficult to sustain. Alcohol and problems in his marriage made the situation worse. Depressed, he took to amusing himself in pool halls. He had always enjoyed the game, but it wasn't enough to divert him fully. Although satisfying for the physics, geometry, and technique involved, pool was too slowly paced for him.

One slushy winter day in Cambridge, in the manic turmoil attending his bouts of writing and drinking, he discovered pinball. More accurately, he re-discovered pinball at a level of importance quite beyond his adolescent trysts with the game. During the two summers prior to his departure for Exeter, he had done his share of lurking in the arcades, a Parliament cigarette stuck James Dean-like in the corner of his mouth, the recessed filter offering an illusory margin of protection against the fiery tobacco. From time to time, he would drop a nickel in some colorful Gottlieb or Williams or Bally machine and put on a show of shaking and pounding the balls along a course they would have followed just as well without his intervention. Shirt collar turned up, he would talk scores and flipper technique with his brother and their cronies, but the machines were secondary then, noisy backdrops to help a teenager act cool. They were a means for him to socialize. He could take or leave the actual playing. But since the day he came upon Royal Flush in a bar in Cambridge, his life changed. He became obsessed with pinball—not obsessed as the term is commonly and lightly used to describe a preoccupation, but obsessed in the clinical sense, where little else mattered. "...for where was that metaphysical consolation now to be found?" Nietzsche had asked in *The Birth of Tragedy*. "Here," answered Kirinski whenever he played Royal Flush. "Right here."

Fortunately, he rediscovered pinball at about the time he was finishing that third book, *Is Change Possible?*, or two years of work would have been abandoned with no product to show for it. In fact, rumors among philosophers had it that the concluding chapter, which collegial consensus said was the book's weakest section, had been drafted mostly by Kirinski's editor, the author himself being insensate in some opium den. His failed bid for tenure and nearly simultaneous resignation from the university shortly after the publication of *Is Change Possible?* only served to reinforce the rumors, as did his repeated refusals throughout the following year to join one or another first-rank faculty. In truth, he had written the chapter himself and had always considered it to be the book's strongest section, his development of the notion that real change is only possible for a gifted and enlightened few. He had rightly predicted that such an elitist pronouncement would attract the knee-jerk wrath of his liberal peers. Whether he was denied tenure for this reason alone was never clear due to the hermetic, medieval secrecy surrounding such decisions at Harvard, decisions that allowed no recourse or appeal.

In any case, by the time he left Harvard neither matters of scholarship nor opprobrium nor status nor security held any importance for him. The principles of change and destiny he had been examining in the abstract over the years found their embodiment in Royal Flush. The machine struck him as the purest of metaphors for the entanglements of his life and the hope that he could find a way to extricate himself from them. It was literally *Deus ex Machina*, the "God from machine" theatrical device by which a playwright brings the drama to a happy ending after a character has painted himself into a corner, when escape can only come about through divine intervention. The metaphor came alive and encouraged Nathan every time he played Royal Flush. The ball ricocheted almost constantly when it was in play. He couldn't know where it would go, nor could he always control it. But the point was to stay awake and be ready to respond as the situation dictated. He'd follow the ball, much like a meditator in the Buddhist mindfulness tradition watches his stream of thoughts and comes to realize their impermanence, much like Einstein came to realize that there is no fixed frame of reference, and that everything is moving relative to everything else. Nothing is assured, but everything is possible.

In the midst of all his troubles, this insight was heartening, and Royal Flush became the practical means for sustaining it. He had fallen for a machine and pledged himself to courting it.

So here he is—after a year in a commune, divorce, and another year traveling abroad, incommunicado even from the Belmar Kirinskis—pursuing his courtship of Royal Flush in Wizard's World Arcade, a musty concrete slab of a building on the corner of Eighth and Ocean Avenues in Belmar. This is generally his favorite arcade—but not on summer weekends with the influx of "Bennies," the inimical inhabitants of Bayonne (B), Elizabeth (E), Newark (N), and New York (NY), outlanders that infest the Shore annually from Memorial Day to Labor Day. He hates their manner and their voices and their accents.

Today there is the usual Friday night invasion of Bennies at Wizard's World. Hardly through the door, his ears are assaulted by "Yeah, mutha fucka, ya think ya can do bedda, mutha fucka, g'wan." He grimaces then chuckles indulgently, already unsettled but intent on maintaining his composure. He goes up to a man dispensing change and hands him a five-dollar bill. "Hello, Jimbo. Pretty crowded with them today."

"Yeah, Nate," Jimbo acknowledges as he hands over two stacks of quarters. "It's already jumpin' here. It's only gonna get worse. They're drivin' into town in hordes." Jimbo considers Kirinski. "Look, Nate, you know how it is on weekends here. It's a small place. Why not do yourself a favor? Go to Playland. It's big. They got videos there to keep the Bennies off pinball. You'll be happier there. Then you can start up again at Wizard's on Monday night. Think about it, Nate."

Kirinski surveys the crowd. "You're probably right. Why get aggravated?" He smiles at Jimbo. "Even Bennies deserve to have fun at the Shore. I'll just look around a little, maybe play some if Flush is open. If not, I'll take your advice and go."

He wanders along the corridors of machines, engrossed by their different lights and sounds and personalities. Wizard's has a good collection of what Nate calls "romance" machines, like Gottlieb's "Sinbad," on whose backdrop picture the dashing hero, turbaned and bare-chested, protects a sultry beauty from villains and monsters. Or Bally's "Mata Hari," which depicts a buxom *femme fatale* lying on a tiger head-and-skin rug while some stud, undoubtedly well-endowed in addition to being a source of state secrets, stands astride her. Nate always enjoys seeing the poor tiger's tongue lolling out of its mouth in what he chooses to interpret as frustrated, reverse bestiality.

But these romance games, while fun and well made, are not of a genre that he can take seriously. In fact, Royal Flush, also known as "Card Whiz" on some machines, a sobriquet he despises, is the only game he'll play. Its backdrop panel shows an unimposing gambler at play with a regular-looking woman in a plumed hat standing behind him, watching. There is no sexual hype, as with Sinbad and Mata Hari. Royal Flush is described in small print on the backdrop panel as "a game of skill." And indeed it is that, a challenging, classic machine with a slightly asymmetrical playfield. Nate loves Flush, and has been carrying the manufacturer's address around with the idea of writing them a letter of appreciation for making such a fine machine. He's already started the letter several times but never gotten beyond "*D. Gottlieb and Co., 165 W. Lake Street, Northlake, Illinois, 60164. Dear Sirs:*". Each time he starts he falls to imagining the pleasure the dear sirs must experience daily as they work in their warehouse on W. Lake Street, surrounded by rows of pinball machines.

Nate comes now to the object of his devotion but finds it unavailable. Flush is being used by three Bennies, pimpled teenagers wearing muscle shirts. The lettering on their shirts reads *Weequahic High School Wrestling Team, Newark, NJ.* They are certainly wrestlers, he acknowledges as they bounce the machine around, taking turns ball by ball like they're in a tag team match, alternately pounding the machine's corners and flailing away with its flippers. They are rough with it, with no sense of timing and obviously no understanding of what the game demands. Nate grows more and more perturbed but controls himself in the expectation that the line of quarters lying on the glass will disappear quickly, since the charge is 25 cents for a game with three balls to try. He rests in the conviction that these louts couldn't get the 75,000 points needed to win a replay if they had thirty balls to shoot. Of course, there is always the chance that they will match the last number of their score with the house number spun out by the machine. But the probability is slim...

A loud pop comes from the machine. The assailants from Newark have matched numbers. The pimply Bennies have won a free game. "Awright!" they scream. "Fuckin' A, Man. D'jya hear the mutha pop, man? Awright!"

Nate turns away in disgust and dejection. A gentleman, at least by arcade standards, he can no longer watch the victimization of Flush. An idealist, he can't bear to witness even a momentary victory for the collusive forces of hazard and fate, when justice says that only artistry and preparation should be rewarded.

He leaves Wizard's World and heads in the direction of Belmar Playland. The day is turning out badly. No Esther, no Flush. He sees only battalions of Bennies and the means for servicing them: hotdog stands, putt-putt golf courses, beer joints, souvenir shops. The outlanders fill the boardwalk benches and the Ocean Avenue parking spaces. Already they are lining up to buy beach badges and bathhouse passes for the weekend. Nate walks in vivid loneliness among the foreigners. *I'm home, but I don't live here anymore. I'm in familiar surroundings, but I don't recognize anyone.*

He reassures himself that summer weekends are aberrations after all, that these crowds will have migrated north by Monday. It's curious to him. There was a time when the forebears of these Bennies now dancing on skateboards to disco were a source of excitement, especially their women, who had a brazenness and allure that was missing in local girls. Local girls popped up from time to time in fantasies of marriage. Dressed in loafers, knee socks, kilts, and crewneck sweaters when they were teenagers, he could imagine that they would make clean and wholesome wives. After a stint as "most popular" or "best personality," these fantasy wives would calmly retire into a life of homemaking and mothering and civic responsibility. But it was the girls of Bergen and Union Counties who ran rampant in his imagination. They were hot summer visions dripping in suntan oil, wearing anklet chains and high-heeled gold pumps. He would never think of marrying them; they were crude and boisterous and aggressive, and their accents were harsh. But he could go giddy with the prospect of fucking them forever, reveling in their wetness, their darkness, their boldness. But that was then. That was the '50s, before Junior's had been replaced by the Saigon Room in the basement of the Mayfair Hotel, before the old Tenth Avenue Arcade with its arsenal of quality pinball machines had burned down and been replaced by a beach pavilion, complete with snack bar and locker rooms, that resembled a concrete mushroom.

Nate's grave mood begins to lift nonetheless as he passes the pavilion. He recalls the fabled man-machine battles that took place in the old arcade, the characters and idiosyncratic strategies. He laughs at the memory of David Lindholm, who for two summers could win games at will on "Eight Ball Deluxe" by tripping a mechanism with a piece of coat-hanger wire. One night, Lindholm found that the hole through which he inserted the wire had been plugged up. Furious, and more than a little drunk, he kicked the side of the machine where the hole had been. His foot went through; to free himself he had to leave his shoe behind, an easy target for the police to apprehend as he limped down the boardwalk. And there was huge Junior Clark, who would lift the front ends of the machine onto his steel-toe boots, thereby reducing both the playfield's incline and the challenge of gravity. Clark could play indefinitely on a nickel. Nate is struck by nostalgia and homage. All those machines gone, destroyed by an errant Lucky Strike. All those wild men gone, replaced by bathers with Jersey City accents...

He is pulled from his ruminations by someone yelling. "Hey, Nate! Nathan Kirinski!" He spots the source of the call and tenses when he recognizes two contemporaries from his Belmar Grammar School and Asbury Park High years. Charles Rossiter and Alexander Garfield approach him with hands outstretched. Né Kalman Rosenzweig and Albert Greenbaum. Rosencrantz and Guildenstern he used to call them. As they greet him, Nate imagines their appraisal of both his girth and clothing. He retaliates with his own condescending appraisal of their bodies—pudgy Alexander, skeletal Charles—and designer shirts, jeans, and shoes.

"Albert, Kalman," he opens, pleased to see them react disapprovingly to his use of their given names. "How've you been?"

"Great. We've been doing great," Garfield answers. "You know we're in business together now in New York, partners at Metro Talent and Literary Agency. Four years after law school, we took a lot of the clientele—you know, actors, athletes, artists, writers—away from the mega agency we started out with before we set up MTLA." The two attorneys smile at each other. "Yeah, we're doing great."

"How about yourself, Nate?" asks Garfield. "You're looking, uh, you've changed," he falters, "You know, from when I ran into you a few years ago in Cambridge, when we were all in school up there." *Yeah, when I was at Harvard and you bozos were at Suffolk Law.*

There is a silence among them that Nate cherishes for the discomfort it appears to be causing the other two. He hates lawyers as a genus for their casuistry and cynicism. To him, they are the nitpicking, amoral, cold-blooded ciphers of the age, the mean-spirited, fault-finding, inquisitorial heirs of Torquemada or von Ribbentrop. He particularly detests these two parasites. They were money-grubbing bastards as kids. What's new?

"We hear you've been back here a long time, Nate," Garfield continues. "We figure that book you're probably working on is pretty far along. Maybe finished? A collection of essays? Maybe even a novel? If you need an agent, MTLA does that type of work. Think about us. We're old friends. We'd give you a reasonable deal."

Nate is quiet for a moment, as if he's considering the offer. "I'm not writing a book," he says. "I don't imagine I'll ever write another book, either non-fiction or fiction. I came home simply because I love the Shore and would rather live here than any other place I can think of."

They look at him as if to say, *Nathan, Nathan, who are you talking to? You make this sound like Nice or Antigua or even Fire Island. This is New Jersey, Nathan, New Jersey. You're a fool for living here. We pity you.*

"So what do you do here, Nate?" asks Rossiter. "Play the market probably, huh? With your mind, you must be scoring big."

"The only thing I score big on, Charlie, is pinball machines. As for a living, my brother helps support me." He pauses before adding, "There's just not much that I care about anymore, except pinball and the Shore."

The two have no way to respond to this revelation. But the telling, somehow, has left Nathan feeling clean about himself, and even somewhat charitable toward Garfield and Rossiter. He has no further need either to shock or ridicule them, or to defend himself. He knows but doesn't care that they'll spread the word among mutual acquaintances about poor Nathan Kirinski, the brilliant bastard who had it all going for him until he had a breakdown or something and just couldn't handle it anymore. So he moved back to the Shore—can you believe it?—and just lives off his family and farts around all day playing arcade games and getting fat.

Maybe I'm kidding myself. Maybe I do care. Maybe I am hurt by what they must think of me. But for the moment, he wishes them well and takes his leave.

Belmar Playland is a mixture of kitsch and class. Kitsch is the larger ingredient. It jumps out at Nate before he ever enters the place. It jumps down on him from the 18-hole miniature golf course strewn with ersatz palm trees on the building's roof. Once inside, he is surrounded by video games and the freaks playing them. His senses are bludgeoned by noises that could have been composed by a cross between Ray Bradbury and Sid Vicious, futuristic noises from Space Invaders, Pongs, Blockbusters, Asteroids, Defenders, Space Furies, and Eliminators. Mostly, the games are played by purple-haired punks from north Jersey. Despite his imposing size and the fact that these kids are too fucked up on their insular weirdness to present a danger, Nate admits to fearing these spacemen. To him, they are video psychotics. Just the other day he read a UPI report about two 15-year-olds who beat up a gas station attendant in Dallas because he was too slow in giving them change to play Defender.

So he's circumspect in his approach to the place and tries to slip in unnoticed, to the extent that a leviathan can go unnoticed, much less one out of water. He moves past the video jungle to the classier part of Playland, where ranks of pinball machines by Bally, Gottlieb, Williams, and Playmatic stand in electric, flashing-lights formation against the dark walls. He makes his way to the darkest corner of the room and approaches Royal Flush. Close by, quiet aficionados stand cool and bent-kneed in isolated pursuit of the perfect game. Nathan is at home.

He places the quarters he received from Jimbo on the glass and spends a number of minutes readying himself. As many times as he's played this machine, he refuses to take it lightly. Flush is a difficult game. It demands alertness, a balance of mental and physical reflexes that his long stint in academia never prepared him for—undergrad and grad programs; prelim exams; dissertation research, writing, and defense; teaching; faculty committees; book publishing and tours and readings. None of it seems worth a damn now. To be good, Nate has learned to approach the machine as if he were playing for keeps every time. In fact, he always comes to the game as if everything, in life and beyond, were riding on the way he handled three silver steel balls.

He studies Royal Flush like a maestro who, already knowing a fugue by heart, searches for new expressions within the piece's formal limits. For the thousandth time, he reacquaints himself with the rules and features of the game: an aggregate score of 75,000 points equals one replay, and 89,000 points gets you a second free game; a straight flush is worth 5000 points, a full boat 4000, three queens 3000, a pair of kings and jacks 2000, and a pair of either kings or jacks are worth 1000 points. The drop targets—an ace, two kings, three queens, two jacks, and a ten—spread from left to right across the middle of the playfield are an excellent source of points.

He drops a quarter in the slot, watches the scores from the previous game regress to scratch, and listens with satisfaction as the balls tumble down an invisible chute before coming to rest in a chamber beneath the launcher. The board is swept clear. All is possible. He feels the exhilaration and gratitude that come with having a fresh start.

After testing the flippers for responsiveness and the duration of their hold, he pushes a ball into the launcher slot and pulls back on the launcher with his right hand. Adding the pressure of his left thumb for more velocity, he fires the ball into the ellipse at the top of the playfield. It is one of his idiosyncrasies to spin the launcher as he thumbs it. He realizes that spinning most likely has no effect, but it's his one finesse move, his one extravagance in an otherwise economical style.

Whatever the real value of the spin, he gets a nice launch. The ball drops from the ellipse and activates a joker, which in turn lights a corresponding rollover. Pounding the corners of the machine with the heels of his hands, he bounces the ball off a thumper-bumper and sends it back up into the ellipse through a second joker slot. He senses the beginnings of a long play when he guides the ball yet again up into the ellipse and watches with glee as it falls back through the third joker slot. He hasn't yet left high ground with the first ball and already has completed a three-joker sequence for a special.

Alternately gentling the machine and punishing it, Nate keeps the ball in play. Working the corners, he reinforces the ball hard off slingshots and bumpers through bonus gates and swinging targets, all the while managing to keep his rebounds from drifting toward the free-ball gate and out of play.

When the ball finally drops to low ground, he guides it along the inner drops, cupping it motionless on the flipper until he's ready to carry it to a target—either a lit rollover or pop bumper for 1000 points, or, goal of goals, the middle-queen drop target, which awards 3000 points when lit. But this requires attentiveness and precision. Except in instances of desperation, when the ball explodes from a slingshot or a kick-out well toward the run-out slot, and technique must give way to whatever luck he can create with a flailing flipper, he plays a delicate and well-timed flipper. Seeing that no accessible bonus is lit, he releases the ball from its cradle until it reaches the end of his flipper, the point of greatest leverage. Then he rockets the ball back up to high ground again, almost to the ellipse, and guides it through a final prodigious scoring run before it rolls down a slot and disappears off the edge of the playfield.

He's winded yet energized. He drove a comet through a galaxy of popping lights, and it reaped 61,000 points before dropping from sight. He's left with a number of specials and lit bonuses to convert and on his second ball scores a workmanlike 34,250. With two free games and a good prospect for several more, he launches the final ball. He hits three lit pop bumpers for a quick 3000 points, then stares in dismay as the ball runs to its death through the abyss between his flippers. Final score: 98,250. He had a chance to vault high and blew it. He needed to stay awake to sustain some quality, and he couldn't. He fell asleep and lost.

Disgusted with himself, he pushes the button to activate his first free game, and then purposely tilts the machine to disqualify himself. As he wastes the second free game in the same way, someone shouts, "This dude is crazy, man. Fat and crazy."

Nate turns to a group of five teenagers standing at the sides of Royal Flush. He hadn't noticed them in his preoccupation with the game. For all he knows, they may have been watching him since he snapped that first remarkable ball into its seminal ellipse.

"Fuck off," he mutters to no one of them in particular. They don't concern him half so much as did his dismal play of the third ball.

"You be 'bout ready to watch your mouth, man, Professor Jew, man," says one, careful to move beyond Nate's reach. "You don't be talkin' to none a Spin's men that way."

He's seen these kids before. They're part of the entourage of Sid "The Spin" Hamlin, a man who is renowned locally both for his past athletic successes and his flashy style of living. As kids, Sid and Nate had been incongruously close, the brilliant Jewish-American scholar and the brilliant African-American jock. They had always understood each other as two kids with special talents, although quite different ones, and been drawn together by their shared distinctiveness. Even their careers had been enacted in a crude sort of parallelism. Sid had been an All-America defensive back at Missouri and a starter for the Oakland Raiders about the time Nate's once-high status was unraveling towards its infamous conclusion at Harvard. Then Sid, after only three years in the pros, had unexpectedly (some say it was drugs, some say injuries) left football, returned to the Shore, and begun feeding his signing bonus, pension, and endorsement proceeds into pinball machines. Nate showed up nine years later, albeit without bonus, pension, or endorsement, to do the same. The two see each other almost daily now at one arcade or another, and although they understand each other better than ever, their interactions are no closer than an occasional nod. Within their equally serious commitments to pinball, their approaches are poles apart. Sid is flashy and promiscuous across a broad spectrum of machines; he plays a freewheeling game and courts followers. Nate plays his deliberate, disciplined, obsessional game for himself alone.

"You hear me, man?" the kid repeats. "I say you don't be talkin' to none a Spin's men that way."

"And I say, you little jerkoff, that if you call me fat, crazy, or a Jew again, I'm going to press your nose against the bottom of this glass like an insect on display."

The rest of the group guffaws. The kid has lost, and he knows it. He is about to attempt a recovery when Sid walks up to intervene. He shakes Nate's hand.

"How you been, Nate?"

"Fine, Sid. You?"

"In great demand, as ever," he laughs, nodding at his groupies. "I saw that first ball you shot. One of the baddest plays ever. I don't think I ever saw one better. Of course," he adds with a smile, "I don't think I ever saw one worse than your number three, either."

Nate allows his own small smile while the entourage erupts with laughter. The vanquished teenager laughs the loudest. "That Spin, man, is cruel," he chortles, "very cruel." He gives Nate a wicked look. "The Spin be too good for this dude—too good lookin' and too good talkin' and too good playin'."

Hamlin and Nate look at each other. They know the repartee has taken a bad turn, that suddenly, through the spitefulness of a punk, the situation is out of their control and now demands something that neither of them wants.

"Look, Nate," Hamlin begins. "For years we've been playing pinball around here. But never against each other, man. Never a match." He sighs apologetically and continues, "It's time we had a match, man, you know?"

Nate nods in resignation. He understands that Sid's style and particular obligations to his fans require that Sid play. Nate also understands that he'll have no peace until they play. "Yeah, Sid, I know. Look, how's tonight, about 10? I'll meet you here and we can go head to head on any machine you want. Right now, I can't. I'm sorry. Is tonight okay?"

"Sounds good, my man," says Sid quietly. Then, more loudly, he tells the crowd, "The champ will defend his title here tonight at 10. Be ready to celebrate."

"Nathan," Fay Kirinski scolds him, "You should take better care of yourself. Look at you. You look exhausted. You're sweating."

"Mom, I'm fine. I was running late. So I rushed over here to be on time. It's summertime, after all. People sweat in summertime." He smiles to show his conviviality, to show he's taken no offense.

"I just want you to look after yourself."

"I will. I promise."

They walk together into the dining room. His father and brother are already seated at the table, which has been set with a white lace cloth, the family's best china and cutlery, and two large brass candlesticks with white candles. Nathan goes up to greet his father, Morton, who gives him a dour look and a reluctant handshake. Morton looks him up and down, then hands him a black skullcap. "Here," he says sarcastically, "I hope this fits."

Nathan tries to take the reference to his size with humor. "It fits fine, although maybe a little big, which is not surprising since I'm only a small chip off the old block."

Arnold and Fay laugh, but Morton regards Nate with no trace of humor. "You are certainly not small. And you are certainly not a chip off this block."

"Look, it's sundown," Arnold intervenes. "Light the candles, Mom."

Fay lights the Sabbath candles, Morton blesses the bread and wine, and the four of them sit down to eat. The dinner conversation is dyadic. Fay tells Arnold to eat more, Morton and Arnold talk about business at the diner, and Arnold tries to draw Nathan into the conversation with harmless, general, "what-was-your-day-like" topics, a ploy which begins to backfire barely midway through the entree when Morton asks to know the reason for Nate's somewhat tardy and disheveled arrival.

Nate feels the guardedness of an eight-year-old whose behavior is about to be punished.

"I had an appointment," he answers. "It took longer than I expected, and I walked here very quickly in the heat to make up time."

"And may I ask," his father persists with exaggerated politeness, "the nature of the appointment?"

Arnold and Nate look at each other with alarm. "Come on, Dad," Arnold mediates. "What's the difference? Besides, it's *Shabbos*. Let's be peaceful and enjoy each other."

"What's the difference?" Morton repeats, the normally slight trace of his Boston accent growing more pronounced with his anger. "The difference is that I had a son who was once handsome and tidy, a respected professor who brought us *nachas*, who made us proud. He had all the chances, all the good things. Then what? He gets kicked out of his professorship in a renowned university. And then what? He loses his wife and child. And then what? He disappears for two years without trace, so that we can't even contact him to come back for..." Morton's voice cracks. He seems unable to continue but then renews his recriminations. "So that we can't tell him that his sister has died, and that he must come to the funeral. The difference, since you ask," he says to Arnie while gesturing disparagingly at Nate, "is that now, I've—you've got a brother who's a freeloader, who does nothing but play games and sleep with *shicksas*. Those were probably his so-called appointments. A bum—he's a bum who came back to shame us."

Nathan rises from the table, barely able to control himself. He puts down his skullcap, shakes hands with his brother, and walks over to kiss his mother on the cheek. No one tries to stop him. "*Gut Shabbos*," he says, before his slight control falters and he rushes for the door. Within moments, he's far enough away to curse, and to cry.

Nathan dreams dreams, and in one dream he moans. There's a sharp probing in this particular dream that he cannot specify. It's elusive, both an object and a sensation. The sharpness moves quickly from his foot to his knee and up his arm to his chest. It lingers over his nipple, alternately pulling and pressing it. Aroused, he arches his back to guide the sharpness toward his groin. It nibbles and glides across the folds of his belly and becomes a soft wetness sliding around the glans and shaft of his penis. In a half sleep now, he begins to move his hips against the sliding. When the wetness engulfs his scrotum, the dream ends as he explodes like a sunburst cap on a pinball machine. He opens his eyes and draws the dark bobbing head of Esther O'Connell to his face. "Dear Esther. You are tender and wonderful and a gift to me in my despair."

"It's equally my pleasure, Nathan." She curls against his side and nestles her head on his shoulder. "Now tell me what's got you despairing. Is it your folks? When I saw Arnie he told me you were supposed to go there for supper tonight."

"It's my folks. It's my life." He tells Esther about his day: the impending match with Sid, the argument with Morton, meeting Garfield and Rossiter, the inability to find anything that interests him except Royal Flush and, "of course, my relationship with you." But even she has become an issue now. "I wonder how Morton ever found out about us. Certainly, Arnold wouldn't have said anything. Fay knows that I date someone named Esther." He smiles. "I think she would like to assume that with a name like Esther, you must be Jewish, the biblical savior of our people, just as she would like to assume that I spend my time working on a terribly important book that will surely be acclaimed. It gives her something to impress them with at Hadassah meetings and the beauty parlor. Why pursue truth if it's inconvenient? Now Mort is different, just the reverse. Mort will pursue the truth with the energy of a quasar. But he assumes that the truth is terrible, and that misery is its only confirmation." Nate pauses, not knowing how to express what he feels. Finally, he settles on "Fucking Mort."

They lie quietly together, Nathan Kirinski, crackpot, and Esther O'Connell, sexpot. They have become lovers only recently, the one-time genius and the one-time model Catholic girl, the virginal student at St. Rose's High School whose reputation was sullied irrevocably after she was slandered by an unrequited suitor from an influential local family. Her devout, conservative parents disowned her, and she set about trying to save enough money as a nanny and waitress to eventually escape the Shore. She met Nathan one day on the boardwalk in Avon, and he began dropping in to see her at Vic's Pizzeria, purposely choosing slow periods at the restaurant so they could talk. The relationship developed, and now they are a couple. Nathan esteems her equally for her undulations and her beauty and her kindness. He's also attracted by the combination of her Irish surname and Jewish-sounding first name. The mixture both soothes his sense of tradition and excites his rebelliousness. Pondering their improbable pairing, Nathan is sure that he is everything Esther never envisioned for herself: fat, poor, divorced, Jewish, and devoted to pinball. Yet for her part, what Esther sees is a smart, entertaining, and generous gentleman, one she has come to love, just as he has come to love her.

"What about the match with Sid? It's getting close to 10 o'clock. You could default, couldn't you?"

"No, I've got to play. Defaulting would only put off the inevitable. One of Sid's cretin groupies would force it again sometime." He shakes his head, frustrated. "Christ, the irony of it is so unsubtle. For years I'd been performing at one school after the other. I got sick with the pressure of it. So it wasn't all bad that I was forced out."

"But don't you miss any of it, Nathan? I mean, you were so respected."

"Sure, I miss being flattered and having a good salary and book deals and speaker fees. But you give up a lot for all that. You give up your freedom. You become dependent on what other people think about you. That's why I understand Sid. He still needs the crowd, even if the crowd is mostly a bunch of asinine teenagers. And that's why we got forced into playing this game. Left to our own devices, we would never compete. But I guess it was bound to happen sometime. Better to get it over with."

Esther looks at him for a long moment. Finally, she asks, "What about Royal Flush? You seem, well, dependent on it, the sort of thing you say you don't want to be. Does being dependent on how a machine measures you make you feel any better than being dependent on what people think of you?"

"The difference is that I really love that machine."

The dark corridor is crowded with spectators when Esther and Nate arrive at the pinball section of Playland. The crowd is mostly Black. The Bennies and punks are captive to the video games at the front of the arcade.

The brat who instigated the match spots Nate and yells to Sid Hamlin, who is standing down the line watching a young woman play Gargon. "Yo, Spin. Spin. It's the professor, man. The professor's here."

Sid comes over to greet them. "Hello, Nate. Esther. It's getting late. I thought you might have decided to skip the fun."

"I had thought of it, to be honest. But then it would have been hard for me to ever play here again. So here I am. What's your choice of machine?"

Sid smiles. "Royal Flush."

Nathan is unprepared for this. He's superb on Royal Flush because he plays it almost exclusively. He would be an easier mark on any other game. Sid knows this, but his choice reflects some hedging of bets. If he doesn't play on Nate's best machine, any victory might be inconclusive to his followers. And if he happens to lose—well, all Kirinski can do is play Flush; he's a specialist; he's unbeatable on that machine.

"Smart, Sid. Smart."

They decide to play the best two out of three. Nate wins the coin toss and elects to go second. There is no wager between them. Victory is the payoff.

Sid plays with a flair that is captivating. He is all body English and reflexes. He plays pinball like he once played cornerback, attacking the machine with hard reinforcements and hits off the slingshots and bumpers that time after time bring him to the perilous edge of a tilt. At the end of two balls in the first game he has run up 58,000 points, an excellent total. His entourage begins to sniff blood until Sid, at 63,300 points, tilts. At the end of his three balls, Nate finishes with a 20,000-point scoring run to win game one at 65,000 plus change.

"Not to fear, Spin," someone yells. "Not to fear, man. You almost won even with the tilt."

"That was just a warm-up, children," Sid tells the crowd. "Just a short practice game to learn the machine." The delighted gallery applauds. They love their Spin, the aplomb and style of the man.

Nate shoots first on the second game. His play is emotionless, spare, and consistent, his launches and flips eschewing any extravagance. Colorlessly, almost abstractedly, he works his way to a respectable 85,000 points before the third ball drops.

Sid smiles at him quizzically. "Nice game, Nate."

When Nate doesn't acknowledge him, Sid gets to work, investing his play with an electric dynamism that had been missing in his opponent's game. He lags behind after the first two balls but finishes the second game by rocketing his own third ball into the ellipse, completing a three-joker sequence, hitting the special, then staying in an up-post position long enough to work his game to 89,000 points. The match is tied at one apiece.

Sid plays the deciding game as if it were an all-out assault on immortality. For the crowd, he gives his launches an exaggerated spin. "Yessir," they yell. "Spin it, Spin!" He flips balls to high ground again and again, and his corner work keeps the kick-out wells popping. He is light on the flippers and strong on the corners, and his dancing at the machine delights the crowd. He is masterful, and at the end of his third ball he has shot 106,000 points.

Yelling and dancing, the crowd focuses on Nate. He starts his final ball at 62,000 points. Until now, he has played serviceable but uninspired pinball. Now, facing what is surely an insurmountable deficit, he experiences an un-nameable change in himself. The lethargy lifts and is replaced by a fierce and pure attention. Time after time he hits the point getters: 5000 points for a Royal Flush, 4000 for a full boat, 3000 for the middle queen—once, twice, three times. Rollovers and sunburst caps pop as he cradles and pounds and coaxes his score upwards until, at 101,000 and with all specials lit, he mistimes a flip and watches his last chance for victory drop from sight at the low end of the playfield.

Sid Hamlin gives him a long, appreciative look. Nate worries that Sid will question him about letting the final balls drop in games two and three. But Sid says nothing as he shakes Nate's hand before walking away amid the high-fives of his juiced-up entourage.

Nathan stands motionless until the pinball corridor is quiet, and only he and Esther are in the vicinity of Royal Flush. Then he pushes the free-game button and runs his first replay to 123,000 points. He activates a second game and builds it, using everything he knows and every bit of concentration he can exert, to 144,000 points. The free games keep popping with firecracker quickness, and when the third ball disappears at the end of the run-out slot, the machine matches numbers. Pop. The Cherry Bomb. The Ashcan. The Roman Candle.

Laughing, he pulls Esther O'Connell over to stand between him and Royal Flush. Together, they rocket ball after ball high into the ellipse. Each taking a flipper, they ride their free games on into the night.

2
Carousel

ARNOLD AWAKENS SLOWLY, RELUCTANT to sacrifice sleep to the obligations that Fridays always bring. But he has no choice.

He carries his clothes to the living room, careful not to disturb Miriam. He wishes he could linger in bed until she awakens, to make love before he leaves for the Shore. But there's no time. Instead, he quietly returns to the bedroom, forced to be content with a lingering, affectionate look. *The time will come when I'll be with you every day, when we're finished with our doctorates and married.* He allows himself to fantasize their lives together as Dr. Arnold Kirinski, Professor of History, and Dr. Miriam Kaplan-Kirinski, Professor of Anthropology. *We'll find research projects we can conduct together, get grants to support our work, travel, co-teach seminars, co-author books, give interviews together....* Arnold interrupts his fantasy. All of that is a long way off. He and Miriam are graduate students, who only met by chance when both signed up for an inter-disciplinary seminar on ethnography. They're in different fields of study, and it's a long-shot that they would ever find teaching positions in the same institution. They've been sleeping together for three years but don't live together. They haven't discussed marriage. They haven't met each other's family, and, among the Kirinskis, only Nate knows that his deeply private brother has a girlfriend. *Save your dreams for later,* Arnold admonishes himself.

He leaves the bedroom, washes at the kitchen sink, and dresses at the window overlooking Riverside Drive and Grant's Tomb. Then he stares for a moment at the lights along the Palisades across the Hudson. New Jersey beckons.

It's nearly dawn, time to leave Manhattan for the 70-mile drive to Asbury Park. He has no concerns about traffic at this hour. If his old Chevy Nova cooperates he'll arrive by six to open the family diner. Three mornings a week it's a burden he can spare his father.

He takes the Henry Hudson Parkway north, crosses the George Washington Bridge, and heads back south, first down the New Jersey Turnpike and then the Garden State Parkway. Once he's on these open roads he turns on a tape recorder and begins dictating his latest stream of thoughts about his doctoral research in history at Columbia University. The focus of his work is the Khazars, a Turkic tribe that dominated the Eurasian steppes for three centuries in the Middle Ages and converted to Judaism. His routine on Fridays, Saturdays, and Sundays is to transcribe the recordings during slow moments at the diner. He returns to the city on Sunday nights and throughout the week incorporates the transcripts into his evolving manuscript. The dictation-to-print process is seamless by now. He's in the final phases of preparing the dissertation for submission to the faculty and so steeped in his knowledge of the topic that there is little difference between the content he speaks and the content he writes.

Arnold turns off the recorder when he exits the Parkway for Asbury Park. Several miles of local roads bring him to Lake Avenue and the Carousel Diner. At 5:50 a.m. he parks in a reserved spot next to Wesley Lake and opens the diner. On time. As usual.

It's mid-afternoon. Except for two or three customers who linger over coffee, the luncheon crowd is long gone. Arnold is cleaning up the kitchen when Nate enters the diner, waves, and sits at the counter. Arnold interrupts his cleaning to serve up Nate's usual repast of eggs, home fries, buttered rye toast, and coffee.

Arnold keeps glancing at his brother as Nate eats, his slouching posture, his ballooning body weight. He worries about Nate's state of mind, his despair over his failed career and broken marriage. And now his obsession with a pinball machine. He doesn't know how to help, other than to support Nate in every way he can and not say anything that fuels more self-loathing.

The brothers banter until Nate has to leave. "Will I see you at Fay and Morton's later?" Arnold asks.

"Of course. Far be it from me to stand up Queen Sabbath on a Friday night date. Speaking of which. If Esther drops by, would you please ask her to meet me at my place tonight, maybe around nine? Okay? Thanks, my brother, my savior. Until tonight."

He turns at the door. "And don't worry, Arnold. I'll be nice."

Arnold nods. "Good, Nate. Put some scores on Flush for me, okay?"

Nathan heads east towards the boardwalk and Arnold returns to his saucepans.

Arnold locks up the diner at 6:30 p.m. and drives to his parents' home in Belmar. He showers, dresses, and at 8:00 joins his mother and father in the dining room. Fay is putting the Sabbath candles in the gold holders her parents brought from the old country. Mort sits at the table, which is already set.

"I hope your brother gets here soon," Fay says. "I have to light the candles before sundown. Do you think he'll be here by then? It's almost time." Arnold reassures her. Morton scoffs but says nothing.

They sit for a few minutes while Arnold tells them about his week and how the day went at the diner. "Thank you, Arnie," says Morton. "These three days a week that I don't have to stand and cook and clean are a lifesaver at my age. I don't know how I'd manage without you. And I don't know how you do it, with school, the commute. It would be a lot easier on you if your brother ever helped. Although I'd be a nervous wreck with him in there, like a bull in a China shop."

Arnold tries to guide the conversation away from Nathan. The evening will be difficult enough without his father's anger gaining too much momentum before Nate arrives. "I enjoy my days at the diner. It's a relief from school, a totally different activity and pace. And you pay me a fair wage. Believe me, it's a great help. The city's not cheap, as you and Mom know from your years living there."

They hear the front door open and close, and Nathan enters the room. He's out of breath and perspiring. Fay expresses concern about his health, but Nate laughs it off. "Don't worry, Mom. It's summer. People sweat. Besides, I had an appointment and rushed so I wouldn't be late."

Nathan goes up to greet his father. Morton grudgingly returns the greeting then hands Nathan a black skullcap. "Here. I hope this fits."

Arnold winces, hoping his brother will ignore the sarcasm. When Nathan's attempt at a humorous retort only serves to stoke Morton's acrimony, Arnold intervenes. "Look, it's sundown. Light the candles, Mom."

Fay welcomes the Sabbath, and Mort blesses the meal. As they eat, the talk is general and harmless and all paired with Arnold: Fay to Arnold, Mort to Arnold, Nathan to Arnold. That changes when Morton turns to Nate to ask why he arrived late and unkempt to dinner.

Again, Arnold tries to head off a clash. "Come on, Dad," he mediates. "What's the difference? Besides, it's *Shabbos*. Let's be peaceful and enjoy one another."

"What's the difference? The difference," Mort splutters, "is that I had a son who was once handsome and tidy, a respected professor who brought us *nachas*, who made us proud. The difference, since you ask, is that now, I've—you've got a brother who's a freeloader, who does nothing but play games and sleep with *shicksas*. Who we couldn't even contact when..." He shakes his fist, starts to stand, then slumps back down, his voice more subdued. "Those were probably his so-called appointments. A bum—he's a bum who came back to shame us."

Arnold realizes there is no saving the evening now. He does nothing to stop his brother from leaving as Nathan rises, kisses his mother, shakes Arnold's hand, and nods to his father. He bids them all a good Sabbath and leaves the house. Arnold follows him to the door, hoping to say something reassuring, something comforting, something that suggests tomorrow will be better. But Nathan has already started down the street, too late for Arnold to talk with him but not too late to hear his brother crying.

When Arnold returns to the dining room, only Fay is there. She tells him that his father is tired and has gone to bed early. They pick at the rest of the dinner but hardly talk. They understand each other's sadness. There is nothing more to say.

After he helps his mother put away the leftovers, Arnold goes upstairs to the bedroom that he and Nate shared full time until they graduated from high school, not counting Nate's year at Exeter. After high school, it was primarily

Arnold's room except for holidays and summer vacations when Nate came home from Harvard. Nothing about the room has changed since they were teenagers: two matching single beds, a shared dresser, a desk they took turns using for homework, two small closets, college pennants, the Revolutionary War-era shot pouch Arnold purchased at the Battle of Monmouth museum store, a Japanese officer's sword given to the boys by a Kirinski relative who served in World War Two, and two snakeskins—a cobra and a South American viper—tacked onto the outside of the door. Arnold uses the room on Friday and Saturday nights, but Nathan, feeling unwelcome, hasn't stayed here since his return to the Shore after his long disappearance. Arnold wishes they were sharing the room now, talking through the night as they often did on weekends, when they could sleep in the next morning, then wake up and lie in bed and talk some more. For Arnold, it was mostly about his anxieties.

"I can't think of a future for myself, Nate, and it depresses me. I'd like to go to college, but my grades are poor, and so far I've bombed every standardized test they've made us take. I guess the diner will be my future. That's as far as I can see." Arnold had appreciated how careful and encouraging Nate was when this topic came up. He never mentioned his own college prospects, which could hardly have been brighter, and he was always supportive.

"Come on, Arnie. Don't give up. I know how smart you are, and nobody's a harder worker. Your brains and persistence will pay off. I'm certain of that."

In those days Morton didn't often ask for their help in the diner, although they typically went there on their own to pitch in once they were out of bed. Arnold remembers how well the three of them, and sometimes their sister Deborah before she married Eddie Martino, worked together, and how much fun they had. "Poached eggs with a side of bacon," the gorgeous waitress Deb would yell. "You got it," the ace short-order chef Arnold would yell back. "Hey, you—Professor Busboy," the faux-stern proprietor Morton would call out affectionately to Nathan. "The floors need sweeping." Team Kirinski, they named themselves, joking and loving and united, they were sure, forever.

Sounds of his mother's crying awaken Arnold. He puts on his bathrobe and walks down the hall to his parents' bedroom. He's hesitant to intrude; it's nearly 11 p.m. But Fay's crying continues, and he knocks. There's no response but he enters anyway. "I'm sorry for bothering you, but I was worried when I heard Mom." Mort gestures towards a chair, and Arnold sits down.

"We don't know what to do, Arnie," Mort begins. "I try to hold my temper, but I can't get over my anger at your brother. And every time I blow up at him, it only makes things worse—for me, for him, and most of all for your mother."

Fay looks up. Her eyes are swollen and red and she holds tissues in both hands. "I think it's different for each of us. Your father can't get past his anger at Nathan, and I can't stop being worried and sad—about what happened to his career, what happened to his marriage, and especially the way he's been separated from his daughter. It's a heartbreak your father and I understand all too well." She looks away and reaches for more tissues. "What worries me most is that he just doesn't seem to have any direction now. He doesn't work, he doesn't study or write anymore. We hear rumors...from friends. They mean well, most of them anyway...that Nathan has a girlfriend with a bad reputation, that he plays arcade games, just like you all did as teenagers. But he's 36 years old! He has a child! Things can't keep going this way..." She starts to cry again. "I worry about him all the time."

"Nate will find himself," Arnold says, desperate to make them feel better. "You'll see. The divorce from Holly...I think he's over that, but he's always depressed about this horrible, 5000-mile separation from Ellen. That can't be helped right now. I can only give you the same advice I give to him when he laments the state of his relationship with you." Arnold hesitates. "And especially you, Dad, if I'm frank. Be patient, try not to react to the things he does or says that bother you. It's pretty standard advice." He pauses again, collecting himself. "But there's a legacy of love and closeness in our family. Things will get better. This too shall pass and all that. And I have to say that you shouldn't worry about his relationship with Esther O'Connell... that's her name, the woman your friends say has such a bad reputation. I've never met a better, more decent person. She's really good for Nate. With time, and once you get to know her, I'm sure you'll come to see her and their relationship the way I do."

They sit together for some time without speaking. Finally, it's Fay who breaks the silence. "You're right, Arnold. Of course you're right. No family could be closer than we are, or used to be, anyway. An hour doesn't go by that I don't remember something that we experienced together. Until recently...Deborah's death," her voice catches, "Nathan's troubles...the memories were mostly happy. How special our Deborah was, how devoted to each other you all were, how you and Nathan—you've always been more than brothers, much more than brothers."

"Believe it or not," Morton offers, "I have those memories, too. I know you both think I dwell on the bad ones, the ones about Deborah's agony and Nathan's decline and long absence, and lately I guess it's true." He pauses, looks down, then looks back up at them. "I wish I could get back to remembering more of the nice times, but your brother makes that hard to do. You, Arnie, have always been more of a known quantity, hard-working and dependable. You might have had a slower start than your brother, but you've persisted and made up for any lost time. Your mother and I are very proud of you. I want you to know that. Very proud. Your brother..."

Mort sighs and shakes his head, "well, we know what happened. But he was never predictable. He has a stubborn streak, which is his greatest strength and weakness. You never know what he'll do when he digs in his heels, or which direction he'll take. It's always been like that. Early on the direction was positive. It took him to Harvard and success. But that's not so anymore, his direction hasn't been positive for a long time." He pauses and looks at Arnold. "You know him the best. What's your opinion of what I'm saying?"

"I don't think I'll ever understand how our lives took such different directions. I ask myself this a lot. Is it all a matter of character, of personality? Back in our childhood, adolescence, and early manhood, the sure bet for success would have been on the brilliant Nate." Arnold stops, grimacing at some memory. "You know that," he continues. "It was just as sure a bet as any predictions against my becoming the more accomplished twin. But that's not how it's turning out. Looking back, I do think it comes down to our personality differences. We're polar opposites. My interest, from the start, has been reading and memorizing history, other people's history. I crave the structure, clear chronologies, seamless sequences, and predictability that history gives me. Nate creates his own history," he laughs, "always trying something new, coloring outside the lines. And it always seemed to me that he thrives on surprise, even confusion. He won't follow a plan or be on time or finish anything he doesn't want to do. I fear surprise. It's my enemy. Everything with me has to be planned and go as planned. I'm driven to finish whatever I start, whether or not I chose to do it, whether or not I wanted to do it. I have to see everything through to its end."

Arnold stops, then looks at Mort. "I'm sorry. I got carried away. To answer your question, Dad, about how I see our differences. I live by a checklist. Nate lives by passions and impulses."

Fay picks up the theme. "I could tell the contrast between the two of you in all sorts of ways, and at every age. Lots of examples come to mind." She takes a breath and smiles, relieved to be entering these memories. "The earliest is when you were two years old. I was pushing you in a stroller along the boardwalk, Arnold—you started walking very late and were timid about taking chances. But Nathan—Nathan kept running ahead. It was hard to get him to stop. He was such a handful. But I never had to worry about you. And I remember when you both used to roller skate around the block with the Goldberg kids, our neighbors when we lived on 12th Avenue."

"I remember those skating parties like they were yesterday," Arnold says. "The sidewalks were fairly level and smooth most of the way around the block, except for a stretch of 20 or so feet on 13th Avenue just before it met E Street. The pavement there was a different texture from the rest, much more pitted and rougher. Remember?" Animated, he speaks faster. "Zooming down 13th from Main Street, the Goldbergs and I would always be careful to stop before this stretch and slowly clomp across the adjacent grass before continuing down E, because you'd be moving fast and had to take care to control your momentum. I would begin dragging my feet to slow my speed before I got to the bad stretch. Then I'd wait at the corner for Nate, who came careening down 13th, screaming with crazy pleasure as he went faster and faster. From the time we began to skate, and it became clear that Nate was not going to follow the same cautions the Goldbergs and I did, my job was to signal him if a car was approaching the intersection. If I raised my arm, Nate would somehow figure out a way to stop, always at the last moment, sometimes by skating onto the grass bordering the sidewalk, sometimes by purposely falling on his bottom, a maneuver I found incredibly daring, but also incredibly stupid for an otherwise smart kid." The parents are laughing now. "The same daring-but-stupid evaluation applied when I didn't raise my arm, which meant that Nate, like a tiny bronco buster, would go flying off one curb, cross E Street, and crash into the opposite curb. Usually he crossed the street upright and unscathed. The exceptions could be frightening, like the time he slid across the asphalt on his chin. At the doctor's, I was in the corner trying not to faint, and you held Nate down while Dr. Schimmelman picked out the asphalt flakes embedded in his left cheek and put in 12 stitches to close the wound. When Nate's not wearing a beard, the scar is still visible. It reminds me of a mountain range's peaks and valleys." He laughs. "Mount Kirinski."

Now Morton joins the reminiscences. *(He looks happy,* Arnold thinks. *Happy.)* "God knows we would try to discipline him, but Nathan had little tolerance for authority, ours or anyone else's. I remember the Hebrew school incident, when your class was preparing for *bar mitzvah* at the Jewish community center on 11th Avenue next to the synagogue. Rabbi Steinman himself was your teacher. The rabbi told your mother and me that, with one exception, the class listened attentively as he explained the significance of confirmation. The exception, of course, was Nathan."

"I know the situation you're talking about," Arnold says. "I can remember the rabbi's lecture that day almost word for word. And I definitely remember what happened next." Arnold stands and inflates his chest. *"'You are all twelve years old,'* the rabbi began. *'Until now, you have not been required to observe the commandments of our faith, commandments that have defined our people, the people of Israel, for thousands of years. Soon, however, that will change. When you complete the bar mitzvah ceremony, you will be obligated—publicly, in the full view of your relatives, your friends, and the whole community—you will be obligated to follow the commandments. But don't think that bar mitzvah is only about what is required of you. It is also about certain rights that you will have as adult Jews: the right to lead services, to count as part of a minyan, the quorum of ten for prayer, to enter into contracts, to testify in religious courts—and to marry and raise a family. According to bar mitzvah's meaning in Hebrew, you will become 'Sons of the Commandments,' and therefore...'"* Arnold exhales, his mimed pomposity over.

"Rabbi Steinman stopped and looked towards the back of the room, where Nate was sitting. The rest of us looked down, knowing what would come next, our embarrassment excruciating. 'So, Nathan,' the rabbi said. 'What do you think you are doing?'

"You know Nate. Always straightforward, he didn't hesitate to answer the question as it was posed. 'Eating peanuts,' he responded. He didn't argue in the least when Steinman told him to leave. Nor did he smile, smirk, show surprise, protest, or ask to be forgiven. He just left, looking much as he might have appeared if class had ended on a normal note."

"Your brother always did march to his own drummer," Morton says, his facial expression somewhere between a grimace and a smile.

Now that these memories of Nathan's antics have been dislodged, his parents and brother aren't ready to stop sharing stories. Morton especially seems to be enjoying the anecdotes. "You realize, don't you," Arnold says, "that Nate's anti-authority streak wasn't limited to interactions with big shots like Rabbi Steinman. It was entirely democratic and applied to any authority figure: clergy, coaches, youth group leaders, teachers, you name it. He just didn't give a damn about rules or expectations other than those he might have created and chosen for himself. I think that's what drove the authorities crazy. They could tell he really didn't care who they were or what they thought."

"I know your mother and I often tore our hair out trying to get Nathan to follow our rules—which we thought were part of our duty to our kids and pretty reasonable. But he obviously disagreed." Morton pauses. "Okay, I'll admit it. These shenanigans of his have got me interested. Your brother has never been boring, that much I can say."

Arnold jumps to take advantage of the opening, hoping these affectionate anecdotes about Nate will evoke a corresponding return to affection from Morton. "I'm thinking of the time our Little League baseball team, Kiwanis, was playing VFW. I know you often came to our games, Dad, but I can't recall if you were at this one. Anyway, Nate and I were 12 at the time. It was our last season. We had hit the age limit. Both of us were starters. I was the catcher, which suited me. It's not the most glamorous position, but you have to be dependable pitch by pitch. Nate, though, was the flashy center fielder who might make a spectacular catch on one play and an inexcusable error on the next. It was the same on offense. I was usually good for a single or a walk. Patience and deliberativeness were my characteristic strengths. But Nate—he was as inconsistent at the plate as he was on defense." Arnold assumes a batter's stance and knocks dirt off imaginary cleats with an imaginary bat. He has his parents laughing. "He might blast a homer in one at bat, stretch a single into a dare-devil triple the next time up, then get picked off base because he wasn't paying attention. After he got picked off a third time within a span of four games, our coach, an otherwise tolerant policeman named Jim Cleary—remember him? —finally blew his stack. Nate was on second base with two outs and our best hitter, Stanley Paduano, at bat—'Stanley the Manly,' we used to call him, our local variation," Arnold explains to his mother, "of the great St. Louis Cardinals player Stan 'the Man' Musial. Anyway, 'What's wrong with you, Kirinski?' Cleary screamed at Nate. 'You just wasted a chance for our team to score, to win. I don't mind mistakes, provided you try. But I hate it when you space out and don't even try to tag up. You're benched.'

"When a player is benched...well, you know, he's supposed to stay on the bench. It's a punishment for bad play and lasts until the coach believes the player has learned his lesson. It's a standard part of the game. But standard and Nathan would not co-exist. He picked up his glove and gym bag and started walking away.

"'Where do you think you're going?'" Coach Cleary yelled.

"Nate turned to face the coach. 'Home,' he said, and walked away."

Fay is laughing so hard she has trouble catching her breath. Mort is shaking his head, but smiling. Arnold continues with another story, relieved to see their moods lifting. "And then the next year, when we were 13, you gave us permission to attend that week-long jamboree with our Boy Scout troop in the Kittatinny Mountains, way up northwest in Sussex County. Remember?" His parents both nod. "The senior patrol leader, a militaristic kid named Glenn Davies, kept harassing one of the new scouts, an 11-year-old whose name I can't remember, by telling him he wasn't allowed to pee or poop until he secured a latrine pass. 'How do I get one?' asked the newbie. 'You'll have to ask around,' Davies told him, knowing of course that there was no such pass. Initiation rituals were not particularly unusual treatment for a new scout, a Tenderfoot. But Davies refused to relent for nearly two days, even when the kid begged him to use the latrine. 'I can't hold it any longer,' he cried." Arnold hobbles around the room, his thighs scrunched together. "Finally, Nate took the kid by the hand and led him to merciful relief. Davies was furious.

"'Who the hell do you think you are?' he confronted Nate. 'His initiation isn't finished yet.'

"Nate was totally unintimidated. He looked directly at Davies, who was 16, the oldest and also biggest kid in the troop. 'Your initiation is stupid,' Nate said. 'It was hurting him. You were hurting him. It needed to stop.' Nate stood there, continuing to look at Davies until Glenn walked away, muttering something about assholes...Sorry for the language, Mom, but that's what I remember. Anyway, that was Nate's last scouting event, by his own choice. When I asked him why he was quitting, he said, 'I don't like it anymore.' Truth be told, I didn't like it anymore, either. But I believed you just couldn't drop something you had signed up for because you didn't like it. Unless you were Nate."

"I like that story," Fay says. "It reminds me of how proud we were of Nathan. Not just for the things he accomplished with his brain but for his character, his morality." Morton doesn't say anything. He looks pensive.

"I'm going on too long. It's getting late. I'd better stop."

"No, please don't," says Fay. She looks at Morton, who nods in agreement.

"I could keep going on and on about Nate and his quirks and the differences between us," Arnold says, "but I'll stop after telling you two incidents that in my mind are closely related, although they happened ten years apart. The first one happened in second grade at Belmar Grammar School. Nate and I were in art class, Nate's favorite and my least favorite subject. The teacher, a pleasant and encouraging woman named Miss Galloway—Remember her? She lived by herself in that rooming house on C Street between 4th and 5th—told us to draw our favorite bird and color it in. I took the path of least resistance with a stationary cardinal, which, at least in my rendition, only required a solid red crayon with no other subtleties. Nate, meanwhile, blasted out an in-flight hawk embellished with a fantastic mix of pure colors and invented shadings that a bird of paradise would have envied, some recognizable in nature but others that I'm sure only existed in his mind. When I glanced over at his work in progress, I remember thinking that I, at least, could never associate his colors—orange, fuchsia, amber, violet, what have you—with any real bird.

"After looking over his shoulder for a while as he worked, Miss Galloway said, 'It's beautiful, Nathan, really beautiful.' Nate kept working. I couldn't tell if he was listening to her or not. Probably not, is my guess. He definitely could concentrate when he liked what he was doing. After another minute, she interrupted him to ask if she could put the drawing on an easel so they could both look at it together. Nate didn't agree or object, which she apparently took for agreement and picked up the drawing. She called the class over to the easel.

"'Nathan has made a beautiful drawing,' she told us. 'All the shapes and colors he has imagined are interesting. But,' she continued, 'it's not really a bird like we can see in nature, is it?' She took a black crayon from the pocket of her artist's smock and began touching up Nate's work to make the hawk's shape more recognizable. Then she applied a variety of other crayons that made the hawk's colors more like you'd expect them to be in nature. To me, the drawing was looking a whole lot better with her changes.

"Miss Galloway finished her touch ups and smiled. All of the students smiled. We liked what she had done. Then she turned to Nate. 'What do you think, Nathan?' she asked, probably expecting him to be as happy with the new work as the rest of us.

"'It wasn't your hawk. It was mine.' He took the drawing off the easel, tore it in pieces, dropped the pieces in a trash can, and walked out of the room."

Arnold stops. "You said there were two more anecdotes," Morton says, "and that they're connected. What's the second one?"

"Ten years after the art class incident, Nate and I were in the same senior English class at Asbury High. The teacher was Mrs. Herkimer—I'm sure you remember her. She had been Deb's teacher, too. She could be quite a crusty, grumpy person. Rumors were that she was an alcoholic, and that she kept a bottle of booze in her desk drawer. But anyway, Mrs. Herkimer assigned us all to write a short story. The subject was up to each of us, and I have no recollection of what I wrote, much less what anyone else wrote. But I do remember what happened a week later when she returned the stories.

"'Nathan Kirinski's story is quite good,' she began. 'The best in the class.' This didn't come as a surprise to any of us. 'But,' she went on, 'the ending doesn't quite work. So I want each of you to take a copy of what Mr. Kirinski wrote and come back next week with your own ending. You, too,' she nodded at Nathan.

"The following week, Mrs. Herkimer had each of us read our revised endings out loud. She turned to Nate last. 'Please read your new ending, Mr. Kirinski.'

"'My ending is the same as it's always been.'

"Mrs. Herkimer was not pleased. 'The assignment was for everyone—I repeat, everyone, including you—to come up with a better ending. Explain yourself.'

"'My original ending is what the story requires. I certainly can't come up with anything better, even if I wanted to, which I don't. And nothing I've heard from anyone else comes close. Besides, it's my story, from start to finish. Other people have their own stories. A story shouldn't ever be a group project.'

"Mrs. Herkimer glared at Nate and then, to the other students' relief, dismissed the class. If rumors about our teacher's having a bottle of liquor in her desk drawer are true, I remember thinking, I can understand why she's letting us out early.

"I don't recall what happened after the second grade or 12th grade incidents, whether Nate was disciplined or whatever. Both times, though, to me he was like a creature from outer space, despite his being my twin. Both times, I had to wonder how much I truly understood him. But those weird and funny and wonderful quirks of his just made me love him more."

Arnold stands. "It's late."

"Thank you, Arnold," Morton says. "You made the Sabbath better for us. Although," he snorts, "I wouldn't exactly call it a day of rest."

Arnold walks over and hugs each of his parents before leaving their bedroom. He lingers for a moment in the hallway after closing the door.

"Okay," he overhears his father say. "Okay already, Fay. I'll try. I promise."

Arnold's alarm clock goes off at 5. He lies in bed for a few minutes listening through the open window to the waves rolling onto shore three blocks away. Then he showers, quietly leaves the house so he won't wake his parents, drives to Asbury, parks next to Wesley Lake, and opens the diner a few minutes before six.

He eats a quick breakfast before the steady stream of customers that is usual on Saturday mornings in the summer begins to arrive. He repeats the basic cook, serve, take money, and clean up routine through lunch, and by two o'clock things are quiet enough for him to resume work on his transcriptions. Around 3 he's happy to be interrupted by Nate and Esther O'Connell, who join him at the counter. Lucky Nate, Arnold thinks as he takes in Esther's thick black hair, hazel eyes, clear skin, angular features, and shapely figure. All of that, plus her extraordinary kindness and authenticity. Then he catches himself, concerned that his admiration will be too obvious.

"We're sorry to interrupt your studies, Arnie," says Esther. "It's my fault. I really wanted to see you."

"I'm glad you stopped by," says Arnold, as he pours three mugs of coffee. "And don't worry that you're keeping me from anything. It's busywork that I can do any time. How have you been, Esther? What have you been up to since I saw you last weekend?"

"There wouldn't be much to tell if last night hadn't happened. Nate and Sid Hamlin had a big pinball-machine match on Royal Flush. It was amazing to watch and went down to the wire."

"So who won? It had to be Nate. No one can outplay him on Royal Flush."

Esther looks at Nate, who takes up the story. "Sid won. It was close, but he was just too good. Last night."

Arnold notes the pause before "last night" and decides not to pursue it. There must be more to the story. He'll ask Nate about it another time. Instead he changes the topic to something he had wanted to say to Nate but had no chance to after the abortive Sabbath dinner. "Speaking of last night...I realize how upset you must have been with what happened, what Dad said and all..."

"It happened, Arnie. Water under the bridge, over the dam, whatever. Wherever water goes. Talking about it isn't going to change the situation."

"Just hear me out, just for a minute, and then I'll let it go. It's the same advice I've offered before. Keep trying, be patient, try not to react to Dad's anger and sarcasm. He does love you. But you hurt him, and it will take time for him to get past that. But he will. Don't give up on him. And don't give up on yourself. You're home now. You've got Esther. You've got me. And you have our folks, even if it doesn't feel like they're in your corner these days. You've been through a lot. You have your own healing to do, your own balance to find. But I know it will all fall together. I'm sure of it. You'll see."

Arnold stops talking, sure that Nate, and probably Esther, too, must think he's blathering. Be patient. Keep trying. Dad loves you. Blah blah blah. "I'm sorry," he tells Nate. "I wish I knew how to help."

"You help all the time, Arnie. Now it's up to me."

Arnold closes the diner after lunch on Sunday and drives back to the city. Miriam doesn't come over that night, but that's not unusual. She has her own place and her own doctoral research going on in the anthropology department. He works for a couple of hours on his dissertation, heats up a Stouffers mac & cheese, and watches TV until bedtime.

He spends all of Monday in the history department at Columbia, reviewing his progress with the faculty on his dissertation committee and meeting with undergraduates who drop by to discuss their term papers for the summer course on research methods he helps teach as part of his assistantship. Whenever he has a spare moment in between he returns to his research on the Khazars.

He feels fortunate to be where he is, to be doing what he's doing. On his walk back from lunch at a nearby café, he wonders at the irony of his life, or more accurately its irony in relation to the way Nate's life has turned out. Nate was the prodigy with unlimited prospects; Arnold was the consensus dullard headed for whatever pedestrian work might happen along on his way to succeeding Mort as proprietor of the Carousel Diner. Nate was like a shooting star, incandescent and spectacular. Even his Hebrew name, *Natan*, reflected this: "gift," or "giver" of prophecy, the leading-edge seer through whom God first delivered the Messianic promise of an eternal kingdom based on King David's descendants. And like a shooting star, his brilliance was short-lived. Arnold, by contrast, was a plodder, a painfully slow starter who was always bringing up the rear. While Nathan went off to Ivy League glory, Arnold could only get admitted to Monmouth College in nearby Long Branch; in the 1950s and '60s, few were ever rejected there. He even got turned down by Rutgers, the state university, which at the time had to accept any New Jersey high school graduate with marginally decent grades. In retrospect, not making the cut likely spared Arnold, since Rutgers was notorious for flunking out a lot of the freshman class to compensate for having had to accept so many kids. From the family's perspective, it was just as well that he ended up at Monmouth so he could help his father at the diner.

His landing at Monmouth also had important long-term effects that might never have happened had he matriculated elsewhere. One day between classes, he read an announcement on a bulletin board about opportunities to study abroad, including in Israel. He can still visualize the flyer that caught his attention, a panoramic view of the Temple Mount and the Old City walls of Jerusalem at sunset. "*Jerusalem the Golden*," the legend read. "*Imagine yourself as a student here, where ancient history is alive every day.*" There was little competition for this sort of thing, at least at Monmouth, back in the 1960s. He applied, was accepted, and even won a travel grant to pay most of his expenses thanks to an encouraging history professor and a recommendation from Belmar's rabbi, Aharon Steinman.

Thus Arnold got to spend his junior year at the Hebrew University in Jerusalem. The romantic come-on from the flyer on Monmouth's bulletin board turned out to be true, although in a somewhat inverted way. Whether ancient history seemed alive every day in the Holy City depended on one's imaginative capacity. What was not imaginary was that Arnold came alive, socially and intellectually, in Jerusalem.

It was there that he had his first serious love affair. Her name was Sinaiya, a native-born Israeli and pre-med student at Hebrew University. They walked the streets of the city together, studied together, and eventually slept together. Although her English was excellent, Sinaiya insisted on their speaking Hebrew. "You must have Hebrew to really study Jewish history," she would challenge him. Mainly thanks to Sinaiya, by the time Arnold was scheduled to return to America he was reasonably fluent in modern Hebrew, and he was sure that her encouragement, along with his formal coursework and some residual knowledge from Belmar's Hebrew school, had a lot to do with his fast progress toward literacy in biblical Hebrew.

And she had inspired more than his linguistic proficiency. "I love you, Sinaiya," he told her as they sat together in an airport lounge waiting for his flight to be called. "I really do. And so I was thinking—maybe I'll transfer to Hebrew University. You know, as a regular student. And we could live together. And..."

"I do love you, too, Arnold," she interrupted him. "But we're too young for anything more right now. Years of medical school are ahead for me, maybe graduate school for you...Let's just stay friends, okay?"

"Okay," he agreed, disappointed but knowing she was right.

"Please, don't look so sad. Being friends is important, especially to an Israeli. *Chaver* is more than a friend. It's a comrade, and sometimes a lover. So I have this gift for you, a gift of our friendship," she continued, handing him an original edition of Jacob Weingreen's authoritative *A Practical Grammar for Classical Hebrew*. It was inscribed "To my dearest Arnold—Something to remember me by. And to remember yourself by.... Love, Sinaiya"

They have stayed in touch, although neither of them holds the expectation that their future relationship will remain other than friendly.

Jerusalem gave life to Arnold's mind as well. A class taught by the famous scholar Gershom Scholem reinforced Arnold's love of history generally and ignited a specific passion for Jewish history. He wrote a couple of good term papers under Professor Scholem's tutelage and made some extra spending money helping Scholem catalog his Kabbalah archives in the National Library, site of the world's largest Jewish studies collection. Professor Scholem's subsequent recommendation was what got Arnold into grad school at Columbia. He got lucky again when, on the considerable strength of Scholem's reference letter, he was accepted as an advisee by Tibor Halasi-Kun, a leading scholar on Turkic culture and a co-founder of Columbia's Department of Near and Middle-East Studies. Through Dr. Halasi-Kun, Arnold has studied with such Khazar specialists as Anatoli Khazanov, Omeljan Pritsak, Peter Golden, and even D. M. Dunlop, the renowned Eurasianist and one of the fathers of Khazar studies. And now, against all early expectations, including his own, here he is: Arnold Kirinski, a budding Khazar scholar himself and, if all continues to go as planned, soon to be Dr. Arnold Kirinski, the recipient of a Ph.D. in history from one of the world's great universities.

By Wednesday afternoon, Arnold still hasn't heard from Miriam. This is unusual. In the three years they've been dating, they meet most days for lunch or at least coffee. When their schedules permit, they have dinner together and stay the night in one or the other's apartment. Arnold could call her but figures she must be busy; she'll get in touch when she can.

At 4:00 p.m., Arnold leaves his small office in Fayerweather Hall and heads towards one of his favorite watering holes, Buster's Café, less than a mile's walk south down Amsterdam Avenue. The street is alive with summer-session students discussing their courses and plans for the coming weekend. Patrons spill out to the sidewalk tables all along his route from 117th Street to the café between 103rd and 104th. He loves this part of university life. In fact, he loves all of it. His pace picks up as he feels a rush of delight—with the day, with the place, with his work and his life.

After coffee and a croissant he walks back up Amsterdam. He'll finish his work for the day and then, if he still hasn't heard from Miriam, he decides he'll phone her after all. Whether or not they get together this evening, he wants to know how she's doing.

Arnold stays on the west side of Amsterdam while he walks north. As he passes the Cathedral of St. John the Divine, he sees Miriam on the other side of the street. She is a half-block ahead, also walking north. But she's not alone. Her arm encircles a man's waist; his arm is around her shoulders. Arnold follows them as they turn right onto West 113th Street, cross Morningside Park, and go up Manhattan Avenue to 118th Street. He watches them enter the apartment building at 444 Manhattan Avenue. Where Miriam lives.

Arnold waits outside the apartment building until he sees them leave an hour later and follows them as they walk for ten minutes to the subway station at 116th Street. He stays hidden behind a pillar on the platform until a train comes. The couple is too engrossed with each other to notice him watching them from an adjacent car. Closer up now and under the car's bright lights, Arnold recognizes the man, a young instructor in the anthropology department whom he has met at a couple of recent parties. Arnold curses his naiveté; from Miriam's casual introduction, he had no inkling of anything between the two, other than their departmental affiliation.

Twenty minutes later, Miriam and the man get out at the 14th Street Station in Greenwich Village. At West 12th Street they walk south for five minutes and enter the Village Vanguard, a jazz club on 7th Avenue South. The marquis says that the trumpeter Blue Mitchell, a favorite of Arnold's, is performing. But tonight he's not here to listen to jazz. As he stands near the club's entrance, he's not at all sure why he's here, or more to the point what he should do now that he is here.

Arnold goes inside and stands at the bar until he spots Miriam and her friend, who are entwined together in a booth along a wall. The show hasn't started yet. Arnold walks over to the booth. "What the hell is going on, Miriam?"

"Arnold…. Shit." She stands up, takes his arm, and pulls him towards the door. "Let's talk outside. Please."

They walk a short way down the street. "So I'm asking you again: What the hell is going on?" He gestures towards the Village Vanguard. "What are you doing here, Miriam? With him?"

"I'm sorry, Arnie. I didn't want you to find out this way. I was waiting for the right time to tell you."

"Find out what? Tell me what?" He stops. "God, what an idiot I am." He looks down at the ground, shaking his head, and then looks at Miriam. "You were waiting to tell me that we're done. Right?"

Miriam nods. "I really like you, Arnie. I…"

Arnold doesn't let her finish. He starts to walk away, then turns back. "I should ask you why, Miriam. But I don't want to know. I'm afraid to know. Anyway…I'll be in New Jersey this weekend. I want you to pick up any of your stuff you have at my place and drop off any of my things—toothbrush, cloths, books, whatever—that are in your apartment. You can slide the key under the door when you're done."

He turns away again, this time for good, struggling to collect himself so he won't fall apart on the subway. *Miriam. Some say the meaning of the name in Hebrew is mistress of the sea. Some say it means wished-for child. That's what I chose to think: Miriam, the one for whom I have wished. Others say it means sea of sorrow.*

Arnold takes the train back to his apartment and labors through most of the night and all of Thursday on his dissertation, compartmentalizing his tasks from his feelings. He drives to Asbury Friday morning and opens the Carousel at the usual time. Nathan enters the diner in mid-afternoon and seats himself at the counter next to Arnold, who interrupts his transcriptions to greet his brother.

"How was your week?"

"Better than the last one. No lost pinball matches, no battles with Morton. And you, Arnie? How was your week?"

"Definitely worse than the last one."

Nathan smiles but turns serious when he sees that Arnold isn't smiling back. He waits for his brother to say more. "Miriam dumped me," Arnold says and gives Nathan a blow by blow account of the Village Vanguard episode. "I'm still trying to take it all in. Three years with this woman I've loved, and who I thought loved me. Christ, just a few days before she's in bed with me! The worst of it was that I was so passive—that I didn't scream at her, or punch out her new boyfriend. Or even ask her for an explanation. All because I was too inhibited to make a scene and risk making a fool of myself at the vaunted Vanguard. Now I'll never know. Was I too nerdy, too homely, lousy in bed?" He shakes his head and smiles. "Do you think it's because I'm not an anthropologist?"

They sit for a while without speaking. Nathan despairs over Arnold's heartbreak. He cannot stand seeing him suffer. Still, he's relieved to see the trace of humor and responds in kind in an attempt to distract his brother from his pain. "I never liked the Village Vanguard," Nathan says. "I'm more of a Café Wha? type of guy, myself." Arnold laughs. He knows that Nathan hates the tourist-filled basement club on the corner of MacDougal Street and Minetta Lane, the Greenwich Village music scene's equivalent, at least from the iconoclastic Nathan's perspective, of a Jersey Shore arcade overrun by Bennies on a Saturday night. Happy that his joking ploy has worked, Nathan again turns serious. "I never told you this, Arnie. After Holly and Ellen left for Alaska, I spent a lot of my long disappearance in Israel—I know, I know. Given your background there, I should have told you that, at least—but the point is that I had a love affair in Israel and got some of my self-respect back. I guess what I'm getting at is maybe you should do something like that. Contact that Israeli woman you used to tell me about—Sinaiya?—and go see her. Go back to Jerusalem."

Arnold often chides Nathan about his impulsivity, his way of making major decisions on the fly, giving no real thought to consequences. Advice of this sort would ordinarily be anathema to the circumspect Arnold. But not this time. This time he realizes that Nathan is right.

"I'll do it. Sinaiya and I have corresponded steadily since I was a student there. I know she isn't married...and anyway she might not be interested in starting something with me again..." He stops himself. It's one thing to be impulsive, another to be stupid. "I'm getting way ahead of myself," he tells Nate, who is grinning now at Arnold's uncharacteristic lack of deliberation. "But whether or not Sinaiya's in the picture, I agree. I should go to Israel. The summer session is almost over at Columbia, and my dissertation is ahead of schedule. I can take several weeks off before the fall term starts, and I've got enough extra money saved from working here..." Working here. The diner. His father has come to rely on him. How can he leave during the height of tourist season?

"I know what you're thinking," Nate says. "That you can't leave Mort in the lurch. But what if I fill in for you while you're away?"

Arnold doubts that their father will accept this arrangement. But it's worth a try. "Okay. I'll bring the idea up with him tonight."

Arnold and his parents have Sabbath dinner together. Afterwards, they linger over brandy. "I've decided to go to Israel for two or three weeks," Arnold tells them, hastening to add that he has an idea for covering his shifts at the diner while he's away. "Nathan. Nathan will fill in for me." He surprises himself with the declarative force of his statement—not "Nathan can" or "Nathan might," but "Nathan will." To his further surprise, his father doesn't object.

"Well, once upon a time he could run the diner," Morton says. "He was actually quite capable. But that was a lot of years ago. You'll have to train him, Arnold, refresh his memory so that he doesn't make a mess of things. But okay. My only condition is that you do the training. Not me."

Arnold phones his brother with the news, and they agree to work together at the diner for the rest of this weekend and all of the next. During the week in between, Arnold calls Sinaiya and books his flight to Israel. Nathan completes his refresher course the following Sunday, two days before Arnold's departure. That evening, the brothers close the Carousel together.

3
Solace

ESTHER AWAKENS FIRST FROM a nap with Nathan the afternoon before his big pinball match with Sid Hamlin. *I could stay like this forever, here in this bed forever, sleeping and making love with Nathan forever, giving him pleasure, being so close, like we're part of each other. I even know when he's dreaming. I can tell he's dreaming now. I hope it's about me. I think it is. Let me make sure. Like this. It's working. He's groaning, writhing around, almost there...There.*

Nathan reaches down and pulls her towards his chest. Esther enjoys this part the most. Nathan is a large man, overweight but very strong. And his skin is so smooth; she feels as if she's sliding over softening ice. She settles against the broad, solid, safe haven of his shoulder. She turns her face to his and they kiss. "Dear Esther—you're tender and wonderful and a gift to me in my despair. Thank you for entering my dream." *He really says this. He really talks this way. I love how he speaks to me, his sweetness.* "It's the same for me," she says, "and I get such pleasure from making you happy."

But she worries that he looks unhappy now. "What's got you down?" She knows he's having troubles with his folks, who are angry at him for going away and not contacting them for two years, for not being there when his sister was dying, for missing her funeral.

"That's part of it."

"What's the rest?" she encourages him. It always seems to lift his mood when he can talk about what's bothering him. He's an emotional man who needs to express his feelings. Esther is happy that she can help him do this.

"It's pretty much my whole life. My parents are down on me, I don't have a job, my daughter is thousands of miles away. Thank God for you, Esther, and for Arnie. And for Royal Flush. At least I'm good at that. You and that machine keep me sane."

Nathan tells her that he and Sid Hamlin got maneuvered into playing a pinball match later tonight, and that he ran into a couple of old high school classmates who made him feel bad about himself. "How did they do that?" she asks.

His answer breaks her heart: "By reminding me what a success I once was, and what a failure I am now."

She does her best to cheer him up and lets him know that she'll go to the pinball match with him. "Of course I will. And I'll be with you all the way through it."

It's Saturday, the morning after the match. Nathan is exhausted, so Esther is careful not to wake him as she leaves his place. She wishes she could spend the day with him, but she's got some shopping and cleaning up to do before her shift starts at Vic's Pizzeria. She pulls in her best tips on Saturday nights in the summer. When the weather's nice, like it is today, it adds up. But at least she'll get to see Nate this afternoon, when the two of them will drop in on his brother Arnold at the Carousel Diner. Esther is very fond of Arnie. Next to Nathan, he's her favorite person in the world. *No exaggeration. The world. Because Nathan and Arnold are my world. I bet if people heard me say that out loud they'd feel sorry for me. But they shouldn't. Two close friends are way better than none, which was what I had before I met Nathan.*

Nathan's place in Ocean Grove is four miles from Esther's bungalow in South Belmar, which the local government is talking about re-naming Lake Como. Esther hopes they do. She thinks it's a much nicer name, and the lake that takes up most of the town is beautiful. It makes her happy to sit on her porch watching the ducks and swans and seagulls. It's a delight when she and Nate sit there in her two Adirondack chairs drinking coffee.

Getting to her bungalow isn't always so great for her, though, because she has to pass through Belmar. Most of Belmar's okay, but passing anywhere near the Saint Rose Parish buildings is the hard part. The church and the school actually take up quite a small area between 6th and 8th Avenues. But when the whole town is only a mile square, it's hard to avoid any area, or avoid seeing the high steeple of Saint Rose Church. Esther sees it now, and it brings back some terrible memories. It always does.

She had worked so hard to be a good girl, to follow all the rules, to obey the priests and nuns and other teachers, to make her parents proud. And up until her third year of high school, that's how things were. Then she met Richie McIlroy. Well, she didn't actually meet him then—they had known each other from the time they were little kids. They had always been friends and playmates. She liked Richie, but not like a boyfriend or anything. He was just this nice guy she grew up with. "Met up with him" is a better way of saying it.

"Hey, Esther," Richie called as they left school for the day. "Can I walk you home?"

"Sure," she said. She and Richie lived close to each other a couple of blocks from school. The McIlroys' house was on South Lake Drive, Esther's was a block further east on 8th Avenue. The McIlroys' place was pretty fancy. Richie's father owned a successful hardware store, and he had been Belmar's mayor for as long as Esther could remember.

"It's a beautiful day," Richie said as they approached her house. "Why don't we walk up to the ocean." He was right. It was beautiful. Nothing could be better than walking on the beach in Belmar on a beautiful October day. "Sure," she said again.

They took off their shoes and walked south along the water, laughing and yelling when the foam from a breaking wave went further than they expected and their feet got wet. It was cold but so much fun. Like being little kids again. At 13th Avenue they walked back towards the boardwalk. When they got next to the pavilion there Richie suddenly grabbed her hand and kissed her. It happened before she could do anything. She was too surprised. Then he pushed her back against the east wall of the Pavilion, where it meets the sand, and started pawing at her breasts. She tried to push him away, crying "Stop it! Stop it!" But he wouldn't, not until she lifted her knee hard between his legs and he fell on the sand, moaning "You bitch" over and over again. She left him there and ran down the boardwalk, shoeless. She didn't care if she got splinters. She just wanted to get home, to get away from Richie McIlroy, the childhood friend who had just assaulted her.

She didn't say anything to her parents about what had happened, or to anyone. It was Richie who did all the talking. She found that out the next day when guys kept coming up to her, whispering that they wanted to meet her after school somewhere. "You know," said one, "to have a little date." "You know," said another, more bluntly, "I'd like to do what you and Richie did. He said you're really hot. You really enjoyed it. You couldn't get enough." The day went on like that, then the next and the next and the next. Girls who had been Esther's friends stopped talking to her, just like the boys did when she rejected their advances. A girl she knew who attended Manasquan High, a public school, had loaned her a book they were reading in English class, Nathaniel Hawthorne's *The Scarlet Letter*. "No way the Saint Rose teachers will let that book into your school," her friend cautioned her, so Esther read it in secret, thinking at the time it was a good story, but old and not much related to modern life. Yet now she understood Hester Prynne, the book's heroine, and what it meant to be shunned. The difference, Esther saw, was that Hester actually did what the Puritans accused her of.

It was the same with her parents. God, that hurt. They believed the rumors, believed that she was a slut and a nympho. Richie McIlroy wouldn't lie, must have been how they saw it: the mayor's son, an altar boy, a good student, an athlete, such a nice kid. After Esther gave her side of the story, the principal and her parents continued to believe Richie's account, which was that Esther had been the one chasing him, that they dated for a while—and "Yes, we did make out," he admitted—but that Esther became jealous of his interest in another girl and was lying about what he had done just to get him in trouble. Esther was ostracized at school and had no support at home. She was so lonely and depressed. When her schoolwork suffered and she started skipping classes, the nuns came down hard—detentions, extra assignments, public scolding, and worse.

Esther tried to put up with it all, but things became impossible after she got on the bad side of Sister Mary Agnes, an older nun who apparently believed the rumors about her. The first incident was bad enough. Esther was sitting in the back row of history class, totally in her own despairing world, when she heard Sister Mary Agnes call out. "Esther O'Connell—Please answer the question I just put to the class."

"I'm sorry, Sister. I didn't hear the question. Could you repeat it, please?"

"No, I won't repeat it. I'm confident you can't answer it anyway because you didn't do the homework assignment. Am I right? Be honest."

"Yes, you're right," Esther replied. But there was no reward for honesty.

Sister Mary Agnes had her come to the front of the room. "Hold out your hands, palms up." Then she hit her with a heavy ruler, ten times across each palm. Esther had heard stories, the kids had all heard stories, of this punishment, but Esther, at least, had never witnessed it, much less experienced it. It stung, but didn't hurt that bad. What hurt was the humiliation. Which only got worse.

A week later, Sister Mary Agnes stopped her as she entered the room at the start of class. "I will not permit unkempt clothing in my classroom," she said, pointing at the skirt of Esther's school uniform.

"I'm sorry, Sister, but I don't understand..."

"Your skirt is wrinkled," the nun interrupted, indicating an iron and ironing board in the corner of the room. "I want you to take it off and iron it. Right now." This was another parochial school punishment that Esther's public school friends always teased her about. She told them it was pure fantasy; such things never happen. But Esther realized she was wrong. By now the whole class was watching, eager, she could tell, to see her shamed again. But after months of unfair treatment and punishment and damage to her very life, Esther had had enough.

"Fuck you, Sister. Go to hell," she said, in two short sentences ending her matriculation at Saint Rose High School. Esther couldn't believe she had done this. She never used language like that with anyone. And what could be worse than using it with an elderly nun, whose entire celibate life had been directed towards heaven?

But there was no taking it back, even if she wanted to. She was suspended indefinitely but didn't care. She never returned to Saint Rose after that day. The school called her parents who, mortified by what she had done and already criticizing her for any and everything since the Richie McIlroy episode, told her they wanted her out of the house as soon as she could arrange to be gone. That meant having money and a place to live, not so easy for a 17-year-old to arrange. But she managed. She got a waitressing job at Vic's, lined up some babysitting work, and rented a room with a shared bath and kitchen in a cheap boarding house in Ocean Grove. Eventually, she saved up enough to buy an old car and move to the rented bungalow in South Belmar.

A few years later, she met Nathan Kirinski.

Esther and Nathan are in Avon, sitting on a boardwalk bench overlooking the Atlantic. It's early afternoon the day after the pinball match with Sid Hamlin. On Saturdays, she and Nate are in the habit of taking the long walk from her bungalow to the Carousel Diner, where they meet Arnie for a late lunch. Avon is more or less mid-way, a convenient spot to rest. After lunch they generally go to Nate's place in Ocean Grove for a nap and a cuddle before walking back to her bungalow. All together it's an eight-mile roundtrip walk, a good one-day-a-week workout. Their daily walks are shorter the rest of the week. Nathan is trying to increase the distances to lose weight and get in shape. Esther doesn't push him one way or the other on this; she wants it to be his choice. But she's glad to see it happening. It means he's getting better, taking the initiative to get out of his funk over Holly and Ellen and his parents and his career and all his bad memories and turn his life around. Esther's issues are different, but she basically understands what he's going through.

"This is close to the spot where we first met," Nathan says. "Do you remember?"

"Of course I remember. Meeting you was the best day of my life. The best."

"I still marvel that it happened," he continues. "For me, it was pure attraction. 'Look at that gorgeous person walking my way,' I remember thinking. 'I can't let her go by without saying anything. But will I frighten her? I'm twice her size. And I can't imagine she'd find me attractive. The only physical thing we have in common is dark hair, but most of mine is on my face.' See, I was already talking myself out of taking the risk that you'd reject me. I had no self-confidence then, none at all. But the bigger risk that day was not trying to talk to you and just letting you walk away."

"It was pure attraction for me, too. Part of it was physical, but there was something more. I wasn't worried in the least by your size, or your long mane of hair—like a dark lion, I thought—or your big beard. I had been alone for ten years, ever since the high school mess I told you about. Trusting guys, or anyone really, was not something I was ready to do, even after so long a time. But there was something about you, something I wanted to know, somebody I wanted to know. It's hard to explain, and I'm not so good with words to begin with."

"For me, the attraction was also more than physical, although I'd be lying not to admit there was a whole lot of that. I swear there was an electrical current between us, and whatever the connection was I knew right away that you were the jolt I needed. It's strange. I've never been insecure about my brain, even when my self-confidence is at its lowest. But the reverse is also true when it comes to my emotions. Whenever I let my emotions and impulses lead the way the results have been terrible. But in this instance, with you—I just knew my feeling was right, that if I could just bring myself to say something to you my life would get better."

"Maybe the attraction between us is like electricity, the attraction of opposites. I have zero trust in my intelligence. I never finished high school, I wait tables in an Italian restaurant...But I do trust my gut. And my gut was saying, 'I sure hope that guy talks to me.' And you did. Right here. And my life has never been better."

They sit for a while longer without speaking. It's all been said. *We're each what the other needs,* Esther thinks. *Finally, we'll be okay.*

4
Child's Talk

ELLEN KIRINSKI, AGE SIX, plays alone in her bedroom. She lives with her mother Holly and her mother's boyfriend Warren in the Fairview neighborhood of Anchorage, Alaska. It's nine o'clock at night, late for a child her age to be awake. But this is July, and the sun doesn't set here until midnight.

Holly lies on a couch in the living room staring at the ceiling. Ellen can see her through the doorway. *Mama looks so sad*, Ellen thinks. At the far end of the trailer, she can see Warren sitting at the kitchen table drinking bourbon. Ellen knows that it's bourbon because Warren told her the drink he likes best is bourbon, and the bourbon he likes best is called Wild Turkey, and you can always tell what's inside the bottle if there's a picture of a turkey on the label. She likes looking at the picture, but she doesn't like it when Warren drinks bourbon, even Wild Turkey. He gets angry sometimes and that frightens her. And his breath smells bad, like he didn't brush his teeth. She hates it when he kisses her when he's drinking bourbon. Ellen is happy that he'll leave soon to meet his friends. When he's gone her mother will be more relaxed. Ellen hopes the grownups don't start arguing before he goes. Warren is so nice when he's not drinking bourbon. He used to play with her a lot and teach her things, like how to fish and ride her bike and catch a ball. That doesn't happen so much anymore.

"I brush my teeth every day after breakfast and supper," Ellen tells Beany and Karen. "And I try not to be angry like Warren or sad like Mommy." Beany and Karen are her two best friends. Beany Bear was her first best friend. He used to be her parents' best friend, too, when her mother and father were married. They used to talk to each other through Beany to make up after arguments. "Oh, Beany," her father would say. "I feel so bad that I yelled at Holly. I want her to know how sorry I am, and that I love her." "Me, too, Beany," her mother would answer. "I know Nathan didn't mean it," and stuff like that. Ellen wishes her mother and Warren would talk to Beany, but they don't. Warren thinks that Beany and Karen are only stuffed animals. Ellen knows they're stuffed animals, but they're not only that. During one of her phone calls with her father, who lives in New Jersey, Ellen told him she was worried that Beany would be lonely when she was at school and he didn't have anyone to talk to, and a week later Karen Rapunzel came in the mail. Ellen named her Karen Rapunzel. She looks a lot like Beany Bear but she's a girl and he's a boy. Ellen thinks Beany and Karen will get married someday, but they'll still be her best friends, and even if they don't get married they can still keep each other company and not get lonely when she's at school.

"My Daddy called a little while ago," she tells them now. "It's very late in New Jersey, he said it was after midnight, but he wanted to tell me about a game he just finished. He didn't win, but he was excited anyway and couldn't sleep. 'Remember the pinball machine I taught you to play the last time you came to Belmar?' he said, 'Royal Flush? That's the game I played against a man named Sid.' I asked my daddy if he was sorry he lost, but he said he wasn't. 'Sid is a really good player. We both played well and had fun, so it didn't matter who won.'" Ellen looks at Beany and Karen. "Daddy lost, but he wasn't sad or angry."

A little later Ellen's mother comes in to read her stories and help her get ready for bed, although Ellen can read now and change into pajamas by herself. But snuggling together before Ellen goes to sleep is one of their favorite times. And Warren is gone so her mom seems a little happier.

It's still light outside when Holly leaves the bedroom. "Goodnight, Sweetie," she says. "I know it's hard to sleep before dark, but try. Maybe you and Beany and Karen can tell each other bedtime stories."

Ellen tries to fall asleep but can't, even though the sun has finally set. She gets up and goes to find her mother, who is sitting on the couch reading. "What's the matter, little one? Can't sleep? Want me to read to you some more?"

"Could you read the story that Daddy just wrote?"

"You mean the one about building sandcastles?"

"The one about me. How I'll build sandcastles when I go to the beach with Daddy and Grandpa and Grandma and Uncle Arnie and Esther next summer. Beany and Karen want to hear it, too."

Holly agrees, and Ellen brings Beany and Karen and the story into the living room. Mother, daughter, and their two stuffed-animal friends curl up together. Holly begins to read.

Sandcastles

Ellen was good at building sandcastles. Actually, she was better than just good at it. She was one of the best sandcastle builders around.

She had had lots of practice that summer on the beach in Belmar, New Jersey, where she was spending a few weeks with her father and grandparents and Uncle Arnie and her father's friend Esther. The sand there was excellent for castles, and the ocean water came up to the same level every day so that Ellen knew just where it was safe to build.

The other kids on the beach admired Ellen for her skill. She knew exactly how to pack the sand into cans and pails and milk cartons to make the towers and walls of a castle. She knew exactly how much water to mix with the sand to make it hold together. And she used all sorts of designs, some that she drew in her mind, others that she had seen in drawings from books of fairy tales. The other kids agreed that she was the best castle builder on the beach, and even the older ones would sometimes help her gather sand and water to build her masterpieces.

One day Ellen built the most beautiful sandcastle imaginable. It had twelve towers, each with special walls for the king's soldiers to hide behind in a battle.

It had sixty windows, all very small and high so that nobody could climb inside. And it had a moat going all the way around it. Ellen even built a drawbridge with cardboard and string that she could lower over the moat, and she made bright flags for the top of each tower by taping colored pieces of paper to toothpicks. She finished it off by building a high tower with a pointed roof right in the middle of the castle. This, she decided, was where the princess would live.

Ellen worked on the wonderful castle all day. She was so busy working that she would have continued right through lunch and never missed it if her dad hadn't called her. By the time she finished, people came from all around the beach to see Ellen's creation. At the very end, she brought water in pails from the ocean and filled up the castle's moat, which she had already lined with plastic to keep the water from disappearing into the sand.

When Ellen finally stood up to look at the finished castle, all the people who had come to watch her, grownups and kids, applauded. She had never been so proud. Happy but exhausted, she had her dinner and went to bed.

Ellen slept so soundly that she never heard the fierce storm which came during the night. Many inches of rain fell, and strong winds created waves so big that the ocean water rose high above its normal level and flooded most of the beach.

When Ellen woke up early the next morning, the storm had passed. Although she could hear the sound of waves, she had no idea that there had ever been a storm at all. Her first thought was of the amazing sandcastle. She could hardly wait to run out onto the porch and look at it.

The sight that greeted her was not the one she expected. Instead of a calm sea, a wide beach, and a blue sky, Ellen saw large rolling waves sweeping across the beach under a gray sky. And instead of a sandcastle, she saw swirling pools of water.

At first, Ellen felt a terrible sadness. Her sandcastle, the best she had ever built, was gone. She was standing there crying when her dad found her. He tried to comfort her, saying, "I know how you feel, Sweetheart. It was a lovely castle. But it had to disappear sometime. At least we all got to see it."

Ellen hardly listened. Her sadness had passed, replaced by anger towards the pounding ocean. "I hate you for taking my beautiful castle," she cried. "I hate you."

Her anger stayed with her. Nothing anybody could say or do seemed to help ease her mind at all. Her father and grandparents and Uncle Arnie and Esther were all troubled to see her that way, as if she were at war with the sea. Every morning she went down to the beach and built sandcastles, each one bigger and farther back on the beach than the one she had built before it. But the bad weather remained, and each day the ocean came and took Ellen's sandcastles away.

Even though she kept losing to the water, Ellen would not stop fighting. She kept building. The people at the beach were amazed as they watched her. Each day her castles got better and better, until one day she made one that was every bit as wonderful as the one with twelve towers, sixty windows, a moat, a drawbridge, and a tower for the princess that had first been destroyed by the storm. If anything, it was better than the earlier castle, because it was stronger and larger and higher. And this one was built a lot farther back on the beach, too, which everyone hoped would keep it safe from the water.

The bad weather passed, and the castle stood for many days. Each morning, Ellen and her friends would put new water in the moat, straighten the flags, and fix any places that the breeze may have disturbed during the night. Ellen's mood seemed to change with the weather, much to the relief of her family and friends. She became her usual cheerful self, working all day on her castles, as well as fixing up her special one.

But after a while she began to lose interest in building and fixing. Ellen's father thought she was losing interest in sandcastles altogether. This surprised him, since she had always been so serious about them. As long as she was happy, however, he wasn't worried. "Ellen's growing up," he told Esther and Arnie. "She's finding other things to do."

In fact, Ellen had a lot going on in her mind. Her problem was the stupendous castle, the second one, she had built many days before. It was still standing, and whenever Ellen saw it she thought that she would never again build one as beautiful. The other castles she built never seemed to be as good. After a while, she didn't even like looking at the stupendous one anymore.

Instead, she found herself picturing the first great castle she had built, the one the ocean had taken away in the storm. In her memory, that castle was the best, the one that gave her the most pleasure. When she thought of it, she grew excited and interested in building castles again that would be just as good or even better. But whenever she began to build, she saw the stupendous one standing nearby. She stopped what she was doing and walked away. The pleasant, soft-and-grainy feel of the sand couldn't make her keep building, and the pictures of new castles disappeared from her mind.

One morning, Ellen walked out on the porch and was greeted by the sight and sound of huge waves. There had been another storm in the night, her dad told her, and he hoped that Ellen would not be too sad because her great castle, which had stood for so many days, was gone. Ellen didn't say anything, but her father thought it was strange when he saw his daughter smile at the news that her second big castle had disappeared. "I love the ocean," she said, almost in a whisper.

By the next morning, the sky was clear, the water level was lower, and the sand was dry. Ellen began again to build sandcastles, each one different from the others and from the ones that had gone before.

When Ellen kisses her mother goodnight, she sees tears on Holly's cheeks. Ellen wonders why "Sandcastles" would make her mother sad. Back in her bedroom, she falls asleep thinking about next summer.

5
Writing

I ENJOYED WRITING "SANDCASTLES" for Ellen. After years of academic books and articles, with their imposed logic and organization and conventions and emphasis on intellectualizing, it was a pleasure just to tell a story. I decided to do more of this kind of writing, to relate experiences—actual and imagined, my own and others'. Beyond "Sandcastles," my motivation for doing this had two unexpected catalysts.

I detest my former classmates and nemeses Alexander Garfield and Charles Rossiter, né Albert Greenbaum and Kalman Rosenzweig. All they stand for and have always stood for offends me—money and status above all, above aesthetics or morality or basic human sympathy. I often challenge myself: Deep down, is my dislike of them the sour grapes of envy at their material success, especially now as I try to rise out of my slough of career despond? No, I don't believe it's that; I despised them even when I was a star at Harvard. But I have to give credit where it's due, however begrudgingly. The stable of celebrities they have attracted to their talent agency is impressive. They couldn't have achieved that if they didn't know what they were doing.

So I've decided to take the advice they offered that day I ran into them on the boardwalk. I'll write again, but this time it won't be anything like my three books of philosophy. This time I'll keep a notebook of stories and reflections about my life. The saga of my early success and sudden collapse is intriguing—and mystifying, even to me. Maybe it will sell. And whether or not it's ever read, I might learn something in the process of writing it down.

Anyway, at this stage what else do I have to do between playing pinball, hanging out with Esther, and helping out at the diner? If nothing else, Fay can at least tell her buddies at the beauty parlor that her brilliant son really is at work on another book. And someday Arnie, Esther, and Ellen might read what I write. I doubt that it will answer all the questions they must have about me—my moods, my reasons, my actions, my decisions. But it should explain a lot.

Part Two

The Inner Lives of Boys

Nathan Kirinski's Memoir
1946 – 1962

1

Provenance

I THINK AUNT ELLA'S bare feet came first as we lay on a bed in the Bronx, on Hull Avenue, near the Grand Concourse and the Fitch Sanitarium where I was born. I put Ella's white wiggly toes in my mouth. They aroused me. But is this possible? I was only two years old.

But maybe the milkman came first. I see myself standing in blue corduroys—pants, coat, hat—also in the Bronx. I remember a milk wagon, horse-drawn. I remember having to pee in the street, right on Hull Avenue, the milk wagon and horse in the background, someone scolding me for wetting my pants. I thought, how did I get to this place? Why am I here? But is this possible? I was two years old.

I remember staring at a huge desk. My mother, her name for it as ponderous as the thing itself, calls it "The Secretary." It stands in our hallway, heavy, wooden, ornate. As I stare, I feel Jewish. Could this be possible either? I was four.

The papers in The Secretary's drawers emit an intimate odor, an odor I am sure I have known before. But from where? From when? Much later, my twin brother Arnold, the historian of Judaism, tells me it's the parchment smell of *Yiddishkeit*, of Jewishness, and that every Jew recognizes it.

Children, I'm convinced, have some intuition of infinity until the adults, who have lost that intuition themselves, step in with all their good intentions to teach the child what to see and what not to see, how to think about things and what conclusions to draw. The Secretary, in addition to giving me a glimpse of my Jewish roots, where I had come from, was also my window on infinity. Where had any of us come from?

Like any child, I soon despaired of finding an answer to the general question and so reverted to more finite and manageable concerns. Where, specifically, had I come from? How did I end up here, in Belmar, New Jersey?

Europe

My grandparents would not say much about their lives before America, no matter how much Arnold and I pestered them for stories. From their silence, we thought something terrible must have happened to them back in Europe. We imagined them there, living in misery, hungry, tormented by Jew haters, praying for escape. When we asked our parents, they would only tell us that our father's family came from Russia and our mother's from Poland. Then they changed the subject. Or they whispered to each other in Yiddish.

So we began to study the history on our own. Over the years we learned quite a lot. But it was too late for many of the personal details to be known. Anyone who could have provided them was dead. True, towards the end of her life Aunt Ella, whose once sensuous toes by then had become too arthritic to wiggle, was generous with what she knew about our mother's side of the family. Our father's side, notorious among my generation of cousins for taciturnity and sarcasm, were of no help, although one of the in-laws, Uncle Joseph, a high school history teacher, was kind to tell us what he knew.

Harry was our father's father, our *zaide*. When he landed in Boston in 1890 at age 13, his official name was Herman Kirinski. He was given the nickname Harry by older laborers when he found work washing dishes in a Roxbury restaurant, an establishment he would eventually manage.

But years later in our Belmar synagogue, when our father Morton was called to say the blessings for the reading of the *Torah*, the rabbi announced him as *Mordechai ben Naftali Tsvi Ha Levi*, Morton the son of Naftali Tsvi from the tribe of Levi. "If *Zaide*'s name is Harry," we asked our father, "why does the rabbi say Naftali Tsvi?" "Because that was his name in Warsaw— Naftali Tsvi Kirinski," he answered. Now we were more confused. "But everyone always says that *Zaide* is from Russia. Warsaw is in Poland." Our father, as was his wont, never explained.

Harry married Mary Marcus in 1899, when they were both 22 years old. We don't know whether they met in the old country or in America. And if they did meet in the old country, which old country? Is our grandmother also Polish, we asked? "No," Dad said. "Your *bobbe* is from Russia." Again, he didn't bother to explain. We asked one of our older relatives to show us on a map where our grandmother had lived in Russia. She pointed to a place called Vieksniai. "The Lithuanians called it that," she told us. "The Jews called it Vexna." We looked closely at the map and saw it, a small dot on the Venta River, near the Baltic Sea and the southern border of Estonia. In big letters we read a name that was new to us, LITHUANIA. Then we noticed the western border of Russia to the right of Vieksniai and again we were confused. "Lithuania was part of Russia when your grandmother lived there," our relative explained. "Then did *Bobbe* have a Russian name?" we asked. "No," we were told. "She was Jewish. Her name was Mirel."

The genealogy was no less confusing on our mother's side. Our research told us that our mother's father embarked from Rotterdam on the passenger ship *Dania* in 1890. He was 17 years old. He processed into Castle Garden, New York City's pre-Ellis Island immigration center, as Pawel Aleksandrowicz and processed out as Paul Alexander. Pawel, now Paul, was from Krakow, Poland's ancient capital. He was conversant in German, the language of the central European Enlightenment, as well as Polish and Yiddish. Inspired by the stunning architecture and cultural splendors of his beautiful birthplace, he was intent on becoming an artist. Painting movie sets in New York City, before the big studios moved to California, was as close as he would come to fulfilling this ambition.

Our maternal grandmother, our *nana*, was born Toba Haufer in West Galicia, now southern Poland but then Austro-Hungary. Nana was born in 1877 in Brzesko, a large provincial town 40 miles or so east of Krakow, and spent part of her youth on the outskirts of Brzesko in the tiny hamlet of Jadownik. At some point, and for reasons never explained to Arnie and me, Toba's family split up. Some moved to Budapest and Szeged in Hungary, and a few of the younger children, Toba among them, were shuttled back and forth between Galicia and Hungary. By circumstances and necessity, Toba became somewhat of a linguist, conversant in Yiddish, Polish, German, and Hungarian. She arrived in New York City in 1894 as a 17-year-old and lived on Sheriff Street in the Lower East Side, not far from the newly named Paul Alexander, who resided in a rooming house on East 4th Street. A relative had paid Toba's way, and she worked off her debt scrubbing floors until she married Paul in 1898.

As with our paternal grandparents, we never knew whether Paul and Toba met in the old country or America. Brzesko and Krakow were little more than an hour's train ride apart; Arnie and I surmised that, at minimum, their families would have known each other and perhaps brokered the marriage either in Galicia or in New York City. In any event, in her thirties Toba became an insurance agent for Equitable Life and started calling herself Toni Alexander, also known as Mrs. Paul Alexander. Whether or not the Anglicized name had anything to do with it, she was successful enough in her business to bring a dozen relatives to America.

These genealogical complexities became increasingly maddening to my brother and me, and there was no one we could turn to for more clarification, either because they didn't know, were hiding things they considered better not shared, or weren't interested in a painful background they wanted to forget. Why, we wondered, did the marriage certificate we found in one of The Secretary's drawers say that Pawel/Paul's and Toba/Toni's nationality was Austrian when they both came from Poland? Why did Harry and Mary's marriage certificate say that they were both Russian, when he came from Poland and she from Lithuania? Our constant questions went unanswered, as I said, so we continued looking for answers on our own. Our frustration at not being able to pin-point our own family's history soon became less of an aggravation as we delved, fascinated, into the broader history of the several old countries that were our provenance. As we assembled the pieces, Arnie showed himself to be a natural-born historian. Having served as his co-researcher, it is no surprise to me that he became the prominent historian he is, or that he has specialized in the particular area he chose. My pride in my brother's success is considerable. He started slowly but has proceeded splendidly. Most of what I know about our origins I know from him. I hope I'm correctly summarizing what he has told me and written.

Our Paternal Forebears

According to Arnie, some historians date the Jewish presence in Lithuania from the reign of Prince Gediminas, the Grand Duke, in the middle of the

14th century, when groups of Jews arrived from Germany and France in flight from blood libels and Crusaders. Others subscribe to the theory that Jews came to Lithuania much earlier, from Babylonia and elsewhere in the Near East in the 9th and 10th centuries A.D. after the decline of the Jewish communities there. Still others emphasize the importance of the migratory flow from the Jewish state of the Khazars, which dominated the Eurasian steppes between the Black and Caspian Seas for nearly three centuries before the Khazars lost their kingdom in 969 and were expelled by Russian princes who had recently converted to Russian Orthodoxy. (I believe that our family is descended from the Khazars. I am much influenced in this belief by my historian brother Arnie, an expert on the Khazars. Even our surname supports my conviction. I recently came across this quote in the American-Jewish novelist Louis Begley's *Wartime Lies*: "She might say she was a Sarmatian tracing her descent from unsullied generations of other Sarmatians, all of whose names ended like her own with the noble 'ski' of Sobieski and Poniatowski: let him prove the contrary." How and when did this suffix become common among Jews? The Sarmatians flourished in the central Eurasian Steppes from the 6th century BC to the 4th century AD, not long before the Khazars. Is there a Sarmartian-Khazar connection?)

After the expulsion, masses of Khazars moved to Grodno, Minsk, Pinsk, and other Lithuanian fortress towns and were joined by other Jews who reached the country as individuals, in groups of merchants, and as prisoners-of-war. These Jews were welcomed by the nobility for their skills as merchants who could help build a country mostly populated until then by serfs bound to ducal estates.

Let's jump ahead five centuries, to 1569 when Poland and Lithuania were united into the Poland-Lithuanian Kingdom. The unity lasted for 200 years. Then, from 1772 to 1795 Poland was partitioned three times by Russia, Austria, and Prussia. After a series of heroic but failed uprisings, by Poles joined by many Jews, Poland-Lithuania disappeared as an independent state. Its three million people were pretty much evenly divided in the third partition in 1795.

Austria appropriated the Krakow area (*thus Pawel's and Toba's designations as Austrian*). Russia acquired all of Lithuania (*thus Mirel's designation as Russian*). Prussia held Mazovia, including Warsaw, until it came under Napoleonic rule in 1807. From Napoleon's defeat in 1815 until 1918, Warsaw was part of Imperial Russia (*thus Naftali Tsvi's designation as Russian*).

Once it had become home to the world's largest Jewish population, czarist Russia had to come to terms with its long-standing Jewish policy, which had prohibited Jews from living in Russia since the end of the 15th century. So Russia created a territory within its borders where Jews were authorized to live—the *Cherta*, or Pale of Settlement, comprised of 15 provinces, or *gubernias*, nine in Russia and six in Lithuania and Belorussia, including Kaunas, where Vexna, the hometown of our grandmother Mary/Mirel, was located. Although its borders were always in flux, the Pale remained in effect from 1791 until the Russian Revolution in 1917, and by 1897 it covered close to 400,000 square miles from the Baltic Sea to the Black Sea and was home to nearly five million Jews.

The czars were absolute monarchs—despotic, reactionary, intolerant, and autocratic. The Imperial policy of the Romanovs was one of discrimination, not only against the Jews but also against Muslims and, in fact, against anyone not affiliated with the Russian Orthodox Church, including Catholics and Protestants. In this respect, the Russian monarchs followed a ruling by the Russian Orthodox Church, even though Catherine II and subsequent czars had promised to grant the minorities all the rights and privileges that they had been promised. Throughout the czarist period, this pattern repeated itself: glimpses of liberalization alternating with discriminatory and frequently violent reactions to liberalization. The Jews had no protection against these reactions—least of all from the authorities, who not only issued increasingly damaging edicts, but encouraged and even organized pogroms. After Alexander II was assassinated in 1881, there was an outburst of hundreds of government-organized pogroms under his son Alexander III.

The upheavals, which continued to erupt over the next 25 years, triggered the mass exodus of Jews from Russia. (*Many Jews fled Lithuania after the 1881 pogroms. I wonder, but have no way of knowing, whether or not our grandfather Naftali Tsvi's family was among the Litvak emigres. Had the Kirinski and Marcus families known each other in Lithuania?*) Finally, during the 1894 to 1917 reign of the last czar, Nicholas II, the resurgence of nationalism and revolutionary movements fueled additional anti-Semitism because of Jewish involvement (sometimes prominent, as in the case of Trotsky) in these movements, even when those Jews did not identify with Judaism or the Jewish people.

The signals had been clear from the time the Polish-Lithuanian Kingdom was divided up in 1795. Naftali Tsvi Kirinski's Warsaw and most of Lithuania, including Mirel Marcus's Vexna, went to the Russian Empire. When these two paternal grandparents of ours were teenagers, pogroms were spreading like a plague. It was time for any Jew who could leave to leave. So Naftali Tsvi and Mirel did, for America.

Our Maternal Forebears

Meanwhile, the Aleksandrowiczes and Haufers were being affected by similar trends in Austria and their part of Poland. Austria annexed Galicia in 1772 and, with the third partition of 1795, acquired the Jewish population of central Poland, or West Galicia, with its significant subset of Hasidim. At about this time, large numbers of Jews began immigrating into Hungary from northern Poland. By 1867, when Emperor Franz Joseph, following a lost war in Germany, reached an agreement with the Hungarian nobility to convert his empire into the Austro-Hungarian Dual Monarchy, the Jewish population in Hungary almost equaled that of the Jewish population in Galicia, and in another 50 years exceeded it. By 1910, there were nearly one million Hungarian Jews.

After the immigration of Jews to Hungary in the mid-1800s, there were still nearly half a million Galician Jews, the vast majority of whom lived in small cities and towns and depended on trade. This included the Haufers of Brzesko and nearby Jadownik. Though her family was not observant, much less Hasidic, it was inevitable that Toba, our maternal grandmother, would rub shoulders with Hasidim, inasmuch as the great Hasidic dynasties were prevalent not only in eastern Galicia, but also were present in the more enlightened West Galicia. And while Hasidism in Hungary never had the size or impact it did in Galicia, Hasids had been a presence in Hungary since the 18th century. So it was natural that Toba, shuttling back and forth between the fragments of her family in Galicia and Hungary, would encounter Hasidism in Budapest and Szeged, as well as in Brzesko and Jadownik.

Besides her proximity to Hasidism, Toba's rearing in Hungary and Galicia made her an interesting mix. By the time she started going to Hungary, an alliance had formed between reformer Jews and the Magyar-speaking nobility; as a result, the Jews had been "emancipated" and Magyar was spoken in Hungarian schools. The Magyarization of Hungarian Jews led to Toba's fluency in Hungarian to go along with her knowledge of Polish, German, and Yiddish. She was a true Habsburg Jew, culturally adaptable and multi-lingual, secular in her upbringing but intrigued by Hasidic mysticism.

As I consider the context in both Galicia and Hungary in the 1870s, when our maternal grandparents Toba and Pawel were born, I can easily understand why they would have emigrated and become the New Yorkers Paul and Toni. In the 30 years prior to their births, divisions within Habsburg Jewry had grown more and more pronounced as Hungarian Jews continued to modernize while Galician Jews lost ground. Just as there was no unifying sense of nationhood in modernized, transnational, multicultural, and multilingual Habsburg society in general, there was now a diminished sense of a unified identity among Habsburg's divided and assimilated Jews. The stock market crash of 1873, blamed on the Jews, triggered anti-Semitism throughout the Austro-Hungarian Empire and in Europe generally. While it never reached the virulent level of the Russian pogroms of the 1880s that led to the exodus of Lithuanian and Polish Jews, including Mirel Marcus and Naftali Tsvi Kirinski, Habsburg Jews were also affected—if not necessarily in body, then in the belated realization that assimilation was an illusory and even dangerous prospect. Christian Europe had only appeared to be ready to accept Jews when times were good. But beneath these appearances, Jew-hatred was always waiting to erupt.

As youngsters, Toba and Pawel directly experienced the divisions within their Jewish communities, disillusion about the prospects for assimilation, and anti-Semitism. And so they emigrated, firm in their belief that everything which had fallen apart in Europe would be resurrected in America, the fabled New World. For the most part, that is what happened. Pawel, now Paul, and Toba, now Toni, established mostly comfortable roots and livelihoods in New York.

Our Mother

Paul and Toni Alexander had five children, three girls and two boys, born over a 20-year period. The oldest, Beatrice, or Bert, came in 1899 and was followed in short and regular intervals by Abraham, called Al, our mother Fay, and Milton. I'm guessing, because it was hinted at rather than said directly, that the fifth child, Ella, ten years younger than Milton, was likely a surprise pregnancy. All of them were born and raised in Manhattan and the Bronx.

Again I'm guessing, but I also had the sense that our mother Fay, born in 1904, was closest to her parents in temperament, and certainly followed Paul's inclination towards painting, which she studied at Washington Irving High School and Hunter College. She danced professionally from her early twenties until her mid-thirties as a member of the original Doris Humphrey-Charles Weidman modern dance company, performing in such Broadway classics as *Lysistrata* and *As Thousands Cheer*, among others. She counted celebrities like Irving Berlin, Ethel Waters, Ruth St. Denis, and José Limón among her acquaintances. Fay returned to painting after her dancing career ended and became well known in New Jersey as a water colorist. In interviews, she often attributed her inspiration and sensibility as a painter to dance.

Our Father

Mary and Harry Kirinski had seven kids, six boys and a girl. All were born, like clockwork, two years apart between 1900 and 1912, first Samuel, then Mordechai (Morton), Sarah (Sadie), Eli (Elliott), Sigmund (Ziggy), Matthew, and Simon (Simmy). Each of the sons took up occupations related, in varying degrees, to their father's restaurant trade, whether as buyers, waiters, chefs, or managers. Sadie taught piano.

Our father, born as Mordechai in 1902, was called Morton from his early teens on. The story goes that he suffered bullying in tough Roxbury in part due to his obviously Jewish name. One day, bruised and bloodied from his latest fight, he complained to his older brother Sam that "my stupid foreigner's name Mordechai will be the death of me." Sam, a student at Boston Latin, suggested that he call himself Morton: "You can call yourself 'Mort' for short, which means 'death' in Latin." The name stuck, though it later came to light that Sam had confused the Latin and French roots.

Mort worked hard to make a living his whole life, starting with milk-bottle deliveries before school as a kid. He studied accounting and worked for restaurants in Boston and New York before purchasing the Carousel Diner in Asbury Park. Why there? Another story goes that Mort was managing a cafeteria in New York City when he made the acquaintance of one Zimel Resnick, a supplier of money and arms in the fight for Israel's founding who also owned the Palace Amusement Park in Asbury, whose famous merry-go-round gave the nearby Carousel Diner its name. Resnick, from Russia and only a few years younger than Mort, considered our father a *landsman*, a compatriot. When the diner went up for sale in 1946, he loaned Mort the down payment and guaranteed the bank loan for the balance of the purchase price.

The diner was never as profitable as Mort expected it to be, but it did provide an adequate livelihood for the family of five. Still, it never seemed to be enough for our father, who was forever trying to strike it rich, dying at age 91 after being hospitalized for a fracture suffered from a fall en route to buying a lottery ticket. To us, his sons, our father was unrelentingly materialistic, the epitome of the merchant. In retrospect, though, I think we underestimated him. Even as he readily admitted to having no artistic bone in his body, he was Fay's most ardent supporter in both her dancing and painting. Over the years, he filled several scrapbooks with memorabilia from her dancing career and personally matted and framed all of her art works.

Intermarriage, 1928

Arnie and I used to joke that we were the products of a mixed marriage, but it's only partly a joke. Our parents' marriage combined genuine multipolar qualities—geographically, ethnically, religiously, temperamentally, and occupationally. Morton was raised by religiously observant "Litvaks," while Fay was the child of secular "Galitzianers." We can see significant fault lines here.

As Arnie explained it to me, Litvaks, the Lithuanian Jews of Belarus, Ukraine, and the northwestern Suwalki region of Poland, were characterized by an intellectual approach to Judaism, an approach most associated with the *Haskala*, the 18th century Jewish Enlightenment influenced primarily by Elijah ben Shlomo Zalman, the famed Gaon of Vilna, who emphasized critical textual examination of the Torah and related technicalities of Hebrew grammar, as well as knowledge of the secular sciences. The Vilna Gaon was at the forefront of Lithuanian Jewry's traditionalist opposition to Hasidism, the ecstatic, prayerful movement spawned farther south in Galicia—western Ukraine and the southeastern corner of Poland—by the equally famous Baal Shem Tov, the "Master of the Good Name." It was not so much that Elijah, the Gaon of Vilna, opposed mysticism per se (his own interests in Kabbala would dispute charges of such prejudice), but rather what he considered the Hasids' grave misunderstanding of Judaism, particularly *Halacha*, or Jewish Law, and *Minhag*, the inviolable (in Elijah's view) traditions, order, and curriculum of Ashkenazi religious practice.

The cultural attitudes separating these two subdivisions of Ashkenazi Jews were deeply entrenched and mutually disdainful. They ridiculed each other's pronunciation of Yiddish and Hebrew. For the Galitzianers, the cerebral Litvaks came across as "cold fish"; over the years, I heard frequent complaints about coldness and sarcasm from my aunts and uncle who had married Kirinski siblings. From their side of the divide, the Litvaks considered their more emotional, spontaneous, and expressive southern brethren irrational and uneducated. Even their cuisines were a source of opposition, the Galitzianers preferring rich, heavily sweetened food and the Litvaks plainer fare. (*I remember refusing to be put in my crib at bedtime during one of Nana's visits. She climbed into the crib, curled up on my mattress, put her thumb in her mouth, and feigned sleep. I screamed until I was allowed to trade places with her. No Kirinski Litvak would have done what the Galician Toba did.*)

Our parents crossed this so-called Gefilte Fish Line when they wed in 1928. These cultural and religious-secular divides were complicated by a fundamental difference in temperament, the difference, essentially, between materialistic and artistic aspirations. Morton—to us, his sons—was a businessman to his core. Fay was an artist to hers. But these categorizations need to be qualified. Morton's forebears were likely not only merchants. The yeshiva in Telz, famous in the Orthodox Jewish world for the quality of teaching and learning, was near Vexna. It's probable that at least some members of an extended religious clan like the Marcuses, our *bobbe* Mary's family, would have studied there. Even girls during the *Haskala*, the Jewish Enlightenment, were encouraged to study, if not in the yeshiva with boys, of course, then in local schools and with tutors. By contrast, neither side of Toba's family was at all religious. Still, they were Galitzianers, and as such would have been influenced by two centuries of exposure to Hasidism.

And so Fay—the dancer, the artist, the child of non-religious Habsburg Jews who could not help but be touched by the mysticism of their Hasidic neighbors—married Morton, the descendent of Talmudists and merchants in the Russian Pale of Settlement.

Home

In 1946 our family moved to New Jersey when my father, finally realizing his dream of owning a restaurant, became proprietor of the Carousel Diner. I imagine he was thrilled, just as I imagine my mother, the born-and-raised New York dancer and artist, was not. I learned later that the move was tough at first on our ten-year-old sister Deborah: big city to small town, leaving behind an extensive network of nearby cousins, new school, no friends at first, her prepubescent hormones beginning to twitch. As a two-year-old, other than missing my grandparents, uncles, and aunts (especially Aunt Ella and her wiggly toes), I don't recall being much affected at all. From the time we moved to the beach town of Belmar, I was all Jersey boy.

Who said it? Maybe Maugham. That he had met some who traveled widely but were uninteresting, while others who never left home lived lives of substance and depth. It's a reasonable but simplistic observation. Whether we travel or stay put, the influence of home is there, wherever we find ourselves, at once anchoring us and weighing us down, rendering us secure yet captive, giving coherence to our perspective, but in the process conditioning and constraining it. I doubt that those of us who travel ever really leave home emotionally or psychologically. We move elliptically, from base camp to summit and back, much like children extending playground borders one Jungle Gym at a time, one swing at a time, one see-saw at a time, all the while casting anxious eyes on the parent standing nearby, vigilant and dependable.

I've traveled widely, but home for me will always be Belmar, New Jersey and not my New York birthplace. Belmar is a scant mile square, bordered on the east by the Atlantic Ocean, on the west by Shark River, on the south by Lake Como, and on the north by Shark River Inlet, which connects the river and the sea. These days, it doesn't take me long to walk the mile-square town. I choose different routes within the perimeter as the spirit moves me. Once I would have aspired to writing a large-scale account of a large-scale terrain, much like Alfred Kazin did in *A Walker in the City*. I'm more modest now in my ambitions and content to write about Belmar's tiny geography, the terrain of which I'm pretty much an expert.

It's not just the geography I know so well. I know the town's history, its stories, its characters and dramas. I should know it well after so many years of growing up, frequently visiting, and now returning to live here. But memories have a proportion of their own, a proportion unrelated to spans of time, and the memories spawned by this town disproportionately exceed, in quantity and influence and meaning, the memories I have from all the other periods of my life combined. Maybe that's the nature of home. A lot gets packed in.

Memory's most important starting point, with all respect to the Bronx and Aunt Ella's wiggly toes and the milkman with his horse and wagon, is Arnold, my twin, my first and best friend, boardwalk buddies from the time we learned to toddle, pushed along the beachfront in tandem prams by our mother. From infancy through high school, except for my aberrant year of private school, we did everything together, pleasant and painful. The town became our shared cauldron, boiling and then melting us in the same rites of passage.

Our first home in Belmar, a duplex, still stands on 12th Avenue and E Street, on the intersection's southwest corner. Many of the main characters in the drama of our upbringing lived nearby, including three whose juxtaposition was certainly incongruous. Eddie Martino lived four houses up 12th Avenue from us. Four houses down the street in the opposite direction, and immediately next-door to Rabbi Steinman, lived Eddie's best friend, Buster Layton. Eddie and Buster were notorious among local Jewish kids as anti-Semites whose favorite demonstration of prejudice took the form of harassing any child both smaller than they and who happened to be out by himself. This pair turned into a double hit for our family: years later Eddie became our brother-in-law, and our sister had to tolerate Buster, who remained Eddie's best friend well into adulthood. (Unrelated to this but as a matter of historical interest, four houses down E Street from us lived the Hoffmans. When they moved away, their house was bought by Mrs. Sancious, who let her son David and his friends Clarence Clemons, Vini Lopez, Danny Federici, Garry Tallent, and Bruce Springsteen use the basement for rehearsals of their fledgling E Street Band.)

Much of my early life in Belmar was compressed into several blocks. Belmar Grammar School was on Main Street, a block west of our corner. Immediately across from the school was Memorial Field with its four baseball diamonds, where Babe Ruth is said to have hit a 500-foot home run that bounced off the post office roof. Our synagogue, Congregation Sons of Israel, was on 11th Avenue, two blocks away from our house. The magnate Jacob Schiff laid the synagogue's cornerstone in 1904, and the writer Sholem Aleichem attended services there when he summered in the town. My beloved public library was on 10th and E. Our parents gave us free rein to go to these places almost from the time we could walk. Unbridled access to more distant places expanded along with our ability to ride our bikes to them: the beachfront and arcades, the railroad tracks, the marina at Shark River where the commercial fishing fleet was harbored, the four draw bridges spanning the inlet into Avon and Neptune, the next towns to the north. All of these places were my playground. They comprised a lovely and intimate world. I was happy and care-free and innocent there.

This changed when I turned twelve. It was 1956, and we moved to 5th Avenue between C and D Streets. Again, in miniscule Belmar scale counted for a lot. Our new house was only eight blocks from our old home, but the divide between the two neighborhoods felt vast to me. Fifth Avenue was more up-scale and affluent than 12th. Our new block was as full of friends as my old one was, but somehow those friends were different, more materialistic, more competitive, more prone to spread gossip and make mean-spirited judgments. Eventually, I adjusted, but at the expense, I came to realize, of what I left behind. I was no longer so happy and care-free and innocent.

In my anxious need to adapt and be popular, I almost left Arnie behind. But I caught myself in time to prevent that from happening. He steadied me. He stayed my best friend. He reminded me of what and who I had been. I welcomed those glimpses as a kind of salvation, even as I sensed that something in my core was irrevocably changing.

2

Adventures in Communion and Solitude

BELMAR IS OUR WORLD-sized town, Arnie's and mine.
It is self-contained; all that we know or care to know is here.
We do most things together, but not everything.
If I were to walk the town with an outsider, there would be a story to tell on each block,
whether about Arnie and me or just me, whether ending well or badly.

Here we are, my brother and I:
- watching "The Howdy Doody Show," avowing its superiority to "Captain Kangaroo";
- building a replica of Captain Video's spaceship in Jasper Lupo's attic;
- splashing in the calm pools between sandbars, protected from the waves;
- practicing our trumpets, mine a cheaper Pedler, Arnie's (he the better player) a superior Bach;
- lifting weights in conscientious but fruitless efforts to lose, or gain, bulk;
- seeing who could read Hebrew the fastest, the prayers unintelligible at any speed;
- eating lunch on school days at Milt Aronis's restaurant, amused that his son is named Champ;
- paying nine cents admission for the matinee on Saturdays at the Rivoli Theater;
- brushing Duke the collie while his owner, Violet Levinson, brushes our hair;
- playing baseball, basketball, football;
- combing the beaches in winter;
- running the beach chair and umbrella concession in summer;
- inhabiting the public library for hours upon hours upon hours.

Yet we are not the same person.
I don't know his separate secrets.
He doesn't know mine.

3
Louie's Charm

LOUIE LERNER, MY BEST friend after Arnie, lived directly across from us on 12th Avenue. Even though Louie was a year younger, throughout our childhood the three of us did everything together. We went to the beach and learned to swim together, played games and sports together, and watched television together. Louie's family had the first TV I can remember watching. A few minutes before five every weekday afternoon, our mother would walk Arnie and me across the street to the Lerners' to watch two kids shows, "Rootie Kazootie" at five and "Howdy Doody" a half-hour later. We particularly loved the old-time movies they showed on "Howdy Doody." We laughed, as the saying accurately describes the condition, until our sides hurt.

There were other kids in the neighborhood with whom we played. One was Gary Holtz. Gary was tough. He was quite strong for his age and did all sorts of daring things, like climb the highest, most challenging trees and jump off garage roofs. He wasn't a mean boy, although he did get into his share of wrestling matches. But Louie, Arnie, and I were a little afraid of him because he played so hard. We tried to keep our distance, but it wasn't always possible because Gary lived right down the street from our houses.

One day Louie showed me a metal charm somebody had given him. Arnie wasn't with us at the time. The charm was round and about twice the size of a quarter. At its center, inside a silver ring, was a gold four-leaf clover. The charm had a thin, removable chain on it that was also gold.

I became obsessed. I couldn't remember having ever wanted anything more than I wanted that charm. When I went to bed that night, I couldn't stop thinking about it. I stayed awake trying to figure out a way to get it for my own. By the time I fell asleep, I had come up with a plan.

The next morning, a Saturday, I snuck across the street without my mother or brother and told Louie his charm was in danger.

"What could happen to my charm?" Louie asked.

"Somebody could steal it. I think it would be safer if you hid it in a secret place where nobody can find it. Especially someone like Gary Holtz."

"How about in my house?"

"No, that wouldn't be safe from Sam," I explained, referring to Louie's younger brother. "I have a better idea. We should bury it in a box in your dad's vegetable garden. It would be like having buried treasure. And you could dig it up whenever you want to play with it."

I suspected that Louie really didn't understand the danger I was talking about, or why a box under the dirt would be a better place to put the charm than a shelf in his room that was too high for Sam. But Louie was a year younger than I; it was natural for a six-year-old kid to follow the lead of a seven-year-old.

Later that day, just before dinner, we put the charm in a small box, dug a hole in a corner of the garden at the back of the house, and buried the box, looking around as we did so to make sure nobody was watching. Louie went inside his house for supper, and I went home for mine.

Or at least I made believe I was going home. As soon as I waved good-bye to Louie and saw him close the door to his house I snuck back to the garden, unburied the box, removed the charm, put the box back in the hole, and covered it up again. Then I went home.

I couldn't wait to finish supper. I shut myself in the bathroom and took the charm with its little chain from my pocket. It was like I was holding a special treasure, and I spent a long time just looking at the golden, silver-encircled, four-leaf clover lying in my hand. At first, it didn't bother me at all that the charm wasn't mine, or that I had stolen it from my second-best friend. I thought of it more as borrowing something, something I just couldn't be without. After a while, though, I started worrying about what I had done and how I would explain things to Louie. Finally, I realized I couldn't keep the charm. In fact, it had already begun to lose a little of its attraction now that I had had a chance to hold it for a few hours. What I needed to do was figure out a way to get it back to Louie and still keep him as a friend.

The next morning I went over to Louie's house and told him I had an important secret to tell him. "Right after you went inside for supper yesterday, I heard Gary telling some kids that he saw us burying a box in your dad's garden, and that after dark he was going to sneak over and dig out the box. I got scared, so I went back and dug up the charm before he could. I took it home with me last night to keep it safe. Here," I continued, removing the charm from my pocket and handing it, with its chain, to Louie. "I guess you were right all along. It would have been safer just to keep it in your house."

Louie looked at me as if he were deciding whether or not to believe me, even though he knew, I was sure, that I was lying. I held my breath, knowing that our friendship depended on what Louie would decide to do.

"Yeah," Louie finally said. "It's better if I just put it in my room when I'm not carrying it in my pocket. Sam won't get it."

We dug the empty shoe box out of the garden and covered up the hole so that Louie's father wouldn't get angry at us. Then we found Arnie and the three of us went off to play.

Louie and I have been close friends for many years. We've both had our separate ups and downs. When we get together we talk quite openly about the difficult times, although we prefer not to dwell on those. Mostly, we like to share happier memories, for example of "The Howdy Doody Show" with its old-time movies. We've never talked about Louie's charm.

4
Tommy

BELMAR HAD TWO MOVIE theaters. One was the Rialto. It was located on Ocean Avenue, right across from the boardwalk on the corner of 8th Avenue. It was only open in the summer. I can't remember having gone there even once. Back in the fifties, polio was the big scare. Parents particularly warned kids away from movie theaters and swimming pools, two places, it was feared, where the disease incubated. There was a swimming pool three blocks from the Rialto. That coincidence did not help the theater's business. The only people I can remember going there were the summer tourists, who the local residents figured just didn't know any better.

The other theater, the Rivoli, was a very different matter. The Rivoli was a year-round place. It was located on Main Street, right in the center of things at the corner of 9th Avenue. It was hugely popular with local kids. The cost of admission was nine cents. It was within quick walking distance of virtually everything, and it was immediately adjacent to the Sugar Bowl, a luncheonette that featured cherry cokes and malted milks and hamburgers and candy, and whose owners had the cleverness to let kids read comic books for free while they were eating at the counter. Parents were still concerned about polio at the Rivoli. But there was no swimming pool nearby, and the customers were predominantly local.

The Rivoli figured into an important incident in my early boyhood. I was ten years old and fixated on Roy Rogers, the cowboy actor. I idolized him in the most serious sense possible, even to the extent of fantasizing my adoption by Rogers and his wife, Dale Evans. I was certain I was meant to be brought up by them on the Lazy R Ranch, the only person entrusted by Roy to care for Trigger, his palomino stallion. I would have done anything, however illicit, to see a Roy Rogers movie.

On the day in question, Rogers' "Pals of the Golden West" was playing at the Rivoli. Although it was a school day, I figured I'd have nearly an hour from the time school let out to make the matinee. Arnie had some chores to do so couldn't go with me. I didn't have to be accompanied in any case, even as a ten-year-old; in the early fifties, things were a lot more innocent, probably because they were, or at least seemed to be, much safer. You just didn't hear about kids getting abducted or assaulted in Belmar. We had the run of the town. Very little was off limits. Besides, the Rivoli was only two blocks from our school, Belmar Grammar School, and only four blocks from our house. So it wasn't odd for a ten-year-old to go alone to a Roy Rogers movie. My parents never appeared to worry about Arnie or me. They just assumed, correctly for the most part, that we were playing with friends.

My routine was to pay the nine-cents admission ticket with a dime, then go next door to the Sugar Bowl to buy a piece of Bazooka bubble gum with my penny's change. I got to the box office early, pulled off my right glove, and reached into my pocket for the money. Only it wasn't there. I searched every pocket in my corduroy pants and fringed-leather Roy Rogers jacket. It just wasn't there. I tried to think through my choices. I still had 45 minutes before the feature would begin. Going home wouldn't work. Neither my parents nor sister would be there, and Arnie and I had no current savings in our shared piggy bank. I thought about taking a dime from my father's underwear and handkerchief drawer, where there was always the possibility of finding spare change. Had I been older, maybe twelve or thirteen, I would have taken that route with no compunction. But I was ten and still afraid to commit an obvious wrong. I decided that my only alternative was to borrow. This was something I knew my parents would not condone. But I was fairly sure they wouldn't condemn me too much. Borrowing was not such an obvious wrong, after all. They would only chide me. I could live with chiding.

Having settled on the wisdom of borrowing as a solution, I just needed to figure out whom I could borrow from and still make it back to the theater within 45 minutes—35 if I wanted to see the news and cartoons and previews. My closest source, I concluded, was Tommy.

Tommy lived only two blocks away from the Rivoli, right off of Main Street at 11th Avenue in a square block of houses immediately adjacent to Belmar Grammar, the school we all attended. This block of homes merits some description. I didn't think much about it then, but in retrospect I realize they would have more accurately qualified as shacks. And all the families living in those shacks were Black. Later, I found it hard to believe I hadn't noticed the difference between this block and the rest of the town. Granted, for a small town in the 1950s Belmar was a relatively mixed community in religious, ethnic, and racial terms. It was also pretty harmonious, with no obviously demarcated enclaves among the residents of mostly Italian, Irish, Anglo, Eastern European, Protestant, Catholic, and Jewish heritages. The town was mixed, too, in socio-economic terms, but not lopsidedly so. There were pockets below the middle-class line and pockets above it. For the most part, though, the town was made up of nice, one-family homes which, in my memory's eye, were almost stereotypically middle-class American and inhabited by...well, just people.

But my memory's eye was a child's eye, which did not register differences of class or color. Those visions took irrevocable root several years later, when the self-consciousness and cliques and snobberies and hostilities of high school altered my pre-adolescent egalitarian worldview forever. Only in retrospect did I understand that the day of the Roy Rogers movie presaged this change. Until that day, my child's eye had not noticed that Tommy's block was all shacks, or that the block was inhabited entirely by Black people, or that Tommy was Black. He was simply a kid in my school, my friend, my playmate. All of that began to change the day I decided to go to Tommy's house to borrow a dime to see the Roy Rogers movie. Because, in fact, I had never actually been to Tommy's house before.

My decision made, I ran from the Rivoli's box office toward Tommy's. I reached his block and encountered a basic obstacle, which was not having the slightest idea where to find Tommy. I had never entered this neighborhood, only seen it from the school playground across 11th Avenue. I now saw that the neighborhood had nothing in common with other parts of town. It had no streets or alleys, only a warren of dirt paths with no discernible pattern or flow. My only point of reference was 11th Avenue. But 11th Avenue had no utility in this new land, except as a border I had crossed and to which I could retreat. And retreat was already on my mind.

The power of Roy Rogers, however, was more compelling than the power of strangeness. I asked a passing woman where I could find Tommy's house. She directed me down a path that took me farther into the cluster of dwellings. I had no idea where I was when I arrived where I thought the woman had indicated. I asked directions of another person, and then another, and then a fourth, intuitively, by my questions, trying to pare down the perimeter of an uncertain territory by the process of elimination. How could I have ever anticipated becoming lost in one tiny area of the town I knew so well, which in its entirety was so small to begin with?

I was becoming desperate and scared. I was also getting cold as the early-winter afternoon began to darken. But I kept traversing the strange neighborhood, searching for a house I had never seen; I had no choice, I realized, by now having lost any sense at all of how to find my way back to 11th Avenue. Then I came upon the woman who had first tried to direct me to Tommy's. This time, she took my hand and walked me to my destination.

I knocked on the door. Tommy opened it, obviously surprised to see me. Cold, I stepped inside, even without Tommy's invitation. I found myself in a tiny room crowded with frayed furniture and piles of what looked like newspapers and cardboard. The light was dim, its main source the glow of fire from a potbellied stove. I smelled its smoke, mixed with the odor of unfamiliar cooking. Tommy's two little sisters were sitting on the bare wooden floor, drawing in the same notebook.

"What do you want?" Tommy asked.

However difficult it had been to find my friend, the purpose of my quest had been clear. Until now. All of sudden—seeing that room, comparing it to my own comfortable home—the idea of borrowing money from Tommy, for a movie no less, seemed like the most selfish act imaginable. Something, even in my child's consciousness, understood that Tommy was poor, that Tommy's family had no money, that asking for the loan of a dime would embarrass my friend, and that it would embarrass me.

"I was across the street at the playground. I thought maybe you'd be able to come play."

Before Tommy could respond his mom came in from what I guessed was the kitchen. We greeted each other. Tommy asked if he could go to the playground with me.

"It's getting late," his mother said. "It's already quarter to four. I have to go out soon. I need for you to watch your sisters and the fire. Not today, Tommy."

When I heard her say "quarter to four" I panicked. My insight of just a few moments ago, that asking for money would be a mutual embarrassment, was completely superseded by my need to be back at the Rivoli in time for the four o'clock feature.

"Okay, Tommy," I said. "We can play another time." Then I looked at Tommy's mom and in my most polite manner said, "I'm sorry that I came so late. I didn't know what time it was."

Tommy's mom nodded and smiled. I turned to go. Then I turned back, the compulsion to see the movie stronger than I could control. "Can I borrow a dime until tomorrow?"

Over the years since I asked that question I've frequently come across the phrase "time stopped." To some, the phrase might be a cliché, an unimaginative literary artifice. Not to me. To me, the phrase will forever mark, with total accuracy, a moment that has held unchanged its photographic reality for more than 50 years. I see Tommy turning to look at his mom, his mouth open, his eyes anxious. I see the two sisters, their eyes no longer on the drawing, but on their mother. I see myself, my expression frozen in the realization that I have said something terribly wrong. The only one I don't see fixed in a photograph is Tommy's mom. Instead, I see her in motion. Her motion begins with a frown. Gradually it turns to a smile. The smile is neutral, neither amused nor derisive. "I'm sorry," she finally says. "I don't have any change. You should wait until you get home and ask your folks."

I said goodbye and went out the door. From the top of their stairs, I could see Belmar Grammar School. Oriented this time, I made my way out of Tommy's strange world and back toward my own safe land. I was staggered and confused by what had just transpired. And I was reconciled, finally, to missing the movie. There was no way around it. I started for home.

On the way through the playground I stopped to use the Jungle Gym. To do so, I needed to take off my fringed jacket and cowboy gloves, the leather kind that also had fringes on the cone-shaped cuffs extending two or three inches up the forearm from the top of the wrist.

Something dropped out of the left-hand glove when I removed it. The dime. It had been there the whole time. I picked up the coin and put it in my pocket, already running as fast as I could toward the Rivoli, praying I could get there in time for the feature.

Roy and Dale Will Adopt Me

A HALF-CENTURY AFTER the Tommy incident, I was reading *Parade Magazine* and saw a photo in Walter Scott's "Personality Parade" column that caught my attention. "Trigger and his longtime companion," read the caption. Trigger was a horse. His longtime companion was Roy Rogers.

Scott's column had a question-and-answer format. The question came from one Ron Riddle of St. Petersburg, Florida: *"Please settle a bet between friends,"* Mr. Riddle began. *"Who starred in more movies and TV shows, Roy Rogers' horse, Trigger, or Gene Autry's Champion? A steak dinner is riding on your answer."* Scott's answer: *"We sure hope that's beef-steak you're talking about, pardner. And you may have to cut it in half, because the answer's plumb complicated. The long-lived palomino Trigger (1932-1965), called 'the smartest horse in the movies,' co-starred with Rogers in some 90 movies and 100 episodes of* The Roy Rogers Show. *Fellow singing cowboy Autry, on the other hand, rode no fewer than seven sorrel-colored horses named Champion (or Champ) during his long movie and TV career. Savvy?"*

Scott's snippet took me back, first to 1998, when I read that Roy (born Leonard Slye) had died at the age of 87, and then back to the late 1940s when, as a kindergartner, I first became aware of him. And a powerful awareness it was, for Roy was the universally acknowledged King of the Cowboys. It must have been the constancy of his sterling character, I thought, that appealed to so many, the essence of American values manifest in, and distilled into, one smiling, handsome man: decency, integrity, honesty, humility, optimism, patriotism, a just-subtle-enough-never-in-your-face reverence for God, the instinctive readiness to stand up for what's right, a demonstrable commitment to protect and champion the down-trodden. And there seemed to be no difference between the public and private Roy Rogers. For kids and adults alike, Roy was both the archetypal and individualized American hero.

There were other contenders for our affection, of course, chief among them, at least in the cowboy realm, Gene Autry and Hopalong Cassidy. Gene and Hopalong were quite admirable in their own right. It's just that...well, they were not Roy. In my estimation, they could not measure up to the King, much as the Brooklyn Dodgers could never measure up to the New York Yankees, Rootie Kazootie to Howdy Doody, Duke Snider to Joe DiMaggio, Jayne Mansfield to Marilyn Monroe, Wilt Chamberlain to Bill Russell, Chryslers to Cadillacs. I remembered an aunt and uncle giving me a pair of Gene Autry cap pistols, a beautiful facsimile of real six-shooters with Gene's patented, orange-handled grips, complete with etched-leather holsters on a belt lined with slots to carry bullets. It would have been unthinkably impolite to refuse the gift or even show disappointment. Instead, I hid them away out of loyalty to Roy and continued to wish for a set of Roy Rogers' pistols, a form of grace that never did alight. But the capacity to have inspired such delayed gratification, such voluntary, agonizing abstention in a six-year-old was no doubt an ultimate hallmark of worship.

All of us kids wanted to be like Roy. I took it a step further, though. I wanted to be adopted by Roy. Make that two steps further: I had moved from desire to fantasy and then conviction that my adoption by Roy and Dale was imminent. I would be sad to leave Arnie and Debbie behind, and, depending on the day, even my parents. But...I had my priorities.

Reflecting on my own traits and inclinations as a boy, I could under-stand why I was able to talk myself into this conviction. Roy's influence on America's youth had been far-reaching before he ever met Dale Evans; once they joined forces, it became pervasive. Over the course of his career, as Walter Scott mentioned, Roy starred in close to a hundred movies and more than a hundred TV episodes. He had already made half of those movies by the time he and Dale married in 1947, and she co-starred in the next 40 starting with "The Cowboy and the Senorita." Together, on December 30, 1951, they launched "The Roy Rogers Show," the TV series that captivated my generation on Sunday evenings for a hundred or so episodes. "Happy Trails," the theme song written and sung by Roy, became our anthem and lullaby.

And what child could fail to be captivated by the wholesome, brave, good-hearted, good-looking Roy and Dale? By the cantankerous but deep-down kindly and ever-faithful Gabby Hayes? By Roy's stupendously beautiful and intelligent golden palomino Trigger (named by Smiley Burnette, a pre-decessor to Gabby as Roy's side-kick, because the horse was able to "turn on a dime and so quick on the trigger")? By Dale's gentle, dependable mare Buttercup? By the rousing musical accompaniment of Roy's long-time group, The Sons of the Pioneers? In one combination or another, in such films as "Southward Ho" (Gabby's first film with Roy following short side-kick stints by Smiley Burnette and Raymond Hatton), "Red River Valley" (the Sons' first film with Roy), "Home in Oklahoma," "Rough Riders Roundup," "Days of Jesse James," "Frontier Pony Express," and "Young Buffalo Bill," to name a few of the more memorable, this company helped to define my childhood—my games, my plots, my reveries, my very conception of the life worth living.

By the time I entered high school in 1958, I had seen most of the movies and TV episodes that Roy had filmed to date, which in themselves would have been enough to nurture my pre-teen worldview. Add to this the commercial reinforcements of Roy Rogers hats, shirts, bandannas, cap pistols, holsters, lassos, furniture, sheets, blankets, clocks, wristwatches, and lunch boxes, and that worldview was virtually commandeered by the Double-R brand.

But the leap to adoption—more accurately, the wishful fantasy and then unshakable expectation of adoption—required certain pre-conditions. First, I knew that Roy and Dale lived on a ranch in California (during my childhood, it was in Chatsworth, much later in Apple Valley). This was the stuff of dreams for me, a kid who lived in a rented duplex with virtually no land in small-town New Jersey. Second, there was my knowledge, gleaned from things Debbie told me from magazine articles she read, of what they did on the ranch: such rapturous activities as riding, trap- and skeet-shooting, hunting, playing with 30-plus coon hounds, motor boating, fishing—the further stuff of dreams for a kid with no dog, no horse, no guns, no boat or, to be honest, any prospects for these emblems of the ideal. Third, there was my intense desire—a Jewish boy whose "greenhorn" immigrant grandparents were still alive, speaking Yiddish, and not all that far removed from the old country—to be "American." And what, instead of being a Kirinski, could be more American than being a Rogers?

Thus it was that my fantasies really went wild when I heard Roy and Dale had adopted several kids to join Linda Lou and Roy, Jr. ("Dusty"), Roy's biological children from his marriage to Arline (who died in 1946) and, for a tragically short time Robin, Roy and Dale's biological daughter who died of Down syndrome at age two. The adoptees were Cheryl Darlene; Deborah Lee ("Debbie," from Korea, who later, at age 12, died in a car crash in Mexico); John David ("Sandy," an American Indian, who died in his sleep while serving in the U.S. Army in Germany); and Mary Little Doe ("Dodie," also Native American). During a trip to the United Kingdom, Roy and Dale met Marion Fleming ("Mimi"), whom they invited to America as their ward and who, for all intents and purposes, became like their own child. With this menagerie of youngsters—natural, orphaned, multicolored, and multicultural—already in the mix, I asked myself, why not me? And once I was part of the Rogers family, maybe I could convince Roy and Dale to adopt Arnie and Deb as well, since I hated the thought of leaving them behind.

In any event, I was sure I would be a perfect addition to the family: I would take excellent care of the horse they would surely give me, help with the chores, train the dogs, develop into an expert marksman, and—perhaps most important—become as dependable and indispensable a partner in Roy's adventures as Gabby and Dale. Over time, my fantasies predicted, my combination of motivation, conscientiousness, and upright character would turn me into an American hero, too, just like Roy.

The problem with my obsession to be adopted by Roy and Dale went beyond my internal fantasies. Soon there were consequences at school, specifically involving my kindergarten teacher, Mrs. Copeland, who, I was sure, had disliked me even before the adoption issue came up. I suppose she had her reasons.

There was the whale-bone incident. Belmar is right on the ocean, and I was an enthusiastic beachcomber. In September of 1950, the year I was in kindergarten, a hurricane beached a whale at 9th Avenue. Despite efforts to push the animal back to sea and save it, the whale died. The populace's humane instincts quickly gave way to baser ones, and the carcass was chopped to pieces for souvenirs over the next couple of days until only some of the biggest bones were left. Several of my friends and I laid claim to the backbone, which was ten or twelve feet long. But where to take it? School, we decided. Teachers and kids alike would be interested, we figured. And the teachers and kids were interested. The presence of the whale's backbone in the corridor outside Mrs. Copeland's classroom caused quite a commotion, and at first everyone was enthusiastic. Gawkers congregated around it throughout the day, and other teachers brought their classes to see it.

The problem became evident on the second day of the bone's presence among us. School opened that morning to a horrendous odor—a dead whale odor. The small group of which I was the ringleader had placed the bone against a radiator. Apparently, the heat unleashed the smell; it wafted all over. Through no fault of her own, Mrs. Copeland, as our teacher, was nonetheless the responsible adult in this episode. I began to sense that she didn't much care for me.

This sense became certain knowledge after my presentations during story time. Some days, story time consisted of classical children's readings by Mrs. Copeland—Spot and Jane, Hiawatha, Paul Bunyan, Johnny Appleseed, and the like. Other days, kids were invited to tell their own stories. I loved this and took every opportunity to raise my hand when Mrs. Copeland asked for volunteers. Usually, mine was the only hand in the air. Even so, probably because of the whale-bone incident, I guessed, or maybe just to spread opportunities around more widely, her eyes kept scanning the crowd waiting for a contender before she reluctantly chose me. My stories were more in the tradition of a saga, a series of adventures that grew out of my love of the Old West, my Roy Rogers-inspired worldview. They were also highly imaginative and extemporaneous—tall tales, some would call them. Others might characterize them as lies, which was the approach Mrs. Copeland took. Even more than the whale-bone incident, I later realized that this was why she was reluctant to choose me. It came to a head over a series of story-telling sessions.

The saga I told was epochal. I would stand in front of the class and go on until Mrs. Copeland called an end to the session. On each subsequent occasion, I picked up right where I had left off, days or even weeks ago. The tale started, appropriately enough, right there on the Jersey Shore where, I informed my enthralled audience, I had organized a wagon train to head west, to California. I populated the wagons with these same classmates and other recognizable Belmar citizenry. I trained the horses, purchased the wagons, oriented the passengers to the hazards of the journey, and commissioned all the supplies from such local merchants as Levi's Bakery, Pat's Diner, Biesky's Luncheonette, Taylor's Hardware, Kedersha's Bootery, and

Larry's Kosher Butcher Shop. I made a special point of noting that I did all this as Assistant Trail Boss—assistant to Roy Rogers, and as such the fourth member of the Roy-Dale-Gabby team. Each chapter of the saga was loaded with adventure and associated diversions: bandits, rustlers, Indians, plague, singing songs around the campfire under the star-studded sky at the end of a hard and dangerous day—all the usual ingredients of Western movies, more specifically Roy Rogers' movies. The other kids were captivated. In hindsight, I suspected that Mrs. Copeland must have recognized this and therefore indulged me longer than she might otherwise have liked.

The saga ground to a halt, along with student presentations generally during story time, at about the time my wagon train crossed the Continental Divide and moved into the high Rockies. It was winter. Food was scarce. Progress was slow. People were cold and depressed. Tempers were high. The travelers could hear the wolves at night, hungry beasts waiting for signs of the train's vulnerability. Indians were undoubtedly waiting for their shot as well. But a hero emerged, a champion. This time it wasn't Roy. It was me, Nathan Kirinski. I found, slaughtered, and dressed several buffalo, thus providing food for the winter. I gathered masses of firewood, ensuring my wagon-train charges could cook, stay warm, and be protected from the wolves. I befriended an Indian chief and negotiated the safety of the entire wagon train. As my reward for these heroics, Roy and Dale adopted me. I was now Nathan Evans-Rogers.

At this point Mrs. Copeland stepped in to interrupt the story, her portly frame poised liked an opera singer about to blast an aria. "Thank you, Nathan. This has been a very interesting story." Looking back with the eyes of the educator I became, I could only admire her restraint and sympathize with her dilemma. She couldn't publicly squash or ridicule me, much as she might have been inclined to do just that. At the same time, she couldn't let the rest of the class believe that this was anything but a tall tale. This was not as easy as it would have been had I not claimed adoption. My classmates were a bunch of six- and seven-year-olds, after all, impressionable, naïve, trusting. "Children," she continued, "Nathan is quite a good storyteller, don't you think? But I hope you all know that the story isn't true."

I was devastated. That my story wasn't "true" meant that I was a liar. She was calling me a liar. I knew it was a story, in the sense that none of the things I described had actually happened. But the part about my adoption was problematic, both for Mrs. Copeland and for me, although in different ways. For her it was an unacceptable lie and not just a harmless adventure story. For me it was—well, it was what I so much wished for and expected. The fantasy had become my truth.

But it didn't end there. There was the matter of my parents—my biological parents, Fay and Morton Kirinski, now about to be usurped, at least in my mind and without their knowledge or permission, by my adoptive parents,

Dale Evans and Roy Rogers, who would take me to the ranch—"our Rogers' family ranch"—in California.

Fay and Mort, my long-suffering parents. Over the years, I came to appreciate them as exemplars, generous and self-sacrificing for their children in the extreme. But at the time...well, they weren't Roy and Dale. They had no ranch, no dogs, no horses, no guns.

My parents arrived at Mrs. Copeland's classroom after school that day, concerned at having been summoned. In my presence, Mrs. Copeland told them about my story and then asked me what I had to say.

"It was just a story," I offered, expressing what I thought should have been obvious. "I didn't mean to lie. Movies don't lie. Books don't lie. They just tell stories. I didn't mean to lie," I repeated.

"But telling the other students that you were adopted is really a bad thing to have done," Mrs. Copeland said, looking to my parents for affirmation and receiving it.

I must have absented myself from the conversation at that point; I have no memory of what was said next. I only remember what I knew. That my teacher was wrong. That everything would turn out okay. That Roy and Dale would adopt me.

6
Miami Beach

"*MOON OVER MIAMI*," ARNIE and I sang in falsetto, imitating Patti Page in her current hit, as we danced around Deb and made up nonsensical lyrics, *"smiling at you from the tallest palm tree, while you sunbathe 'til dawn in your new bikini..."*

"You two are so infantile," Deb chided us, but we knew she didn't mean it. She was as excited by what our parents had just told us as Arnie and I were. The whole family was excited. We were going to Miami Beach for the three-week school break in the winter of 1956, five days down, ten days there, five days back. None of us kids had ever been farther away from New Jersey than Boston. Our parents had been to Quebec for their honeymoon in 1928, and Mom had traveled as far as Chicago during her professional dancing days. But Miami Beach! This was special.

Our father put some glossy brochures on the table and pointed to the photo of a seven-story, beige building circled by balconies. "The Sorrento," he said. "Right on the beach, just off Collins Avenue. Brand new." He pointed to a photo of the Sorrento's famous neighbor. "And we get to use the Fontainebleau's pool and beach."

I couldn't believe what I was hearing. "But what about the Carousel?" I asked.

"We'll close it down." He saw my shock. "It's a once-in-a-lifetime deal. Would you rather work over the holidays?"

"No!" we all yelled in unison. "*Moon over Miami*," Arnie and I sang again, "*as we lounge by the pool, with no thoughts about school...*"

"Idiots," Deb laughed.

Three months later, my parents, Arnie, and I made the drive south in our '54 Ford. Deb was finishing up her exams at Boston University and would fly down to meet us. En route, I most loved the Smithsonian in Washington, DC, where I obsessed over the stuffed body of Baldy, lead dog of the famous Alaskan dog musher Scotty Allan, who inspired the protagonist in Jack London's *The Call of the Wild*. Baltimore Harbor, with its echoes of "The Star-Spangled Banner," made an impression, as did the Coca Cola mansions on West Paces Ferry Road in Atlanta. From there, even Cape Canaveral, Daytona, and Palm Beach were blurs. We could hardly wait to be in Miami Beach.

And it was wonderful at first—Parrot Jungle, the flamingoes at Hialeah, Seminoles wrestling alligators, Jai Lai exhibitions, swimming at the Fontainebleau. A 12-year-old's paradise. Then Deb arrived. I was thrilled to see her when she got off the plane. Arnie and I adored her, and she, despite the seven-year age difference, mostly adored us. Even when we crossed her, she was never mean. She was our big sister, a college student, our idol. Now that she had joined us, paradise would be complete.

The problem presented itself when we went to the front desk to register Deb. "I'm very sorry, Mr. Kirinski," said the clerk, "but the room you reserved for your daughter can't be occupied."

"What are you talking about?"

"Well, a pipe burst, and the room flooded. Everything's soaked—carpet, bed, furniture. It'll take days to fix it up. It's just not habitable."

"Okay, too bad. Just give us a different room."

"That's the problem. It's Christmas season. We're totally booked. There are no other rooms available."

"So where's that leave my daughter?"

"We can put an extra bed in your room or," the clerk gestured toward Arnie and me, "your sons'."

"No way," sputtered the distraught Deb. "Never!"

The manager came up. Mort cajoled, threatened, even hinted at a bribe. In the end it didn't matter. Arnie and I were rooming with our 19-year-old sister.

The situation was manageable during most of our days there, when Arnie and I only came out of the ocean for meals. But a two-day infestation of Portuguese man o' war jellyfish, notorious for their painful sting, forced us to use the pool. That shouldn't have been anything but wonderful (the Fontainebleau's pool was a marvel for its size, architecture, dipping pools, and cabanas) if it weren't for the sights around the pool. By this I mean bodies: shapely, tanned, oiled, bikini-clad female bodies. I would lie there, face down, on a chaise lounge trying not to ogle, but failing; hoping my erection would subside before I had to walk to the restaurant to join my family for meals; wondering what in the world was happening to me "down there"; wishing that I could stop looking at, and thinking about, the bodies all around me. Bodies that included Deb's, whose opulent shape, beautiful face, Irish Setter-red hair, and vibrant personality attracted the handsomest young men around. Furtively, I would watch her cavort with one or another of them in the pool, lying in their arms, sitting on their shoulders, wrestling for a beach ball...

Nights were more excruciating. There lay Deb, her curvaceous contours visible under the sheet, illuminated just enough to torture me by the hotel's ambient lights. I put Arnie on the side of the bed we shared closest to Deb. I turned to face the opposite direction. Still, I couldn't stop visualizing her in her bikini, couldn't help imagining her without it. My sister! How bad could I be? Biblically bad. So bad that I couldn't share the cause of my distress even with Arnie.

I avoided interactions with my sister. At meals, I couldn't bring myself to have eye contact with her. My parents and Arnie didn't seem to notice any of this, but Deb did. "You've been weird these last couple of days, Nathan. What's going on?" I looked down, not answering. "Actually," she continued, "I think I know what's happening, why you're avoiding me." *You couldn't possibly*, I thought, but just sat there, eyes averted.

"It's sex, isn't it?" Now I looked up, shocked by the word and her clairvoyance but also, somehow, relieved that at least someone *knew*, even if that someone was the object of my perversity.

"Am I right? Come on, Nathan. You know I am. Don't think I haven't seen that bulge in your bathing suit," she laughed, "and don't think I haven't seen boners before." I must have groaned or something. She turned more serious. "What you're going through is natural. One day you're a kid with no interest in sex. Maybe you're even disgusted by the idea of it. Then out of nowhere these thoughts and urges come over you like a wave. You imagine all girls, or boys if you're me, naked. You imagine kissing them, touching them, being touched. Believe me, it's natural. And it's good."

My God. Here was my sister not only creeping into my innermost mind, but pretty much telling me that she had "done it," done the thing I had only heard about in gym locker rooms, or conjured up from suggestive pictures in celebrity magazines, or read about in books like the newly published *Peyton Place* I found on my parents' bedside table.

She smiled and stood up. "You're a handsome fella, Nate, and I can tell you've got a lot of fun times ahead of you. Too bad you're twelve. And my brother. But you are."

I sat there for a few minutes after she left the room. The ache in my groin that had been there since Deb arrived in Miami Beach was still there. But having it was okay now.

We left Miami Beach two days later, all five of us together this time. We stopped along the way in Saint Augustine, Charleston, Chapel Hill, and, for two days, in Washington so that Deb could visit all the sites. Arnie and I shared a room each night. Deb had her own.

7

The Skylight

MY FRIEND RALPH FICANO had a reputation for mischief. No one in Belmar would have disagreed that the reputation was well deserved, although opinion was split whether or not he was basically a good kid despite the trouble he caused. During the couple of years that Arnie and I hung out with Ralph, some people had the same split opinion about us.

"Those three are hoodlums," old Mrs. Anderson ranted to police investigating the broken windows in the garage behind her house on 6th Avenue. "I watched them throwing stones from Helen Murphy's backyard, laughing and congratulating each other whenever they broke a pane. I yelled at them and they ran. Then I called you. They should be in jail."

But Mrs. Anderson was the only witness. When questioned, we not only pleaded innocence, but acted incensed that anyone would accuse us of such vandalism. The police had no choice but to reject Mrs. Anderson's charges. The fact that Ralph's uncle, Phil Gugliermo, was police chief had no bearing. If anything, the opposite was true.

"There's no proof, but I know you guys did it," Chief Gugliermo told us. "You better be careful," he warned us. "You're headed in a bad direction."

There was no absence of proof with our next adventure, when we broke into an unoccupied summer residence on 12th Avenue one winter's afternoon. People in Belmar rarely locked their windows or doors; it was a very safe town, especially in the mid-1950s, when this incident occurred, and the town was small enough that most people knew one another. All Ralph, Arnie, and I had to do was climb onto a shed attached to the house, raise a window, and enter. We thought about taking some items to justify this incursion; but really, we were doing this purely for the fun of it; there was no reason to take anything, so we didn't. This ended up being a smart decision. Breaking and entering was one thing, burglary quite another. And there was no way we could deny the former charge. We were caught red-handed when we climbed back onto the shed and were greeted by Officer Mike Cleary, who also happened to be our Little League baseball coach. "I couldn't be more disappointed in you boys," Cleary said as he loaded us into his patrol car.

Down at the station, there was nothing avuncular about Ralph's Uncle Phil. Chief Gugliermo was all cop as he had us fingerprinted and placed in a cell for an hour of "reflection" before releasing us to our parents' custody.

"Nothing was damaged," Phil told the families, "and these guys are only eleven. So I'm not going to press charges. This time," he added pointedly. "If you ever break the law in this town again, get ready for Jamesburg." He was referring to the site of the notorious New Jersey Training School for Boys, a juvenile reformatory that was the stuff of nightmares among local kids. We could tell that he was entirely serious.

We never broke the law after that. More accurately, we never got caught for what were more on the order of "moral indiscretions" than anything qualifying as outright criminal behavior. From time to time, we would play hooky from school to walk the railroad tracks out to the old Jersey Central terminus in Wall Township, where we would explore the abandoned freight cars. In this and other out-of-the-way places we would smoke whatever cigarettes we had been able to filch from our parents and older kids. Once, we did flirt with actual crime when we shoplifted from Berman's Five and Dime, but had a change of heart and replaced the merchandise, undetected, before we left the store. On two other occasions, we "borrowed" items from friends' homes but managed to return them before being found out.

When we turned 12, puberty took our mischief-making in new directions, directions we couldn't understand or control. Most of these were innocent enough, like the tickling fights with Gail Morton, a 14-year-old whose squirmy fingers ranged all over our bodies, just as ours ranged all over hers. In the afternoons after school, games of spin-the-bottle with Betty Lou Stillwell in the garage behind Ralph's house began to take the place of basketball. And there were the wrestling matches with Ruth Fairbanks, a young married woman whose husband was often absent on business trips and who treated us like sons. We wondered at Mrs. Fairbanks' closed-eye grimaces as she applied her favorite hold, what she called her "leg-scissor squeeze," around our hips.

As 13-year-olds puberty took on an elevated dimension, so to speak, when some older members of our Boy Scout troop introduced us to the mechanics of masturbation. From that crucial learning juncture onward, sex became life's center. The urge for sexual experiences was constant and overwhelming. The lack of opportunity to have such experiences was equally constant and overwhelming. This was not for any laziness on our part. We invited Gail to renew the tickling bouts, but she, now 15 and dating high school boys, rebuffed us as "immature." We tried raising the stakes in spin-the-bottle from kissing to stripping, but Betty Lou could not be persuaded to play that game. We even resumed dropping in on Mrs. Fairbanks, but she was pregnant now and not inclined, or in any condition, to wrestle. So we limped off to find other outlets.

The one we settled on was voyeurism, although this was not a term most 13-year-olds would know. We did know the term Peeping Tom, and that's what we became. Our first foray in this activity was a nightly vigil outside Betty Lou's house. We knew where her bedroom window was, and we could catch fleeting glimpses of her when the lights were on. But there were obstacles: it was difficult to see into a second-story window; we ran the risk of being discovered; it was too cold to spend hours watching; there was no guarantee that watching would yield anything worth seeing; and, just when we thought Betty Lou was undressing for bed, she invariably closed the blinds and turned off the light.

As titillating as it was to continue imagining Betty Lou in the nude, our frustration at never actually seeing her naked drove us to seek other venues for spying. We roamed all over town looking for promising peeps. There was the occasional success, a glimpse here and there of naked bodies. These fleeting moments heightened our craving to see more.

One evening, as we were crossing the drawbridge over the inlet separating Belmar from Avon, the neighboring borough to the north, we stopped to look back at the lights of our town. That was when we saw the line of five attached row houses near Inlet Terrace, a stretch we hadn't yet reconnoitered. Here was another venue for spying, another set of windows that might offer a special sighting if the circumstances were right. But the necessary conditions for special sightings were rarely aligned, in our experience. It needed to be dark enough outside for the lights to be turned on, but not quite late enough for the shades to have been drawn. And even if these conditions were satisfied, it was unlikely that something worth seeing would fill the transparent, backlit window.

But Arnie, Ralph, and I were limited by a traditional idea about windows, which as far as we knew were always on the side of a house. This was the 1950s; unless you had been to Europe, you would have no concept of any other kind of window, which was why we were intrigued by the light coming from the top of one of the row houses. This was something we hadn't previously come across. We decided to investigate.

The row houses were connected by a common roof, which we reached by climbing a tree at one end of the complex. The light was coming from the other end of the row. It was easy to walk there; the roof was only slightly pitched.

We found a flat, rectangular, transparent piece of glass, maybe three feet square. We lay prone at its edge and peered in. We saw a brightly lit bathroom. A bath tub. A woman bathing. She wasn't young by our standards, in her thirties, we guessed. But she was pretty. A brunette. With large breasts and dark nipples. We didn't dare move as we watched her soap herself, her actions at once languid and sensual. After washing her breasts, she put her hands under the water. It was a bubble bath; we could only see her head and upper torso. But we could tell she was washing between her legs. Soon, she showed the same closed-eye grimace Mrs. Fairbanks had on her face when she performed the "leg-scissor squeeze." Ralph, Arnie, and I were two years past those wrestling matches; at thirteen, now Boy Scout masturbatory initiates, we had a pretty good idea of what was going on, although we had never considered that girls did such things.

It was too much for Arnie. He crawled back across the roof and was already climbing down the tree before I, a breathless captive to what I was witnessing, realized he was gone. Leaving Ralph at the skylight, I reluctantly followed my brother and joined him on the ground. "What's the matter with you? I can't believe you left. Let's go back."

"It's wrong, Nate," Arnie said as he turned to walk home. "We shouldn't be doing this. It's bad."

"It's not bad," I called after him. "It's not."

I considered returning to the roof but figured the bath would likely be over by now. I jogged after Arnie. "It's not bad," I repeated when I caught up. "It's the best thing I've ever seen."

I kept going back to the window on the roof, which I had learned from a library book was a new invention called a skylight. But Ralph and I went without Arnie now. He said he would have nothing to do with peeping anymore, either through the skylight or anywhere else. He refused to cross a boundary, while Ralph and I clearly reveled in the territory on the other side. Except for when it rained or snowed, we went back to the skylight almost every night. It was always the same routine. Fully dressed, the woman came into the bathroom, turned on the lights, poured in some bubble bath, and ran the water. She left while the tub was filling and returned wearing a silk bath robe. She turned off the water, took off the robe, and stood naked in front of a full-length mirror, looking at her body from different angles. Once a week or so, she would shave her legs and armpits. Occasionally, she would trim her pubis, first running a comb through the thick, curled hair, then clipping it a bit, and finally running her razor along the edges of her dark triangle. This was one of my favorite moments.

But it was only a build up to the rest of the routine, in which Ralph and I now participated, imagining ourselves to be the woman's actual, if not actually interacting, lovers. As she bathed her breasts and pulled at her nipples with her fingertips, we each massaged our penis and scrotum. As she submerged her hands and began to masturbate, we did as well. As her grimace of pleasure intensified, our hands moved more and more rapidly along the shafts of our erections. As the woman's grimace turned into an open-mouthed gasp, Ralph and I, kneeling so we could continue looking into the skylight, arched our backs and caught our discharges in the tissues we were never without these days. And as the woman relaxed back into the water, we fastened our pants, crawled quietly back across the roof, lowered ourselves down the tree, and made our way home.

Ralph, Arnie, and I played on the same Babe Ruth League baseball team that summer, and Arnie resumed hanging out with us after practices and games. Ralph's and my trips to the roof were no longer an issue for Arnie; they were on hold, because it stayed light too late for Ralph and me to go back to the skylight without the risk of being discovered—and likely for no reward, since surely the woman's bath would be over. Instead, the three of us walked the boardwalk in the evenings, played pinball in the several arcades along Belmar's beach front, and flirted with the girls our age whose families were summering at the Shore. Every so often we scored, if not an elusive home run, at least to the extent of some heavy petting under the boards. But heavy petting takes its toll. By the end of the summer, even Arnie's scruples were compromised. As the days grew shorter, Ralph and I resumed our visits to the skylight, now joined by Arnie.

One autumn evening, as we looked down at her while she relaxed in the tub, the woman's eyes shot open. We pulled back from the edge of the skylight. Had we been spotted? How, after all the months of Ralph's and my undetected voyeurism, and then in recent weeks with Arnie? But clearly, something had agitated her. When we peeked back in, she was gone.

We gave it a month before venturing back to the roof. When we reached the skylight, we looked in only to see our reflections in what was now opaque glass. But we could tell there was a light on in the bathroom. Was the woman there—bathing, fondling herself, climaxing? We chose to think she was, and that she could see us.

8
Denny

MY FRIEND DENNY GALLAGHER was sturdy and well proportioned, but he was also short for his age. If you didn't know him, you might be tempted to call him Shorty (or Squirt, after he urinated on Grover Dern's lit cigarette while yelling "Put out the fire!"). But anyone who did so wouldn't repeat the mistake. Denny was tough, and he would never back down. Quite the opposite: he was typically the aggressor, goading bigger kids to fight. If they were too big, he was fast enough to evade them, laughing over his shoulder, somehow staying the aggressor, the victor, even in retreat.

But everyone (except for Grover) loved Denny. Grown-ups invariably described him as "cute," and he was—the diminutive, blond, freckled, buzz-cut Irish child, smart, skilled at sports, saucy and swaggering, always laughing and joking. Even other kids described him as "cute," but we meant it as a compliment. We wanted to be like him. We envied him his looks and abilities and sweet nature, even his short stature, which, if anything, enhanced his attractiveness to adults and brought him the lion's share of their doting attention. We especially envied him his two older brothers, James, a New Jersey State Trooper, and Mike, a high school football coach. Even his father, a conductor on the Jersey Central Railroad, evoked envy. How cool to have that adventurous job riding the rails, in contrast to the office-bound or laborer occupations of most of our dads.

Yet our envy was never mean-spirited. None of us begrudged Denny his good fortune; he was too well-liked. And from all appearances, he was the happiest kid in the world.

It's not that happiness was rare among my friends. Looking back on that summer of 1957, I'd say it was the prevailing disposition in my group. We were 12- and 13-year-olds, and the turmoil of high school was a year or two away. Our time during the summer was mostly our own. Until the age of 14, when we could apply for working papers, we didn't have to worry about jobs. And we were virtually unsupervised. Crime in our community was rare, and our small town was like a miniature kingdom whose borders we, the princes of the realm, could patrol from end to end in a matter of minutes on our bicycles. The town's size and absence of danger lulled our parents into giving us free rein, and we took full advantage of the latitude. Mornings were spent at the beach, riding waves. Afternoons were devoted to baseball, our common obsession. Most of us played organized ball, either Babe Ruth League for the 13-year-olds or Little League for the 12-year-olds. On the days when there were no league practices or games, we filled our afternoons with sandlot games. Evenings were spent following our newly aroused hormones to the boardwalk, where we would play miniature golf and pinball and make believe we weren't interested in the girls from North Jersey as they roamed the arcades. We checked in at home for meals, of course, as much to reassure our parents as to eat. Who had time to eat with everything else there was to do?

We all realized this would likely be one of our last unfettered summers. Most of us would start working in the summer of '58, the rest in '59. It's not that we didn't want to work. In Belmar, summer jobs were a rite of passage for 14-year-olds, a key maturity marker, and we were keen to accept its responsibilities. But we had watched our older siblings enough to know that maturity must come at the price of the nearly unconditional liberty we presently enjoyed. So we were intent on experiencing this summer to the fullest. At times, our pursuit of fun and adventure took us in dangerous directions, but even on those occasions our seize-the-day attitude prevailed.

Whether the circumstances were pleasurable or risky, Denny, with his combination of charisma, ability, wit, and good-natured swagger, led the way. When Marty Reiser got caught in a rip tide off the 11th Avenue beach after the lifeguards had gone off-duty, Denny organized the rest of us into a hand-holding chain that saved our gasping, exhausted friend from almost certain drowning. When Denny and two others took an eight-foot dingy with a stalling, barely functioning outboard motor out into the Atlantic—way past the breakwaters and nearly to the half-mile buoy, where the swells had grown to five feet—it was Denny who kept his head, somehow managing to keep the engine running long enough to bring the trio back to the safety of Shark River Inlet. When the sullen, over-sized, 15-year-old Desmond Clark bullied one of Denny's friends, Denny confronted Clark and actually made him apologize. When a group of us accepted Glenn Bowditch's dare to follow the same route through Shark River he claimed to have taken, then watched with fear as the water rose to our chests when we were only half-way across, it was Denny—whose shorter body was submerged up to his chin—who kept us calm until we reached shore. After the police let Ralph Ficano, Arnie, and me off with only a warning for vandalizing eccentric old Mrs. Anderson's garage, it was Denny who persuaded us at least to clean up the mess. And when David Lindholm, enraged when he tilted a pinball machine on the way to a big score, kicked the machine so hard his foot got stuck, Denny was the only one of the group of friends who stayed behind to help David extricate himself.

Except, you could say, for pissing on Grover Dern, Denny Gallagher really was a fine and special kid—solid, valorous, right-minded; a person with singular potential who had everything going for him.

One afternoon towards the end of that memorable swan song of a summer, Denny forgot to take his baseball glove when he left my house to go home for dinner. It was getting dark by the time I saw it lying in a chair, but I decided to return it to Denny that evening. Denny loved that glove, a Phil Rizzuto model he cared for as if it were a baby, rubbing it with Neatsfoot Oil and tying it up around a baseball over night to form a good pocket and keep the mitt flexible. I wanted to save my friend from worrying and prevent him from being tempted to go out to look for it after dark.

The Gallaghers lived on 13th Avenue, on the block between the railroad and the river. It took no more than ten minutes to get there from my house if I walked diagonally across the several baseball diamonds on Memorial Field. I heard screaming as I approached the Gallaghers' house. I recognized Mr. Gallagher's voice. He was bawling someone out. James and Mike no longer lived there, and Mrs. Gallagher had passed away, so I guessed the screams were directed at Denny. My folks yelled at me from time to time as well. What parents didn't take off after their kids? But this was louder and angrier and more profane than anything I had ever heard. I knew I should have turned for home right away. I knew I shouldn't have looked through the window. It was wrong. But Denny was my friend. I thought I might be able to help him, if not in that moment, then with moral support the next day. But I did look through the window. Mr. Gallagher was standing behind a shirtless Denny beating him with a belt, more accurately with the belt buckle. There were welts and several bloody scratches on Denny's shoulders and back. I could tell Denny was crying; I could see him shuddering. But he continued to stand there and take it, a Denny so unlike the feisty kid who would never take shit from anyone.

I finally did turn away, feeling helpless and shamefully voyeuristic, but only after Mr. Gallagher appeared to lose the strength to continue beating his son. And only after Mr. Gallagher threw himself down on a sofa and started crying himself. And only after I watched Denny gently cover his father with a blanket, stoop to pick something up off the floor, walk to the kitchen and throw away what I could then see was a bottle.

Denny entered his bedroom and closed the door. I walked home across Memorial Field.

I lost touch with Denny after grade school, when we enrolled in different high schools. Years later, I heard that he had suffered a nervous breakdown the summer before our crowd's first year of college and was confined to the mental health facility at Marlboro. But Denny must have recovered. He became a legendary baseball coach in Belmar. I don't know what he did the rest of the year. But Denny was a star in the summer: a cute, well built, self-assured little guy, always smiling, always happy.

9
American Pogrom

I WALKED TO A corner of the synagogue and ducked down the stairs to the men's room. My plan was to stay there until I had a chance to slip across the hall and out the cellar door without being seen. In less than a minute I began to retch from the odors of ammonia and urine. The nausea propelled me from my hiding place and into the hall. I passed the refectory where the kids under 13 years of age held their separate services, opened the outside door, and stepped into the hedges bordering the east side of the building. Above me, I could hear the *hazan* begin to chant the *Shema*, the essential expression of a Jew's faith: "Hear, Oh Israel, the Lord our God, the Lord is one." I waited until the rest of the congregation joined in, then made my way directly to an indentation at the base of the hedge. I reached inside and felt around until I held the knotted laces of my sneakers. Then I screamed as someone grabbed me hard around the back of my neck and yanked me to my feet. I tried to free myself. It was no use. Harry Krakauer, the congregation's sexton, was a strong man.

"So, *Boychik*," Krakauer said sarcastically as he pulled me toward the synagogue. "Is the House of God such a prison that you are always trying to escape? On *Shabbos* a Jew should pray, not play basketball with *goyim*." He pinched my cheek until I grimaced. "Especially you," the sexton continued, "one of our few *Levi*. You'll learn to serve our priests, the *Kohanim*. You'll be called to the *Torah*. You'll make your parents proud."

Krakauer led me back past the men's room and up the stairs to the main synagogue. Fantasies of game-winning heroics were punctured by the visage of Rabbi Steinman, who glared at me as the sexton whispered an account of my latest transgression. The rabbi motioned for me to sit next to him. There was no escape. There was no basketball game for me that day, only incomprehensible prayers and complicated, interminable rituals I would never get right. I hated this place. It confused me with its combination of intimacy and foreignness. I could not understand what it had to do with me, or with America. In that respect, anyway, old Krakauer had things right: to me the synagogue—the whole religion—was a prison. I was imprisoned by services twice a day, by Hebrew school after public school, by prayer shawls and phylacteries and laws upon laws upon laws. And by expectations that were beyond my choice or control or personality. I could not stand the unfairness of being indentured to all of this merely through an accident of birth. There will be more to my life, I told myself, than this foolishness of being a Jew.

At the end of the *Amidah*, the Silent Devotion, I watched enviously as my brother Arnie and our friends Howie Dorfman and Richard Marner began walking to the main door at the back of the synagogue. I looked expectantly at the rabbi, who was still swaying in the plumage of his prayer shawl, a somber bird of prey circling the object of its hunger. The rabbi unwrapped himself. He looked at me and then at the departing boys. "Go," he said gruffly.

I caught up with Arnie, Howie, and Richard as they were leaving the synagogue. We had started down the stairs when Richard screamed and grabbed his leg. Disorientation turned to panic when we realized that five teenagers standing directly across the street from the synagogue were bombarding us with stones. Arnie, Howie, and I helped Richard to cover behind the thick columns at the building's entrance. The stones kept coming, along with shouts of "Jewboys" and "Kike bastards."

I felt paralyzed. This was my town, my snug haven of a town. I went to Belmar Grammar School and played with non-Jews as much as I played with Jews. I sang Christmas carols and painted Easter eggs with them. True, they did not as a rule return the interest on Hanukah and Passover, and envious references were made now and again to the extra days I got off from school on Jewish holidays. But I could never remember having been called a Jew, much less having been punished for being one. Now I was being called a Jewboy and some kind of bastard I had never heard of before.

The stones kept landing on the stairs and portico. We were afraid to go back into the synagogue and risk being injured as we left our cover, so we remained crouching there, involuntary combatants in an incomprehensible war. From our bunker, I recognized one of the assailants as Pat Knowles. Knowles was a punk, a bully from St. Rose High School who occasionally invaded our elementary school yard to give the younger kids a hard time, calling us names and pushing us around if we talked back. But Knowles' meanness had been mostly harmless and democratic, set loose upon smaller children of all denominations. Now his assault was both violent and specific, for some reason, to Jews.

Krakauer the sexton came out the door. When he saw what was happening he started screaming at the attackers. They stopped for a moment and then resumed their assault. Enraged, Krakauer started down the stairs after them, still wearing his prayer shawl and skull cap. As they retreated, the gang continued to shout insults and throw rocks. A stone struck Krakauer on the head before he ever reached the street. Laughing, Knowles and his friends rode away on their bicycles, their departure punctuated by the strident sound of the chain sirens attached to the bike frames.

Krakauer stood on the sidewalk with his head bowed. He covered the wound with his right hand. His left hand was raised in a fist, but to me he seemed puny and innocuous there in his religious regalia, a pushover had the gang decided to push. Krakauer climbed back up the stairs, winded and trembling. As he approached, we left the protection of the columns like small civilians in the aftermath of a bombing who emerge, shell-shocked and hesitant, to watch the dust settle over their city. The sexton was dabbing at his bleeding forehead with his handkerchief. "Bastards," he said as he opened the door and entered the synagogue. "Hoodlums."

The four of us sat on the stairs. Richard raised his trouser leg to reveal a red welt where the first stone had hit him. None of us spoke for a while. Then Howie broke the silence. "If they hadn't surprised us like that we would've gotten rid of them real fast. We didn't even have anything to throw back at them." The rest of us were quick to agree with him. How could we fight back when we didn't have any ammunition, when we were outnumbered and surprised? As for the attack on Mr. Krakauer, it had been a lucky throw by a coward who was running away.

We decided to walk to Arnie's and my house on 5th Avenue, to which we had recently moved from 12th Avenue, where we would hang around until we had to return to services later in the afternoon. On the way, Richard and Howie predicted that a time would come when we would get even with Knowles; the bully wouldn't always be able to get away with picking on younger kids.

I had been quiet through most of the discussion about Knowles' eventual retribution. Then I interrupted. "What's a kike?"

Richard told us it was a kind of Jewish person, but it wasn't a nice thing to call someone. It was like saying wop or spic, and being called one could make a person very angry. Richard recalled when his father, a real estate broker, had gotten into an argument with a client about money. The man had said kike, and Mr. Marner had pushed the man and yelled at him never to set foot in his office again. Later, Richard had asked his sister what the word meant, and she told him it was like calling a person a dirty Jew.

I wondered why Knowles had called us dirty Jews. Knowles hardly knew us.

To get from the synagogue on 11th Avenue to my house on 5th we had to go through an area I called No-Man's Land. It was a forbidding neighborhood primarily because St. Rose Church and its elementary and high schools were located there. While all the rest of Belmar felt intimate and friendly, the area around St. Rose had always presented a vague sense of threat. Belmar Rescue Squad's headquarters, basically a garage with two ambulances surrounded by a grass field, was on the outskirts of No-Man's Land. The field was a short-cut to my house, so we took that route. As we started to cross the field, we saw that Knowles and his friends were gathered at its far end, their vigilante bikes corralled nearby against a cyclone fence. I assumed they had spotted us, and I experienced an even greater fear than I had during the bombardment of stones, when we could have retreated to the synagogue as a last resort. But now we had no place to go, no recourse. We were four 13-year-olds against five 15-year-olds. The enemies' arsenal included initiative, size, and a hatred of Jews. Our arsenal was limited to the 50 yards that separated us from them.

We stood at the border of the field, paralyzed, sure we would be attacked. But the gang had yet to notice us. They were preoccupied in tormenting a fat little boy who was lying supine in the dirt. "Look," Richard whispered. "They've got Steinman. They've got Akiva."

Knowles sat on the rabbi's son, whose crying could be heard across the field. One of the gang was holding a small dog in his arms. He stooped with it now, pushing the dog's backside, tail lifted, towards Akiva's face. Mimicking a girl's voice, Knowles said, "Come on, little fatty, you like to eat. This doggie's ass will taste just delicious. Lick it right here, little fat Jew."

Akiva was screaming now. He twisted his face away in an effort to avoid the animal. Knowles grabbed the younger boy's hair and started to pull his head up. It was then that Akiva saw us standing on the far periphery of the field, heaven-sent comrades come to end his travails. "Help me, you guys," he called to us. "Help me."

His captors looked at us. "Yeah," Knowles said, still imitating a girl's voice, "come on and help him, you guys."

Howie yelled out then, his own voice an unfortunate falsetto. "Leave him alone, you jerks. You'll get in a lot of trouble for this."

Knowles made Akiva get to his feet. He spoke quietly to his friends, one of whom grabbed Akiva's tie and began pulling him in our direction. The gang came within a few yards of us and threw Akiva down on the grass. Knowles straddled him as he lay on his back. "Okay, we'll leave him alone. We just wanted to clean him up a little before he goes to your church." To the guffaws of his friends, Knowles unzipped his pants and began urinating. Sobbing, Akiva tried to roll out of the way, but he was pinioned between Knowles' feet.

My terror was insuppressible. I broke away, running spastically back in the direction of the synagogue. I cried as I ran, well beyond the power of shame. The others bolted immediately behind me. We sprinted in a pack for over a block until, fighting for air and certain we were not being chased, we stopped. We looked back towards the field. Knowles and his friends were walking back to their bicycles. Each of them took a parting punch at Akiva, who still sat in the dirt whimpering. The chain sirens sounded as the posse of bikes disappeared towards the Church of St. Rose.

When the gang was gone, we walked back to the field. Akiva stood up slowly as we approached him. His shirt was ripped, his tie undone, his jacket filthy. The dirt on his face was lined from tears and urine. His shoulders and chest were heaving. When we had almost reached him, he turned and walked away. We caught up with him, and I put my hand on his shoulder. Akiva shook it off and continued walking, resolute and silent. We stopped following him and just stood there as he moved away, isolated and untouchable now in a dirty sort of dignity. We were afraid of him, of his anger and of what he knew about us and about himself. We had abandoned him. He had suffered, and he had survived. For him, the worst had come directly to pass and by its reality had moved him beyond the fear of its potential. Akiva's knowledge still lay in wait for the rest of us.

1987

Thirty years later and the smell was the same. It was a smell that had assaulted me in synagogues from Manila to London to Silver Spring, Maryland. It was the smell of prayer books and Talmuds, of old men wearing dentures, of schnapps and herring and parchment and mildew. I was sure I could have been set down blindfolded in any Ashkenazi synagogue in the world and known beyond doubt where I was by the smell. A Jew who converted would be plagued unmercifully by this smell. The apostate must literally cut off his nose in the spiting of his faith.

I arrived early and was alone in the synagogue. I reacquainted myself now with the details of this small building that continued to factor so heavily in the dramas of my memory: the cornerstone, donated and laid 80 years earlier by some vacationing grandee; the display board commemorating the dead; the stained-glass windows, dedicated to the memory of one or another founding congregant; the worn benches, whose discomfort still served the cause of wakeful worship; the *m'chitzah*, the curtain separating the sexes, one of Orthodoxy's less subtle methods for keeping men's minds on God's work; and the sacred Ark, repository of the *Torah*, the scrolls of Mosaic law which may have accounted for more order and more confusion, for more meaning and more suffering, than any other collection of words in the history of humankind.

As ever, I was ambivalent about these odors and artifacts of Judaism. I felt captive to their influence. I wanted to get away. In reality, I was free to go. I was not bound. But my senses and associations had been unalterably conditioned. My mind had crystallized into the mentality of a slave, and despite my objective liberty I did not feel entirely free.

An old man entered the room. He looked at me suspiciously, as if he were calculating his chances of escape should this stranger standing near the *bimah*, the prayer platform, become aggressive. Thirty years earlier I would have tensed at the sight of the man, who had had an unfortunate penchant for pinching small boys' cheeks until their eyes teared. Now it was the old man who was nervous. I recognized his anxiety and approached him slowly, offering my hand. "Mr. Krakauer, don't you remember me?"

Krakauer rubbed a small scar on his forehead as he scanned my face. Then, ignoring my outstretched hand, he took me by the shoulders. For a moment, Krakauer looked as if he were going to cry. Instead he whispered, "*Boychik*, you're back. It's been a long time since we had a young *Levi*."

I left synagogue after morning services to pick up Arnie at our parents' house. He was visiting for the weekend and would join Esther and me for a late lunch at our apartment in Ocean Grove, where I now worked for the post office. On the way, I entered No-Man's Land and took the short-cut across the field surrounding the rescue building. Most of it had been paved over with asphalt since my youth. Only a small rectangle of grass, perhaps 40 square feet, remained. In the middle of this plot I noticed a stone-mounted plaque I had never seen before. Its commemoration date was 1985. *Belmar Rescue Squad,* it read. *Organized in 1952 to provide succor and service in times of need.*

In my memory's eye I saw Akiva, beaten, splashed with urine, abandoned but oddly proud. Then I left No-Man's Land and made my way home.

10
The School Bus

NINTH GRADE AT ASBURY PARK High School was a challenging transition year. Accustomed from kindergarten through eighth grade to the small size, familiarity, and security of Belmar Grammar School, I was now in a large, less personal institution that drew its students from multiple communities. There were a lot of different groups; I was confused about which groups I wanted to belong to and worried whether any of them would accept me. Maybe that's the way high school is most places, especially in the first year. You're totally concerned about being cool, being liked, belonging. And if acceptance isn't in the cards, you at least don't want to be hassled.

Arnie and I had to take a bus to get to Asbury High. Each weekday morning we'd wait on Main Street in Belmar to get picked up along with the other kids in our neighborhood. The ride took about a half-hour. The bus was an unsettling experience, mostly because we had heard from the older kids that every freshman boy had to be initiated. The most common initiation was called "de-pantsing." This was when the junior and senior boys took off a younger kid's pants in the back of the bus and threw them to the front of the bus, where all the girls sat. To get your pants back, you'd have to walk up front in your underwear. The fear I had of being de-pantsed, the threat of being humiliated in front of girls whom I had known most of my life, was even greater than the fear I had of some of the more brutal forms of initiation, like when they put out cigarettes on Eugene Bergman's hands. The kids who had done that had gotten in a lot of trouble for it. Something like that was not likely to happen again, I figured. But de-pantsing was a definite possibility.

The possibility affected my whole outlook on life, and I went to school anxious every day. The half-hour bus ride each way was hell, and my sense of relief whenever I got off the bus without having been initiated was tremendous. I suspected all the younger kids felt the same way, although we never talked about it. We never talked about our fears.

Nothing happened on the bus at first. There were no initiations. Could be, I thought wishfully, they were a thing of the past and the current group of older kids didn't have an interest in such foolishness. Among this group of older kids were three who played a role in this story. One was Donald Perkins, a smolderingly angry 19-year-old who had been left back a couple of grades in elementary school. Don had been an excellent athlete in baseball and basketball when he was in grade school. In the seventh grade he had broken his leg, shattered it, actually. It had healed badly and stopped growing; Don walked and ran with a worsening limp thereafter. Although he continued his involvement in sports—he played Junior Varsity basketball in high school—he was never the same person after his accident. Basically, he turned mean.

The same didn't go for Raymond Dupree, the kid who followed Don wherever he went. He didn't turn mean; Raymond had always been mean. But he was the type of bully who would pick his spots tactically and never try to beat up on anybody from whom there was a risk of serious retaliation.

A third senior on the bus was a guy named Mike. He had a Jewish-sounding surname, but I can't remember what it was. Mike had only been in Belmar, living with an uncle, for a few months. Nobody seemed to know much about him, except that he came from New York City. He kept to himself, an average-looking guy, on the tall side, who didn't attract much attention. Whenever I looked at Mike, I thought how difficult it must have been to enter a new town and a new high school as a senior, and how particularly difficult it must have been to leave the city behind.

One day in early December, after three months with no incident, what I feared came to pass. Perkins and Dupree, from their seats in the back of the bus, started talking noisily about the little bookworm kids with their corduroy pants and white buck shoes and eyeglasses. At that point, we were all potential targets. Then Don and Raymond focused their attention on Andy Baron. Safe for another day, I thought.

The strange thing was that Andy wasn't a freshman but a sophomore. It obviously didn't matter. He was an easy target: small, pudgy, and studious, with curly hair and glasses. He was sitting three seats in front of his tormenters, who began by throwing crumpled up pieces of paper at him and saying things like, "What's the matter, Andy? Chicken shit?" when he wouldn't respond. The rest of us just sat there, motionlessness our form of self-protection.

Raymond took a textbook from a nearby kid and threw it hard at Andy. It hit him on the head, and he cried out. Then Raymond got up, walked over to Andy's seat, and began pulling him to his feet. Andy struggled, but Raymond was strong and held the terrible authority of fear over the younger boy.

Raymond drew back his fist to hit Andy when a voice from the back of the bus on the opposite side said, "Leave him alone." Startled, Raymond looked up. He never did hit Andy. Something sudden and subtle had changed in the balance of power. Even slight opposition was enough to make Raymond lose the advantage of pure intimidation.

But Donald Perkins was a different story. He was a bully, certainly, but his toughness was authentic. He looked over at Mike. "What did you say, man?"

"I told your friend to leave him alone."

The rest of us didn't move or look in their direction. I had the impression of listening to a radio drama, where you could imagine the action without actually seeing it. I was amazed at Mike's having the guts to say anything, but I had no doubt that it would end badly for this new guy, despite his boldness. Better, I thought, had he just stayed low and kept looking straight ahead.

Don always had talked like a hood. "You think you're so tough, man, so cool. Ray," he ordered Dupree, "go ahead and hit Baron. Break the little faggot's head."

What happened next happened very quickly, and the drama moved right into my passive line of vision. Mike grabbed Raymond's arm, punched him in the mouth, and knocked him to the floor of the bus aisle. Then Don came forward and hit Mike, bloodying his nose. Don was built like a truck, he was angry, and he had struck first. I was sure this guy Mike was in trouble. But Mike was already hitting Don, knocking him towards the back of the bus. Don threw a roundhouse that missed, and Mike caught him under the arms and slammed him to the aisle floor on his back. I had never seen such compressed violence and skill. Mike was on top of Don, punching his face. At one point, Don was able to use his great strength to throw Mike off and get up. I heard Raymond saying in a soft, worried, insistent voice, "Get him, Don. Get him." It was as if Raymond's hero and support in life were falling, beaten by a superior force, and Raymond himself was going down with him.

Don's white shirt was covered with blood. His face looked all mashed up as he stood there saying, "You think you're so tough. I don't care how good you are, how tall. I'll get you, man. I'll take you down." I was struck by how odd it was for Don to have said "how tall," until it occurred to me much later that a guy whose shattered leg had stopped growing might have been jealous of anyone taller.

Mike had blood on him, too, most of it Don's with the exception of the damage from Don's first hit to Mike's nose. Since then, it had all been Mike's fight. I was awed. A slim kid, a quiet guy who minded his business had out of nowhere come to the rescue of not just Andy Baron, but every other frightened underclassman on the bus. I wanted to identify with Mike, to share some power and self-esteem. Isn't that what heroes are for, to bring you something you can't get for yourself? But it was impossible to fool myself about this situation. Mike had the skill and the courage to do what the rest of us could not do. It was Mike's day alone. The rest of us had been saved, but we had not changed.

Belatedly, as the action was dying down, Mr. Laird, the bus driver, came back and pulled Mike off Don, who was again on his back in the aisle. Don kept screaming something about not caring and taking Mike down. Raymond was mumbling something like, "You'll get him, Don. You'll get him."

Mike tucked in his shirt, took his seat, and stared out the window. He was impassive and totally still. Glancing back at him, I found him as much a mystery in repose as he had been in action.

11

Interlude

I DON'T BLAME MY parents. They wanted the best for me, and a full scholarship to Phillips Exeter Academy is as good as it gets in terms of faculty, the quality of education, and career prospects. But the rest of my life there was another matter.

I didn't want to leave the Shore. It was familiar, personal, and mostly secure despite incidents like what happened on the school bus, which were infrequent. But high test scores led to an exceptional opportunity, so in September of 1959 I went to Exeter for my sophomore year. It was mostly a mismatch from the start, except for the academics, in which I did well. The schooling was excellent; my teachers in every subject had graduate degrees and to a person were intellectually stimulating. But I could never adjust to a culture that was, at least compared to Asbury Park High School, so homogeneous in ethnicity, race, religion, and socio-economic privilege. And my classmates, through snide remarks about my clothes, accent, and religion, made it clear they weren't going to get used to me either. Ostracized outside of class, I languished, terribly lonely and constantly homesick. I understood that I was embarking on a sure-fire successful career just by virtue of being at Exeter. But the long-term advantages of a promising career were an abstraction. The only future I could bring myself to care about was the next holiday away from prep school, my next trip home.

Just as I couldn't fault my parents for sending me to prep school, I couldn't thank them enough for allowing me to withdraw from Exeter at the end of my sophomore year and return to Asbury Park High. It had to have been a hard decision for them, but my obvious misery outweighed their own disappointment in the end. Now I was back, elated to be with my brother and friends, elated too that they were happy to have me with them again.

12

Greenbaum and Rosenzweig

THERE WERE TWO MEMBERS of our group I could have done without after I returned from Exeter. I say, "members of our group," which they were in the sense that they were my classmates at Belmar Grammar School and part of the small contingent of Hebrew school students preparing together for *bar mitzvah*. But they were never my friends.

Albert Greenbaum entered my life mid-way through our 6th grade year of elementary school. I was focused on an assignment at my desk one morning and only vaguely aware of the door opening at the back of the room. "Oh, he's cute!" I heard the girl sitting in front of me whisper. I glanced up and saw her turned in her seat looking at the door. When other girls joined the "he's cute" chorus, I also turned. The school principal was introducing a new kid to our teacher, who walked the boy to an empty desk near the front of the room. "Class, this is your new classmate, Albert Greenbaum. He comes to us from Queens in New York City. Please say hello to Albert."

"Hello, Albert," we dutifully called out.

I had mixed feelings as class resumed. There was the sympathy I would have for any kid entering a new school and community. I knew how difficult the transition from New York City to Belmar had been for my sister Deb at about this age. Then there was the jealousy I felt when I heard the girls' whispered evaluations of Albert, who, I had to admit, was quite cute. Male competition, age-eleven style. I had a sense of foreboding, of anxiety: my small and intimate world was changing; it was no longer filled with people I had always known; like him or not, there was a new kid in town.

I didn't like him from the beginning. The dislike, which soon became mutual, extended across all sectors of our childhood and teenage years— academic, athletic, social, and economic. Until he arrived on the scene (and I know I'm being immodest, though nonetheless honest), I sat unchallenged on top of the academic heap. But Albert's intelligence was soon apparent, and I had to contend with it. Daily, we vied for highest grades, most number of times called on in class discussions, and most effusive compliments received from teachers. Neither of us was a stand-out athlete, but that didn't stop us from being the most cut-throat, head-to-head competitors in Belmar Grammar School, whether in official basketball, baseball, and track contests or pick-up sandlot games. Before Albert, my puppy-love crushes on girls were the most private and protected aspect of my life. They were no one else's business; had they been publicly known, I would have been mortified. Once Albert was in the picture, these little affairs joined grades

and sports as tallies in the Greenbaum versus Kirinski columns of wins and
losses. Our competition even extended to summer jobs: who would make
the most money? If you added things up over the years, I had the edge on
everything but money. On that dimension, Albert had no peer. Success in
academics and sports came from a mixture of native ability and hard work.
Social success depended on how much people liked you. Making lots of
money required skill and persistence and luck, but also something more:
a certain attitude and temperament, a way of dealing with the world and
other people that put calculations of winning above all else. Albert had that
mindset in spades. He would do anything to come out on top—including
collusion with his biggest rival.

I was wary but also flattered when Albert tried to befriend me soon after I
returned from Exeter in the fall of our junior year. He came up to me as I was
organizing books in my newly-assigned locker. "It's good to have you back,
Nate. But I gotta say, for the life of me I can't believe you gave up Exeter
Academy for APHS."

"Thanks. It's nice to be back. Exeter had obvious advantages, but I'm
just more comfortable here. And I gotta say," I mimicked him, "that I'm surprised by your welcome. We haven't exactly been buddies over the years."

"Oh, come on. Let bygones be bygones and all that. We were kids.
Plus, I'm looking at things selfishly. You're a brain. Like the marketing people
would say, you'll raise the school's profile. The Ivies will be looking at us, and
I'll be right next to you in the picture."

I turned back to my locker, but Albert remained standing there. "Kalman and I are going to the flicks this Friday night. Alfred Hitchcock's new
movie 'Psycho' is playing. How about joining us? We'll meet at the Palace at
seven and have pizza at Vic's afterwards. "

I didn't want to. Greenbaum was a turd, and Kalman Rosenzweig was
like a fly on a turd—a sycophant who did Albert's every bidding. But what the
hell, perhaps both of them had changed. I doubted it, but at least Albert was
trying. And they couldn't be worse than the Exeter snobs, who never invited
me to do anything.

"Okay. I'll see you then."

During the week I wondered about this odd turn of events. Albert had
only ever been my nemesis, and serving as his factotum and accomplice
seemed to be Kalman's principal role in life. Together they had been the
source of much aggravation. I recalled bitterly how they had spread rumors
that I enlisted my sister, older by seven years, to conduct the research, write
the essays, and create the illustrations I submitted for the *Ner Tamid*, or
Eternal Light, award, a high distinction testifying to religious study and practice that can be earned by Boy Scouts who are Jewish. The rumors were
patently false, and I eventually won the award. But the lies made the process

quite stressful. Albert Greenbaum, it should be noted, was also a candidate for the award until he dropped out when it became clear that I would fulfill the requirements first.

Then there were the poker games. Throughout our freshman year of high school, three or four kids whose parents were often away on weekends would convene for invitation-only games that had frighteningly high stakes, especially for 14- and 15-year-olds. I enjoyed playing poker and was enthusiastic to try my hand when Rosenzweig asked me to attend a game he was hosting at his house. In the beginning I did well, building up a nice pile of chips. Gradually, though, the stakes got higher and I began to lose. It was natural enough to lose hands. But I was losing every hand, even when I drew really good cards and despite being a cautious bettor. Too late, by the time I had run out of chips it occurred to me that each hand I lost was either to Albert or Kalman. One or the other of them would raise the stakes until the other players were forced to drop out, leaving only Albert and Kalman. By then, the pot was so big that I couldn't help but feel envious of the winner and sorry for the loser, regardless of my equal disdain for them both. Those feelings were replaced by anger when I was leaving the house and spotted the two of them in another room dividing up their winnings. When I confronted them, they were unapologetic. "It's just smart tactics," Greenbaum said. "We didn't do anything illegal or against the rules. Why don't you join us next time? We'll split the winnings three ways." Fat chance, I thought to myself as I walked home, broke. For me there would be no next poker game with them, much less any intention of teaming up with these two fuckers for anything.

Yet there I was, little more than a year later, about to spend an evening with them, giving them the benefit of the doubt as I tried to make my return to the Shore as ripple-free as possible. The movie part of the evening went pretty well. We shared popcorn and screamed along with everyone else during the film's gruesome shower scene. But things turned bad over pizza. First, they tried to enlist me in a scheme to steal the final exam questions from a locked drawer in our biology teacher's desk. During the weekly after-school teachers meeting, they proposed, when the corridors were mostly empty, Kalman would be at the end of the hall and act as a sentry. I would stand just outside the classroom door, and he would signal me if anyone were coming. In turn, I would alert Albert, who had discovered that there was an unlocked drawer above the locked drawer that could be removed to give access to the test booklet, which he would quickly duplicate on the copy machine in the classroom.

"Count me out, guys."

"What's the problem?" Albert persisted. "It'll be a sure hundred on a really hard test."

I should have walked out then. I don't know why I didn't. Maybe I didn't want to look like a holier-than-thou prude. "It's too dangerous," I said instead. "A perfect grade isn't worth the risk."

"Okay, that's up to you. But you won't say anything, will you?"

"No."

We took the bus back to Belmar and got off at the corner of 5th Avenue and Main Street, the closest stop to our three homes. As we were walking down 5th, Kalman said something to Albert that Albert apparently didn't like. The next thing I knew, Albert slapped Kalman hard across the face. Why? I was used to wrestling matches, or even punches to settle an argument. But a slap was different, somehow more humiliating. And these were two close friends, an inseparable pair since childhood, equal in size. I expected Kalman to hit him back, equal to equal. But he didn't. The last I saw of them as I walked away was Kalman, his head hanging down as Albert stood there berating him.

13
Intimations of Something More

IN THE FALL OF 1961, the beginning of my senior year, I came across *The Asiatics*, a 1935 novel by Frederic Prokosch. It happened while I was waiting for the school bus in Biesky's Luncheonette near the corner of 7th Avenue and Main Street in Belmar. Biesky's was owned by Arthur Biesky, whose son Bruce was a classmate of mine. On cold mornings, Mr. Biesky would let us kids wait for the bus inside the restaurant to keep warm. Usually, I would spend the time talking with my friends, but sometimes I would find a way to separate from the group and look through the paperback novels on the rotating wire bookrack near the front of the store. A book with an orange cover depicting an intense young man wearing a khaki work shirt caught my eye. The man in the picture was standing against a backdrop of mostly darker-skinned people, each wearing the colorful garb of a different land. One was a beautiful woman whom I surmised from her dress to be Chinese. She was looking at the young man.

The bus came and I had to leave. The image of the orange-colored book with the young man and beautiful woman occupied me that entire day and evening. I lay awake with it. Finally, I fell asleep with it.

I left the house early the next morning and made my way to Biesky's. Taking down the book, I studied the cover. There were two testimonials in quotation marks, one by André Gide (whose name I pronounced to myself as "Ander Guide"), the other by Thomas Mann. I had no idea who these critics were, but I was taken over by what they wrote in assessing Prokosch's story of a young American who hitchhikes his way across Asia, from Beirut to the southern border of China. "*An authentic masterpiece,*" wrote Gide. "*Astonishing,*" wrote Mann. "*Among the most brilliant and original achievements of the young literary generation.*"

I opened the book with reverent care and read Prokosch's first paragraph:

> Far down the street I saw the night watchman slowly approaching with his lantern. He was singing to himself in a soft grief-stricken voice. When he saw me he grew silent, his wrinkled-apple face grew intent and solemn. He passed me quietly. And then when he reached the corner he began singing again, chanting, I should have gathered from his tone, about the coming of disasters, the grief of old men, the end of love.

I rushed to the counter and purchased the book. Then I hid it among the gear in my gym bag before boarding the bus for Asbury Park High School.

I spent most of that night reading, following the nameless narrator to places I had mostly never heard of but somehow felt I knew intimately. It was as if a
part of me, always essential but asleep until now, had been stirred into feeling.
Prokosch and his young hero led me out of Lebanon through Syria and Iraq;
over the Transcaucasus and down into Iran and Afghanistan; and finally across
India, Burma, Siam, and French Indo-China en route (as the novel ended and
the protagonist and I parted) to China and the promise of Japan. The adventures
were exotic, at times dangerous. The encounters were mysterious and often sensual. And as I read, I had no doubt that my experiences with Prokosch's hero, my
new great friend, though physically fleeting and confined to numbered chapters,
would endure emotionally. There were moments of quiet as well, moments of
exquisite aloneness and contemplation and recognition in a hotel room in Tre-
bizond or a caravanserai in Meshed or a palace garden in Badrapur.

Prokosch's language and vision formed my personal Asia. The formation
was irrevocable. Years of subsequent traveling and living in Asia never shook
it. Upheaval, development, modernization, and westernization did nothing in
the least to modify the continent that Prokosch's prose implanted inside me.
In later years, with the wisdom of academic hindsight, I recognized the book's
pervasive Orientalism. But I also recognized that for me, both as a boy and
later as a grown man, the novel's enduring influence has little to do with what
might be called objective. It has only to do with what might be called true.

Beyond stirring rhapsodic currents in my emotions and imagination, the
book re-aroused my interest years later, after I learned that Prokosch had never been to Asia when he wrote the novel in the 1930s. The author's personal
history struck me as more than a little enigmatic. Born in 1908, dead in 1989,
Prokosch's life had been privileged. According to *World Authors 1900-1950*,
his father was a distinguished academic, a linguist and philologist, his mother
a concert pianist. There was money in the family, and Prokosch himself had a
varied education at schools in Austria, Germany, and France before receiving
a B.A. from Haverford College and a Ph.D. from Yale with a specialization
in Chaucer. He taught English at Yale, spent two years at Cambridge, and
then taught for a year at New York University. There is some suggestion that
Prokosch may have trafficked in Chaucerian and Audenian manuscripts, both
private editions and forgeries—more "for fun and not for money" as his brief
biographical entry puts it. He was cultural attaché in Stockholm during World
War II. Thereafter, "he lived in a well-appointed house, 'La Trouvaille,' in Plan
de Grasse, Alpes Maritimes, France." He published several collections of poetry, translations of Hölderlin and Labé, an autobiography, and sixteen novels.
Presaged in his earlier work, he addressed his homosexuality directly in a 1968
novel, *The Missolonghi Manuscript*, and the 1983 autobiography, *Voices.* His
first two works of fiction, *The Asiatics* and *The Seven Who Fled*, were critical and commercial successes. However, "the fourteen novels that Prokosch
wrote after this did not fare so well, commercially or otherwise."

Years later, I came across a single-paragraph entry about Prokosch in *Merriam-Webster's Encyclopedia of Literature*. There was a tacit quality to the introductory sentence that was as poignant, intriguing, and mysterious as *The Asiatics* itself. "American writer," it read, "who became famous for his early novels and whose literary stature subsequently rose as his fame declined." Whatever the facts of his life, whatever its fictions, failures, successes, and predilections, the 27-year-old Prokosch, who imagined and then shared his imagination in *The Asiatics*, had an important and premonitory influence on my own life. Few things have been more personal for me than this novel, few things more important and formative.

At some point I lost the 1960 Signet paperback edition I purchased from Biesky's. A couple of ironies surround that loss. The first is that I later took the book on a sojourn to Asia, but the box containing it and other books that I mailed from Japan to my brother's apartment in New York City never got there. I guess I hadn't packed the box securely enough for overseas handling, that it likely fell apart and never made it past the docks of Yokohama, that it likely never left Asia. The second irony is that I found an original edition of *The Asiatics* among my parents' belongings after they died. It was hardcover, used but not abused. It had our surname written inside the front cover in my mother's beautiful, Palmer Method cursive hand: *Property of the Kirinskis*, the inscription read. How long did my parents have the book? How could I have missed seeing it over the years? Had they read it, this imagined series of adventures that meant so much to their son? Might they and I, unbeknown to them or me, have actually shared all of this?

This was all hard for me to reconcile. *The Asiatics* was of my essence, and I did not want it—did not want myself—fully shared, even with my parents. Which is foolishness, I scolded myself. A work of literature is there for whoever wishes and is able to benefit from it. I could not claim co-ownership of Prokosch's imagination. *The Asiatics* was not about me, nor was it mine.

With this new sense of charity in tow, after discovering my parents' copy I went to a bookstore to order *The Asiatics* as a gift for a friend, although I didn't know if the novel was still in print or even available in a used copy. The book seller sat at his computer, searching the possibilities. "I can get it for you new in paper, new in clothbound, or look for a used edition, hard or soft," he informed me. "Your choice."

"Who publishes the softcover?"

"Signet."

I planned to give my friend an unused, softbound Signet edition of *The Asiatics* for his birthday. While the book was on order, before I ever saw it, I wondered whether it would be a later version of the Signet edition I had bought at Biesky's in 1961, the one with the exotic woman looking at the American hitchhiker, the one with such promise of romances to come.

Part Three

The Excruciating Confusions of Youth

Nathan's Memoir
1962- 1980

Sand-smeared, bathing
in dreams,
the young leap against each other.

–Shinkichi Takahashi

1
Liberal Learning

IF MY SOCIAL LIFE in high school had bordered on moribund, my intellectual life there hardly had a pulse. One of the few times I felt excited about schoolwork at Asbury Park High was when I wrote a story for Mrs. Herkimer's class, only to have her tell me that my ending wasn't good enough. It's not that I didn't have some life of the mind and a reflective bent. I read constantly and would have taken up residence in the public library had they let me. But little of that was nurtured in the classroom.

At Harvard, a bastion of the traditional liberal arts, the reverse was true. New Jersey had been liberal in terms of the unfettered freedom I had to explore and experience. But the freedom was mostly extra-curricular, outside the classroom and unrelated to curriculum or pedagogy. Harvard was liberal in the more formal educational sense, in that it offered a structured interdisciplinary approach designed to free one through revelation—to understand and actually "see" the essence of a given historical period in the relationships among the era's prevailing religious worldview, philosophical orientation, literature, politics, visual arts, and architecture. This broadening approach was in welcome contrast to high school, in which 14- and 15-year-old freshmen were encouraged to "specialize" from the outset by defining, and thus further dividing, themselves and their futures according to explicit college prep or vocational tracks, and implicitly according to one's supposed aptitude (as if that were synonymous with interest) in science or the humanities.

College didn't force a binary choice—quite the contrary, as I discovered when the book assigned as summer reading to all new students for discussion during freshman week was C.P. Snow's *The Two Cultures and the Scientific Revolution*, a provocative argument for multiple ways of knowing through interdisciplinary approaches, the idea that different fields of knowledge are complementary components of a greater knowledge. In high school, differences—of status, wealth, race, ethnicity, religion, ability, personality—were often a source of separation, tension, and, sometimes, open conflict. In college, differences were the basis for a philosophy of liberal learning that emphasized reflecting, comparing, and delving into our shaping traditions and attitudes. The faculty members were consistent in their commitment to this approach, and I gradually came to understand and appreciate the Socratic, Aristotelian, and Stoic tenets of the path they were encouraging us to follow. First and foremost, we were exhorted to lead the examined life, to know ourselves in order to liberate our minds from the bondage of habit and custom. Such critical self-examination was meant to bring us face to face with our attitudes and biases toward difference—a compelling matter for me, whose life to date had been all about differences, albeit it in a negative way.

The assumption was that the resulting pluralistic perspective would inform an enlightened sense of citizenship, a sense which would lead us to consider ourselves as citizens of the whole world, people who could appreciate and value local loyalties yet balance these with a primary loyalty to human beings everywhere. This would require the development of our imaginative capacity, our ability to venture beyond our individual backgrounds and empathize with others' realities, both in their similarities and differences. All of these characteristics of liberal education—the examined life, a pluralistic perspective, an enlightened conception of citizenship, the capacity to imagine realities not our own—were bundled into Harvard's interdisciplinary curriculum and teaching approach. At first, I resented all the required courses that filled up much of the first two years. But gradually I came to understand the curriculum-guiding Deweyan assumption that the goal of education is to make students' experiences more intelligent and satisfying, and that this required prerequisite knowledge one could build upon.

This approach to learning was not something I could appreciate at first or in the abstract. It took practice, as well as inspiration. The faculty provided both. To a person, I could see their commitment to helping students learn from, versus just have, experiences. Through their different disciplinary perspectives, they gave us what we needed to transform our experiences—in Dewey's terms, to "intelligize" us toward a more "consummatory" life. In my case, three professors led the way.

Sergio Ferretti, a literature professor, taught me to utilize comparative perspectives, "comparative" being defined in both disciplinary and geographical terms. A well-known poet born in Italy, raised in America, educated at Columbia and Florence, an instructor at universities in the Middle East, Asia, and Europe, Professor Ferretti taught—and lived—world literature. The year before my matriculation at Harvard, he had been a Fulbright scholar in Japan. I was one of the beneficiaries of his fascination with other countries generally and Japan in particular. The descriptions of the place in his poetry, journals, lectures, and conversations struck an irresistible and enduring chord. Later, I would go to Japan due in no small part to Professor Ferretti's influence. But it was his person more than anything else that made him so compelling. He vibrated with emotion and passion. When I first experienced this, I was in equal parts enthralled and put off. I had never seen so expressive a man. He would surely have been ridiculed for this in New Jersey. That—my upbringing—is what put me off at first. A man should hold his feelings in check. A man should be cool, even cold, at times even cruel. But Professor Ferretti was the Anti-New Jersey Man, and this gigantic contrast was what eventually enthralled me.

My first college classroom experience was Freshman English with Professor Ferretti. Twenty students were in the room, all very quiet and, I guessed, apprehensive like me. The professor was writing on the blackboard. He struck me as bizarre, his clothes and hair in particular. He wore an unfashionable jacket, frayed and ill-fitting. His shoes were scuffed, one was untied. His black hair, hardly combed, fell over his collar. When he turned to face us, I couldn't believe what I was seeing: his black pupils were the pupils of a cat, actually vertical. I thought he looked deranged. This impression was reinforced when he spoke. The last quotation he had written on the board was by Gerard Manley Hopkins. "Gerard, oh Gerard," Ferretti moaned, his cat's eyes tearing, his cheeks wet. My first college professor in my first college class was crying.

In New Jersey, an important manifestation of cool was your body—how it looked, how smoothly you controlled it. Here, too, Professor Ferretti came up short. We were taking the mid-term exam for his course. I was engrossed in an answer I was writing in my bluebook when I heard a crash. Startled, I looked around and saw Ferretti sprawled face down on the floor. He had been reading a collection of Andrew Marvel's poems as he walked up and down the aisles separating our desk-chairs and tripped on a briefcase a student had left in the aisle. Before any of us could go to help him, our professor rose to continue walking—still reading, never taking his eyes off the book, as if a mishap had never occurred. Not cool according to the criteria of physical appearance or coordination, but far cooler than those superficialities in terms of nonchalance, imperturbability, and pure self-containment.

Winston Broadwell was a prominent, University of Chicago-educated historian. His seminar on the history of ideas was demanding and feared: demanding because of its long reading list and feared because of its challenging writing assignments, which emphasized one's abilities first to analyze and then synthesize a particular epoch's cultural interdependencies as those were embedded in the many readings. The course was structured in historical chronology, beginning with ancient texts from various world regions and ending with contemporary texts, also from around the world and drawn from the humanities, sciences, and social sciences.

Dr. Broadwell was a dynamic and charismatic teacher who had a talent for integrating an era's various elements under a kind of overriding cultural umbrella. Despite his obvious braininess and expository ability, however, for the first weeks of the course I had a hell of a time getting what he was trying to convey. In part, this was because of the trouble I had completing, much less absorbing, the assigned readings. But I think it was more the fear—a lack of trust and self-confidence, really—of making my own connections and hazarding my own conclusions about the readings.

Then came the epiphany. We had been wending our way through St. Thomas Aquinas's *Summa Theologica*. At the same time, we were also exploring other aspects of the period's context—its science, literature, and material culture. On this particular day, Dr. Broadwell brought in a pile of poster boards. One by one he placed them on an easel in front of the class. Each was a blown-up photo of a cathedral. As the series of images played out before me—an exterior front, an exterior side, the roof, an interior front, an interior side, the ceiling—I suddenly saw it: how the architecture of a medieval cathedral reflected the ideational structure of the *Summa Theologica*. For the first time in the course I raised my hand to speak. Dr. Broadwell was silent for a long moment after I shared my observation, and my initial enthusiasm and confidence quickly ebbed. I lowered my head, cursing myself for taking a chance, promising I would never expose myself so impulsively and carelessly again. I was staring at the floor when I heard Dr. Broadwell shout "Yes!" And again: "Yes!"

My relationship with him from that point on was like a tutorial. I would visit him whenever I had a question I couldn't answer or was inspired by an insight I couldn't contain. He became a mentor, a guide to the connectivity between ideas and events and phenomena, a weaver and clarifier of gigantic narratives.

When I was an undergraduate, you could not declare a major until you had finished your sophomore year. This was meant to provide ample time to explore many of the disciplines that offered majors through a series of required courses across the humanities, sciences, and social sciences. At first, because of the esteem in which I held Professor Ferretti and Professor Broadwell, I thought I might be a literature or history major, but certain of the other professors in those departments did not appeal to me, either by reputation or from my direct experiences with them. Then I considered psychology, a field that genuinely interested me until I discovered that psychology as I conceived of it through its literal definition as the study of the soul actually had nothing to do with the soul. In hindsight, this was a premature conclusion, one based on a single course in experimental psychology. Statistical descriptions of rodents blundering around mazes searching for food turned me off. But that was the required course, after all, and on its basis I decided against psychology as my major.

Then, as a sophomore, I encountered Martin Murray, a philosophy professor and chair of the department. He was a short, round, bald man, physically unimposing except for his inordinately large head. I came to believe that he needed such a capacious cranium to house his inordinately large intellect. Except for his moving lips and alert, darting eyes Murray sat, otherwise still and with his hands folded on the desktop in front of him for a full hour as he talked, softly and without notes, about the problems and methods of philosophy. I was captivated by both: the perennial inconclusiveness of the problems and the beauty of the methods, so logical and multi-layered and bottomless. That the problems would likely never be solved made it all the more compelling.

This was life: mysterious, moving, and elusive—heavy with intimations of deep meaning that kept skirting just beyond reach. And I was captivated by Professor Murray, his incisive brilliance of mind, kindliness, and air of real wisdom.

It was with Murray, who became my academic adviser, that I had my most satisfying collegiate success experience. Throughout high school and most of college, I procrastinated until the eleventh hour before studying for an exam or writing a paper, I think because few topics or assignments excited me. But in Professor Murray's courses it was the opposite. In one instance, his ethics course, I began researching and writing my term paper after the first class session of the semester. I can remember the title: "Suicide, Sacrifice, and Self-Realization," although I have no memory of what the paper said. I only know that the project became a labor of love, a preoccupation that I worked on for hours every night. Murray gave it an A+, the only such grade, he wrote in a note on the title page, that he had awarded in his many years of teaching. On the flip side, I also remember a note that he wrote on another of my papers, this one on a comparison between Existentialism and Zen Buddhism. "Having only been trained in Western philosophy," he commented next to the grade of A, "I have no idea whether this deserves an A or an F. So I'm giving you the benefit of the doubt." I felt at once terrible and lucky, terrible because I had obviously disappointed my esteemed teacher, lucky because he chose not to penalize me.

During my sophomore year, the job I had as part of my scholarship package was to sweep the floors, straighten the chairs, clean the blackboards, and empty the trash bins at six each morning in the building where the philosophy department was located. My first class on one particular November day, taught by Dr. Murray, wasn't until 10:00 a.m., so I went back to bed for a couple of hours. I overslept and was barely able to get to class on time. I rushed in and sat down, unaware that President Kennedy had been shot. Afterwards, I wrote this:

Philosophy Class, November 22, 1963

He has an incongruously Buddhistic look for a professor of Western philosophy. Today, although impassive as always, his face is wet. He looks like the Buddha crying. Only the tears move. His head, big and round and hairless, could be a statue. His folded hands, motionless as a mudra, lie on a desk that sits on a raised platform between the blackboard and the class. The room is uncharacteristically still for a college lecture hall. The teacher, without doing anything but sit and cry, has the students' full attention.

"Democracy," he finally says, "is based on the premise of equal intelligence. Class dismissed."

That was the day I decided to major in philosophy.

2
Holly

HOLLY MACDONALD, A FRENCH literature major at Radcliffe from Worcester, Massachusetts who had spent her junior year at the Sorbonne, was vivacious, intelligent, beautiful, and sexy. By Thanksgiving of my senior year, I was dating her exclusively, and towards the end of fall term my grade-point-average was in danger of plummeting. Rationally, I couldn't blame Holly for this; she was a Dean's List student, so I couldn't say it was our heavy dating schedule that caused my unravelling. But I could attribute it to the intensity of our relationship—more precisely, Holly's intensity. I had never been with someone who demanded such constant attention. She had to be at the center of things, the life of the party, and she mostly was. She was a highly compelling person: lively, dramatic, quick-witted, and utterly charming. When she felt she had all your attention, being with her was pure pleasure.

But she could quickly flip into a different personality when the focus wasn't on her, and that's where the intensity came in. She constantly needed approval and appreciation, and if you weren't right there with it she had a whole arsenal of tactics to bring you back. The hardest of these to manage was her excessive flirtatiousness. This could quickly turn into hypersexual behavior, and in some very risky circumstances.

For example, we often studied together in the library stacks. When Holly had finished for the evening, but I was still working, she didn't care. To get my attention, she would grab my hand and put it on her breast or in her pants. If that weren't enough to divert me, she'd put her hand in my pants. Inevitably, we'd start fucking, sometimes against the bookshelves, sometimes on a table, sometimes on the floor. Luckily, the stacks weren't much used by others as late at night as we studied there, and we were never caught.

Another example is when we were walking the mile-and-a-half from a movie theater in Somerville to South House, Holly's dorm in the Radcliffe Quadrangle on Linnaean Street in Cambridge. I was totally worked up about the film, Jean Luc Goddard's *Breathless*. I couldn't stop raving about Jean-Paul Belmondo and Jean Seberg. Maybe it was the attention I was giving the actress in particular that soon had Holly demanding that we make love right then and there, "there" being in the shadows of the garage belonging to Radcliffe's dean of students.

Riskiest of all was the Saturday night we got drunk with a group of friends at a bar near Harvard Square. When we got off the bus a few minutes' walk away from South House, Holly started complaining that I had danced once or twice with one of the friends, a woman I had dated for a while before I met Holly. I tried to reassure her that it had been innocent, a polite thing to do for old time's sake. But she wouldn't accept my protestations, so I gave up and just walked along without saying anything. My silence set off all her insecurities. Holly pulled me into the bushes outside her dorm and did everything she could to arouse me. Drunk though I was, it worked. And because I was aroused, and drunk, I accepted her invitation, her dare, more accurately, to go up to her dorm room. Had we been caught in those conservative days before the sexual revolution, we both might have been expelled. But Holly was Holly, and the only senses I seemed to have available were the ones under my belt. Somehow, we made it to her room without being seen—except by her roommate Gwen, who was reading in bed. Gwen, as it happened, was a lot like Holly and had also roomed with her in Paris. Our getting it on in the next bed did not faze Gwen at all. Later, the two women teamed up to help me get down the stairs and out of South House without being seen. When I got to the street, I puked my guts out from a combination of alcohol and released anxiety. Then I sat on the curb, debating whether or not to end my relationship with Holly MacDonald. The problem was that I was falling in love with her. The pleasures of being with her outweighed the troubles. At least that was my conclusion by the time I managed to stand up and navigate the 20-minute walk to my room at Eliot House.

I managed to salvage the semester by sequestering myself from Holly long enough to cram for finals and complete term papers. We resumed dating after Winter break, and by the time we left for Spring break I was working myself up to ask if she wanted to get engaged. This thinking made me nervous, not because I was especially concerned about Holly's idiosyncrasies after six months of going out, but because I hadn't even turned 22 yet; there were so many experiences I wanted to have, so many places I wanted to go. Did I really want to be bogged down in a formal relationship? But maybe, I reasoned, being engaged would add a deeper level of seriousness to my decisions about life after college. And maybe, given Holly's contagious vivacity when she was at her best, being with her would make whatever experiences I had in store all the livelier. I had a lot to think about during the ten-day break.

By the time I left New Jersey, where I had spent much of my time walking the empty beaches, I decided to propose to Holly when we got together the next weekend. As it happened, she wasn't available that Saturday night, so I went out drinking with one of my Boston cousins, a senior at MIT. We decided to venture into the notorious Combat Zone, the adult entertainment district centered on lower Washington Street between Boylston and Kneeland. Created in the early 1960s when Scollay Square, Boston's former red light district, was demolished to make way for the new Government Center, the Combat Zone's bars, strip shows, and brothels were a magnet for newly legalized 21-year-old drinkers like us. It was also a magnet for soldiers and sailors from the nearby Boston Navy Yard, whose military uniforms, along with the area's high incidence of violence and crime, gave the Combat Zone its name. In case you needed the dangers to be explicitly emphasized in order to take them seriously, you could read the sign in a window at one of the neighborhood's borders: *You are now entering the Combat Zone. You have nothing to fear but fear itself.*

We entered one of the more famous clubs, the Two O'Clock, settled into a table near the stage and ordered beers. Not surprising for workers in a place as dangerous as the Combat Zone, the strippers were attractive enough, but hard-looking. Except for one, who wasn't at all hard-looking, only attractive. Holly MacDonald. My prospective fiancée. My cousin was too engrossed in the scenery to notice my consternation. When Holly left the stage to go back to the dressing rooms, I followed. A bouncer intercepted me, but Holly told him it was okay, I was a friend. Not wanting to cause a scene in the club, I asked her to meet me outside after she got dressed. When we met, I confronted her. She laughed, not at all embarrassed, and chided me about my conservatism. I guess I was conservative, if conservatism is defined as being upset to learn that your girlfriend, to whom you are about to propose marriage, is a stripper, eye-candy for legions of horny men.

"But why, Holly? Why are you doing this, and in the Combat Zone of all places?"

"It's fun, Nate. I feel so alive there on the stage. So...desired. That's it. Desired."

"But what about the dangers? Physical dangers, certainly. And social. Worcester's only an hour away, and school's just across the river. What if someone you know sees you?"

Holly laughed. "You did."

I told her I would never be able to reconcile this, that I was ending our affair. She seemed uncomprehending of my reaction and genuinely hurt. "Too bad," she said as she turned toward the dressing room. "You and I have had a lot of fun."

After Holly, I pretty much gave up my dating life. I tried to get her out of my mind, but it was difficult. We'd run into each other around Cambridge and say our polite hellos. From time to time I'd catch a look from her that I could only interpret as an invitation, a silent "If you ever want to call me..." But I never did.

As the semester wound down, I was accepted to Harvard's graduate program in philosophy with a teaching assistantship. Arnie, who had come into his own academically at Monmouth College and his junior year at Hebrew University in Jerusalem, was working on a similar deal to study history at Columbia. It was a time of both pride and relief for Fay and Morton Kirinski: two sons in the Ivy League; two sons who would be eligible for extended military deferments.

Meanwhile, Holly would return to Paris to do graduate work at the Sorbonne. Not for the first time, it occurred to me that she was by far more like my literary hero Henry Miller than I could ever be. Like him, she would be an ex pat in France. Whether consciously or not, I expected she would also follow the same maxim, trying her best, as Miller wrote in *Sunday After the War*, "to put my hands on everything and leave a stain."

In those days, Harvard and Radcliffe hadn't yet merged and held separate graduations. As befitted old friends, I invited Holly to my ceremony and later attended hers. Afterwards, I gave Holly a congratulatory hug. Her chest was soft against mine, and I couldn't feel any straps across her back when we embraced. I had the impression she was naked under her gown, but thought that was probably just my imagination.

"Good luck in Paris."

I expected her to wish me luck at Harvard in return. "Come with me," she said instead. "Seriously, Nate. Come with me. We'll have a blast."

Despite my never having been to Paris, I could envision it: walks along the Seine, picnics in the Bois de Boulogne, aperitifs at Les Deux Magots, love-making in our Montmartre atelier. She would study. I would...What? Wonder where she was and whom she was with if I couldn't give her all my attention? Worry about her well-being, become crazy with jealousy? I saw myself searching for her in countless Left Bank bistros and dives. And then finding her, unharmed if we were lucky. Until the next time.

"I'm sorry, Holly. I can't." I pulled her to me for a last hug to soften my rejection. As we separated, she lowered the zipper down the front of her gown a foot or so then quickly raised it. I had not been imagining her nakedness underneath.

"Good luck in Paris," I said again, forcing my thoughts toward graduate school.

3
Halls of Tangled Ivy

...grant me a nature having two contrary forces, the one of which tends
to expand infinitely, while the other strives to apprehend or find itself
in this infinity, and I will cause the whole world of intelligences with the
whole system of their representations to rise up before you.

–Samuel Taylor Coleridge

Had he a foreboding of what he was losing on that day? European civ-
ilization with its comforts and achievements, its living successes called
careers?

–Jiri Langer

NINETEEN-SIXTY-NINE WAS a banner year for me at Harvard. I received my doctorate, a faculty appointment in philosophy, and a contract
from a major university press to publish my dissertation. The contract provided ample funds to prepare it for publication in book form, which would
not require much editing or new writing. My teaching load was only two
courses a semester; since I had already taught these courses as a teaching
fellow, very little time would have to be devoted to the courses beyond actually teaching them and grading. It was traditional to protect new faculty
from committee work, so I would have few service requirements during my
first year. I had already begun developing the outline for a second book, and
I was optimistic about the progress I would make on it given my otherwise
undemanding schedule. I was happy.

With biblical propitiousness, my contentment continued for nearly sev-
en years. In 1970 Holly returned from Paris with a graduate degree from
the Sorbonne and a year-to-year appointment to teach French literature at
Boston University. We resumed dating, and it wasn't long before Holly started talking about marriage. I loved her, but the same misgivings I had about
her four years earlier were still with me. Nothing I could think of was more
enjoyable than sex with Holly. But that was what gave me pause; I just didn't
know if I could satisfy her over a marriage's long haul. True, she didn't seem
to be as hyper-sexual and adventurous as she had been, but I couldn't help
having the concern. I chided myself for being pseudo-clinical; I was no psychologist after all. Maybe it was just Holly's frenetic zest for life that threatened me. In the end, though, my misgivings lost out to Holly's allure.

Marrying outside Judaism was a consideration as well. I didn't want to
hurt or disappointment my parents. They had been down this road before
with my sister Debbie and had been very unhappy about her marriage to

Eddie Martino. But at least that ground had been broken. Still, I decided not to rub it in by having a formal wedding, which was fine with Holly, who wasn't at all sure how the MacDonalds of Worcester would react to her marrying a Jew. Instead, to save our parents from an immediate struggle with choices about religious ceremonies or conversions, we had a civil ceremony in Boston attended only by Arnie as our witness.

Late in 1971 Holly and I moved into an apartment on Brattle Street, "Historic Brattle Street," as the guidebooks referred to it. The Department of Philosophy was in Emerson Hall at 25 Quincy Street, a pleasant ten-minute walk for me across Massachusetts Avenue, then past Harvard Square, Harvard Yard, and Widener Library. Holly's commute was equally pleasant and almost as convenient, a two-mile walk or half-hour "T" ride across the Charles River to BU's French Studies department on Commonwealth Avenue.

By the time Ellen was born in the summer of 1974, I had finished writing two books and was well into a third. I had received several teaching awards and was a sought-after and well-paid speaker. Money wasn't an issue for us, and Holly had enthusiastically given up teaching to be a full-time mother. We were so happy, the kind of family you'd expect to read about in *Parade Magazine* or *McCall's*.

But by 1976, our trajectory took a nosedive. Explaining why is complicated. Perhaps the best way I can approach it is in the chronological order of my three books, or more accurately in the context of our changing marital relationship as each of the books was written.

The Language of Art, the Language of Science, and the Epistemology of Portrayal was published in 1972. The book is a re-titled, somewhat expanded revision of my doctoral dissertation, *Merging Epistemic Approaches: Implications for an Art-Science Synthesis*. Basically, the book explores characteristics of artistic and scientific writing styles and then argues that philosophers, as well as intellectuals in hybrid fields such as the social and behavioral sciences, need to become conversant, if not fluent, in both languages.

This first book, written so many years ago, remains the most meaningful of the three for me, and I ask myself why. Why is the topic so compelling, especially now that I am no longer a professional philosopher? I sometimes consider that the tension between polar opposites is what the entirety of my mental and emotional lives rests on. By this I mean that I'm always struggling to find some balance point, some satisfying reconciliation between contentious opposites. I have come to attribute the origins of this life-long preoccupation to my parents, who themselves represented a kind of art-science divide: Fay, the whimsical, intuitive dancer and painter marries Mort, the practical businessman and accountant who would only accept what was empirically evident.

One practical and concrete manifestation of my commitment to reconciliation was the conviction that miscegenation, or blood mixture, would be the only "cure" to humanity's conflicts and violence. Beyond my love for Holly on the emotional and physical levels, marrying a non-Jew satisfied my philosophical inclination as well.

I had heard horror stories of what authors went through to satisfy major academic presses, but getting the volume ready for publication was unexpectedly stress-free. The relative ease of it made the first two years of marriage pretty much of an extended honeymoon. We had plenty of time and money to enjoy ourselves in vibrant Boston—walking its streets, taking advantage of its museums and concerts and lectures, hobnobbing with the intelligentsia populating the multitude of universities in the area, and hanging out in cafes. For Holly, it was like being back in her beloved Paris—"Paris on the Charles," she called it. Her contentment was reinforced by the theme of my first book as well, particularly the language of art part. Literature was her passion; she knew a great deal about it and was a genuine help to me throughout key sections of the book, which I dedicated to her. The science part was not so familiar or interesting to her, but her intellectual prowess made her an astute reader and critic even for those sections. Up until this point in our lives together, my work didn't interfere with or detract from our marriage. If anything, it reinforced our contentment.

My second book, published in 1974 at about the time Ellen was born and dedicated to her, extended my ruminations on language, portrayal, and reality. *Useful Fictions and Fictions as Truths* focuses on the work of Hans Vaihinger, a once-influential thinker who in the early part of the 20th century developed the "As If" philosophy, which suggests that even knowing that our thoughts and ideas might be false, they are nevertheless useful coping mechanisms in the face of the overwhelming complexity of our existence.

As I was writing this second book, Arnie was deeply engrossed in his doctoral work in history at Columbia. From time to time I would visit him in New York, but more frequently he would come to Cambridge to stay with us while he utilized special collections in Boston-area university libraries. These were immensely vibrant and invigorating visits, not only for Arnie and me but also for Holly, whose own academic background was as deep as anyone's when it came to matters of methodology in general and deeper than most on the topic of "fictions" specifically.

But it was a particular pleasure to have Arnie in these discussions, which went on into the early morning hours over several pizzas and more than several bottles of wine. In my experience, no one is more steeped in the current intellectual literature than a doctoral candidate who has recently passed his comprehensive exams, defended his dissertation proposal, and embarked on his research. Arnie was no exception to this generalization, and what's more I was pleased to see that his commitment to being an historian was total. When it came to matters of "truth-seeking," Arnie—whom I enjoyed goading with sarcastic accusations that his view of methodology was too orthodox, doctrinaire, and imprisoned by convention—was invariably cogent and reasoned in his critiques of my Vaihinger project. Our disagreements revolved around our different starting points. Mine valued free-wheeling speculation and theorizing, while Arnie was committed to the historical method that was standard in academic circles in his field. First, the historian should recognize an historical "problem" and the need for certain knowledge about it. Next, he should gather as much relevant information about the topic as possible as the basis for forming hypotheses that tentatively explain relationships between historical factors. Then he collects and organizes evidence, and in the process verifies the authenticity and veracity of information and sources. Finally, after selecting, organizing, and analyzing the most pertinent of the collected evidence and drawing conclusions based on same, the historian records the conclusions in a meaningful narrative.

It was the prospect of the last step that intrigued me the most, but it was also the juncture that led to the most heated arguments between Arnie and me, as well as with Holly, whose methodological orientation was closer to my own. While I was writing *Useful Fictions*, I became a proponent of what the novelist Bernard Malamud termed "fictive biography." Earlier in my career, I had adopted the prevailing positivistic worldview in academia across most disciplines at the time: that there is a singular reality "out there," objective, independent of any observer, governed by cause-effect, visible, measurable, and manageable. Later, while not having succumbed entirely to the more extreme articulations of post-modernism, a trend that became increasingly and, in my view, disturbingly popular, I nevertheless admit to having inched closer to the belief that all knowledge, particularly social and psychological knowledge, is relative: there are multiple realities; these are subjective and dependent on the particular observer; nothing is simply true or good; we are subject to multiple causes and our beliefs are affected by our unique circumstances.

And, of course, there was the issue of "objectivity" in our discussions, an overblown and ultimately elusive ideal, in my opinion, even in the empirical sciences, but a goal of scholarship to which Arnie was totally committed. I didn't want to dampen his enthusiasm for what he considered to be the ideal. But in good conscience I couldn't leave him with the impression that I believed in it. I recall a debate in which Arnie called me to task for what he called my "unbridled, undisciplined, and unfounded idea that 'truth' can be other than singular and objective. Seriously, Nate," he argued, "think about it. How can there be more than one factually based truth about a single event? I mean, from my point of view a 'reality' is singular, it can't be filled up by more than one actuality. If a thing is true, it's true. I don't accept the idea of competing truths."

"Okay, Arnie," I countered. "I get that you're the aspiring positivist historian who can't accept the idea of competing truths. But here's my problem with the idea that reality is finite, bridled, confined to one possibility. From my perspective, the truth is never singular or objective. It's subject to, I guess you might say even victim to, worldviews and interpretations that vary with whoever is painting the picture—the person's experiences, habits, psychological makeup, and cultural influences. Which truth? is my retort. Told by whom? Heard by whom?"

But Arnie was game. Cogently and logically, he kept countering my arguments, and Holly's. Finally, we went to bed. Several hours later I awoke and enlisted Holly's help to write a mischievous rejoinder, which I left in a book Arnie had in his overnight bag. No doubt he would find it, but I hoped not until he got back to New York. It was Holly's and my way of accentuating the idea that there is a multiplicity of ways to apprehend and describe realities in the plural.

An Inventory of Methods

being apprehending perceiving noticing selecting observing intuiting

sensing listening absorbing feeling thinking reflecting comparing interpreting judging evaluating doubting appreciating fearing braving forgetting concentrating

inquiring analyzing categorizing reading studying conceptualizing theorizing learning synthesizing integrating knowing realizing understanding

describing portraying conveying repeating restating condensing summarizing planning acting controlling

imagining dreaming desiring wishing hoping praying expecting worshipping

resisting remembering regretting despairing atoning accepting respecting releasing relinquishing advancing retreating meditating practicing penetrating pervading uniting resting emptying dying

resuming adding continuing
Ad infinitum?

> Love you, Brother and Brother-in-Law. Keep at it.
> Nate & Holly

So you see, at this point Holly was still my friend, my partner, my happy helpmate. The process of writing my third book ruined all of that.

Looking back, I'm amazed that *Is Change Possible?* ever made it to publication, which it did in 1976. When I began writing the book two years earlier, I was confident it was destined to be not only my most important work, but a philosophical classic, a work that would inspire readers to take the fruits of sedentary contemplation and reflection into realms of constructive action. I saw it as a book that would be a natural and seamless progression from Vaihinger's philosophy of "As If" to my conception of "Useful Fictions"—mental inventions that, in addition to helping us make sense of the world, could be employed to make it better.

So why do I say I'm amazed it was ever published? For one thing, the book was ambitious in substance and challenging methodologically (in retrospect, perhaps too ambitious and challenging). A second reason was that it contained a number of ideas (in retrospect, perhaps too many) that were difficult to connect. A third reason was that the ideas themselves were quite controversial and vulnerable to criticism, particularly in academia. And probably most important, the process of writing the book was so hellaciously stressful that I could barely finish.

My thesis was that real and permanent social change depends on real and permanent individual change; the former is impossible without the latter. If I had stopped there, the largely negative reaction to the book would certainly have been more muted than the loud outcry that greeted it. One problem was that I extended my argument to suggest that genuine personal change is also likely impossible for all but a few who, by virtue of relentless work on themselves, might transcend the bounds of egotism and self-interest to function at a higher, more enlightened level of being. That aspect of my proposal really riled people up, and I was bludgeoned with charges of elitism and "soft-headed mysticism." It didn't help that, in my concluding section, "A Very Practical Approach to Change," I invoked the system of personal and spiritual development most associated with G. I. Gurdjieff, a mysterious Central Asian savant whose work, at least in the popular press of the mid-1970s, seemed either to be exalted by flaky seekers, or reviled by conventional religious authorities and anti-"occult" intellectuals alike.

In fact, I had Holly to thank for this influence. She had joined a Gurdjieff discussion group in Boston. At first I was skeptical of the ideas as I was hearing her describe them. But when I started reading the books she was reading and attending lectures on the ideas of Gurdjieff and P.D. Ouspensky, his best-known follower and interpreter, I not only became intensely interested but saw immediately the connection between their ideas and my own project. Still, these were not the type of ideas that had much prospect for acceptance among academic philosophers, and my prominent use of them became easy fodder for criticism of the book.

A second problem involved the examples I presented to support my thesis. Basically, I centered on the history of anti-Semitism to show that it was patently wrong to assume any prevailing altruistic instinct in the overwhelming portion of humanity when it came to inter-group relations, particularly in the areas of race, religion, and ethnicity. Altruism and compassion, I argued, are only possible for those who have made the long, hard effort to develop such capacities. When you really look into most people's motivations, what many of us think of as compassionate behavior is entirely ego-driven and self-interested and stuck within the superficial surface of personality. Beyond charges of cynicism regarding this piece of my argument, philosophers from various quarters berated me for intellectual inconsistency, claiming that my third book, in its insistence on the reality of the unbridgeable gaps that separate us, directly contradicted my first two books, which had featured synthesis and reconciliation. "Come on, Kirinski," I could hear them saying. "You're a philosopher (or you used to be). You can't have it both ways. Re-read Kierkegaard's *Either/Or*, or Aristotle's Law of Non-Contradiction. Remember? A thing can't be both true and not true in the same instant. Make up your mind."

There was a third problem that, in the politically correct climate of academia circa 1975, was probably the most disastrously consequential for me: I was accused of purveying Zionism. This part of the saga is complicated. As sympathetic as I tried to be toward the plight of the Palestinians, and as ecumenical as I was when it came to organized religions and my own marriage to a Christian, I was nevertheless an unabashed supporter of the State of Israel. My Jewish identity had been important to me from the time I first "felt" Jewish at the age of four as I looked at "The Secretary" in my parents' foyer. Anti-Semitic episodes I experienced personally during my elementary and high school years accentuated this identity, as did the genealogical research I began to conduct as a teenager into my family's roots in Europe. Arnie's accounts of his time in Israel and our discussions about his doctoral studies had a profoundly expansive effect on my knowledge of Jewish history, at once challenging my assumptions and informing my opinions. Arnie's graduate work at Columbia between 1971 and 1975 coincided with an increase in criticisms of Israel on U.S. campuses, and his tutelage on the issues involved emboldened me to defend Israel in debates at Harvard. This provoked the wrath of many liberals within the faculty and the student body who were overwhelmingly pro-Palestinian. Some of these were my immediate colleagues and students, people who had previously been among my admirers. This former allegiance in no way prevented them from turning against me. Quite the contrary, I would say, since they considered me a traitor to one of the century's principal Leftist causes, Palestinian sovereignty over their ancestral lands.

The final debate in which I participated was so heated that I feared for my personal safety. I admit to making matters worse at three junctures in the debate. The first was when I implicitly framed the Israel-Palestine situation in terms of anti-Semitism by quoting Isaiah Berlin's observation of "... the unbelievable cost in blood and tears which has made the history of the Jews for two thousand years a dreadful martyrology." My intent here was to highlight the mutuality of the Palestinian-Israeli tragedy, but it back-fired. The second juncture was when I shared an apocalyptic dream I had of Jews being massacred by Yasser Arafat's followers screaming "Throw the Jews into the sea and destroy them!" This blunder was also well-intentioned; I merely meant to show how organized political players on both sides were not helping the situation. The third juncture was when I shared the gist of the conclusion of my soon-to-be-published book. Basically, I told the hostile audience, this time explicitly citing anti-Semitism, I could envision no prospect for reconciliation. The combined power of anti-Jewish history, emotion, and habit was too intractable, I argued, for there to be any lasting resolution to the conflict at social, cultural, or national levels. This was not what the mostly progressive, pro-Palestinian audience wanted to hear. What they did choose to hear, despite my never saying it, was that I was advocating for the status quo. In other words, I was supporting the continuing expansion of Jewish numbers and power in the country. I was, in essence, a hateful Zionist.

My struggles on all of these levels—conceptual, methodological, political— nearly did me in emotionally. I would leave the house to walk for hours, stopping off from time to time to play pool or watch movies in an effort to clear my head and get my thoughts straight. Holly grew resentful as these amblings became more frequent, and Ellen was distraught by my long absences. The worst of it was that the walks didn't much help at first, and I started dropping in for one, then two, then who knows how many drinks at bars I passed along the way. When I got home I was usually drunk, and our home life started to fall apart. Things hit their low point the night I stumbled in, barely ambulatory, while Holly was reading to Ellen before putting her to bed. As our 18-month-old came toddling up in her footed pajamas squealing "Daddy! Daddy!" I had to run in the other direction, barely making it to the kitchen sink before puking up my evening's store of Jim Beam. When I turned back to Ellen, she was curled in a fetal position on the living room floor with her thumb in her mouth, silent and shuddering. Holly, cooing soothingly, picked her up, walked into the baby's bedroom, and angrily slammed the door shut. I collapsed into the easy chair in my study, sober enough to hate myself but not enough to stay awake. I didn't see either of them until the next morning, when only Ellen would speak to me.

I went cold turkey that day. A week later, I was feeling much better, and Holly and I were doing much better. We decided to take advantage of the upswing and visit the Shore for a few days. This is something we had been doing fairly regularly before I started to fall apart, and it was always a particularly exciting visit for Ellen, who was diligently spoiled by her grandparents and uncle. It was fun to watch the three of them argue over whose turn it was to take care of Ellen. Usually, when the weather allowed it, they ended up wandering off together, pushing the stroller around town, stopping at Belmar's several playgrounds, and building sandcastles on the beach. The abundance of babysitters gave Holly and me a chance to sleep in, read, and just enjoy each other's company before my parents and Arnie returned with a tired but happy Ellen. Then the three would argue again over who would put Ellen down for her nap, and the same process repeated itself at bedtime. During those visits, things couldn't have been better on the extended family front, and it was gratifying to see Ellen thrive on her relatives' doting affection.

Back in Boston, with Holly's encouragement I took long walks to lower my stress level. It was during one of these walks that I entered an arcade in nearby Somerville and discovered Royal Flush, the pinball machine that became my obsession. Now it was pinball that kept me away from home as I tried to manage my anxiety about the upcoming tenure decision. But at least I wasn't drinking, Holly and I weren't fighting, and Ellen had my full, playful attention when I was home.

I was denied tenure in the spring of 1976. The decision, by Harvard's president, was delivered to me by the glum chairman of the philosophy department, the successor to Martin Murray, my retired mentor. The chairman said it pained him terribly to convey this conclusion. "I hired you, after all, and saw such promise ahead in your career."

He went on to say that he was bound by rules of confidentiality so was not at liberty to give details of the deliberative process. "I can give you my personal perspective, though, in the interest of any changes you might want to make in your future scholarly projects."

I could have cared less at this point, sure that the real reasons for the denial had more to do with accumulated collegial jealousy at my success during my first years at Harvard and resentment of my politics during the past year. But he continued, as much for his sake, I guessed, as mine.

"We in the department have witnessed a trend in your articles and books towards increasing speculation, by which I mean that your conclusions, particularly in your last book, are not well supported by your examples and logic." He stopped there, apparently waiting for me to react and argue. I had no energy to do either. He went on.

"The other problem I see, in all your work, frankly, is a tendency toward syncretism. You try to bring too many disparate ideas and theories into a unified whole. It's an admirable ambition, but a dangerous one in our world. Philosophical propositions require precision and depth and tightness. Your work is astounding and enviable in its imaginative creativity. But you lose other things in the process, things that are important to professional philosophers."

Again, I was sure he expected me to respond. When I didn't, he sighed and got down to basics. "As I think you know, our policies allow you to keep your position for another year, specifically the 1978-1979 academic year. You'll have the same salary, benefits, and course load, but there are no expectations for you to serve on committees or that sort of thing. This will give you more time to secure another position elsewhere."

"I won't stay beyond this semester. I worked so hard to..." I stopped myself. Venting wasn't going to change anything. "I'll send you a formal letter stating that I'll leave the university as soon as I've submitted my grades."

The chairman looked dumfounded that I was rejecting this lifeline year. After a few moments he sighed again, rose, wished me luck, and shook my hand. I had a moment of sympathy for him, an odd emotion, perhaps, under the circumstances, since I was the wounded party. But in fact the chairman's hands were tied by the entirely closed system governing promotions at Harvard then, its utter lack of transparency or recourse. Appeal was not an option. Indeed, the chairman had been generous in conveying any reason at all for what might have led to my denial. Harvard's "system" at the time allowed for none of that. There was no defined tenure process. Junior professors were hired with no guarantee of tenure or promotion. Quite the contrary. Internal promotion and tenure were exceedingly rare, with most tenured positions being filled at the full-professor level by academics who had earned big reputations elsewhere. New hires were warned of this and advised to make the most of their seven or eight assistant-professor years so that they might well be hired by other institutions, there to make a name for themselves and with the prospect of later being invited, often out of the blue, to return to Harvard as full professors with tenure. I knew this. Yet I was self-important and naïve enough to believe my star quality would make me an exception, to believe that I would be offered what exceedingly few were ever offered. My ruined expectations were what made this outcome so devastating.

I walked home more slowly than usual, wondering how I would tell Holly both pieces of news: first, that I didn't get tenure; second, that I refused the normal grace year and its recompense.

She surprised me. "I feel bad for you, Nate, really bad. I know how much your career means to you. But to be honest, I'm relieved. Our lives together, yours and mine, have not been going well for more than a year, and I think that's had an unhealthy effect on Ellen. I say fine—let's get out of here and do something totally different. Maybe it will bring us back to where we were before you started writing *Change*."

Holly surprised me again the next morning when she suggested that we move to Claymont, a community and school in West Virginia based on Gurdjieff's philosophy. We had visited there for a time in the summer of 1975. And I surprised myself by immediately agreeing to the idea. The decision was so liberating, the prospect so new and exciting, so promising for us as a family.

But now we had to explain our plans to our Kirinski and MacDonald parents. We doubted that any reason we gave would satisfy them, so we left things fairly vague. We both touted the external aspects of Claymont. It was a place where we could learn how to be more self-sufficient, grow our own food, build and repair our own house. This was true as far as it went, and it was something that many people our age were gravitating towards in the mid-1970s. Holly added that she needed something new, something deeper and more meaningful than what life offered in Cambridge, and it would be a wonderful experience for Ellen.

In my case? I needed a way to discount and make light of my Harvard exit. "It was bullshit every day there," I told anyone who would listen. "Constraining. Political. A place to be rid of." At least that was my public rationale. Internally, and more honestly, I was devastated by my failure. If Harvard had called and said, "Professor Kirinski: We've reconsidered. It was a mistake. Please accept our offer of tenure. Please come back," I would have returned in a moment, damaged dignity and hurt feelings be damned.

But they didn't, and I couldn't.

"For the life of me, I don't understand. I can't," my father said after I told my parents, Arnie, and Deb that I was leaving Harvard. The five of us were sitting in the living room after dinner. Holly was putting Ellen to sleep, and Eddie was on rotation at the hospital.

"I don't know how else to say it, Dad. I didn't get tenure, so I would have to leave in a year in any case. Holly and I figure it's better for us to leave now, to take a year and figure out what we want to do next, you know, for the longer term."

"But why West Virginia, Nathan?" my mother asked. My father seemed merely baffled, but her question had an edge of desperation. "Why in the world? I mean, this place you're going to, this farm—how can this be good for you, for your career, for your family? And what about money? What will you do for money?"

"We have a lot of savings, and it will hardly cost anything to live there. It's a beautiful place near the Blue Ridge Mountains. We have friends there. We'll learn a lot of practical skills—building, carpentry, plumbing, electrical work, pottery, gardening. Someday we want to buy some land of our own and build our own house. At Claymont, we'll learn how to do it. And there are lots of kids. Ellen will be in heaven—there's childcare, healthy food and air..." I didn't get into the esoteric aspect of Claymont, not even with Arnie and Deborah. Although this was the real reason we were going to Claymont, I knew that anything that might be characterized as spiritual development or mysticism would absolutely freak my parents out. I was pretty sure that Arnie and Deb wouldn't be judgmental, at least openly, but why risk it? It wasn't something I wanted or needed to get into.

In any event, I realized that all my explanations and enthusiasm wouldn't allay my parents' concerns and disappointment. As they saw it, we were dropping out, joining the unwashed masses of Hippies and protesters that threatened to overturn American society as Morton and Fay's generation had come to know and cherish it: the orderly, upwardly mobile, materially comfortable world that they and their parents had done everything possible to insure for their progeny. The Kirinski family had survived Vietnam and the accompanying upheavals of the late '60s and early '70s intact. So how could it be that a child of theirs was falling prey to a similar madness now, when they thought those dangers were past?

"I think it sounds interesting," my sister said. "All the reasons you gave make sense to me. A welcome break for you and Holly and a wonderful life for Ellen."

I looked at her with all the appreciation a look can convey. Deb's life with Eddie was an unhappy mess. Arnie and I knew this, although our parents didn't. The move Holly and I were about to make was probably the stuff of dreams for Deb.

"I'm probably not the best one to give an opinion," Arnie said, "first," he laughed, "because you didn't ask for one. But mainly because I'm still in the process you just opted out of—trying to climb the same academic ladder that you've been on. So, yeah, I share Mom's concerns about a lapse in your career. I wish things had turned out differently at Harvard for you, that you could stay there. I'll miss our conversations about philosophy and history and methodology. All of that."

Arnie turned to our parents. "But I also agree with Deb. It sounds like it will be a very interesting experience. Nate and Holly will learn a lot of useful skills, and I'll bet it will be paradise for Ellen. What kid wouldn't want to live on a farm? And it's only for a year. As Nate explained, it will give them a chance to figure out what comes next."

I didn't voice what I felt: Arnold Kirinski, you're the best.

Mort stood up. "Obviously, I'm not happy about any of this. But I hope I'm wrong and your brother and sister are right. You don't have my blessing, but I do wish you luck," he said as he left the room.

Fay came over and took my hands. "I'm your mother. Mothers always worry. I hope this will all work out okay." Then she kissed me on the cheek and followed her husband.

4

West Virginia

HOLLY, ELLEN, AND I left Cambridge in September of 1976 and moved to Claymont Court, a 400-acre estate on the outskirts of Charles Town, West Virginia. We would be there for ten months as students in a course offered by the Claymont Society for Continuous Education, a school started by John G. Bennett, who had worked directly with both Gurdjieff and Ouspensky, whom I mentioned earlier. Shortly before he died, in 1974, Bennett purchased Claymont with plans to establish the intensive course he had previously run at Sherborne House in Gloucestershire, England. In a prospectus titled *A Call for a New Society*, Bennett articulated his vision for Claymont as a "self-sufficient, psycho-kinetic community," a venue for continuous education along the lines of schools of wisdom that have existed since ancient times to provide seekers with the conditions and methods for their bodily, mental, and spiritual development. Such schools, he went on to write, are especially important in times of global crisis, times, in fact, like our own, when self-interest takes precedence over concerns for humanity as a whole. A new society, service-oriented and worshipful, is required, a community dedicated to the divine, to nature, and to our fellow human beings.

Laurent Ambrose, who had been with Gurdjieff, Ouspensky, and Bennett, took over as director of studies after Bennett's death. Based on a long visit to Claymont that Holly and I made in the summer of 1975, sooner than I had anticipated but in no way against my will, I was happy to have this opportunity to work with Laurent, now in his sixties and one of a dwindling number of first-line Gurdjieff disciples.

To call my time at Claymont eventful would qualify as my life's greatest understatement.

Even chatty Ellen stopped talking as we drove through the outskirts of Charles Town and approached Claymont. We parked at the mansion, Claymont Court, a handsome, Georgian-style structure built in 1820 by Bushrod Corbin Washington, grandnephew of George Washington. The registrar signed us in and directed us to the Great Barn. This football field-sized building, originally used to house show horses, had been converted into family and dormitory living accommodations, kitchen facilities, bathrooms, a child-care center, meeting rooms, and the Octagon, a huge, open, three-story venue on whose polished wooden floor many of the course's activities would be held.

We settled into our room along a corridor of private accommodations for couples and families. It was small but spacious enough for the three of us, the dresser we brought for our clothes, and the mattresses on the floor that came with the room. We hung a curtain to make a separate space for Ellen, which she immediately populated with the few stuffed animals, toys, and children's books we brought.

While Holly got things organized, I put Ellen in our backpack carrier and took her for a walk through the part of the property that housed the animals. "Daddy, Daddy! Look!" she screamed with excitement at every stop. "Look—chickens!" "Look—pigs!" "Look—cows!" "Look—horsies!" We had made the right choice to bring her here. I was sure of it.

At dinner, we began meeting our fellow students. Most of us were American, but there were also a few from France, Germany, Canada, Australia, the U. K., and Israel. We were pretty evenly split between women and men, and almost all white with a couple of Native- and Asian-American exceptions. The course was open to all religious traditions, although the majority of us had Jewish and Christian backgrounds. A number of the students had been in Gurdjieff-Ouspensky groups, others not. There were a dozen or so families, with kids ranging from newborns to teenagers. Several were Ellen's age. It was a comfort to assume that we shared certain counter-cultural values of the 1960s and 70s: pro-peace, pro-civil rights, pro-environment, and anti-establishment. And at the deepest level, whatever other differences there might be among us as individuals we could believe that we were at Claymont with the same intent: to develop ourselves and better serve the world. We were all seekers, searching for ourselves, for wisdom, for something essential, for the deeper meaning of life.

Holly and I knew some of the residents from our earlier visit to Claymont, and their welcome to us was gratifying. We were also pleased to reunite with a few of the other visitors who had been there with us that summer, particularly Mitchell and Edie.

Mitchell was an exuberant, witty man my age and half my weight. "God," he said as we hugged. "Are we gluttons for punishment, or what, coming back to try this penal colony again?"

"Yeah," I laughed, "and as volunteer convicts, no less, offering up our bodies and minds for some mysterious purpose with no guarantee that we'll ever figure out what that purpose is. But based on all the weight I lost here in a matter of weeks last time, at least I can anticipate that the diet will curb my gluttony."

"Right. Because our appetites will never be satisfied. Think what I'll look like a year from now."

"I can just see it—I'll become your size, and you'll be the latest Claymont poster boy when starvation turns you into pure spirit."

It all seemed so right just then. For the second time that day, I had no misgivings about having made the choice to come here. I had a powerful feeling of having come home—not just home in some déjà vu physical sense, since I had been here before, but home in the sense that I was fated to live here.

The course officially began after dinner that night—Monday, September 20, 1976—with an introductory meeting with Laurent. Holly and I were both able to attend when a resident who had a child Ellen's age agreed to baby sit for us. Roughly one-hundred students and several residential staff were gathered in front of Laurent. All of us, Laurent included, sat cross-legged on cushions. Anxious, excited, quiet, I waited for him to speak. At Claymont, I had learned during my previous visit, if it were necessary to talk at all it was important to do so without wasting words and to avoid "idle chatter"; long silences before utterances were a style I would become used to and adopt myself.

"Normally," Laurent began in his upper-class British accent, "we would begin with a talk. But I've decided to alter that approach tonight and instead invite your questions. This will give us all a better sense of one another."

I raised my hand. "May we take notes?"

"I ask that you refrain from taking notes, either during this or any talk for the remainder of the course. That way, one becomes more concentrated and attentive. Whether or not you write anything down afterwards will be up to you."

"I've read a lot of books about the Gurdjieff Work," said an intense-looking woman, "and came here believing that I know what it's about and why I'm here. But when I arrived yesterday I started to doubt myself and ask, why am I really here?"

Laurent looked down and nodded, giving me the impression that he approved of this question. "My assumption is that all of us here share a common attitude regarding change. This attitude is the hope for transformation. There are two types of change: apparent change and real change. Apparent change is deterministic, subject to accident, and temporal. Real change is purposeful and permanent. The two types of change can occur at various levels and in various ways. Temporal change occurs at the level of personality, which is comprised of our habit patterns. An important part of our work here is devoted to developing the capacity to observe these patterns. Permanent change occurs at the level of eternity. It requires that we have developed the capacity to be aware of eternity. For most of us, the second-level capacity is a long way off, and might never come to pass at all. But it is always out there, waiting for those who work hard enough to approach it."

A hand shot up. "You don't sound very optimistic about our prospects," said a young man in the row behind me. He was obviously agitated. "I mean, if what you call *real* change is so elusive, where does that leave those of us who don't have the capacity for it? How should we proceed? *Why* should we try?"

"The two levels of change are not separable, nor is the preparation for them separable, although there are subtle levels of difference. Here at Claymont it will be preparation in the psychological notions of Gurdjieff, Ouspensky, and Bennett. This is the level at which one must deal with one's barriers or hindrances. Thus one must often go back before one can progress—to the level of development, the level at which new power can be acquired. We must begin by observing ourselves with sincerity. We come here wishing to work, but after a while we may have a curious observation: that we cannot work, that we don't even have the wish to work."

"In addition to wish," my friend Mitchell asked, "what else is required?"

"Part of the essence of Gurdjieff's teaching is that we cannot work alone. Perhaps eventually we will learn to accept one another. There are those of us that are weak and those that are strong. Strong and weak complement each other, need each other. We must get beyond thinking in terms of 'we' and 'they,' of 'my' possessions or 'your' possessions or whatever. We're all in the same boat and must get beyond the barriers we set up. And we must learn to use restraint, particularly now in terms of our food and not eat more than we need, and in terms of silence. Silence is more communicative than words. In our culture we talk and think too much. For that reason, we will devote a lot of time to the Movements, or 'sacred dances.' For those not familiar with the Movements, they are precisely scripted dance-like exercises, performed to music, which Mr. Gurdjieff devised or adapted from a number of spiritual traditions as a way to harmonize one's intellectual, emotional, and physical aspects, or 'centers.' The Movements require tremendous attention, energy, and practice, and in the process of learning them one might see one's habitual postures and the psychological states those postures mirror."

Laurent paused, waiting for more questions. "Right," he said after a long silence, seeing no hands go up. "Let me give you a basic idea of how the course will proceed." We were not to leave the property without permission, he continued, although there would be scheduled opportunities to leave every two weeks or so on what he called exeat days, as well as some time around Christmas. We could expect a range of activities during the course—some held daily, others periodically, still others only rarely or once.

We would convene in the Octagon every day at 6:00 a.m. for an hour of Morning Exercises. "These are guided inner exercises to develop concentration and powers of attention," he explained, "but I won't say more at the moment. The instructions for doing them are very precise, and those must be transmitted directly in person." He then made the distinction between these proactive efforts in Morning Exercises and meditation, which he called Evening Exercises. "Meditation is receptive rather than active work. To meditate, use the idea of air, which is limitless and boundless. Find a position, with your back straight, that is comfortable enough to maintain for 35 to 40 minutes. Let air flow into you. When your mind begins to chatter or go elsewhere, gently nudge it back to the idea of limitless air."

Prior to Morning Exercises we were expected to do preparatory ablutions, or ritual bodily cleansings, much as Muslims perform before prayers. He then described how to do these by washing our hands, mouth (three times), nose (with three inhalations of water far into the nostrils, each followed by a forceful nasal exhalation), eyes (three times), ears (three times), genitals, feet, hands again, and forearms.

We would be split into three groups, he continued. "On a rotational basis, one group will be responsible for housekeeping each day while the other two attend classes and maintain the property and garden. Each of those in the housekeeping group will be responsible for particular daily maintenance chores, such as housecleaning, cooking, and childcare. Also on a rotational basis, one of those in the housekeeping group will be designated as the primary supervisor overseeing all chores. As a combined, large group, you'll do a variety of what are called Practical Work projects, for example, clearing foliage, cutting wood, planting fields, harvesting crops, demolishing old barns and other structures in the local area in return for reusable materials, and building or repairing structures on the property itself. Some of you, of course, have more of a background in this sort of work than others. But those who can teach are expected to teach, and all of you, in any event, will be taught carpentry, pottery, and weaving along the way. Practical Work, and indeed every activity in every moment but particularly Practical Work, should be seen as opportunities to 'Work' in the inner sense, which is the reason for our being here at all."

Laurent went on to mention certain aspects of inner work. "Throughout the course, you'll be given themes to guide your efforts, and there will be frequent Question & Answer sessions to discuss your observations in relation to each theme. The themes will provide an important structure for our day-to-day work. Detailed instructions for working with a theme will be given when the theme is introduced, but examples of themes you might anticipate could include, among others, *'Talking,' 'Experiencing,' 'Relaxation,' 'Objections,' 'Procrastination,' 'Blame,' 'The neglect of other people,' 'Being, versus having and doing,' 'Preparation,' 'What is my work this week?,' 'Air as food,' 'Suggestibility,' 'Persistence,' 'Help,' 'Stillness,' 'Never do as others do,'* and *'Temptation.'* Well, perhaps these topics have given you a bit of an idea."

We would practice the Sacred Movements relentlessly as a major component of the inner work, he said, and we would all participate in special activities and projects during the course, such as Morris Dancing, a Shakespearean play, and presenting two training sessions on topics of our own choosing to our fellow students. In the evenings we would hear readings from Gurdjieff's *Beelzebub's Tales to His Grandson* and readings from, as well as tapes of, Bennett's lectures. From time to time there would be Work Weekends open to people from outside our residential community. These typically would include people experienced in the Work as well as newcomers. In addition, we could expect to have a number of guests and guides from such traditions as Sufism and Buddhism, among others, as well as visiting Gurdjieff-system teachers.

"Are there any questions?" There were none, and Laurent brought the session to a conclusion. "Throughout, we must keep asking ourselves: Why were we given this life? What are we here for?"

I felt inspired as I left the session. My imagination was fueled by the prospect of realizing the possibilities I had been reading about in the Gurdjieff and related literature: of attaining harmony; learning equanimity, dispassion, and non-attachment; cultivating stillness; moving towards ever greater awareness; and, finally, fulfilling the mystic's ultimate aim of transcending all dualistic relationships to become one with the Universal Mind, the Absolute in which there would be no divide between subject and object, you and me, inner and outer, this and that. I was pumped, as we used to say, anxious to get started. I was about to be taught ancient, and often secret, methods of transformation and was sure I would take every opportunity to make the most of these "skillful means," as Buddhism puts it. Now it was up to me. I was ready to change in whichever ways the answers to Laurent's questions might require: Why was I given this life? What am I here for?

5

Almost Heaven: A Diary

The soul which has apatheia is not simply the one which is not disturbed by changing events, but the one which remains unmoved at the memory of them as well.

–Evagrius Ponticus

I CONSCIENTIOUSLY DOCUMENTED SEVEN of the nine months I spent in West Virginia in a diary that grew to a couple of hundred pages before I stopped recording daily events on April 17, 1977. By then the exercise had become a compulsion, a rigidly self-imposed mandate to jot down each detail, the sort of mindless and automatic behavior, I chastised myself, I was at Claymont to learn to change. But in moments of honesty, I knew the real reason for stopping was that my life had gotten too confusing and depressing for words. Living the experiences was bad enough; re-living them by writing about them almost immediately after they happened was torture.

At the same time, I was bereft to be giving up one of only two activities I felt I had any control over. The other was morning ablutions. Every morning until the end of the course in June, I would wake at five o'clock and make my way to the communal bathroom, a half-hour before anyone else awoke, to beat the crowd lining up to wash before Morning Exercises. No longer keeping a diary, solitary ablutions would now have to suffice as my primary solace.

Going to Claymont had seemed so right back in September. How had things come to this? Obviously, there was a process at work. But what process? Reading back over some of my diary entries from that year in West Virginia leaves me undecided whether the process was one of important personal evolution or just a badly misguided life-style choice.

I spent the first day of the course in the garden. As an inner exercise, we were to put our attention in our little finger. Attention would be a key emphasis in the course: to remember we have this faculty to begin with, to develop the capacity to place and sustain it, to move towards an ever-finer quality of awareness: from basic, personal awareness to what various writers refer to as Pure Awareness, the impersonal, eternal witness, or watcher, behind one's personal awareness.

My group, Group A, had house duty all day. Any time we had house duty I hoped my assignment would be childcare so that I could spend more time with Ellen. But that had to remain a private wish; sometimes it worked out that way, other times not. And because Holly was in a different group with different house days, the chances that one of us would be on childcare doubled.

But this morning I was the kitchen boy, the chief chef's assistant, and in the evening I was on dining room service. The theme we are working on is "The Food We Eat." Within this theme we are to pay particular attention to "the food we waste." It occurs to me that there are many forms of food—energy, air, impressions, and sensations, for example—and many types of waste. The amount of energy I waste on idle chatter, fantasizing, holding grudges, and so much more is extraordinary and alarming.

We had a demolition project today tearing down an old barn on nearby Blakeley Farms. Throughout the day we were to pause every 15 minutes to sense whichever hand we were using at the time. The supervisor for practical work at Claymont is a Sherborne alumnus named Conrad Broderick, a dark, hulking, menacing figure fond of giving oracular pronouncements. "Brody" reminds me of Popeye the Sailor's nemesis Bluto. The caricature would be amusing if Brody himself weren't so sinister. I don't like this man.

Laurent gave us an exercise connected to the food-we-eat theme. We are to eat our first mouthful of food at each meal consciously, to be present then. We are to continue this exercise for a week, longer if we like. He went on to say something about vegetarianism and special diets, as there are a number of us who follow such regimens and who have raised questions about how we are to continue following them at Claymont.

Laurent was merciless, telling us it is a form of self-centeredness and egoism for us to insist on these preferences. "It is sentimental nonsense. All food that can be eaten and assimilated is good food. And man is the only being who transforms his food. There is a responsibility that goes with this capacity." As a vegetarian, I spent all day pondering his words while I picked tomatoes and started a compost of rotten tomatoes.

That night, Holly and I agreed to give up vegetarianism for the duration of the course. "We're here to change," Holly said, "and we trust Laurent's guidance." My decision was practical. "We'll need whatever nourishment we can get to make it through this year. Better not to be picky."

We thought it would be hard for Ellen to make the adjustment, but eating animal products didn't seem to bother her physically. And she was two; ethical dilemmas weren't part of her world.

I worked all day with Steve, a senior resident and instructor whom I like very much. Part of the time was spent organizing tools and supplies in one of the property's workshops, and the rest of the time we repaired a boiler pipe. As I worked on these specific tasks, Steve suggested that I try to get an idea of the overall process I was involved in: where my predecessor who had worked on the task had left off, where I picked it up, where I left it for the next person. "Try to connect with a larger pattern," Steve encouraged me.

That Holly and I are in different groups is presenting a bigger-than-usual problem today. So far, we've had the flexibility to spell each other to be with Ellen when she's not in childcare. But today we both have particularly challenging responsibilities that neither of us feels we can shirk. Eventually, we decided that I had more leeway, today at least, to leave my group's work in the garden and the pottery than she had to take time from her role as Group C's house supervisor.

But we need to agree on how we're going to divide the labor from now on. As a start, we decide to alternate attendance at Morning Exercises, Meditation, Talks, and Movements; one will attend while the other takes care of Ellen, and it will be up to the one who attends to fill in the one who couldn't attend. We know this is far from ideal, but we also knew from the time we applied for the course that the problem would inevitably arise. We'll just have to negotiate and make do.

Right now, our time with Ellen is especially important. She's adjusting well enough, but there have been some difficult moments. A key reason for this is that she has orthopedic shoes, the kind that force her feet outward. This has really held her back from learning to walk. Meanwhile, the other kids are running around all barefoot and happy. By contrast, it's hard to watch my kid struggle to stand, much less walk. I also have the sense that the other parents think we're pampering Ellen.

"There is a substance," Laurent said at Morning Exercises, "that pervades the universe, one that allows us to connect the natural and the spiritual worlds. This is attention. It is the only tool available to us."

I was on childcare all day. While I was talking with Joe, the other student sharing the assignment, I placed my attention in my left hand and was able to maintain a strong sensation there. As long as I applied my attention and sensed, I was aware of a definite difference between this and my usual conversations—paradoxically, perhaps, a feeling of detachment along with a feeling of presence. I did not exactly *remember* to sense; rather, sensation *came* to me. I was aware of myself sitting there and talking, and at the same time I was aware of the sensation, primarily in my hand but elsewhere as well. Normally I don't look at people's eyes when I talk with them, I'm not sure why, probably because looking away gives me time to think about what is being said and how I might respond. But on this occasion I looked right into Joe's eyes, very naturally and entirely cognizant of doing so.

I spent most of the day in the woods, clearing cut lumber and stacking it for sale. I also served as kitchen boy preparing the dinner salad. I love both of these jobs. Neither requires any leadership or responsibility. Neither is easy to screw up. Their less-demanding nature made it easier for me to work with the day's exercise, which was to consider the idea that "man is asleep." Yet this same un-demanding nature made it easier to fall asleep through sheer routinization.

At one point, Brody came by and told us to remove a giant tree trunk with a dense network of roots. I and several others began chopping away with no prior assessment of what might be required. An hour later we were still hacking away. That we had hammered the trunk into mush only made our task more frustrating. We were three exasperated woodsmen whose in-creasing expenditures of effort were obviously getting us nowhere.

Laurent came by and watched us for a while. Then he borrowed a long-handled ax and within minutes had managed to cleave the trunk into several clean sections and separate the roots. From there it was easy enough for us to remove both the trunk and the roots. I was impressed by Laurent's deliberative assessment of the situation before he moved into action, and then by the efficiency of his action. I felt more than a little inadequate by comparison, not only because of his more intelligent, incisive approach to the problem, but also because here was a 60-year-old man of unremarkable build who clearly had more strength and energy than I and my fellow woods-men, all of us 30 years younger and physically larger than Laurent. I wasn't surprised at this, as I had seen him on several occasions hold his arms out horizontally, parallel to the ground for long periods of time, only to lower them slowly when all the rest of us, who tried to follow his lead, had dropped our arms in pain and fatigue. Was this purely a matter of muscular strength? I doubt it; there are some impressive physical specimens among the students. I think Laurent just has much greater discipline and powers of concentration.

During a theme discussion this evening, Laurent laid into us about the mind-less quantity and quality of the observations most of us were offering.

"You are driven by idle curiosity," he said, "thus it's no surprise that your comments reflect this in idle chatter. Instead, you should ask questions you have worked to answer for yourselves— honest questions, as opposed to the dishonest questions you ask just to show off, or to get someone else to do what you're too lazy to do, or because of the self-indulgent pleasure you get from asking frivolous questions."

After he left we just sat there, chastised and stunned. To a person, I have no doubt we were privately resolving to be more careful with our speech from then on.

Laurent gave us the following topic: Observe likes and dislikes. He added that "we cannot be free if we avoid what we dislike."

At dinner, he announced that we would have an exeat the next day, starting after lunch and ending at 6:30 p.m. Until lunch, we would work in the garden or do practical work. "Free" time, he explained, is meant to do something useful, to remember what we are here for. Accordingly, he gave us two tasks for the following day: first, to contrive somehow to be awake at the stroke of noon; and second, to be conscious of our first mouthful of food after noon. It occurred to me then how seductive of old habits a day away from Claymont would be, a day where I would be able to eat as much as I wanted after the austere Claymont diet; a day when I would be back in the material clutches of the outside world; a day in which the struggle to stay awake would easily succumb to the lure of sleep.

As dinner proceeded, I was very aware of the weightiness and clarity of all that I saw—flowers, mugs, plates, benches, people. It was as if, all of a sudden and despite lifelong myopia, I had excellent and precise vision. I was most aware of the food I was eating, and this was quite a striking experience. Each mouthful seemed like a distinct and entire meal. I ate much more slowly and was satisfied with less food than usual.

During exeat, Holly, Ellen, and I went to Charles Town to purchase necessary personal supplies and treat ourselves to some indulgences—beer for me, chocolate for Holly, ice cream for Ellen. I enjoyed being with my family, just the three of us.

On the way to my 8:30 a.m. to 12:30 p.m. stint in the garden, I read the following notice on the bulletin board from Laurent.

To all on the course:
Would all of you write me a few lines to describe how you observed yourself working throughout this morning.
For instance, mention specifically whether you were there at all, or all the time, or part of the time. How did you start? Was it on time? How did you end and how would you describe the way in which you worked—was it energetically, as lazily as possible, spasmodically, continuously, well at the start but poorly at the end, or the reverse, etc.?
Please let me have your observations by 12:00 noon tomorrow, Saturday.

I replied that evening after returning from exeat.

Dear Laurent,
I worked in the truck garden this morning harvesting black-eyed peas and observed the following:
I arrived two minutes late due to delivering Ellen to childcare, and aside from those two minutes I was at that site until 12:15 pm. Because I came late, I needed to have the instructions repeated.
In general, I worked steadily. For the first 15 minutes, however, I had difficulty getting started; consequently my pace was slow, although I eventually

got into an accelerated and steady rhythm. I decelerated to a very slow pace for the last 15 minutes as my thoughts turned to returning early so that I'd have time to wash up for lunch.

More specifically, I have an observation concerning this morning's work which is connected to the like-dislike theme. I was feeling quite disgruntled when I arrived at the garden. It had begun to rain fairly hard, and my rain gear was not adequate for the downpour. It was difficult enough to find the plants; the rain drops on my glasses made the job even more frustrating. I was able to reach a relatively steady work rhythm, one powered, I'm afraid, by some anger and resentment towards all sorts of slights, actual and imagined, as well as by the proximity of others—I didn't want to slack off in front of them. By 10:15 I was thoroughly soaked. Even my boots were full of water. I considered leaving. Then the urge came to me to sense. I did, half-heartedly at first. However, the urges became persistent. No sooner would I leave off my efforts to sense and move to day-dreaming than another urge would arise. I can best describe it as being visited by the impulse to sense. I remembered the Q & A period of the preceding day. In answer to one of my questions, Steve remarked that one's remembering that one can sense at a given moment is a gift. To choose not to sense at that instant is a sin. I put all my efforts into sensing then as I worked, in whichever limbs—usually my hands—seemed most accessible to those efforts.

At about 10:45 or 11:00, I can say only that the discomforts of the rain, my coldness and wetness, ceased to matter. I experienced a deep thankfulness that I was there and alive. The condition of my boots, my feet, my clothing—none of that mattered. When the rain stopped a few minutes later, it was all the same to me. I was still able to work steadily, but this no longer required that I do so in order to impress the others who were nearby, or that the intensity of my labors be driven by resentment and anger. It seemed natural and important to work in this neutral, unaffected way. I wished to continue working in this way.

This lasted for about half an hour. I managed to remember to try to be awake at the stroke of noon, but all I can say is that I only remembered to pause at noon. I have no other observations about that pause. Sometime between 11:30 and 11:50, however, I remember starting to daydream again, mostly about how fine a person I was to have labored so contentedly in the awful rain. My attempts to sense became more sporadic, half-hearted, and perfunctory between 11:50 to 12:10 or so, when I left.

Sincerely,
Nathan Kirinski

Theme: "To observe the multitude of 'I's within us." We were told this topic is not at all time-limited. Working with it would be an on-going task.

In Psychology class this morning, Laurent responded to an observation I made regarding the multitude of "I"s and how my "I"s often contradicted one another. They had me on a roller coaster: some were uppers and some were downers; some seemed motivated to work, others bent on obstructing work.

"There are many aspects of us," he said, "many 'I's which do not want to change." Then he dismissed the class by asking us to continue the theme, this time by trying to catch ourselves saying "I."

Later in the day, I was setting things up in the dining room between meals. I had given myself the task of catching myself saying "I" at least once before I went to bed. But so far I hadn't been able to do it. Exasperated, I decided to go up to a person and start a conversation quite purposely with "I...."

Harold, a Canadian student, came in to set cups on the table. "Were any of the cups you made at the pottery the other day accepted for glazing? We need more cups."

Ha! Here was my chance. I replied with exceeding deliberation. "*I* made two cups. And *I* am pleased to say that both of the cups *I* made were acceptable, and *I* have been told by Eric [the head of the pottery] that the two cups *I* made will be glazed." I emphasized "I" so obviously in order to make sure I caught myself saying it. I was proud to have done so, but not so proud when I realized I hadn't caught the "I" which was so goddamned pompous and self-congratulatory.

The more I work with the multitude of "I"s theme and try to catch my various "I"s, the more I get the Buddhist idea of impermanence. Einsteinian physics provides the same insight: there is no fixed frame of reference in the universe; everything is moving relative to everything else. The analogy that comes to mind is pinball: the steel balls ricochet continually, unpredictably, subject to no discernible rhyme or reason and following trajectories that even the most skilled players can't always control. All you can do is be alert; watch and be ready to activate your flipper before the field changes and you've missed your chance.

In a discussion with Laurent on the like-dislike theme, I offered my observation on my rainy-day-in-the-garden experience. It was a summary version of what I had described at length in my letter to him. He made no comment on what I said, but I had the impression that he was receptive to it. To me, however, what I said was stale and non-explicit compared to the vitality of what had actually happened.

During the session Laurent made several points about likes and dislikes. The main thing, he said, is that we be free. The only way something can occur towards this end is when struggle is present. It means little to go and do something just because one dislikes it—in fact, it is important to learn to enjoy what we do. It is also important that we actually *retain* strong likes and dislikes. To be otherwise is to be apathetic. We need strong preferences in order to "observe, observe, observe." Freedom from likes and dislikes does not mean being able to do what we don't want to do. *It means to be detached from either state.* He ended by saying we are to continue this theme, with those who did not speak this time doing so the next, and those who did refraining.

I strained my back, and the pain became severe enough that, at Holly's urging, I went to talk with Steve. He referred me to Laurent, even calling him for me. When I met with Laurent, he suggested a stretching exercise: hang from a door sill, sense my spine, and recover from this position very slowly to prevent spasms. He asked that I try to locate the pain quite precisely, with the notion that if it proves to be, say, a pinched sciatic nerve, a possibility he considered likely, he will give me more specific exercises.

He also suggested that I rest the back and not do certain activities, particularly Practical Work and Movements: I am to sit in the back of the room and "do" the Movements inwardly, an effort that Laurent says can be just as effective as actually assuming the postures. I said I was reluctant to do this, since I don't want to be seen as lazy or favored. Laurent replied that this is precisely the Work that is significant—it is genuine work and offers possibilities, whereas actually participating in activities means nothing. I must use this experience of people saying, for example, "What's this fellow doing lazing about?"

Laurent said, and I could only concur, that my attitude to all this is a projection of my own reaction to people whom I judge as lazy and not working: "What's that so-and-so doing or not doing?" Laurent went on to say that the world truly is upside down. Often enough, what looks like Work is nothing, and vice versa. The important thing is to be free from people's reactions to my "lazing about." I said I would try, though it would be difficult to abide their negative judgements.

"We're so mechanical," Laurent replied. "The fact that we can't even catch ourselves saying 'I' is horrifying. Yet we go around talking about 'Work.'" He paused. "Some others," he continued, "have been putting me on about their so-called back injuries. Remember *Galatians*: 'You cannot mock God.' Think of God as the Work. It knows what is inside. What good is outward change if you are still the same phony inside?"

Laurent then asked me how I was getting on. (At this point I was getting a welling up, weepy feeling just because he was being so nice to me.) He asked me this with what seemed like a very different expression in his eyes than earlier. He was graver and more intense. I was doing my best to put my attention into my hands and sense them. As I made this effort, I looked directly into his eyes and he was looking directly into mine. I'm certain that each of his eyes was different from the other—one appeared to be further away, the other closer. I believe we had some authentic contact then.

I told him that things were difficult in my relationship with Holly, but not beyond coping. I chose not to elaborate; instead, for some reason I couldn't identify, I blurted out that I often experienced what I could only describe as "feeling" stirring in me. (I was ready to cry then; it must have been noticeable.)

"This is quite good," Laurent told me. "Emotion is important. Something different is happening."

This morning I was breakfast cook. I couldn't sleep past 4 a.m. so I got up, had a long bath, and went to the kitchen at 5. All went well; I prepared a nice meal and arranged a nice set up.

At breakfast I was contentedly ladling out oatmeal when a loud voice said, "Boy, are you slow." It was Brody. I continued ladling at the same speed, then glanced at him and replied, "I know it."

"I'm very serious in my comment," he said.

I paused in serving. "I know you're serious. I'm very serious in my response, too." I looked down and resumed dishing out oatmeal.

Later, as I sat down to eat after everyone else had finished, I wanted to cry. I realized that Brody is "The Coach," my most inimical archetype, all the shop teachers and sports authorities and performance evaluators of my past. I loathe him just as I loathed them.

Something else in me, though, thanks him for saying what he did. Lots of material there. Much of me wanted to justify and explain myself to him, to say: "If you realized how bad my back is, you'd know why I'm slow." But the truth is that I am slow, bad back or not, particularly around food; I never learned to cook even for myself, much less for a hundred hungry people needing a solid meal before going off to perform strenuous tasks. My father took care of that at the Carousel Diner, and Arnie became his backup. I was content to sweep floors and wash dishes. When it comes to cooking I'm fearful because I don't know what I'm doing, and I'm nearly paralyzed by the prospect of screwing things up. So I go slowly, carefully, to avoid mistakes. Bad Brody has stepped on a corn, and the corn can be valuable in that so many emotional storage tanks are connected to my fear of failure. Holly has pointed out that I'm too thin-skinned. I need somehow to get over that.

Unlike me, Ellen is physically thriving. I have no doubt this is because we got rid of her orthopedic shoes. Her feet have straightened out on their own, and she's learning to get around as well as the other kids her age. I took a certain pride today in watching her deal with Jason, a kid who has tried to bully her since we got here. This afternoon in childcare, he tried to snatch a toy out of her hands as she was sitting on the floor. Ellen grabbed his wrist and refused to let go. Judging from Jason's grimace, whines, and eventual sobs, her grip must have been very strong. Go, Ellen!

It's a work weekend, and many outside visitors are here. As he is the rest of the time, Brody is in charge of Practical Work during these weekends, too.

At the end of the day, the visitors and course participants convened in the garden to share observations around a special exercise we had been given, something along the lines of our connection with other people. In summing up, Brody said that we can experience powerful and striking states when we work with intense effort and concentration, "as you did today." But, he added, "it's an illusion to think that we have achieved such states individually. There are things that come with group effort, things that can never come to us alone." I doubt that I could ever bring myself to like this person, but I can bring myself to appreciate certain of his insights.

I was premature even to think of cutting Brody a break. The guy's an asshole. Three days ago I was chief cook for supper. Cooking even for myself is a struggle; being responsible for feeding others is pure trauma. Fortunately, the menu Walter, the kitchen chief, gave me was macaroni and cheese. Simple enough, even for me. Unfortunately, Brody was in a punitive mood, apparently because the groups working in the woods were not performing to his satisfaction. So he kept them going. I had prepared the meal for serving at 6:00 p.m., the scheduled time. When no one came, I kept it warm until 7. Then 8, 9, and 10. By the time they arrived to eat at 11:00 p.m. the mac and cheese was dried out and unappetizing. What made the whole fiasco worse was that, with the best of intentions and sympathetic fellow-feeling, I had prepared pots of coffee and trays of chocolate chip cookies and had my serving assistants deliver those to the work site. It all came back, uneaten. According to the servers, Brody was really pissed by "Kirinski's misguided, unsolicited pretense at compassion."

Well, I'm just as pissed by his cavalier arrogance and poor judgement. He takes our lives in his hands whenever we go off to demolish a barn or other structure in order to salvage its materials for Claymont use or re-sale. It's amazing to me that no one has been killed walking along decaying roofs or handling old wires. I have yet to hear Brody offer any safety reminders, much less prevent people from being in these derelict structures to begin with.

Today was an all-day exeat. Holly, Ellen, and I pigged out on breakfast at Howard Johnsons with Mitchell and Edie. I bought toiletries for several of the teens whose parents are on the course, then went to Harper's Ferry with Holly and Ellen to have strawberry ice cream and look around a little. We ended the day, to Ellen's adorable delight, with Baclava.

Observations on my back problems and incapacity to do physical work: At first, it was extremely difficult—a struggle to follow Laurent's advice to rest because I didn't want to be considered a malingerer. To avoid this impression, I started justifying myself to anyone who would listen, telling them of my condition and making it known that Laurent was working with me in this—that he knows about, fully approves, and has even ordered my inactivity. But I still can't bring myself to lie down in meetings and during readings, as Laurent suggested. I tried to do so once, along with Joan, another student with back problems. But when she fell asleep and began to snore during a reading, I woke her at once so that people wouldn't think it was I who was snoring. I resolved never to lie down in these gatherings again, regardless of what Laurent said.

I have to admit that I occasionally like missing activities, no less than I used to abhor missing them. I realize that one preference is just as automatic and conditioned as the other. But today, missing activities has become very difficult again. I am in charge of supplies, and people are coming in to get cleansers, sponges, and what have you. I feel guilty to have them see me lying on the floor while everyone else is out working. "I have a pinched nerve in my back, you see," I insist on explaining.

I don't want Laurent to see me doing any work, but neither do I want him to see me lying down, especially in Movements class. Fantasies of his disapproval abound, despite his recommendation that I should rest. In my mind, at least, I have set it up to be inevitable that he'll disapprove: "Nathan is not lying down, as I told him. He doesn't have the strength to suffer the disapproval of others." Or: "He is lying down still. He overdoes this 'infirmed' condition. It's been days now." The classic, albeit self-imposed, double bind.

At dinner, Laurent introduced the theme of Noticing. "If you don't notice something, it doesn't exist—not for you. You can transform the world you live in by noticing. It's a very important topic. I urge you not to take it lightly. When we notice different things, we live in different worlds."

On the theme of Noticing: Yesterday, I was carrying and stacking tomato posts, piling six at a time on my right shoulder, stooping low to lift and holding my right arm around them as I carried. When the pile was off-balance, I needed to use both arms to stabilize the posts. I enjoyed this activity, both as exercise on a lovely day and because my back finally felt strong. As I was stacking the posts, two by two, I noticed quite clearly that I was doing it exactly as I used to carry beach umbrellas for the concession that employed me as a teenager in Belmar. That pattern of physical functioning has not changed in 20 years.

Our new theme is "Tearing down and giving in." The "tearing down" part perfectly describes what's happening to me lately—to my defenses, self-image, confidence, and ego. The second part, "giving in," does not yet apply. I fight like crazy to hold onto my identity, the permanent, wishfully eternal Nathan Kirinski.

I'm sure that part of this fight to hold on involves Holly. Day by day she seems more distant from me, less interested in talking or even being together. Intellectually, I can understand that she must be going through her own identity struggles, her own tearing downs and giving ins. But it hurts my feelings when she's like this.

The following note "To All Students" is on the bulletin board:

<u>Thanksgiving</u>
I asked one of you who was inquiring about plans for "Thanksgiving" what it was all about, and I was given the usual historical explanation. But when I further inquired what it meant on a personal level, I was told that it was just an occasion for a 'good nosh.'

It is more than this! Thanksgiving is part of our response when we receive something. For instance, glimpses of the real world should be for us a summons to set out on a pilgrimage to find and enter it. But they are not given to us for our private benefit as St. Paul so clearly says in Corinthians in describing charismata. Everything that we receive gratuitously without having earned it—as for instance one's U.S. heritage, since this occasion is the American Thanksgiving—should arouse in us not only gratitude but determination to pass it on to our children and children's children.

I suggest that we should observe Thanksgiving Day, Thursday 25th November by individually doing something towards this— and to help us in so doing, that instead of gorging ourselves we should fast for 24 hours. What do you think?

Laurent

Laurent introduced the Decision Exercise. It is to extend for 30 days. The task is to choose something quite specific and simple to accomplish each day, and the exercise consists of seven steps for each decision process:
1) Review what needs to be done during the day.
2) Review what you might do on the following day.
3) Ask why.
4) Ask how you might do it.
5) At the end of Morning Exercise, ask "Have I made my decision?"
6) Visualize it.
7) Review what you did at day's end.

When the time comes actually to make the decision, he continued, don't do so in the affirmative unless it feels right to do so. If you make the decision and fail to fulfill it, punish yourself for not doing it. "Train yourself, train your body, to accomplish what you set yourself."

At today's Q & A session with Steve, I was continually on the verge of saying: "I find myself, in answer to the question 'Why am I here?' having nothing except the usual responses, for example, to perfect myself, to change, to work, etc. Honestly, I don't know what 'Work' means. Occasionally I experience a longing, but when I try to specify for what, I come up with nothing. Can you comment on this?"

As it turned out, I never got to ask this question, which was just as well considering how uncomfortable I was with the ambiguity of it. At one point I nearly did ask, but Harold and I both started to speak at once and I deferred to him. Towards the end of the session, however, after I had decided not to ask the question, someone brought up that she had the sense of being watched, to which Steve replied that it would be a useful exercise in the midst of this situation to try and see *from where* one is being watched. He then went on to say that reality is the reverse of what we think it is. That *we* don't do the watching, that we are nothing; that something *over there* is "we," or "I." This, he said, is supposed to be a terrifying experience for some, but for him it was wondrous. It takes only a few seconds to change everything, and the experience will stay with one for years to come.

At this point I jumped in. "Steve! How can we make this contact? How can this contact come to us? What can we do?"

"It takes a certain intensity. If you work intensely long enough, if you struggle enough, it may come. It's a mixture of intensity and grace. Here at Claymont, we've tried to provide the conditions for this intense work on oneself. Many people never use this opportunity."

Working with the animals has been one of my most challenging but satisfying activities. Part of the reason for this is because I get on very well with James, a born-and-raised Nebraska farm boy and Sherborne alumnus who oversees all of Claymont's farming and animal husbandry operations. Thanks to James, the cerebral Nathan Kirinski, Ph.D. has learned to birth calves and piglets, put nose rings in sows, castrate boars, coddle neurotic Guinea hens, and generally care for the whole lot. Just as with children and plants, the animals can't be expected to take care of themselves; we have a special responsibility for them—night, day, all year round. There is no room to let them down, there are no acceptable excuses.

James and I spend many hours talking during frigid Blue Ridge nights as we wait together, like expectant fathers, to help with the births of our charges. Our conversations are often quite personal—sharing details of our histories, the influences of family and friends and places when we were growing up, our highs and lows, our plans. As my relationship with James deepens, I'm tempted to tell him about what's going on between Holly and me: how the distance between us keeps increasing, my sense that she might actually dislike me, my confusion and distress at what's happening. But in the end I decide not to divulge such intimacies. This community is too damned close, too damned public.

I have been trying hard to observe the functioning of my "machine." What I see is a constant chain of associative links among my physical, emotional, and intellectual centers—where a thought provokes an emotion and an emotion leads to an action, or at least an imagined action. Here's an example. I cut myself in the kitchen and wrap my finger in a paper towel. As I watch it absorb the blood, I'm reminded of what an elderly professor friend, Dr. X, told me *eight years ago* about his battle with cancer and the blood he daily saw after he defecated and wiped himself. But he kept working despite this. "Why doesn't he retire?" I had asked Holly. "He's having too much fun," she answered. "He has his institute and lucrative consulting projects. He's making lots of money and turning out articles and books." Anyway, Dr. X co-authored a book with a junior professor, Dr. Z. Young Dr. Z gave me a copy. I could see that Dr. X was pissed: *Why Kirinski?* I imagined he was thinking. *Kirinski didn't help. He had nothing to do with this book. Why waste a complimentary copy?* I never actually heard Dr. X say this. I imagined it. And what I imagined I felt, and the feeling was rejection.

There's lots to observe in this and numerous other examples of the workings of associative thinking, lots to catch. But I seldom do. And if I do catch a part of the associative sequence, it's hard to retrace all the steps: How did I get *here?* It's hard to catch thoughts as they arise or the emotions those thoughts generate. The rapidity with which these associations occur is staggering.

Here's a more immediate example. Morning Exercises are held in the Octagon, where dozens of us sit in the pre-sunrise darkness following the guided instructions of Laurent or a senior instructor. Virtually every morning Andrew Petrossian, one of my fellow students, breaks noticeable wind. I've become accustomed to it. But on this particular morning, the smell is more obvious and pungent than usual. I can't help but focus on it. Then I think, *Fucking Andy. What a terrible odor. It's so bad I can't concentrate on the exercise. Why can't he control his eating? But maybe it's not something he can help. Maybe he's got a problem with the food or the cooking. Maybe it's Claymont's fault. Either way, Andy's obnoxious flatulence is screwing up my ability to concentrate on this exercise and impeding my development. Not that much of that's happening. Fucking Claymont. Can't wait to get out of here.*

So here it is: a smell has set me off against Andy, the choice of food, the cook, and the place itself. I'm angry enough to think about leaving this session, and possibly getting out of damned Claymont altogether. In just a few seconds, all because of a simple fart, one thing associates with the next in a chain reaction that has me thinking about quitting the course.

Things between Holly and me are falling apart. For a while I've been seeing signs that she's growing impatient with me; whatever I do or say obviously annoys her. Now it seems that she actively dislikes me. I don't understand what's happening. Every interaction ends in an argument. Yesterday I blew my stack. In the middle of my tantrum I glanced over at Ellen, who was curled up like a fetus with her thumb in her mouth, frightened by my rage, much as she was that terrible, drunken night back in Boston.

I was mortified. My chagrin settled me down enough to have a reasoned conversation with Holly. We agreed to separate for a while.

Today I had a talk with Laurent to discuss my moving into the men's dorm. He started by saying that he'd been keeping his eye on me, watching my face get longer and longer every day. I was involved in a process, he went on, that I could not see the end of. He advised me to be patient, for I was on a knife's edge with traps all around. "All of oneself is phoniness," he said, "all of one's past life has been phony. People join the Work and say they want to see themselves, but when they do see something, they don't want to admit it. Instead they say, 'Oh, that terrible Work that has gone and messed up my life.' It's not the Work at all that has done that. Consider this: What looks like an end may in reality be a beginning. Be patient. Don't do anything spectacular."

He read to me from *The Egyptians* by St. Macharias, who exhorted his community of brethren to practice both charity and cheerfulness: "The brother who prays must know that the brother who labors is laboring for him, and the one who labors must know that the one who prays is praying for him. All serve one another. And they should do so cheerfully!"

I remarked that cheerfulness is not a ready part of my repertoire, but I would try. He said I must build some confidence in myself, some strength. I'm not sure what this was in reference to. I took it to be the Work, but it may have been just as much a reference to Holly and our relationship. Or maybe it was his sense of me, of my underlying insecurities.

In what probably seemed a *non sequitur* to Laurent, although I thought it was absolutely appropriate, I blurted out that I feel on the verge of something, but that I keep getting in the way of it and prevent it from coming. "Be patient," he repeated, and referenced the Slough of Despond in John Bunyan's *Pilgrim's Progress*. "It's dangerous to push these things. A time might come when you are doing a small thing, a job or something, and suddenly it will be just right."

We left it that I am to live in the men's dorm, temporarily and indefinitely. Holly would surely agree to this, I told him, since we needed some distance from each other to sort things out. He offered to let me "off the hook" with respect to what others may think of me by changing the composition of groups A, B, and C and also instructing some people, including me, to live elsewhere. I said I would prefer that people think what they will, and I'll struggle with that.

"Good," he responded. "But try not to be too proud of yourself for choosing the harder way."

I was sitting in Morning Exercises today, trying to concentrate on our inner task and keep my thoughts from wandering, when something brushed against my leg. I jumped, thinking it might be a rat wandering through the barn. It was Ellen, who was normally asleep at 6 a.m. She curled up in my lap and just lay there. When the session ended, I carried her to the dining room for breakfast and sat down next to Holly. I couldn't remember having felt so estranged, so alone, so helpless and inadequate.

Tonight I talked with Walter, one of the senior residents who often serves as chief chef and is a Movements instructor. He asked how the course was going for me.

"To be honest, some days I don't know why I'm here. I don't think I'm making much progress, and I worry about how little time is left. I want to change, but will I? Can I? Am I just wasting this opportunity? And what does 'change' even mean? Lots of questions. Lots of concerns. Lots of frustration."

"The value of the course might occur in 30 minutes or less," Walter said. "One of the 'true' experiences I had at Sherborne happened when I was doing the Mevlevi *sema*, the Dervish turn. That was when I truly understood the meaning of 'Wish.' Until that experience, I had pretty much been where you just described yourself. One moment changed everything."

I repeated what I had said to Laurent about my sense that I was on the verge of something, but that I kept frightening it away.

"Certain experiences need to sneak up on you," Walter said.

This morning, Laurent gave us a new theme: "We live in a world of illusion."

Frankly, this whole Claymont process is beginning to strike me as illusory, if not delusory. First, we're told that we can't expect help from external conditions, and that work and any results are up to us. Then we keep hearing the tiresome and ambiguous refrain that "we cannot do." Finally, as Steve keeps emphasizing, we must wait for something else to come in—"Call it Grace"—and when it does make sure that we don't get in its way.

So, to sum up, I'm fucked: I can't expect help from changes in the external environment, there is nothing I can do, and I'm not open enough, it seems, to receive any gifts. I'm angry at this "Work" and everything associated with it.

Dear Laurent,

My best wishes to you for this season and New Year. I hope your visit to England is going well, and I look forward very much to seeing you here again.

I have several things I want to relate about my situation these days. First, I'm realizing more and more what an awful, book-fed romantic I am. My head is full of preconceptions of what the "Path" should be and what experiences should be awaiting me at every turn. Whenever I walk between the barn and the mansion in beautiful weather, for example, I expect something profound and significant to occur—illumination, a deep sense of gratitude or longing, a glimpse of unity or eternity, etc.—and can't remain content with just enjoying the walk. What strikes me, however, is that I began the walk with appreciation for the weather and the view, and then lost even that to my thoughts. Depression and self-criticism are the consequences, since nothing ever happens in accord with the expectations I have for my "inner life."

In relation to this, I remember the meeting we had several weeks ago when you spoke to me of cheerfulness. Cheerfulness is a difficult state for me to assume, particularly these days when my marriage—or the complex of role patterns that have passed for a marriage—is falling apart at the seams. In my clearer moments, i.e., when not in the heat of an interaction with Holly, I can see how much more sense it would make to be different than I am, to give up my old reactions and associated agonies. And yet I find it nearly impossible to do this, to "sacrifice my suffering." Maybe I enjoy depression too much?

I talked with Steve about ways to catch my reactions when I'm with Holly. He emphasized sensing, as well as trying not to think about an interchange after it has happened. His advice hasn't helped much, I'm afraid. Intellectually, I can see what an opportunity this whole situation presents to do something with my-self, but on a practical level it doesn't seem that I'm getting anywhere, although I guess I do manage to catch a glimpse of myself now and then. For example, I don't keep up as many appearances as usual and don't care so much about whether or not people see me as dependable, diligent, sensitive, or whatever.

Also, I'm nastier. I'm sure this is due in part to my anger towards Hol-ly, myself, and our state of affairs, as well as living in the dorm, where life among a bunch of single men is more basic and expressive than it is in the family quarters. And I realize that much of my anger, as you warned me is often what happens to people, is directed at "the Work": it is so exasperating and inexplicable and impossible an undertaking. I can't change the simplest things, and, really, my life since I came to Claymont is certainly worse than it was before. My world and the images I have of myself as a nice guy, a sound family man, and the like are shattering.

Then I think "Okay, I'll make the best of this," only to find myself running around compulsively collecting and ordering the pieces, trying to force them into the same old picture. This confuses me. On the one hand, I take this to be con-vincing evidence that I am not cut out for this awful Work, that I will never devel-op the amount of will and persistence and intensity required. And yet on the other hand, the more fury I experience in relation to it, the more essential it feels to me. At these times, I want more than anything to learn to work. At these times, my only wish is that I have the potential for being something, someone, more. And then my anger returns, along with a great sadness, because I don't even know what "Work" is or what I need or why I should try or what "Being" means.

                                        Sincerely,
                                        Nathan

Theme: "Ask yourself 'Why?'"

Given my feelings about the Work, my disintegrating marriage, and the seeming futility for me personally of this whole Claymont enterprise, I wonder if there's some cosmic sense of humor responsible for putting this particular theme out there now. And the succession of themes following this one strike me as extensions of the same comedy: "Go against the flow," "Keep the pot boiling," "What is help?," "Attitude (learning to work with it)," "Payment," "Necessity: Only doing what is necessary," and finally, "What does it mean, 'Paying the debt of our existence?'"

In introducing the theme "Attitude (learning to work with it)," Laurent said that with this topic there is a real chance for success. We are totally self-defended and that affects everything we do—our criticalness, feelings of superiority, etc. If we can see that our attitudes get us nowhere, we can change. If we can say, for example, "I don't need to be critical," we can change.

At a conceptual level, as usual, I can get this. We can get beyond personality to something more essential, the "Real I." In the abstract, I can understand Zen master Shunryu Suzuki's distinction between the little mind and the big mind; I can see that personality, self-image, ego, my limited self, whatever you want to call it, is not who I really am, is not my true and eternal self. But in my day-to-day efforts at grappling with the world, I badly need my personality and ego. These have developed over the course of my life to protect me, to make me feel safe. They are doing their job. I'm not at all sure that I want to transcend and be free from ego. I admire its spunk, its dedication to little old me.

On the theme of "Paying the debt of our existence," Laurent stated that "You don't get something for nothing; you can give up some of these habits of yours in order to get something else." He quoted Gurdjieff: "There's a new bank, but only people who can write checks with six zeros can use it." In the discussion, I offered the observation that "I have never paid for anything. I've lived my whole life on credit, thinking that I can always begin paying tomorrow. I can often see what's required in a given moment, for example controlling my negative reactions, but I don't give them up, I don't pay *then*."

Laurent's response to me was sobering. "The only certainty we have is death. Nothing else is certain. You're really talking about death and resurrection. But you haven't truly seen it—if you had seen something, if you had seen the certainty of death, you would understand what's required and could not choose other than to work. You would do what is necessary. You would do everything you can to pay the debt of your existence. You would do so *now*."

I was happy and optimistic yesterday morning when Holly said she would like me to spend the night with her. Next day was an exeat, so there would be no pressure to wake up early. She had arranged for Ellen to stay the night in the room of our friends Edie and Mitchell, whom Ellen adored.

Would this turn things around? I bathed and perfumed myself like a teenager on his first date. Horny and hopeful, I broke open a bag of new jockey shorts, sure that this would be a pleasant and enticing surprise to Holly, who over all the years of our relationship had only seen me in what must have been very un-sexy boxer shorts. I preened in front of the mirror, sure that my now muscular physique, hardened by months of labor and trimmed down by a spartan diet, would advance my hopes for reconciliation.

I arrived in a romantic mood, looking forward to an affectionate conversation over the bottle of wine I had brought. But Holly had other ideas. She was impatient to get into bed. Well, okay; after months of celibacy I couldn't object to that. We'd exhaust our ardor and then make softer love until morning.

But that's not how it played out. I felt like I was involved in a sexual audition, and Holly would make her casting decisions accordingly. Obviously, I didn't get the part, despite my buff physique and bright white Fruit of the Looms. We never even got to a conversation—affectionate, cordial, or rancorous. We fucked, enjoyably enough, I thought, and then she asked me to leave. That was it.

Holly and I have resumed our stand-off. Interactions have become increasingly unpleasant, and they all end in disagreement. Holly tells me that I lack understanding, and for support in this criticism cites Laurent who, she claims, says that understanding equals agreement.

"Don't say you understand," she yells. "You don't understand me at all. If you don't agree with me, it shows you don't understand."

This "logic" drives me crazy. "Bullshit," I respond. "These are totally different ideas. That's why we have two different words for them. Two different spellings and sounds, two different definitions in the dictionary. Do I need to agree with XYZ in order to say I understand XYZ? If you play your 'logic' out, you can't expect any useful communication or interaction at all."

I feel vindicated a few days later after we both have separate interviews with Bhante Mahathera V Dharmawara, a prominent Cambodian Theravadan Buddhist priest who visits Claymont annually to teach meditation. In desperation, I had arranged to seek Bhante's counsel for myself and had also persuaded Holly to see him. Bhante told me I was absolutely correct to try to keep the marriage intact. Marriage is a give-and-take, he said, an on-going negotiation. What should not be negotiable in most conceivable circumstances was ending the marriage. I sat outside Bhante's chambers while Holly had her interview, which hardly lasted five minutes before she came storming out. It was hard to conceal a smirk of vindication when I learned that he had scolded Holly for considering separation. But even I had to admit, albeit only to myself, that Bhante, being an 85-year-old Cambodian monk, might not be entirely in sync with changes in generational attitudes and life-styles in America.

I have begun to blame Laurent and the "Work" for my situation. But in rare moments of clarity I can admit my central responsibility in my marriage's dissolution. With every tantrum and mood swing I'm only pushing Holly further away.

And when it comes down to it I do trust Laurent, despite a lapse now and again when I blame him and "the Work" for my travails. But I know this is out of frustration, helplessness, and anger. And I know I can rely on Laurent, that in his own mysterious, impersonal way he is looking out for my best interests. I recall, for example, the advice he gave me when things started unraveling with Holly: "Don't do anything spectacular." Sound counsel. If only I were able to follow it.

And I know it sounds weird, but Laurent has given me sound advice in dreams. "Learn to make people less willing to like you," he said in one, capturing a strength (likeability) and weakness (needing to be liked) in a single, uncanny, paradoxical statement.

The dream with Laurent's advice comes at an interesting juncture of certain experiences and the introduction of certain psychological ideas, including one that the Work calls "Chief Feature." As Kathleen Speeth explains in *The Gurdjieff Work*,

> ...although there are many 'I's each person has one central attribute, a pillar on which the personality structure rests or around which it could be said to revolve. This 'chief feature' is almost always invisible to oneself but other people can often give accurate enough information about it....Once chief feature is known it can provide the key to the invalidation of the personality so that essence is relatively stronger in its struggle against it.

Gurdjieff, as recounted by Ouspensky in *In Search of the Miraculous*, elaborates on the distinction between essence and personality.

> Essence in man is what is *his own*. Personality in man is what is 'not his own.' 'Not his own' means what has come from outside, what he has learned....Essence [which manifests more and more rarely as personality grows] is the truth in man; personality is the false... A man's real I, his individuality, can grow only from his essence....But in order to enable essence to grow up, it is first of all necessary to weaken the constant pressure of personality upon it, because the obstacles to the growth of essence are contained in the personality.

In *Warrior's Way*, Robert de Ropp, another Work commentator, accentuates both the promise and the difficulty of this growth process and how it all relates to chief feature. "One who has seen his chief feature and learned to separate from it is on the way to real liberty.... [But] It is a real showdown, at which Dr. Jekyll meets Mr. Hyde, at which all the rotting monsters in one's personal cesspool come crawling out into the light of day. The process is not without its dangers..."

When Laurent first spoke with us as a group about chief feature, he told us that he would eventually disclose our specific chief feature to each of us individually. But before that, we would have to do some groundwork in preparation for learning it. Over several weeks, I developed a list of what I assessed to be my primary strengths and weaknesses, and then pared those down to what I considered to be my chief feature. Under strengths I listed three items: (1) ability to conceptualize and articulate, (2) laying out step-by-step processes to get things done, and (3) getting people to like me. My self-identified weaknesses numbered six: (1) self-pity, especially manifest in believing that people owe me respect, recognition, and deference; (2) wanting to appear "good" (reliable, talented, ethical) to others; (3) resentment, and a general inability to let go of negative reactions to others; (4) worrying, and letting my worries distract and pre-occupy me; (5) inability to stop thinking and projecting; and (6) intolerance of my own imperfections and mistakes. I winnowed all of this down to conclude that my chief feature is fear of failure.

I sent Laurent a summary of my self-assessment process and my conclusion in advance of my interview with him to discuss chief feature. I was confident of what I had come to, and also proud of the analysis I had done leading up to it. I expected praise when I walked in the door.

Laurent wasted no time: "You're a coward," he told me. "Cowardice is your chief feature."

He said more, but I wasn't listening. I was too shocked by what he told me. In my personal hierarchy of values, cowardice lies at the bottom. I couldn't absorb this characterization. Nor could I say anything. I stood up and left.

Since the meeting with Laurent, I haven't asked him to elaborate on what he means by cowardice, or what his evidence is to describe me that way. Nor has he taken the initiative to explain. Perhaps he did so immediately after he dropped the bombshell and thinks that I heard him. If he did explain, I was too much in shock to listen. There are variations of cowardice: physical, moral, emotional, motivational, decision-making. Which does he think I am? More importantly, I haven't asked him how to work with this chief feature. So I'm left trying to figure out the definition and the method for myself. Maybe that's how it's supposed to be.

Some of my things are still in Holly and Ellen's room. This afternoon I went to pick something up. Brody was there. He and Holly were talking, yards apart and likely innocent. But who knows? I went through my stuff and got what I needed as quickly as possible to avoid any perception that I was performing some kind of surveillance. Brody left before I finished, and I left without saying anything. Had I said something, it would have been to warn Holly that Brody, in addition to all his other virtues, is a notorious sexual predator. But maybe she knows that. Maybe, like the hypersexual Holly of yore, that's what she has in mind. Maybe he just showed up, and she had nothing to do with the coincidence. I don't know what's what at this point.

I was wrong. Brody isn't the predator, Ben Griscom is. Ben: a nice fellow whom I befriended early in the course and who has been an occasional drinking buddy ever since. I inadvertently discovered that he and Holly have started an affair when I saw them get in his car and drive away on an exeat day. The day before, she had asked if I could take Ellen for the day, she had some things she needed to catch up on and could use the uninterrupted time. Sure, I readily agreed. Happy to do it.

Now it's clear to me that Holly and Ben are getting it on. I can't stand it. I finally snap and rush around trying to find Ben, intent on...What? Scolding him? Cursing him? Shaming him? Pummeling him? I find him, of all ironic places, in the childcare room, where he is assigned for the day. Ellen loves him.

I wait until he comes out of the room, alone, and slam him against the wall. I'm shaking with rage. To his credit, he stays impassive, resigned, perhaps, to a beating by a jealous husband. But something stops me. Judgement? Incurable civility? Fear that he might retaliate? Whatever the reason, I don't hit him. I merely shake him, saying something brilliant, like "Argh!", and walk away, totally befuddled at what is happening to my life and amazed at my ineptitude in dealing with it.

A timely new theme: "Respect (What am I missing?)." It occurs to me that I must be missing a lot, since the bulk of my existence these days is taken up with fits of jealousy and anger towards Holly and Ben, along with a general sense of helplessness about the whole situation. Nothing seems under my control—neither the situation nor my emotional reactions to it. To retain some sense of control, however illusory, I continue what I can of my routine by waking every morning at 5:00, straightening my bed, and doing ablutions ahead of the others. Then I either go to Morning Exercises or, on alternate mornings, to Holly's room to take care of Ellen. I had been scrupulous throughout the course to stop at the bulletin board and copy the daily schedule right after breakfast, but I'm doing that less and less consistently since discovering that Holly and Ben are having an affair. It's hard enough for me to keep investing in the activities themselves; writing down their names—Morning Exercises, Movements, Lunch, whatever—now strikes me as useless and irrelevant.

Still, there are moments in which I am able to calm myself down and dredge up some modicum of perspective. In these moments, I try to appreciate Holly's side of things. I can see and admit that I missed a lot, that I never paid serious attention to what was happening with her almost from the time we first met back in Cambridge. I had never realized the extent to which she is terrified by the prospect of repeating her parents' relationship, which in her mind is a quintessential example of male chauvinism: the husband's needs, wants, and agenda are primary. Then I came along and, in her eyes, fell into her businessman father's male-first mold, pursuing my career as a rising, tenure-bound professor first and foremost while expecting her, if only implicitly, to subordinate hers as a term-limited, contract-hire instructor; constantly writing or teaching when in Cambridge and otherwise traveling the world to give speeches and interviews while she stayed home; reveling in my status as media darling and co-ed idol; never cooking or cleaning; withholding the full attention her temperament required; and so much more that made her feel like a non-factor. I would guess that we were only equal and a real team when it involved Ellen.

In Holly's mind the accumulated resentments apparently are past the point of any possible rapprochement. I, on the other hand, am desperately focused on the hope that we can sort things out. The problem is that my moments of reasonable, undramatic behavior are so rare. My jealousy and anger have made me emotionally unhinged, even in my own eyes, and I must look a whole lot worse to Holly. So why would she want to reconcile, other than for our daughter's sake? But a child, although a hugely important consideration in a marriage, cannot be the whole of it.

And while it might not be connected to the *respect/what am I missing* theme in anyone's mind except mine, I'm aware that Laurent has been ramping up the frequency of the Sufi "Stop Exercise." This is a method for self-remembering, for seeing ourselves in habitual positions and attitudes of which we're largely unaware. In this exercise, the teacher gives a command, and an in-progress or incipient movement is interrupted. The body comes to a halt in an unaccustomed position, a standstill that offers an opportunity for enhanced self-observation and a break in one's automatic functioning.

I can say that on several occasions when Laurent has called out "Stop!"—once during Movements, once during a Practical Work Project, and once while I was walking between chores—I saw myself: both the usual me, beset by depression and hostility, and a non-automatic me, momentarily on the verge of freedom. I cannot say that I went past the verge, only that I saw myself with that possibility. Unfortunately, I could not sustain enough appetite to turn these three tastes into a full meal.

I struggle on, setting up experiments for myself in a desperate effort to change and not merely react.

- *Experiment 1: Whenever I see them together, I will step back and watch my reactions <u>then</u>*. The work here is to let go enough, to free myself enough, from my attachments to enable a separation to occur.
- *Experiment 2: To manifest cheerfully and energetically when I see them together or imagine them together*. The work here is to be a

man. That is, to hold my head up and be present and sacrifice the suffering reaction. This is particularly important: to manifest cheerfully with other people and not carry my hurt feelings with me.

- *Experiment 3: When we are together, I will not talk about us.* The work here is not to speak about our relationship at all for a given period, to hold that constant reaction in check, to sacrifice the pleasure I get from beating a dead horse.
- *Experiment 4: <u>Never</u> react negatively, but only manifest cheer and good wishes from this day on.* Although I have yet to ask Laurent what he meant by "cowardice" when he revealed my chief feature, I believe it relates to this experiment: I have to struggle against my propensities to be glum, sad, fearful, anxious, pessimistic. To act like a warrior, the opposite of a coward, I need to learn to be cheerful, open, optimistic. On the surface, this seems redundant of Experiments 1, 2, and 3. The difference is an adjustment to specific circumstances versus the development of a general attitude: Experiments 1-3 concern my overt reactions to Holly and Ben; Experiment 4 requires an entirely new and pervasive way of being.

Ellen is a major part of my struggle. Although I see her every day, I feel like an absentee father, a type of person I have always despised: *Short of physical force*, I would judge, *how can a father allow himself to be separate from his child?* I could not come to grips with this, with my conception of what a father ought to be versus my reality. I began to loathe myself for allowing the situation to dictate what I had become, and for my sense of helplessness in not knowing how to change it.

At the start of the course, I resented the alternate days when I had to skip morning exercises and evening events in order to watch Ellen. Now I cherish those times when I can curl up with my daughter and her stuffed animals while Holly does the Gurdjieff stuff. I can tell that Ellen enjoys these times as well, snuggling with her father, reading stories, napping in each other's arms. Being parent and child.

Work is pain. It is agony to push for the demise of a self-image that does not want to die. It refuses to die, and the torment is prolonged. At times, the self-image nearly goes, and I say, "Thank God." But it's not to be. So the struggle continues between the forces that want to see its end and those that want it to survive intact.

And then there are moments of deep joy—infrequent, fleeting, yet the only source of hope I have. For a day or so these moments nourish a yearning so strong that I feel sure my heart will explode from the intensity of it.

But then it comes full circle. I enter weeks of misery. I'm the wretched man of Romans 7:15 in the *New Testament*, who despairs: "I do not understand what I do. For what I want to do I do not do, but what I hate I do." Struggle again. Joy again. Tears. Hope. Forward and back in equal measure. But there is no turning back, no escaping the longing that draws me towards whatever or whoever is waiting beyond the veil of the father, the husband, the man I thought I was. This damned "Work." It is agony. It's a low today, a high tomorrow. It is clarity and gibberish, hope and despair, redeemer and destroyer. And for all its ridiculous contradictions, there is a strangely reassuring inevitability about it, the only thing now that lends any sense to my life.

(Even to me, dear Diary, this paragraph reads like it was written by a very troubled person.)

Thanks to Ellen, today I experienced a rare enjoyable moment, a comic interlude in the midst of my deepening depression. All of us, the entire course, were gathered to celebrate the completion of a bridge we had constructed over a gully that flooded in heavy rain. Brody, as Claymont's Practical Work supervisor, was facilitating our observations on the day's inner-work theme. Someone had just offered an observation. In response, Alma, a student who has a chip on her shoulder and a tendency to be aggressively judgmental in these sessions, said: "It sounds like bull shit to me!" A voice, tiny but very audible, immediately echoed: "It sounds like boool sheeet to me!" The voice was Ellen's, who had somehow managed to leave childcare and make her way, unseen, down to the bridge. We all cracked up, except Alma and Brody. A little kid had pretty much summed things up.

After lunch today I stayed in the dining room to meet with Irma and Raphael, two of the other Jewish students on the course, to discuss a possible Passover *seder* we'd like to conduct the following week. There are other Jews here, but none shows any interest in joining us to organize the event.

We divided up tasks. "I'll oversee the food," volunteered Rafi, who has professional restaurant experience as well as an observant Jewish upbringing. "Basically, I'll work with what we already have on hand, and I have a cousin in DC who will bring us matzos, horseradish, and a few bottles of kosher-for-Passover wine."

"And I'll take care of pulling the materials together," Irma said. "You know, the basic prayers and songs. I can get them Xeroxed in town."

They both looked at me and laughed. "I guess," Rafi said, "that leaves you, by the process of elimination, to get permission for us to do this. While you're at it, what about some money for matzos and wine?"

Getting permission meant going to see Laurent, which I did that evening in his cottage. "I'm here to ask your approval to conduct a Passover ceremony next week."

"Why do you want to do this?"

"We draw a lot here from Moslem, Christian, Buddhist, and Hindu traditions. Judaism is hardly represented at all, except for the occasional Old Testament reference. Irma, Raphael, and I would like to bring some of our tradition into the mix by conducting a *seder* for the whole community on Sunday, April 3ʳᵈ, the first day of Passover this year. If possible, although the three of us can take care of it ourselves if necessary, any contribution we get for food and materials would be appreciated."

"All right. I'll put it on the schedule and arrange for you to get reimbursed for whatever you need to purchase."

More than a hundred students and residents gathered in the dining room for the Passover *seder*. I don't know whether to call the event a success or a failure. Maybe that's not how to look at such things in any case. My main misgiving is that it went on too long, although the one-and-a-half hours it took weren't as long as a traditional *seder*. Irma, Rafi, and I had argued about this. "We should do an abbreviated version," I said. "People won't want to sit through the whole thing. You know how it is: the group works hard and will be starving. Eating will be their priority, not listening to a bunch of Hebrew prayers and songs they won't understand even with our explanations."

But it was two against one. Rafi and Irma prevailed, arguing that people would recognize and appreciate the spiritual dimensions of the *seder*, and that the food, even if served in slow courses, would be filling. "Besides," Rafi said, "we're supposed to be attentive and mindful here, especially over meals. This is an obvious opportunity for that." But during the *seder* itself, after more than an hour of explaining the rituals and trying to teach people prayers and songs in Hebrew, we could sense people's impatience and hostility building. Even Laurent, usually inscrutable, looked irked.

I made a unilateral decision. "Well," I said, standing up to address the gathering, "I think we've given you enough of the basics, at least of Passover's exoteric dimension—the historical story, the liturgy, what the foods symbolize. But the reason that Irma, Rafi, and I organized the *seder* was to introduce some of the inner significance of at least one Jewish holiday." The gathering seemed to perk up. This was the kind of thing they were at Claymont to experience—esoterica, inner meanings and practices. Now it was up to me to try and provide that. What the hell, I thought. I'm used to winging it. It's kind of like being back at Harvard.

I took a deep breath and waited for inspiration. And then something happened. I said things that felt real, things I hadn't realized I even knew: how leavened bread is like the inflated ego, bloated with mindless, automatic thinking; how matzah, flat and simple, brings us back down to basics and away from distracted, endlessly associative thinking, back to the true self not obscured by ignorance, illusion, and delusion; how the land of Egypt represents our captivity by its king, the Pharaoh, who keeps us from seeing and experiencing the greater world of human possibilities; how the Exodus of the Jews from Egypt represents the potentiality we all have to become free; how the plagues that were visited upon Egypt were God's way of teaching Pharaoh the factuality of karma, that every action has consequences, and the need for compassion towards others if one is to end his or her own suffering; how the horseradish reminds us of slavery's bitterness; and, finally, why we leave a glass of wine inviting the presence of the Prophet Elijah, who reminds us to be open and alert, at every moment and in every place, to the Divine in each human being.

Raphael, Irma, and I ended the *seder* singing the traditional Hebrew song to Elijah: next year in Jerusalem, next year in freedom. When we finished, I looked out and saw Laurent staring at me. He nodded once. And again. And a third time. Then we adjourned.

I understand much better now what the social-psychologist Kurt Lewin was getting at back in graduate school when he wrote, "If you want truly to understand something, try to change it." This gets right at my state of mind and echoes what I quoted earlier from *Romans* 7:15 regarding the man who wants to change yet realizes, again and again, the utter impossibility of doing so. He can neither give himself up nor maintain what he imagined he was. I am trying so hard to change. But I can't. And I despair. Over and over again.

Things keep deteriorating. I keep deteriorating. I stock up on bourbon during exeat days and drink myself to sleep most nights.

John, a senior associate of Bennett's visiting from England while Laurent is traveling in Turkey, draws me aside to show me a chakra exercise meant to transform negative emotions. First he explains the emotion associated with each chakra: (1) throat with worry; (2) solar plexus with self-pity; (3) sex (behind or below the gonads) with fantasy; (4) spine with excessive physical energy; (5) base of the skull with criticism and excessive talking; and (6) the center of the head with destructive thoughts. "When emotion arises," John then instructs me, "direct seven breaths to the appropriate chakra. For protection against energy stealers, draw one breath through all chakras saying, 'Let me be purified.'"

I work on this daily. I can't say my energy has improved, much less that I have been purified. But who knows?

John has us work on what he calls "Active Looking," in which the effort is to *purposefully direct* the attention of one's eyes, rather than passively receive visual impressions as we ordinarily do.

I have been devoting myself to this exercise intensely for the past week. I have no expectations that anything will happen or be achieved; by now, I have pretty much given up any thoughts of "advancing" in this stupid

Work. More than anything, I want to survive the anguish I'm experiencing. At least these exercises distract me and divert my attention away from my emotional pain.

Our group is working in the orchard this afternoon, gathering apples. I have to take care of Ellen for a while after lunch, so I join them late. On the path to the orchard I focus all my attention on the Active Looking exercise, so much so that my eyes hurt from the effort. Fifty or so yards from the group I direct my sight towards Jim, the student nearest to me as I approach. Something happens. I watch myself from behind as I watch Jim. No. Wait. I am *seeing* myself from behind, seeing myself and Jim and everyone else. It's clear that I'm doing the seeing, but it's also clear that a presence other than I does the watching. This continues as I keep walking. And then this realization strikes: nothing belongs to me, I possess nothing, nothing is owed me, everything is given to me, nothing is stable, and everything can be taken away. Not even these clothes I am wearing are mine. Not even this body is my own. There are no classifications. No mine, no yours. No this or that. It's all the same. I feel a gush of what I can only describe as a profoundly joyous loosening, and for this moment I am free from possessiveness. I want nothing. I claim nothing.

I can't say how long this state lasts. Maybe seconds, maybe minutes. Soon I'm talking to Jim with no one watching or seeing from behind. Nathan and Jim are next to each other but separate now, each with his own body and clothes and name.

Afterwards, I do my best to convey all of this in the theme discussion. My description seems feeble and inadequate to me, and John, who is leading the discussions, doesn't respond. But I don't care; the power of the experience is still with me. Later, Holly tells me that John mentioned to her how happy he was for me. I think she is happy, too, if only to believe I have relinquished my jealous possessiveness, however temporarily.

The course will end soon. I can't for the life of me evaluate what it has all meant. Certainly, there have been some ups along with the downs. A major saving grace has been my involvement in Morris Dance, whose origins are in 15th century England. I was captivated by Morris the first time I saw it performed and heard its music. I'm reluctant to sound melodramatic, but I had the distinct sense that I had done this before, long, long before. At Claymont, I became the Fool of the seven-member troupe, the key role, the dancer who leads and chides and ridicules and encourages, the one person who is free to improvise and dance outside the structure to which the others must adhere. We performed many times, both at Claymont and at festivals in the greater Charles Town region.

Lord knows I have had more than my share of disastrous moments. I played the exiled Duke Senior in Shakespeare's *As You Like It*, and Holly played Rosalind—Duke Senior's daughter, who loves the handsome Orlando.

Irony of ironies, this is the play that features the famous speech about the seven ages of man, from infancy to old age: "All the world's a stage, and all the men and women merely players; they have their exits and their entrances, and one man in his time plays many parts..." The whole production seemed to mirror my personal saga, my many "I"s.

We rehearsed for months and gave three scheduled performances, two at Claymont and the other at a nearby theater for the surrounding community. I was relieved when the last scheduled performance ended. I had made it through without blowing my lines or otherwise embarrassing myself. Then Laurent told us we must do one more for another community. This must have been too anti-climactic for me. I got to my final lines, almost the last lines of the play, and totally spaced out. I forgot them. The actor who was opposite me, who had listened to me innumerable times, had to remind me of my lines in a whisper. I recovered, but the play's dramatic momentum was interrupted when it should have been most powerful. A frightening lesson about inattention and mindlessness.

But the worst instance was during our performance of the Movements to the entire Claymont community and associated Work visitors. In the middle of a movement, I forget which one, I basically stopped. The rest of the students continued, but I stood there motionless while my peers did their best to go around me and salvage the effort. Considering the centrality of the Movements—the Sacred Movements—in the Work, this was no small failure.

"Make people less willing to like you," Laurent had said in my dream. Well, I did, although not in a dream. Right after the last performance of the play and just before this Movements demonstration, I had shaved off my impressive, truly full and regal beard. Thus I stood there, lost amidst the swirling sacred dancers—diminished in appearance, devoid of gravitas, past any pretensions, unveiled and naked in my public collapse.

A letter to my closest friend in graduate school, Eliezar Ben-Dor, an Israeli:

Dear Eli,

It's been too many months since we've been in touch. I hope things are going well for you in Tel Aviv.

Much has happened with Holly, Ellen, and me. Living at Claymont is proving to be an excruciatingly intense experience, which is understandable considering that part of the aim of this place is to establish something real in people—and the roles we assume, our automatic reactions, our ego are what get rocked the most. In consequence, relationships also get rocked. My relationship with Holly is no exception. We're evaluating our marriage, its basis and prospects, with the realization that there is a good deal of phoniness to get beyond. If we can do that, only then is there the potential to be what we should for each other.

We'll be here until June 12. What life will be for us after that is anyone's guess. I can say that I have no plans, although my preferences, realistic or not, include: (1) not returning to academia, and (2) traveling. Preference 2 brings me to the possibility of visiting Israel, among other places. Most likely I'll be alone on that visit, given that a trial separation of three to six months seems called for so that each of us can sort things out individually. I'd like to pay you a visit if the timing—yet to be determined, of course—is convenient for you. And please don't think that I'm contacting you to finagle a place to stay. Not at all! I'll be totally independent as far as logistics are concerned. But I very much hope that we'll be able to spend some good conversational time together. I miss that from our Cambridge days. Really, it's even doubtful that this trip will ever happen, but you never know. Please just consider this an alert in case it does.

Life is a curious process, to paraphrase centuries of cliché wisdom. More than anything, I want to pull it all together, to establish a worthwhile relationship with Holly and the basis for a strong, sustainable marriage with solidity for Ellen. I can only hope that Holly feels the same way. But honestly, I just don't know.

Warm regards,
Nathan

P.S. With the exception of the short first paragraph, I realize that this letter is all about me. My apologies. I can't seem to focus on much besides my own situation these days.

Laurent has recently returned from Turkey, where, we are told, he was made a sheikh of Sufism's Mevlevi order. We had been introduced to the Mevlevi s*ema* (turn) and *zikr* (practice of remembrance) earlier in the course, but now, as the end of the course approaches, we practice both every day.

Zikr is an invocation, a mantra repeated rhythmically in time with breathing, and the repetition builds to strong effect, especially when done in a group. The strong effect for me is emotional: an indescribable, peculiar feeling invades my heart. And the *sema*—how can I put it?—opens me. As I turn and turn I go higher and higher; I begin to connect to something—an energy, a higher force and presence—that I have never experienced before. The combined effect of the turn and *zikr* is profound and inexplicable. It makes me cry, but not from sadness or despair. Something is moving, uniting. I am nearly there, nearly there. Nearly...Nearly...

When the course ended, Holly stayed on for an additional week to attend a seminar, and I took Ellen to Belmar. Arnie came down from the city to see us. The first night, I went for a walk on the boards after dinner while Ellen's uncle and grandparents argued over the privilege of putting her to bed.

When I returned, my parents and Arnie were in the living room, obviously waiting for me.

"You look great," Arnie began. "Trim. Strong. But why so subdued?"

I sat with my head down, not speaking for a while. In part, it was a hold-over from Claymont, where the act of talking was deliberate and purposeful in the interest of not being mechanical. In larger part, it was the difficulty of the subject matter. Finally, I looked up. "Holly and I are separated. We might get a divorce. It's looking that way."

My father walked to a window, clenching his fists and shaking his head with angry energy, his back to the room. My mother, mouth open in a parody of shock, threw herself back against the sofa cushions. But I knew it wasn't a parody. It was grief. "Poor Ellen," she sighed. "Poor child."

My brother, usually so contained and undemonstrative, began to cry. "I can't believe it. It was a marriage made in heaven. I was sure of it."

6
Fathers Without Children

RIGHT AFTER CLAYMONT I spent most days in public libraries around Belmar, reading self-help magazines to help me with depression, with anger, with drinking. But the ploy backfired as I came across article after article about the plight of single mothers. I had sympathy for them. I did. But I couldn't find anything about people like me, fathers who are separated from their children.

It could have gone either way. Holly was a good mother, I was a good father. Ellen was equally close to us both, and we were equal in the division of our parenting time and duties during the year we were in West Virginia. But despite the turmoil between us, Holly and I did at least agree that her motherly influence would likely be more important than mine for the immediate future. Then something unexpected and unimaginable happened: Holly and Ellen moved to Alaska.

Should I have been so reasonable, so accommodating? I stewed about this a lot. Holly was the one who had triggered our split, after all. On the other hand, I had primed the trigger by my prior actions. My neglect, distraction, absences, and moodiness in Cambridge were the real precipitating factors. Intellectually, I realized that. But I couldn't get past the emotional sticking point that Holly had made the last, irrevocable move. That she had taken our daughter away—and to Alaska, goddammit. I couldn't get past my fury, bewilderment, and heartbreak at what she had done.

I tried to get past it. I really did. I ran, meditated, and prayed. And when those didn't work, I drank. I drank every night, more and more bourbon each night as I tried to erase the visions that kept assaulting me: of Holly driving away from her parents' house in Worcester; of Ellen staring out the back window, crying as she mouthed "Daddy, Daddy, Daddy"; of me standing there, helpless and bereft, until they were no longer in sight; of Holly's anguished parents hugging me for the last time; of my drive back to the Shore, the past, present, and future equal blurs.

7

Sunshine

I DECIDED TO LEAVE America, for how long I didn't know, because my life was in a shambles. I was 33, unemployed, and divorced now from Holly, who had primary custody of Ellen in Alaska. My self-confidence was shattered. I could not muster the will or energy to work, despite having unsolicited offers from three universities that had heard about my leaving Harvard. I worried that I was too fragile and depressed to manage a new job. To my way of thinking, spending some of my remaining funds on a trip to Israel was not only an attractive option, but one I hoped would save me. I figured I had enough to cover child support for ten months; weekly phone calls, postcards, and the occasional gift to Ellen; and one trip to Anchorage, from Tel Aviv or wherever else this adventure might take me.

So on January 10, 1978, three months after Anwar Sadat's historic démarche to Jerusalem, I took a limo to Kennedy Airport from the Crystal Inn, the inexpensive motel across the street from Fort Monmouth in Eatontown, New Jersey where I had been living incommunicado from everyone I had ever known. If Sadat, a mortal enemy of the Jews, an Egyptian nationalist responsible for innumerable Israeli deaths could make such a trip, I mused, why not a gentle Jewish boy from New Jersey?

During the 90-minute drive the chauffer, George, and I conversed with an intensity and sympathy I had been finding was common among men going through divorce and its aftermath, an intensity and sympathy that were almost—how else to describe it?— female in their intimacy. Thirty minutes into the trip, after I told George my story, I asked him to stop the car so I could ride next to him up front. By now he felt like my friend, not my driver.

"I don't know who it's tougher on," George said, "the one who gets left or the one who does the leaving. You got left. That must hurt like crazy, especially when you lose your kid. But it's no picnic the other way, either. That's how I did it. My ex had a gambling problem. That's the short of it. There wasn't a day throughout the whole racing season that she wasn't at the racetrack, blowing her money and mine, or at off-track sites the rest of the year. Then it was drugs and...well, she got in with some bad people. After a while, I just gave up. I didn't have it in me to try and help her anymore, you know, to try and save her. So one day I just left. No forwarding address, no nothing. I don't know if she's dead or what. I loved her once. A lot. But I couldn't do it anymore. I feel bad some days. Most days. Maybe I should've stuck with her. But I couldn't. At least we don't have kids."

George would not accept a tip when we arrived at the entrance to El Al Airlines, only a handshake.

Check-in went quickly enough, but there were long lines awaiting clearance by El Al's vaunted security personnel. "Going with a group?" the middle-age woman asked in accented English as she examined my passport.

"No."

"Do you speak Hebrew?"

"No, I only had a little in Hebrew school many years ago. I can read some. Biblical."

"Where are you staying when you arrive?"

"I don't know. I'll find a hotel in Tel Aviv at first."

"Your return ticket is open-ended. How long do you intend to stay?"

"As long as my money lasts."

"And how much money is that?" I showed her my cash and travelers checks.

"What kind of name is Kirinski?"

"A Jewish name," I answered, trying not to sound sarcastic or show annoyance.

"Yes? From where?"

"My grandparents came from Poland and Lithuania a hundred years ago. My parents were born here. New York and Boston."

"Have you been to Israel before?"

"No."

"Then why now?"

"It's something I feel I have to do. If not now, when?"

The allusion to Rabbi Hillel's famous saying was not meant to be clever, and my inquisitor did not seem to take it that way. I figured she was used to come-lately American Jews seeking roots, identity, and pride by visiting Israel. I could have said more about my motivation but decided not to: that I was sick of lying around, self-pitying, vacillating, and stymied; that I had recently read Carlos Castaneda's *Journey to Ixtlan*, in which Carlos's teacher, the shaman Don Juan, suggests using death as one's advisor; that I had asked myself: If I were to die tomorrow, what would I have missed most? The answer was never having gone to Israel.

Without knowing such things about me, which I doubted would have made my clearance easier in any event, the security agent directed me to a curtained booth where two polite but intimidating men in unmarked khaki fatigues repeated many of the same questions while leafing through my books, searching my clothes, squeezing my toothpaste, and frisking me. Finally, they wished me a pleasant trip and pointed the way to my gate.

The El Al plane was a madhouse of 400 people. It was nothing like a U.S. airlines flight. People were running all over visiting one another, crowding the aisles. There was a "Bibleland Tour" conducted by Dr. Wayne Dehoney. Or was it Duane Mahoney? Whomever, these holy rollers were not dull or stereotypical. For several hours, a group of them sitting near me surreptitiously poured whiskey from one large bottle into smaller bottles of Log Cabin Maple Syrup, which were then further distributed around the group along with Styrofoam cups.

A man walked by, winking and patting my shoulder before escaping back to the first-class cabin. This was Sam, whom I had met in the departure lounge after each of us was approached in turn by a Lubavitcher Hasid politely inquiring, "Excuse me. Are you a Jew? Yes? Then perhaps you would care to lay *tefillin*, you know, phylacteries, with me? I'll teach you how."

"Thank you, but no," I had replied, equally courteous until the Hasid persisted to the point where I had to turn away, refusing to engage him any longer.

Sam declined the Hasid's request even as the man was voicing it. "Get away from me, damn you! I hate your kind." I was shocked. Sam noticed my reaction, which led to a long and intense conversation—nothing unusual, I was to discover repeatedly, in conversations with Israelis. An immigrant born in Austria, 31 years old, Sam was just coming from Mexico, where he owned a business that had made him a millionaire. He was traveling with his wife, a dark-skinned *Sabra*, or native-born Israeli, and his sister-in-law Dahlia, with whom I instantly fell in love, knowing, alas, that my feelings would go unrequited and I would never see her again. She was married, after all. But I was thankful nevertheless for having seen her, however briefly: her delicate, sharp, thrusting profile that led me to imagine an Old Testament princess; hair hanging to her lovely ass in thick black waves; her intelligent smile that, all at once, made me feel caught in some naughty act yet the subject of her compassion, even affection. Dahlia was only one of several women I had fallen for that day as a result of my long loneliness—stewardesses, security guards, and fellow passengers who may or may not have been aware of my furtive, needy glances.

During our two-hour wait in the departure lounge, Sam had commented that if a wife goes screwing around with another man, it's because she needed to. What is the husband to do? I asked. Give her space, Sam told me. "Say: 'Go do what you feel impelled to do, whatever your reasons and whatever the consequences.' And this is very important: Be her friend across the space." One must be a real man to do that, I reflected, to relinquish one's moodiness and suffering. I wished I had met Sam before my marriage began to fail, but I doubted the advice would have saved it. How can advice you haven't the emotional capacity to follow do any good? But you never know.

The plane flew over Newfoundland, England, France, the Alps, Italy, the Peloponnesus, and Rhodes. As the sun rose over the eastern Mediterranean, a group of men, mostly old, gathered one another and carried their phylacteries and shawls to the back of the plane to pray. And there, finally, lay Israel along the right wing. I saw the breakers off Jaffa. Inland, green fields and small manicured woods were set up in protective shields around settlements and farming clusters. I wanted to be moved at this moment. Hadn't I prepared myself for it over many years, and somehow been prepared for it over many centuries? So of course, with all these expectations riding on the moment my emotions went into deep freeze. I tried to recover from the missed opportunity, reminding myself to be alive, to be aware and awake when my feet hit the ground. So, also of course, I forgot, my high-minded intentions diverted by a lovely blond apparition in uniform standing on the tarmac. Then I came to, angry at myself for wasting the moment's possibilities.

But I was not angry for long. As I made my way through Immigration and Customs, I exulted with the realization that I was actually in Israel, land of my Fathers whose capacity for courage I had come here to learn. My elation lasted as long as it took to get to baggage claim. The sense of belonging and camaraderie I had begun to feel on the plane gave way to a palpable isolation. I allowed all my uncertainties and insecurities to fester into a frenzy of anxiety. I tried to harness myself, making the effort, as a man should, not to succumb to hysteria. And there! With the effort I felt myself growing inside, then outside. Elation returned. I was strong, physically and inwardly. I had the unmistakable sensation that I was filling the moment, that it was inevitable to be standing here, growing into myself, that the air was full of possibilities, that I was solid and powerful, yet open and warm towards people at the same time.

The usual conditions for anxiety—a new situation, a crowd, not knowing anyone—were momentarily irrelevant, and I did something entirely out of character. A worker, a thin, middle-age Israeli, jumped off the moving conveyer belt and stumbled. I anticipated his fall as it was unfolding and was there to catch him in my arms. The bystanders applauded. The man and I smiled at each other. "Pardon. Thank you," he said in English. The incident was an omen to me, the harbinger of my new self.

Outside the terminal I lined up for a "sheroot" taxi, a revamped, cigar-shaped De Soto limo once fashionable in New York City. The ride from Ben-Gurion Airport in Lod to Tel Aviv turned hilarious. The driver was in his late thirties, blunt and cynically funny in broken English. There were three other passengers. One woman, she looked more than 80 years old to me, was going to a private residence. A couple from Miami Beach, in their mid-60s I guessed, completed our quartet.

The couple was incorrigible, expert in the arts of negative comparison and the back-handed compliment. First example: The driver said, "Look at sun! Beautiful!" as we exited the airport and drove through acres of orange groves on the outskirts of Tel Aviv. "And fantastic oranges on trees!" the driver continued. "They're so *small*, those oranges," responded the woman, "not like the ones we have in Florida. And look! They're all falling off the trees!"

Second example: The couple tried to get the driver to speak Yiddish, apparently not realizing the stigma often attached to that language in Israel.

"I'm a *Polish-a* boy too," he said good-humoredly, "but born in Israel." In a *non sequitur* but for the subject of language, the woman exclaimed, "I've been to Israel six times and speak five words of Hebrew." This came as an assertion, prideful I thought, without apology. "It's like that old joke," she continued, "the one about a mother on a Tel Aviv bus talking to her son in Yiddish, but he keeps answering in Hebrew. She keeps trying until someone sitting next to them says, 'Why don't you just let the kid speak in Hebrew?' The mother says, 'Because I don't want him to forget he's a Jew.' Ha!"

Third example: The driver shot through traffic. "I bet this guy drove a tank in the war, the way he drives this thing," said the husband. "Hey," he called to the driver. "Did you drive a tank in the army?" The Floridian turned to me. "These Israelis are something. You have to admire them."

After every put down, side swipe, and innuendo, the couple exclaimed to me how much I would love it here, what a great country it was.

The driver dropped me off on Hayarkon Street, which ran along the Mediterranean and was where most of the hotels were situated, from the Hilton, Ramada, Sheraton, Dan, and Diplomat at the south end to the cheaper pensions on the north end. I started walking north, having narrowed my selection of prospects from Frommer's *Israel on $10 and $15 a Day* to three with Hayarkon addresses. Even in mid-morning, Hayarkon's whores were soliciting. In my naiveté and idealism, I had never considered the possibility that there were Jewish whores anywhere, least of all in Israel. Some of them, I learned later, lived in the Imperial Hotel at 69 Hayarkon, where I eventually registered.

The cats in Israel cry differently at night, I thought. Instead of "meow," they just left it as "ow" and protested as if they were being unconscionably treated by some monster among the garbage cans, some anti-Semitic oppressor from the trash heap of history. How did I come to this observation? It was 1:00 a.m., the dark hours of my first night in *Eretz Yisrael*, the Land of Israel. I was buried under quilts and blankets against the surprising coldness of Tel Aviv in winter. A curious, self-destructive, worrying fellow I am, I chastised myself: I hardly sleep for 30 hours, then, after three hours of deep sleep, I awaken long enough to allow the prankster Thought to sneak in and have his way, like a satyr on a virgin. Variously, I thought: I'm nuts for being here. What do I do next? I miss my child terribly. Poor lonely me. I need to get work. Should I abandon this foolishness and return to the U.S. immediately? Et cetera. Ad nauseam. And then, like a savior, a constructive admonition descended out of the darkness to say: "Turn it off. Stop giving power to the machine, don't allow it to keep idling away. You're listening to the wrong voice anyway." Yes, I agreed. The only important question was: "How to be a Man?" A Man, I told myself, should be able to remove idle thoughts, breathe deeply, discipline himself not to indulge fears, and thereby come to himself, to be present. Then everything will change, I assured myself. And it happened: a quietness, free from associations, filled the moment, which before had been a troubled space, a maelstrom whirling with anxious, extraneous considerations. The moment gave me a boost of badly needed energy and confidence. Like a lop-sided sandbag, my weight had been redistributed and a proper balance restored.

I phoned my graduate school friend, Eliezar Ben-Dor. Eli's mother answered but spoke no English. The hotel's bellhop, whom I beckoned for help, ascertained from Eli's mother that her son would return in an hour. In the meantime, I walked to the sea, the Mediterranean that had figured frequently in my fantasies over the years. Here it is, the real thing, I told myself with faux, self-manufactured ecstasy. But as on the tarmac when I disembarked at Ben-Gurion, I stood there unmoved. Shit. When faced with a real thing, the replaced fantasy takes its vengeance on me. I recalled Camus's character Meursault in *The Stranger*, unemotional after committing murder on another Mediterranean beach.

On my way back to the hotel I met a dog. Stooping to pat her, I was surprised when she immediately came to me and offered her paw. It felt strange to speak to an Israeli dog in English, but she was unfazed. She even followed me, but I escaped the attachment by ducking out of sight. *I would love to take you, dog. Loneliness does not seem to suit you anymore than it suits me.*

An encroaching sense of desolation propelled me into the gift shop of the five-star Hotel Dan.

Dear Ellen, I wrote on my first post card to her from Israel. *How are you? I am fine, except that I miss you so much! I just met a dog walking along the beach front here. (The water is a beautiful, shiny blue, as you can see in the photo.) The dog and I liked each other but couldn't really have a conversation. I think she only spoke Hebrew! I love you, Daddy.*

I picked up an envelope and airmail stamp from the front desk, inserted the card and a child-support check to Holly, and found a mailbox on Hayarkon. The Dan's embossed return address will make Holly curious, I mused. Was I actually staying in such a fancy hotel?

I reached Eli, who was flabbergasted at my unanticipated presence in Israel. "Your letter from West Virginia was so vague. There was no final decision, no schedule. But I'm very happy you're here."

We met for dinner at a vegetarian place and talked for hours, about our lives, our disappointments, our memories of graduate school's persecutions.

"I remember that day you became my friend," he said. "You know the one I'm talking about, don't you?"

"Oh, yeah. It's still clear in my mind, ten years later. We were in one of those never-ending Vietnam War debates. I can't remember who was arguing what, it was all such a confusion on campus those days. But what I do remember is you going at it with some guy who kept getting in your face. At first, you were polite. You kept backing up, physically, trying to keep things from getting more heated. But he wouldn't let up, and then—wham. You went nuts, absolutely nuts, yelling and gesturing and moving right back at him. Your intensity freaked him out. It freaked us all out, actually, everyone who witnessed the interaction. I didn't understand exactly what had set you off until you explained it to me later."

"Right. The son of a bitch—See? I can still curse in English—wouldn't stop pointing his finger at me, jabbing it. Like a gun. That was what did it. When you've seen frontline action in the Israeli Defense Forces, you don't want to feel like someone's coming at you with a gun. I snapped. I still feel bad about it. No, that's not true. I don't feel bad about it at all. I had asked him to stop."

"And he did, Eli. He did. You certainly won that argument."

We walked here and there, stopping three times for coffee. Eli didn't approve of my being at the Imperial, which according to him was a notorious hangout for lowlifes. He introduced me to the Nes Ziona, a small hotel on a quiet street of the same name two blocks from the sea. I moved in the next morning, spending four U. S. dollars a night for a single, half the cost of the Imperial. My ensuing two weeks in Tel Aviv were restful. It was winter; there were few tourists; the temperatures were cool enough for a sweater at night; the strong sun at the beach healed and replenished me during the day. I took long walks each morning, several times including the six-mile round trip to meet Eli in Ramat Aviv, where he taught in the philosophy department of Tel Aviv University.

I had dinner twice with Eli and his parents, immigrants many years ago from Riga. Other evenings we got together with Eli's sister Rivka, with whom I surely would have sought a deeper relationship had she not been my friend's sister. It was all too close. The siblings complained about each other to me when the other was out of earshot.

"She'll drive me crazy," Eli fumed while Rivka was in the ladies' room at a café on Dizengoff Street, Tel Aviv's hippest boulevard. "You know that course we took together in the Psych department, when we were exploring different disciplinary perspectives on Existentialism? As soon as I read the description of Narcissistic Personality Disorder, it was like a light shining on my family. Specifically on my sister, who made the rest of us miserable for years. She's so self-centered and demanding and manipulative. 'Look at Me. Me. Me.' She's impossible."

Eli got up to go to the men's room as soon as he saw Rivka on her way back to our table. "It's amazing to me that my brother has you as a friend. I could never be his friend. If I had a choice I wouldn't be his sister. He doesn't give a damn for anybody but himself. But you—obviously, you're loyal to him, in spite of the way he is, grumpy, superior, always critical. That's something I like in a person, by the way—loyalty." She looked at me, her beautiful green eyes staring right into mine. "Will you be loyal like that to me?"

Lonely as I was, I considered accepting Rivka's come-on, even risking the possibility she was the narcissist Eli claimed her to be. But no, I decided. It was all too close.

I ate only twice a day to save money, taking both meals at Hamozeg, on the corner of Ben Yehuda and Shalom Aleichem. Meals there were plentiful, healthy, and a pittance at an exchange rate of seven Israeli liras to the U.S. dollar, less than a dollar for breakfast and about two dollars for the late meal. Once, when leaving Hamozeg, I was approached by a bearded, middle-age man.

"Where are you from?" the man asked in un-accented English.

"America."

We walked together along Ben Yehuda. The man introduced himself as Avram Elon. He was from Toronto and had been living in Israel for 20 years, working as a copy editor for a publisher specializing in Hebrew-to-English translations. He invited me to stop in for a cup of tea at his place, a ground-floor apartment nearby. The apartment was modest but pleasant, full of books and art posters throughout the two small rooms.

The conversation took an uncomfortable turn. Avram talked about his sense of estrangement despite his two decades in Israel, his aloneness. It was clear he was about to make advances. I pointedly looked at my watch and said I had better leave, I was supposed to meet a friend on Jabotinsky Street, a 15-minute walk away. "I'll just be on time if I leave now."

Avram acceded courteously, not pushing the matter. I returned the politeness, leaving what could be said unsaid. I sympathized with the other's obvious loneliness. But Avram's remedy for loneliness was not mine.

I walked daily along Tel Aviv's shoreline on the Herbert Samuel Esplanade. Every afternoon, I spent an hour or more looking out over the beach and sea with Aharon Peretz. Raised in a Polish *shtetl*, complete with side-curls and caftan and the product of strict religious training, he had survived the concentration camps and come to Israel in 1946 aboard an illegal refugee ship—"a pale, weak, scared young boy," as he described himself. Now he was a rugged, healthy, exuberant retired construction worker, a straightforward, earthy man who loved sports, particularly basketball, and English, his broken version of which he learned while working in a U.S. Army post-exchange in Germany after the war.

Peretz told me many stories, but nothing about the camps, only about his life in Israel—stories about his being in the Israeli army during the 1948 war; about his family ("My daughter's a sergeant," he laughed. "I only rose to private"); his sorrows (a brother in Florida who never returned his frequent letters and another brother who lived in Israel but, being Orthodox and kosher, wouldn't eat in Peretz's home); the period of his post-army early life he spent as a boxer; his desire to visit the United States and listen all day to "the beautiful sounds of English."

In our final meeting before I left Tel Aviv, Peretz spoke about his love for Israel—just being in its cleanliness and warmth, feeling like a man, not being called a fucking Jew, his love of physical labor and his concomitant disappointment at not being an educated man. But a happier, sunnier man I had never met. His robustness and good humor were contagious. And all this after the life he has endured, I thought. The physically indelible tattooed numbers on Peretz's right forearm left an indelible mental and emotional imprint on me, saying to me something about character and choice. Thousands in this country, and elsewhere, suffered a similar trauma. I had met several of them, but none so alive and joyful as Peretz.

I recalled something Castaneda's Don Juan said, that one can choose to be happy or sad, it's all the same. *If I can bring myself to remember Mr. Peretz when I am in the throes of despondency,* I encouraged myself, *usually over nothing, nothing at all, I hope I can choose his way. But how to do it? What does it take to be like this man?*

As if in answer, Peretz broke into spontaneous song in his comical, heartfelt, beloved English.

"You too, *Natan*," he interrupted himself, using my Hebrew name. "You sing too. 'You Are My Sunshine'. It's my favorite song."

What the hell, I surrendered, overcoming any fear of making a fool of myself so I wouldn't disappoint him. Reinforced by the smiles and applause of passersby, Peretz and I sang verse after verse, my voice gradually becoming as forceful as my partner's. As we sang I gazed at Peretz, whose face was lifted toward the sky. His eyes were closed. He swayed to the music. The chorus became a chant—*"Please don't take my sunshine away."* I closed my eyes and lifted my face toward the sky, the same Israeli sky. Then both of us swayed as we sang, two Jews joined in common prayer.

8
Jerusalem the Golden

Jerusalem the golden, with milk and honey blest....
Even now by faith I see thee, even here thy walls discern.
To thee my thoughts are kindled, and strive, and pant, and yearn.

–Bernard of Cluny, 1146

Jerusalem the golden,
Fount of myths and dreams:
Please be my answer.

–Nathan Kirinski, 1978

AFTER TWO WEEKS IN Tel Aviv, it was time to make the ascent to Jerusalem. Tel Aviv had become a holding pattern. I knew this. I was becoming comfortable there. How not to be comfortable walking its clean boulevards, lingering in its sleek cafes, warming myself daily in the Mediterranean sun? But there was no answer to be found there, I was sure. Why I was sure, I couldn't say. I didn't know what answer I sought, or even the question to be answered. I only knew it was time to leave, and that Jerusalem was where I must go. I hoped I would somehow—what?—cohere there. And I was determined not to worry—not yet—that it might turn out otherwise.

I boarded a seven-passenger sheroot taxi for the two-hour drive from Tel Aviv to Jerusalem. In my imaginings over many years of this very trip, I had not expected the landscape's diversity, the quick transitions from flat, sandy coastal plain to orchards, farmlands, industrial areas, the outskirts of towns and settlements, Arab villages, and Bedouin camps. Conversation in the sheroot stopped as we climbed higher and higher through terraced hills, here and there strewn with the wreckage of trucks and tanks rusting in the sun, grim and silent reminders of the sacrifices made to save Jerusalem from isolation and starvation during the 1948 war. Could there be a more historical and blood-stained stretch of earth anywhere?

I asked to be dropped off at the Central Bus Station in order to walk the last two miles down the Jaffa Road toward the Old City; I wanted to absorb this long-anticipated ambience at my own pace, in my own time. I passed the stores and market at Ben Yehuda and stopped at the corner of Shlomzion, my throat catching with emotion as the ancient walls loomed into sight. Gathering myself, I crossed Shivte Yisroel and entered the Jaffa Gate. Hardly aware of the weight of my belongings in their small canvas bag, I wandered for two hours before being able to impose a break on myself when I reached Tiferet

Israel Street. More accurately, it was the view that made me stop, the view of *Ha Kotel*, the Western Wall and the Temple Mount, Judaism's holiest site.

As I stood there, captivated, I realized I was being watched by a bearded, grizzled old man dressed in a caftan and leaning on a cane. He spoke to me in Hebrew, but I couldn't understand. Then in Yiddish, with the same result. "I'm sorry," I said, raising my hands in apology.

"Not understanding is okay," he said in accented but fluent English. "Especially here, in front of *Ha Kotel*. It's not so easy to understand thousands of years of history. If you said you understood, you'd be pretending." He laughed. "But watching you I see no pretense. I see a man who has come home."

Then he turned and walked away, his cane tapping the cobblestones. "Please, wait!" I called after him, but he didn't stop. He rounded a corner into an alleyway and was gone. My imagination leaped. Elijah. Was he Elijah, the ancient, immortal prophet who wanders the world unseen until he suddenly reveals himself to rescue someone or bestow a blessing? According to legend, he might appear anywhere. Why not here? "Especially here," he had said.

I made my way through the alleyways of the Christian Quarter towards the Church of the Holy Sepulcher and booked a room for 35 liras, the equivalent of five dollars a day, including breakfast, at The Knights Palace Hotel. Avram Elon, the ex-Canadian who flirted with me in Tel Aviv, told me about this place, a huge stone building, built in 1847, with steep stairways, heavily carved furniture, gothic arches and high ceilings. Originally part of the Latin Patriarchate, it later became a religious seminary, then a pilgrimage hostel for Knights of the Holy Sepulcher, a Roman Catholic order with roots in the First Crusade, and finally a hotel that welcomed all visitors. The desk clerk asked how long I intended to stay.

"I don't know. Maybe a long time. Let's start with two weeks."

My first morning in Jerusalem I walked down the road from Mt. Herzl, past Har Hazikaron, the Hill of Remembrance dedicated to the six million Jews murdered by the Nazis during World War II, and the Avenue of the Righteous Gentiles planted with trees in tribute to those who helped save Jewish lives in the Holocaust. Then I entered the cluster of buildings at the top of the hill. What can I say about Yad Vashem, Israel's memorial to the victims of the Holocaust? What can I say I felt? The sanctuary's effect was instantaneous, insistent, and terrible. The photos and displays froze my emotions. Such atrocities cohabiting a world of breath and sky and earth and animals and families and aspirations and....It was not comprehensible. I walked along, past exhibit and exhibit and exhibit. Four or five times my mind yelled, *Stop. What is the point of all this? It's too much, far too much.* Yet I walked on through the gauntlet of exhibits, my incomprehension building. Toward the end of the displays were posts with inscriptions reading "Rumania, X number killed," "Poland, X number killed," on and on. At the last post, my confusion dissolved in an instant of grotesque clarity and understanding as I read, "Children: 1,500,000" and saw, beneath the legend, a display that moved me beyond rage and hatred to a sigh and a prayer. There I saw a glass case, a cube. In it rested the crushed, high leather shoe of a five-year-old. I thought of my daughter.

I continued to Yad Vashem's memorial hall. Inside, I stood alone, reading the names of the camps and killing fields set out on the floor according to some geographical logic. A flame burned toward the back of the room. I walked along the L-shaped banister. Abruptly, somewhere near Treblinka, Sobibor, Theresienstadt, and Baba Yar, I felt pulled to a stop. Despite having been distant from observant Judaism for some years, I recited the entire *Kaddish*, the mourner's prayer, from memory. Then I left Yad Vashem.

I wandered for a long time through the streets of M'ea Shearim, the ultra-Orthodox quarter of Jerusalem. I was both drawn to and repelled by the people there. Drawn because they were part of my history and my blood. Repelled because it was possible to "see" pogromists throughout the centuries come along and destroy these men wearing side curls, come along and have their way with these women in wigs and kerchiefs, and not meet a protest. The kids currently living there ran down the alleys with their own bouncing side curls, chattering in Yiddish, lugging books. I turned a corner and "saw" my sister as a beautiful, redheaded eight-year-old smiling there on a street of a neighborhood that would have looked the same 200 years ago. And she existed all those years ago, in Poland, Ukraine, Italy, just as she existed these days in Crown Heights and Williamsburg, just as she faced me today, a child in M'ea Shearim. Who can say that time runs in a straight line, in a logical sequence? Who can say that my American sister and daughter could not be here, laughing and talking with friends in a language neither ever learned in America, their loveliness shining in this anachronistic ghetto of Jerusalem?

> *Dear Ellen, I am in Jerusalem now, one of the oldest cities in the world. It's beautiful, and many of the buildings are a golden color, as you can see from the picture. I miss you very much and think of you all the time, and especially when I see children. I wish I could walk around Jerusalem with you and show you all the old churches and markets and other interesting places. Love, Daddy*

As I prayed one night at the Western Wall, two prayers came to me: the one, "Lord, have mercy," in English; the other, the *Shema*—"Hear Oh Israel, the Lord our God, the Lord is One"—in Hebrew. My hands on the Wall, eyes closed, feet together, body swaying, I prayed. It's called the Wailing Wall for good reason; my tears fell within seconds of my touching it. There was no willing this, just as there was no willing the prayers. The words came, the tears came. There was no thought, no expectation, no aim. There was only this person, this constellation of feelings drawn tightly together, meeting for a moment the Beloved who dwelled there that night. Only that. No more.

Another night I walked the Stations of the Cross along the Via Dolorosa. During the day, the Church of the Holy Sepulcher was a madhouse of visitors milling through the Roman Catholic, Armenian Orthodox, Greek Orthodox, Russian Orthodox, Abyssinian Coptic, and Syrian Orthodox custodianships. That night it was nearly free of people. I sat upstairs, at the putative site of Calgary, reciting the Prayer of the Heart. From a nearby minaret the muezzin intoned *"Allah Ho Akbar,"* slowly, melodiously, gently, to mark the end of the Muslim Sabbath, which coincides with the Friday evening start of the Jewish Sabbath. As I left the church, the streets were full of ultra-Orthodox Jews returning from their Sabbath evening services at the Wall. Inside me, a quiet moment, a joyous moment. All is one.

I visited the famous Rockefeller Museum, whose display cases were crowded with antiquities representing archaeological finds from 150,000 to 1,000 B.C. But I had little interest in artifacts, little patience for staring at relics. My interest was in Jerusalem's people more than its antiquities. Jerusalem, the Eternal City, truly seemed to evoke the gamut of time. For me, its eternity dwelled most tangibly in what was current. It was in its neighborhoods, and not its museums, that the material symbols of man's long history there—walls, cobblestones, buildings—were most meaningful. The inorganic and the organic, the past and the present, mixed naturally and had a special symmetry in the streets of Jerusalem.

> *Dear Ellen, there are so many ancient things to see in Jerusalem. (Ask your mom to explain what "ancient" means.) The picture shows some of the oldest things they keep in a museum here. (Ask your mom what a museum is.) Someday I hope you'll be able to come here and see them for yourself. Love, Daddy*

For quite some time I had been searching through the ruins and partially rebuilt streets of the old Jewish Quarter for the ancient Churva (Ruin) Synagogue. The map indicated it was to be found off Ha-Yehudim, the Street of the Jews. But there were many ruins there and nothing indicated the Churva's exact whereabouts.

I noticed a Hasid and, not knowing which language to try, muttered greetings and a request for directions in my minimal Hebrew. *"Shalom. Boker tov. Bevakasha, Ay fo Churva Shul?"* The man, about 50 years old, surprised me with a New York-accented, "We'd do better in English." A Brooklynite, he too, it turned out, was looking for the Churva. We poked around together saying, "This must be it" or "This certainly must be the place" until another

Hasid appeared. My companion and the newcomer spoke in animated Yiddish, of which I could follow very little.

The first Hasid translated while the second led us to the Churva. "It took 600,000 rubles to build it originally," he told us, his reference to Russian money striking me as more oddly atavistic than charming.

The two Hasids exchanged names, touched hands. The Jerusalemite asked where I was from. "New Jersey," the New York Hasid replied on my behalf. No recognition. "Asbury Park." No recognition. "Belmar." Still no recognition. Then I said, "Bradley Beach," the mention of which stimulated happy head nods, probably in recognition of the well-known Congregation Agudath Achim, the Orthodox synagogue established in Bradley in the 1920s.

We three went our separate ways. *"Shalom." "Shalom." "Shalom."* I moved alone about the ruins, wondering at it all.

An outlook on Ha Yehudim offered a breathtaking view of the Wall and, against the blue sky above it, the golden-domed Mosque of Omar, the Dome of the Rock. For Jews, the rock is the traditional spot where Abraham prepared to sacrifice his son Isaac at the Lord's command. The rock is holy to Muslims as well, Islam's third most important site after Mecca and Medina. I had already spent many hours there and in the neighboring Al-Aqsa Mosque but had never looked at them from this vantage point.

I was absorbed in the vista when a young Arab boy approached and tried to sell me a stack of postcards. I tried to put him off, telling him I had been to those places and had pictures of them. One by one, the boy covered the legend on each card and in passable English asked me the names of the sites depicted. I got most of them right. Then the boy asked if I wanted to be guided through the Jewish, Arab, Christian, and Armenian Quarters, or perhaps just one of them. When I answered no, that I had been through them already, the boy asked if I really knew what I had seen. "Of course," I responded.

The boy then pointed to a building pictured in one of the postcards. "Question 1: What's that?"

"I don't know."

The boy repeated the exercise, pointing to a different building. "Question 2: What's that?"

Again, I admitted that I didn't know. The boy repeated the examination two more times with other landmarks. I knew the names of none.

"Four questions I ask you," the kid exclaimed. "You don't know any. You fail test. You need guide."

Dear Ellen, I bought this postcard from a boy who is very smart. He knows all about the famous places in Jerusalem. I bet you're just as smart as he is, and some day when I visit you in Anchorage you can tell me all about places there. Love, Daddy

A man approached me in the street. "Pardon me," he said, in accented English. "Are you English perhaps? American?"

I told him I was American. "Oh, good," he said, and introduced himself as Ilyas Taimoar, a stateless Muslim refugee from Pakistan. "I wonder if you would help me write a letter, as my written English is not smooth."

He looked destitute to me, beaten down, which was understandable given his circumstances. He evoked my sympathy. And his name, Ilyas—I recalled the old man I encountered near the Western Wall my first day in Jerusalem, the one I imagined might be the prophet Elijah. Saint Elias to Christians. Ilyas to Muslims. Be alert, I reminded myself. He can appear any time, any place. To provide help. To bring blessings.

We went to a tea house in a back alley of the Arab Quarter. The letter Ilyas had me write was addressed to the chairman of the International Christian Community and the Red Cross of Nazareth, the ICCN. We explained that Ilyas had 1,500 Israeli liras, about 215 U.S. dollars, towards the purchase of an oscilloscope and hoped to borrow the remaining 1,500 liras from the ICCN. He proposed to repay the loan at 200 liras a month, offering as collateral 2,500 liras worth of his present equipment. He stated that he already had 15 loyal customers in Nazareth Illit, Eksal, and Ein Mahal. Once he established himself in his trade as a medical technician, he planned to marry and apply for Israeli citizenship.

It was mighty ironic for me, a Jew, to be helping a Muslim in the city of Jesus, Christianity's archetypal Helper. It was also humbling: in my fractured state, I felt hardly up to helping anyone. Well, at least I had a serviceable skill and could write a decent letter. I hoped Ilyas would get what he needed.

Three weeks into my stay there, I was sure I would be happy to remain in Jerusalem forever. I also realized that I needed to shake myself free from the city for a while in order to experience more of the country. I headed back to the Mediterranean, intending to loop north by bus, sheroot, and thumb through Natanya, Caesarea, Beit Shearim, Haifa, Acre, Nahariya, the Golan Heights, Safed, Tiberias, Nazareth, the West Bank, the Dead Sea, the Negev, Sinai, and Eilat, and return, at the end, to Jerusalem.

Days later, while sitting in a café in Acre mapping my onward journey, a man my age interrupted me, in American English, to ask directions. This was Lawrence Carter, an archaeologist from the state of Washington who, as it happened, was driving a rental car and visiting sites not easily accessible without an automobile. We conversed for a while, and he invited me to join him on a trip along the Lebanese border and through the Golan Heights.

One of our stops was Gamalah, a recently discovered dig, well off the beaten track, far up in the Golan Heights and close to Syria. Along the way we passed military installations and were questioned at military checkpoints, each of which commanded a seemingly impenetrable spot and stunning view of snow-covered Mt. Kinneret. Gamalah, the last town to be taken by the Romans under Vespacius (later the emperor) in 67 A.D. of Nero's reign, was a strange combination of ancient fortress, modern warfare (we could hear sniping at the nearby border and see jets zooming overhead), and nature's beauty (six eagles soared 50 feet above us on strong winds). Lawrence carried a copy of the complete works of Josephus, including *The Wars of the Jews*, which we referred to now. As we read out loud the historian's vivid account of the battle that took place at Gamalah, it was as if I were in the middle of it.

Several days later, I was in Safed and feeling quite at ease again after a morning of wandering around and talking with people in that lovely, clean, and cool town high in the mountains. I had parted from Lawrence Carter and was glad to be on my own again. Although I was thankful to have met the archaeologist, I was relieved to be done with him. After traveling in the Middle East for over a year, Lawrence was abrupt and hostile toward any "native." He was convinced he was being cheated and would squabble over a few liras, despite being able to shell out 25 dollars a day for a rental car. In this respect, the value of going with him was that his negativity offered me a real-time reminder to counteract any such paranoid tendencies of my own. It had been difficult not to be swayed by his distrustful attitude. It required intentional effort and vigilance. All of that said, Lawrence was quite knowledgeable about the history of the Holy Land sites we visited. He was better than a tour guide for that sort of thing, and thanks to his car we were able to explore a number of unmarked, un-touristed places that I otherwise would never have heard of, much less been able to visit: Gamalah, Kfar Bar Am, Ksariat, Tel Dan, and others. But I found Lawrence's *blitzkrieg* mode of travel tiring and overstuffed with information, and my impressions of places began to overlap by lunch (which we never took much time to enjoy on Lawrence's driven, single-minded schedule). Lawrence had become prisoner to a rent-a-car; historical facts and antiquities were of more concern to him than encounters with the living.

By contrast, soon after Lawrence dropped me off in Safed I checked into the Pension Hadar and had an enjoyable, leisurely conversation in an art gallery with its owner, an elderly woman who had settled in this mountainous town after fleeing Germany 40 years earlier. Then I wandered the alleys of Ha Kirya Knessetim, the synagogue section, taking in the still-palpable ambiance of the great Kabbalist rabbis—Isaac Luria, Isaac Aboad, Moses Alshek, Yosef Ha Banai, Mendel of Vitebsk. I left stones of commemorative respect on their tombs in the nearby cemetery and sat on satin cushions conversing with the sextons of the Kabbalists' ancient Sephardic prayer houses. At the monument to the heroes of 1948, I joked around with a class of 10th grade girls who wanted to practice their English and get my autograph. I delighted in their company. I was open to people again, which was the main point for me now—and not ruins, however impressive. With Lawrence, I could never have had these meetings, both because of the archaeologist's suspiciousness of the locals and his compulsion to get his money's worth—to see absolutely every Holy Land site ever written about by Josephus and other historians. And to hell with the living.

> *Dear Ellen, this is a picture of Safed. It's a very old town and one of the highest places in Israel. The air is so clean and fresh and cool. I like it here very much. I know that Alaska is also clean and fresh and cool, and I hope that you and your mommy are having a good time there. Love, Daddy*

I stayed in Haifa for three days, moving to a different hotel each night—The Lea, The Nesher, The Daphne—all midway up the mountain in Hadar Ha'Carmel, "the Glory of the Carmel," to take advantage of the city's splendid views. Carmel, from the two Hebrew words *Kerem-El*, "Vineyard of the Lord": the mountain is well named, I thought. The cave of the Prophet Elijah, the Baha'i Temple, and the neighboring Druze villages of Daliat-El-Carmel and Isfiya were of particular interest.

Elijah had been an intriguing figure for me since I was a kid. My most memorable moment at Passover *seders* was when a cup of wine was placed at a designated setting with an empty chair to welcome the Prophet. I especially loved the haunting song that conveyed the welcome: "Elijah, Elijah the Prophet. Come quickly to us with the Messiah, the son of David." I thought of Ilyas Taimoar, my letter-writing partner, and wished I had asked him about Elijah, or Ilyas, in Islam. I had read somewhere that Ilyas is also known by Muslims as al-Khidr, a green-cloaked presence who might come upon you at any moment and in any guise, like Judaism's Elijah, to test the quality of your being. When I read André Schwarz-Bart's *The Last of the Just*, I wondered if Elijah were somehow related to the *Lamed Vav*, the 36 righteous souls—ever present, never known or recognized—whose existence justifies the purpose of humankind to God. Each bears the world's pain; when they are no more, humankind will lose its justification in God's eyes.

I went to Elijah's Cave, a holy site for Jews, Muslims, and Christians where the prophet was supposed to have shamed and disgraced the priests and worshippers of the idol Ba'al, and where Elijah was said to have hidden from King Ahab and his wife Jezebel, who sought to kill the prophet. On the way in, I met a young religious Jew who introduced himself as Josh. Eight years in Israel, originally from Woodmere, Long Island, Josh was a member of the new Haifa Torah Center of the Diaspora Yeshiva, quartered right above the cave. I spent an hour with him and Benjamin, a Californian who had been in Haifa for a year or so after six years in Kyoto and spiritual sojourns to the Sri Aurobindo Ashram in Pondicherry, among other places in India. The conversation was relaxed and informative, over two cups of coffee, with no proselytizing. Josh gave me a list of books about Judaism in English to look up, intriguing titles like *Ways of the Righteous*, *Path of the Just*, *Ways of G-d*, *Duties of the Heart*, and *Book of Knowledge*.

Leaving the cave, I made my way down Carmel to the Baha'i Temple and Persian Garden. Had I some compelling desire or need to be an adherent of an organized religion, Baha'i might have been my choice. Its message emphasizing the essential unity of all religions and universal brotherhood seemed genuine and was actually practiced, from all I had read and heard. Christ, Buddha, Mohammed, Moses—all were messengers of God in Baha'i's theology, each sent at a different time in history with a doctrine suited to the needs of humankind's contemporary situation. The most recent of the heavenly teachers, according to Baha'i, was Baha'Ullah, who was exiled in the mid-19th century from Persia to Palestine, where he wrote his doctrines and died. I was moved, too, by Bahai's history, a history filled with persecution and genocide, commitment and survival. Much like Judaism. Much like early Christianity. The Baha'i Temple's shrines and the neighboring Persian Gardens rivaled Jerusalem's golden dome and the Zen garden in Kyoto's Ryōan-ji Temple as the most beautiful man-made sites I had ever seen.

The next day I took the half-hour bus ride along the uppermost rim of Carmel to the Druze villages of Daliat and Isfiya. As a teenager reading Leon Uris's *Exodus*, I had been enthralled by the Druze, an Arabic-speaking, non-Muslim people who were loyal to Israel and fought fiercely on the new state's behalf in 1948. Though Arabic in appearance, a number of the Druze I saw were blond, the genetic influence, no doubt, of Romans, Crusaders, and other "parents" of the Holy Land. The Druze religion was obscure and curious to me, for example their veneration of Moses' father-in-law Jethro and St. George, whom they also call Elijah the Prophet. I spent the afternoon walking through Daliat and Isfiya, browsing in shops and sitting in a café talking with a Druze teenager who in clothing and mannerisms was like any other modern Israeli kid, all the while observing the older men walk by, mustached and clad in flowing robes.

On my last evening in Haifa I had dinner with the Cohens, an elderly couple from Paterson, New Jersey with whom I had struck up a conversation in the Persian Gardens. They were visiting their daughter Karen and her husband Amos Wexler. The younger Wexlers lived in an upscale neighborhood high on the Carmel. I felt intimidated. Karen and Amos were my age; they lived in a lovely home; they were gainfully employed, both lawyers; they dressed well, like the parents, while I could assemble no better than jeans, boots, and a threadbare turtleneck sweater under a thin and spotted ski jacket. They not only had a child but were with their child. I temporized when they asked me about my plans, telling them I might accept one of the university jobs I had been offered, even though I had no such intention. "Or," I added, "I might stay in Israel."

"How long would you be here?" Mrs. Cohen asked.

"I'm not sure. I'm thinking of studying Hebrew intensively. I'm considering living in Israel for good at some point."

Courteously, their conversation accommodated my vagueness for the rest of the evening. After leaving them I stopped at the end of their street, Margalit, breathing deeply in relief to be by myself again, subject only to my self-judgments, which God knew were harsh enough. I walked along Habroshim on the way back to my room at The Daphne. An attractive woman my age approached, asking for the time in Hebrew. Nonplussed, I held up my watch, unable, without preparation, to respond in the same language. She thanked me and walked away. I had the impulse to run after her yelling "Ten o'clock!" in Hebrew, but didn't have the nerve.

> *Dear Ellen, this is a picture of a famous temple in Haifa. Isn't it beautiful? Haifa is a city right next to the sea, and it is built on high hills. Remember the Passover dinner we had in West Virginia, when we put a glass of wine out for the Prophet Elijah? Well, Haifa is one of the places he lived. Maybe he's still here now! Love, Daddy*

Weeks later, many adventures and encounters and reflections later, I returned to Jerusalem. Things seemed different, or rather, I felt different. I was happy to be there. It was home in some essential and historical sense. But I was strangely empty, jaded, dull. My determination to meditate, to stop smoking, to pray—I couldn't summon up the energy to do any of these.

During my first weeks in Jerusalem, I had gone to the Wall to pray every day and fully intended to resume the practice now that I was back. But I ended up viewing it from a distance this time, not approaching the Wall itself. Something in me felt unready, inadequate—unclean, to put it biblically. Early on, like multitudes of visitors have done over the centuries, I had written a message on a small piece of paper and placed it in one of the Wall's crevices. The message was a supplication, a prayer asking that I be reunited with Holly and Ellen. My action then was filled with energy, and I was filled with hope. Now I worried that my lethargy would invalidate the prayer I had inscribed.

During my first stay in Jerusalem, I had developed several routines beyond my visits to the Wall. Now that I was back, I resumed these other habits. I walked to Kikar Zion, or Zion Square, a small, central area in Western Jerusalem circumscribed by King George Avenue, Jaffa Road, and Ben Yehuda Street. After a falafel sandwich at one of the numerous food stands, I stopped for coffee at a cafe on Jaffa Road where I would sit for an hour or more sipping espressos, reading, and writing one of my frequent post cards to Ellen, my only correspondent. (I was incommunicado with my family, who had no idea where I was, or if I were still alive. I don't know why I did this. Shame?

Cowardice?) I always went to the same place, whose name was the Alaska Café. Now I sat there reviewing the post card I had just written.

> *Dear Ellen, I hope you like this picture of a desert next to a sea. I just came back from there. The desert is called the Judean Desert. It's very, very old. People have walked across it for many years, but nothing really lives there except for camels and cute little animals called prairie dogs. The sea is called the Dead Sea because nothing lives there either. It is too hot and salty—so salty that you can float on it without ever sinking into the water. It's a funny feeling. Now I'm back in Jerusalem and trying to decide where I'll visit next. Love, Daddy*

I put the card in an envelope along with a check to Holly. I would mail it when I got back to my hotel. But meanwhile, where to go next? What to do next? I left the café and phoned Malka, a woman I had met on my travels. We arranged to meet at her office, a social services agency, after she finished work. *Maybe this will shake me out of my lethargy. Please!*, I thought as I walked there that evening. We were joined by her friend Yaki, an agriculture student. We all had coffee together, a fine time, stimulating conversation. They invited me to a party the following weekend.

As I stood up to leave I traded looks with a striking woman, about 30 years old, I guessed, who had just entered the office. In a burst of energy, without thinking, I approached her and introduced myself. "*Shalom*," I said, offering my hand. "Hello. I'm Nathan. Nathan Kirinski. I'm pleased to meet you." Already I was embarrassed by my impetuosity and schoolboy greeting, the type of thing we were taught as children.

"*Shalom*," she replied, taking my hand. "Hello. I'm Hannah. Hannah Gordon. I'm pleased to meet you, too." She gave this imitation in unaccented English, and with kindly humor. We both laughed.

Hannah told me she was Canadian, originally from Ottawa, and had been living in Jerusalem for eight years. She attracted me very much. Her smile was lovely. I experienced a surge of glee when she invited me to stop by the following afternoon at the King David Hotel, where she managed the souvenir shop. I decided the invitation was sincere. *You can feel that sort of thing*, I reassured myself. *You can feel the movement between you.*

"Sure," I said.

Later, I began to doubt she actually expected me to show up. But then I decided there was no way I would miss making that visit. I thought of her that night as I huddled against the cold in my spartan room at the Knights Palace. Her smile.

The weather the next day was perfect. I went to the Temple Mount, not to enter the mosque as I had often taken to doing during my first days in Jerusalem, but just to sit in the brilliant sun, in the quiet against a far wall of the courtyard where worshippers conducted their ablutions. I took in the gold of Omar's dome and the silver of neighboring Al-Aqsa. There was no pretense of spiritual aspiration in me now. I was content merely to sit in the sun, in its reflections off the dome, to be warmed and bide the time until I could go to see Hannah at four that afternoon.

I arrived early to pay uneasy homage to the history of the King David Hotel. The Jewish Irgun's bombing of the hotel in 1946 certainly accelerated Britain's departure from Palestine and the advent of the State of Israel two years later, but the explosion was massive and deadly. I thought of the many that perished there—British, Arabs, Jews, and others—for whom history ceased in a flash. I found "trade-offs" like this impossible to evaluate, much as I had been unable to sustain thoughts about the beginning and end of things, the timed and the eternal, when I was a kid.

Hannah seemed happy I had come. "*Shalom*," she said, offering her hand. "Hello. You must be Nathan, Nathan Kirinski. I'm pleased to see you."

"Touché," I responded, holding her hand and laughing.

It wasn't tourist season; few customers interrupted us as we sat and talked until closing time at 10:00 p.m. We went to her apartment in nearby Rehavia and continued talking over coffee until I left at 12:30 a.m. I was entirely taken by her, her intelligence, her genuine warmth. And I knew I could learn from her, an observant Jew, but in no way doctrinaire. I outlined my own connection with Judaism—from Orthodox origins to spiritual ecumenism to intermarriage to my present struggles with Jewish identity, the tension between a particular ethnic identity and a broader American one. From her own experience growing up in predominantly Christian Canada, Hannah understood my ambivalence and resistance. "It's much easier not being the Other," she said.

All the while, under the veneer of earnest conversation, I so wanted to touch her, to kiss her, to be with her. In romance, the first move had never been easy for me. This evening was no different; the best I could muster was a cordial "good night." But I could still luxuriate in racing feelings of attraction as I made my way down Ramban and Agron, through the Jaffa Gate and back to my room in the Christian Quarter, where sleep came with difficulty.

On our first date, Hannah and I dined together at a high-end restaurant. It was a memorable evening for me. It was natural and easy to be with this woman, so open in her spontaneity and humor and self-doubts and vulnerability.

"Do you ever miss Canada?"

"No. Not Canada the country. It's a convenient place to live—clean, beautiful, universal health care, affordable education. It's progressive in many ways. But if you're a Jew, you're aware of an uncomfortable undercurrent. At least that was true for me. I often felt like a stranger there, an outsider, especially in school. Mostly, the anti-Semitism was subtle. But I was always aware of it. From an early age, I knew that I would leave Canada for Israel someday. So no, I don't miss Canada the country."

"But what about family? Are they here or there?"

Hannah went silent for a while, and I was afraid I had overstepped some boundary. "I'm sorry. I don't mean to pry..."

"It's okay. Don't worry. It's just that I do have family there, whom I miss terribly. Well, one relative actually, but a very close one. Both of my parents died when I was a little girl, and I was brought up by my mother's brother and his wife. Uncle Bernie and Aunt Selma. I had planned on moving to Israel right after high school, but I couldn't bring myself to leave them. When Selma died during my university years in Toronto, I thought I'd never be able to leave Uncle Bernie alone. But he surprised me. 'Hannah,' he kept urging, 'you should go to Israel. It's the only place on earth you can truly be a Jew. I didn't encourage this when Selma was alive because not having you here would have been devastating for her. I'll miss you, certainly, but I'll be fine. I have my business, my clubs and friends, the synagogue. You don't have to worry about me.' So I made *Aliyah* and immigrated."

"That must have been hard."

"It was. It is. But my uncle and I talk on the phone every week, I go to Ottawa once a year, and he spends Passover with me here every year. I keep asking him to move here permanently, but he just repeats what he told me when he urged me to leave—his business, friends, and synagogue are all there. He reminds me all the time how lucky I was to have no strong ties in Canada, nothing to keep me from living, as he said, in the only place on earth where you can truly be a Jew."

By our fourth date we were in love. Now there was Hannah. She took several days off from work, and we spent almost every moment of that time together, sharing deeper and deeper intimacies as we walked Jerusalem's streets, and finally, inevitably, sleeping together. I checked out of the Knights Palace and moved into her apartment, thankful that I had been given these days to be with her, these days in Jerusalem, the happiest I had been after a long and empty time.

In the Old City one day, before going to meet Hannah at the King David, two things happened. In the Church of the Holy Sepulcher, as usual when I went there, I recited the Jesus Prayer, the Prayer of the Heart. Midway down the ancient stone stairs leading to the deepest catacomb, mechanically repeating the prayer, I tripped and nearly fell. Later, resuming my recitation of the prayer, I walked through the Suq El Bazaar. As I looked through a shop window I heard a noise, like a person walking, on the roof overhanging the alley. Thinking nothing of it, I continued walking and reciting the prayer. A rock rolled off the roof and hit me on the head, raising a welt. In both instances, in the church and the suq, I had experienced a shock, the type of shock described by Gurdjieff that transforms and redirects energy into mindful witnessing of our immediate experience. In both instances, it was clear to me that mechanically saying the prayer, *Lord, have mercy*, had provoked a necessary jolt—stumbling, the rock—to shake me out of mindlessness. I had fallen asleep. I was sure I was being awakened.

One Saturday morning I accompanied Hannah to her synagogue, an Orthodox Ashkenazi congregation on Ibn Ezra Street, a short walk from her apartment on Rehov Ramban. I had shied away from temples, especially Orthodox synagogues, from the time I married Holly. Out of guilt from leaving my ancestral faith? Yes, in part. But more, I think, because my ecumenical, let's-bridge-all-differences mindset bridled at the expectations imposed by organized religion. But this day was special. "It's my mother's *yahrzeit*," she told me, the annual remembrance of the date of her death.

"Okay," I agreed, and put on my only presentable shirt and pants.

The synagogue was much like Belmar's, including a *mechitzah*, the curtain separating men from women. Hannah went to her side of it and I took a seat in the men's section, as off to the side as I could find. But they did find me. The *shammes*, the sexton, came over to ask my Hebrew name. "You're our guest. We'd like to call you up to raise the Torah after it's been read and put it back in the Holy Arc." This was the last thing I wanted to do. But it was an honor I couldn't easily refuse. I agreed to do it for Hannah.

After the service, Hannah introduced me to some of her friends. I held out my hand to the first one, but when I noticed her hesitation I apologized and didn't repeat the overture with the others. I also noticed that some wore wigs over their shaved heads—*sheitels*, the Orthodox Ashkenazic custom aimed at ensuring modesty among married women and not distracting men from their prayers with sensual provocations. The wigs, the touch avoidance, the curtain—this would just be the beginning, I thought, of the proscriptions I would have to conform to if I stayed with Hannah and ever entered this world. And if I didn't conform? She and I would both be in untenable positions, a prospect that didn't auger well for the long term.

The next day I would leave Israel. A light rain was falling in Tel Aviv, only the fourth rainy day of my months-long trip. Literally and figuratively, the sun had shined on me. Leaving Jerusalem two days before, I had not looked back. Out of respect for the place, I fought against being sentimental towards it. The Law of Return, the legislated right for any Jew to enter, reside, and have citizenship in Israel, had personal meaning for me now. I felt it was inevitable that I would be here again.

But there had been sentimentality despite my resolve. Leaving Hannah at the shop in the King David and again when I locked up her apartment and slid the key under the door, tears welled, my throat caught. She had given me so much. The days and nights together, talking, walking, loving, knowing that our time together must run out but grateful for the circumstances that had brought us together. The big bed, the special meals, the records and baths and strolls through the parks and suburbs of West Jerusalem. And especially walking the alleys of East Jerusalem: the Jewish Quarter; the Wall; the café overlooking Temple Mount; the movies; the orphanage I visited, with Hannah as translator, at the request of old man Feigler back in New Jersey, another resident of the Crystal Inn in Eatontown, who had been contributing to the charity for years and wanted me to visit it for him when I mentioned I was going to Israel, to be witness to the concrete results of his generosity.

Above all I would remember our communication—humorous, intellectually stimulating, respectful, and emotionally honest. Honesty about my feelings had never been my strong suit, but when I was with Hannah being so seemed natural and unavoidable. Her intuition was so finely tuned, her emotions so responsive. She read me like the proverbial open book. My primary concern was that she would hurt too much after we parted. Life had hurt her enough—orphaned at an early age, struggling to make her way as an immigrant and single woman in a new country. I didn't want to add to her pains and disappointments.

"You have a *Yiddishe neshamah*," Hannah told me as we lay in bed one morning, "a Jewish soul."

"With you, I believe I do. You've touched and nurtured it, and now I feel Jewish in a way I never did before."

"How is that?" she pushed.

"It's hard to explain. I feel part of a history now, a legacy and lineage that stretches back past the arbitrary time markings by which history is normally defined. Being in this country, especially in Jerusalem, I'm convinced now that I'm connected to all of that...Eternally, I guess I can say."

"Just as I said, Nathan. You have a Jewish soul."

But underlying all of this was the question that had begun to bother me since the day I accompanied her to synagogue: Did Jewish soul mean the same to her as to me?

"When you told me that the first time, I agreed. But I had better ask: What does *Yiddishe neshamah* mean to you?"

"That you have a Jewish identity grounded in this land. That you remember, every day, our people's unique covenant with God. And that you will come to abide, every day, with the commandments and customs created to insure the survival of the covenant."

That was a lot for me to unpack, and I said so. "Okay," she asked, "so what does it mean to you?"

"It means having a feeling of connection, like I said. And while I value the connection and shared memories among Jews, I don't buy the covenant part, or the idea that we're chosen or special, or that we need to follow rabbinical strictures to be soulful, or that God is Jewish. When it comes down to it, I guess I place more importance on my human soul than my Jewish one."

"If you come back to stay, Nathan, which I hope you will, I'll do my best to change your mind."

I couldn't know whether or not I'd be back. I only knew that I was leaving for now, carrying the same small suitcase I had arrived with and a whole lot of memories, the most cherished of them associated with Hannah. I thought of her friend Ephraim Mizrachi, for example, the barber at the King David whom Saul Bellow wrote about in *To Jerusalem and Back*, who was born 70 years ago in the Old Jewish Quarter and who had a collection of more than 200 letters from Hubert Humphrey, whom he considered his closest friend. Ephraim, that proud, intense, and beautiful old yeshiva student who lived alone in a tiny room by the Central Bus Station, grabbed and kissed me when we parted. Where would I have met such people had it not been for Hannah?

But I could acknowledge that I made my own way, too. I found my own experiences and relationships. I thought of the many people who had befriended and engaged me. Uncle Kamel, who shared his water pipe with me many afternoons in his carpet-lined room near the suq, telling me stories about an older Palestine. The antique store owner on Christian Quarter Road who invited me in for tea every time I passed by, even knowing I was not a prospective customer. The jeweler in the Jewish Quarter, who told me what it was like in Jerusalem when he had emigrated from Vienna 40 years ago. The West Bank Arab who gave me cigarettes on the bus to Hebron, smiling delightedly when I offered some sentences in Arabic. Uncle Moustache, the kind, happy man whose hole-in-the-wall restaurant near Herod's Gate in the Arab Quarter served bountiful meals for the equivalent of 75 cents to a ragged but fascinating assortment of hippies, backpackers, vagabonds, and the local poor. Abu Seif and his sons, who allowed me to browse their kitchen near Jaffa Gate and choose from the variety of foods cooking in numerous saucepans. The Knights Palace Hotel keeper, Muhammed, who told me that one's religion doesn't matter; it only matters that one be religious. Asher, Anat, Racheli, Malka, Yaki, and Gabi, young Jerusalemites who shared their world with me. The Indian and Filipino seamen with whom I conversed and drank at the pension Lea in Haifa. Uri, the concierge at my hotel in Tel Aviv, the Nes Ziona, whose kindnesses to me at the homesick start of my Israel sojourn eased my transition. The patient woman who answered my naïve questions about her religion's history and theology at the Greek Catholic Patriarchate. Simon the Bokharian. Yusuf, the Yemeni masseur. Marty, an alumnus of my U.S. college and an employee of the Mt. Beatitudes Hospice, where I stayed on the Sea of Galilee.

Probably because of my own anxieties about returning to America, my thoughts turned particularly to the strange, lonely, long-haired Japanese boy I met in the unheated, cavernous dormitory we shared at the Sisters of Nazareth. He and I were the hostel's only inhabitants, and he latched onto me for two days after I greeted him with one of the few Japanese phrases I knew.

"*Konnichi-wa.* Hello. The nun at the desk told me you're from Japan. My name is Nathan. I'm from America. How do you do?"

"Oh! *Konnichi-wa,*" he replied. "You speak Japanese! I do not hear my language very often. Thank you. My name is Junichiro Watanabe. Please call me Jun."

Jun and I did everything together, touring Nazareth, eating meals, and sharing the otherwise empty dorm.

"My parents are unhappy with me for taking this trip," he told me over dinner the first night.

"How long will your trip be? And why are they unhappy?"

"I have been away from Japan, from my home in Tokyo, for two years, and I don't know how much longer I'll be gone. Until I have no more money, I think. I don't want to go home."

"Why?"

"Because I will have to become an office worker, a *salariman,* we say in Japan, a man who works for a salary. I will have to spend all my time indoors, all day, sometimes all night, doing the same thing with the same people. That will be my life until I die. I did not want to do that. So I left. That's why my parents are unhappy. They think the *salariman* life is the right life, the only life. I don't know yet what I want, only what I don't want. That life."

I had deep admiration for this young man who had the courage to travel the world for as long as his money held out, a voluntary refugee from a culture that could not abide such an extreme individualist, a culture to which he knew he must someday return, much as a sailor must return from shore leave to the confines of his ship.

But these experiences in my life—with strangers, a country, a people, a city, a woman—were over. I had to leave, just as Jun would have to leave some day, to meet obligations.

> *Dear Ellen,* I wrote on the last postcard I would mail from Israel, *Today I'll be getting on an airplane to fly back to New Jersey. Then I'll find a job to earn enough money to visit you in Alaska. I don't know when that will be, but I'll do it as soon as I can. I hope you're having a good time in school, and that you're making lots of snowmen this winter. Please say hello to your mom for me. Love, love, love, Daddy*

The El Al jet departed Ben-Gurion. Once in the air, I had no discernible emotions. Transitions usually stimulated me, but I was numbed by this one. I only knew that Israel was behind me. Better to let it go. For now. For now...

I drifted towards sleep, mercifully empty of thoughts. The magnet of Jerusalem had ceased pulling me. I let the clipped sounds of the pilot's Hebrew-accented English run over my ears. I marveled at the cleanliness of the plane.

But when I awoke on the descent into New York, I thought immediately of Jerusalem, of Hannah in Rehavia, the Wall, the markets, the mosques and churches and synagogues, the streets and alleys, the golden shimmer that seemed to color everything, the life of it all. Again, I had to remind myself: Acknowledge the past but leave it. Prepare for the future but don't obsess over it. Find the present.

As luck would have it, George was my chauffer from Kennedy back to the Shore.

"You look good," George observed as I dropped my bag in the back seat and climbed into the passenger seat beside him. "Tan. In shape. More calm. I'm guessing you had a successful trip. Am I right?"

"It was wonderful. Just what I needed—hiking, swimming, the Mediterranean sun, meeting people, getting out of my own head and troubles for a while. The country's incredible, George. There really is history around every corner, just like the guidebook says. The place is alive with it. Food and lodging are inexpensive, and in most parts of the country it's fairly easy to get around. In fact, I thought of you a number of times. They have these limos, like yours but older, that they call sheroots because they're shaped like a cigar. You see them all over. They're popular on longer trips, from the airport, from city to city, that sort of thing."

He laughed when I told him the story of my first sheroot trip, from the airport to Tel Aviv, with the elderly couple from Florida. "Yeah, they sound familiar. Maybe I gave them a ride the other day. Or someone like them. You get some real doozies in this business."

I told him more stories during the 90-minute drive to Eatontown, short versions of my love affair with Hannah, encounters with soldiers, survivors, Arabs, Hasids, artists, intellectuals, students, workers, Zionists, anti-Zionists, moderates, fanatics, *Sabras*, ex-pats, and tourists.

As we pulled up to the Crystal Inn across the road from Fort Monmouth, he said he was glad that the trip had gone so well. "Now I'm thinking of doing the same. Not going to Israel or another country. But maybe to Miami or Vegas or LA. Some place warm. Some place new."

"I recommend it," I said. Israel had restored my perspective. I was ready to try again in the United States. Israel, after all, had redeemed me.

9
Hawaii

MY SENSE OF REDEMPTION was short-lived. Soon after I entered my 40-dollar a night room at the Crystal Inn, I sank back into the same pit of despair that had been my life right before Israel. The psychological strength I had recouped in Jerusalem was gone. I was nearly broke and without obvious prospects, since I had taken no steps during the months I had been away to figure out what I would do next. The worst of it was being back at the Shore. In my fragile, easily threatened state of mind, I began to obsess about status and money, which in my mind were the prevailing local criteria for success. My present inability to fulfill either standard only reinforced the extent and depth of my depression. Status and money: without these in tow, how could I possibly face my family? I knew this continuing avoidance was a reprehensible way to treat them, but I couldn't bring myself to contact them.

Desperate for job leads, I compiled a list of academicians to contact, despite my earlier resolve to stay away from universities. I had no illusions that the several top-ranked schools interested in hiring me when I left Harvard would still have a position for me, and I figured I'd be lucky if any place would want someone two years removed from teaching who was applying unsolicited. But I did get lucky on just my second call, when a former colleague at Harvard said he knew a professor at the University of Hawaii who was scheduled to leave soon on sabbatical and was looking for someone to fill in for him while he was away. Hawaii... I had often fantasized about going there; what better place to spend a half-year. And the department there was excellent, even renowned in the field of comparative East-West philosophy.

"It sounds perfect," I told my Harvard friend. "There are dimensions of Eastern philosophy that I have an intense interest in exploring. I'd really look forward to working with certain of the faculty there."

There was a pause at the other end of the line. "The thing is, the position is not at the main Manoa campus in Honolulu. It's at the University of Hawaii in Hilo, on the island of Hawaii. But there's some interesting stuff going on there, academically and socially. The Hilo campus has excellent facilities, and the Big Island, as it's called, is an extraordinary place. I've been there."

Now it was my turn to pause. So much for the idea of status regained. But I needed a job. "It sounds intriguing," I said.

My friend promised to phone the departing Hawaii professor, Fred Harrington, on my behalf that evening. Late the next day Harrington called me, and within 15 minutes we worked out the salary and course-load details he would propose to Edgar Shiba, his department chair. Two days later, a contract and plane ticket arrived by special delivery at the Crystal Inn. The following week, I would fly to Honolulu, spend the night in a hotel, and catch a flight the following day to Hilo. I was scheduled to teach two undergraduate courses I still knew by heart from my Harvard years, and in any case there was ample time to request and receive the course syllabi I needed from Harvard's registrar. As an additional bonus, my letter of hire from Dr. Shiba stated that I would house sit, rent-free, for Professor Harrington while he was on sabbatical.

I was in happy shock now, both from my unexpected good fortune and the speed with which it had come my way. I considered calling my family to let them know my situation. But I didn't. What reason could I possibly have not to tell them I was okay, that I was healthy and employed? Basically, I chickened out. I was ashamed of myself on so many levels: as a wash out, a drop out, a divorcee, an absentee father, and a son and brother who hadn't the fucking decency to be in touch with them for a fucking year. That's it. I plain chickened out.

With Ellen it was different. During the time we'd been apart I mailed her postcards at least once a week and telephoned her whenever I could. Our conversations were animated and filled with stories about my latest adventures in Israel and hers in Anchorage. "How are Beanie and Karen doing?" I would always ask, priming her for the response I loved to get and she loved to give about her two stuffed-animal friends: "They're good, Daddy. We read your postcards together and they ask about you every day." Invariably, she would add that she read the postcards with her mother as well. "Mama loves them, too, Daddy." With all my heart I wished that the sentiment applied to the writer as much as the postcards. Was there any chance that my wish to be reunited as a family would ever be fulfilled, the wish I had stuffed as a prayer into a crevice in the Western Wall?

But I wasn't very effective at furthering my cause with Holly. I couldn't keep myself from being curt when she answered the phone. I couldn't get past my anger. And I was vague about my whereabouts, so even if my parents or Arnie had contacted her, which was highly improbable given our divorce, she wouldn't have been able to tell them anything other than that I was alive, as far a she knew, and last heard from somewhere in Israel. It might have been enough to have had that assurance. At least.

Dr. Shiba's letter had instructed me to pick up a courtesy van from Honolulu International Airport to the Kaimana Beach Hotel, where I was to spend a night before continuing on to Hilo. All expenses would be covered by the university, for which I was grateful. But the trip exhausted me, not so much because it took 11 hours, but more because of all the time it gave me to think and worry and second-guess my decision to have accepted this job. I couldn't shake this pessimistic frame of mind even as the van doors closed.

The driver informed me and several other passengers that the ten-mile drive down Nimitz Highway would take 20 minutes or so. Rolling through the dingy industrial landscape in that part of Honolulu, as well as seeing the wreckage of the ships in Pearl Harbor that had been sunk by the Japanese in 1941 and then turned into a macabre aquatic museum after the war, didn't help my mood. My unrelenting romanticism—reinforced by the South Pacific tales of James Michener, Mark Twain, Robert Louis Stevenson, Paul Gauguin, Sterling Hayden, and the TV series *Adventures in Paradise*—had led me to expect so much more. But the scenery gradually improved until, at the end of Kalakaua Avenue, the bus pulled up to a splendid, eight-story building whose sign read *Kaimana Beach Hotel.* The surrounding area, flanked by Diamond Head, was lush with palm trees and flowers. I could hear waves, even though the entrance was not on the hotel's ocean side. That view would have to wait, not that I was hopeful. What I had seen of the Pacific from the bus disappointed me. I had expected huge waves rolling in from the far horizon, but the swells I watched from the bus didn't look much different from what I had grown up with on the Atlantic, although I acknowledged that the view from Nimitz Highway was probably too distant to make a fair judgment. But my disabused pre-conceptions hardly mattered now; all I cared about was showering and sleeping.

My gloom lifted when I entered my room on the top floor. It was a corner suite with a balcony on two sides. One side overlooked the ocean. The waves I had dreamed of were there, all right, not especially high but so much longer in the intervals between swelling and breaking and reaching the shore than anything I had ever seen. And the Pacific's crystalline blue-green color, shimmering and transparent down to the underlying reefs interspersed with patches of blazing white sand, was also unlike any color I had ever seen. From the other balcony, I could see Diamond Head in one direction; in another, I had a long and unobstructed view over the zoo, past Kuhio Beach Park, and all the way back along the shoreline to the cluster of more established tourist hotels on Waikiki. I showered, ordered dinner from room service with my voucher from United, and spent the hours of remaining daylight and long into the evening lying on a lounge chair, amidst fragrances and breezes and sounds that exceeded any previous idea I had of paradise from books or movies. I was smitten by Hawaii.

The Aloha Airlines flight from Honolulu to Hilo the next morning took less than an hour. The Hilo region, on the windward side of the Big Island, was in a tropical rainforest, one of the wettest locales on earth with an average annual rainfall of 130 inches. But today it was as clear and bright, reinforcing the surge of optimism I had begun to feel at the Kaimana Beach. The views during the plane's descent over Hilo Bay were like a triptych lifted from *National Geographic.* Panel one featured the 14,000-foot Mauna Kea, the snow-capped dormant volcano which, if measured from its base on the ocean's floor, was higher than Mt. Everest. Panel two showed the two-mile long breakwater constructed in the 1920s to impede earthquake-generated tsunamis. It was more reassuring in appearance than effect, at least to judge from the hundreds I read about in my guidebook who had been killed by the devastating tidal waves of 1946 and 1960. Panel three was like a landscape painting which, without having seen the actual model, one could only attribute to the artist's fanciful imagination: impossibly blue water and lush green forests; waterfalls cascading down perfectly vertical cliffs; high-rising spumes of pure-white foam from waves breaking all along the shoreline; vast fields of hardened lava, textured and thick like frozen, metallic rivers—the creations, Hawaiians would say, of Pele, goddess of fire, lightening, wind, and volcanos, whose eruptions were Pele's way of expressing her longing to be with her own true love.

Hilo was the second-largest city in Hawaii, although "second-largest" was misleading in a state whose entire population numbered 750,000; Honolulu accounted for 600,000 of the total, Hilo 25,000. Despite the distinction of being Number 2, the town was in most ways the classic backwater: close-knit, slow-moving, quiet, safe, pleasant, and unpretentious. At the same time, somewhat incongruously, its airport was designated as international, and it was home to the second-biggest campus of the state university, my new, albeit temporary, place of employ. "Professor Kirinski?" someone hailed me as I waited for my one suitcase in the baggage claim area among a dozen or so other passengers. "Nathan Kirinski?"

"Here," I answered, turning to see an Asian man walk toward me with his hand extended. He had a necklace of flowers in the crook of his left arm.

"I'm Edgar Shiba," he said as we shook hands. "Welcome to Hawaii," he added as he put the lea over my head and laughed. "Sorry you got me instead of a hula dancer. I hope you had a good flight and pleasant stopover in Honolulu."

"It was a perfect trip from start to finish. I can't thank you enough for making the arrangements. The Kaimana Beach was paradise."

"I know I'm chauvinistic in saying that you'll find the Big Island even more of a paradise, but I have the excuse of being from here. If you're not too tired, I can show you around town a bit on our way to campus. Once you've filled out the standard personnel paperwork, I'll take you over to Professor Harrington's office—your office—and introduce you to whichever departmental colleagues are around. Once those niceties are over, I'll take you over to Fred's place—your place—to get settled."

"I never expected such a welcome, and from the department chair, no less."

"And I could never have anticipated our good fortune in having you join our faculty, even if it's only for the semester. I've read all of your books and articles. I'm still pinching myself in disbelief that you're here." He laughed. "Please stop me from waking up if it's a dream."

"I'm the one who doesn't want the dream to end."

Shiba's personable, laid-back, and sincere manner invited confidences. I decided to be straightforward. "You know that I was denied tenure two years ago, and I haven't taught or written anything since. Just having a job is a big deal for me now. I'm sorry. I mean..."

He laughed again. "No apologies necessary. This isn't exactly Harvard. On the other hand, it's as comfortable a setting to teach in as one can imagine. Not too many brilliant students, and they're all undergrads. But you'll find they work hard for the most part and want to make something of their lives. I'm anticipating that you'll enjoy your time here. You'll have three colleagues in the department, including me, and not a one of us is competitive. Besides...," he smiled here, "tenure's not an issue. So please, just enjoy yourself."

We began to get to know each other a little during the five-mile drive from the airport along Kekuanaoa Street to the building on West Kawili Street where the philosophy department was located. I learned that he had a doctorate from the University of Minnesota with a specialization in ethics. I asked the predictable question of how a Hawaiian had chosen to go to the frigid Twin Cities.

"The lure of a fellowship overcame my good sense." Again, the attractive laugh. "It was hard at first, I admit. Most of my stipend that first year went for parkas, blankets, and space heaters. But by the time I defended my dissertation and became Dr. Shiba five years later, I had come to like the place quite a bit—not enough, I hasten to add, to have a second lapse of good sense and remain there. The Hilo campus was expanding, state resources were being devoted to it, and having a successful local boy come back to teach and eventually chair a department was a very attractive profile builder for the school. I'm glad I made the choice to forego fame and fortune."

Edgar Shiba had become an inspiration to me in the 20 minutes it had taken us to reach campus.

After filling out my paperwork under the guidance of the departmental secretary, Dr. Shiba introduced me to the other two philosophy faculty members. Both were gracious and apparently as pleased to have me with them as Shiba said he was. I left the several books and files I had brought with me in my new office, a sunny, airy, spacious corner room full of Fred Harrington's books. It would be a fine place to work.

Dr. Shiba drove me the three miles to Harrington's home at 340 Lehua Street, a small but beautifully efficient place with a screened-in porch, koa wood-floored living room, modern kitchen and bathroom, and bedroom with a queen-sized mattress on the tatami floor. It had a small back yard with papaya, guava, and mango trees and its own driveway. A VW was parked there.

"Fred's beetle," Dr. Shiba said. He dug in his pocket and handed me a set of keys. "You don't really need house keys here. There's rarely any crime and almost never a break in. But here are the front and back door keys in the event you ever want to lock up. And you will need this third key for the car."

I must have looked confused. I had expected to take public transportation or walk the three miles each way to save money. "Fred wants you to use his car as well as his house, pots and pans, telephone, TV, linens, office, books, and whatever else you need."

This time I must have looked amazed. "Call it the Aloha Spirit," he explained. "What's ours is yours. You're one of us for as long as you're here. In Hawaii, 'paradise' is no abstraction." He laughed his friendly laugh. "Even for philosophers."

Despite my having been out of the academic saddle for two years, teaching was a breeze. There were no obvious Hegels, Hobbeses, or Heideggers among my students, but to a person they were earnest, polite, and easy to teach. And there was Ailani Kaluhiwa.

I was closing up for the day during the first week of classes when there was a knock on my office door. "Come in," I said, thinking it was one of the several attentive departmental assistants wanting to help and make me feel welcome. Instead, a hulking figure walked through the door.

"I'm sorry to bother you so late in the day, Professor Kirinski." His speech was slow, courteous, and correct but heavily accented. I soon learned to recognize the accent as Pidgin English. "My name is Ailani Kaluhiwa."

"Hello, Ailani. It's nice to meet you. Are you in one of my classes?"

"I'm not, but I'd like to study with you. You know, independently. A directed study."

In my experience, these weren't a responsibility to take on lightly. They could be time-consuming, burdensomely so with some students. And they were not included in one's course load. But something in Ailani's manner interested me—a thoughtfulness, an earnestness— and I decided to hear him out. I invited him to sit down. "What do you have in mind?"

The invitation seemed to animate him. Maybe he had been prepared for me to refuse. "I have an outline," he said, pulling a sheet of paper from a notebook and handing it to me. The project he proposed was titled *How I Want to Live My Life*, and the reading list included philosophers ranging from Plato to Buber and cultural sources spanning the globe. The topic struck me as perfect, one that every human being would benefit from exploring. When I told Ailani this, he beamed. "But what you're proposing is ambitious, and I'm only here for a semester. Still, I'm willing to work with you."

We spent the next hour brainstorming ideas for the project, and I asked him to come back in a week with a detailed outline of the paper he would submit at the end of the term. We also agreed to meet weekly to review his progress and discuss the readings. "I'm very grateful, Professor Kirinski. I won't disappoint you for taking me on."

I told Edgar Shiba about this the next day. "I hope I'm not making a mistake. I had never met the guy, and he's not one of my regular students.

I'm sorry if I overstepped any local bounds. But Ailani seems so sincere. And it's a more interesting and relevant project than any I can recall at the undergraduate level."

"It's a fine topic, especially in the local context, where the career you choose is never prioritized over the general quality of your life. I'm glad you agreed to do it, and I think you'll be pleased with the result. Ailani has definite promise. I'd love to see him go on to graduate school, preferably in philosophy. I can envision our catalogue now," he said, his distinctive smile amused but kind. "*Dr. Ailani Kaluhiwa, first homegrown, Polynesian Ph.D. in philosophy*. It would be a boon for the school and the department. But in any case, Ailani's not your standard Big Island student. He's not any place's standard student, for that matter."

However much time Ailani's directed study would require from me, I knew I could accommodate it. My two regular courses, "The Pre-Socratics" and "Introduction to Metaphysics," each required only three instructional hours a week. Best of all, my total six-hours a week of teaching, plus my meeting with Ailani and general office hours, were loaded into a Monday-Thursday schedule, which allowed me three full days each week to explore the Big Island. And the sobriquet "Big" is no exaggeration, both in terms of the island's size and diversity: 4,000 miles square, 95 miles from north to south, 80 miles from east to west, 266 miles of coastline, more than two and half miles from sea level to its highest point, and a topography transiting tropical rain forests, sugar plantations, macadamia nut farms, one of America's largest cattle ranches, vast lava fields, and archetypal Polynesian beaches.

Just as Israel had redeemed me, so did Hawaii. The diet, scenery, climate, pace of and attitude toward life restored my physical and emotional reserves. I enjoyed my students generally, and I learned as much as I taught in the directed study I did with Ailani Kaluhiwa. I grew to love the place and was tempted by the idea of living there forever. Half-way through my five-month stay, I approached Edgar Shiba with that thought in mind. He was diplomatic, but also clear.

"I'd love to have you here, Nate. The students like you, and so do the staff. But Fred and I are ten or more years from retirement, and the two younger faculty, who I'm hoping will be granted tenure, have much longer careers ahead of them. And as generous as the university has been to us, it's not likely that Hilo's philosophy department will ever get more faculty lines."

He tried to soften the message. "If a regular position ever opens up, you'll be the first person I contact to see if you're interested."

I thanked him for considering the idea and turned to leave his office. "Look, Nate," he stopped me. "You're a star. You've got important books and ideas ahead of you, but not if you stay here. You know how much I love this place. That plus the fact that I'm a professional philosopher gives me the basis for pointing out what should be obvious. Hawaii nurtures contentment, not philosophy. The place is soporific. It lulls you into such a pleasurable complacency that you never really want to do anything but wallow in the enjoyment. You're going through a rough patch now—I'm sorry. I know I'm being a bit personal here—but I have no doubt that your career will pick right back up when you're ready for that to happen. And that wouldn't happen here even if there were a position. Possibly at the Manoa campus. But more likely one of the big-name schools on the Mainland."

I thanked him again, without adding that the prospect of going back into that world filled me with a dread equivalent to dying.

In November, Hannah came for a two-week visit. Our time together was paradise within paradise. I had afternoons free in addition to full days on Friday, Saturday, and Sunday. We put hundreds of miles on Fred's car crossing the island and driving its perimeter: up the Hamakua Coast along the Mamalahoa Highway through places with names we delighted in trying to pronounce, names that had no relationship to English or Hebrew or any of the European languages we had studied—soft, vowel-laden names like Papaikou, Pepeekeo, Kawainui, Honomu, Wailea, Hakalau, Honohina, Ninole, Laupahoehoe, Kukaiau, Honokaa, and Waipio. Then along the Kohala coast through Pololu and Hawi before turning down the island's sunny leeward side through Kawaihae, Kaunaoa, Hapuna, Puako, Anaehoomalu, and Kailua-Kona to Kealakekua Bay. Then to and fro across the island, once via the high Saddle Road skirted on the north by Mauna Kea and the south by Mauna Loa, once via the ranch country surrounding Waimea, and once through the volcanoes and lava flows in the Puna district south of Hilo. We lolled on beaches and made nightly love. And we talked, concluding by the end of her visit that ours would not be a relationship for the long term, even if I did return to Israel. Or rather, that's what I concluded.

"But why?" she asked, hurt and confused.

I tried to explain. "Do you remember that day I went to synagogue with you?" She nodded, and I continued. "That's when I realized it would never work. The *mechitzah* separating the sexes, the *sheitels* hiding women's sexuality to protect the men from their masculine urges—the whole proscriptive, guarded world of Orthodox Judaism. And there's the prevailing mindset of that world, especially in Israel. It's far more nationalistic and self-referential and rigid than I would ever be able to accept. And the flip side would be true for you. How could you ever tolerate my conciliatory, compromising approach to things—Jews befriending Arabs, Jews marrying Christians, Jews being apologetic about or even surrendering their designation as God's Chosen People, much less surrendering certain portions of land occupied by Israel—would be more than you could abide."

"I understand our political differences, Nathan. And I honestly don't see those as the main problem. Jews with different ideologies have always been able to unite when it comes to our people's survival."

"So what is the main problem, then?"

"That deep down you want to be reunited with Holly and Ellen."

Hannah was the last to board her plane to Honolulu, where she would catch a flight to Toronto and a three-day visit with her uncle in Ottawa before returning to Israel. Our farewell was affectionate and wistful. Affectionate for all we had shared and enjoyed together. Wistful for what would not continue.

"I wish you well, my beloved *Natan*," she said before walking into the plane. "With whatever comes next, I wish you *shalom*, I wish you peace. Or maybe," she added with what I knew was genuine kindness, "I should say *Ma shlomkha?*"

Ma shlomkha—What is your peace?

10
Anchorage

IT WAS MID-DECEMBER and Anchorage was under snow. The plane landed while the sun was still high and shining off the south face of Denali, which was visible nearly 200 miles away. By the time the plane rolled up to the terminal my nerves had settled down to the point of numbness. The reunion I had carefully choreographed in fantasy during the flight decomposed before it could ever be enacted. My imagined heroic poise, strength of character, kindliness, and wisdom had evaporated somewhere over the Kenai Peninsula. I was left instead with the embarrassing realization that, after five months in the blood-thinning climate of Hawaii, I had come to Alaska ten days before Christmas without a coat. The imposing personality I had mentally created for myself unraveled against the fact of such an oversight.

Ellen, five years old now, was the first person I saw as I left the ramp and entered the terminal. Christ, she had grown in the months I'd been away from her. She came running toward me, a 41-inch version of the Michelin Tire Man all bundled up in a white quilted snow suit, her oversized rubber boots shuffling across the airport linoleum. I had feared she would be shy with me, but we took to each other immediately and fully, as if, like in the old days, I had just returned from a brief conference or speaking engagement. And then I was holding her, feeling the comforting weight of her. We stayed like that for a long moment while I kept my back to Holly and her boyfriend. *Idiot*, I told myself. *Don't ever let them see you cry.*

I jerked my head back to look at the child hugging my neck. "Gosh, it's wonderful to see you," I said, marveling at who my daughter had become during our months apart. "It's been so long." I could tell she was moved, too, and happy.

"Daddy, I've got so many things to tell you about," she began with a rush. "I've got a new cat named Calico who just came out of the street one day to live with me and I go to kindergarten now where my best friend's name is Lisa and where this boy named Shad is always bothering us because his lips are dirty when he tries to kiss us."

By then I had set her down and was stooping next to her, trying to take in her avalanche of words and handle my own implosion of feelings. I knelt there revering the details of her—the blond, soft hair grown several inches longer; the slightly epicanthic eyes (a trait mysteriously born, Holly and I used to joke, from my fascination with Asia); her precocious vocabulary.

The others came up to greet me.

"You must be cold," Holly said, indicating my bare arms.

"Freezing," I replied as I gave her a hug. "And I haven't gotten past the airport yet. I'm probably the only person in Anchorage daring and dumb enough to try and get by with a tan and a short-sleeve shirt." It was a good try at recovering a largely irrecoverable dignity.

"Don't worry about it," said Warren the boyfriend as he offered his hand in greeting and gestured at my small backpack. "We figured you wouldn't be carrying winter clothes around for all your months in warm weather just to make a two-day visit here. Try these on." Warren handed me a high-necked rag sweater, a wool scarf, mittens, and a bulky down coat with hood. After I put all that on, Warren added wool socks and a pair of white bunny boots, the air-insulated rubber moon shoes that are as warm as they are unwieldy. Clad in these, I took Ellen's hand and followed Warren and Holly toward the exit. On the way, I glanced empathetically at the airport's landmark, a stuffed polar bear in a glass case standing on its hind legs in some taxidermist's vision of ferocity.

By the time we left the airport it was 3:00 p.m. and already dark. We slid across the ice-covered parking lot to the car, where I received an exuberant greeting from Jake, Warren's Golden Retriever. We drove to Fairview, the residential section where Holly and Warren's small house was situated. The ride was mostly taken up with Ellen's headlong chatter about Lisa, school, and the dirty-lipped Shad who, aside from being uncouth, "is the same race as me, half Jewish and half other stuff."

I was comfortable in that car, sitting in the back between Ellen and Jake. I was enjoying her monologue, the questions they all had about Israel and Hawaii and my own voluble and amusing answers to those questions. Objectively, I thought, this whole setting is not something I ought to be enjoying. It's too cold. It's prematurely dark. My ex-wife sitting in the front seat next to her boyfriend is an emotional risk for me. But I'm here with my child. For two days and a night I'm a father again.

After an early dinner, Ellen and I played and read together until her bedtime. She had accumulated a lot of books and toys, including a number I had sent her. I had tape recorded some of the books so that she would at least have my voice around. Knowing that helped allay my fear she would forget me. Now, she said, she would like to go through the taped books with me in person, "the real thing."

"I'll be happy to be the real thing for you, Ellen," I laughed. "Let's see if you like me as much in person as you do on the tape."

We had been reading together for some time when, in the middle of a story about Leo the Lop, a bunny whose life and adventures demonstrated a seemingly endless procession of moral lessons, she closed the book and asked, "Why aren't you and Mama married anymore?"

I tried to talk around the question. "I don't know, sweetheart. We still really like each other. You know, as people. We're still friends. We just ended up wanting to do different things and live in different places. So we stopped being married."

She looked at me as if I were telling a Leo the Lop story, a story where everything ends, if not always happily, then at least for the good, where life exists for the sake of presenting us with persuasive maxims, a child's Book of Job. Halfheartedly, I gave it another try. "We just live such different lives now that it's too hard to stay together." Christ, I thought. What am I supposed to say to her? That it didn't happen all at once? That through a combination of thoughtlessness and sullen moods, mostly mine, we fell from devotion to disaffection in a matter of seven years? Or that Ellen's own birth, which came midway along the descent, had not been enough to turn things around?

"Are we all ever going to be together again?"

"No, sweetheart. I'm afraid we never will."

She started to cry, very quietly. I held her, crying even more quietly. We stayed like that until, trembling at intervals, she fell asleep, brought up and then down by the expectations and disillusions of the day.

When she was asleep, breathing regularly, I disentangled myself from her arms and walked to the door. I went into the bathroom to collect myself. It took some posturing in front of the mirror before I felt prepared to join the others.

Holly and Warren were sitting at the kitchen table.

"How'd it go?" Holly asked. She seemed both sympathetic and nervous.

"Fine. She's hopped up, so it took a while for her to fall asleep. It's amazing to me that she's asleep at all. I remember those first years in Cambridge when it seemed like she was always awake. She's a lot calmer now. And polite. You guys have done a nice job with her."

Holly smiled at the compliment, an appreciative smile that told me I had just become less of an enemy. "Thanks," she said. I would have understood if she had added, "I needed that." Instead, she changed the subject and told me that some friends would be stopping by to see me. I was happy about that. They were people I liked. Holly asked me if that would be a problem, if I'd be too tired. In truth, I was exhausted. I'd been awake full time since turning in my grades the day before. But I was keyed up past the point of sleep. "I'm okay. I'm glad they're coming."

We traded news of family and friends until the others arrived. Holly's sister Kate and her boyfriend Chuck got there first. They were partners in a small trailer repair business and were going to be married soon. Leonard Richardson, a bisexual piano teacher with an alcohol problem and a very large heart, showed up next. We caught up on one another's lives until Walter, Dee, and Julia got there. Walter was Warren's younger brother, Dee was Walter's fiancée, Julia was Walter's former wife. Walter, Julia, Holly, and I had all lived together during our year in West Virginia. Marital discord had hit us all at about the same time, and it was primarily through Julia's influence that Holly had decided to try Anchorage. Holly's sister Kate had followed Holly there. Walter, Warren, and Chuck were Alaska natives, and Leonard, as far as I could tell, appeared in Alaska at the tail end of a drunk that had started somewhere in Massachusetts. It had always been disconcerting to me that I liked them all as much as I did. It was an incestuous assortment who could be rowdy, unreliable, uncouth, and alcoholic. They were also generous, exuberant, and un-pompous, and it was only when I was not with them that I thought of them in any negative way, a judgement formed by the circumstantial fact that they had been witnesses to the dissolution of my marriage. Now I was enjoying them. By the time I left Anchorage, though, I predicted that I would resent and dislike them merely for being Alaskans and friends of Holly, unwitting accomplices against my wishful self-image as a husband and conventional father.

We stayed up listening to music and talking about travel, gurus, and old friends from West Virginia. And we drank. I tried to pace myself. I had tried to cut back on booze in Israel and Hawaii and had attended AA meetings in Hilo. In the company of this crowd, I was worried that I'd slide back into the heavy drinking habits I had been fighting since Claymont. I wasn't fighting them very well at the moment.

By 2:30 a.m., everybody except Warren and me had either left or fallen asleep.

"You must be ready to drop," Warren said.

"I should be unconscious or even dead by now," I joked. "I don't know what it is. Alcohol and exhaustion stimulate me. I need sleep, but I'm too wound up, like I've been on Benzedrine for days. Probably when I get back to Hawaii I'll end up sleeping around the clock. Maybe not, though. I've been a real light, four-hours a night sleeper ever since Ellen was born. Even now, long after I last lived with her, I keep listening for her to cry."

I thought for a moment, and then added, "Ellen obviously likes you a lot. I'm jealous of that and your time with her. But I also want you to know that in my better moments I'm glad it's you and that you're good to them."

We were quiet for a while, aware of the irony of this confidence between rivals.

Warren poured us each a drink. "It's been hard with them," he began. "When we first started living together last year, Ellen wouldn't have anything to do with me. She kept saying that she was going to kill me, that she wanted her daddy back."

Knowing I should be distressed, I instead silently thanked her for her homicidal threats in my behalf.

"Things are an awful lot better now between us, though," Warren continued. "Not too long ago I was putting her to bed when she started to cry and asked if I'd be her daddy. I told her no, and never to forget that she has a daddy—You."

I wanted to kill Warren for telling me that. I hated all of them at that moment: the mother for going away, the kid for giving me up, and the boyfriend for just being there and talking. Warren looked like he knew he had said something stupid. I knew he meant no harm and that he cared about Ellen. "It's been hard on her," I offered. "We screwed up her world and now she has to put it back together however she can. Your help is as important as mine is for her. More, because you're with her every day. Just keep being good to her."

We sat there drinking for a few minutes, each in our own thoughts. Warren broke the silence. "Holly is going through a lot of troubles now," he began, "and I don't know what to do about it. She's getting more and more depressed about what happened between you two, the breakup and all. She feels a lot of guilt about her part in it and is always talking about wanting to die so she can be in another world, she says, where she'll be happy. I'm worried about her, that she'll just stay this way or even kill herself."

Warren was obviously hurting as he related this, all slouched down in his chair and discouraged. But shit, I thought. Truth be known, I welcomed the news of her depression and guilt. Damn right, I told myself. She took my kid away. She deserves a dose of agony and second thoughts. But thoughts don't have to be words. "She's always been hard on herself," I said. "We were too much alike that way. We think we're directly to blame for everything bad and nothing good. Give her time. She'll be okay. And her share of blame is the smaller part for sure. Believe me, she'll recognize that and be okay."

It was 4:00 a.m. when we said goodnight. I felt close to Warren by then and had to admit I liked him. I recalled having the same reaction to Ben, Holly's previous boyfriend, the one in West Virginia who, if not responsible for our breakup, certainly helped catalyze it. How did I get to be so goddamned civilized and forgiving, I asked myself as I spread a sleeping bag out on the living room carpet. It was a rhetorical question. I had never developed the capacity for overt violence or the ability to channel my anger away from myself. Other people called the inability gentleness. After Claymont and Laurent's revelation of my chief feature, I thought of it as cowardice.

I turned off the light and crawled into the bedroll, where I was attacked by an armada of memories and feelings. Mostly, as I lay there in the godforsaken Alaska night, 20 feet from where my one-time wife was bedded down with her boyfriend, 10 feet from the room of the child I so rarely got to see, I wondered at the awful incongruity of it all while I drifted into sleep.

When I woke up Ellen was lying there looking at me. "Hi, Babes," I said, nuzzling her. "How'd you sleep?"

"Fine," she answered, turning around and putting her back against my stomach. She paused and then added in a playfully accusatory tone, "Daddy, your breath smells."

"What's it smell like today? Peppermint or spearmint or cotton candy?"

"More like a Big Mac," she retorted, giggling.

"That sounds serious. I better do something about it, or I may only get to talk to the back of your head from now on." I looked at my watch by the rays of electric light coming from the hallway. It was 8:30. I felt like hell, but I needed to make the most of this day with my daughter. "What time do you have to be at school?"

"I don't know. I better go ask my mom." She shuffled away in her footed flannel pajamas while I sat on the bedroll looking towards the window, wondering how it would affect you if you had to wake up each morning and go to work in pitch blackness. No thanks, I thought. That is far from my idea of the good life, and I knew I would be a sure casualty in the war against cabin fever.

Ellen ran back in. "I have to be there at ten o'clock. Mama says you better get up now if you're going to get me there on time."

I shaved and spent fully five minutes in the shower washing two days of accumulated grit out of my hair. I felt much better, confirmed in my conviction that shampooing is the great curative of our times, the event that renders millions of lives more bearable each day.

I helped Ellen get dressed and ready for school. By the time I got to the breakfast table, Warren had already left for work and Holly was about to leave. She gave me directions to the school, handed me the house key, and said she would meet me back here at three so I could use the car, if I preferred not to walk in the descending darkness, to pick up Ellen. Just before she got to the door she asked me to make sure the woodstove in the living room kept going all day. I had little idea what that would entail but was too proud to say so. "Sure. See you at three."

Ellen and I left the house at 9:30 for the mile walk to her pre-school. The temperature was average for Anchorage that time of year, about ten degrees Fahrenheit. Away from the water and across the mountains it would be 15 below zero. Thank God for little mercies, I thought, wondering how my thin blood, accustomed as it was to Hawaii, would fare through the trauma this climate was bound to cause it.

The snow wasn't deep at all; I figured we could make it to the school by ten without much problem. And I was glad to see that the sky held the beginnings of daylight. We walked holding hands, conversing as easily as I might with a fluent adult. I remembered an incident from the last time I saw Ellen, just before she and Holly left for Alaska. Ellen and I were playing a word game we had made up where one person says, for example, "I'm thinking of something you can see in the kitchen that begins with the letter 'S.'" An obvious answer is stove. "I'm thinking of something that begins with the letter 'U', and it's close to your mom," I said, guessing she might answer umbrella or underwear. "Uterus," she exclaimed with no hesitation.

Now we were describing to each other what we noticed around us as we walked to the school. "I see a white and gray world," I said, "with some brown houses here and there adding some color. It's not very colorful out there, is it? At least it's not to me."

"It's because you're not used to it here. So you don't know how to see all the colors. There are really lots of them. Some are left over from the summer, too, when I used a tall piece of grass to take colors from one place and brush them onto another. Now I can see those colors around us. Once they're painted on like that, they never disappear." I felt like Charlie Brown in a Peanuts cartoon I once read, where Charlie and Linus and Lucy are all lying on a hill looking up at clouds against a blue sky. Lucy observes, "Clouds always look like something to me. What do you see, Linus?" Linus says something like, "I'm reminded of the advent of the Four Horsemen of the Apocalypse over there on the left, while that cumulus mass straight above us is a fair facsimile of the lower panels in Rodin's Gates of Hell." After one silent frame Lucy says, "That's interesting. What do you see up there, Charlie Brown?" "I was going to say a donkey or a horsey," he allows, "but I changed my mind."

At the school, I helped Ellen get out of her winter paraphernalia and then let her show me around the facilities. I got to meet her teacher, her Korean-American friend Lisa, and the notorious Shad, whose lips did look like they were still at breakfast. When I was ready to leave, I kissed her goodbye and told her I would pick her up that afternoon. As I walked back to the house I relished, however temporarily, the sense I had of myself as a routine father.

I was disconcerted by the darkness that persisted through the morning, lifted for a couple of hours, and returned by mid-afternoon. I had heard that Alaskans were as likely to drink in the morning as they were in the evening. This morning it made perfect sense, so I poured myself a glass of bourbon to drink as I explored the house. I walked into Ellen's room and sat on her bed, slowly scanning the toys, books, and other belongings that lined the shelves. I was happy to see a neatly arranged collage of various picture postcards I had mailed from Israel and Hawaii: Marc Chagall's stained glass windows; the Pension Hadar, where I stayed in Safed; the clock tower, mosque, and harbor in Acre; the Wall, the Mosque of Omar, and the Church of the Holy Sepulcher in Jerusalem; the Yoram Youth Hostel where I stayed in Kare Deshe, on the Sea of Galilee; the excavations at Qumran, where the Dead Sea scrolls were discovered; Bedouins with their camels in the Sinai Desert; the Kaimana Beach Hotel in Honolulu; Rainbow Falls, Akaka Falls, Waipio Valley, Mauna Kea, and the volcano at Mauna Loa on the Big Island.

My eyes came to rest on a group of old stuffed-animal friends from our years together: Beanie Bear and his wife Karen Rapunzel; Peony, the purple lion; Flutterby, the magical flying horse. I took Beanie down and snuggled up with him on the narrow kid's bed. "Hello, Beaner. We're a long way from

Massachusetts." The bear had this quizzical, sympathetic look sewn on its face, a look that always used to make me think I had a friend in the world. Beanie was a masterpiece of consolation, and I was grateful to the geniuses at Pillow Pets responsible for the design. When things were beginning to accelerate toward disaster between Holly and me, we turned more and more towards Beanie as an emotional mediator. He was cute and cuddly and easy to talk to, and we were able to air our emotions through him in the other's presence, emotions we had trouble expressing directly to each other. Thank you, Beanie, for your patience and goodness in a world gone awry. You did your best.

I dozed off, and when I awoke the house was noticeably colder. Only a few coals were still lit under the grate in the woodstove. I put on my borrowed winter gear and went out to the porch to look for some wood. I could only find some shavings so took the ax that was propped against the wall, walked out into the yard, and went to work on a giant slab of tree trunk. In a half hour I was sweating from an effort that yielded barely enough wood to get a fire started. I was thinking of the embarrassment involved in spending the next few hours reading magazines in the drugstore to avoid freezing when I noticed some split logs under the stairs. I thanked whatever patron saint was in charge of green-horns as I got a passable fire going. Jake and Calico must have been feeling the cold, since they immediately curled up near the stove and went to sleep. I sat there on the floor watching them for a while and recalled how shattered I had been when Ellen phoned with the news that Warren had given her Jake as her dog. I wanted to be the one to give her a pet, just like I wanted to be the one to give her a bicycle. Now I looked ruefully at the bike with training wheels resting against the wall in the corner, while the tricycle I had given her for her third birthday sat in a corner of her maternal grandparents' basement back East. It had been there in the driveway when, two weeks after I bought it, Holly and Ellen drove away in our old VW wagon bound for Alaska. I had the clearest image of myself standing on that Worcester sidewalk, trying to get a last glimpse of them as they receded from my life.

I sat around drinking, reading, and stoking until, earlier than expected, Holly came home. She was friendly and energetic, although I sensed she'd had to gear up to be that way with me.

"How was your day?" she asked as she put her groceries away.

"Perfectly restful, except for a close brush with hypothermia. I'm no Daniel Boone when it comes to woodstoves and axes."

We had a cup of coffee while she told me about her job teaching French literature at the Anchorage campus of the University of Alaska and about Ellen's social and academic progress at school. I told her I would spend the following week in Hilo packing up my belongings before returning to the Jersey Shore. Shamed by how I had disappointed them, I also told her, I had not been in touch with my family almost from the time I left West Virginia, not even with my brother or sister. Now that I was feeling a bit more solid, I was ready to reconnect with them. I knew the reunion with Debbie and Arnie would be okay, that they'd forgive me. But I was anxious about the welcome I might, or might not, receive from my parents. That brief disclosure was as personal as the conversation would get. Holly and I had little to say to each other anymore, but we were polite enough to give it a try. The politeness and distance bothered me. Back in Hilo, I knew Hannah had been correct in her surmise that I still wanted to get back together with Holly, and not just because it would mean being with Ellen again. Now I realized that surmise was out of date. The wish to be with Ellen would always be there, but any desire to reunite with Holly was gone. Strange. I had spent seven years with this woman. Seven years. The time it purportedly takes the body's cells to die and regenerate. Some cells may never regenerate. I had to let it go. There would be no reconciliation. An accumulation of insuperable causes, large and small, obvious and subtle, had seen to that. In retrospect, it may have been the little things that proved the hardest to overcome. A poem I wrote soon after Holly and Ellen drove off to Alaska came to mind.

Slip of the Tongue

Young mother
on a Boston bench
baby at her breast.

Young father
feelings moved
expresses his affection.
You look so matronly
he says
confused when she cries.

I meant to say maternal
he reassures her
convinced it is a small thing
not understanding this omen
of the irreparable future.

I finished my coffee and walked to the school. Ellen had obviously been waiting; when I opened the classroom door, she was right there to greet me with a hug. As we got her clothing together, it was also obvious she was making sure the other kids got to see me with her. I was touched by that, and feeling guilty because I understood that today was her one chance to show off in this particular way.

When she was dressed, we headed out to the road. It was 3:00 p.m., but the streetlights were already on. A light snow began to fall as we crossed the overpass and made our way to a nearby shopping center. I had two surprises planned for her. The first was a visit to a novelty store where I let her pick out twenty dollars' worth of whatever toys she wished. She chose a set of multi-colored magic markers, a wild animal coloring book, a bag of balloons, a jar of liquid for blowing bubbles, and a slinky. To carry it all, I threw in a Snoopy backpack. For the second surprise, we went to Swensen's Ice Cream Parlor where she had a strawberry cheesecake, her favorite flavor. She observed that Swensen's was very tasty, and certainly less expensive than Häagen-Dazs, but that neither was quite up to her favorite flavors at Day's in Ocean Grove, New Jersey. She loved their ice cream, she said, and at every opportunity wore the "Day's Ice Cream" tee shirt I had sent on her previous birthday.

As we were finishing up our treats she said, "Daddy, I've been thinking a lot about how when I'm older I'd like to spend the school year with you sometimes and the summer with Mama. Mama says we'll see what's a good thing to do in a few years, maybe when I'm a ten-year-old. I sure hope I can get to do that."

"I hope we can arrange that, too. It would be wonderful to have you with me that long. It would be different, though. Now, whenever I'm with you I spoil you like crazy because we have such a short time together. If we lived together for most of the year you'd have chores to do, and I'd have to be strict with you sometimes. That's just part of being a father." She looked at me skeptically, as if she might want to qualify her plan to stay with me given this unanticipated possibility of strictness on my part. I laughed and added that, in spite of chores and discipline, our time together would be mostly fun. "Just remember," I went on, "that whether you live here or with me, you're the most important person in my life and I love you." The words sounded feeble even to me. I wondered what must be going through her mind, a bright mind but nevertheless a child's mind. Did our family situation seem as out of joint and frustrating to her as it did to me? If so, then no words would put things back in order. I could only hope that my feelings for her were getting through.

When we left Swensen's she said she now had a surprise for me, a special place called the Gravel Pit that she wanted me to see on the way home. I asked her why it was a special place. "Well," she said, "it's real quiet and private there. It's like my own country, and it has a hill of stones right in the middle of it. Sometimes I take Lisa there and I let her be the princess of the Gravel Pit Kingdom. But mostly I go there alone. It's safe because my mom can see it from our house and can hear me if I yell. The only times I can't go there are when the big trucks are picking up and dropping off gravel."

"It sounds like a good spot."

"It is good, Daddy. And certain very special things happen there."

"Like what?"

"Well, at the end of last summer I was playing there by myself after supper. I was sitting on the gravel hill counting stones and pretending they were gold when a moose came and stood real close to me for a long time."

"Weren't you afraid? I mean, a moose can be dangerous."

"No, I wasn't scared at all. I just knew that moose wasn't going to hurt me. He was there for company. He knew that I wouldn't try to hurt him, either."

"What happened then?"

"Nothing much. We just stayed there looking at each other for a while, until it was time to say goodbye. Then he walked away toward the trees over past Walter and Dee's house. I was real, real sorry to see him go, and I could tell he didn't really want to go. He seemed like a very sad moose. But I've seen him a lot since then."

I didn't want to deflate her and point out that the city of Anchorage, nearly a quarter of a million strong, was an unlikely habitat for a moose. So I side-stepped the topic by saying I had only seen moose in zoos, and that once I had been at a zoo when a moose had fallen through the ice over the pond in his enclosure and had to be pulled out by ropes around his antlers. Someday, I added, I would like to see a moose in the wild.

"That's the surprise I have for you. I've never seen a moose in a zoo. I've only ever seen this one I told you about. But I can see him whenever I want, because I know when he'll be in the Gravel Pit. He's going to be there today. That's why I'm taking you there."

As we walked, I thought about what I would say to her when her moose didn't appear. That the animal had to go elsewhere to find food. Or that some people probably scared him away. I didn't want to dampen what she obviously meant as a gift for me, however odd and improbable an offering it was.

The Gravel Pit was an area about 150 yards in circumference. It was surrounded by empty fields on two sides, several houses, including Ellen's, and a grove of evergreen, presumably the woods the moose entered after he left Ellen. The ground had been rutted by the wheels of front-end loaders and dump trucks. The ruts were frosted white and looked like spokes emanating from the hub of the gravel mound. We walked to the mound and sat down after climbing ten feet or so up the side facing the woods.

"We'll just sit here for a while," she said. "The moose will be coming soon."

I knew it was a farce but was prepared to stay there with her until she called it off. After a few minutes she grabbed my hand and whispered, "Daddy. Look. My moose."

A moose, his outline clear and definite against the snow, was walking toward us. I sat without moving, startled but unafraid; there was something strangely poignant and personal and unintimidating about the animal. The moose stopped for a moment about 50 feet from us, then continued his approach until he stood at the foot of the hill where we were sitting, the tips of his antlers nearly level with my eyes.

Everything was quiet for what must have been 30 seconds. Then the moose tossed his head and began climbing the hill. He stumbled in the loose gravel and nearly went down, only regaining his balance as one of his knees hit the stones. He backed off the hill and stood there staring at us. I was transfixed. Before I could react, Ellen slid down the hill to within a few feet of the animal. Standing there next to him in her quilted suit and tasseled ski cap, she looked like a gnome whose magic made her invulnerable to the natural giants in her domain.

I held back a yell when she walked up to the moose and rubbed her mitten over his muzzle as he stood with his head bowed. When she stopped, the moose tossed its head another time, turned, and walked slowly back toward the grove of evergreen. The spell broken, I slid down and joined Ellen. I took her in my arms and began to shake with released tension. She was quite still as she watched the animal move away. Finally, I set her down and we walked without speaking toward the house.

After dinner I helped Ellen get ready for bed. She knew I would be leaving that night after she was asleep, and during her bath we spent a lot of time talking about the two planes I would be riding and how long it would take to get to Honolulu and then Hilo.

"Someday, I want to take a long trip with you on a plane to one of those places you go to, like Israel or Hawaii."

"I want you to see Israel especially," I said as I toweled her off. "I'd like to live there for a while. When you're older, you could live there with me."

"And I wouldn't have to go to school there," she proposed. "You could teach me, and I could just travel around seeing things with you."

I laughed and helped her into her pajamas. As I zipped them up she watched my face intently, her expression both serious and timid. "Daddy, please don't leave," she began. "You could stay here in Alaska and live with us and get a job here and that way I would see you every day and not miss you." She put her arms around my neck. "Please don't leave me again."

I carried her into her room and sat her on the bed, holding her tightly for a while before I said anything. What could I say? That Alaska was not for me? That I didn't have the inclination to be more than an infrequent visitor in my ex-wife's new life? That her mother was equally disinclined to have me around? But hell, if I were a little kid no reason in the world would suffice to explain the departure of a parent. Even death wouldn't explain it.

"I have to go, Ellen. I'm out of place here in Alaska. It's not my home." She didn't say anything, so I continued. "Look, sweetheart. I'm like that moose in the Gravel Pit, out of place and clumsy. I came here only because you're here. I came to see you and nobody else. There's nothing else here for me. I can't stay or I'll start stumbling around like he did when he tried to climb the hill. It was no place for him. He knew he had to leave, and I know I have to leave."

I put her under the covers and lay down next to her. There was no way to know what she was thinking. After several minutes she stirred and held my face in her hands. "Daddy, after you go will you promise to keep doing our special exercise, the one you taught me the summer before I came to Alaska?"

"I promise. Whenever I'm lonely for you, I'll close my eyes and picture your smiling face and breathe that picture down deep into my heart. It'll be my way of calling you and having you with me whenever I miss you and feel sad."

Again there was a long silence until she said, "I want to do that special exercise now." We both closed our eyes and breathed deeply. I pictured her, laughing and happy, until the image was as definite as her shape beside me. I took that face deep into my heart, to be kept there and peered at like a photo in a locket.

Soon she was asleep. I stood up as quietly as I could and looked down at her. I had a strong urge to kidnap her then, to bundle her up and jump out the window and take a plane to some untraceable spot. The urge passed and I went over to bid a silent goodbye to Beanie before walking out the door.

Fifty minutes later I was once again passing the stuffed polar bear in its glass case at Anchorage Airport. I had just bid goodbye to Holly and given her the borrowed winter gear to return to Warren. I was leaving as I had arrived, wearing shirt-sleeves and a tan.

At 10:00 p.m. I boarded my flight to Honolulu. Twenty minutes later the plane lifted out of Anchorage. Yesterday I had been exhausted and apprehensive. Tonight I was merely exhausted.

I closed my eyes, hoping for sleep to descend and obliterate all emotion. Instead, a terrible sadness invaded my chest and rose up into my throat as I was assaulted by the image of the moose. He walked back toward the evergreens and then turned to look at me, high-antlered and dignified, before stepping into the woods.

11
Deborah

ON NEW YEAR'S DAY of 1980, I phoned Arnie from Hilo to tell him I was returning to the Shore. My brother is not an emotionally expressive person. For some moments he was silent, and I could only guess that his inner reaction to hearing from me after two years of no contact was a mixture of surprise, relief, and anger. But he showed none of this. I would have preferred it by far to his coldness.

"So what's your plan?" he finally asked.

I told him I would fly into Newark in two days, take a limo to the Crystal Inn in Eatontown, and settle into whatever rental I could find in the Belmar area before contacting our family. Then I'd figure things out from there.

"You'd better come to my place in New York City first. I'll pick you up at the airport. There are some things you'll need to know before you see the folks."

He didn't elaborate; it was a long-distance call after all, and there would be plenty of time to catch up on family news. I gave him my itinerary. "See you on the 3rd," I said. There was no answer. He must have already hung up.

He was waiting for me in the arrival area. I rushed to hug him, kiss him, but he would only shake hands. "Look. I imagine you'll have some explanation to offer for two years of silence. What might be explainable, though, likely won't ever be excusable from my point of view. But let's address all that another time. Now the important thing for you to know is that Deb is dead."

I sat down hard in the nearest chair. Arnie relented. "I'm sorry, Nate. I shouldn't have been so abrupt, and I certainly should never have mixed up my anger at your absence with what I had to tell you. I'll fill you in when we get to my place."

We hardly spoke during the hour-long drive to his apartment on Riverside Drive, but once inside we talked late into the night. Deborah had died six months before from pancreatic cancer, he told me. "It's a rapid-onset cancer with no method of early detection. You know she smoked a lot from the time she was a teenager. That may have been a cause. Who knows?" She had the best of care, Arnie assured me, thanks mainly to her husband's professional contacts. Eddie was a cardio-vascular surgeon, not an oncologist, but a former medical school professor of his was high up in the Sloan-Kettering hierarchy, and he had taken a personal interest in Deb.

"Still," Arnie added. "It was a horrific, painful demise. Towards the end, morphine hardly helped, and she was begging Eddie to euthanize her. Honestly, I don't know whether or not he did. Probably not, or some authority would have figured it out and taken punitive action by now. It was awful for Fay and Mort. They couldn't help. They watched her die in the worst agony. I tried to help..." he stopped and turned away, his facial muscles twitching, then collect-ed himself and continued. "But the agony went beyond physical pain. Deb told me that Eddie had been having an affair, before and even during her illness. I don't know if it was true. She was so screwed up and delusional from the pain and drugs. Probably it was true, knowing Ed. I also don't know whether Deb said anything about it to our parents. I hope not. Losing a 42-year-old daugh-ter was hard enough. Thinking the circumstances at the end of her life were emotionally devastating, whether the cause was real or imagined, would have made it that much worse. In the end, both her body and mind were ravaged. The degeneration of her appearance deeply bothered her, and she insisted on being cremated. As you can guess, with our family's Orthodox background, however distant, cremation roiled things up more."

And I was absent through it all. Disappeared. Inaccessible. Uninvolved. Not only of no help whatsoever, but an extra burden of concern to my whole family.

Arnie never asked about my long disappearance, and I didn't introduce the topic. Instead, we talked about Debbie. She had been our shared hero-ine for all of our years together. We worshipped her, despite the inevitable episodes of mostly humorous discord between older and younger siblings. "Do you remember the shit-and-hell incident, Nate? That was pure Deb. And pure you."

"How could I forget? The scene, the Calvary Baptist Church a block down from our house on E Street, is still perfectly clear to me. Deb was baby-sitting both of us, but you were such an easy kid. She could trust you to stay put in our room reading baseball biographies. I even remember the title of the book you had just taken out of the library, *Ralph Kiner: Timber Unlimited*. Poor Deb. She still had me to bother her, but at least she could devote all her attention to my latest acting-out behavior. That day, I tried my first curse words on her. 'Shit and hell,' I said." Arnold was smiling. I rushed on with the story to take advantage of the thaw. "Deb stared at me threat-eningly. 'What did you say?' 'Shit and hell,' I repeated. 'You better not say that again,' she warned. 'Or else.' We were in our living room. I began to ma-neuver away from her. I walked through the kitchen. When I got to the back door I turned and screamed, 'Shit and hell!' and tore out of the house, run-ning south down E Street. Deb caught me when I reached the sidewalk next to the church—you remember how strong and athletic she was." Arnie was laughing now. "Already exhausted, I fell. She swooped in on me, hand raised to strike, when a woman leaving the church walked past. She and Deb ex-changed greetings, as if I weren't there or about to be walloped. The woman passed. 'Now, what did you say?' our sister repeated. 'Nothing,' I answered, in apparent defeat and contrition. She let me up and walked back toward our house. I went in the other direction, towards 13th. I got to the corner, turned, yelled 'Shit and hell!' and was gone." We were both laughing now. Together.

"She was tough on me, too, from time to time," Arnie said. "Remember when I was stressing out that the Asbury Park draft board wouldn't grant me a student deferment? You had already received yours, and I was sure they would never give two to the same family. Deb, a practicing physical therapist by then, had the most forthright, if frightening, idea. She offered to tear my knee cartilage. Remember? She had me stand in the doorway between our parents' kitchen and dining room, my leg braced against the threshold in such a way, she assured me, that a crisp tackle by her would do the job. "This will hurt, but not as much as Vietnam." As I stood there, getting ready for her to charge, I couldn't help thinking of the Charles Schulz annual fall *Peanuts* cartoon, where Lucy holds the football and moves it just as Charlie Brown rushes in to kick it. In this case, I was Lucy, my leg was the ball, and Deb was Charlie. Every time she came in for the kill I chickened out and pulled my leg away. Unlike Charlie, Deb gave up trying, disgusted that I hadn't the courage to follow through with her plan to destroy my knee and save me from the army. If the roles had been reversed, you know Deb would have seen it through and not moved her leg."

I had to agree. "She was courageous, for sure, especially when it came to trying out new things and making friends with types who were not part of the conventional Jewish social fold. Maybe it was because she never felt part of that fold herself. You and I were barely toddlers when we moved from the Bronx in 1946. Belmar was always home to us. We never had to adjust. We were always part of the place. It was different for Deb, really rough, as she later told us. She was ten at the time. She had been happy and successful in vibrant New York, surrounded by relatives and friends. Belmar was tiny and in-bred. All of her classmates had grown up together. She was the lone and lonely outsider. In the beginning, they spread gossip about her, I think out of jealousy that she was so smart and pretty, and later because she chose to have friends—non-Jewish, Black, whoever—beyond the acceptable in-group. There were compensations, of course. The attractions of the beach and the marina boosted the population to 50,000 in the summer back then, and things came alive. In addition to the pleasures of sand and surf, what youngster could resist the excitement of the concerts, arcades, amusement parks, and eateries that were there to accommodate the influx? After a socially unhappy first school year in Belmar, she began to thrive the following summer, when she had the chance to meet city kids who felt as out of place as she did. And the dreaded New York State Regents exams had no analog in New Jersey. Belmar Grammar School was a relative cinch for Debbie academically. Eventually, she adjusted and thrived in Belmar's society, despite her classmates' periodic mean-spirit-edness. But I always had the feeling that she continued to like New York the most, and that she had a particular affinity for outsiders."

"She certainly accepted and made friends with all sorts of people," Arnie said. "She had a great capacity for that. It was a big part of the courageousness

I mentioned. I'm thinking of the incident with Captain Butler of the *Early Bird*. Remember him?"

"Oh yeah. He was the only African-American commercial boat owner and skipper in the Belmar fishing fleet. I can still picture a tall, thin, friendly man whose ability to step from boat to upper dock without stepping on the intervening five feet of lower dock totally impressed me. And Captain Butler was exceedingly generous in taking kids out for short sails on the *Early Bird*. You and I got to know him because Deb and two or three of her girlfriends started sailing with Butler as part of their membership in Sea Scouts. Occasionally, younger siblings were allowed to tag along. These forays ended quickly after the girls' parents began expressing qualms about Captain Butler's 'personality,' which was code then for the parents' suspicions, valid or not, about what might motivate a man—a Black man, at that—to spend so much time, at least once on a fishing trip that extended well into the evening, with an attractive group of teenage White girls. I'll never forget the night Deb charged into a meeting the parents had in our house to discuss their qualms. We could hear it all from our bedroom. She really blew them out. She actually called them racists. It didn't change their thinking, though, and we know from what Deb told us later that it all added up to lasting disappointment and anger at the adults for removing the *Early Bird* and Captain Butler from her life."

"A paragon of tolerance, our sister," Arnie said, "a real trend-setter for a young girl in the 1950s. The Captain Butler situation was about race. But the bigger issue was Deb's willingness to welcome religious differences. What a head-ache for our parents. Deb definitely broke the mold when she began dating non-Jews in high school. Remember Joe Stillwell, her date for the Junior Prom, the guy from the sticks of Wayside who picked her up in his black Chevy hot rod? I can still hear Mort and Fay's groans when they saw his sideburns and duck's ass hairdo."

"Right," I said. "And it didn't get much better when she dated Costas Lambros all of her senior year. I used to overhear our parents' whispered concerns whenever she was out with Costas, and they thought we were asleep. Would she get pregnant? Elope? Convert to Greek Orthodoxy? Spend the rest of her life living over the Lambros family's Parthenon Restaurant in Asbury?"

We sat quietly for a while, sipping bourbon and privately reminiscing. "I can't get the long red hair out of my mind, Arnie. Or her beauty, talent, brains, and incredible gift for attracting friends. She had it all, I always thought."

"She did. At least for a while. But remember, too, how complicated she was, and how emotional and self-defeating, especially in her relationships with men. In a lot of ways, I think she was just too high strung, too intense. I'm only saying this now because I'm a little drunk. After tonight, I'll deny what I'm about to say: that she was too intense to last, and that her life had become such a disappointment to her that she didn't want to live it anymore.

She had an absolutely shitty marriage, the disappointment of being childless, and the sure knowledge that everything she had wanted to do earlier in her life—travel, romance—would never happen. The life she had in mind to live pretty much came to an end at age 26, when she married Ed. By then, her tolerance had extended too far, too late."

I had to concur. Basically put, Eddie—the future Dr. Edward Martino—was a racist and an anti-Semite. This was something Arnie and I weren't aware of as kids; Ed was eight years older, and the only contact we ever had with him until he started dating Debbie was visual, an occasional sighting from across the street. We only learned of our brother-in-law's prejudices years later from Jews in Eddie's peer group, kids whom he had terrorized on their way home from school with name-calling, threats, and punches, and also from comments Deb made to me, after she married, about Eddie's reaction to one of her Black co-workers. Ed's partner in persecution was Buster Layton, whom all of us kids knew to be a hater of Jews. The Laytons lived kitty-corner across 12th Avenue from us and, in another neighborhood irony, immediately next door to Rabbi Steinman.

But I had to consider that Ed Martino might have changed as a result of living with Deb. Had he gotten beyond all that? I hoped so. I liked him in some ways—his sense of humor; his intelligence; the hilarious stories he told about Belmar and its characters; his compassion, only in rare and unexpected moments with humans but (when he wasn't out hunting) unfailingly with animals, as with the gunshot-wounded Canadian geese he treated and harbored. In other ways, though, I detested him. His humor could turn to hurtful sarcasm in an instant. His sullenness could put a damper on any gathering or encounter. His momentary demonstrations of compassion morphed quickly into morose sentimentality, especially when some sad ballad was playing in the background. He hunted the same species he rehabilitated. He never gave up smoking non-filtered cigarettes despite being a cardio-vascular surgeon. He was abrupt and disrespectful to our parents. And then to find out he might have been cheating on Deb while she was dying.

My relationship with Ed troubled me, just as I know his own relationship with Ed troubled Arnie, although I doubt that anyone would have suspected any problems among the three of us from outward appearances. I was invariably cordial to Ed, and on occasion our interactions were personal, even affectionate. But I think that was the issue: I felt I needed to disguise my antipathy toward him in response to my parents' ardent wish—their constant beseeching, in fact—for me to be nice to him in order to keep our ties with Deb.

The sky was brightening over Manhattan by the time Arnie and I finished the bottle of Jim Beam and tried to catch a few hours of sleep before driving to the Shore for what was bound to be a tough reunion with Mort and Fay.

We continued reminiscing about Deb as Arnie made up the couch for me in his study. "I'll never forget the Shalimar perfume she always wore," I said. "I think of Deb whenever someone walks by wearing that fragrance. Sweet Deb. But do you remember the St. John's Bay Rum she insisted we use? 'The girls will like it,' she promised. 'And it will clear up your pimples.' That stuff stung like lye. And I don't recall that it attracted girls or cured acne. The Shalimar-St. John's Bay Rum dichotomy was an apt metaphor for Deb, wasn't it? Fragrant most of the time, but she could sting."

"The old Shalimar-St. John's Bay Rum dichotomy," Arnie laughed, and then became serious. "You know I can't help being an inveterate historian of Judaism. Much of the way I see the world comes from that, including the way I think about Deb, her temperament, her actions, the way she was. Even her scent—Shalimar is a concoction of Middle Eastern ingredients, you know. And her name in Hebrew, *Devorah*, has a related etymology. Basically it means 'bee,' which is a perfect representation: she really was like a bee, whose sting could be painful but whose honey was sweet. There's also a profound irony to her name. You remember Deborah in the Old Testament, the hugely influential prophetess who urged the Jews to return to God and who led a Jewish army against their godless Canaanite oppressors? Deb could have used the help of her biblical namesake, someone who could have protected her from her path of self-destruction, the path she took away from her people."

I couldn't tell whether or not Arnie was implying that there was a parallel between my sister and me, that we both might have benefited from a protector—she from leaving the entire nation of Jews, I from leaving four of them.

12
Morton and Fay

"AS YOUR FATHER, MY only emotion should be delight that you're alive. But that's not what I feel. What I feel is pure anger. Until today, we were afraid that we had lost two children. So the good news is that we only lost one. The bad news is that it was our Deborah."

My father walked into the bedroom and closed the door. I looked at my mother, hoping for some opening, some possibility of connection. Fay's expression was as sorrowful as Mort's had been angry.

"What he said was cruel. But it's his anger talking. And his concern for you. You have to understand this is as true for me as for you father. We've been worried sick not hearing from you. What else but to think that you were dead? How could you have done that to us? Why didn't you contact us? Or your brother? Or De..." She began to cry.

I looked over at Arnie, who had moved off to the side as soon as we entered my parents' living room, and then turned back to my mother. "I have trouble explaining it, my disappearance, even to myself. I'm sorry. So very sorry."

She walked up to me and raised her hand. I flinched, expecting her to strike me. Instead she touched my cheek. "We're both glad you're safe," she said, before following her husband into the bedroom.

Part Four

Householder Again

Nathan's Memoir
1980 – 1990

The next twenty-five years...were to be lived as a householder, as the head of a family, a prop to the old, a supporter to the wife, and a sound teacher to the children.

–Kirpal Singh

The householder must always please his wife with money, clothes, love, faith, and words like nectar, and never do anything to disturb her.

–Vivekananda

I've often thought I was never meant to be a householder. Maybe I should have become a monastic right out of high school, much as many Thai boys become Theravada bhikkhus when they turn 18. But then there would never have been Esther, who nullified all the maybes.

–Nathan Kirinski

1
Helpmates

"WE'RE SORRY THIS IS so impromptu," I told Arnie as he, Esther, and I sat in the waiting room of the City Clerk's Office on Worth Street in Lower Manhattan. It was a few minutes before noon on January 8, 1981, and Esther and I were about to be married in a civil ceremony.

"Please. There's no need to apologize. I'm thrilled that this is happening and honored to be your witness."

"We wouldn't have wanted anyone else," said Esther. "Thank you, Arnie, for agreeing to do this at such short notice. The application process is so quick and simple in New York, and there's no residency requirement here. And I hope you understand—if you hadn't been able to be here, we would have postponed our marriage until you could be here. You're that important to us. To both of us. It would have been wonderful to have your parents here, too. And I had thought about inviting my parents, but in the end decided not to go there. My family and I are estranged far past the point of any return. But I did have hopes for your folks..."

"Just so you know, Arnie," I jumped in, "I did invite Fay and Morton to be here, but they declined. It's disappointing, but hardly surprising."

"Give them time," Arnie said. "I know they'll come around. And in a broad historical sense—you know me—there is some connection to family in the vicinity other than me. Our maternal grandparents were married a mile and a half from here 83 years ago, also in January, in a temple that was once on East 4th Street."

A secretary called us into an office, and ten minutes later I was the husband of Esther O'Connell Kirinski. The official who married us—a judge or justice of the peace whose name I don't recall—offered each of us a congratulatory handshake, gave us our legal certificate, and left for lunch. The ceremony didn't quite have the pomp and circumstance of a Jewish or Irish-Catholic extravaganza, but neither of us cared. We were married. We experienced a special unity nearly from the moment we met. Now we had the letter to go along with the spirit.

When we got to the street Arnie handed me two keys. "What's this?" I asked.

"The silver one is the key to my building. The gold one is for my apartment. It's my gift to you. A three-day honeymoon in the Big Apple while I toil away in the grease and heat of Morton's Carousel Diner." He hugged Esther, who was crying. "Congratulations. I was getting impatient to have you become my sister-in-law." Then he turned to me. "*Mazel Tov*, my brother. With Esther as your helpmate, I couldn't be happier for you."

While Arnie took the subway uptown to pack a bag and get his car, my helpmate and I walked the ten miles through the city to his apartment off Riverside Drive, hand in hand the whole way.

We moved into a small, inexpensive, but comfortably furnished apartment on Bath Avenue in Ocean Grove, a literal stone's throw from the beach and not too far from the rooming house I had been living in since my return from Israel. It was hard at first for Esther. She loved her bungalow in South Belmar. But I planned to apply for work with the Ocean Grove post office, and we figured my chances of getting a job there would be improved with Ocean Grove residency.

At the same time, it felt odd for me to continue living there. Ocean Grove, despite its proximity to Belmar, was a foreign country to me when I was growing up. I had always thought of it as Holy Roller Central, even before I learned that it was actually called "The Queen of Religious Resorts." It was a camp meeting site founded by the Methodists in the mid-1800s, and in the summer months it's still a magnet for pilgrims, many of whom reside in tents surrounding "The Great Auditorium." And it was frighteningly prohibitive from my vantage point. The Camp Meeting Association owned most of the properties. They could be leased out, but for no more than 99 years. And it closed down, I mean actually closed down, on Sundays. You couldn't drive, bike, or (holy) roller skate. I still laugh when I remember an article in the *Asbury Park Press* reporting a Sunday accident, when the only two vehicles authorized to drive on the Sabbath, an ambulance and a police car, crashed into each other.

Gradually, though, Esther and I began to appreciate the town: its small population of three thousand; the walkability of its one square mile, the same size as Belmar; its impressive Victorian architecture; its history of celebrity visitors, including six U.S. presidents; it's uncluttered beaches and boardwalk; its proximity to my potential job and Esther's actual job, a mile and a half away, waiting tables and tending bar at Vic's Italian Restaurant on the corner of Evergreen and Main in Bradley Beach; and, especially for me, the fact that Southside Johnny, one of the originators of the Jersey Shore Sound in rock music, grew up there. We were content. Now it only remained for me to find work.

When I applied for a mail carrier position with the Ocean Grove post office, it looked easy enough to fulfill the requirements: I was over 18, a U.S. citizen, had a good command of English, could show proof of Selective Service registration, had submitted positive recommendations from several local residents, and had already passed the written exam. Now I only needed to get through the interview.

A short, wiry man stood up to shake my hand when I entered his office on Main Avenue in Ocean Grove. He introduced himself as Ralph Crandall, Director of Human Resources. "Thank you for your application,

Mr. Kirinski," he said, as he looked through the pages of a file on his desk. "Your resume, recommendation letters, and score on the written exam are all very impressive. But I'll cut straight to the point and tell you that, even supposing our interview goes well—I have no reason to think it won't, by the way—I've decided to defer action on your application."

"Why? Is my application incomplete? Is there something wrong?"

"Your application is fine. Very thorough. But there are two things that have to be addressed. We can cover the first in this interview. It's not often—make that never—that we have a Ph.D. apply for a mail carrier position, especially a Ph.D. with your accomplishments. Harvard. Books. I mean, the educational requirement here is a high school diploma. Why in the world are you applying for this job?"

"It's a long story, Mr. Crandall. But basically, I'm newly married, have a child to help support, and need a job. And yes, I could go back to academia, but I feel like that phase of my life is past. I didn't like the politics and stress of that life and don't want to go back to it. I love the Shore—we moved here when I was two—and want to stay here. I like to be outdoors, I'm sociable, and I like to be of service. To my mind, being a mail carrier here would be the perfect job. And I'll be good at it, I promise."

Crandall took notes as I spoke and then looked up. "Okay, you've answered my question. You seem sincere, and I have no reason to doubt your motivation."

"But you said there were two reasons you've decided to put my application on hold. May I ask the second?"

"To be blunt," said the short and wiry Mr. Crandall, "you're too heavy to be a mail carrier. I see from your paperwork that you weigh 250 pounds. True, you're tall, six feet two. But that still makes you about forty pounds too heavy. You'll have to trim down to 210. This is as much to protect you as it is to limit the postal service's liability. Being a mail carrier is strenuous work, especially in the heat of summer. We can't knowingly put someone on the job who's at risk of a heart attack or stroke any more than I think you'd want to take that risk. In any case," he said, standing up, "we're open to reconsidering your application when you get down to 210."

"Come on, Nathan, you can do it. Another half mile, five minutes at most, and we'll be there."

Esther and I were jogging south along the Belmar boardwalk as part of my six-day-a-week exercise routine. On alternate days I would swim and work out with weights at the Y in Asbury. The next day I would run the four miles from our Bath Avenue apartment to 20th Avenue in South Belmar. Esther, a devoted jogger, helped me get through the runs, and then we would walk the four miles back to our place together. It was a killer workout for me. I doubt I could have seen it through without her. But along with the mostly vegetarian diet we followed, it was working. Twelve weeks after the post office interview, I was within a few pounds of the target weight Crandall had set for me.

"Today's harder than most days," I complained. "I hate running against the wind."

"But think how easy it will be in a few minutes when we walk home with the wind at our backs, drinking water, taking a hot shower—together—and then a delicious soup-and-salad lunch."

Talking was part of the program. Esther had taught me that joggers shouldn't go into oxygen debt, where you're gasping for breath and can only manage short distances. If you could maintain a conversation while you ran at a reasonable pace, you'd avoid this and could continue indefinitely.

"It's a huge help that you do this with me...encourage me...push me," I huffed as we ran. "I know I piss and moan too much...but I actually enjoy the running days...because I'm with you...and it's a good balance with... those lonely workouts at the Y... I think the old Chinese Taoists would... have approved of the lifestyle we have...thanks to you... Balance in all things...was their advice... The fusion between opposites... Naturalness, simplicity... Run and walk...Lift and swim...Veggies and water...God I can't wait... to get to the walking part...And maybe a pizza...one of these days...as a reward for our discipline?"

Esther returned to my old Taoists comment on the walk home. "Don't get me wrong, Nathan. I'm glad you're not thinking about going back into academia. All that competition and stress you've told me about. But you have all sorts of ideas, and I love it when we talk about them. I don't want to push you on this, but if you ever decide to write some of your thoughts down. Like what you just said about the Taoists, or whatever...I don't mean in a book or anything, or in the notebook you're writing your memories in...but just for me. Ideas you've found to be useful. Then I can think about what you've written and give you my own thoughts about them in return."

We walked for a while without speaking. "There's a lot I've been thinking about lately," she continued. "Basically, I want to know why I have my life, and how I should live it. These are the things I really want to talk about."

Remarkable questions from a remarkable woman, the identical questions Laurent Ambrose had posed at the beginning of the Claymont course as the over-arching guidelines for reflection during the year ahead, the same questions that guided Ailani Kaluhiwa's project back in Hilo.

"It's a good idea," I said. "It would be fun. And doing it with you would be valuable for me, too, a real give-and-take. The things you have to say—about life, people, us—blow me away, Esther. I love our conversations. So yeah. I'll write some thoughts down. But only after I hit 210 and get the damn job."

At the end of April 1981, two weeks before my 37th birthday, I reached fighting weight and then took it five pounds further. I couldn't disguise my pride and satisfaction when I handed in the results of my updated medical exam.

"Wow. I'm impressed," the wiry Mr. Crandall exclaimed after he read the results. "Forty-five pounds in less than four months. You've got incredible motivation and discipline, Mr. Kirinski. Can I call you Nate? Please call me Ralph. Fill out this paperwork, a week of training starting Monday, and the job is yours. Welcome to the Ocean Grove Post Office."

Now that I could do it, I ran the mile and a half to Vic's, where Esther was on the daytime shift. It was a weekday mid-afternoon before tourist season, and hardly anyone was there. I ordered a pizza with all the trimmings, Esther joined me at the table, and Vic Giunco's son John, who owned the place now, delivered our pie himself.

When I went to the cash register to pay, he wouldn't accept any money. "I've known you and Esther since you were kids, Nate. It's a pleasure to see you together and so happy. This pizza's on the house. Congratulations on your new job."

A voice called out as I was finishing my route on a blistering day in August. "Up here, Mr. Postman!"

I looked up to see an elderly woman on the second floor porch of a big home on Ocean Pathway, one of the many turn-of-the-century Victorian structures lining my mail carrier's route. "Good afternoon," I waved. "What can I do for you?"

"Please meet me on the porch. I'll be down in a minute with some water. You must be roasting."

As I waited, I took out the mail for this address. Mrs. Theresa Glendening was the name on two envelopes. "Mrs. Glendening?" I asked as she handed me the glass of water. I didn't recognize the name, but there was something familiar about her.

"No. Theresa's my daughter. Do you have any mail for me, Gladys Herkimer?"

"Mrs. Herkimer! I thought you looked familiar. I'm one of your former students at Asbury Park High. Nathan Kirinski, class of '62."

"My word. Nathan Kirinski. It's a delight to see you. But I'll admit you're about the last person I would have expected to see delivering mail."

She invited me to sit down while I drank the water. "What led you here?"

"It's a long story," I said, my usual preface to explaining, or avoid explaining, my situation. "Basically, I spent some fruitful years in academia, then left, went through a divorce, and am now happily re-married and living here, over on Bath."

"Well, that's certainly an outline that leaves much to my imagination. But I won't pry. Except to ask if you're still active intellectually. You were among the best students I ever had. Although I do recall an awkward moment with you in my senior English class..."

"Right. It was uncomfortable. I could have handled myself better. I was rude. I should have apologized for what I said then. I hope you'll accept my apology now."

"I'm the one who should apologize. It was your story, and an excellent story at that. I had no right to open it up to experimentation by the other students. Your ending should have remained your ending."

"Thank you for saying so. But I'll have to say, after some years of being a teacher myself, I can understand what you were trying to do as an educational exercise. But I just didn't have the background to see it with that perspective at the time, and I was thin-skinned in general those days."

"Excellent. We're mutually forgiven. Let's toast the reconciliation," she said, holding up her glass, which obviously wasn't water. "The rumors of a bottle of booze in my desk drawer at school weren't true, by the way." She smiled. "But we're not in school now."

Esther and I had everything we needed: an adequate combined income, excellent government benefits, and, but for the continuing sadness of my separation from Ellen and my parents, a lifestyle largely free of stress. A year into our marriage, I found an additional source of satisfaction as a volunteer teaching elementary school kids to read and tutoring at-risk teenagers in whatever subjects they were failing. I had always enjoyed teaching and was glad to see that I was still good at it. That these kids weren't philosophy students at Harvard or the University of Hawaii didn't lessen in the least the sense of satisfaction I got from working with them. My experience with Nolan Jamison was especially gratifying, although our tutoring sessions started out badly.

"Please come in," I called in answer to a knock on the door of the room that was reserved for volunteers at the high school. It was 7:00 p.m. on a warm Tuesday evening in early June. I had worked late that day and hadn't had a chance to shower at home and change out of my mail carrier's uniform. A tall, muscular teenager walked in and sat down across the table from me, although I was standing and extending my hand, which he didn't take.

"Shit, it stinks in here. Like a damn gym."

I seated myself slowly, trying not to react to his rudeness. "Yeah, well, sorry. It was a hot day for delivering mail, and I didn't have a chance to clean up before I got here."

"What the hell? So how's a mailman gonna help me pass English? How's a mailman supposed to teach me 'literature'?"

"I wasn't always a mailman. And if I had always been one, what makes you think I wouldn't know about 'literature'?" I said, mimicking his sarcasm. "Anyway, I'm not the one failing English. You are. So, if you're still interested in learning something, I suggest we start again. My name is Nathan Kirinski," I said, standing up and offering my hand across the table. "And you are...?"

He glared at me for a moment, but then stood up and took my hand. "Nolan Jamison." I thought we would be okay, but he stayed sullen and aggressive. "How you gonna teach me, man? This English stuff they have us read. It's for fags, man. Especially the poetry. God, I hate that shit. It don't make no sense. And why in the hell would I ever want to learn stuff that ain't gonna get me nowhere, that's got nothin' to do with my life."

"What do you want to do after high school, Nolan—assuming you can pass this course and graduate?"

For the first time he seemed to let his guard down and show some animation that wasn't negative. "The military. I'm gonna be a soldier, or a marine. That's what I want my career to be, and the recruiter told me if that's what I want for a career, I'd have a leg up if I graduated. Dropouts don't usually get too far. That's what he told me. So that's why I'm here. And that's why I wanna know how you gonna teach me."

"I'm from Belmar and graduated from Asbury High back in the sixties, just before our country got involved in Vietnam. I went on to college and graduate school—like I said, I wasn't always a mailman. Anyway, I had a buddy back then, a friend from Belmar who went to Manasquan High. They were our big rivals, but we stayed friends. His name was Bobby Shannon."

Nolan came alive. "Bobby Shannon. THE Bobby Shannon?" I nodded, pleased to see that Bobby's name was still recognized locally 20 years after he was selected New Jersey's top scholastic athlete two years in a row for his accomplishments in football and track and field. "He's still my dad's hero. He's always talkin' about all the stuff that dude could do, all his records. I do the same field events Shannon did—shotput and discus—and play tight end like he did. And I'm good, but no way I'm as good as Bobby Shannon was. My dad says he coulda been All Pro. But my dad doesn't know what happened to him. You say you're still friends. What happened?"

"I agree with your father. Bobby could have been a big time sports star. He could have gone onto college with an athletic scholarship. But he never had much interest in school. He always wanted to join the army, to serve his country. Like you. So he enlisted and ended up being one of the early Green Beret advisers in Vietnam."

"No shit! What happened to him?"

"He left the service as a Master Sargent and with a Silver Star after doing two tours in 'Nam. He and I corresponded during those years. I still have his letters. I'm sure he wouldn't mind if I shared them with you. Maybe you could even have your own correspondence with him. I could ask him."

The guardedness returned to Nolan's face. "Why would you do that for me?"

"You said you want to go in the service, and Bobby might have some advice to offer about that. But the bigger reason is that I think you might re-evaluate your attitude about 'literature' under Bobby's influence."

"And why would I do that?"

"The letters from him that I want to share with you are mostly poetry, beautifully written poetry about his experiences in Vietnam. The writing is clear as a bell. And powerful. And hard to read sometimes because of the violence he encountered, both in the battles he fought against the enemy and within himself. Poetry, Bobby told me, was a big factor in helping him get through the war, in helping him to make some sense of it all. Are you game to read it? If you are, I bet it will give you a whole new perspective on the material we'll be working on together for your course. "

Nolan thought for a moment. "Yeah. I'm game."

"Good. I'll contact Bobby and ask his permission to share his letters with you, and to see if he's willing to correspond with you."

We spent the rest of that first meeting reviewing Nolan's required reading list and how we would proceed in our tutoring sessions. As he got up to leave, he asked me what Bobby Shannon did after he left the service.

"He went to college and became a coach and teacher at a high school in Oregon. He teaches English literature."

When I wasn't delivering mail or tutoring and Esther wasn't at Vic's, we spent every moment we could together. Mostly, we walked. I doubt there is any better place for walking than the Shore, especially for those who know it as intimately as Esther and I did. At one time or another, we covered most of the 140 miles of boardwalks and beaches lining the coast from Cape May in the south to the Atlantic Highlands in the north, but on a day-to-day basis we concentrated on the towns of Belmar, Avon, Bradley, Ocean Grove, and Asbury Park—what we thought of as "our" section of the Shore.

Soon after I returned to the Shore and learned of my sister's death, I established a monthly routine of walking inland along county highways to Monmouth Memorial Park in Tinton Falls, where Deborah's ashes are interred. The ten-mile round trip was both my homage and amends to my sister for being absent during her illness and passing.

"I'm going to walk out to Deborah's grave," I told Esther one day soon after we moved in together.

"I'd like to go with you. If that would be okay."

"Of course it would be okay. Anytime I'm with you is 'okay.' But really, I'm fine making the trek alone. And I do it from a sense of duty, and guilt, and love. But it's ten miles, Esther. Please don't feel you should go with me."

"I'm your helpmate, Nate. Where you go, I go. And going to the cemetery would make me feel close to Deborah. I'm sorry we didn't know each other. From all you and Arnie have told me about her, I'm sure it would have been a real friendship."

My monthly visits became our monthly visits, Esther's and mine. I taught her to join me in saying *Kaddish*, in Hebrew and then English, after which we would sit quietly for half an hour or so and then walk the five miles back home.

One day, as we walked along Lake Avenue in Asbury, we passed Morton's Carousel Diner. It was closed at the time, so I didn't have to worry about any inadvertent sighting or encounter with my father. The diner was across the street from Wesley Lake, which divided Asbury from Ocean Grove. A short way down the street were Palace Amusements and, a little farther toward the ocean, the Casino. Both were closed now, but during their 100 years of operation they had been home to two of history's great hand-carved carousels and, in the case of the Palace, a famous Ferris wheel. I told Esther how Arnie and I always joked that "Morton's Carousel Diner" should have been called "The KKK Diner"—short for "The Krazy Kirinski Karousel Diner." I felt affectionate toward all of my family when I said this, but the feeling was short lived, replaced by the sadness I always experienced when I thought about my dead sister and estranged parents.

Esther knew what was going on inside me. "I'm sorry that marrying me has only made your relationship with your folks worse, Nate. I wish I could do something to help. I hope I'll get to meet them some day. I keep thinking they might like me, and the situation might improve, at least a little."

"Maybe," I said, privately convinced that such a meeting would never occur, much less make things better.

Thanks to Arnie, though, a meeting was eventually arranged. He tried to prepare me. "It was a hard negotiation, Nate, I have to tell you that, and I have no confidence that this will go well. Mort was dead set against meeting Esther. And frankly, the prospect of seeing you doesn't appeal to him either. 'Dad,' I implored him. 'Esther's a wonderful person. You'll see. And she's perfect for Nate. You'll see that, too.' So they both finally agreed, and tonight's the night. It won't surprise you to know that they're very nervous about meeting Esther. For Fay, the anxiety is motherly: 'How can this woman,' she asked me, 'how can this woman—not only a gentile, we're used to that with Holly and Eddie, but wanton from what we've heard in the gossip around town—be perfect for Nathan? He's never shown good judgement. A look at the way his life has gone is proof of that. But he's a decent man, however confused. He only needs to find the right person, to settle down, to stop wasting his time and talents, to get back on the track that once made us so proud. Still, Arnold, you speak well of Esther O'Connell. You're steady. I trust your opinion. If you say this woman is good for Nathan, I'm ready to meet her.' For Morton, though..."

"It's okay, Arnie," I cut in. "Let me save you from having to hint around at what I already know and can say more bluntly. For Mort, it's not just nerves. It's agitation. It's anger—at his brilliant failure of a son, who squandered genius and achievement and fame and position to become a wastrel, a mailman. 'And now he goes a step further, this blimp of disappointment,' I can hear our father complaining, 'now he takes up with another gentile, a slut from what my pinochle-playing cronies tell me. Now he goes beyond embarrassing us. Now he shames us. And you, Arnold—thank God at least for you—you're always the gentleman who sees the best in everyone. It's no surprise you would speak well of the woman, whatever the truth of the situation. But it's the Sabbath. We are Jews. The woman will be a guest at our table.' And I can hear Fay sighing at this point. 'I hope you're right, Arnie. Your brother's life has been a disaster since he left Harvard. If she can help him, she'll be a blessing, whatever else she might be.' And I can imagine her turning to her husband: 'You'll behave?' she challenges. And Mort snorts in reply. 'Of course I'll behave. She's a guest, as I already said. How I deal with her husband, though, I refuse to promise or predict.'"

The anxieties my parents must have been feeling could not have been more severe than those Esther and I would bring to the Kirinski elders' house in Belmar that evening. Arnie and I choreographed things ahead of time, so that he would bring Esther to the house to introduce her to our parents, and I would arrive a half-hour later with the excuse that I got a last-minute summons from the postmaster to help sort an unusually large amount of mail for the next day's deliveries. Esther deferred to us on this, accepting our concern that my presence at the crucial introductory junction might make a difficult situation even more uncomfortable.

As logical as this approach was, I couldn't help berating my lack of courage as I watched my much braver wife and brother walk to the front door. From my hiding place in our parked car down the darkened street, I saw Esther hand my mother the bottle of high-quality wine she had specially picked out as a gift.

Thirty minutes later I knocked on the front door. Arnie answered, gave me a thumbs-up, and beckoned me into the living room. My relief was tremendous as I witnessed my wife and parents in cordial, smiling conversation. Esther's charm and sincerity seemed already to have registered with Fay and Morton. My mother rose and came over to kiss me. Then my father—my father!—walked over and shook my hand.

"*Gut Shabbos,*" he greeted me and continued to hold my hand. "I've been reading the Ramban lately, Maimonides." Although he was typically blunt, my father had an occasional flare for the cryptic. I waited. "The Ramban asked, 'Who has reached complete repentance?' Then he answered his own question: 'A person who confronts the same situation in which he sinned, but this time abstains and does not commit it again.'"

My father released my hand and turned to Esther. "I'm glad that we're finally getting to meet you." He paused and then looked at me again. "I'm glad, too, that we're all together."

The evening wore on, stilted at times but always polite. Stilted but polite was a vast improvement over my relationship with my parents until this evening. Someday, I dared to hope, with Esther by my side perhaps I could follow the Kirpal Singh exhortation I quoted and be a prop and blessing to them after all.

2
Visits

"DADDY! DADDY!" ELLEN SCREAMED across the boarding area as she let go of the airline staff member's hand and ran to meet me. Thirty days from now the scene, minus exuberance, would unfold in reverse when I handed her over to another attendant for the flight back to Anchorage. But until then we would be a normal father and child.

Holly and I had agreed that Ellen would stay with me for a month every summer. I would fly to Seattle to meet her and return her to Seattle, where she would connect to her accompanied trip back to Anchorage. We typically spent a day and night sightseeing in Seattle on both ends of the journey. Although the flights and overnights and time off from work were an expensive arrangement for me, it was well worth it for the fun and bonding opportunities the month provided. At least early on.

During that first visit to Seattle we started a game that would become a tradition for the two of us. Actually, Ellen started it. "Between now and the time we come back to Seattle, let's try to find car license plates from every state."

"That sounds challenging. But okay. Let's try."

By the time we boarded our flight the next morning, we had only spotted plates from the far-western states of Washington, Oregon, California, Nevada, and Idaho. "This will be hard, Daddy. We have to find 45 more. But we have 29 days left, so we shouldn't give up." I assured her I would be with her in this game all the way.

Esther was at Newark Airport to greet us. She was nervous, and so was I; she and Ellen hadn't met before. On the drive to Ocean Grove I was relieved to see that they were getting along just fine. I drove while they sat in the back seat together looking for license plates. By the end of the trip, New York, Pennsylvania, and New Jersey had been added to the evolving total. "Esther and I found three more, Daddy. Only 42 states to go."

When Ellen phoned Holly to tell her we had arrived, I overheard her describing the license-plate game she had invented. "Esther helped me find three, Mama. She's really nice." I was happy when I fell asleep that night. My daughter, my new wife, our cozy apartment with its open windows letting in the sound of the rollers breaking against the shore one block away...

The next day was a joyous reunion for Ellen with my parents and Arnie. They doted on her just as they used to, when she was a pre-Alaskan infant and toddler. Had I been the year-round custodial parent, I'm sure I would have chided them for spoiling her. But I was intent on establishing positive associations for Ellen, and I only had a few weeks to do it. Letting my family feed her sweets and give her more presents than a kid would ever need supported this strategy.

Our days together soon fell into a routine. Esther, who had arranged to work only night shifts for the month, took Ellen to the beach or the pool and the several local playgrounds every day, and I would join them on weekends. The three of us ate an early dinner when I finished work and before Esther left for Vic's, and then Ellen and I would spend the evening playing miniature golf and riding merry-go-rounds. Esther had Sunday nights off, and we'd all have dinner together at my parents, including Arnie, who would wait until Ellen's bedtime before returning to the city.

By the time we arrived at our Seattle-Tacoma Airport departure gate, I knew it had been a perfect summer. And it had a perfect ending, although one that nearly didn't happen. Before we had checked into our motel near the airport the day before, we still hadn't met our license-plate goal. Ellen was distraught. "We failed, Daddy," she sobbed. "We have three more states to go, but I'm leaving soon. And one of them is Hawaii."

I couldn't stand the idea of our month together ending on a sour note. "Remember you told me we shouldn't give up?" She nodded. "Well, let's go into the city and look around." Which is what we did, and spotted two of the three: Montana and North Dakota.

"But we still have Hawaii, Daddy. How will we do it?"

"We'll go to the airport early tomorrow and walk around the parking garage near Hawaiian Air. We'll find it."

We trudged through four floors and multiple aisles of parked cars the next day. I was giving up hope when Ellen yelled, "Hawaii! We did it, Daddy. Fifty states." We danced around celebrating as if we had just won a million dollars. I thought of Edgar Shiba. The Aloha spirit. The goddess Pele.

An hour later our time together was up. "I don't want us to say goodbye, Daddy."

"Me either," I said, hugging her hard before she had to take the flight attendant's hand and board the plane.

So, yes, Ellen's first visit from Anchorage to the Shore, in 1980, when she was six, had been perfect. And it was more of the same until she was ten.

"Can I have some privacy, please? PLEASE?" she actually yelled at me one morning as I tiptoed across the living room a couple of days into her 1984 visit.

"I'm sorry, Sweetie. But I have to get to work, and this is the only way out to the street."

"I can't stand it," she muttered, burying her face in the pillow.

Later that day, Esther and I strung up some wire for curtains that would at least give Ellen some control over her space and visibility. "It doesn't make it any more of a room," she said by way of thanks.

"I wish we had a separate bedroom. I'm sorry."

From there, the issues only intensified. "Don't you dare!" she screamed when Esther knocked on the bathroom door for the third time.

"I'm sorry, Ellen, but I need to get ready for work."

"In Anchorage, I get to lie in the tub and soak as long as I want. It relaxes me."

Esther turned to me with an exasperated look. *You're her father,* she seemed to be saying. *Do something.*

"We only have the one bathroom, Sweetie," I said through the door. "How about we work out a schedule so that we can each have our private bath time?" There was no answer. "But for now, you need to come out."

The door swung open and Ellen, wrapped in a bath towel, pushed past me. "This stinks," she said as she pulled the curtain around her makeshift bedroom.

Then there was the telephone. Ellen called her mother every day. I let it go for a while, figuring it was easier just to eat the long-distance costs in the interests of peace. But the bigger problem was Ellen's demand that Esther and I not be around during the calls. "Can I please have some privacy?" she would huff if we were anywhere in the vicinity, a demand that was hardly tenable in a small apartment, especially when one of us worked at night and was home during the day, and the other worked during the day and was home at night. It began to piss me off, and I showed it, which didn't help. "Look, Ellen," I finally complained. "What do you expect? That we'll have to go outside every time you talk with your mother? Which are never short conversations, by the way."

She started to cry. "I need to talk with my mom. I really do," she said as she ran out the door.

Running out the door became a common occurrence that summer. This was a serious concern. We couldn't predict her comings and goings, or where she went. And who knows what dangers lurk around beach towns in the summer? Again, I let my temper show. "Damn it, Ellen. You have to stop doing this. I don't want to have to worry about you. You're grounded."

"We need to make another arrangement," Holly told me on the phone after Ellen returned to Anchorage from the visit of '84.

"What are you talking about?"

"Ellen's not happy about spending the month there anymore. She wants to stay in Anchorage with me."

"I don't get it. Why?"

"She just says she doesn't like it there anymore, sleeping on the couch, without her own room, no privacy, leaving her friends and her cat and her dog back here."

I saw no point in pushing it. In the end, we decided to split the difference and have her come for two weeks. If that didn't work, I was willing to cut it down to one week, plus two days for round-trip travel.

"I'm shattered," I told Esther. "I don't know what happened, how it went from such delightful times four years ago to this."

"She's growing older, a girl growing older."

"Growing older without a cat, a dog, or a room of her own. I don't know how two weeks instead of four will change any of that, how I can make things better."

"We, Nathan. How we can make things better."

But we never had the chance. Ellen refused to come east after that summer. I kept up my practice of phoning her on Saturdays, and until she was 13 I took vacation days two times a year for trips to Anchorage. But by then Ellen had entered teendom, and it was obvious that her friends held more interest for her than her father. After three years I stopped going, and our communications eventually dwindled down to answering machine messages—mine to Ellen, who never called me back.

"Let's not give up," Esther encouraged me every week.

"No," I said, and dialed.

3
Days of Awe

"DAD, PLEASE, COME WITH me tonight," I begged. "We haven't been to the synagogue together in 15 years. You haven't been there in nine. It's Erev Rosh Hashanah, the eve of a new year, a time to forgive. Try to put aside your feelings for the rabbi."

I knew my pleading would be useless, an annual failure of good intentions. True, my father was still treasurer of the synagogue, one of the three or four men whose efforts kept the congregation alive and functioning from year to year. He would go to meetings, he would file financial reports and tax statements, he would even deliver the rabbi's paycheck to his door every two weeks. But Morton Kirinski would never attend services as long as Aharon Steinman was rabbi, not even on the eve of Rosh Hashanah, and definitely not when I was the one trying to persuade him. But I doubted my father would have changed his mind about going to the service even if his favored son Arnie, who was abroad on this occasion, had been the one exhorting him to attend.

"I'll pray alone," he told me, "like I always do. The Almighty hears prayers from my kitchen as clearly as He does from some wooden bench on 11th Avenue. Better, I think. I'm calmer here, less distracted."

He turned away. The conversation was over. I was putting on my coat, resigned to go to the service alone, when my father spoke again, in obvious anguish. "Look, don't you think I'd love more than anything to go? But I won't, I can't, so don't make me feel worse than I already do by trying to persuade me. I can't take the rabbi. That's all there is to it. I refuse to be around him during a service of any kind. High Holy Days or not, I cannot find it in me to forgive him."

He turned away again and opened his prayer book. I watched him for a moment as he rocked back and forth, enveloped in the privacy of his prayer shawl, murmuring Hebrew words, an old man, alone in his kitchen, supplicating God. I guessed—no, I knew—that my father was immersed less in prayer than in the despair and humiliation and anger of that Rosh Hashanah eve years before when Rabbi Steinman ordered him not to say *Kaddish*, the mourner's prayer for my sister Deborah, who had recently died, at age 42, and been cremated at her own request. "The Law forbids it," the rabbi had previously pronounced privately to my father in Steinman's office before they joined the others in the synagogue. As the other mourners stood up to pray, my father sat. All around him his cronies, unaware of the rabbi's ruling, stared at him like he was a crazy man. "Mort!" they hissed. "What's wrong with you? It's the *Kaddish*. Get up and pray for Deborah." All the while Morton Kirinski sat there, unmoving, his face red with shame. At the end of the *Kaddish* he walked stiffly up the aisle and out of the sanctuary, never to return or explain what had transpired between him and Steinman.

I knew no details beyond my father's anger at the rabbi for exercising what I understood to be the formal prohibition against reciting the *Kaddish* for one who chose to be cremated. Though I would never say so, I thought the rabbi made the better point: if you bought into Orthodoxy, the Law must prevail. But I had come to accept my father's obsessive nurturing of his anger. There was no more to be said. He would not be swayed. I didn't try to enlist the support of my mother, who was bent over something in the kitchen and pretending not to listen. She detested Rabbi Steinman as much as her husband did. I left them and made my way alone to the synagogue.

Belmar's Congregation Sons of Israel, which in recent years had never attracted more than a tiny gathering even on the Days of Awe, finally achieved a quorum this Rosh Hashanah eve when congregant number ten, Rabbi Steinman himself, walked in. Except for me, the *minyan* was drawn entirely from geriatric remnants: Rochelson, Himmelman, Sklar, Oster, Krakauer, Weinstein, Resnik, Belding—all of them pale, rheumatic, barely ambulatory octogenarians, a far cry from the community's golden age of 30 and 40 years ago, when lithe Norman Sklar coached the Junior Maccabees basketball team and dexterous Max Oster taught the kids to make crystal radio sets; when Jake Resnik, a professional gambler and numbers runner when he wasn't praying for redemption, tutored us in five-card draw, and Al Rochelson, with all the credibility of his scarred face and knuckles, showed us how to box and do whatever else might be necessary to defend ourselves in a Jew-hating world. At moments, I was still the admiring child as I pictured these men back in the midst of their energetic middle age. At other moments, adult, real-time moments, I fought the ungenerous impulse to see these former heroes as dotards. Nor did they seem to be viewing me through the prism of a glorious past. I was greeted warily, with reluctant, limp handshakes and barely nodded hellos. I understood their coldness. How else to greet the rabbi's one-time protégé—a potential rabbi myself or at least, with my once-sweet singing voice, a cantor—who had twice married out of the faith? How else to greet one whose father sat praying alone, implacably alone, at his kitchen table on Erev Rosh Hashanah out of some mysterious distaste for the rabbi?

Just as the smell of the place, the aromas of *Yiddishkeit*, of Jewishness, hadn't changed in the years since I had been away, the routines surrounding the prayers, much less the prayers themselves, hadn't changed either—no surprise in the tightly ordered, millennial arena of Orthodox Judaism. The men sat in the same seats that had been assigned to them when they first joined the congregation, although that now meant they sat mostly one man to a row, and only in a very few of the available rows at that. As soon as the service began, I found myself moving automatically to the seat next to the one my father had occupied until he made his break.

Nor had the show changed. Harry Krakauer served as *shammes*, the sergeant-at-arms who would bang his fist on his prayer stand and yell for quiet at periodic intervals. Belding and Sklar, chatting with each other incessantly, were incessantly shushed, to no avail, by those around them. As two or three late-comers straggled in, Krakauer became more and more zealous in his attempts to impose order, finally extending his admonitions to the handful of women in the balcony hidden behind the *mechitza*, the curtain separating the sexes, who nevertheless continued to talk throughout the service, behavioral clones of their menfolk.

Mr. Oster, the *hazan*, his voice raspy and down an octave since his tenor heyday in the 1950s, still chanted the Hebrew liturgy as fast as I could manage merely to scan and turn the pages. During the *Amidah*, the Silent Prayer, I felt frozen in eternity as I watched—for the hundredth time? The thousandth?—Rabbi Steinman, wrapped in the folds of his vast shawl, sway in concentric circles of devotion. Resnik stood in his usual spot near the *bimah*, the pulpit, praying with more and more fervor as the service wore on. I noticed the smelling salts in their accustomed place on Resnik's prayer stand. By late afternoon the following day, everyone knew from annual experience that Resnik would faint from his penitential fervor, and whoever was nearest him at the time would use these salts to revive him. Fainting, it had always been assumed, was his repentance for running numbers and making book.

Oster stopped singing and left the podium. He was replaced by the rabbi, who began his sermon. I was immediately at home with the cadences, if not the content, of the preaching. Even after many years of absence from the shul, I knew Steinman's formula by heart, just as I knew by heart the words and tunes of the service after years of not having recited them. As a child, I would stay in the synagogue to listen to the rabbi's talks while my friends went outside to play on the front steps. My ten-year-old's sense of morality was invariably inspired by Steinman's persuasive righteousness. Had our forceful rabbi been secretary general of the United Nations instead of the Nordic, mild Dag Hammarskjold, I used to tell anyone who would listen, the world would be a far safer place.

But from my teenage years on, I began to discern in Steinman a disquieting tendency to combine good sense with extremism, thoughtfulness with pomposity. Tonight's sermon was more of the same, a confusing yet strangely compelling mixture of erudition, charisma, self-aggrandizement, and fanaticism. The rabbi spoke first of the brotherhood of man and how important it was, especially for Jews, to counteract prejudice in all its manifestations. Then he tried to illustrate the real-life relevance of this message by describing how, as a child, he experienced prejudice when he was surrounded and pushed around by "a gang of Irish micks!" and how the experience had made an enduring, indelible impression on his sense of the world.

He pursued his strangely reasoned theme of anti-prejudice into the realm of current events. "There is a battle going on this very day," he inveighed, "over the ownership of Jerusalem, over which nation of people can claim the Holy

City as its own." Steinman stopped to survey his sparse but rapt audience. "Who can possibly claim it? Jerusalem," he thundered, his chest heaving, "is not Arafat's city. It is not Hussein's city or Saud's city or Carter's city or even Menachem Begin's city! It is the Lord's City, and as such it is everyone's city."

Following this passionate universalist argument for brotherhood came the Judaeo-centric sucker punch, the formulaic twist of a-logic so familiar to me from my teenage years and the beginning of my disenchantment with the rabbi as a desirable world leader. "But the Jews," Steinman nearly whispered, "the Jews are the Children of the Lord. This is the claim the Children of Israel have on the Holy City, for we are the first-chosen of our Father. *This*," he fairly bellowed, "is what the Belmar Rebbe says to you. And you can tell your friends and your relatives and your co-workers and especially, *especially*, our enemies that *this* is what the Belmar Rebbe says to you."

Amazing, I thought, as the rabbi, drained and somber, collected himself. He calls himself the Belmar Rebbe as if the designation, the self-designation, were comparable to the Bratslaver Rebbe or the Lubuvitcher Rebbe or the Saint of Lublin or the Baal Shem Tov himself. As if one's friends and relatives and co-workers, much less one's enemies, would be swayed in their thinking by the pronouncements of the Belmar Rebbe. As if the dozen or so congregants were an audience of hundreds. Amazing that this man had once been my candidate for secretary general.

I was not sure what the sermon's message was supposed to have been, but I had to admit that the rabbi's oratorical power had the effect of leaving his audience in a respectful, anticipatory silence for the kind of convoluted but compelling punch-line which, based on years of hearing Steinman's sermons, we all knew would come next. "My friends," he began. "Wrestling with difficult issues is the essence of Judaism. You'll remember from the Book of Genesis that God, blessed be He, gave the name Israel to our patriarch Jacob after Jacob spent all night in combat with an angel, who was in fact the Almighty. 'You shall no longer be called Jacob but Israel, for you have striven with God and with humans, and have prevailed.' So you see, my dear friends," the rabbi continued, "we wrestle, we struggle. It is what Jews do. Whether we ultimately prevail remains to be seen, but we must nevertheless keep at it. Tonight, Erev Rosh Hashanah, reminds us, the God-wrestlers, of this obligation. For without struggling—with our problems, with our relationships, with our habits, with our oversights and transgressions, with our successes and the pride we take in them, even with, especially with, our lapses in faith itself—our petitions for forgiveness during the entirety of the High Holy Days are useless."

Steinman stopped, sighed, and looked down, obviously weary from the weight of the message he must convey. All congregational chatter had ceased. After a long pause, somehow refreshed and reinvigorated he looked up and resumed, this time rhetorically. "'So, Rabbi,' I can hear you asking, 'be concrete. What does it mean to struggle?' Fair enough. You deserve an example of a problem, and one that we all have in common. It is true we are a small community. And this truth is painful to those of us who have spent our efforts over the years to help our community expand rather than shrink. But," he conceded, the most reasonable and straightforward of men, "we *have* shrunk. Although, thanks be to God, our children have grown up the way we wanted them to grow up—as lawyers, doctors, businessmen, teachers, professionals—our pain is that they have not grown up *here*. They have moved away to the cities, where their talents have made them successful. And yet," he acknowledged, smiling and nodding his head toward me, "they do come home to us from time to time. These returns of our children to their roots are what justify the existence of our community. More, that our community, small though it is, persists as a link in the continuity of traditional Judaism in this country is a fact that is significant beyond expression."

Here he paused, dipping his head, shrugging his shoulders, raising his upturned hands apologetically. "But to continue," he explained, "to survive, we must have funds. To have a house of prayer, we must pay a mortgage. To heat and cool and light and maintain a house of prayer, we must pay bills. To staff a house of prayer, we must pay salaries." Now Steinman grimaced, as if suffering—again—from the weight of his responsibility to convey an unwelcome but inescapable message. "My dear friends, our community is in jeopardy. And it is solely up to us," he artfully beseeched the audience as he stepped down from the podium, "up to each one of us in this sanctified room of God's house—in front of His *oren ha-kodesh*, His Sacred Ark—to insure our very survival."

After Myer Weinstein, president of the synagogue's Men's Club, took the donation pledges, the service continued. At the end, Steinman mounted the *bimah* once more, this time to urge the congregation to "cooperate" on the following morning by arriving at nine o'clock sharp so that services could begin as scheduled. "If you want to leave early," the rabbi instructed us, "you have to come early. The sooner we have a *minyan*, the sooner we can start and eventually finish services. And another thing," he added, stern and glowering. "Don't rush off now. Linger and talk for a few more minutes. Connect with one another. Judaism is a collective effort. We are a community. Our essence as a people is each individual's responsibility to the community. So you'll be a little late for part four of *Shogun*," he grinned slyly, conspiratorially. "You're surprised? Don't I know you after all these years? We've been praying hard together. Don't waste the effort. Don't run out the door to watch TV. Collect yourselves. Leave like Jews."

Chastened, the congregation at first seemed ready to linger. But the shame at having been caught out was soon superseded by curiosity as nearly everyone hastened away ("Don't I know you?" he had said) to watch part four of *Shogun*.

Having missed the first three parts of *Shogun*, I was in no hurry to return home. I was among the last to leave the building and was unprepared to encounter the rabbi and Mrs. Steinman standing by the door.

"I'm glad you were able to join us for services this year," Steinman began. "But I'm surprised you're not with your family."

Ever since the death of my sister Deborah, in 1979, the rabbi had chosen to believe my father when he said he and my mother would henceforth spend the High Holy Days with his brothers and sister in Boston, his hometown, or with Arnie in New York City. For both my father and the rabbi, collusion in this myth was preferable to confrontation.

"I've been meaning to be here for Rosh Hashanah for some years," I deflected. "I'm happy to have finally been able to arrange it."

"We all have a lot of catching up to do," Mrs. Steinman said. "Can you join us tonight for dinner? We can talk at our leisure."

I was mortified by the prospect of being with them, both because of my father's feelings toward the rabbi and because I had a pretty fair idea of what I was in their eyes: a lost son, non-observant, divorced from one gentile woman and re-married to another, an over-educated mailman. To them, I must myself seem a gentile. I gave a politely pre-emptive excuse. "It's a gracious invitation. When I remember how delicious your cooking used to be, it makes me all the more sorry that I've made previous arrangements. But I want to thank you very much for asking me."

The Steinmans accepted my regrets, I suspected with as much relief as I felt when I came up with the reasonable-sounding excuse. All faces now saved, we parted with the traditional Erev Rosh Hashanah greeting: *L'Shanah tovah tikatevu*, "May you be inscribed in the Book of Life for a good year."

By now I was the only one left in front of the shul. As I reached the sidewalk, I noticed the hedges bordering the street. I went over to them, drawn by an indentation just above their roots. This had been my cache, the place where I used to hide my sneakers on Saturday mornings so that I could grab them on the run as I left *Shabbos* services en route to the Belmar Community Center, where I played in a basketball league. Every Saturday had been filled with a conflict between guilt and desire. The guilt was powerful, and it subsequently proved to be the longer-lasting emotion. But in the heart of a 12-year-old the desire to play proved unconquerable, and it prevailed from week to week. I stooped and put my hand in the indentation. Did I expect my shoes to still be there? No, it was just another reflex, like remembering Hebrew prayers and Ashkenazi melodies, holdover habits that had somehow managed to survive my decades-old descent into non-observance, a descent traceable, I was sure, to a confluence of three factors: the victory of basketball over piety; the deterioration of my once pleasing, pre-pubescent singing voice; and my disillusion with Rabbi Steinman.

I started out for my parents' home, my close brush with dinner at the Steinmans making me thankful for my freedom. I decided to take my time and meander. The service, the people, and the building had all put me in a mood to remember. The evening, cool and still not totally dark in mid-September, conspired to do the same. Even now, on the cusp of middle-age, even though I had been away from Belmar for much of my life, the town continued to have power over me. I was no longer part of it, but it would always be part of me. I could never expect to excise it, though I had been trying for years to remove at least some of its more burdensome and unhappy aspects. It was like the cliché about the sore tooth, an attraction as well as an agony. Tonight, I thought, I'm here. So I'll push my tongue against the tooth. If it hurts, I'll will myself to withstand the pain. If it doesn't hurt...I'll be surprised.

When I returned to my parents' home I found my father asleep in the old reclining chair he used for reading and watching TV. My mother put her finger to her lips to prevent me from speaking and waved goodnight as she walked into their bedroom. My father still wore his skull cap and prayer shawl. When I leaned over to turn off the reading lamp, I saw a file folder on his lap titled *Steinman Correspondence*. I hesitated before picking it up, worried, practically, about waking my father and concerned, morally, about violating his privacy. Careful to avoid the former and overcoming my compunctions about the latter, I inched the folder off his lap, glided softly into the kitchen, turned on the dim light over the range, and began to read.

The file consisted of a series of letters ordered chronologically, earliest to most recent, and one addendum. The first letter was from my father's brother-in-law Sam—the family intellectual, a Hebrew school teacher in Boston with a Master's in history from Tufts—to the Union of Orthodox Jewish Congregations of America, the largest such association of synagogues in the country.

Gentlemen:

I respectfully request an answer to the following question which is of the utmost importance to a close relative of mine. What is the law or rule relating to a father's saying Kaddish for a departed daughter who was cremated in respect to her own specific wish? (Services were held, I should add, in a Jewish Reform temple. They, at least, provided some solace to my grieving relative.)

Please do not suggest that he consult his own rabbi unless your answer is "each rabbi makes his own ruling."

I would greatly appreciate a direct answer as soon as possible.

Very Sincerely,
Samuel Lieberman

One week later Sam received the following reply from the Rabbinical Council of America, the most authoritative association of Orthodox rabbis.

Dear Mr. Lieberman:

The Union of Orthodox Jewish Congregations of America has forwarded your letter to us for reply. The fact is that this is a question that should be addressed to one's Rabbi, but I infer from what you say that your relative is reluctant to do this.

At any rate, the obligation to recite the Kaddish for the deceased person devolves only upon a child for his parent. In all other instances it is voluntary. If the individual concerning whom you inquire wishes to recite the Kaddish for his daughter, the nature of her burial, etc. does not prohibit him from doing so.

Sincerely yours,
Rabbi Isaac Lapidus
Executive Vice-President

A few days after Sam received Rabbi Lapidus's reply, my father sent the whole packet to Steinman with this hand-written note:

Dear Rabbi,

Enclosed please find a copy of a letter sent by my brother-in-law to the Union of Orthodox Jewish Congregations of America and a Photostat of the letter from the Rabbinical Council in answer.

I am sending this to you for your consideration as I feel that you and the rabbinical authority whom you told me you consulted were wrong to issue the edict that I should not say Kaddish for my daughter. The hurt done to me cannot be undone but if another family should be faced with the same misfortune under similar circumstances as mine, then perhaps you would pass judgment according to the recommendation of the Rabbinical Council.

The file copy of the note was unsigned, although the original may have been; other than asking my father, which I was reluctant to do since I was reading all of this without his permission, I had no way of knowing. In any event, on the file copy of the draft that preceded his final message to Steinman, my father had written and then crossed out, after the phrase *then perhaps you would pass judgment according to the recommendation of the Rabbinical Council,* "and not according to the cruel decision of the so-called authority who passed judgment on me." He also had crossed out "Very Sincerely" in the file-copy draft, which, as with the signature, may have been part of the note actually mailed to Rabbi Steinman.

My father received this hand-written response from Steinman, dated three days later, on the synagogue's letterhead:

My dear friend Mordechai,

Your personal letter of the 9th and the copies of correspondence exchanged, I did receive today.

Believe me sincerely, that as a Rabbi in Israel committed to the uphold-ing of "Halacha," or Jewish law, I could not rule differently in the matter of saying Kaddish for your beloved daughter.

I thoroughly researched all the sources dealing with cremation. Not satisfied with my own conclusion I did further speak via phone for almost a full hour with an out-of-town senior rabbi—a great Talmudic scholar and authoritative expert in Jewish law, to whom many turn for definitive rulings in questions of Halacha. After much pro and con he concurred in my opinion that the Kaddish should not be recited in the case of cremation. There are, he says, one or two circumstances and minor rulings which permit Kaddish to be considered in a cremation case. But even these are a compromise of sorts, and even in such instances the Kaddish should be recited by someone other than the father.

Truthfully speaking, dear Mort, I was radically lenient as an orthodox rabbi and I really bent all the way in permitting your family's shiva observance and myself participating in this mourning period. If I did so, it was purely from a sense of infinite compassion, of humane empathy to spare any embarrassing questions from outsiders who were not privy to the matter of your daughter's expressed wish.

I beg you to bear no animosity against me, for my spiritual advice and ruling were neither capricious nor arbitrary. It was according to Jewish teaching where I seek the easing of hardship where it is lawfully possible.

I know, my dear friend, a little of your deep hurt and pain, your frustrating sorrow and heartbreak over a tragedy that is constantly crushing on your mind. May the Lord send you of his sweet healing balm to soothe and calm you.

I do not wish to enter into any Halachic disputation with Rabbi Lapidus of RCA on his ruling. If you wish, Mort, to pursue this matter further then please obtain from Rabbi Lapidus the authoritative source in Jewish codes—chapter and verse—on which he bases his opinion. If it is in black or white for him, then I too will have access to that information. We both use the same law books.

Yours,
Rabbi Aharon Steinman

I saw that my father had made a photocopy of Steinman's letter and added two comments in the margin. Next to the rabbi's statement "Not satisfied with my own conclusion I did further speak via phone for almost a full hour with an out-of-town senior rabbi...After much pro and con he concurred in my opinion," my father wrote: *Why pros and cons for so long? Who was trying to influence whom?* Later in the letter, next to Steinman's protestations of being "radically lenient as an orthodox rabbi" and acting "from a sense of infinite compassion, of humane empathy to spare any embarrassing questions from outsiders not privy to the matter of your daughter's expressed wish," my father wrote: *Why should outsiders have any bearing? What about their thoughts about my not saying Kaddish? I think the rabbi is a phony.*

I found this addendum in my Uncle Sam's handwriting:

Dear Mort,

    I spoke to my cousin Menachem, executive secretary to the Lubuvitch-er Rebbe, as you know. He says: "The Rebbe's chief assistant totally opposes the edict of Steinman and his authority. In other words, your brother-in-law is allowed to say Kaddish for his daughter. The problem is that we cannot, for the sake of inter-denominational amity, go on record with this result. I'm sorry. I asked the chief assistant what he would advise your brother-in-law to do. 'Pray elsewhere,' he said. 'When the mourners are called to stand and recite the Kaddish, he should do so without hesitation, for he is in the right. Only not in his home synagogue.'" Menachem also said: "Please, please do not quote me on this."

                                            Love,
                                            Sam

    Quietly, gently, I replaced the folder on my father's lap. To my relief, he snored on.

    A half-hour later, my father came into the living room and apologetically interrupted my reading. "So how was the service?" he asked.

    "You didn't miss much. You were smart to stay home."

4
Useful Ideas

"I DON'T THINK I could ever live away from the ocean," Esther said as we walked along the boards one Sunday morning through Ocean Grove, Bradley Beach, Avon, Belmar, and Spring Lake. "It's hard to describe what it means to me. The water is always moving, on the surface and underneath. Like me. Like us. And how intimate and vast it is, both at once. That it's rolling, right now, on this shore, our shore, and every other shore in the world. If I close my eyes, I can actually picture people walking along other shorelines. Maybe a couple in love, just like us, in England or France or Brazil or Ghana or Japan. I have this strong sense of connection with them, whoever they are. Somehow...I don't know. I can't really grasp it. But I can feel it, and I'm just about to cry from what I feel. Not in a sad way. Not at all in a sad way. It's just the opposite. It's like I'm all around the world right now, and that I know everyone. Even though in real life I've never been much farther away from here than New York City."

I didn't say anything for a while. I was sure I knew what Esther was talking about, what she was feeling. She was getting at some elusive, ineffable truth, something neither of us could describe but both of us understood. "Remember," I finally said, "how I told you about the times I would look eastward from here and imagine I could see people directly across the Atlantic? I didn't know them personally, not yet anyway. But I had this sense—I still have this sense—that I'm destined to meet them someday, all of them, just like I'll meet everyone on all the other shores of the world. Damn. That's so badly put. But it's what I think as I listen to you. Is that the kind of thing you mean?"

"It's exactly what I mean. It's like closeness and infinity at the same time. It reminds me of an idea you once shared with me—'differentiation and integration' you called it, how everything, everyone, is unique and universal, a distinct individual as well as a tiny part of the whole, both at the same time. Like the separate waves on the ocean's surface, what we're looking at now, and the vast world below, which we can't see but we know is always there. Each wave is different from the next, but they all flow back into the deeper sea."

We walked a little further before she continued. "It helps me, Nathan, when we put names to these feelings and ideas. Which leads me to the question: How's that piece of writing you promised me once upon a time coming along?"

On Friday evening, March 16, 1990, I finished what Esther had asked me to do years earlier, which was to write down certain ideas from my academic past that were still meaningful to me. I titled the piece "Useful Ideas." In one way or another, all of the ideas, like differentiation and integration, had come up in our casual, husband-wife discussions—in walks along the beach, over meals, in bed, wherever, a sort of 'Conversations with the Kirinskis' series, she had joked. But she had wanted something more formal. "Why?" I had asked.

"My education, or whatever you want to call it, stopped at high school. I'm tired of cheating myself, and being cheated. There are things I'd like to study and learn—books, philosophies, concepts I can reflect on and then discuss with you. I might even want to go back to school, maybe to Monmouth, like Arnie. We'll see. But for now, I could at least be reading what you write."

I couldn't ignore her pointed second request, and now that it was finished I was anxious to give her what I had written when she got home from work. I envisioned handing the typewritten pages to her after she changed clothes and poured a glass of wine.

"Here," I would say. "I'm sorry it took me so long. Please read it when you can, whenever you're in the mood."

"I'll read it right now," she would say, excited.

"Okay. I'll take a long midnight walk on the boards while you do." I would be worried about her reaction. "See you later," I would say as I put on my coat and walked out the door.

Dear Esther,

I apologize for taking so long to give you this. It's been a challenge, I can tell you. Not because of what's in it—these are all topics we've discussed at one time or another. So the content is nothing new. I'm just adding some concepts that have been useful to me over the years as a way to organize and think about things. I'm sure I've put off writing it because the process reminds me of academia, and you know about my troubled times there. For all that, though, it's been a helpful challenge, and I thank you for asking me to do this.

I've grouped the ideas into six categories: (1) knowledge & learning, (2) psychology, (3) self-development, (4) meditation, (5) energy, and (6) unity. I'm anxious to hear what you think of what I've written, and to explore it all with you in the days ahead.

Love,
Nate

IDEAS ABOUT KNOWLEDGE AND LEARNING

On approximating truth.

I first heard the term "triangulation" when I was taking a research methods course in graduate school. The general topic of discussion one day was how to go about validating theoretical constructs. The professor brought up the example of artillery fire in warfare: the first shot at the target might be wide to the left, the second wide right, and the third too low or high. But eventually the circumference within which the target sat would tighten, and so would your presumed accuracy on subsequent shots. The professor went on to talk about convergent validity, which I understood to be a research approach analogous to the idea of triangulation: the more discrete means used to measure a construct, in effect to converge on it, the more accurate would be your assessment and understanding of it.

The idea that elusive "truth" could be surrounded, approached more closely, and perhaps even captured by tightening the perimeter from several different methodological directions seems so obvious to me now, but at the time it was revelatory. And "obvious" is not the same as "elementary": in the humanities and social sciences, at least, truth is more likely relative than absolute. The research task is not to find *The Truth* in any singular sense, but rather to find something close to it by considering as many perspectives, measures, and coordinates as possible. In effect, you seek a consensus among subjectivities in an effort to get as close as you can to truth.

As an example, do you remember that time a couple of years ago when we were having morale problems at the post office? It worked out well in the end, and I credit Ralph Crandall, the human resources director, for that. He brought in a consultant, a psychologist from Monmouth College. Basically, the psychologist interviewed people individually to get our perspectives on what was going on and then interviewed small groups of people. He also had us complete a questionnaire anonymously. This gave him three sets of data which, when put together, offered highly detailed information. Then he reported the results back to everyone in a large staff meeting and facilitated a discussion. It was a really constructive give-and-take that brought different points of view to light, as well as some shared points of view about problems and possible solutions. I think his mixed-methods research approach made this possible. The individual, group, and survey data reinforced each other and gave the results more richness and credibility—much more than if he had only relied on anecdotes from the interviews or numbers from the questionnaire.

On tacit knowing and dwelling within.

The philosopher and scientist Michael Polanyi was required reading for the research methods course I mentioned earlier. The students in the course were quite a mixed bag when it came to levels of research sophistication and conceptions of the research process. But I think we all shared the then-prevailing idea that the conduct of inquiry should be scientific in the positivistic sense: one should systematically build theoretical structures, make sure they're internally consistent, generate hypotheses, test them empirically to control for or rule out variables that are possible causes of the effects under examination and not the hypothesized causes, explain relationships among phenomena, and insist that these relationships be testable and publicly observable.

But most of us in the class were humanists and social scientists, after all, not hard scientists. Much of social reality, certainly subjective psychological realities, couldn't be observed, much less tested. Yes, we could conduct surveys and run experiments. But the bulk of our understanding must come from less stringent or controlled measures: from personal observation, interaction, and intuition. Under the influence of positivism, we insisted on asking how results from such approaches could be trusted. They provided no certainty. They were too soft and dependent on subjective judgement.

Then along came Polanyi. We relished his disputes with positivism, whose characterizations of science and knowledge in general he considered faulty: for example, that knowledge should be objective, detached, impersonal, and wholly explicit, and that everything should be explainable by the mechanistic, universal laws of chemistry and physics. For Polanyi, applying such objectivist and reductionist criteria to the study of human beings is inadequate at best and absurd at worst. He in no way rejected science—he was a prominent physical chemist himself—only the positivistic conception of science, whose ideal of absolute objectivity he rejected as false and even delusional.

Instead, he proposed that personal knowledge, by which he meant personal participation of the researcher in shaping knowledge, is indispensable in science. The knower must be involved and cannot be detached. Furthermore, he argued that the preponderance of knowledge must be tacit; things cannot be wholly explicit as the positivists insist; it's impossible to tell the entire story of anything.

The most influential of Polanyi's ideas for me is his notion of indwelling: any genuine understanding of individuals and human societies will depend on our ability to put ourselves in their position, to dwell deeply within their situations and share their thoughts and feelings. Clearly, this idea flew in the face of the positivistic insistence on detachment. We graduate students loved it. Polanyi's proposals gave us a whole new understanding, both of the process of knowing and the scientific enterprise. We applauded his humane and humanistic perspective. It encouraged us to treat the conduct of inquiry in more flexible and metaphysical ways than we might otherwise have done.

Still, I have to acknowledge this: I took Polanyi so much to heart because he was a scientist and had earned his stripes in the demanding tradition of positivism. He had the credibility to challenge its tenets. Had the same arguments been offered by someone without this background, I likely would have rejected them.

I wonder what you think of these ideas about tacitness and indwelling. Is the traditional scientific approach I described above the only sure way of knowing something? If you get personally involved with someone or something, does that reduce your objectivity? On the flip side, does too much detachment from something, or someone, reduce your ability to truly understand?

On linguistic relativity.

This idea assumes that different languages produce different observations and evaluations—in effect, different views of the world. A language does not simply report experience; rather, it *defines* experience for its speakers by directing habitual ways of perceiving, analyzing, and categorizing experience. Thus language differences are *reality* differences that can create barriers to communication and understanding.

The principle of linguistic relativity is most closely associated with the linguists Edward Sapir and Benjamin Whorf. Their Sapir-Whorf Hypothesis is a classical theoretical formulation which is also important in its practical implications: i.e., that culture is relative; we express ourselves differently and thus understand things differently depending on the ways our cultures have taught us; and in order to bridge differences, we have to learn to see and describe reality in ways additional to what we have been brought up to see and describe.

Sapir and Whorf were Western scholars. What I find interesting is the correspondence of the principle of linguistic relativity with certain other traditions. For example, Lopon Tenzin Namdak, a Tibetan religious leader of the indigenous Bon, or Bonpo, tradition suggests a similar relationship between language and reality: "...we think that what we name must exist and be real.... We give the world a structure according to our use of language." I'm drawn to this idea of linguistic relativity, but I don't always buy it. Deep down, maybe I'm still that graduate student positivist I was making fun of earlier. Namdak again: "We falsely think that language mirrors reality. But we mislead ourselves." Maybe reality is something "out there," something that exists independent from me, my thoughts, my language. Or maybe the insistence on objectivity is all wrong, after all. I think of that old Zen question: *If a tree falls in a forest and no one is around to hear it, does it make a sound?* I'd like to hear your thoughts about this. I've been struggling with it for years.

IDEAS ABOUT PSYCHOLOGY

On projection.

Freud has been admired, debunked, accepted uncritically and rejected uncritically. Whatever one's position on his theories, they are clearly at the center of modern thinking about the human mind. I have always marveled at the airtight internal consistency of his explanatory system, even when I couldn't agree with certain concepts within the system. But more often than not, the concepts have made sense, particularly the dynamic of personality Freud termed "projection"—our tendency to endow others with attributes that we ourselves possess, and which in some instances may even be unacceptable to us.

When I first heard about the idea, I couldn't get it. It was too abstract for me to see how it actually played out in behaviors. Then one summer day I was on a bus in Boston when a young woman with a lovely, scantily-clad figure boarded. I guessed her age to be about 20. She paid the fare and stood in the aisle, no more than 15 feet from where I was seated. I concentrated on looking down at the floor so that no one, myself (especially myself) included, could have accused me of watching her, when in fact I was trying to take in every detail with practiced peripheral vision.

A man was seated mid-way between her and me. He was about my age, 10 or 12 years older than the woman. He stared at her with no attempt to disguise what he was doing. This enraged me. How could he? Pervert. Dirty old man...At once I "saw" myself in him. Or, more accurately, I saw myself *on* him. I was the projector, he the screen. Two dirty old men starred in that movie.

Have you experienced anything like this? (Not the dirty-old-men part...)

On autonomy and homonomy.

Andras Angyal was another personality theorist whose ideas have influenced me. He analyzed and explained the person as a holistic system, an organism which can't be separated from its surrounding environment without destroying the natural unity of the whole. Angyal called this indivisible entity the biosphere. (Please hang in here with me, Esther. I know it sounds jargon-y, but that's how Angyal presented it.)

He described certain processes that characterize the biospheric system's organization and dynamics. The most meaningful of these processes for me consists in the energy of the biosphere being fueled by the tension between the organismic pole and the environmental pole. Essentially, these are two opposite directional trends. One he called *autonomy*, the individual's movement toward self-determination by controlling the environment to satisfy one's desires and interests. Angyal called the contrary trend *homonomy*, the movement toward self-surrender in which the person seeks to participate in something larger than the individual self—a social group, nature, or an omnipotent being, for example.

Angyal went on to say that, while the two trends might appear to be opposed, they are actually two aspects of a more transcendent biospheric trend, which he termed self-expansion. In this conception, the person is an open system that both takes from the environment (autonomy) to expand the self and at the same time expands the environment by contributing to it. Seeing things as a complementary push and pull between self-determination and self-submersion continues to make perfect sense to me. Does it to you?

On chief feature.

My year in West Virginia was difficult, to be sure. But it was also very productive in the sense of gaining a deeper level of insight into myself specifically and human behavior generally. One significant psychological concept I learned there is Chief Feature.

In his *Psychological Commentaries on the Teachings of Gurdjieff & Ouspensky*, Maurice Nicoll recalled Gurdjieff's having "defined Chief Feature as the axle round which everything turns. He said: 'A man must work against Chief Feature in order to change himself.'" If the central axle goes unaddressed, change can't happen. But if working against it becomes one's primary aim, an entirely new psychology and perspective can develop in one's life. However, a person can't discover his or her chief feature suddenly. It takes long and earnest efforts at self-observation to do this, and until that work is well advanced, having someone identify it for you won't result in anything other than your unwillingness to accept what you're told. ("No! I'm not like that! I'm not defensive. You're wrong!") With effort, though, Nicoll says that "you can at least become conscious of how you are behaving," even if you can't change yourself. However, "This daily work builds up new memory which can begin to change you." Eventually, Nicoll continues, this hard-earned "work memory" developed by self-observation can help you discover your chief feature, and you'll begin to see "things in yourself that have been controlling you your whole life....Remember that the Work says that only an increase in consciousness can change you."

In my experience, recognizing chief feature depended on two things: first, sincere efforts at observing myself, and second, Laurent Ambrose's actually naming the feature that I had come close to identifying for myself, but not close enough to give it a label. Had I not devoted the self-observational work ahead of time, I would have rejected what he had to say because, as Nicoll points out with elegant sarcasm, "your picture of yourself is quite contrary to such an idea. There is of course nothing much wrong with you."

Thanks to Claymont, some hard personal work, and Laurent, I think I have a pretty good sense of what my "central axle" is. To be honest, I'm not at all proud of my chief feature and have never shared it with anyone. But I will with you. And maybe you'll share thoughts about what yours might be with me?

IDEAS ABOUT SELF-DEVELOPMENT

On one's decisions, and finding perspective.

"When you are still fragmented, lacking certainty, what difference does it make what your decisions are?" This quote by Hakim Sanai, an 11th century Persian Sufi mystic, comes from his *The Walled Garden of Truth*. I came across the passage, quoted in Idries Shah's *The Sufis*, during a troubled and searching time of my life. I wonder what you think of it.

At first, the idea he seemed to be proposing annoyed me. *What's he talking about?* I asked myself. *Every decision has a consequence, damn it. If you make the wrong one, it can really screw things up. Is he saying you shouldn't care? Or that you may as well punt and be reckless until your head is straight?*

But the quote got me thinking, and I concluded that of course I should care. Decisions often can't wait and absolutely do have consequences. You might be screwed up, but you still have to choose and act, wherever those choices and actions might lead. But at the same time, I think I recognized the essence of what Sanai was proposing: in order to make fundamentally *right* decisions, I needed to gain some solidity. I needed to strive for self-knowledge by working hard on myself, by doing all I could to find my ground and have faith that destiny might treat me kindly. And if it didn't? Well, I had done what I could.

But what I just wrote begs three questions: How to get a sense of oneself? How to define one's ground? From what point of view should one work hard and do one's best? These have been exceedingly difficult questions for me, and I don't pretend to have anything approaching full answers, although I have come to a few tentative conclusions.

The first conclusion is that memory is both a valuable friend and a ferocious enemy. In his book *Warrior's Way*, Robert de Ropp catches the enemy part well. "Nostalgia practically destroyed me," he writes. "It cut me off from the real world, weakened me, confused me, brought me to the edge of suicide. Nostalgia is fatal to the spirit of the warrior, whose task is to live in the here and now, not hankering after the past or fussing about the future." I think what de Ropp is pointing to here is the danger of letting yourself wallow in memories. Memories are inescapable phenomena in the human make-up. If used intelligently and unsentimentally, they can be of tremendous value in helping us to identify our habitual patterns, understand our personal psychology, and remind us of what we want to change. The danger is in allowing ourselves to be imprisoned by our memories and obsessively keep returning to them. Thwarting this danger requires that we see the memories without identifying with them, that we don't let them take over and drag us into useless depression, self-recrimination, second-guessing, self-justification, resentment, or other energy-depleting fantasies. You and I have shared a lot of memories—difficult ones about some very hard times. Do I dwell on those too much? I know that I do but can't help it. As de Ropp rightly says, such wallowing can be a real trap.

My second conclusion relates to the other part of de Ropp's statement about "the spirit of the warrior, whose task is to live in the here and now, not hankering after the past or fussing about the future." Finding perspective, in other words, depends on our capacity to cut out and cut through the things I mentioned in my first conclusion—to de-fang the past, which can't be changed in any event, and ignore at least those fruitless, anxious projections into a future that can't be known or controlled. Of all the people I've known, if anyone has a warrior's spirit, it's you. I can hear you now: "Cut the crap,

Nathan." But it's true and no idle compliment. I think you've pretty much de-fanged the past. How? I badly want to know; I'm such a prisoner of my past.

My third conclusion concerning perspective is to concentrate on doing, to the best of one's ability, what's required in a situation. Again, this depends on being able to focus on the here and now, without allowing one's energies to be siphoned off into preoccupations with the irreparable past or the un-controllable future. (Easy to say...) Sure, the past, properly considered, can help prevent mistakes or offer a better way forward in the present situation. And implications for the future are important to identify and consider. But the emphasis should be on sizing needs up right now.

My fourth conclusion on perspective is that I'm not unique or spe-cial. My self is no better, or worse, than anyone else's. We're all in the same boat—impermanent, doomed to die, and thus worthy of mutual compassion in equal measure.

And my fifth and final conclusion is this: pause, whenever the instinct comes to you, and remember yourself—remember that there is someone more than the automaton of habit, someone who has, by grace, luck, ac-cident, what have you, the capacity to be aware and present and open to a greater possibility. How to realize that possibility?

I've had fleeting experiences with each of these five conclusions; they're not entirely theoretical. But I want to make the phenomena they describe more regular and active parts of myself. I'd like for this to be a project we can approach together.

IDEAS ABOUT MEDITATION

On the reasons for doing it.

I've been a meditator for as long as you've known me. Yet you've never once asked me why I do it. Out of politeness, I'd guess. But I'd also guess you might think it's a strange, Nathan-type waste of time and wonder: *Why does he sit there for an hour or more every day, sometimes on a chair, sometimes on a cushion, doing nothing?* It's a legitimate question with more than one answer, because meditation works at different, and often interacting, levels—physiological, psychological, and spiritual.

For example, it's been shown to help with stress reduction, slower heart-beat, lower blood pressure, and overall relaxation, and it's not unusual for med-itators to experience increases in gentleness, patience, and sense of humor. The Buddhist teacher Pema Chödrön identified these five qualities nurtured by meditation: (1) *steadfastness*, or the ability to stay with an experience; (2) *clear-seeing*, which refers to a nonjudgmental, unbiased clarity in seeing our-selves and our patterns; (3) *courage*, which is the capacity to experience discom-fort, trials, and tribulations and gradually to shake up our habitual patterns; (4) *attention*, the ability to be in the present moment, awake to our lives, ready to meet the unknown wholeheartedly and good-humoredly, and then to welcome the next moment; and (5) the attitude that *it's no big deal,* life happens, my highs and lows aren't special—the attitude that says "see it all, love it all."

Chögyam Trungpa Rinpoche, Chödrön's teacher, described yet another dimension. "Meditation," he said, "is not a matter of trying to achieve ecstasy, spiritual bliss or tranquility, nor is it attempting to become a better person. It is simply the creation of a space in which we are able to expose and undo our neurotic games, our self-deceptions, our hidden fears and hopes. We provide space through the simple discipline of doing nothing."

So: through the discipline of meditation, of doing nothing, we relax, stay present, quiet the mind, and see ourselves. And, depending on how ardently we practice, we might experience something that meditators from varied traditions have pointed to for centuries. In his autobiography *A Voice at the Borders of Silence,* the Fourth Way teacher and Zen practitioner William Segal writes, "There are no associations, the mind and body are stilled... It could be called a state of absolute equilibrium, a balance of all parts of oneself...an acceptance of the 'Is-ness' of things."

This is all closely related to what I wrote earlier about finding perspective. Is meditation something you'd be interested in doing with me? If so, here are some methods we might explore together.

On breathing.

How does one get to this acceptance that Segal mentions? The literature on meditation is vast, and many methods of practice specific to one or another tradition have been suggested and systematized. Much depends on the purposes of meditation in the particular tradition, its modes of instruction, the style of the instructor, and the level of the individual student. But many of the approaches I've surveyed have in common, at least as a starting point, the focus on breath: becoming aware of it, following it, counting its cycles of inhalation and exhalation, then losing and returning to it time and again as one moves, according to the degree of diligence in one's practice, towards deepening concentration, insight, and stillness.

On just sitting.

Certain other aspects of meditation also seem to be basic across traditions. Posture, for example, should be erect. As a practical matter, this will help prevent drowsiness. Another consideration is energy flow (a topic I'll return to later). "Sit with your back straight," Eva Wong advises in *Seven Taoist Masters,* "because only with a vertical spine can the energy rise to the head."

A second common aspect in meditative approaches is scanning, by which I mean moving one's attention from place to place in the body in order to identify tensions and then try to relax them. Scanning can also be applied to sensations and feelings. Until recently, I had settled on the view that the aim of meditation is unity with the divine, to which the senses are obstacles; one should rid oneself of them, disregard and transcend them. It consoles me to hope that unity might await me, should my efforts be earnest and sincere enough. But then I began to think about it differently: why would the Unity, God, the Tao, the Great Spirit, or what have you give us the senses if we're to disregard them? They're wonderful—sometimes painful, sometimes pleasurable, but full of wonder and alive. Unity may or may not be in my future. But this life—what I see, hear, feel, smell, taste, touch, sense—is now. The body is the gateway to presence, I remember reading somewhere. And this was reinforced the other day when I came across this quote from Chip Hartranft's editorial commentary on *The Yoga-Sūtra of Patañjali*: "The yogas of both Patañjali and Siddhartha Gautama regard bodily sensation as a foundation of mindfulness and therefore a direct path to understanding the nature of consciousness." Instead of rejecting this gift, we should relish it. Be thankful for what has been given us. Enjoy this body and the things of the world it allows us to experience. And if it's really all one—non-duality—in the end what's the difference? When we die and the senses, presumably, are gone we can abide in the unity. But for now, we have the gift of our senses. Let's do our best to attend to them, to what we have.

A third common aspect of meditation is the emphasis on detaching from thoughts when they arise. There's nothing wrong with having thoughts; how can we not have them? The issue is not identifying with them, not becoming them. In the state of calm and equilibrium, when the roiling mind has been tamed, you're neutral with respect to the Eight Worldly Concerns mentioned in the ancient Buddhist philosopher Nāgārjuna's *Letter to a Friend*: neither pleasure nor pain, gain or no gain, fame or disgrace, praise or blame will affect you.

As always, we are pulled back to the crucial question: How? How do we dissociate? How do we manage to be unperturbed and unaffected? How do we *proceed* in this practice called meditation? Lately, I've found suggestions from two sources, one ancient and the other modern, who have been helpful. The ancient source is the 11th century Tantric Buddhist Tilopa, who offered "Six Words of Advice": 1. *Don't recall*, let go of what has passed. 2. *Don't imagine*, let go of what may come. 3. *Don't think*, let go of what is happening now. 4. *Don't examine*, don't try to figure anything out. 5. *Don't control*, don't try to make anything happen. 6. *Rest*, relax right now.

The modern suggestions come from the Zen teacher Dharmachari Subhuti (Alex Kennedy), who recommends "The Five Justs" for meditators: (1) *Just Settle* (calm your mind). (2) *Just Wait* (for whatever arises). (3) *Just Watch* (what comes and goes). (4) *Just Enjoy* (the flow, the show). (5) *Just Sit*; there is nothing more you need to do.

I love the simplicity and memorize-ability of both sets of suggestions. They help me a lot. And some days, when I'm having trouble even with these few words of advice, I boil it down to two suggestions, one from each list: Just rest. Just sit.

IDEAS ABOUT ENERGY

On the work of Wilhelm Reich.

I first heard of the psychoanalyst Wilhelm Reich during college. The outlines of Dr. Reich's life immediately fascinated me—his ground-breaking work *Character Analysis*, his insights into the biological basis of neurosis, his discovery of what he called cosmic orgone energy, his close relationship with and then painful break from Freud, the harassment and slander he suffered at the hands of the psychoanalytic community, and his death in a U. S. Federal prison. But it wasn't until several years after college that I began to grasp Reich's significance, particularly with respect to his work on Life Energy.

I remember the day well. My parents invited me to join a group of their friends at a barbeque in one friend's back yard. That friend's son, a guy my age, was there as well. Let's call him John, which isn't his real name because what he told me that day was quite personal. I had known John for years, and we spent most of the afternoon talking with each other. Somewhere in the conversation he pointed to a man I had also known for most of my life, the husband of one of my mother's closest friends. I knew he was a psychiatrist who was originally from Italy, but few other details. We'll call him Dr. X.

"Dr. X saved my life," John said, and described a psychological malady he had suffered from as an adolescent. He had been unable to stop swallowing, and it was literally driving him crazy. Dr. X agreed to accept John as a patient and soon stopped the problem, which never recurred.

"How did he stop the problem? What did he do?"

"He taught me to throw up every morning. Not that food would necessarily come up. That was rare. But the important thing was to create a gag reflex, the idea being that my throat muscles were preventing a healthy flow of energy."

I couldn't understand what John was talking about and told him so. "Think of a tree," he explained. "That's the analogy Dr. X used. The sap flows unimpeded from the roots to the leaves. If that vertical flow is cut off, the sap is cut off, nourishment stops, energy diminishes, and the tree eventually dies. That's what was happening to me. I was running out of energy. What Dr. X called Life Energy. He got it moving again. 'Think of the tree,' he told me in his infectious Italian enthusiasm. 'Whoosh! Whoosh! The sap, its food and energy, flows up its trunk—Free! Free!—from the earth to the sky.' I haven't missed a single morning of putting my finger in my mouth to provoke my gag reflex ever since."

Later that day, I spoke with Dr. X and learned that his therapeutic approach was modeled on something called bioenergetics. The next day, I looked it up and learned that the therapy was based on the work of Wilhelm Reich, who claimed that psychological traumas create muscular armaments which, much as John had described, cut off our normal, vertical flow of energy. These blockages can be buried in various places—the groin, the solar plexus, or the throat, for example.

Subsequently I read much more about Reich, the details of whose life and work are endlessly informative, poignant, and cautionary. But the basic image of the tree never left me, and intuition tells me that life or cosmic energy, Orgone energy in Reich's terminology, is at the root of things, and I'm sure that understanding it would reveal many secrets.

On the transformation of energy.

In readings that range from Thermodynamics to Kabbalah to Kriya Yoga to Taoism, I have often been reminded of Dr. X's image of sap rising up from the tree's roots to its canopy and then on into the atmosphere. These and other traditions describe how energy similarly ascends, both in the universe ("As above") and the human body ("so below"), and becomes increasingly refined along the way. This example, again from Eva Wong's *Seven Taoist Masters*, is especially descriptive:

> I am not very learned [said Sun Yuan-chen], but I have read a few Taoist classics of internal alchemy. They describe how the generative energy [in the groin area] can be transformed into vital energy [the heart area], how the vital energy can be transformed into spiritual energy [the head and eyes], how the spirit can be cultivated to return to the void, and how the void can be cultivated to merge with the Tao.

The Gurdjieff system might see a connection between generative energy and the physical center, vital energy and the emotions, and spiritual energy and the intellect. Yoga might describe the process in terms of energy's ascent along seven *chakras*, or energy centers, via the *nāḍī*, or energy channels. Likewise, opening the "seven seals" of spiritual perception is mentioned in Christianty's *Book of Revelation*. In Sufism, the *lataif* (plural, *latifa* in the singular) comprise a system of six centers, or organs, of psycho-spiritual perception. Kabbalistic Judaism speaks of the ten *sefiroth*, or divine emanations.

None of these systems can be perfectly equated; there are certainly differences among them. But there are significant similarities as well, and they all seem to be describing a process of cerebrospinal movement in which energies are transformed—from coarser to finer, from physical to spiritual.

There's so much more I'd like to explore and understand about the transformation of energy. Maybe this is a topic we can take on together?

IDEAS ABOUT UNITY

On differentiation and integration.

On one of our walks, you recalled that we had discussed this idea. You said it was an example of the kind of thing you wanted me to write about, and it has led to this letter. Here it is in more detail.

I enjoyed college and graduate school for the freedom I had to explore. I took advantage of every opportunity to take courses over a range of disciplines, including several in which I had no intrinsic interest, much less aptitude. Management was one of those no-interest areas. I signed up for a course in organizational behavior largely because classmates spoke highly of the two professors who co-taught it, Paul Lawrence and Jay Lorsch of the business school at Harvard. The course was based primarily on a comparative study they had recently completed of six organizations operating in the same industrial environment. The deadly dryness of the topic nearly led me to drop the course on the first day. But I decided to give it a chance, and I was happy I did, because during the second session Lawrence and Lorsch presented the pivotal concepts underlying their research and further theory building: differentiation and integration. It took me a while to absorb the concept because of the convoluted way they defined it. (Honestly, Esther, we all would have benefitted from having you in class. I'll always be guided now by how you said you understood the idea when I first mentioned it to you: "how everything, everyone," you said, "is unique and universal, a distinct individual as well as a tiny part of the whole, both at the same time. Like the separate waves on the ocean's surface, what we're looking at now, and the vast world below, which we can't see but we know is always there. Each wave is different from the next, but they all flow back into the deeper sea." So beautiful. So clear.) Once I got past the opaque language Lawrence and Lorsch used, the concept itself was exciting and revelatory. And despite its being grounded in the unappealing context of industry, it inspired the philosopher in me to consider the broader implications and applications of the idea, something I have been doing ever since I took the course back in 1967. There's the connection to Taoism, for example, a philosophy I've been quite taken with lately. Eva Wong, in *Taoism: An Essential Guide*, writes that

> Before we were born, we were part of the Tao. Formless and undifferentiated from the Tao, we were not subject to birth and death, and growth and decay. In this state, there is no form, no mind, no body, no sense, and no feeling...The fetus represents a break, or separation, from the Tao: it has taken a form and is no longer undifferentiated from the Tao....When the physical body dies, the yuan-shen [original spirit] is liberated and is once again merged with the undifferentiated energy of the Tao. This is the final stage of internal alchemy—returning to where we were before we were born.

The Hindu *Upanishads* poetically echo the Taoist perspective. "This is the truth: the sparks, though of one nature with the fire, leap from it; uncounted beings leap from the Everlasting, but these, my son, merge into It again."

As powerful as the concept is on the intellectual and spiritual levels, differentiation-integration also has significant practical implications, inasmuch as it helps us to relate different phenomena and aspects of reality that are at work, often simultaneously, in real-life situations. Paramahansa Yogananda, for example, addresses this in the most basic humanitarian terms in *The Yoga of Jesus*:

> Truth, in and of itself is the ultimate 'religion'....The sectarian stamp of human affiliation is of little meaning. It is not the religious denomination in which one's name is registered, nor the culture or creed in which one was born, that gives salvation. The essence of truth goes beyond all outer form...We are all children of God, from our inception unto eternity. Differences come from prejudices, and prejudice is the child of ignorance. We should not proudly identify ourselves as Americans or Indians or Italians or any other nationality, for that is but an accident of birth.

And David Shulman, in his afterword to the Israeli novelist S. Yizhar's *Khirbet Khizeh* (the title is the name of a fictional Palestinian village in the late 1940s), describes the differentiation-integration relationship clearly and concretely in the tumultuous context of modern inter-ethnic conflict. "Morality," Shulman writes, "in the usual sense of the word is perhaps the least of it. Rather, the choice has something to do with extricating oneself from the thick envelope of one's tribe and neighbors and colleagues...so as to touch, at least in passing, that elusive, unsentimental freedom that defines the human being. It is from this point that one can act."

I think all of this boils down to how we relate the individual to the whole, the particular to the universal. This strikes me as so important in our troubled world, where our prejudices and inability to cooperate threaten survival some place or another every single day. This brings me to two useful ideas from the social sciences, a set of disciplines whose courses I appreciated at Harvard for their applied value. First is the distinction between a stereotype and a generalization. Second is the idea of the superordinate goal.

On stereotypes and generalizations.

Stereotyping occurs when we take a characteristic that we have come to associate with people from a particular culture (based on media images and personal experiences), apply it to all members of the culture (e.g., "Italians are highly emotional"), treat the characterization as a truth, and fail to acknowledge that some people in the culture will differ from the (perceived) norm. Stereotypes, in other words, mask differences among individuals. As such, whether positive or negative, they are distortions of other cultures.

A generalization is when we take a characteristic derived from the same media and experiential sources and treat it cautiously as a hypothesis rather than a fact. A generalization recognizes that there is diversity within a cultural group and not all members possess particular attributes. Generalizations, then, can be considered provisional statements—for example, "Based on what I know at this point, Italians are likely, but not necessarily in every case, to be more expressive and emotional than we are."

On superordinate goals.

This idea is most associated with the Turkish-American social psychologist Muzafer Sherif. He posited that more positive intergroup relations will occur if goals can be identified that are not only desired by each of the groups (i.e., common goals), but in fact cannot be attained without all of their cooperative efforts. The goals must certainly be held in common, at minimum. But the chances of success are improved to the extent that the desired result (a problem to be solved, the establishment of a program, etc.) stimulates the necessary commitment, resources, and efforts of all concerned parties.

In this conflict-ridden world, I believe that the identification of superordinate goals has important implications for improved communication, reduced competition, increased cooperation, and a modification of negative inter-group stereotypes. We're both big news readers. Maybe discussing daily world events in terms of these ideas will put a whole new slant on things. I can see the headline now in the *New York Times*: **Kirinskis Win Nobel Peace Prize!**

On balance and harmony.

Given my tumultuous history, I'm hardly the one to talk about the "Middle Way," but it's a philosophy I deeply admire, and I wish I had the temperament and capacity to attain it in my life. In my view, polarity is a fundamental characteristic of the universe at every level of human existence. The pendulum never ceases to swing in politics, economies, fashions, social conventions, one's emotions—you name it. Depending on degree, the swings can be creative or destructive. But the ideal for me are the moderates, those who can navigate constructively between opposites and avoid extremes. Being able to walk the Middle Way, the way of harmony and balance, is truly an art.

The Middle Way has been an ideal and objective in various traditions: Eastern, Western, philosophical, religious, and scientific. Taoism centers on the principle of balance and fusion between opposites (Yin and Yang) and the ideal of human nature aligning with great nature and the cosmos. Buddhism's Middle Way is a path of moderation that rejects the extremes of austerity and self-mortification, on the one hand, and sensual indulgence on the other. The ancient Greeks espoused the Golden Mean, the desirable, symmetrical, proportional, and harmonious middle between extremes. Later European philosophers valued dialogue between opposite sides and often sought a synthesis, a moderate position between opposites, from the dialogue as well. In Gurdjieff's teaching, balance is defined by the harmonious interaction and operation of the intellect, the emotions, and the body. And both the sciences and social sciences refer to homeostasis, or the processes by which living things seek to survive by maintaining stable, steady-state conditions in the face of conflicting phenomena (psychological stress in an individual, political upheavals in society, chemical imbalances in the body, etc.).

In college I was introduced to Lao-tzu's *Tao Te Ching*—in English, *The Way and Its Power*. I loved it, and memorized a quotation I recite to this day whenever I see moving bodies of water: "Those who flow as water flows know they need no other force. Feel no wear, feel no tear, need no mending, no repair." When I die I want to be cremated and have my ashes poured into the Atlantic. That way, despite my inability to have walked the Middle Way in life, perhaps I can at least swim it in death.

Please, Esther: Throw me in!

Would she have liked what I wrote? Would she have found the ideas useful? I like to imagine she would. Imagining is all I can do.

Vic's Italian Restaurant, where Esther worked, closed at 11:00 p.m., and it was Esther's routine to phone me when she left the pizzeria for the ten-minute drive home. Closing up sometimes took longer after a busy night, so I wasn't worried when her call didn't come until midnight or so. But it wasn't Esther. It was the dispatcher from the Neptune City Police Department telling me that my wife had been in an accident and was in the emergency room at Jersey Shore Medical Center. A drunken driver had run a red light at the corner of Corlies Avenue and Main Street in Neptune and smashed into the driver's-side door. The dispatcher had no information about Esther's condition. I was at the hospital within minutes. A doctor came out to tell me that my wife was dead.

I spent the next month walking robotically through the logistics of death: funeral arrangements, death certificate, bank accounts, insurance, car titles, leases, notifying people and agencies, selling and giving things away, probate, and dealing with legal issues stemming from the accident. I applied for, and was quickly granted, an indefinite leave of absence from the post office.

Arnie and my parents joined me at Monmouth Memorial Park for the interment of Esther's ashes in a plot I had secured near Deb's. The plaque I had commissioned read:

Esther O'Connell Kirinski
Beloved Wife and Friend
February 14, 1948 – March 16, 1990

"The same age as our Deborah," Morton observed as he patted my shoulder.

"She was a true Valentine," Fay said, referring to Esther's birthdate as she hugged me. "A sweet, lovely Valentine."

I told my family that I planned to travel for a while to get my thoughts together. I also told them I would be in touch. At the time I said this, such was my intention.

Part Five

Leaving, Returning, Leaving

Nathan's Memoir
1990 - 2012

1
Ellen

I HAD PHONED ANCHORAGE before the funeral to tell Ellen and Holly about Esther. There was no answer, so I left a detailed message on their answering machine and asked them to call me back. They never did, which didn't surprise me. Up until the time she was 10 years old, the arrangement for Ellen to come east every summer was in effect. But those visits came to an end at Holly and Ellen's urging. And by the time Ellen turned 14, my twice-a-year trips to Alaska became such unendurable exercises in recriminations from Holly and disinterest from Ellen that it no longer made sense for me to go there. By the time Esther died, Ellen was 16, and I hadn't been in contact with her for quite a while. My letters, except for a monthly child-support check to Holly, and packages came back unopened, and my phone calls went unanswered. I was in despair about my daughter's estrangement and at a loss over what I could do.

Holly had married Warren in 1982, when Ellen was eight, and they divorced two years later. There were suggestions by people I knew in Alaska that Warren had gotten into drugs and become physically abusive to both Holly and Ellen. The same people also told me that Holly had developed a serious drinking problem, and during her frequent binges she would blame me for the way her life had turned out, complaining in one breath that "If he hadn't screwed up his career, we'd still be an intact family living the good life in Boston," and in the next that I had only cared about my career, and never about the family. Inevitably, Ellen was influenced by these diatribes. How could she not have been? I became the villain, the reason she and her mother were stuck in Alaska, living in a trailer, struggling to make ends meet.

When I failed again to contact Holly and Ellen after the funeral I phoned Leonard Richardson, one of Holly's and my mutual friends in Anchorage, to ask him to get word to Ellen that Esther was dead. He promised to contact Holly and get back to me. When he did, he told me that Ellen was now a runaway. According to Holly, she had left home two months before, and no one had any idea where she was.

I walked the three miles to my parents' home and entered without knocking. My mother, father, and brother were in the living room.

"I don't know what to do. Without Esther. And now Ellen. She ran away. No one knows where she is. I don't..."

The three of them embraced me as I stood there sobbing.

After Esther's funeral, I terminated our rental lease, gave away whatever hadn't already been sold or thrown out, and arranged for all mail to be forwarded to Arnie's. He agreed to take care of whatever bills hadn't been debited automatically from the substantial checking account I set up for that purpose. Aside from necessary clothes and several favorite books, I kept only our second car; Esther's had been totaled.

I headed west with no particular plan, inspired by William Least-Heat Moon's *Blue Highways* and Clancy Sigal's *Going Away*, books that resonated closely with my needs to mourn, ponder, wander, and re-group. I had no sense of how long I might be gone, nor did I have any intention of being out of contact with my family for any extended period of time. As it happened, I was away for the next 12 years, and once again incommunicado except for a phone call to the post office six months into my sojourn to terminate my employment there. My sympathetic supervisor encouraged me to call it an indefinite leave of absence, apply for reinstatement when I returned, and, if I didn't return, make sure I got whatever retirement money I had coming to me after nine years of service. He also gave me advice on health insurance options.

My travels took me across America from 1990 to 1993 and for nine years after that to Japan, Korea, Thailand, Nepal, India, and China. My financial reserves were enough for my spartan lifestyle and the places I visited. I had my car for most of my three years in America. When it died after two and a half years I was content to take buses, hitchhike, and walk. I was also content to be homeless when necessary. For several stretches of time, I lived in communes and religious communities across the U.S. During my nine years in Asia, I frequented monasteries or took English teaching jobs that came with room and board.

I began those wanderings burdened with regret about my ex-wife's disintegration, grief over my late-wife's demise, and now fear, to go along with my long-standing remorse, about my teenage daughter. There was nothing I could do about Holly. Or Esther. But Ellen....

The World Wide Web became publicly and freely available in 1993. Everywhere I went from then on, from Brooklyn to Seattle, Laramie to San Antonio, wherever, I made it a habit to use the computers in public libraries to catch up on news and examine my bank statements, but principally to search for Ellen. I finally got a lead during a stopover at the local library in Coeur d'Alene, Idaho. An 18-year-old named Ellen Kirinski had been picked up for loitering in Sparks, Nevada. She was released on her own recognizance but had also been assigned a liaison in a local social service agency who would be responsible for helping her navigate her way through various legal and other processes before she was to appear in court three days later. This in itself was not especially newsworthy. But the reason it had made the Sparks and Reno newspapers was a heated public complaint by one of the involved court clerks. It was not just that Ms. Kirinski had failed to show up in court, something that wasn't so unusual. But somewhere in the process the agency, unidentified in the article, lost track of her person as well as her file. This had all occurred less than a week before I read the account. Slight though it was, I had a lead. And at that point I still had my car, so I headed for Sparks, a 12-hour, 800-mile drive south.

I spent a week looking for more leads. Between Internet searches and inquiries at shelters and agencies, I picked up a few bucks doing day labor in Reno—clearing rocks from a pasture for show horses, distributing advertisements for a new pizza parlor, bagging debris littering the grounds surrounding a salvage company. The first two nights, I slept in my car in an expanse of prairieland down the road from South Valleys Public Library, a nice, uncrowded facility with mostly open computer terminals and friendly librarians who had no problem with my presence or my use of the restrooms. The library was only ten miles from downtown Reno, where most of the regional agencies had offices, and 20 miles from Carson City, the state capital—perfectly located, I thought, for following up any leads I might discover.

But I got worried the second night when several cars slowed down as they passed the site where I was parked. Maybe there was nothing to worry about, but I decided to move 15 miles up the highway toward Lake Tahoe and stay at Mt. Rose Campground, a 9000-foot high site maintained by the U.S. Forest Service. It was farther out, 25 miles from downtown Reno in one direction and 30 from Carson City in another, but at $15 a night it was cheap, safe, beautiful, and, since peak season had just ended when I arrived, almost empty of other campers. The September temperatures got down into the 40s at night, but I had a high-quality sleeping bag. I could also use electricity at the campground and cook on my Coleman stove. Best of all, the public restrooms had hot-water showers. In a month, the campground would close down until spring, but I was confident that my search would conclude by then, whether successfully or not was an open question. And there would always be other places to sleep if there were still leads to follow, even if not so well-suited as Mt. Rose.

By the end of my first week in the area, I was frustrated. I had exhausted whatever Internet searches I could think of, and none of the agency personnel I spoke with knew anything more about the possible whereabouts of Ellen Kirinski than I had learned from reading the article back in Coeur d'Alene. Frustration turned to depression by the end of the second week. I bought a bottle of bourbon, telling myself a drink or two in the evenings would soothe my nerves and feelings of failure and self-loathing. Soon it was three, four, and five drinks a night, and then a bottle. I was relapsing into the alcohol abuse triggered by Cambridge, Claymont, and the breakup of my family. I decided to look for an Alcoholics Anonymous meeting. A guy I traded life stories with during one of my day-labor jobs told me about a meeting he went to from time to time in downtown Reno, a two-minute walk from City Hall.

The next evening I drove the 25 miles from Mt. Rose Campground to the address he had given me on West 1st Street. But the night I picked was an Al-Anon session primarily attended by families of alcoholics, not an AA meeting. Still, I decided to stay. I was drowning in self-recrimination as well as in bourbon. I needed something, some support, some company, some perspective.

I sat in the back of the large basement room listening to a series of accounts, each interesting in its own way and a poignant mixture, I thought, of optimism and desperation. After a while, though, the testimonies to patience, non-judgment, love, and compassion were starting to sound the same, and I began to tune out. Then a young woman stood up, hardly more than a girl, tall and thin with short, dyed-pink hair. She wore a plaid, lumberjack-type shirt and faded, patched dungarees.

"Hi, my name is Ellen," she told the 30 or so of us sitting there. "Right now I'm a runaway from my alcoholic mother. I love my mother. She did her best to take care of me after we'd been abandoned by my father and then by my stepfather. I'm still struggling to come to grips with the father part, which happened a long time ago, but we were actually lucky more recently when my stepfather left. He was an alcoholic himself and beat us up whenever he got drunk. But Mom and I were in it together, and as I said, I love her for always being there, in spite of her own problems. But I had to run away. I couldn't take the screaming and arguments anymore." She stopped. Her eyes were wet. We waited.

"Sometime I want to go back to her, though, and that's why I'm here. I need tools to work with when I do go back. I want to learn to forgive my mom, to understand and support her. I have so many questions." Her voice broke and she stopped again. Again we waited. "How can I let go of the anger I feel towards all of them, my mom included? How can I stay sane when I'm around her? How can I learn to actually show her my love, and not just tell myself that I love her when we're apart?

"I don't expect to change her. Her issues are so deep, her illness is so serious. And the father part. How can I change my attitude and stop blaming him? How can I get past my anger, which right now doesn't feel possible? He really let me down.

"Thank you for this chance to share," she finished to applause. "Thank you for listening."

The meeting ended a half-hour later, and most people stayed behind for coffee and snacks. I walked up to the girl named Ellen, who was standing by herself in a corner.

"Ellen Kirinski?" I don't know what I expected: that she would turn away or yell at me or hit me or hug me seemed like the most likely possibilities. But she did none of those.

"It's weird to see you here," she said calmly. "What do you want?"

"I came here tonight for my own needs. I had no way of knowing you'd be here, not in this specific building, anyway, and not tonight. But I saw a Sparks newspaper article several weeks ago about a runaway named Ellen Kirinski, so

I drove here from Idaho to see if I could find you. I've been anxious to recon-nect since we lost touch four years ago. And I kept trying to contact you, but I never heard back when I wrote and left messages on your answering machine. In one message I told you that Esther was killed in an accident. That was two years ago. When I didn't hear anything after that, I found out from Leonard Richardson back in Anchorage that you were gone and started searching for you. Now that I've found you, I hope we can renew our relationship. Can we?"

She didn't speak for a while. "I'm sorry about Esther. I didn't know. Two years ago was about the time I left Anchorage or I would have contacted you for something as important as that, and my mother wouldn't have called you back for any reason, assuming she even got the message. But as for re-newing our relationship—no, not yet. Maybe never. But not yet anyhow."

"Can we go talk somewhere, at least? I'd like to explain things, give my own version of what led up to your mom and I splitting up, and what hap-pened afterward."

"I already said not yet, if ever. What part of that don't you get?"

"But why?" I persisted.

"You were my father. I really," her voice broke, "loved you. Then you let me down. You never came to get me, to get me away from fucking Warren. You abandoned me," she said, then added, with obvious sarcasm, "—Dad. And those times I came to visit you, sleeping on the couch, no room of my own, no privacy when I was on the phone with my mom or even to take a bath. It was fun when I was a little kid—the beach, the playgrounds, grandma and grandpa and Uncle Arnie doting on me all the time...I miss them a lot...Privacy didn't matter then, but it did as I got old-er. The worst of it, though, was that I never felt part of things, part of you and Esther. I always felt like an add-on, kind of an obligation you couldn't wait to see leave so you could return to your life as a couple. With you, it was all about Esther. And Esther—it was pretty clear that she resented me for taking your time and attention away from her. I didn't much like her either after a while, but I don't blame her. She didn't know what to do with me except to assign me chores or tell me to hurry up with my bath. And I wasn't her kid. But I was your kid, and I do blame you. First you let me down. Then you left me out."

I was stung by the past-tense use of "were my father" and "loved you" and "was your kid," her repetition of the complaint she had shared with the group about my having let her down, and by the way she said 'Dad.' But I decided not to push things. Better not to be defensive. Better not to force an explanation of why I did what I did, or my feelings about what her mother did. Ellen's reservoir of resentment seemed too deep. Instead I asked, "Can I at least give you a way to contact me if you need anything?"

After some thought, she agreed. I had no address or phone number, so I gave her Arnie's. Then she walked away.

2
Korea, 1995

I LEFT AMERICA IN 1993, lived in Japan for two years, and then spent 1995 to 1997 in Korea. The first year I taught English at an institute connected with a university in Seoul.

One of my students was a woman, in her early 30s, I guessed, named Kim Ju Ok. Her English was already proficient. She had been sent to the institute by her company, she told me, for a short-term, intensive "brush-up" so that she could translate for and correspond with her company's prospective foreign clients. Her company was a small but growing electronics firm in Chunchon, a provincial city 60 miles northeast of Seoul near the de-militarized zone between North and South Korea. "Now," Ms. Kim told me, "we have few foreign clients. But soon we hope to have many."

We met for coffee several times during her three-week course. This wasn't unusual; institute students tried to take advantage of every opportunity to practice their English with native English-speakers generally and, better yet, institute instructors, who had the professional knowledge to guide learning as well as converse.

"Please tell me a little about yourself," I asked at our first get-together. "Where are you from?"

"I am from Hyoja-dong, a small town near the city of Chunchon. I went to Chunchon to work after I graduated from high school in Hyoja-dong."

"Do you have a family?"

"Kirinski *Sunsengnim*, Professor Kirinski—Are you asking if I'm married?" She laughed as I blushed. "No, I am not married, and I am 32 years old. In English, I think you say I'm an old maid."

"Do you live in Chunchon City?"

"Yes, in a *hasuk chip*, a boarding house that belongs to my company."

I asked a few more pedestrian questions under the guise of conversational practice, which she clearly didn't need. And I didn't need to learn that she was very attractive. That much I knew by looking at her.

"How did you learn English? It's excellent."

"In school. I studied English for many years."

This was the answer I typically got from students I complimented in response to my equally typical question. But she's unusual, I thought. Granted that Korean high school graduates have studied English for years. But the pedagogical approach was right out of Imperial Japan, which had occupied Korea from the early 1900s until the end of World War II and deeply influenced the educational system for decades thereafter. The attention was on grammar, reading, and writing. It was not so common to find products of that education who could actually speak English. Things were changing as Korea

adapted to the requirements, first of internationalization and then globaliza-
tion, but the changes in English-language pedagogy were slow.

Towards the end of her course, Miss Kim offered to show me around
her "beautiful" city during my upcoming winter break. I was quick to accept.
"You're kind to invite me. I haven't had a chance to see anything of Korea yet
outside of Seoul. And Seoul is so huge and busy. A smaller, quieter setting
is just what I need."

Left unsaid was my deeper need for a relationship with a woman, even
a Platonic one. Esther had died five years before; I had been "chaste," both
emotionally and physically, ever since. We traded phone numbers. She gave
me the name and address of a Chunchon *tabang*, or tea house, where we
would meet on the Saturday after I turned in my grades.

On the appointed day I took the subway to Kangbyeon Station, across
from Dong-Seoul Bus Terminal. I had come to enjoy public transportation
in Seoul for the moments of incongruity that often presented themselves
during my rides, such as my sighting on this particular morning of an old
man in traditional Korean clothing in this modern subway car, sitting amidst
advertisements of laptops and liqueurs and jetliners and, a few minutes later,
of a Buddhist monk, in full religious regalia complete with wide basket hat,
speaking on a cell phone.

I had been steeping myself in Korean history since my first day in country. T. R. Fehrenbach's 1963 book about the Korean conflict, *This Kind of
War*, was one of the resources I turned to most often, not only because of its
quality as a written account but also because of the striking photos the book
contained. I thought of those photos throughout the hour and 40-minute
ride to Chunchon, my first foray into the Korean countryside. The mountains we were driving through had been starkly beautiful 40 years ago, but
it was a different, bleaker beauty then because there were no trees. Four
decades of Japanese occupation, the Korean War, and the desperate need for
fuel conspired to defoliate much of the country. Seeing this new lushness, I
felt admiration for this nation's accomplishments since its days, not so long
ago, as one of the world's poorest countries.

The well-engineered highways and tunnels the bus was transiting now
manifested Korea's progress, I reflected as I looked out the window of this
luxury bus at the sports fishermen, power boats, and water skiers populating
the broad, lovely river that bordered the road. Where there had only been
impoverished and wasted hamlets, I saw from the photos in Fehrenbach's
book, sleek resorts now lined the road along the way.

In Chunchon, I decided to walk the couple of miles from the bus station
into the city. I crossed the Kong Ji Chan River and began climbing the hill to
the city center. The gradual incline became quite steep as I continued past
the center up the hill to the Chunchon Sejong Hotel, where I had booked
a room. The hotel, which had a long, low, two-story layout, was built on a

mountainside—*Bonguisan*, according to the map I had picked up at the bus station. It was an exquisite place, with a sweeping view of the valley looking back over the city in the direction of Seoul. I was happy in this setting, happy with my room, happy to have come to Chunchon.

I followed the front desk clerk's directions back down the hill to the tea house where I was to meet Miss Kim. She was waiting for me, as relieved that I had actually come to the meeting, I imagined, as I was to see her there. We spent all of that afternoon, a two-hour dinner, and another two hours back at the *tabang* that evening talking. If anything, her English proficiency, already advanced, had improved since our last get-together. She gave me a long, guided walking tour of Chunchon the next day, then accompanied me on the taxi ride to the terminal that afternoon to catch my bus back to Seoul. We arranged to meet again in Chunchon the following weekend. Watching Ju Ok wave to me as the bus pulled away, I offered a momentary mental apology to Esther, who I was sure would understand and encourage my attraction.

I returned to Chunchon almost weekly throughout that winter and spring. I would take the bus on Saturday morning, stay the night at the Chunchon Sejong Hotel, and return to Seoul Sunday evening. After four or five weeks, Ju Ok and I started sleeping together. She was careful to come to my hotel when the lobby was least crowded. Dating a Westerner still posed difficulties for a Korean woman. Foreigners attracted constant attention, some of it intrusive and unwanted. Centuries of victimization by a constant series of invaders had formed a markedly xenophobic mentality among Koreans, especially in the provinces, and the more so in a town like Chunchon, which had a large U.S. military base nearby. A woman in the company of a foreigner was often seen, and sometimes addressed, as a whore. The unwanted visibility was a burden that obviously weighed on Ju Ok, as it did on me. But our moments of happiness were acute and made any social discomfort we encountered bearable.

Chunchon became a lovely cocoon for me. It was the capital of Kangwon Province, a region noted for its scenic mountains, rivers, and coastline. In 1995, it had a population of 240,000—a town compared with Seoul's ten million. Ju Ok and I spent our days together walking through the snowy streets and surrounding hills, hills which 40 years before had been victims of shellings and fires and marching boots. The land had been ravaged, the trees destroyed. Even now, well after the modernization of the country's infrastructure and explosive economic recovery, a palpable sadness still seemed to permeate the once-vanquished landscape. This was particularly so in winter and early spring. Yet the land was beautiful for all its harshness in those seasons. Much like the Korean people, I thought, the enduring Korean people.

That summer, I went to Japan for several weeks after my contract with the institute ended. I hadn't decided yet whether or not to renew for a second year. Immediately upon my return to Korea, I wrote to Ju Ok to say I would be in Chunchon the following weekend. When I saw her at the *tabang*, our standard meeting place since my first visit to Chunchon, she was subdued. In the hotel room, I asked her what was wrong.

"I'm just tired. I work in a new place now. I am trying to do a good job, so I am working many hours." She was vague about her new place of employment. Another office, she said.

As we lay in bed that night, she began to cry. I pulled her to me. "Tell me truthfully," I encouraged her. "What's wrong?"

"I'm pregnant," she replied, almost too softly for me to hear. "What will we do?"

My first reaction, internal and selfish, was panic. This will seal my fate, I remember thinking, for my remaining time alive. I'm 52 years old, already a failed father once. Another child at this age? I'm not ready. I can never be ready.

I struggled to compose myself, to be humane and upright, to support this person whom I claimed to love. "We'll get married," I said, suddenly resolute. "We'll have the baby."

I was surprised when this didn't reassure and relieve her. She was more morose the next morning. "I know a way not to have the baby," she said.

"No," I persisted in my new-found certainty. "We'll be fine. Everything will be okay."

"I don't want to have a baby this way," she responded angrily. "People here will say bad things about me. And you love me now. But that won't last. Someday, you'll hate me. I'm Korean. I'll live here. You'll have your own life in America."

We continued in that vein all day. Nothing I said comforted her. I rode back to Seoul that night in despair. It was a complicated, multi-layered despair, marked irreconcilably by a desire to do what I believed would be right—to marry and give fatherhood a second chance—and the desire for Ju Ok to do what she had threatened and have the abortion.

I had planned to return to Chunchon the following weekend but on Friday received a letter from Ju Ok saying not to come. She had had the abortion, she wrote, and was weak.

My emotions vacillated between anguish and relief. The result of the conflict was guilt. Why hadn't I been more careful in our lovemaking? Why hadn't I been more insistent that she have the baby, that we marry? How could I be feeling relief when I should only be feeling loss? How was Ju Ok? Why the hell did she make the decision without me? Wasn't I an equal part of all this? Why hadn't she just agreed to get married? We loved each other. It would have worked. It might still work...

But I never had a chance to test that possibility. I never saw or heard from Ju Ok after I received the letter informing me about the abortion. My letters were returned unopened. Her phone at the boarding house was disconnected, and I never had learned the name of her new company. I had few tangible connections to her. One was a black-and-white photo showing Ju Ok—wearing a cocktail dress, her long hair elegantly piled atop her head—posing on a staircase against a wall that looked to be in some sort of establishment. A Western-style restaurant, perhaps. Or a bar.

Questions have continued to plague me: Did Ju Ok have the baby? Was the baby mine? Is there a child in Korea now that is mine? If so, had Ju Ok been trying to protect me—to safeguard my future at the expense of hers and the child's? Or...Or...

Lately, I have taken to visiting genealogical sites on the Internet. I came across one where children were searching for their American fathers. I looked up "Chunchon, Korea" and noticed inquiries by a number of individuals with the common surname Kim who were born in Chunchon in the mid-1990s. When I saw that none of the mothers was named Ju Ok, my relief and sadness were indistinguishable.

3

Return

WELL, DEAR NOTEBOOK, IT'S been an extensive interlude, and I apologize for the lack of entries. For several years, I just haven't had the energy, the will, to do much. It's been hard enough to live my life, much less write about it. But I've managed to recoup some reserves, and I owe you an update.

After losing touch with Ju Ok, I decided not to renew my teaching contract at the institute in Seoul. I felt I was disintegrating, literally disintegrating, much as I had done during and immediately following my breakup with Holly in West Virginia. I knew I needed to find some peace in my inner life. I also knew I needed help for that to happen, and so spent the next five years in an ever-deepening meditation practice that took me to monasteries and retreat centers of varying traditions, first Sŏn in Korea, then Zen in Japan, Chan and Taoism in China, Tibetan Buddhism (which I had been introduced to before leaving America by a lama who, after a year of teaching me, encouraged me to visit Asia) in Nepal, Theravada in Thailand, and variants of Yoga and Sufism in India. I still had enough savings to cover travel and incidental expenses, and room and board were covered in many of the places I lived in return for the chores I did as a member of those communities. From time to time I would pick up work as an English teacher, but I purposely kept those jobs to a minimum in order to concentrate on the inner practices I was learning, practices I realized were, at least early on, my desperate attempt to make amends for my relentless proclivity to disappoint people—parents, partners, siblings, child. Gradually, though, I began to detach from the feelings of guilt and failure that seemed always to lead to the idea that I must redeem myself, to atone somehow for the bad things I had done and the good things I had not done to those I had been closest to in my life.

I sat with Marei one evening on the roof of the Ganges View, a guest house overlooking Assi Ghat in Varanasi, the Holy City of Benares. It was toward the end of my years-long sojourn during which Marei, a Swiss-German woman my age, and I would occasionally travel together. She was a hard-core spiritual vagabond, a person of independent means who had been steeping herself in Asian and Middle Eastern religious traditions throughout her adult life.

"Where will you go after India?" she asked.

"Home, I think. Back to America."

"Why?"

I didn't answer immediately. Why indeed? "I don't know," I finally said. "It just feels like it's time for me to return. Lame reasoning, huh?"

"Very," she agreed. "I can't imagine giving up moments like this"—she gestured toward the sun setting over the river and the worshippers bathing and praying on its bank—"for the staleness of Zurich. But maybe New Jersey is different? At least it's by the water," she laughed. "But seriously, Nathan. You must have a reason."

"As I said, it just feels like it's time. I've been away for 12 years, out of touch with my daughter, my brother, my parents. I don't anticipate they'll welcome me with open arms. I want to see them, though. Very badly. Even if they reject me."

"And if they do reject you, what then? How do you think you'll react?"

"With equanimity, I hope. I've experienced a lot in the time I've been away. I've had a number of wise teachers, first in America and then over here. I have to think I've internalized some of their lessons."

"Which ones?"

"Damn it, Marei, you can be difficult. But okay. It's a fair question. Let me think about it."

The next evening we sat again on the roof of the Ganges View. "So, tell me, Nathan: Which lessons?"

I handed her the three sheets of handwritten notes I had prepared.

"In addition to several meditative practices and the guidance of the monastic and retreat advisers," she read out loud, *"I've been helped along the way by the wisdom of various traditions, wisdom that I can easily remember because it's usually packaged in numbered formats. Here are the ones that are the most meaningful to me.*

▶ *The Toltec shaman Don Miguel Ruiz's Four Agreements:*

1.   Be impeccable with your word.
2.   Don't take anything personally.
3.   Don't assume.
4.   Do your best.

▶ *Emphases of several Buddhist traditions:*

1.   Don't harm others (Hinayana)
2.   Help others (Mahayana)
3.   See everything's natural purity (Vajrayana)—In their essence, all sentient beings are Buddhas.

▶ *Be indifferent to the Eight Worldly Concerns (as articulated by Nāgārjuna):*

1.   Gain
2.   and Loss
3.   Fame
4.   and Disgrace
5.   Praise
6.   and Blame
7.   Pleasure
8.   and Pain

▶ *Heed Tilopa's Six Words of Advice:*
1.   *Don't recall. (Let go of what has passed.)*
2.   *Don't imagine. (Let go of what may come.)*
3.   *Don't think. (Let go of what is happening now.)*
4.   *Don't examine. (Don't try to figure anything out.)*
5.   *Don't control. (Don't try to make anything happen.)*
6.   *Rest. (Relax. Right now.)*
▶ *While meditating, as suggested in the Zen Shikantaza, or "just sitting" tradition:*
1.   *Just settle.*
2.   *Just wait.*
3.   *Just watch.*
4.   *Just enjoy.*
5.   *Just sit.*

Inspired by these and dozens more advisements, I also came up with my own bromidic, self-help formulations. For example:
1.   *Fresh breath*
2.   *New start*
3.   *Anytime*
4.   *Right now*
And:
1.   *Be grateful for this precious, fleeting life.*
3.   *Every action has a result. Use your life well. Don't be discouraged. Get up. Be cheerful. It's up to you.*
4.   *Leap into life. Never give up.*
5.   *Relax. Be open. Be soft. Be interested. Be friendly."*

"It's a good list," Marei said when she finished reading. "I hope it serves you well."

At that moment, I felt fortified by my years of diligent practice and these encouragements, fortified enough to return home and face the understandable criticism I could expect because of my 12-year disappearance. I was not so worried about Arnie, my ever-tolerant brother. It was my parents' likely reactions that concerned me. Would I be strong enough to weather their opprobrium? Strong enough not to slide back into the habitual depressions that had always resulted from my self-loathing after having let people down? And Ellen. What would I do about Ellen? Could I even find her? And if I couldn't, would I somehow be able to keep myself from falling back into the paralyzing self-recrimination and despair that have plagued me since the day she and her mother left for Alaska?

I'll be okay this time, I told myself. I've worked hard on my attitude. And I'm 58 years old now, certainly mature enough by virtue of age alone to avoid falling back into the habit patterns of the past.

But was I? As I gave myself this pep talk, I recalled a story about John Bennett, the senior Gurdjieff disciple and Claymont founder, who toward the end of his life concluded that he had, after all of his protean psychological and spiritual efforts, developed the emotional maturity of a 17-year-old. So where did that leave me?

I arrived at Newark International Airport less than a year after 9/11. Not surprisingly, it took me hours to clear immigration and customs. I had been out of the U.S. for nine years and spent much more than the usual tourist's time in a half-dozen countries. I had also gone back and forth from those to neighboring countries to renew my short-term visitor's visas. After a series of security interviews and X-rays, I did what I had done 22 years before when I returned from Anchorage to this airport and phoned Arnie at his apartment in New York City.

When he answered, pure nerves took over as I blurted out what I had been practicing for hours to say to him. "Arnie, it's Nate." Silence. I rushed on. "I don't expect you to accept my apologies for disappearing again. But I'm eternally sorry for any worry and trouble I've caused. I'm just a really troubled person is all I can say as an explanation. But I've been working hard at pulling myself together. Now I'm back for the long term. Do you think the folks will see me? Do you think they'll forgive me?"

"Enough apologies. Enough explanations. I'm glad you're safe, though at this moment I can't say that I'm glad you're back. I'm guessing I will be when all this sinks in. As for the folks, you're too late. This is something better said face-to-face, but you may as well know now that they're dead. It's just you and me."

We agreed that I'd take a limo to Belmar that day and meet him the next afternoon at our parents' home. Fay had died eight years ago and Mort followed a year later, but Arnie hadn't gotten around to doing anything about the house and their belongings. "I've been dragging my feet on the estate stuff, except for the diner, which I sold and put the proceeds in an account under both our names. But I kept the house. I'm not sure why. Probably a combination of unfinished grieving and hopes that you'd reappear so that I wouldn't have to carry the logistical load alone. Anyway, the key is under the mat where it's always been, and the utilities are still on. I'll see you there tomorrow."

Within minutes after entering the house I was debating whether to get a motel room. An unrelenting surge of vivid memories assaulted me as I walked through the rooms and passed objects that had been in our family at least from the time we moved to Belmar. The easy chair in which my father was napping when my mischievous sister urged me, a three-year-old, to hit him with my heavy toy rowboat; the blood streaming from the gash in his forehead; Debbie running up the stairs to lock herself in the bathroom as Mort,

bellowing, went after her; Fay, screaming, trying to hold him back; Arnie and
I bawling our little hearts out. The twin beds Arnie and I used, springboards
for the hide-and-seek game our sister and two of her friends played one night
when they were supposed to be baby-sitting us; Arnie and I crying whenever
one of the girls stepped on us as we cringed under the covers. The image of
Fay, still young, undressing down to the full nudity of her dancer's body as
Arnie and I, supposedly fast asleep, gaped at her reflection in the mirror on
her half-open bedroom door. The balustrade Arnie and I hid behind as we
observed our parents holding each other and weeping the day they learned
that Debbie had eloped with Eddie Martino. The foyer in which my parents
and I celebrated as we read my acceptance letter from Harvard; the same
foyer, a week later, in which Arnie, with only me there for company, opened
his acceptance letter from Monmouth College. The wrought-iron, glass-
topped kitchen table that had been silent witness to decades of episodes,
joyous and tragic, in the Kirinski family saga.

　　When Arnie joined me the next afternoon, we went directly to our parents' and sister's cemeteries. Fay, who had died from congestive heart failure,
and Mort, who died from septicemia after being hospitalized with multiple
maladies, were buried side by side in Chesed Shel Ames Hebrew Cemetery
in Neptune. Their grave markers had simple inscriptions: *Fay Alexander Kirinski, Beloved Wife and Mother, 1904 – 1994* and *Mordechai "Morton"
Kirinski, Beloved Husband and Father, 1902 –1995.* We picked up stones
we found nearby and placed them on each marker in remembrance. Arnie
began to recite the mourner's *Kaddish*, and I joined in. When we got to the
end—*O-seh sha-lom bi-me-ro-mav, hu ya-a-seh shalom a-lei-nu ve-al kol
Yis-ra-eil, ve-i-me-ru, a-mein,* "May He who causes peace to reign in the
high heavens, let peace descend on us, on all Israel, and all the worlds, and
let us say: Amen"—we both broke down. Whether or not for the same reasons, I cannot say.

　　We repeated our devotions at our sister's grave site in Monmouth Memorial Park in Tinton Falls, a five-mile drive from our parents' cemetery. Eddie had died during my absence, and his ashes and marker were immediately
next to Deborah's. Arnie and I recited the Lord's Prayer for Eddie. We tried
to do so without ambivalence.

　　When we recited the *Kaddish* for Deb, we did so for ourselves but also
as surrogates for our father, who had been denied this sacred privilege by
Rabbi Aharon Steinman.

Arnie and I spent most of the next month arranging to sell the house and
furniture, since neither of us had plans to reside in the former nor make use
of the latter. After separating out the photos, estate and genealogical documents, and a few other memorabilia we wanted to keep, we dropped off,
as dispassionately as we could, the remainder of our parents' belongings at

local charities. Arnie and our parents' attorney had already taken the estate through probate. All that we had to do now was divide up the estate once the house was sold, which would be a modest amount in total, even including what was left from the net that Morton had received for the Carousel Diner a number of years before.

Meanwhile, I took steps to collect the retirement funds I was due from the post office. When I contacted my former supervisor to initiate the process, I was gratified when he encouraged me to apply for re-instatement as an Ocean Grove mail carrier. My application was approved. I decided to work for four more years and take early retirement when I turned 62. Whatever pension accumulation and Social Security I was due, added to my half of the inheritance from our parents, would easily support the modest lifestyle I had in mind for the rest of my days. This lifestyle would include a year-to-year rental of two furnished rooms with kitchen and bath at Las Palmas, a rooming house in Belmar.

Why Belmar? It was my hometown, full of mostly affectionate memories that easily outweighed any tribulations I had experienced there. But why Las Palmas? It was a low-end establishment by many standards, and I could have afforded more than the tiny and basic apartment I leased. Still, it was adequate for my needs and could easily accommodate the few belongings I had packed into two suitcases: one full of clothing and photos and the other containing some favorite books, including the constantly expanding notebook I had been lugging around for decades in a thick, three-ring binder. My new home was near the ocean, more importantly a section of the ocean at 12th Avenue where I had some of my best experiences: as a child chasing minnows, collecting shells, and building sandcastles with Arnie and Louie Lerner; as a pre-teen body surfing for hours and then basking, exhausted, under the rejuvenating sun; as a high school student courting North Jersey girls by day and making out with them at night.

As an additional advantage, Las Palmas was in walking distance of a retro arcade whose pinball collection, I had learned, included Royal Flush. I spent my first day in Las Palmas cleaning the apartment, had an early dinner of a sub and beer at a bar on Main Street, and then went to see what shape the machine was in. The establishment had little of the ambience of the old-style arcades like Wizard's World or even the Benny-ridden Playland, both of which had closed during my years away. But I was no longer the purist I had been then, and I was anxious to renew my acquaintance with Flush regardless of the setting. There were few customers, and I was pleased to find Flush available and in good condition. I put my first quarter into the coin slot and felt a sharp thrill as the board was swept clear of the previous player's score and Flush's lights came on—popping, crackling, waiting to bear their dazzling electric witness to my game. My excitement grew with the distinct, separate thumping sound of each metal ball dropping down the chute into the chamber under the launcher slot. I told myself to slow down, to remember to breathe, as I tested the flippers. Satisfied with their give and responsiveness, I pushed the first ball into the launcher slot and fired it into the ellipse at the top of the playfield. Tentative at first, I was soon playing as if I had never been away, my confidence and happiness growing apace as my flipper shots and hard reinforcements hit off bumpers and slingshots, as rollovers and bonus gates and specials lit up like fireflies all over the game board, from the machine's inner drops to its high ground.

The free games kept coming and I played on until, an hour later, my last redeemed ball disappeared down the slot and off the playfield. I taunted myself: Beginner's luck? No. Returner's luck. I was back.

"Twelve years is a lot of mail," Arnie said as he carried two boxes into Las Palmas the next day. "I paid all the bills out of the account you left. I hope you don't mind that I also opened envelopes that were personal mail. I didn't really read them, of course. But I thought I should at least give the contents a quick look in case anything needed attention—you know, legal, insurance, that kind of thing. As far as I could tell, there's been nothing that needed a response. Except maybe this," he said, handing me a book titled *The Value of Philosophy: A Practical Guide for Students*. The author was Ailani Kaluhiwa, the undergraduate I had worked with on a directed study back in Hilo, now Dr. Ailani Kaluhiwa, professor of philosophy at the University of Hawaii's main campus in Honolulu. "You might want to look at the dedication," Arnie suggested.

To Professor Nathan Kirinski. For his confidence in me, and his nurturance.

I thanked Arnie repeatedly for all he had done to take care of my affairs for so many years. Until I called him from Newark, for all he knew he might have had to do this forever.

I spent some time looking at the envelopes in the personal mail pile Arnie had separated out from everything else. I saw there was nothing from Ellen.

"You know, I did see Ellen about ten years ago," I told him, describing the painful scene in Reno with my then 18-year-old runaway daughter. "I gave her your address and phone number in case she needed anything. I guess you never heard from her..."

"I never did."

4
Reunions

I RETIRED, AS PLANNED, in 2006 and spent the next six years reading, continuing these notebook entries, walking, and playing pinball. It was a satisfying enough existence, and Belmar was a satisfying place to lead it. Daily, I walked the boards and reflected on things against the soothing sounds of the ocean. My life had had its ups and downs, its ebbs and flows. The Atlantic's tides and waves were a reminder to keep the changes in perspective: Nothing stays the same. Pay attention to the fleeting moment. When memories and regrets invade, acknowledge but don't entertain them. They'll come and they'll go. Don't follow them up or down.

I could manage to follow this self-generated advice most of the time in my insular, isolated life. Aside from Arnie's visits and interactions with my landlord, fellow arcade rats, and a couple of merchants, I didn't have to contend with much human stimulation, which to my way of thinking was all to the good. Relationships did not interest me, and I was wary of their unpredictability. I was content to be alone.

This self-contained space was trespassed in the fall of 2012. It was time for my 50th high school reunion. A horde of classmates would gather at the Shore to celebrate. Unless I left home, it would be difficult to avoid them. And if I did manage to stay out of the way, Arnie would once again be left holding the bag, fielding the inevitable "Where's Nate? Tell us about Nate" questions. He could handle this, I knew; my multiple disappearances over the years had given him lots of practice in making up explanations and offering excuses for me. But the idea of leaving him with this responsibility 67 years into our paired lives did not sit well with me. Hadn't I worked hard on myself all these years, meditating, trying to come to terms with who I had been, trying to resolve my insecurities and act like the steadier Nathan I believed I had now become? I would attend the reunion, damn it, and hazard any consequences.

Despite my decision, I still tried to understand what made me so reluctant to participate, while my classmates, as far as I could tell from the e-mail chatter on the reunion website, were so enthusiastic. I concluded, perhaps simplistically, that class reunions provoke mixed emotions. The anxiety of comparison is certainly one such emotion: How much have I changed? Do I look older than my classmates? Am I heavier? Balder? Handsomer? Happier? Healthier? Wealthier? More procreative? More accomplished? More enviable? More content with my life? I guess for some the anxiety is outweighed by curiosity and positive anticipations: the pleasures of sharing memories, catching up on the past half-century, meeting spouses and partners, reviving old friendships. But for me there were no mixed emotions. There was only the anxiety of comparison. I judged my life a failure in too many ways and had little doubt that this group would make the same judgement. How could they not? Most of my classmates last knew me as Harvard Professor Nathan Kirinski, Ph.D., author, talk-show guest, husband of beautiful, brainy Holly, father of adorable Ellen. A man to be envied.

Two scenes flashed through my mind, one an actual memory, the other an imagined event. In the first, Holly and I were pushing Ellen along the Belmar boardwalk in her stroller when we ran into the Seligmans. "Well, hello Dr. and Mrs. Seligman," I said, full of feigned bonhomie. "So wonderful to see you. Have you met my wife Holly and daughter Ellen? No? Please, let me introduce you." In fact, my enthusiasm hid a deep distaste for this couple. Dr. Seligman, a dentist, exemplified for me what it meant to be *nouveau riche*, a man who never tired of letting people know how wealthy he was, a man who couldn't be content to make large donations to the synagogue, for example, but had to brag about the amounts. And Mrs. Seligman was his perfect partner, a social climber and snob who, whether people had heard her husband spout dollar amounts, would continually remind us of their generosity. "And how," I asked after the introductions, oohs and aahs over Ellen, and a brief re-cap of our lives in Boston, "is Harold doing?" Harold Seligman, their son, had been a year ahead of me in school, the apple of his parents' eye until the realization set in that he didn't have the brains or talent or drive to get beyond a bank teller's position at a local bank. If they, and Harold, too, hadn't been such pricks I would have had more sympathy and compassion for their disappointment. But I couldn't stop myself from rubbing it in. "Harold's just fine, thank you," said Mrs. Seligman. "And what's he up to these days?" I persisted. "Still at the bank? Married yet?" The couple looked pained. "He's doing just fine, Nathan, thank you," said Dr. Seligman, obviously avoiding specifics. "That's good," I said. "Please give him my regards." As we parted I could feel their envy and luxuriated in it. "Those Kirinskis," I pictured them saying. "How the hell did they get all the *nachas?*," using the Yiddish word for the joy one gets from one's kids, the pride one takes in their accomplishments. "Greasy spoon proprietors, for God's sake. But sons with Ivy League doctorates. In reputable positions. And now a grandchild." I was confident that this envy was not limited to the Seligmans. We Kirinskis were riding high, and everyone knew it.

"Did I imagine it, Nathan?" Holly asked as we continued down the boardwalk. "I don't know how to describe it. You were sarcastic with them. Biting. Gloating."

"They deserve it," I answered, without offering any explanation.

But now the tables had turned. I imagined my classmates' whispered questions at the upcoming reunion: –"Whatever happened to him? You're kidding. A mailman, for Christ's sake." –"What about his wife? You mean he's had two?" –"And didn't he have a child? She'd be 40 by now. What's she up to? –What do you mean he doesn't know? How could he not know about his daughter?" Ellen. That would be the worst of it. They'd be right. How could I not know? And when would I get around to finding out?

Amid these worries, Arnie eased my mind a little by reminding me that there would be two reunions during the weekend. Our Hebrew school's *bar mitzvah* class of 1957 would gather on Friday evening at La Dolce Vita, a restaurant on the corner of 4th and Ocean in Belmar. This reunion I could look forward to without qualms. The small group of attendees would represent my pure Belmar, the idyllic and innocent town that was my happy home until I entered Asbury Park High School in 1958. And so it happened. The *bar mitzvah* reunion was joyous. The much bigger high school reunion following it was another matter.

We were 12, I wrote in remembrance the day before our confirmation class of 1957 gathered, *12 in number and 12 in age. The rabbi proclaimed us the town's Jewish future—12 about to go from childhood to manhood, all bar mitzvah in the same year. The old men who were the core of the synagogue's daily quorum of worshippers were elated to have us as reinforcements, their expectation being that we 12 would show up to pray two times a day for the short remainder of their lives, and that they would no longer have to cajole and badger our middle-age, work-a-day fathers to form a minyan.*

From the time the financier Jacob Schiff laid the temple's cornerstone in 1904, no one could remember such a bullish manpower market. The future seemed secure. But of course, as with any market nothing is guaranteed. To a person, we 12 moved away, to college and then to careers that we could not pursue in the small town. The congregation languished. The old men died. Our parents died. The synagogue is closed now, ghosts its only parishioners.

Now we were all back in town, and our evening together was a delight. Our banter was entirely affectionate, never competitive, never mean-spirited. Our singular frame of reference was the experiences we shared as boys on the cusp of becoming men, at least as Judaism defines such things. It was an evening devoted to story-telling, to the mostly hilarious tales about our struggles to learn Hebrew and memorize prayers, our encounters with the rabbi and old-men congregants, our ambivalence about having to observe the Sabbath, the dietary laws, and any customs that differentiated us from our non-Jewish peers.

"Do you remember," Howie Dorfman asked, "our embarrassment when we had to undress in the school locker room and reveal our *tzitzis?*"

Laughing, we did indeed remember. "What the hell you wearin'?" the bully Junior Clark had challenged us, pointing at Howie and the fringed garment observant Jewish males wore under their street clothes in accordance with the commandment in *Deuteronomy* to "Make yourself bound tassels on the four corners of the garment with which you cover yourself."

"It's a special undershirt that only Jews can wear," Howie had replied.

His response was really no explanation at all and could easily have backfired if Clark had taken offense at being excluded from the strange attire. But it seemed to satisfy Junie, or at least keep him sufficiently mystified to end his questioning.

"And you, Nathan," recounted Louis Lerner, "always our model, a leader, even when it came to performing the *bar mitzvah* ceremony. But we never resented you for your talents, were never jealous. Why? Because we could always count on your human touch."

"What are you talking about?"

"On your *bar mitzvah* day, as one example. You didn't do the minimum like most of the class—you know, the basic blessings and our particular *Torah* portion. You ran the whole, three-hour service. The rest of us sat through it in awe, looking at each other, shaking our heads: How does Kirinski do it? But the human touch came at the end of the show. Remember?" I nodded and grimaced as Louie continued. "The *Torah* scrolls had been put back in the Ark, the mourners had finished reciting the *Kaddish* for the last time, and you were leading the congregation in the final prayers, your voice as powerful and lovely as a young cantor's. And then your voice gave out. It literally dropped an octave and cracked. It was a horrible sound, especially in contrast to what had been going on until then. It was like going from Caruso to Joe Cocker." By now we were all laughing in collective remembrance. "I thought," Louie finished, "how this was *bar mitzvah*—the transition from boyhood to manhood—in real-time action. And I also thought how much I loved you, Nathan, for fucking up."

We recounted story after story like this for hours, right up to the restaurant's closing time. La Dolce Vita is well named, I thought as we all parted. These guys made my life so sweet.

I dreaded the class of '62 high school reunion. High school had launched such great expectations, propelling me to Exeter and Harvard. But then I retreated from the first and failed at the second. Basically, I was embarrassed to be back in the social setting that had witnessed these risings and fallings. But the reunion went unexpectedly well for the most part. Out of a graduating class of 400 close to 100 alumni attended, and many were accompanied by spouses. It could have been overwhelming but wasn't. During the casual wine and beer receptions, the one formal dinner, and the guided tour of the modernized high school building, people gravitated to classmates they had known and liked. Despite my initial apprehension, I was enjoying myself. As with the *bar mitzvah* group's tales of an earlier time, the stories and laughter about our high school years went on and on, and for most of the weekend I was fully engaged.

"Remember Miss Romero," asked Dino Pierrakos, "our elderly Latin teacher?" Those few of us who took Latin nodded in fond recollection. "Of course," I said. "She was by far the oldest teacher on the faculty. She had never married, which was the reason we always speculated that she kept drilling us on *amo, amas, amat...*'I love, you love, we love...' We were mean, joking that this was her compensation for never having had a love of her own."

"Mean is right," Dino resumed. "I still have the clearest picture of our last class day with her in Latin II. There stood Miss Romero, the bright June sun lighting up her perfectly coifed white hair, which we were sure was a wig. She knew about the gossip and was absolutely defiant when she dared us to come up and pull her hair. No one had the nerve, so Miss Romero did it herself. 'See, wise guys? It's real.'"

"And then there was the guy," Arnie said, "I think his name was Gregg, Mr. Gregg, who always taught the odds-and-ends types of subjects like health and sex education and driving. There was that crazy day when he brought in a machine that simulated a car's controls—the steering wheel, gear shift, clutch, and brakes. He had each of us, in alphabetical order, sit in the driver's seat. Jimmy Ahearn was first. 'Okay, Jimmy,' Mr. Gregg instructed him. 'I'm going to set the car in motion. As soon as you see me hold up this signal,' he said, pointing to a bright amber cardboard placard nailed to the end of a yard stick, 'I want you to brake the car to a stop, just as you would when a traffic light changes in real life. I'll time you, and when everyone has had a turn we'll see who has the best reflexes.'" We were all cracking up by now. We had all been in that class. "Poor Jimmy," Arnie resumed. "He was so anxious to do well that he kept slamming on the brakes before Gregg lifted the prompt. Three times, four times. After the fifth false start, Jimmy broke the pedal and the class was dismissed."

"But you know," Doug Horton pointed out, "the things that happened back then weren't all funny. So let's not get too sentimental. I'm thinking about that day in gym class our senior year. Remember?" We all nodded as Doug began describing a scene we'd never forget. "Things were tense for a while racially. There had been some fights, and on a couple of occasions kids were even frisked for knives coming into school. Anyway, we were given a so-called study break that period and were all sitting in the bleachers, some of us reading but most talking and horsing around. The teacher didn't care. It was close to graduation. There was this one guy, Reggie Coombs, who had been picking on certain kids, taking their lunch one day, then demanding 'protection money' the next. Coombs' main victim was a small, skinny kid named Landon Bartlett. Coombs would take that poor kid's money every day—and let's be honest, guys, not one of us ever intervened or told the teacher what was going on. Well, that day I'm talking about, that day we all remember, Reggie came up to Landon as usual— 'Your money or your lunch, little faggot, your choice'—and Landon actually pulled out a gun. We all hit the floor, except Reggie, who held up his hands and began to back away. 'I'm sorry, man,' he kept saying. 'I won't hassle you again. I promise.' I can't remember all that happened next, other than that I heard Reggie ended up in jail and Landon went to a psychiatric facility. So let's be truthful, guys, it wasn't all fun and games, was it?"

Doug was right to remind us. There had been some bad times. But it was our 50th reunion, and the good times were our justifiable focus. Even for me. Except at the end.

I went to the brunch that had been arranged for our class at the Berkeley-Carteret Hotel in Asbury Park on Sunday, the last day of the reunion. A number of people had already left because Hurricane Sandy was moving up the coast. Strong winds were gusting. The surf was getting ominously higher and beginning to surge over the beaches. So it was a much smaller group than had attended the previous two days of events. The heightened intimacy could have made for a very pleasant moment.

But for me it was the reverse of that, because I had the misfortune of being at the same table with my nemeses Alexander Garfield, formerly known as Albert Greenbaum, and his talent-agency partner Charles Rossiter, formerly known as Kalman Rosenzweig. They had been at the *bar mitzvah* reunion but seated at the opposite end of the long table from me. Now I was right next to them. The conversation started out mildly enough as we and several others at the table reminisced about teachers and mutual acquaintances. Then the talk turned to life paths, families, and careers since we graduated. These were precisely the topics that comprised my no-trespassing zone. I began to bid my farewells before things became more uncomfortable, but I was too slow. Garfield and Rossiter turned their lawyerly lazars on me. They loudly noted how they could not get over the "novelty" of my life. "Pinball and the post office, for Christ's sake," exclaimed Charlie. "It's an incredible story. You were the one consensus genius among us all, the Harvard-bound, sure-fire success. Then..."

"That's when the story gets so interesting," said Al, intuitively picking up the thread of his partner's narrative the way they must have done it hundreds of times in their practice. "You had it made. You dropped out and disappeared. You traveled who knows where doing who knows what and who knows why. Then you came back, settled down, lived conventionally, and— wow, this is what grabs my interest—disappeared again before showing up one more time to hang out in this area the rest of us couldn't wait to leave."

Seamlessly, Charlie took over, making the same pitch the pair had used that day back in 1980 when I encountered them on the boardwalk in Belmar. "It's a great story, Nate. It'll make a great book. We can draw up a contract and arrange an advance to support your writing. If you'd like, we can get a top-flight writer to work with you or even ghost-write it. With our L.A. contacts, I have no doubt we could sell the film rights for a bundle. To say nothing of all the book tours and lectures. What do you say?"

I didn't say anything. They were embarrassing me. To them, the story of my life was amusing, quirky, a potential money-maker because it was so weird and curious. To me, my life story was a long chain of humiliations, a testament to failure, squandered potential, bad choices, and plain stupidity.

"Thanks, guys," I said as I made another move to extricate myself from my chair, this table, these people and their world. "I appreciate your interest but think I'll pass."

Then Al came in for the closing argument. "Come on, Nate," he badgered me. "Think of your daughter. Ellen, isn't that her name? You're not getting any younger," he added gratuitously. "Think of the money that could come her way. You could leave her with a decent inheritance, especially the way we draw up wills and manage our clients' estates and taxes and investments. Come on, Nate," he said again, concluding his spiel the same way he had introduced it. "Don't let your daughter down."

Now I entertained no niceties. I left the reunion without saying goodbye to anyone, even Arnie. I walked into the building storm with Garfield's last words echoing in my head, just as Ellen's had twenty years earlier in Reno: "You really let me down."

5

On Disappearing: A Farewell

Forget the past. The vanished lives of all men are dark with many shames. Human conduct is ever unreliable until man is anchored in the Divine. Everything in future will improve if you are making a spiritual effort now.

–Sri Yukteswar Giri

THIS ENTRY WILL BE the last I ever make in my notebook. I'm leaving as soon as the storm passes. To where, I don't know. But I'm leaving for sure, and the notebook is too big, in bulk and memories, to take with me. I hope you're the one who finds it, Arnie, as I wrote in my letter to you inside the notebook's front cover. Or maybe the flooding caused by Sandy will wash it away. That would be okay, too.

It's all too regrettable—and weird, even to me—that I never accounted for my absences, never provided reasons for them. I'm not talking about making excuses. I don't expect or want to be let off the hook for the worry and pain I've caused our parents, our sister, my daughter, and you. It's too late to explain myself to our parents and Debbie, and I don't know whether I'll ever have the chance to do so with Ellen, or if she'd care after so many years of separation from me. But you...I hope you read this, Arnie. You in particular deserve an explanation, not only because I missed so many opportunities over the years to say something to you, but even more because of the practical consequences my disappearances have had for you.

I know you were always perplexed by me, why I never traveled a straighter and more conventional road, why I kept disappearing. And you had every right to take me to task for my irresponsibility, though you hardly ever did. You've been picking up after me for years, the good boy compensating for the bad boy, the dutiful son helping our parents, the brother who was there for our sister, the brother who never stopped being there for me.

The facile answer is that I never provided an explanation because even I couldn't understand my behavior. True enough, as far as it goes; lack of self-knowledge was certainly part of it. But the more honest answer, while more complicated, can still be boiled down to these basics: a hatred of obligation, an emotional tendency, a habit of mind, and a fundamental trait of character.

From the time I was a kid I fought against expectations, especially our parents' presumption that we ought to do this or that just because they said so. However arbitrary or frivolous their requirements, it never seemed to bother you. Your calm and easy nature never bridled at it, and you made it through with no obvious damage. I wish I could have been more like you—accepting, good-humored, slow to take offense. But I couldn't keep myself from rebelling. The more I felt obliged to do something that had nothing to do with my needs or wishes, the more I resisted.

The pattern started very early on. Remember our grandparents' golden wedding anniversary, when Fay insisted that you and I pose for a photo kissing our cousin Suzie? You puckered up while I kept turning away. "Oh, it will be so cute," Fay cajoled, but to no avail. The photographer gave up, and Fay gave me a smack on the ass. Christ, we were only five. Even then, I remember thinking that if our mother thought it would be so cute to kiss Suzie, she could do it herself. And if I had wanted to do it, I would have done it. My volition, and my volition only, was my criterion for action. What someone else thought I should do was their problem.

There were so many instances like that, from childhood through adolescence and early adulthood. It still hurts to recall coming home for Thanksgiving vacation our first year of college. I thought it would be kind and polite to visit a couple of elderly, widowed family friends. So I did. When the two women told Mort and Fay about the visits, our parents praised me for my thoughtfulness, and I was happy that they were pleased. But by Christmas break the obligatory pattern had already set in. "When are you going to visit Mrs. Berger and Mrs. Kalin?" our parents kept pestering me. It was maddening, particularly because the visits had been my idea in the first place, but now they had somehow been turned into a tradition. After Spring break of my freshman year I never visited the two old ladies again. I couldn't stand it—what had begun as a sincere gesture on my part had become yet another example of "Nathan's selfishness." I doubt that Mrs. Berger or Mrs. Kalin felt deprived when I didn't return, but I certainly suffered from my unwillingness to be obligated. The recriminations from Mort and Fay distanced me to the extent that I looked for ways to avoid being home during subsequent holidays so I wouldn't have to answer to anyone's expectations, or feel any guilt or regret or need to apologize. Disappearing became a useful tactic.

The tactic took different forms. What I just described was physical—I took off to avoid conflict with Morton and Fay, and to escape their coercion and disapproval. In other circumstances, I vanished by distancing myself emotionally. Holly complained about this tendency, and it definitely had a lot to do with our ultimate break up. "Your needs always come first," she would say. "Your writing, your career, your speaking engagements and trips to conferences." Proclaiming the age-old male rationale, I defended myself by pointing out that I was the primary breadwinner, and these activities were for the well-being of our family. How else was I supposed to support her and Ellen? "But you don't have to block us out in the process," she'd reply. "When you're not working, you plead exhaustion and insist on not being bothered. You watch television. You play pinball and come home late most days and miss meals and Ellen's bedtime. I go to bed and you stay up reading,

and drinking, in your study. You put in appearances for sex but not cud-
dling. When we first started dating, I could count on both. But no more. I
can expect the fucking but not the feeling. Being with you is a very lonely
proposition, Nathan. You're just not there." I would storm off during these
conversations with parting words about how misunderstood I was. In hindsight, though, I know she was right. The lack of understanding was mine, not
Holly's. Until Esther, I didn't understand what it meant to be a householder;
or rather, I only understood the part about material support. But my new
understanding came too late for Holly and Ellen.

This tendency to be emotionally distant had a close cousin in my mental
habit of zoning out in the middle of conversations. I remember an incident back
in graduate school during a seminar on comparative East-West philosophical
systems. The professor, an Oxford-educated Turkish Sufi named Aslan Burakgazi, was a charismatic, forceful man who kept us all on edge, not so much because of his formidable challenges to our comments at an intellectual level (by
then we were adept at dialectical argumentation), but because of his uncanny way
of penetrating our psychological armor. On the occasion in question, a heated
discussion on whether or not logical frameworks are culturally dissimilar, I was
mentally replaying an interaction with another student a few minutes earlier. In
the replay, I elaborated on what had actually happened by fantasizing the devastating rebuke I should have given. As I gloated to myself over the perfection of
my imagined comment, Professor Burakgazi cut in. "Mr. Kirinski," he said, black
eyes squinting with mischief and insight. "You have a habit of absenting yourself.
I don't like it. It's disrespectful, to all of us and especially to you, yourself. I urge
you to defeat this habit," he added cryptically, "before it's too late." And soon it
was too late, at least for Holly and me. In Holly's eyes, I would disappear emotionally. Burakgazi pointed out a correlative pattern of mind.

I can't think that I'm unique in wanting to back away from people to
avoid the practical and emotional obligations that are inevitable in relationships. Who hasn't felt the urge to be gone and free from all that? But I have to
think that such urges are fleeting for most people, and they don't make a habit, as I have, of acting on nearly every arising instinct to escape. I also think
there's something in my core that makes me this way, something deeper than
an emotional or mental aversion to committing myself fully to a situation and
seeing it through. I'm convinced that it involves cowardice, my chief feature
as identified by Laurent Ambrose back at Claymont, the central attribute or
pillar of my personality. I was devastated by what he told me that day so many
years ago. Few things can be more demoralizing than being called a coward. I
was so nonplussed that I walked away without asking Laurent what he meant
by cowardice, or how to work with this fundamental feature of my nature.
Was the manifestation he observed physical? Relational? Moral? The timid-
ity of indecision? All of the above? If physical, should I purposely put myself
in dangerous predicaments and directly contend with any fear? If relational,

should I labor through each emotional interaction and entanglement, regardless of how distasteful or dysfunctional? If moral, would acting with less than perfect "goodness" in every life instance be evidence of cowardly choices? If by cowardice he meant my tendency to equivocate and reluctance to act (except for disappearing...) before looking at aspects of a situation, would I have demonstrated more courage by abandoning circumspection?

Assuming Laurent meant all of the above, I've struggled ever since to fight against my multiple fears and make use of them. In the process, I've concluded that my cowardice is a two-edge sword, or in other words an attribute with both negative and positive potential. The negative side is easy enough to understand: it takes the form of running away from worldly duties, requirements, relationships, and concerns. I was practiced at this, as has been repeatedly established. But the positive side of cowardice is more complicated and quite the reverse of escapism. On this edge of the sword, "cowardice" is more akin to bravery—the courage to turn away from the lure of worldly concerns with wealth, status, and reputation and instead give one's all to inner growth. This tension was always with me: to satisfy the requirements of the external, material world, or to follow some inner path seeking...what? Spiritual realization? Enlightenment? Salvation? God? Whatever its end point, the path demands sincere and whole-hearted effort on the part of the seeker. At first in small and then gradually larger increments, this path became my singular priority. And I have to say that it takes courage to follow this path, to relinquish our worldly part—and, at times tragically, those loved ones who inhabit that part—so that it won't smother the part of us that seeks to be free. This is the choice I continued to make. This is why I would vanish—when the urge for salvation was dominant. Was this cowardice or courage? From the spiritual perspective, I was a coward whenever I would return to the world of temptation and obligation. From the worldly perspective, I was a coward whenever I disappeared.

It's natural to ask what led me to commit myself to the interior world. As my meditation practice progressed, the choice was inspired by the gradual realization that everything and everyone in the material world, the world of the senses, is temporary and fated to die. With this realization came the recognition that all our successes, which at the time we chase and achieve them seem so important, are also temporary. Death will destroy them, always and inevitably. So don't put your stake on the sensible world, I concluded, its gains and losses, its accomplishments and failures. Put it on the interior world instead.

I've known success and failure, but never real and lasting happiness. Now I hope to find something more, if indeed there is anything other than this life, this person. But at least the seeking of it—which I think of as an expedition into the interior, my final frontier—may take me into realms I've never visited before. Will I find genuine happiness there? Or will happiness reside in the seeking?

Well, we'll see. Here I go.

Part Six

Hurricane Sandy

2012

So much that happens happens in small ways
That someone was going to get around to tabulate, and then never did,
Yet it all bespeaks freshness, clarity and an even motor drive
To coax us out of sleep and start us wondering what the new round
Of impressions and salutations is going to leave in its wake
This time. And the form, the precepts, are yours to dispose of as you will,
As the ocean makes grasses, and in doing so refurbishes a lighthouse
On a distant hill, or else lets the whole picture slip into foam.

–John Ashbery
"Someone You Have Seen Before"

ARNOLD SITS WITH NINE classmates who are all that's left of the re-union. Nearly 100 alumni of the Asbury Park High School class of 1962 had attended the first two days of the three-day affair. But now it's Sunday morning, and this brunch at the old Berkeley-Carteret Hotel, across the street from the ocean, is the last event commemorating their graduation 50 years ago. It's clear from the numerous empty tables with "reserved" plac-ards on them that the organizers had expected many more guests to be here this morning. But a hurricane is approaching the New Jersey coast, and the bulk of the class has fled.

The remaining ten are equally divided between two tables. Arnold is at one, and Nathan is at the other. The storm, Sandy, hasn't made landfall yet. Even so, the combined roar of gusting winds and crashing surf makes conversations difficult to hear at each table and impossible to hear from one table to the next.

Arnold sees his brother rise from one of the tables, visibly upset. Nate grabs his jacket from the back of a chair, lurches through the lobby, and exits the hotel on Sunset Avenue. Minutes earlier, Nate had been talking with Alexander Garfield and Charlie Rossiter. Those two are staring at him now. They look confused by his sudden departure.

Concerned by Nathan's behavior, Arnold offers a rushed farewell to his classmates and follows his brother across Ocean Avenue, up the ramp to the boardwalk, and south into the approaching hurricane. Sand blows up from the beach, punishing Arnold's face until he enters the lobby of Convention Hall's Grand Arcade from the north, just as his brother leaves its south end. Arnold calls out but Nate doesn't turn around. By the time Arnold follows him back into the storm, the wind has already picked up. He has trouble making head-way, and Nathan, much heavier than Arnold, is gaining distance. "Nathan!" he screams. "Damn it, Nathan. Turn around!" His brother doesn't hear him. Or won't. *If it's only that he can't,* Arnold tells himself, *I understand—we're in a freaking hurricane. Then my only concern is for his safety. But if he won't hear, then I have to worry about Nate's state of mind as well as his safety.*

An image flashes of the first time he followed his brother on the board-walk, 66 years ago. Nathan ran ahead as their mother pushed Arnold, barely able to walk yet at two, in a stroller. She called for Nathan to stop, to come back, but he didn't. Or wouldn't. That much about Nathan hasn't changed.

Nathan is a hundred yards ahead by now, and Arnold has a last glimpse of him as he enters the ruins of the Asbury Park Casino, whose walkway links Asbury Park with Ocean Grove, the next town to the south. Arnold ends the futile chase in front of the Empress Motel, another near-derelict landmark just across the street from the Casino. *Nate will make his way back to his apartment in Belmar,* he reassures himself. *I'll check on him before I return to New York City to see that he's all right. But first I want to find out why he left the reunion so abruptly.*

When he gets back to the Berkeley-Carteret the restaurant is empty except for a couple of cleaning staff and Victor Perreira, the classmate who chaired the reunion committee.

"You better get going, Arnie," Victor says, speaking loudly to be heard over the storm. "Governor Christie just declared a state of emergency. The tunnels and bridges back into the city might not be open for long. I live nearby, in Wanamassa. It's inland enough that I'll be okay. Plus this is what I get for taking on this job. The final clean up."

"You were at the table with my brother, Vic. Do you know why he left?"

"I only know that he was talking with Alex and Charlie. But they were at the other end of the table. I couldn't hear what they were saying. The way he looked when he stood up, it must have been something Nate didn't like."

Arnold drives the four miles south to Belmar and pulls into the driveway at Las Palmas, Nathan's boarding house at the intersection of 12th Avenue near A Street, a block from the ocean. He takes the stairs to Nate's rooms on the second floor. No one answers when he knocks. "Where the hell are you, Nate?" He shouts through the door. "This is a serious storm, goddammit." He takes a breath to calm himself. *We grew up at the Shore*, he reasons, *where hurricanes are a periodic reality. Nate will be careful. He'll know what to do and what not to do.*

He goes back downstairs to look for Freddie Milbank, the landlord, and finds him out front, shuttering the windows facing the Atlantic. "I haven't seen him," Freddie says, "but as soon as I do I'll ask him to phone you."

"Thanks, Freddie. And maybe you could phone me, too?"

"No problem, Arnie."

"I should take a quick look inside his apartment before I leave."

"Sure," Freddie says and fishes around for the key. "Here."

Arnold walks through Nate's rooms. *No surprise he's not here*, he thinks, *and I can't find any new clues. It's futile to have looked, I know, and probably obsessive. But I feel better for having done it.* For good measure, after locking up he slides a note back under the door. *Call me, Nate. Please.* He returns the key to Freddie and heads north.

He's reluctant to leave, but the storm warnings on his car radio are as dire for New York City as they are for the Shore, and anticipated closures to the tunnels and the George Washington Bridge will soon make access to the city impossible. Instinct tells him to take the GW, to brave its above-ground winds rather than drive under a river in a hurricane. Heavy traffic on the New Jersey Turnpike crawls, and he second-guesses his decision to avoid the tunnels as he fights gusts of wind over the Hudson. It takes him more than triple the usual time to get home, but he feels fortunate to have left when he did, judging from broadcasted weather and transportation updates.

Shoulders hunched, arms exhausted, eyes squinting from tension, he creeps along Riverside Drive, on guard against pooling water, flying debris, and fallen limbs. He only begins to relax after pulling into his building's parking garage. He pours a glass of straight bourbon as soon as he enters his apartment, happy to be in this warm, cozy sanctuary of soft furniture, carpeted floors, a stereo, a TV, and expensive appliances—so unlike Nate's drafty and minimalist rooms, he thinks with some guilt. He stays in his apartment for the next two days watching the storm through the picture window that looks out over Grant's Tomb and the Hudson. As it turns out, Arnold's part of Manhattan, the Upper West Side, goes largely unscathed, the main damage being to cars from tree branches downed by the wind. But the Jersey Shore is another matter. He follows the news coverage of Sandy obsessively, hour after hour. Horrific video clips show that Belmar is especially hard hit, and he has yet to hear from Nathan or Freddie. Not that it's unusual for Nate to be incommunicado. But Sandy is a mega-storm, and he's desperate to know how his brother is doing.

Even if Nate were in a position and inclined to answer, the trunk lines are constantly busy and cell phones aren't operable. Still, Arnold keeps trying to reach him, and Freddie as well. Frustrated, he briefly considers going to Belmar to see what he can learn but realizes there would be too much turmoil to accomplish anything other than getting in the way of all the rescue crews he sees on TV. *Okay. I'll wait a day, two at most. Surely Nate will call when communication systems return to normal. For now, though, I don't know what else to do.*

He reaches Freddie that night. "Nate hasn't called you?" Freddie asks.

"No. I was hoping he would. Or you would."

"I'm sorry, Arnie. I've been rushing around dealing with the other places I manage. It's a fucking mess here. Flooding, power outages, major property damage, people in shelters...Total chaos. I'm not at Las Palmas now, but I can be there within an hour. I'll check on his apartment and call you back."

Freddie phones 45 minutes later. "He's not there. But everything looks okay, no worse than usual. I didn't see any food in the kitchen cupboards or the refrigerator that could spoil. There've been some break-ins and looting, but it doesn't look like anything's been ransacked, and I didn't notice any water damage."

"I put a note under his door before I left on Sunday. Was it on the floor?"

"No."

Arnold drives to the Shore the next day and goes as close to the ocean as he can, first through Bradley Beach and then Avon, the two towns immediately to the north of Belmar. The once-broad beaches are narrow strips now. Much of the sand has either been swept to sea or blown inland, where it covers streets a quarter mile or more from the ocean. The boardwalks are mostly gone, and the few surviving benches from the hundreds arrayed along the boards before the storm are piled up in heaps against the remnants of ruined buildings.

In Belmar, it's worse. The pavilions that had helped to define the summers of his youth—5th Avenue, 10th Avenue, 13th Avenue—are gone. Silver Lake, two short blocks from the house where he and Nate spent their teenage years, is unapproachable, walled in by acres of mud and stretches of stagnant, foul-smelling water with no channels for egress.

He parks on 12th Avenue and C Street and walks east toward Las Palmas, two blocks away. As he approaches the area near the beach a uniformed officer stops him at a barricade.

"I'm sorry, sir, but my orders are to keep people away from the ocean front."

"But you're not a Belmar cop. I haven't seen that insignia around here."

"Right. I'm with the Newark Port Authority. Hundreds of police are on loan from agencies in northern New Jersey, Pennsylvania, New York, even New England. We're posted all along the Shore to prevent looting. We're also here to keep 'catastrophe tourists'—I don't mean you, sir—from hurting themselves. So I'm asking you not to go any farther."

"I'm here to look for my brother, who lives just up the street at Las Palmas. He and I grew up in Belmar. I'd like to go check on him."

The officer asks for Arnold's I.D. and writes down the information. "Well, okay," he relents. "It's just that we don't want to have any more injuries or casualties."

"Casualties?" This doesn't ease Arnold's worries.

"A few that we know of, and I won't be surprised if there are more. There were 30-foot waves crashing over Ocean Avenue when the storm was at its worst. It was dangerous even for trained first responders. Rescue operations were a nightmare, and not always successful. Wind isn't a problem anymore. But you can see for yourself how much debris there is, and who knows how long it will take for the flooding caused by the storm surge to recede. Sandy's gone, but it's still not safe around here." The officer stops, obviously aware of the concern on Arnold's face. "I'm sorry...I know you must be worried about your brother and all...I hope he turns up okay."

Arnold thanks him and continues walking. Had Nate braved the storm, walked the boards, and been pulled out to sea? He tries to reassure himself just as he had after first losing contact with his brother: *He grew up at the Shore. Hurricanes aren't an unusual occurrence. He'd be careful. He'd know what to do and what not to do.* So Arnold hopes.

The porch at Las Palmas is covered by three inches of sand, and the yard is a pool of salt water. Freddie Milbank answers when Arnold knocks on the door. The landlord is wearing rolled up jeans and rubber boots. He puts aside a sodden mop when he lets Arnold in. "A disaster," Freddie says by way of welcome, repeating the earlier assessment he had given during their phone conversation after Sandy hit. "A fucking disaster. Your brother's lucky. There was no damage to the second-floor rooms when I check a couple of days ago. Not even mold. I've been back and forth between my other properties, so I can't say whether or not he's been here. And his mail's been piling up since they restarted deliveries—'neither rain, sleet, snow' nor hurricane—so I'm guessing he hasn't been back here, at least when I've been around. Although that note you mentioned you left under his door is missing..."

They share a worried silence. "What are you going to do?" Freddie finally asks.

"You said his place looked okay when you checked, and you didn't see my note. But that was a couple of days ago. Do you mind if I take a look around?"

"Of course not," he says, handing Arnold a key.

Nothing he finds, or fails to find, contradicts Freddie. The place smells like a mausoleum, but that's to be expected. From his earlier visits here, Arnold recalls how stuffy and clammy the rooms were even before the storm. But he can't detect any mold or rot, and he doesn't see any food that can spoil when he looks into the refrigerator and cupboards. He can't tell if any clothes are missing, since he doesn't know what Nate's wardrobe consisted of to begin with. He sees a suitcase. But who knows? Maybe he has more than one. He looks around for his note, thinking that wind from Sandy seeping through the old windows could have blown it anywhere. But he doesn't find it.

"It's just as you said," he tells Freddie when he goes back downstairs. "It's impossible to say whether or not he's been here." He stops to think for a minute. "I better go file a missing person's report. I have no choice. It's been a week with no word from him. I'll be back later to talk about the rent and his possessions. Thanks for keeping an eye out."

He goes to the Belmar Municipal Building at 6th Avenue and Main Street, where the police department and several other borough agencies are located. The reception area is crowded with people concerned about their property, their relatives, their safety, their pets, their electricity, their water supply, their garbage—all the things that take over a community's world in the aftermath of disaster. It's hard to get anyone's attention. He makes his way to a clerk who sends him back outside and around to the Belmar Police Department's separate entrance on the west side of the building facing Shark River. The officer at the front desk directs him down a corridor. "Last office on the right." The nameplate on the door reads *Lieutenant John G. Burns, Detective.*

Arnold knocks and a short, muscular man in his early 40s beckons him in. The man is clearly preoccupied. "Detective Burns," he introduces himself without offering his hand. "What can I do for you?"

"My name is Arnold Kirinski. I'm here to file a missing person's report. I haven't been able to contact my brother, Nathan Kirinski, since Sandy hit."

"We'll do what we can to help you, Mr...Kirinski, is it? But only when we can get to it. I'm afraid there are a number of others in line ahead of you right now..." Burns pauses. "I'm sorry to be curt, Mr. Kirinski. Things here have been busy. Please have a seat." Burns sits at his desk and takes out a notebook. "When, exactly, did you last see or hear from your brother?"

"Sunday morning, October 28th. It was the end of our Asbury High class reunion. We had breakfast with some classmates at the Berkeley-Carteret. We were at two separate tables. He stood up and walked out without saying good-bye to any of us, which was strange. I went after him and kept calling his name, but he kept walking south down the boardwalk and never turned around. The last I saw of him was when he entered the Casino walkway between Asbury and Ocean Grove. I checked his apartment in Belmar that same day before I returned to New York City, where I live. Just before I came here, I checked the apartment again and spoke with his landlord, who hasn't seen my brother."

"Any idea why Nathan would have left the reunion breakfast the way he did?"

"I don't know. He seemed happy until then. Earlier that morning, he told me how much he had enjoyed the reunion, much more than he had anticipated. By the expression on his face and the fact that he left so abruptly, my guess is that something was said during breakfast that bothered him. But I have no way of knowing for sure, because I never heard from him after he walked away."

"Did you try to contact him from the city?"

"Yes, many times. I couldn't connect by phone. The lines were always busy or out of order because of the storm. I was finally able to talk, first by phone and later in person, with Freddie Milbank, Nate's landlord at Las Palmas. Freddie hasn't seen Nate either, as I mentioned. Nate hasn't picked up his mail, but a note I left for him on the floor of his apartment the Sunday he went missing is no longer there, so I guess he went back to the apartment at some point. He was obviously upset when he left the reunion brunch, but my brother's never been suicidal and has no enemies I know of. That's all I can tell you."

"I'm sorry you're going through this, Mr. Kirinski. But Belmar is like a war zone now, and a lot of people have been traumatized. Your brother can't be a priority for us until basic services and needs are under control. I can only promise to call you with any news."

As Arnie stands up to leave, he hands Burns a sheet of paper. "I put together some background information for you about Nate in case it will help."

Nathan Kirinski. Residence: Las Palmas Apartments, Belmar. Born May 15, 1944 in New York City to Morton and Fay Kirinski (both deceased 2002). Two siblings: Deborah Kirinski Martino (m. Edward Martino, deceased 1979) and fraternal twin brother Arnold Kirinski, professor of history at Columbia University. Two marriages: Holly (MacDonald) Kirinski (divorced 1978) and Esther (O'Connell) Kirinski (deceased 1990). One child (with Holly): Ellen Kirinski (born 1974, estranged from Nathan and whereabouts unknown since 1992). Education: Belmar Grammar School, graduated 1958; Exeter Academy (one year); Asbury Park High School, graduated 1962; Harvard College, BA in philosophy, 1966; Harvard University, Ph.D. in philosophy, 1969. Career:

Harvard University professor, author of three books and numerous articles, 1969-1978; postal carrier, Ocean Grove, New Jersey, 1981-1990, 2002-2006; now retired. Hobbies: reading, walking, playing pinball machines. Additional information: Many years of travel in the US (including residence in a West Virginia commune 1976-77), Europe, Asia, and the Middle East. Out of touch with his family for years at a time after his divorce from Holly and the death of Esther. For additional information, please contact Arnold Kirinski, Department of History, Columbia University, Fayerweather Hall, 1180 Amsterdam Avenue, New York, NY, 10027. Telephone: (212)854-4646.

"Now I can place you," Burns says when he finishes reading the sheet. "Your brother-in-law, Ed Martino, was the nephew of Larry Martino, the former police chief here who hired and mentored me. And you and your brother were in the same Belmar Grammar School class as my uncle, Mike Burns."

"I remember Mike. Great guy. How's he doing? Please say hello for me."

"I will. Uncle Mike is fine and happily retired. He'll be glad I saw you."

Burns walks Arnold to the door and shakes his hand this time. "We'll do our best to find your brother," he says, cordiality now holding sway in their tight, small-town world.

The name "Las Palmas" has always amused Arnold for its idiosyncratic New Jersey mix of bravado, self-satire, and wishful thinking—as in wishing for something beyond the Garden State. Did the person who named it, he wonders, do so out of longing for the Spanish city of that name, or as a joke in the service of incongruity, since the only palms in Belmar are either plastic or the potted variety imported from Florida? For most of the year, Las Palmas is a low-rent place. Nate pays a dirt-cheap $150 a month for two furnished rooms with a kitchenette and a bath. From Memorial Day through Labor Day, his rent skyrockets to $700 a month, which is still pretty much the lowest available so close to the sea. Nate's combined income from Social Security and his post office pension would allow something nicer. But he likes being here: 12th Avenue has a particularly fond place in both brothers' hearts; their first Belmar home after the family migrated from the Bronx had been on 12th, and their happiest memories are here. When they moved to the more upscale 5th Avenue at the age of twelve, life took less pleasant turns. Maybe it was an automatic part of childhood's end and the onset of adolescence, a turbulent transition everyone goes through. But in their case, the transition was clearly demarcated by the house on 12th, which they continue to associate with bliss and innocence, and the often-tumultuous times that followed after they moved to 5th Avenue. Arnold knows that for Nate the location of Las Palmas, shabby as the rooming house itself might be, is a reminder of the good times.

He runs into Freddie, who is mopping up the building's small foyer. He gives the landlord a check to cover the rent through April, and Freddie hands him a duplicate key to Nate's rooms after Arnold reminds Freddie that he's co-signatory with Nate on the lease. Then Arnold takes another quick run through the apartment to satisfy himself that everything is all right.

"I'll be back from time to time to check on the place," he tells Freddie on the way out. "Meanwhile, I'd appreciate it if you could hold his mail. I'll collect it when I stop by and...You know, until Nate returns."

"When's that likely to be? I mean, do you think that will happen?"

The second question bothers Arnold. Is Freddie implying that Nate might be dead? But Freddie is only saying what Arnold himself already fears: that Nate, due to death by storm, or for whatever other reason, might not return.

"I don't know. I expect him to come back. But you know Nate. If he does return, it'll be on his own schedule. When I know something, I'll let you know. I hope you'll do the same for me."

"Sure. I'll call you as soon as I find anything out," Freddie says, then looks away, obviously uncomfortable.

"What?"

"About the rent after April..."

"I'll be in touch well before April with a decision whether or not to continue the lease through the summer. This will give you time to find a new tenant, if you have to, at the high-season rate."

Arnold begins walking to his car for the drive back to the city, then stops and turns back.

"Freddie," he asks, "where did the name Las Palmas come from?"

"After just one lousy winter here," the landlord laughs, wringing out his mop, "I really needed something to remind me of Miami Beach."

It's been two months since the reunion and Nathan is still missing. Arnold's moods swing from frenzied worry to resignation. Now that he's filed a missing person's report with the police and held onto the apartment at Las Palmas, he can't think of anything else to do other than refusing to conclude the worst, that his brother is dead. *But this isn't the first time Nathan has disappeared,* he keeps telling himself. *The last time he was gone we didn't hear from him for 12 years.*

It's mid-December, and Arnold's classes are over. Spring term won't start until January 22, and he decides to spend the first two weeks of the university's long winter break in Nate's apartment. Who can know? Maybe Nate will return while he's there. He fantasizes such a moment. Nathan walks in and sees Arnie sitting in the tiny living room. "So, Arnie," he would say, moved that his brother is there for him but deflecting the emotion, along with his embarrassment at the trouble he has caused, with humor. "Where the hell am I gonna sit?"

As soon as Arnold enters the apartment he questions his decision to stay here, even for a short time. The whole feel of it is stultifying, like a heated, indoor swimming pool in too small a space with too low a ceiling. Whenever he visited Nathan here he was focused on his brother, on their conversations, never on the place itself. He never thought, like he does now without Nate here, *God, how depressing*. He never thought, like he does now, *Poor Nate*. Nate would be devastated to know Arnold's reaction to his home, but he can't help it; the place brings to Arnold's mind the kind of tenement their grandparents might have inhabited more than a century ago on the Lower East Side.

His feelings of oppression, sadness, and pity increase as he walks through the several rooms and takes in the worn hand-me-down furniture, linoleum floors, chipped and mismatched kitchenware, stained sinks, grimy bathtub, and dirty windows. There are no rugs on the floors and no curtains, only pull-down shades on the apartment's four windows, one each in the living room, kitchen, bedroom, and bathroom. He thinks of the carpeting on the floors of his own Upper West Side apartment, how it adds to the place's warmth and quietness. He thinks how cold it must be to live here, how exposed. How lonely.

The living room is dominated by an over-stuffed sofa and a recliner easy chair. These, at least, must provide Nate with a modicum of comfort, and Arnie is happy to see them. But then he notices two collapsible bridge tables. One, presumably used for eating, is set in the middle of the apartment. He assumes the other, judging from its placement against a wall and next to a well-packed bookcase, must function as Nate's desk. A single straight-backed chair appears to service both. Again, he is struck by how lonely it all feels.

The kitchen, a monument to singularity, reinforces this feeling: one knife, one fork, one spoon, one set of chopsticks, one dinner plate, one soup bowl, one mug, one glass, one frying pan, one spatula, a potholder, a dish brush, a bottle of Dawn, and a can of Comet. It's the same in the bedroom and bathroom—a single-width mattress on the floor, a low chest of drawers, a towel, a washcloth, and a sponge.

He thinks how mortified their neatnik mother would be to see her son in these minimal, forlorn circumstances. And Deborah. And Esther. And Holly in the years before West Virginia. They would have ordered Nate to leave for however many hours or days it took to make the place livable—to scrub it down, to bring in some decent furniture and accessories. *But they're not here. It's just me.*

He walks over to Nate's bridge-table desk. At least there's an element of personalization here from the photos hanging on the wall above it. He turns the framed pictures over one by one and finds a penciled caption on the back of each in Nathan's handwriting.

– "Paternal grandparents at their Golden wedding anniversary, Boston, 1949, with their seven children and spouses."

– "Arnold, Deborah, and I with our ten Kirinski first cousins and our grandparents at their home in Roxbury, Passover, 1952."

– "Morton and Fay at their wedding reception, New York City, 1928."

– "Fay in dancer's costume at Broadway performance of 'As Thousands Cheer,' 1930."

– "Arnie and I, age 2, chaperoned by Deborah on Grand Concourse, Bronx, 1946."

– "Arnie and I, age 5, at our Oakhurst Country Day School graduation."

– "Arnie and I forced to kiss little cousin Suzie at maternal grandparents' Golden wedding celebration, Manhattan, 1948. Ugh."

– "Arnie and I lifting weights in Louie Lerner's garage, E Street in Belmar, 1957."

– "With Esther and Arnie on the Costa Brava, Hotel Blaumar (sounds like Belmar!), Cadaqués, Spain, 1985."

– "Our Kiwanis Little League team, Belmar, 1955."

– "Bar Mitzvah class, Congregation Sons of Israel, Belmar, 1957."

– "Graduating class of 1958, Belmar Grammar School."

– "With classmates, in full regalia, Asbury Park High School diplomas in hand, Convention Hall, 1962."

Some pictures, though also inscribed and dated, are more ambiguous. Unlike the photos of family and friends, Arnold doesn't know the people, or, with the exception of Israel, the places depicted. The caption on the back of the earliest photo, which is in color, reads: "Morris Dance performance, Claymont Court, West Virginia, 1976. (I am the Fool.)" A bearded, trim, and muscular Nathan, as thin as Arnold has ever seen him, is dressed in white shirt and trousers and a multicolored patch-work vest. The photo conveys a sense of dynamism, with Nathan swirling around six other dancers who are formed in two rows of three. The posture and position of the six dancers are different from Nathan's, more erect and lockstep, with one leg bent at the knee, drawn high up towards the chest. Unlike the other dancers, who wear red sashes around their waists, black Homburg-style hats, and shiny black shoes, Nathan is shoeless and hatless. His long hair, tied in a thick ponytail, flows behind him. He carries a short stick; a balloon and streamers are attached. Arnold makes a mental note to look this up. What's Morris Dance? What's the meaning of "Fool"?

The caption on the back of the Israel picture shows Nate standing with his arm around a striking, dark-haired woman. Arnold recognizes the golden roof of the Dome of the Rock in the distance behind them. "With Hannah in Jerusalem, 1978" is the only description.

One photo shows Nate dressed in a martial arts outfit drawing a long bow and arrow. An older Asian man stands behind him, observing. "Kyudo lesson with Shibata Kanjuro Sensei, Kyoto, 1994." On Nate's shelves, Arnold finds a book titled *One Arrow, One Life*, and learns that *kyudo* means the way of the bow in Japanese and refers to Zen archery. A second Asian photo is of Nate sitting on what looks like a picnic blanket with an attractive, smiling woman. Nate is laughing, clearly happy. The caption on the back reads "With Kim Ju Ok, Chunchon, Korea, 1995."

Two photos are of India. In one, Nate is seated with a group of bearded men, musicians judging from the instruments in front of them. "With the Chishti Sufis," the long caption begins, "in the holy city of Benares, 1998. The Qawwali tabla drum rhythms—dramatic, emotive—constantly change (like me). The stringed instrument keeps a steady, unvarying beat, on and on (as I would wish to be, more like Arnie)." The second photo is a long-distance shot of a crowd milling around amid bon fires and smoke. The description on the back says, "Pyres of burning bodies at Manikarnika Ghat on the Ganges, Benares, 1998." Below the caption are a reference note and a quotation:

Buddhaghosa's second contemplation on death in *The Path of Purification*—
"As the ruin of success: here success shines as long as failure does not overcome it. And the success does not exist that might endure out of reach of failure. Accordingly:
'He gave with joy a hundred millions
After conquering all the earth,
Till in the end his realm came down
To less than half a gall-nut's worth.
Yet when his merit was used up,
His body breathing its last breath,
The Sorrowless Asoka too
Felt sorrow face to face with death.'"

He notices a small, framed photo standing separately on the desk. A child sits on Nathan's lap. She and Nathan are smiling at each other. The note on the back reads *Ellen, age 2, Cambridge, 1976.*

Arnold returns to several of the photos. The parenthetical phrase in the first caption about Benares, *"(as I would wish to be, more like Arnie),"* is flattering but ironical. Arnold has always wanted to be more like Nate. True, Nathan's outsized personal qualities often got him in trouble. He is thinking specifically of Nate's emotionality, which for Arnold was so genuine and affectionate but could be intimidating and overpowering if one weren't used to it. Like the time he and Nate shared a three-man tent, on a Boy Scout camping weekend, with Jerry Landau. Jerry was a new kid in the troop, but his sweetness made him popular from the start. The bugler had just played Taps and the three tent mates were in their sleeping bags, Jerry and Arnold on either side of Nate. "I'm so happy to have you as my brother and tent mate," Nate exclaimed with his usual exuberance as he rolled over to give Arnold an affectionate hug goodnight. "And I'm so happy to have you as my new friend and tent mate," he said, turning to do the same to Jerry.

There was a crunching sound. "God damn it!" Jerry screamed. "You broke my glasses! God damn you!"

Nate actually began crying. "I always ruin things. I just don't think. I move too fast. I ruin everything."

Arnold looks back at the photo of them lifting weights in their friend Louie's garage. Nate was lifting primarily to get stronger. As the photo shows, his teenage body was already nicely muscled and well-proportioned, neither too heavy nor too thin; his corpulence came much later. Arnold, on the other hand, was there to bulk up. He was skinny and would have given anything to be built and look like his handsome brother. Arnold's physique has been the source of certain early and even life-long insecurities. As when kids would call him "chicken bones." As when the rabbi, teaching him to put on phylacteries in front of his giggling Hebrew school classmates, commented in frustration that Arnold's arm was too thin to hold up the leather strap. As when Wendy Adler, Arnold's first lay, ruined the wondrous experience by insisting on counting his protruding ribs and vertebrae. That was the worst following the best, the best having just been an orgasm so delicious and tiring that he felt he could stay under that blanket on the beach entwined with Wendy forever. She said it was pleasurable for her, too, but then ruined the wondrous moment. "Jeez, Arnie. It's amazing how your bones stand out: one, two, three, four..." She kept counting while he plummeted from exhilaration to humiliation before she got to ten.

If only I could look more like Nate, he used to muse. I'd be...What? Happier. More courageous. Less afraid of making mistakes. More willing to risk disapproval. Less prone to taking the safe, conventional way. More willing to step out there and not hide. I'd ask girls out and fight back against bullies. I'd stick up for myself and anyone else who needed help. Look like Nate, be like Nate.

After two days of scouring and airing, the place is livable, even pleasant. And despite the devastation that's still obvious as soon as he walks outside Las Palmas, Arnold is happy to be in Belmar. Fall and winter have always been his favorite seasons here. The 60,000 vacationers and seasonal renters are gone, and the population drops back to 5,000 year-round residents. He recalls the sense of merciful stillness and isolation annually accompanying their departure. His roiling hormones, over-stimulated by a summer of ogling sun-bathers by day and trying to court them at night, settled down. He became himself again. The town became his again. He could walk its streets, as familiar as family, without worrying about his looks, his body, his clothes. There was no one to impress. The beaches, empty in the colder weather, no longer tableaus for preening and parading, became enjoyable again. Standing by the water, with no boisterous crowds to distract him, he imagined— sometimes actually felt—he could see the coast of Spain. Nate used to say the same. Summer, disturbing summer, stirred them physically. Quiet winter stirred them emotionally, romantically. It stirred them to yearn.

Since his youth, though, parts of the Shore have stirred more pity in Arnold than yearning. On one of his walks, he retraces the steps he took following Nathan after his brother left the reunion brunch. Arnold's not sure why he does this. He doubts that he'll encounter Nate or magically conjure up his reappearance. Maybe it's just his current fixation on Shore memories, now that he's back. Whatever his motivation, from the Berkeley-Carteret he crosses Ocean Avenue, climbs the ramp to the boardwalk, turns south, and enters the lobby of Convention Hall, the vast 1920s-era venue that has hosted hundreds of performances by the likes of Glenn Miller, Sinatra, the Temptations, Ray Charles, the Rolling Stones, Janis Joplin, and Bob Dylan. The class of '62 had its commencement in the Hall. Robed and jubilant, diplomas in hand, Arnold and his fellow graduates marched down a marble staircase to the applause of their waiting families. Five steps from the bottom Nathan, still feeling the effects of the pint of rye he and a friend had consumed before the ceremony, tripped on the hem of his regalia and fell.

Arnold enters the Hall's Grand Arcade from the north and passes the Asbury Park Roastery, The Mermaid Haberdashery, The Anchor's Bend, Carla Gizzi's, The Asbury Oyster Bar, Belly's Icebox, and the old Paramount Theatre, where as many as 1,500 people at a time once flocked for movies, circuses, roller derbies, basketball games, and cotillions. Then he continues down the boardwalk. It's a depressing walk, even if there had been no Hurricane Sandy. The stores he passes have some vitality in summer, but after Labor Day there are few tourists and little business even when the weather is pleasant. This wasn't always the case. At the turn of the 20th century, Asbury

Park rivaled Atlantic City as a recreational destination well into autumn. Race riots in the late 1960s changed all that as sections of Asbury fell into ruin. Fifty years later, many buildings are still boarded up, vacant and decrepit. The iconic Stone Pony, made famous by Springsteen, Southside Johnny, and Bon Jovi, has also gone in and out of business over the years. Arnold goes by the forlorn Pony now, remembering the periodic good spells when crowds lined up for blocks waiting for admission to some name-band concert, when the surrounding boardwalk concessions were alive with paying customers, when the beaches and swimming areas were crowded with fun-lovers happy to be in exciting Asbury Park, New Jersey.

At the city's southern border he enters the ruins of the Asbury Park Casino, whose walkway links Asbury Park with Ocean Grove, the next town to the south. The Casino exemplifies Asbury's rise and fall. Built in 1929 with the same architects that designed New York City's Grand Central Station, the beaux-arts casino, arcade, and carousel were left to decay years before, along with much of the rest of the entertainment district. The concrete and limestone building's ruin remains standing—a gaping skeleton, haunting and huge, its poignancy heightened by the original, still-visible polished terrazzo and plasterwork. Arnold tries not to think of the ruin as a symbol for the whole city. Better to be optimistic, he tells himself, to believe that Asbury's future will be more like its distant past than its immediate present. It could be that now, post-Sandy, there will be nowhere to go but up.

Back at Las Palmas, stuck between the cushions on the couch he finds a copy of a *Harvard Crimson* issue that contains an article written by Nate when he was still the university's golden boy. Part of it is about New Jersey, and Arnold's re-reading it now is timely. Its affectionate sense of place re-establishes his own sense of connection to their hometown. He's especially struck by the article's ending: "As for those of us who were fortunate enough to have grown up at the Shore," Nate wrote, "I cannot do other than predict that we shall at one time or another be drawn back. It is a place for returning and settling in...."

Nate did come back. Then he left again. And now Arnold has returned to take his place.

Arnold spends a lot of time during the term break reflecting on Nate's life and, by extension, his own. Up until the time they went to college, Arnold felt that they were twins not only genetically, but also spiritually. As different as they were physically, intellectually, and temperamentally, their affection for each other was transcendent. They were brothers and best friends. They enjoyed each other's company more than anyone else's. They did nearly everything together. This psychic closeness never lessened, even when they lived in different places, even when their lives took entirely different directions. In college, they phoned each other weekly, spent holidays and vacations together, and visited whenever they could in between. They were steady correspondents during Arnold's junior year in Israel, and Arnold relied on Nate often for advice when he was a graduate student at Columbia. And while he didn't know any specifics about the troubles Nate was having at Harvard, Arnold was gratified to be his brother's principal moral support at the time. Much later, he was flattered to be invited to vacation with Nate and Esther on several occasions during their marriage, as the photo of the three of them in Cadaqués, Spain now reminds him, and Arnold, a bachelor, was never made to feel the slightest bit awkward or intrusive. And although they weren't in contact during Nate's disappearances, Arnold never—because they are twins? — lost his strong sense of being connected and somehow "present" to each other.

He wishes he could talk with Nate now. The psychic connection won't answer the questions Arnold has. On his own, he doubts he'll ever understand how their lives took such different directions, despite their common starting point.

As he dusts off Nate's books, Arnold notices a black three-ring binder he had somehow overlooked during his earlier walk-throughs, probably because it wasn't a book with a title. But it's certainly a book, Arnold realizes as he riffles through its hundreds of pages. A hand-written note is taped to the front.

For Arnie,

With deepest love, thanks, and remorse as I embark on a new life.

Nate
October 30, 2012

October 30th. Tuesday. Two days after Nate left the reunion breakfast at the Berkeley-Carteret and disappeared.

Arnold settles into Nate's over-stuffed chair and begins to read.

Part Seven

Which Way Now?

2012 – 2016

When you are still fragmented, lacking certainty, what difference does it make what your decisions are?

–Hakim Sanai

ARNOLD DREAMS DREAMS THAT are staid and uneventful, much like his waking life. Tonight's dream is different, more dramatic. In tonight's dream a hurricane's waters reach Nathan's notebook, leaving its pages sodden and unreadable. "No!" Arnold laments. "No! All of that wasted. All of it gone." He wades through the flooded streets of Belmar, muttering out loud like someone with Tourette's. "Goddammit, Nathan, where are you? Are you dead? Gone for good? Or is this just another of your crazy disappearances?"

He comes out of his dream feeling cheated. He has a lot of questions but no one to ask. He's got a lot of reactions but no target for expressing them. He thought he understood Nate, despite their many differences and the years they've been apart. But the notebook has forced him to conclude otherwise. After reading it, he realizes that there have been gaps all along. He recalls a quotation he was fond of using in a Columbia course he taught on the use of primary sources. "It is only as if one found disordered papers in a drawer and just happened for the present to find no more and had to be content," Rainer Maria Rilke wrote in *The Notebooks of Malte Laurids Brigge*. "What arises behind it is nevertheless the sketch of an existence and a shadow-network of forces astir." Yes. The sketch of an existence, a shadow-network of forces astir.

By the fall of 2013 Nathan is still missing. Arnold resists concluding that his brother is gone for good, choosing instead to consider this as just the latest in Nate's compulsive string of temporary absences.

Meanwhile, Arnold has moved to Washington, DC to spend a sabbatical year at the Holocaust Museum as distinguished scholar-in-residence. He's received a grant that provides office space, secretarial and research assistance, a travel stipend, and rent for a small row house in the city's Capitol Hill area. With his half-salary from Columbia, the norm for year-long sabbaticals, he's able to keep his place in New York City. He plans to return to Columbia for one more academic year following the sabbatical and then retire. Arnold is enthusiastic. The arrangement is a fine opportunity to put the finishing touches on a career devoted to Jewish historiography, particularly to his continuing research on the aftermath of the medieval Khazar Empire. He anticipates finishing a book, tentatively titled *The Khazar Controversy and Jewish Identities*, by the end of the grant period, and he has already signed a publication agreement with a prestigious university press. Beyond the project's inherent professional advantages, the focus required by the work and the stimulation of a new place should ease his preoccupation with Nathan. This work will be the capstone of many years of scholarly effort, his own and others', to discover and scrutinize the evidence supporting or disproving several competing theories which have preoccupied historians for decades. Are Ashkenazi Jews actually from the Land of Israel, genuine descendants of the biblical patriarch Abraham? Are Ashkenazi Jews descended from the Khazars, a Turkic tribe from Central Asia that wielded significant regional power between the 7th and 10th centuries A. D. and whose leaders converted to Judaism? Are Ashkenazi Jews non-Khazars from Central Europe? The relevance of such questions extends well beyond academic and historical interest. The answers have serious contemporary and practical implications with respect to the perennial questions of what defines a Jew; the logic or illogic of anti-Semitism in purely racial terms; and the validity or invalidity of claims to the Holy Land, whether historical, ethnic, or theological. Arnold knows that his examination and discussion of these questions are eagerly awaited by his colleagues. He also realizes that he'll be walking a political tightrope since only some will agree with his answers. But at least he'll have the satisfaction of ending his career in the highest echelons of his specialty.

For the umpteenth time he asks himself how it could be that he is here, while Nate is...Who knows where Nate is. No longer at the top of his specialty, in any case.

Mid-way through the year, Arnold uses his travel stipend for a 10-day trip to Israel to consult with two senior scholars who represent diametrically opposing views on the Khazar question. One, a professor at Tel Aviv University, claims that Ashkenazi Jews are descended from the Khazar Empire in Medieval Europe, while the other, a faculty member at the Hebrew University of Jerusalem, concludes that there is no evidence to support the Khazar "myth" but argues instead that the People of Israel are literally that: descendants of the Biblical Hebrews. The two individuals are leading historians of Judaism, and Arnold reckons that their polarized reactions to his own conclusions will provide useful bellwethers for anticipating and addressing criticisms from scholars in both camps.

While in Israel Arnold stays with Sinaiya, his long-time friend and occasional lover who is an oncologist at the Hadassah Medical Center in Ein Kerem, an ancient hillside village several miles west of Jerusalem where Sinaiya also lives.

"It's beautiful here," Arnold says as the two walk arm in arm along Ein Kerem's charming cobblestone streets. "The views, the cypress trees, the upscale restaurants, shops, and art galleries. Your lovely home and garden. It's perfect."

"And you, of all people, shouldn't forget the history here," Sinaiya chides him as they pass archaeological sites, monasteries, and churches, including the Church of Saint John the Baptist, who was born in Ein Kerem, and Mary's Well, the stone-age spring commemorating Mary's visit to Zachariah and Elizabeth before Jesus was born. They stop to look back over Jerusalem. "We'll both retire soon, Arnold," Sinaiya continues, "and the obstacles that have kept us mostly apart since our student days will be gone then. So why not make Aliyah? Why not come here to live? With me...And don't say something stupid, like 'Oh, such an attractive offer! Thank you, I'll think about it.'"

"But that's exactly what I was going to say," Arnold laughs. Then he turns serious. "You know I've been in love with you since we met 50 years ago. We always had the excuse of distance and our careers for never having stayed together. So you're right. Retirement removes those obstacles. It's an extraordinarily attractive offer. And I do thank you. But it's a huge move psychologically, and I do have to think about it."

"Is it that the move would be so difficult, or worries about your brother?"

"It's complicated, and it's both. I'm devoted to Israel and all things Jewish. But I'm not Israeli. I'm an American Jew. And the twin brother of a man who I believe is alive and will need me. And the uncle of his daughter, who may or may not be alive, who may or may not need me some day. I don't know. As I said, Sinaiya, it's complicated, and I need to think about it."

After his grant ends Arnold returns to Columbia and announces his retirement, effective at the conclusion of the 2014-2015 academic year. He sends the first draft of his manuscript to the publisher and, in between lectures and advising, incorporates reviewers' suggestions into the book's final version, which goes to press in May of 2015.

This grand accomplishment coincides with his 71st birthday. With a bottle of merlot and a box of carryout pizza, Arnold sits alone on his tiny balcony going through the motions of celebrating both occasions. Halfway through the bottle, the pizza hardly touched, he sinks into despair so deep it frightens him: *What will I do now?*

Arnold is unsettled by a palpable sense of isolation. After decades in this city, in this apartment, at this moment he feels a stranger. Grant's Tomb, a constant presence across Riverside Drive and a comforting reminder of the importance of historians, tonight provokes another feeling he can't quite specify. Dread? Desperation? He flashes on one of the pictures in Nate's apartment, the photo of burning funeral pyres in India with the inscription about death as the ruin of success. He looks past Grant's Tomb at the lights on the New Jersey side of the Hudson. At this moment he only wants one thing: to return home, to the Shore, where he will move into Las Palmas, wait for Nate, and decide what to do next.

It takes Arnold two weeks to exit the university, a process combining file purges, consolidation, farewell parties, and personnel forms. He is fond of Columbia and honored to have been on its faculty. The university has treated him well, and he has done his best to serve it conscientiously for 40 years. It's strange to leave it with only six tightly packed boxes of essential books and documents. It takes him another week to sell his furniture, donate most of his clothes, and close up the apartment, which he leaves with one suitcase and three additional boxes of photographs and memorabilia. He drives out of Manhattan and down the Jersey Turnpike—trunk packed, seats crammed, roof rack loaded—amazed and ambivalent to realize that he's been able to fit the remnants of his life into a Honda Civic.

Arnold is confident that he has made the right decision, at least temporarily, by returning to Belmar, but the move still leaves unanswered the question which caused his troubled mix of emotions that night on the balcony:
What next? Age 71, fully retired, with no institutional structure or routine or
goal, what will he do from now on?

The busy work of moving in—lugging, scrubbing, scouring, vacuuming,
dusting, windexing, bleaching, purchasing, refurbishing, arranging utilities—
takes up the first week. Daily, Freddie Millbank comes up to gab. "The place
is looking better and better," Freddie says as he watches Arnold work. "I'm
glad it's occupied again, and by you. I've gotten used to Kirinskis being here
over the years. Nate will be happy to find it all in such good shape when he
returns."

"Thanks, Freddie," Arnold replies, knowing that the landlord's comment is meant more as a reinforcement of the hope that Nate is still alive than
a landlord's evaluation of Arnold's housekeeping. "I'll keep things tidy while
we await the great day."

Most days, Arnold visits his sister's and parents' graves at two different but
nearby cemeteries. Deborah Kirinski Martino's ashes are next to her husband Ed's in the non-denominational Monmouth Memorial Park in Tinton
Falls. Morton and Fay are buried in the Chesed Shel Ames Hebrew Cemetery in Neptune. At both sites, Arnold recites the mourner's prayer and
observes the traditional Jewish custom of laying stones of remembrance on
their individual markers. The actions evoke strong associations: of his visit
to the graves with Nathan after his brother's return to the Shore in 2002, of
his father's agonizing dispute with Rabbi Steinman over the permissibility of
saying the *Kaddish* for Deborah, who had been cremated. *I wish you were
here to do this with me, Nate,* Arnold says to himself on each visit. *I feel so
lonely, so terribly sad and lonely. Am I the only Kirinski left?*

"Hello, Deb," he greets his sister out loud as he approaches her marker.
"I hope you can hear me. I miss you as much as ever. You meant so much to
me in life, and that hasn't changed in death." He tells her this each time he
visits, and then brings her up to date about Nate ("still missing, our unpre-
dictable brother"), Ellen ("I just don't know"), and himself ("retired now and
back in Belmar, trying to decide on my future. I always valued your advice. I
wish I had the benefit of it these days."). He recites the *Kaddish* for Deb and
the Lord's Prayer for both her and Ed before taking his leave. "I'm off to visit
Mort and Fay now. I love you, and will come here again soon."

He communes with his parents much the same way at their graves in
Chesed Shel Ames, but adds: "I read in Nathan's notebook the correspondence between you and Rabbi Steinman, and the letters between Uncle
Samuel and the Rabbinical Council of America. Steinman was wrong when
he told you that saying *Kaddish* for Debbie was forbidden because she chose

cremation. I want you to know that I recite the prayer every year on the anniversary of her death and whenever I go to her cemetery."

Arnold walks through Belmar and its neighboring towns trying to figure out what to do next. Inspired by Nate's notebook, he begins recording certain of his own walking experiences and reflections in impressionistic sketches as the impulse strikes him. Most of the episodes are observed in the present, but some are retrospective and psychological, past moments and states of mind that come to him as he walks. He thinks of these impressions as his version of photography, without the burdens of equipment and expense. It's an exuberant experiment for Arnold, something he hadn't done or even considered doing before. He never saw himself as remotely artistic or innovative, but with these sketches he manages to step outside his usual ways for a while.

When he isn't walking and jotting down impressions, Arnold reads. And now that he's retired, for the first time since elementary school he has time to read beyond some set curriculum or canon. Perhaps because the pressure is off, he also has a new attitude toward reading to go along with his experiments in writing sketches and impressions. He revels in the unaccustomed serendipity of the process. Unlike his schooldays, when all reading felt like it was required, or during his efforts to develop in his discipline and then advance his career through ever more rigorously focused and specialized research and writing, as a retiree he can follow leads wherever they take him, entirely at his leisure and with no pressure to produce.

At first he borrows books, usually poetry and fiction, from the Monmouth College and Belmar Public libraries. Then he begins to explore the volumes on Nate's shelves. The authors are mostly unfamiliar to him. But the titles, along with Nate's allusions to a number of them in his notebook, are intriguing to Arnold—even the ones that strike him as "mystical," a designation that would once have been anathema to him. When a title strikes him as flaky or weird, as many do, he reminds himself that he's no longer a scholastic, and perhaps it's time for him to branch out. But it doesn't look easy. He can't imagine how Nathan could have read all this, which makes his own ability to do so seem unlikely. And if he does somehow manage to get through them all, he worries about his capacity to comprehend them. He wishes he could avail himself of Nate's philosophical training to help him navigate this material. *What do I,* Arnold asks himself, *a historian, know about consciousness, natural mind, no-mind, emptiness, conditions arising, original face, and so many other esoteric concepts, to say nothing of all the words, at their roots inseparable from the concepts, in Sanskrit, Pali, Hindi, Tibetan, Chinese, Japanese, and Korean?*

The titles are daunting, but Arnold is ready to give the books a try in the interest of self-expansion. He's especially enthusiastic to read Nate's collection of books and monographs on Jewish mysticism, including the works of Isaac Abarbanel, Abraham Abulafia, Bahya ibn Paquda, Joseph Caro, Moses Chayim

Luzzatto, Josef ibn Saya, Abraham ben Eliezer Halevi, and Kalonymous Kal-man Shapira; collections of Hasidic tales by Martin Buber, Jiri Langer, and Eli Weisel; and scholarly treatments by Nehemia Polen, Ernst Müller, Perle Epstein, Daniel Matt, and his own former teacher Gershom Scholem. By vir-tue of his training, this is a literature he can at least access in historical and linguistic terms, although he's entirely ignorant of its esoteric aspects.

Time to branch out indeed. He's had a successful career. His new book is being well received in academic circles. His reputation as a scholar is firmly es-tablished. That Nate apparently found the books on these shelves to be useful is recommendation enough for Arnold. But now he worries about the rigorous standards of his own training, and how difficult it will be not to apply schol-arly criteria to topics for which such standards might be unfair or irrelevant. He's thinking of the conversation with the Harvard philosophy department chairman that Nate reported in his notebook, specifically the part about the syncretism in Nate's writings. Honestly, having read his brother's books and articles Arnold has to agree with the chairman's criticism. In addition to his historian's mania for objectivity and demonstrable evidence, a principal reason Arnold has shied away from what's called "New Age" literature is the tendency he's seen for writers in that genre to collapse the spiritual experiences reported in various traditions into one undifferentiated clump and apply one explana-tion to everything. Syncretism, in other words. Arnold is much influenced by Professor Scholem in this regard. In the scholarship on mysticism, Scholem detested conclusions drawn hastily, without sufficient demonstrable, factual, and historical grounds. "What is plausible can do without proof," as he put it with elegant sarcasm in the introduction to his translation of the *Zohar*.

But Arnold is game to give these books a try in his commitment to explore new approaches, ideas, and experiences, to apply some of what he's reading to what he observes and records on his walks. He begins with a phrase he finds in a book Nate has by the Buddhist teacher Pema Chödrön: *the propensity to be bothered.*

Arnold walks through the local Shore communities, engrossed in his efforts not to be bothered. Each person or situation he encounters gives him an opportunity to defeat his propensity to be annoyed by the way someone looks, walks, talks, or behaves. He knows this, and he tries. But he fails in every instance. Why? He determines that it's a matter of lapsed attention: if he can remind himself not to be bothered as the instance is about to arise, or even be aware of it once it has arisen, he's sure he'll win the battle, at least in that instance. And if he wins once, he reasons, he'll know what to do next time, and the time after that until, ultimately, he'll have established the ca-pacity not to be bothered. He's sure of this.

Two figures approach, and he steels himself not to get caught up in the way they walk, talk, or look. He doesn't recognize them until they wave, and one calls out. "Arnold? Is that you, Kirinski? It's Al. And Charlie."

Albert Greenbaum and Kalman Rosenzweig, now Alexander Garfield and Charles Rossiter. Arnold recalls what Nate wrote about them, their influence on his early life and his confrontation with them at the reunion brunch in the Berkeley-Carteret. But Arnold has his own history with these two, and the early resolve of his intention not to be bothered is already fading against the force of this history. But still, he tries.

"Alex, Charlie. It's been a while." He will always think of them as Albert and Kalman, but goes with their adopted names in an effort to be civil.

"Since the 50th," says Alex. "We didn't get to talk with you much then. How have you been?" He tells them he recently retired.

"Are you still living near the university, over on Riverside Drive? It's a beautiful spot."

"No. I live in Belmar now."

Alex and Charlie look at each other. Getting out of Belmar had been the priority for many of their peers. Coming back for family visits, which the two tell Arnold is why they're in town now, and the occasional reunion, is natural and understandable. Leaving New York City to live here again is hardly conceivable. "So you're both here now. You and Nate. Nate was in some rooming house, wasn't he? Where do you live? Back in your parents' place?"

Arnold is bothered by the lawyer-ish questions. He dislikes these guys and only wants to get away. Keep working at it, he reminds himself, working against the propensity to be bothered. "No, we sold the folks' house. I'm living in Las Palmas, over on 12th near the ocean."

"And Nate?"

He decides not to deflect or temporize. "I'm living in Nate's apartment. Nate's been gone for three years."

"Where is he? Is he okay?"

"I don't know where he is, or how he is. He hasn't been in contact with me."

"My God. What happened?"

Fuck it, Arnold decides, reprising what Nate had written. "You two happened. You said some things to him at the reunion brunch that really upset him. How he wouldn't be looking out for his daughter if he didn't revive his career and make money off his past celebrity. How he was being irresponsible." The propensity to be bothered, Arnold reminds himself. Don't get upset. Settle down. Breathe.

"We were only trying to help him out," Garfield says. "For old times' sake. Out of friendship. We..."

Arnold smacks Garfield hard across his face, shocking even himself. Garfield is holding his cheek, his expression disbelief. Arnold looks at Rossiter, whose initial surprise gives way—Arnold is sure of it—to a slight smile. Arnold remembers Nate's description of the time Alex had slapped Charlie. Charlie's payback for Alex's past humiliations of him, he wonders, however indirect and vicarious?

"What the hell was that for?" Garfield asks.

"That was for Nate, who isn't here to do it himself. For all the years you've been such a prick. And for..." Arnold pauses, searching for something. Some words, some emotions, "...for the times you bullied me, Albert, punching me, making fun of my skinny arms, asking how I could be such a dumbass when my twin brother was so smart. Nate never knew any of that. I never told him. He would have killed you. Which wouldn't have bothered me at all. But I didn't want him to feel he had to stick up for me. And I needed to learn how to deal with crap like that, assholes like you, by myself. Like I just did. Finally."

Arnold walks away, no longer bothered but in no way less inclined to become so. The encounter was cathartic on an emotional level. But he realizes that's not all he needs.

He comes across a piece of advice that spurs his optimism. It's from another of Nate's books, a suggestion from Dae Gak, a teacher of Korean Zen, who proposes what he calls bowing meditation. When you're bothered, or catch yourself about to be bothered by walkers, drivers, or whatever, incline your head. Dae Gak claims that a sense of respect, patience, and tolerance will ensue.

He takes Dae Gak's advice on the road the next morning as he embarks on the three-mile walk along the beachfront from Belmar to Asbury. At the Casino, just before he's about to turn around for the walk home, he sees a distinctive figure coming toward him. As he has done so often in recent days, albeit mostly with failed results, he prepares himself not to be bothered, in this case by the man's confident, athletic gait, or his muscular build, or his shaved head, or his black skin. When the man gets closer Arnold breathes deeply and, as Dae Gak advised, inclines his head in a slight bow. The man returns his nod and smiles.

"It's been years, but I recognize you. Your Nate Kirinski's brother..."

"Right. Arnold. And you're Sid Hamlin. I'd know you anywhere."

"Well, thanks for that. I'll take it as a compliment," Sid says, shaking Arnold's hand. "Where are you headed? Mind if I walk with you?"

"I'd like that. But let's go in the direction you were walking. I live in Belmar anyway."

"Good. That's where I'm going. I don't live in this area anymore. I'm in Basking Ridge now. But I come back to the Shore once in a while to walk around. Nostalgia, I guess, although the memories are not all pleasant."

"Why Basking Ridge, if you don't mind my curiosity?"

"It's beautiful, private, upscale, and an easy commute to the city. I'm a stockbroker these days. Actually for the past 30 years and more, from about the time I last saw your brother. We played pinball together."

"I remember hearing about it. The great Royal Flush match. You won."

Sid laughs. "Yeah, I did. But the whole thing was so strange. Honestly, Nate and I were the last people you'd think would be in that situation. I mean, a Harvard professor and an NFL star. Both former, but still. What a comedown for both of us. I never talked with Nate about it. But it seemed to me that he was as screwed up then as I was, two local success stories who had fallen on hard times and turned to pinball, of all things. We both needed something to be good at to bury our depression. But the weirdest part about it is that I won that match. Royal Flush was Nate's game. No one could beat him on it. To this day I'm convinced that he threw it my way. Why would he do that? I never got to ask him."

"I don't know. He never talked about it. He was so private and guarded then. My guess is that he wanted to keep things that way, to be invisible. If he had won, the rivalry would have had to continue."

"That sounds right. And I was the reverse. I needed to be in the lime-light. After football, I could only do that with a bunch of hangers on. Groupies. God, I was so fucked up then. But the thing I've always thought is that Nate understood that about me, and part of his throwing the match was so I'd keep being idolized by my followers. I really appreciated him for doing that, whether or not he meant it to work out that way. Is he in Belmar, too? I'd like to ask him."

"I wish you could. I don't know where he is."

Arnold fills Sid in on Nate's story as they walk through Ocean Grove, Bradley Beach, and Avon. Sid tells Arnold about his post-pinball work on Wall Street, how he was able to pull his life together, get an MBA at NYU, and parlay that with his football renown into a successful career. "Lots of money, a big place in the 'burbs, a wife and three grown kids who could care less about pinball machines. They'd laugh at the person I was then."

At 11th and Ocean Avenues in Belmar, they part. Arnold will return to Las Palmas, Sid will walk over to Main Street "to take care of something" before getting a cab back to Asbury, where his car is parked. Arnold has to ask: "What's on Main Street?"

"*Go Play!* It's kind of a retro arcade with classic games. You know. Skeeball, air hockey. And pinball."

Two weeks after the slapping episode with Alexander Garfield, Arnold receives a handwritten letter postmarked New York City with a return address in Chelsea.

Dear Arnie,

Initially, I thought you should be the one to apologize to me, and maybe I should even sue you for assault. But I've since reconsidered. I deserved that slap for the pain I caused you as a kid, caused Nate at the reunion, and caused Charlie Rossiter throughout the years. In fact, Charlie and I had it out right after you left us standing on the boardwalk a couple of weeks ago. Your retribution freed him up to lay into me with a litany of complaints about the various ways I've bullied him since the time we all first met in 6th grade. I'd like to see you and apologize personally some time when I'm at the Shore, but I'll understand if you'd rather not get together. If that's the case, I hope you'll accept this written apology as the very sincere one that it is.

With best wishes,
Alex

Dear Alex,

Thank you for your letter. I appreciate your apology and certainly accept it. But I've also had time to think about our encounter. I don't doubt that I've been right to feel angry about the things that happened between us when we were kids; feelings are feelings. But I was wrong—and too old—to have expressed those feelings as I did. I had no right to touch you, much less to hit you, and I'm sorry. So—Please don't sue me! Instead, I suggest that we chalk it all up to bygones being bygones on both our parts. And yes: I look forward to getting together when you're at the Shore. There were a lot of good times and friends that we can talk about, and then let's take things from there. You can reach me at 732-681-1226.

Sincerely,
Arnie

Arnold begins meditating, an activity he had never considered doing until he moved into Las Palmas. He's not sure, but he thinks his daily sittings and Dae Gak's bowing exercise are having a positive effect on his attitude. He's more patient, more cheerful, more forgiving, less bothered.

As he makes his way through the books on Nate's shelves, he has new appreciation for his brother's inclination toward syncretism, especially as he recognizes significant areas of convergence in the various religious traditions' descriptions of meditative practice. Still, his training compels him to resist any idea of a Unified Theory or Grand Explanation. He has a lot more to read before he'll venture a conclusion on this. But at least he's open to the possibility, which would never have been the case until recently. He's also open to Nate's notion of useful fictions, albeit grudgingly. As Nate put it in his notebook when he described Vaihinger's "As if" philosophy, "even though we know that our thoughts and ideas are false, they are nevertheless useful coping mechanisms in the face of the overwhelming complexity of our existence." Arnold can never completely buy this as an approach to life; he's too much of a realist, a hardline historian whose maxim is to find and then accept the unvarnished truth. (He can hear Nate's rejoinder from their discussions back in graduate school: "Whose truth, Arnie, told by whom?")

But now, maybe he can meet Nate in the Solomonic middle on this. He can't bring himself to embrace useful fictions—for a positivist historian, no fiction is useful except in novels or movies. But how about useful ideas? In addition to the "Useful Ideas" essay Nate wrote for Esther, Arnold is thinking particularly about Nate's attraction to the utility of numbered formulations of wisdom—"Six Words of Advice," "Four Agreements," "Eight Worldly Concerns," and the like. Along these lines, he also recalls a conversation, not long before the 50th reunion, when Nate told him about the "Nine Rs."

"Remember the Three Rs in grade school—readin', 'ritin', and 'rithmetic? Well, I kept the letter R but came up with my own version of that formulation: Remembrance, Regret, Remorse, Repentance, Reconciliation, Redemption, Ruin, Release, and Repeat. Acknowledging these Nine Rs," Nate went on, "put many of my disappointments in perspective and freed me, at long last, from self-castigation. They've been very useful."

"Okay," Arnold had replied, "but I don't understand the 'ruin' part. What does that mean?"

"That we're all the same boat when we come down to it."

"What boat is that?"

"Death. Every success is destined for extinction if you only define things in the worldly sense."

Arnold recalls getting exasperated at that point. "What other sense is there?"

"Who really knows? We only know that death is for sure. The best we can do is to get ready for it. Put aside any other strivings—to acquire this, to accomplish that. What will you do, Arnie? How will you get ready?"

"I honestly don't know. Do you have any of those numbered pieces of advice for me?"

Nate ignored the sarcasm. "There's a quote from *The Practice of the Presence of God* that I like. Brother Lawrence, a 17th century Carmelite monk, wrote it. 'Death follows us close; let us be well prepared for it; for we die but once, and a miscarriage *there* is irretrievable. I say again, let us enter into ourselves. The time presses, there is no room for delay; our souls are at stake.' No numbers this time, Arnie, but something we both might want to think about."

Arnold replied that the quote was insipid, more on the order of a platitude than an expression of authentic wisdom. "Honestly, 'souls at stake...' I have no way of knowing what that means, and I'm disappointed it has meaning for you."

Nate shrugged, Arnold shrugged back, and they parted.

But it was weird. That night Arnold had a dream he chose not to share with his brother, probably because he was afraid it would look like he was moving too close to Nate's world—the world of esoteric mumbo jumbo that Arnold had no use for. In the dream, he was visiting Nate in his office at

Harvard. Nate handed him a plastic container full of papers. "These are the letters of Yosef ben Ephraim Caro," he said, referring to the 16th century Kabbalist. "A student of mine has been looking through them to find what's missing. But we need you, a professional researcher, to do this." Then Nate rushed off, leaving him with the box.

As Arnold stood there, wondering what to do next, a colleague of Nate's approached. "We're happy that you have the box and will do this," the man said.

"But there must be conditions to this search," Arnold replied, adamant. "These are original papers, irreplaceable archives. I insist that they be kept in a designated room. You, my brother, his student, I—no one can remove them, and whoever touches them must wear plastic gloves."

The man gave Arnold a look so stern and intense that it frightened him. "But the bigger issue," he said, "is to know: What are you searching for, Arnold Kirinski? What do you think is missing? What constitutes BINGO?"

As Arnold pores over Nate's books, he remembers that dream and his conversation with Nate about preparing to die. He had begun to think about dying that night on his Riverside Drive balcony, as he looked out over Grant's Tomb toward the lights along the Palisades in New Jersey. The next morning, following his decision to move to Las Palmas, he began to re-read the entries on death and dying in Nate's notebook and concluded it was time to get serious. To do something. To get ready. To clear the deck. Another dream he had just a few weeks later reinforced the realization, although the only detail he remembers from the dream is a road sign, a kind of billboard with the number "444"—a triply inauspicious omen for impending death, he reads somewhere, if you're Chinese. Which Arnold is not. But in this as well, he tells himself, who knows? Then came another weird, dream-relevant coincidence. The morning after the 444 dream, he randomly pulled the *Dhammapada*, a collection of the Buddha's sayings, from Nate's shelves and just as randomly opened it to this quote: "You are now like a withered leaf; even the messengers of death have come near you. You stand at the threshold of departure at the gate of death and you have made no provision for the journey."

Okay. Arnold gets the point. Now the question is how to start, assuming it's not too late. And what other assumption is worth proceeding from? In a practical, day-to-day sense (proceeding from the corollary assumption that he will not die suddenly in his sleep, under a bus, in a thunderstorm, or in a hold-up), time is less of an issue. As a retiree, his days are mostly unfettered. The question is what to do with the time. Arnold knows himself. He needs a specific project. Walking, reading, and taking notes are too general.

The impetus for the project is the phrase from the *Dhammapada* passage he had read, "...and you have made no provision for the journey." "Prepare to Die," becomes his guiding mantra, and on most days its convincing weight and necessity propel him to follow it. When his commitment to the project flags from time to time, he challenges himself with Rabbi Hillel's rhetorical question (the way his brother, as he recalls from one of Nate's notebook entries, responded to the security officer in the El Al terminal at JFK, who had asked his reasons for going to Israel): *If not now, when?* The timing, then, shouldn't be ambiguous. "When" must be considered immediate. The recurring question for Arnold is how—how to die well, at peace and reconciled with what he has done and failed to do in life. Despite the absence of a method, which remains to be determined, the very act of identifying the task has catapulted Arnold forward. Its compelling nature will keep him moving, much as his research on the Khazars kept him going over a 40-year career. He knows he has the will.

He resolves to prepare for death by treating each day as his last, by following the guidance of Carlos Castaneda's Don Juan, in yet another of Nate's books, to use death as his adviser, to live in a way that projects no future, that forces him to be in the moment, to live, and die, with presence.

But his resolution is immediately shaken. It's a fiction, he scolds himself, because I can't know that today will be my last day alive. And even if I could know, how could I all of a sudden have acquired the hitherto undeveloped capacity to live fully and die well? Then he scolds himself again, telling himself he should do what he can. He goes to the second book Nate authored, the one on Hans Vaihinger's philosophy. I'll live each day *as if* it's my last day alive, he resolves. A fiction, perhaps, but a useful one. And one day it will no longer be a fiction.

Here he's confronted with a competing fiction, or, more accurately, a simultaneous possibility: he can't help but consider that he'll have a future beyond today. The possibility that he won't live past today is easy enough to consider intellectually, but emotionally he can't get past the expectation that he'll be here tomorrow. So he lies in bed thinking, flip-flopping between the two possibilities. Then he castigates himself for his life-long habit of over-analyzing. He forces himself out of bed, washes in the coldest water he can get the old faucet to produce, and approaches his meditation pillow. Soon he's entirely present within his sitting posture, his breath, his sensations, this moment. Analysis stops. *"What's this?"* as the Zen guys would put it. *"Don't know. Just this."*

This works for a bit, until thoughts of breakfast, shopping, walking, and reading intrude. Thoughts upon thoughts. Memories upon memories. Regrets, desires, the future: he can't stay present, even on his last day alive. The lesson seems to be that he can't change simply by thinking or imagining. Or expecting. He tells himself not to expect to be more awake, aware, present, kind, compassionate, attuned, attentive, harmonious, balanced, or integrated. Maybe he'll reach these states, maybe not. Meanwhile, he also tells himself, don't expect anything to happen. Meditation is helping. Just breathe and observe the breath. Just sit and settle. Wait, watch, and possibly even enjoy the show. For this truly could be his last day alive.

Back to the how of it. Along with his sitting practice, Arnold continues reading to find inspiration, to ask useful questions, to get some help—help in gaining a perspective on death and dying, help in mapping out a system for getting ready to die. He's come across some good stuff—at least he thinks it's good stuff; never having died, how could he know? But that's the whole point, isn't it? He doesn't know. He has to rely on intuition, on what makes sense. But there are so many things to consider, so many practical and theological alternatives. Where to start? Should he be talking about the here-after, the there-after, the no-after, the ever-after, the never-after? What to do about unfinished business? Paying debts? Settling accounts? Making amends? Redeeming himself? Accepting what is at once unacceptable (how could he possibly cease to exist?) and (everyone says so) unavoidable? Should he be buried? Cremated? Set adrift on an ice-flow? Left in the wild? A suicide? How should he go about quieting his fears? Building up his soul, his being, his...whatever? What comprises the good death—*ars moriendi*, dying well? And what, when all is said and done, has it been for? As Hannah and Esther said to Nate, it's a wide-open question: Why do you have your life?

He laughs. The range of possible answers to consider is itself enough to kill you. He thinks of the sanguine Socrates and his mastery of the final scene: acceptance of an unjust verdict, compassion shown to his jailer as well as to his friends, his fearlessness and adherence to his principles until the end, his capacity to restrain his tears, his peaceful state of mind, and his sense of humor. "When a man has reached my age," Socrates said, "he ought not to be repining at the prospect of death." He thinks of the Buddhist advice to calm oneself, to observe, to realize *samadhi*, the undistracted mind, en route to enlightenment, and of the Taoist exhortation to become aware of your original nature, your original face—the creation of the immortal body that separates from the mortal body at death and returns to The Way. Then there is Sri Ramakrishna, who tells us that we simply step from one room to another at the time of death. Or the no-nonsense Louis Begley, whose eponymous protagonist in *Mistler's Exit* captures the haunting concern Arnold has harbored since witnessing his sister, mother, and father suffer the attentions of biomedical caregivers: "I'd like to get out painlessly before I become too weak or fuzzy in the head to stop these well-meaning fellows with Hippocratic oaths and funny initials after their names from showing me the marvels of modern medicine." Thomas Mistler's might be a pedestrian sentiment compared with the Buddha's or Lao-tzu's or Sri Ramakrishna's. But it's more personal for Arnold because it gets at his physical fear of death, and the cowardice he worries he'll reveal should his death be painful. Will he, as he hopes, be like Socrates, graceful, serene, dignified, brave, and still mischievous? Or will he be, as he expects, a whining, complaining, sniveling embarrassment to whoever might witness his death. And to himself.

So much for his fear of dying. Then there's the fear of being dead. Truth be told, Arnold is scared to death of death, as is so for most of us, he's sure. Will it hurt? Will he go to a bad place, like Dante's Purgatory or Inferno? Or (better? Worse?) will there be nothing, neither the prospect of hell nor the promise of heaven?

He has another, more subtle fear. Although a number of his peers have died, he's troubled that he still hasn't accepted the inevitability of it all, the idea much less the fact that he'll be no different from every other creature since time began, that he won't live forever. Living for a year in Washington should have been a helpful reminder. Every day he passed the homes and monuments of famous historical figures. Fame aside, they're dead. Yet he could never apply that inevitability to himself. On the other hand, at some level it could be that the realization is beginning to take hold, else why is he now so intent on preparing to die? Perhaps he's less driven by what it all means—or doesn't mean—for him; he is immortal in his own mind after all. But somehow that misconception doesn't have traction when it comes to Nate and Ellen—assuming, as he insists on doing, that they're alive—for whom he's intent on making responsible logistical, financial, and legal arrangements while he's still able. He also wants to make sure he writes his obituary before he runs out of time or capacity, so that others won't have to figure out who he was for some newspaper. He acknowledges this could also be a form of control that he's exercising over his legacy and others' memory of him. Why not?

So he starts writing his obituary to help Nate and Ellen if they ever reappear, or, if they're still out of the picture when he dies, the newspapers. As he writes, he realizes what should have been obvious: one's life has both subjective psychological and overtly factual dimensions. Should an obituary deal with one, the other, or both? Unable to answer even this basic question, his efforts grind to a halt. But in the process he comes to a second realization. One would think, as he had, that trying to write one's obituary would make death less of an abstraction. But it didn't. Death—*his* death—is as abstract to him as ever. He sees how divorced he is from the inevitability of it all. This insight is valuable. It brings him to the conclusion that, whether motivated by spiritual yearning, existential dread, dutifulness, or obsessive compulsion, he could not have landed on a more important project.

As a habitual researcher, his way of starting any project has been to read, and he takes the same approach now. This proves both helpful and frustrating. So much has been written about death. What does it all boil down to? What's right and what's wrong? What does he himself think? Does it matter what he thinks? Does it matter what anyone thinks? Not only does he need to get started, but he also concludes that he needs to develop an approach, a system. He needs to get started *somewhere*. Ever the analyst, he begins by categorizing theories and hypotheses about death that he has gleaned from his readings and experiences.

But again, Arnold persists, how to do it? How, specifically, theories aside, should he practice inner detachment and prepare to die?

Arnold reads *Gurdjieff: Making a New World,* in which John Bennett reports an account in Gurdjieff's unpublished writings of a man who awakes after dying and realizes he's lost the chief instrument of his life, his body, and recalls all he could have done with it while he was alive. Arnold shares that sense of regret more and more these days. But he also realizes his advantage over the man just described: Arnold is still alive. Yet the recognition of this amounts to nothing if he doesn't appreciate and act upon this advantage. He knows he won't experience this life again. Ever again. He won't feel or see or hear or smell or taste or sense this *particular* life ever again. Savor it, he urges himself. It's the last time. You've had your life and chances. Be thankful. Appreciate. Accept. Above all, don't be negative. Don't be grumpy. Don't be bothered. Don't regret. Don't worry about insignificant things—appearances, schedules, things to do, people to please.

All of these advisements bring Arnold to an emphatic conclusion. Enough planning. It's not about preparing to die so much as learning to live, to master, as Kirpal Singh puts it, the art of dying daily. I need to get it all down to the absolute basics, Arnold tells himself: wake up, get out of bed with a minimum of lingering and thinking, walk one step at a time, one foot in front of the other. Then sit. Breathe. Relax. Attend. Observe. Thoughts come, thoughts go. The watcher watches. And waits. *But for what?* Arnold asks. Spiritual fulfillment as death nears? And where? Perhaps in the distant Holy Land, where the prayers and practices of Abulafia, Shapira, and all the rest are directed and anchored? Could he find a life for himself within that land, perhaps by resuming his relationship with Sinaiya, if the offer he told her he would "think about" is still good? Or maybe the "promise" in Promised Land has nothing to do with tangibles or geographical locations. Maybe it's something beyond the land and beyond the prospect of making a life there that he should be seeking. Something more essential. More internal. More eternal. Is "Promised" another word for karma—the irrevocable price we must pay for our deeds?

Oddly, coincidentally, Sinaiya writes to say that she'll be attending a medical conference in New York later in the month and wonders if she can stay with him after her work ends. He immediately phones her to say of course. She has never been to the Shore, although she knows a lot about it through the prism of Arnold's stories and recollections.

"Las Palmas and the other residences near the ocean remind me of sections of Tel Aviv," she says as they walk along Ocean Avenue. "Just like the miles of—what do you call *hatayelet?*" Promenade, boardwalk, he translates. "Just like the boardwalk through Belmar and the other towns here remind me of promenades in certain Israeli towns along the Mediterranean coastline.

But the feeling, you know, is quite different. This is so contained, so small and peaceful, but also—what's a good word? —a bit stagnant. Stuck in time. No movement except for the ocean. Israel, the whole world knows, is anything but peaceful. But it's—again, what word? —dynamic. Alive. Ready to change. In Israel, we all expect something, good or bad we don't know. But it won't stay the same. Here, I think it will stay the same...for good or bad we also don't know."

Sinaiya spends hours looking through the books on Nate's shelves, more in wonderment at the two brothers' interest in them, Arnold guesses, than out of her own intrinsic interest. "So what do you make of them?" he asks.

"Well, there's not much here in my specialty," she laughs. "Or, I would think, for the type of historian you are. From what you've told me about your brother—his field of study, his personality, his problems at Harvard and with his first wife and their daughter and with your parents—I can understand his preoccupation with these philosophical and religious topics. But what do you get from them?"

"What do you mean by 'his preoccupation'?" Arnold asks, deflecting the focus of the question.

"Okay, I'm no psychologist, just a cancer doctor. But from what you told me your brother is desperate for—again, I don't know the damn word in English. Desperate for *ga'al.*"

"Redemption. I believe you're right. He wants to be redeemed for all the people he's disappointed. For much of his life—starting from the time his academic career and first marriage ended until he vanished several years ago—in his own mind he's a failure. The attitudes toward life these books describe and the meditation practices they lay out must have helped him with that, helped him put things in some bigger perspective, helped him to be kinder to himself. At least that's what I thought after reading his notebook."

"The books were useful to him, then, and I'm glad. But you're avoiding the question I asked you. What do you get from these books?"

"They're helping me with my own preoccupation—with death, with dying. Honestly, Sinaiya, I'm afraid. Here I am, retired, financially comfortable, well educated, still healthy—but afraid. I guess I'm hoping these books will make me easier with the inevitability of dying, less fearful of both the process and the end result. My impression of Nate just before he disappeared this last time was that he had come to terms with it, that he was ready. Now I want the same for myself."

Sinaiya is quiet for a while. Arnold can't tell from her expression whether she feels dismissive of his fretfulness or sympathetic to it. "Remember my question to you before we parted last time?" she finally asks.

"I do. It was the clearest, bluntest, most unanswerable question I've ever been asked: 'Why do you have your life?' And it's odd: I read in Nate's notebook that he was presented with the same question in almost the same wording by several different people, including his second wife, Esther. Anyway, I've thought about the question a lot. I think it's directly tied to this late-breaking concern I have about dying. I've spent my whole life on a very narrow path. Until recently, I didn't question the direction I chose. But now I wonder. Did I miss the point? And if I did, is it too late to do anything about it? I find myself envying Nate. He's had a troubled and tumultuous life. From the outside, and from his vantage point as well, it also must look like an irresponsible life, particularly because of his habit of disappearing and staying out of touch. But now I see its advantages. It's given him time to reflect and search. Looking at his choices now from my fearful perch, I believe he's done the right thing by putting all his effort into finding some peace before he dies."

"Again, I'm an oncologist, not a psychologist, and I don't know him. But I wonder if there is more to it. Your brother, as intellectually brilliant as you describe him, also sounds like he's quite emotional. From everything you've told me, I have the picture of a man who leads with his feelings, and his mind follows. You're totally different. You're the most analytical person I have ever known—so calm, so linear, so...disengaged. But I see a change in you, dear Arik," she continues, using the diminutive of his Hebrew name. "What I see happening now is that you're going deeper than intellect, that you're moving towards your feelings—concerns about death, questions about 'ultimate meaning,' the desire to be ready before you die. What I'm saying, Arik, is that you're finding your other nature. It only seems like your mind is still in front. All these readings—they're intellectual modes on the surface, but they're leading you to deep feelings. You are like my patients who are near dying. Very reflective, very aware—that's your intellect. Yet underneath, in your feelings, very afraid. But you have the important advantage over my patients of not having cancer. All other things being equal—is that the right expression? — you have some time to find some answers. So this brings me back to that first, quite philosophical, question: Why do you have your life? Which leads me to the second, quite practical, question: What will you do with the rest of your life?"

Arnold shrugs, offering no response. He knew this topic would come up. He had told her he would think about her offer to come live with her in Israel. Sinaiya shakes her head at his silence, as if to say, *I'll give you a little more time. But just a little.*

They go on to talk about the section of Jewish books on Nate's shelves. Sinaiya, the trained and accomplished scientist, surprises Arnold with her knowledge of the Jewish esoteric tradition. "Did you know that my family's Israeli roots were in Safed?" He tells her he hadn't known that. He thought her roots were in Jerusalem.

"My grandparents on both sides lived their whole lives in Safed. My parents left as young newlyweds and went to Jerusalem to study, work, and raise a family. We would visit Safed on holidays, and my siblings and I would spend the cool summers there when we were young. It's so high up. My family is Sephardic, and my older relatives were very—what do you say in English? Soaked? Okay, thanks. They were very *steeped* in Kabbalah. From my bed at night, I would hear them talking about 'mysteries.' But I was by instinct a scientist even as a child. Mysticism intrigues but doesn't capture me. Still, I see that it does both for you. So maybe it's this mystical Jewish tradition that will help you understand why you have your life. What I'm getting around to saying, again, is that you should think about moving to Israel. If you do, I invite you, again, to live with me in Ein Kerem. You'll have the historical sites of Jerusalem, and then we'll go to Safed for the rest of it."

"The rest of it?"

"Your new interest in mysticism and concerns about dying. You can meditate your heart out with the other mystics up there, the highest town in the country, the closest to heaven. Then, when it's your time, you may as well be in Safed, although any place in the Holy Land will do. 'For to a man who dies in the land of Israel,' the Talmud says, 'it is as though he breathes his last in the arms of his mother.' Or if you prefer," she adds with a laugh, "in the arms of your lover."

When he drops Sinaiya off at JFK's El Al check-in area, he knows that she is departing with the impression that he'll soon be following her to Israel. At first, Arnold is buoyant with the same expectation.

He feels an especially deep connection with his brother as he begins to make arrangements for an indefinite absence. In part, Nate framed his disappearances as a need to embark on a new life, by which Arnold assumed Nate meant an existence unburdened by possessions or any lingering regrets about the past. Arnold imagines that the new life Nate had in mind was to have been a homeless freedom, an existence with nothing and no one to tie him down, nothing and no one to distract him from his spiritual explorations. Arnold's new life would be different. It would also be a life of fewer possessions and, he hopes, a minimum of regrets and concerns. But unlike Nate's, the life Arnold is ready to embark upon is now very much predicated on having a home in Israel.

Arnold's life is already minimal in material terms. He'll only need a couple of weeks, he figures, to make banking and postal arrangements, give Freddie Millhouse some months' rent and notice, give away what he can't carry or mail to Israel, and book travel. But the two weeks turn out to be an underestimation. Not that the things he has to do should take more than that. What he has miscalculated are his motivation and energy to make a change.

The decision about Israel begins to weigh heavily on Arnold. Even his dreams concern Israel. In one, he finds himself in a long screening line at Ben-Gurion Airport in Tel Aviv. The other passengers are processed rapidly, with no problem. But Arnold is sent to an immigration officer, a kindly, pudgy man his own age whose badge identifies him as Uri Martz.

Martz wonders about Arnold's financial means.

"I'm retired, independent, single," Arnold replies. "Means are not an issue."

Later, a second screener asks Arnold who had interviewed him. "Martz," he says.

"Uri Martz," the screener nods. "Good."

In the dream, Arnold remembers how Nathan, in his notebook, described his experience at this same airport many years before, when he was grilled about his reasons for visiting Israel. It was a time of genuine optimism. Egypt's Anwar Sadat had recently journeyed to Jerusalem in an unprecedented overture of friendship and conciliation. Now, Arnold wonders in his dream, in this age of terrorism, why neither screener has bothered to ask him his reasons for coming to Israel.

He goes back to Martz. "Why haven't you asked me why I want to come to Israel?"

"Okay. So why are you here?"

"I came here as a young man searching for Jewish identity," Arnold responds, excited to explain himself. "Now, as an old man, I'm here with a renewed search for my identity."

Martz looks at him, whether with disdain or sympathy Arnold cannot tell. "You're a fool," says Martz, turning his attention to the next arriving passenger.

In another dream, Arnold walks unnoticed through a small Israeli village on the first morning of the latest war with the Arabs. When the Arabs attack the village, they are astonished to find the entire settlement of Jews standing in a solemn line without arms, offering no resistance. Why? Arnold asks a villager. "We're so terribly weary," the man answers. "We meet the enemy without arms not to be symbols of non-violence or anything like that, but because we are tired." Arnold watches, helpless, as the villagers are slaughtered. He reads the newspapers in the days that follow. The world's reaction is predictable at first: screams and condemnations, as with the Holocaust. But the outcry quickly subsides, and Jewish greed and intransigence are blamed for causing the violence. Arnold returns to the village and reads the inscription on a plaque commemorating the dead: *They neither lived nor died in vain. They just lived, and then they just died.*

The dreams are deeply troubling to Arnold. Or rather, his reaction to them is what troubles him. He realizes how conflicted he is, how ambivalent. He is an American Jew, not an Israeli Jew, that's the identity part of it. America is home, not Israel. But another part of it is that he detests what is happening in Israeli politics, which he blames for making the Arab-Israeli situation basically unresolvable. David Ben-Gurion, Arnold recalls, couldn't envision the possibility of peace even before he became Israel's first prime minister, even when the vision of a Jewish state was so idealistic. "Everyone sees the difficulty of relations between Jews and Arabs," Ben-Gurion said in 1919, "but not everyone sees that there is no solution to that question. There is no solution. There is an abyss and nothing can fill that abyss ... We want Palestine to be ours, as a nation. The Arabs want it to be theirs, as a nation." A century later the possibility of peace is even more remote, Arnold believes, because of what the State of Israel has become. This belief is reinforced for Arnold when he reads an interview with the Israeli historian Tom Segev, a colleague he greatly respects. "The situation is very bad in the occupied territories," Segev said. "There's a systematic violation of Palestinians' human rights. Our government is more and more right wing, racist, anti-Arab. If they were members of a government in Austria, we'd recall our ambassador in protest."

Can I live there? Arnold keeps asking himself.

Two weeks extend to a month. Arnold can't bring himself to set a deadline for leaving, or to reach a decision about leaving at all. He has spoken with Sinaiya four times since she returned to Israel. His enthusiasm was evident in the first two conversations, but those were early on, in the first week. She hears his ambivalence in the subsequent calls.

"I'm pretty sure I'll make the move," he tells her during the third call.

"So why only 'pretty sure'?"

He hems and haws but has no good answer. A week later, Sinaiya phones him. This time there isn't even a nod, like "pretty sure," on Arnold's part. "I'm sorry, Sinaiya. I just don't know anymore."

"But why?" she explodes.

Why indeed. He tries his best to answer. "Look, Judaism has defined my life, and no Jew's life can be defined without some personal reckoning about Israel. But how much weight should I, Arnold Kirinski, give it? Where does Israel's part in my life's drama end? Where does my life—only my life—begin?"

"It's not all about Judaism," Sinaiya says after a long silence. "Or about Israel. Or about Arnold Kirinski."

This is their last conversation. She hasn't called him again, nor has he, out of embarrassment and paralysis, tried to contact her.

Arnold asks himself what happened to take him from such a strong, initial excitement to where he finds himself today, still at Las Palmas six weeks after Sinaiya's departure. The question is with him daily as he walks the beaches and especially as he tries to clear his head of thoughts in meditation. He concludes that there are three things at work: the town itself, with all its attendant memories and associations; his calcified nature; and the influence of his brother, whose inner struggle to seek out the meaning of his life has motivated Arnold to look inward as well.

Memory assails him in Belmar. How could it be otherwise? The mile-square geography is dense with experiences and relationships, and each place he passes has the potential to trigger some emotion: the two schools, Belmar Grammar and St. Rose's; the several churches and single synagogue; the homes of his puppy-love girlfriends; the manicured playing fields and make-shift sandlots; the arcades and pavilions, most destroyed by Sandy but a couple still standing; the two lakes, Como and Silver, one bordering Belmar on the south, the other a few blocks short of the town's northern boundary; Shark River to the west; the ocean to the east. But the memories for Arnold, unlike for his brother whose local experiences, according to Nate's notebook, were more mixed, are mostly positive.

And there are other reasons not to leave. Arnold feels secure here, content and comfortable. He knows the terrain, an important kind of knowledge to have at his age. Still, as an historian he's mindful of the dangers of being satisfied with the security and comfort of the past. He recalls what the Israeli historian Yosef Hayim Yerushalmi wrote: "In the metaphysics and epistemology of some of the most sophisticated of Far Eastern civilizations, both time and history are deprecated as illusory, and to be liberated from such illusions is a condition for true knowledge and ultimate salvation."

But Arnold believes that his character is the main reason for his loss of heart as he struggles with the decision about Israel. In his notebook, Nate wrote about the idea, in the Gurdjieff system, of chief feature, the one central attribute or pillar around which one's personality structure revolves. As identified by Laurent Ambrose at Claymont, Nate's chief feature was cowardice. When Arnold first read the entry he was surprised by this attribution; he had never thought of his brother as anything less than a courageous risk-taker who shunned convention and most definitions of normalcy. But now, considering Nate's serial disappearances, Arnold can understand what Laurent might have been getting at. And he wonders, without at all meaning to be cute, if a chief feature might apply genetically in some degree to twins, even though it might manifest differently in each individual. Nate's cowardice was that he kept leaving. Arnold's is that he stays on.

But perhaps staying on is what I most need, Arnold tells himself. Why seek a new life out there when the life I claim to seek is within? Israel would be exciting, full of new experiences and relationships. The history embedded in every stone would never leave room for boredom, just as my friendship with Sinaiya could never leave room for boredom. Belmar, by contrast, will be laden with sameness. But at this stage of my life, assuming I'm sincere about following an inward path, the boredom of Belmar seems a better choice than the diversions of Israel. I hope I'm choosing the right Promised Land.

Part Eight

This Way Now

2017

In the midst of the muddy world, he remained true to himself, and in simplicity and stillness he spent the rest of his life.

–Lieh-tzu

THE MORE ARNOLD READS and thinks about the idea of karma, the more he's persuaded by its doctrine of cause and effect, that every action—past, present, and future—has an effect. As Jamgön Kongtrül summarizes it in one of Nate's books, "In brief: the result of wholesome action is happiness; the result of unwholesome action is suffering, and nothing else. The results are not interchangeable; when you plant buckwheat, you get buckwheat; when you plant barley, you get barley."

But the persuasion comes with mixed feelings. On the one hand, it's consoling for Arnold to believe that he's responsible for his future, that he's free to determine this future by each action in each moment, that there is no external authority, no god or higher power, predetermining his fate. He himself is the highest authority when it comes to his actions and the choices he makes and, by extension, the future he creates. On the other hand, this freedom and responsibility have terrifying implications when he considers what "the future" really means in the full karmic sense. A book on Nate's shelves, *Buddhism Without Beliefs* by Stephen Batchelor, captures the enormity of what's at stake. "The consequences of what we do now will outlive us," Batchelor writes. "The irrevocability of our actions implies that we are responsible not only for our own conduct in this life but for the impact of our actions after our death....For in the very moment we think, speak, or act, we are creating the conditions which will unfold as our personal and collective futures." The impact of one's behavior, in other words, is inter-generational. One's burden of responsibility goes beyond one's own life.

Arnold experiences the full weight of this realization when he makes the rounds of his family members' graves. Reading their markers—Mort's, Fay's, Deb's, Esther's, even Eddie's—he has a strong sense of unfinished business. Other than Nathan, assuming he's alive, Ellen is Arnold's only immediate heir. But is this even true anymore? The last word about her was in 1992, when Nate described his conversation with her after an Al-Anon meeting in Reno, Nevada. She was 18 then; if alive, she would be 41 now. If the concept of karma is right and "The consequences of what we do now will outlive us," as Batchelor suggests, then Arnold has the freedom, and the responsibility, to affect the future one way or another. He can assume Ellen is unreachable, or even dead, and be content to live out his life regretting her disaffection from her father and separation from the rest of the Kirinski family. Or he can assume that she is alive, find her, interact with her, and not be content with mere regret. And if he finds her—what then? What, concretely, would he do? He would give her a copy of her father's notebook. He would apologize for the family's lapse of attention and communication. He would make her his beneficiary and insure her material future.

Perhaps this is the most essential practical import of karma, Arnold concludes. On the spot, he coins a term: *Anticipatory Regret.* Learning to think around corners. To consider what the future might be before it arrives.

To evaluate the effect an action might have on someone before you commit it. To experience regret, to actually feel regret about what you might have done before you do it—or fail to do it.

Arnold decides to look for his niece. He focuses his search on Reno, where Nate encountered her 23 years before. At that time, although he had pinned her likely whereabouts down to the Sparks-Reno area after weeks of looking, it was only by accident that Nate found her at all. With the advances in technology and the Internet since then, within an hour Arnold is able to locate an Ellen Kirinski—age 41, previous domiciles in Cambridge, Charles Town, Anchorage, and Reno—at an address on the Nevada side of Lake Tahoe. He finds a phone number as well, but based on the reception Nate reported and the fact that Ellen never used Arnold's contact information, he's wary about calling her. Instead, he decides to go see her with no advance warning. It's a gamble, surely. But he figures that the surprise face-to-face contact will get him further than a phone call. In any event, he has recently been invited to discuss his book on the relationship between the medieval Jewish Khazars and modern Jewish identities in a symposium at the Simon Wiesenthal Center in Los Angeles. From there he'll drive to Ellen's.

Arnold drives north from Los Angeles on Route 385 through the Sierra Nevada mountains and across the California-Nevada state line to Genoa. From there he makes the 3,000 foot climb on Route 207 toward Tahoe. Then he sees it, the staggeringly beautiful body of high-mountain water he had only ever heard or read about: the largest Alpine Lake in North America, according to his guidebook, 195 square miles in area, 71 miles around, 12 miles wide, 21 miles long, more than 1600 feet deep in places. It's 6200 feet at its highest elevation, and the nearby summits—Mt. Watson, Mt. Pluto, Squaw Valley's peaks, and others—reach as high as 11,000 feet. The statistics, impressive as they are, don't do justice to the visual impact of the lake and its surroundings. He envies Ellen her vantage point.

But at first he can't figure out how to get to the lake itself. It's surrounded by developments, and there seems to be no shore road. So he heads toward Incline Village on Route 28, which takes him through Tahoe National Forest. He parks at the edge of a 1,000 foot long row of lakeside residences between the park and Incline Village and climbs down to the lake shore for a better view of the houses against their backdrop of Agate Bay, Camelian Bay, and Dollar Point. A silver Lexus SUV with a University of Nevada-Reno Wolfpack bumper sticker is parked in the pull-in driveway of the address he had identified as Ellen's. He walks up to the door and knocks.

A trim woman of medium height answers. She could be his sister Deborah: red-headed and hazel-eyed, pale freckled skin over a Slavic facial structure. A Kirinski, certainly.

"My name is Arnold Kirinski. I'm looking for my niece, Ellen Kirinski. Might that be you?"

He doesn't know what to expect—the door slammed in his face, screams, something more violent. Instead, showing no surprise she beckons him in and leads the way to a long sofa facing sliding glass doors that look out over the lake. They sit at the sofa's two far ends.

"Uncle Arnold. So what's it been? Thirty years anyway. What brings you—let me rephrase the question—whatever in the world brings you to town?"

"It's long past time that I'm here, that I tried to find you. You and I might be the only ones left from our immediate Kirinski family. Everyone else—your grandparents, aunt, step-mother, maybe your father—is dead." She gives him a quizzical, even slightly alarmed look. "So, to answer your question, I came here to reconnect, and hopefully reconcile, with you."

"How is it that my father 'may be' dead?" she asks after a few moments, and he gives her the details of Nate's disappearance.

"Okay. We've reconnected. That happened when I let you in the door. But reconciling? Not likely. My father abandoned me. Even when I'd come to visit as a kid, after a while I began to feel like an add-on that he and Esther were relieved to put back on the plane when my 'vacation' was over. I was just as glad to see the visits—mine to him, my father's to me—stop when I turned ten. And the rest of you..." She stops and looks out at the lake. Her lips are trembling. "The rest of you," she continues, "never reached out to me after that, never made me feel part of the family. So 'reconcile'? What the hell could that word possibly mean in this situation?"

"Maybe it's the wrong word. I wish we can put the past, at least some of the past, to rest. But if that's not possible, I still want you to know how sorry I am—and, please believe me, how bereft your father was about losing you. His sadness over losing you—as a child, and then as a teenager—has been one of the few constants in his life. So I guess I'm here as an emissary, an emissary of apology for all of us—and especially, most especially, for your father. From my conversations with him before he went missing, I know what he felt for you, and also what he felt about the past. He's been in continual repentance. In Hebrew—you remember that I taught Jewish history? — it's called *teshuvah*, a word that carries the sense of making sincere apologies and amends to the person one has wronged."

Arnold reaches into his backpack. "Here," he says, taking out Nate's notebook and handing it to her. "This will tell you a lot about your father in his own words. It pretty much covers his whole life, including the parts that your mom and you played in it. It won't be an easy read. Some of it might be painful for you. But it's very truthful. And I have to tell you—your father never wanted the split with your mother, although he understood her reasons for wanting a divorce and never spoke badly of her. In fact, he held out hope for reuniting until it was clear that it just wasn't in the cards, and he would have to move on."

He debates whether to tell her that Nate, during his Jerusalem sojourn, had put his handwritten supplication in a crevice of the Western Wall praying for the family to reunite. But he decides it would be too melodramatic and serve no purpose at the moment. Besides, she'll see it if she reads the notebook. "Anyway, giving you this account of the past, at least your father's version of it, and apologizing for aspects of that past are two of the reasons I'm here."

Ellen looks down at the notebook in her lap. It's a long time before she speaks. "Jeez. Where to start? Where to end? It doesn't speak well of me, but I have to admit that I do take some satisfaction in knowing he was so affected by our estrangement. I sure was. I guess neither of us ever recovered. You said you don't know about him, whether he's even alive. But at least I'm alive and can still work on it. I hope what he's written will help me."

They sit without talking for a while. Ellen speaks first.

"You said that apologizing and giving me the notebook are two of the reasons you're here. Are there more?"

"There's this," he says, reaching into his backpack again. "It's a copy of my will. You're my only beneficiary. You'll inherit my entire estate when I die. I never married and have had a fairly remunerative career, so...."

Her eyes moisten. "Thank you...Uncle Arnie. Thank you for coming, for making the effort. For giving me my dad's notebook. And for looking out for me in your will. It means a lot, although," she gestures with one arm to indicate the ample space they're sitting in, "I'm doing quite well financially. I never married either. After my mother's experiences, I'm a staunch bachelorette. It's all been about my career ever since my father found me during my runaway period back in the early '90s. I went to college, got my MBA, and now I'm a cheese, I guess you could say, in the Reno corporate headquarters of a huge casino and resort operation. High salary, lots of stock options, this place, and a condo downtown. Life is good."

"It'll be even better when my will goes into effect," Arnold jokes, "which, in actuarial terms, likely won't be that long in coming."

Ellen smiles and then turns serious. "I hope it is long in coming. My mom died last year...," she rushes past his expression of condolence, "so you and I are both orphans. Kirinski orphans."

"Right. Unless your father's alive."

Arnold heads for Reno Airport, an hour away, down from the 9,000 foot high summit of Mt. Rose and right past the area where Nate camped out all those years ago during his search for Ellen. The road is winding and treacherous, with warning signs like "No Parking Avalanche," "20 Miles Per Hour MAXIMUM Speed on Curve," "Turnout Ahead," and "Congested Area" for skiing and snowmobiles. But he feels immune to any dangers, cushioned against them by a suffusion of warmth for all Kirinskis, living and dead.

Two months later, in the early afternoon Eastern Time, Ellen phones. Nathan is alive. A Reno hospital just called her about a homeless man named Nathan Kirinski who had been admitted for hypothermia and pneumonia. Further tests showed inoperable Stage 4 lung cancer. Attendants found her Tahoe address among his belongings and tracked her down. The doctors have recommended hospice care. Ellen puts a hospital administrator on the phone and Arnold, who has medical power of attorney and will fax the document to prove it, tells the man that he agrees with the recommendation. Ellen makes arrangements with a local hospice for Nathan to be moved that day. "From what they're telling me, Uncle Arnold, you better get out here right away."

Arnold sends the power of attorney and manages to catch a flight at 5:00 p.m. from Newark. He arrives in Reno, after a stop in Phoenix, close to midnight local time. He rents a car and drives to the address Ellen had given him, a hospice facility not far from the airport. A receptionist takes Arnold to Nathan's room. Ellen is there with a nurse. Nathan lies in a hospital bed with his eyes closed. He is barely recognizable, bearded, long-haired, skeletal. Arnold sits on the side of the bed, holds Nate's hand, and begins talking to him. There is no response. Arnold looks at Ellen, whose eyes are red, then the nurse. "He's in a coma now," the nurse says. "I'm sorry."

Arnold stands and embraces Ellen. They hold each other for a long while, then sit in the two chairs the nurse has placed next to Nathan's bed. They each take one of his hands and stay that way, hardly talking, for the next three hours. Nathan dies at 4 a.m. The hospice staff helps Arnold and Ellen get through the immediate post-mortem logistics. Arnold abides by Nathan's wish for cremation, which he schedules for the following day. Paperwork complete, Nate's brother and daughter sit in vigil with his body. At sunup, Arnold recites the *Kaddish*.

The next afternoon, they pick up the urn containing Nate's ashes. Arnold has told Ellen about Nate's wish to have them spread in the Atlantic off the 12th Avenue beach in Belmar. Ellen decides to be there when that happens. They fly back to New Jersey together. Ellen stays for the next week, sleeping on her father's couch in Las Palmas.

Uncle and niece spend many hours talking. "My father was awake," Ellen tells him, "from the time I got to the hospice until he lapsed into a coma an hour or so before you got there. He was mostly lucid and intent on talking. 'That's why I came to Reno,' he said. 'To find you. To talk with you. I found your address, but then I got too sick...' I tried to get him to rest but he wouldn't. He said there was just too much he needed to share to help make up for all the time we'd been apart. He told me a lot about the past and his regrets, especially his regrets about my mom and me. He was rushing to get stuff out, and it was hard to follow parts of it because he was on morphine and struggling to breathe. It was so important that you had given me his notebook when you came to see me at Tahoe. Most of what he was telling me I already knew from what he had written. And because of that, I had already made my peace and forgiven him. I was able to let him know that before he went into the coma." Ellen pauses, trying to collect herself. "It was an emotional moment for both of us, to say the least."

Ellen tells Arnold that she and her father talked quite a bit about the year in West Virginia. "Mostly, my dad shared his perspective on what had happened there and the time leading up to it, you know, the things that led to my parents' divorce. This was also what I had read about in his notebook, but it was important to hear it all again and be able to ask questions. But there was one moment when I told him something he never knew about the West Virginia year. It happened when I related what my mother told me about Laurent Ambrose, that Laurent had hit on her when she went to see him for advice. It was weird. When he heard this—I mean, there he was on his death bed!—my father started laughing. 'That saintly little asshole,' he said. 'All these years I thought that Ben Griscom and Brody were the threats to our marriage. Jesus. Well, Laurent had warned me. We're all phonies.'"

Arnold and Ellen sit on a bench on the 12th Avenue boardwalk. Arnold had recently donated the bench to the Borough of Belmar and installed a plaque:

In memory of the Kirinski family. They loved the Shore.

Uncle and niece look out over the Atlantic, where moments before they had deposited Nathan's ashes. Arnold had recited the *Kaddish*, and Ellen read a passage from *Once the Shore*, by Paul Yoon, a Korean-American writer. The passage, she told Arnold, reminded her of Nathan's story about Kim Ju Ok and the Korean-American child who may or may not have ever been born in Chunchon, the child who would have been Ellen's sibling.

"In water," Ellen read, "time was not linear. It was, in her mind, a globe, spherical. Death was perhaps less important in that space because it remained inseparable from the living. Within the world of the sea, all was enclosed, all was present. The ritual of burial and mourning seemed nonexistent."

The next day Arnold drives Ellen back to Newark Airport for her return flight to Reno. As they wait for her row to be called for boarding Arnold hands her a framed photo, the one of Ellen sitting on her father's lap, the one with the inscription on the back reading *"Ellen, age 2, Cambridge, 1976."*

Arnold sits daily on the family bench at 12th Avenue, gazing at the breaking waves 100 yards distant. Then he closes his eyes, and the waves are no longer out there, only inside him, the backdrop for a lifetime of memories. He hears them from his stroller as he watches Nate venture ahead on the boardwalk. He hears their consoling sound from his bed at night, the window open, even in winter, an anxious, insecure adolescent concerned about school and girls and a future that doesn't seem to hold much promise. He hears them almost as music as he reaches orgasm with Wendy Adler, his Junior Prom date, at 3:00 a.m. behind a dune near the 1st Avenue jetty. He hears their crashing violence as Sandy approaches and Nate, walking into the storm, disappears from sight.

Appendices

I.   Nathan Kirinski's Summary of His Books
II. Nathan Kirinski's Overview of the Gurdjieff Work
III. Arnold Kirinski's Efforts at a Different Kind of Writing
IV. Arnold Kirinski's Interest in Meditation
V.   Arnold Kirinski's Typology of Death And Dying Theories

Appendix I
Nathan Kirinski's Summary of His Books

THE LANGUAGE OF ART, the Language of Science, and the Epistemology of Portrayal was published in 1972. The book is a re-titled, somewhat expanded revision of my doctoral dissertation, *Merging Epistemic Approaches: Implications for an Art-Science Synthesis.* Basically, the book explores characteristics of artistic and scientific writing styles and then argues that intellectuals, particularly those in hybrid fields such as the social and behavioral sciences, need to become conversant, if not fluent, in both languages. In support of my argument, first I propose that, while most academic writers tend toward one or the other mode of writing, neither is sufficient in itself to attend to the heterogeneity of "reality" (be it mental, emotional, or social). Second, I propose that the language of art and the language of science represent essentially complementary perspectives which converge on the reality portrayed and increase our descriptive approximation of that reality. Each spurs a different level of recognition in the reader, and thus the contours left unexplored by one of the languages may be illuminated more readily by the other. Third, I propose that bilingualism in the languages of art and science will serve to increase both the scholar's access to reality as others portray it and his ability to communicate what he himself knows. And fourth, insofar as language and knowledge are related, I suggest that bilingualism serves to increase the validity of portrayal by increasing linguistic sufficiency.

The book provides a detailed comparative examination of examples in the arts and sciences, of which there are numerous mono-lingual examples, and the few examples I know of that actually are bilingual. In the process of this examination, I identify what to me is the key epistemological question about the relationship between language and reality, namely, as Benjamin Whorf proposed in his famous linguistic-relativity hypothesis, that our languages create our realities. If this is the case, I go on to ask, how can we possibly understand one another? The book concludes, first, with an in-depth exploration of the principle of complementarity, the idea that artistic and scientific worldviews are not contradictory, but rather inhabit a fluid continuum of perspectives; and second, with a suggested "program" by which one can become bilingual and thus a better portrayer and communicator across linguistic divides, at least in the realm of intellectual discourse.

To my mind, this point about complementarity is the work's singular philosophical contribution, an attempt to show that the "two cultures," to use C.P. Snow's famous characterization of the divide between science and the humanities, are actually inseparable; that they are reciprocal in their functions with respect to revealing reality's underlying unitary structure; and that synthesizing or bridging them requires the ability on the part of intellectuals to translate the two cultures' distinctive vocabularies, syntaxes, and grammars.

This first book, written so many years ago, is still the most meaningful of the three for me, and I ask myself why. Why is the topic so compelling, especially now that I am no longer a professional philosopher, just a retired postman and continuing pinball junkie? I sometimes consider that the tension between polar opposites is what the entirety of my mental and emotional lives rests on. By this I mean that I seem always to be struggling to find some balance point, some satisfying reconciliation between contentious opposites. I have come to attribute the origins of this life-long preoccupation to my parents, who themselves represented a kind of art-science divide: Fay, the whimsical, intuitive dancer and painter marries Mort, the practical business-man and accountant who would only accept what was empirically evident. As Debbie, Arnie, and I often joked about the similarities among the three of us, "A little of Fay, a little of Mort."

Beyond this propensity, inherent in my nature from an early age, I gravitated for support to established thinkers who shared my inclination to reconcile differences and influenced me to develop it further in my academic projects—influences like Snow's two cultures; Severyn Bruyn's follow-up suggestion that there may well be a third culture evolving that accentuates the differential value and need to retain both the artistic and scientific languages; the organismic psychologist Andras Angyal's autonomy-homonomy continuum (at one end of which the individual expands by assimilating and mastering the environment, and at the other end submerges his individuality by forming harmonious unions with social groups, nature, or deities); the polymath Arthur Koestler's holon concept (some units are self-contained and relatively independent while simultaneously being dependent parts of a greater whole); the biologist Ludwig von Bertalanffy's general system theory (the idea that living systems should be studied as organized, interacting wholes); the biologist J. G. Miller's idea of the cross-level hypothesis (a supposition or possible explanation that may be applicable to two or more levels of living systems); the sociologist Kurt Back's effort to reconcile the estrangement between adherents of the "game" language (rigorous control and precise definition) and the "myth" language (less denotable "transcendental" concepts) within the social sciences; and, more generally, the dialectical method of Hegel, Marx, Engel, and Lenin, which features logical discussion of opposing points of view in order to arrive at the truth.

Despite these antecedent thinkers, my quest for complementarity left me vulnerable in academia to charges of Syncretism, the effort to blend and harmonize different doctrines into a unified point of view. In philosophy, such a project is rarely seen in a positive light. Combining doctrines, orthodox critics (including the chair of my department at Harvard) say, leads to imprecision and superficiality. My counter argument featured Einstein's persistent effort in the later years of his life to articulate an elusive "Unified

Field Theory" capable of describing and explaining all and everything in one fully integrated, over-arching construct.

My second book, published in 1974 at about the time Ellen was born and dedicated to her, extends my ruminations on language, portrayal, and reality. *Useful Fictions and Fictions as Truths* focuses on the work of Hans Vaihinger, who in the early part of the 20th century developed the "As If" philosophy, which suggests that even though we know that our thoughts and ideas are inadequate, or outright wrong, they provide us with important coping mechanisms. In his autobiography *Janus: A Summing Up*, Arthur Koestler provides this concise overview of Vaihinger's system of 'fictionalism":

> Briefly, it means that man has no choice but to live by 'fictions'; as if the illusory world of the senses represented ultimate Reality; as if he had a free will which made him responsible for his actions; as if there was a God to reward virtuous conduct, and so on. Similarly, the individual must live as if he were not under sentence of death, and humanity must plan for its future as if its days were not counted. It is only by virtue of these fictions that the mind of man fabricated a habitable universe, and endowed it with meaning.

Vaihinger's philosophy resonated strongly with me for its emphasis on the positive power of imagination: that we might invent our futures *as if* we were free and not determined by forces outside ourselves; that we might construct our realities *as if* they were meaningful, purposeful, and worthwhile; and that we might change the world by imposing whatever fictions we choose to adopt, *as if* we were the novel's author and not its subject. In expounding on Vaihinger's argument, I devote a good part of *Useful Fictions and Fictions as Truths* to exploring the literature of the Second World War Holocaust to show how writers—journalistic, historical, interpretive, and novelistic—typically impose their particular "fictions" on the events of the tragedy in order to somehow make sense of what happened. In my discussion, I pay special attention to poets and novelists who do not feel constrained to understand the inexplicable, which in itself is a fictive strategy. All of us, I conclude, will do what we need to do to avoid acknowledging the possibility that we live in a random universe and instead, consciously or not, construct the world *as if* our individual existence in it is somehow designed to be significant. As the critic Frank Kermode put it in his discussion of Vaihinger in *The Sense of an Ending*, "Novels...have beginnings, middles, ends, and potentiality, even if the world has not."

My third book, *Is Change Possible?*, was published in 1976. In sum, I propose that real and permanent social change is likely impossible precisely because it is conditional on real and permanent individual change. I extend my argument to suggest that genuine personal change is also likely impossible for all but a few who, by virtue of relentless work on themselves, might transcend the bounds of egotism and self-interest and function at a higher, more enlightened level of being. In my concluding section, "A Very Practical Approach to Change," I invoke the system of personal and spiritual development most associated with G. I. Gurdjieff, a mysterious Central Asian savant whose ideas, I believe, strongly reinforce my book's thesis.

The primary example I use to support my thesis is the history of anti-Semitism, an example which shows, in my view, that it is patently wrong to assume any prevailing altruistic instinct in the overwhelming portion of humanity when it comes to inter-group relations, especially in the areas of race, religion, and ethnicity. Altruism and compassion, I argue, are only possible for those who have made the long, hard effort to develop such capacities. When you look closely into most people's motivations, what most of us think of as compassionate behavior is ego-driven and self-interested and stuck within the superficial surface of personality.

Appendix II
Nathan Kirinski's Overview of the Gurdjieff Work

G. I. GURDJIEFF'S PHILOSOPHY has been of central practical significance in my life, both because of its role in my controversial third book and
the year I spent at Claymont, the school in West Virginia based on Gurdjieff's
system of self-development. The literature on his system is extensive. This is
my attempt to boil it down, or at least the aspects of it that have been most
meaningful to me and in the particular context of my Claymont experience.

I make this attempt with more than a little insecurity, since much of
Gurdjieff's system—known also as "The Fourth Way" and "the Work"—was
then and still is beyond my personal capacities of comprehension. (Without
getting into unnecessary detail, I need to note that "the Work" lies at the
core of various traditions of spiritual development and should not be equated
solely with Gurdjieff's system.) But I'll do my best based on what modicum
of knowledge and understanding I have: "knowledge" being what I have read
and been told, "understanding" being what I have come to realize as a result
of personal experience.

The most useful starting point for me is what is encapsulated in the
phrase "The Fourth Way." The first way, or path, is that of the fakir, or as-
cetic, which emphasizes struggle with and eventual mastery over the physical
body through painful postures and exercises. The second path, the way of the
monk, develops the emotions; the focus here is devotion, faith, and religious
feeling. The way of the yogi, the third path, refers to the development of intellect and knowledge. As ordinary human beings, each of us will find one or
another of these paths more congenial based on our particular nature, namely our individual proclivity to work from the body (Gurdjieff's Man Number
One), the heart (Man Number Two), or the head (Man Number Three).

But full development in each of these ways requires years of total effort
and in fact may rarely occur in a typical lifespan. Even if it does occur, the
person will be left incomplete as a human being in the sense of imbalance.
The fakir's emotions and intellect, having been superseded by the emphasis
on physical control, will remain undeveloped. Similarly, to progress further
the emotionally refined monk will need to develop his neglected physical
and thinking capacities, just as the yogi, who may know a great deal in the
intellectual sense, will have to develop his physical and emotional capacities
to utilize the knowledge he has gained. Genuine development along any of
these three paths requires sacrifice and renunciation of home, family, worldly
duties, and pleasures.

This brings us to the fourth way, which not only allows but actually ne-
cessitates that the person work within whatever realities the world presents.
This is the way of Man Number 4, in Gurdjieff's characterization the way of

the "Sly Man" who avails himself of every life situation to meet his aims. Here the struggles are certainly with body, emotions, and mind, but the struggles must take place in all three directions simultaneously. They must also take place within the usual material, psychological, and social conditions of one's life. There is no retreating from or renunciation of one's circumstances in this sense. Quite the contrary.

But why struggle at all? To what purpose? The aim, according to the Gurdjieff work, is to be the master of oneself—to be independent of external influences and free from inner slavery. This inner slavery comes from ignorance of oneself. It is this ignorance that prevents freedom, and overcoming it requires self-knowledge: we must study ourselves to understand how our human machine is structured, how it functions, which laws and conditions affect it.

The path to freedom requires, first, that we realize we are in a state of walking sleep and mechanical habits. Only when we have awakened and observed these habits can we attempt to oppose them. But any possibility of seeing our own mechanicalness, much less changing it, depends on our having methods of study by which we might develop the ability to observe ourselves. Without such methods, we are doomed to failure. We think we are a unitary, consistent, continuous self when in reality we are a hodge-podge of momentary desires, thoughts, fantasies, and feelings that sap our energies and pull us in one direction or another, like puppets with no real consciousness or will power or control. So, in the midst of these passing states, this multiplicity of ephemera which we mistake for a solid and cohesive "I," we must struggle to stay awake, to be attentive, and to remember the aim of our *real* self, which is to be free.

Being present enough to accomplish this in everyday life is very difficult. It's easy enough to get excited by Gurdjieff's ideas and generate the initial enthusiasm to begin improving ourselves. But we soon find that our energy dissipates, and we can't sustain our intention. This is because we are as we are—asleep—and have not yet developed the capacity to be awake to our existence. To use Gurdjieff's diagnosis, "Man cannot do." Subject to what he calls the "disease of tomorrow," we procrastinate. Subject to what he laments as our suggestibility, we follow convention automatically and do not think for ourselves. Subject to the prevalent human illusion that we are immortal, we don't realize the gravity of our mortal situation. Then how, in the face of these misconceptions, might we proceed?

The Fourth Way's method—the Work, "the Sly Man's way"—begins with self-observation using the material of everyday life. Principally, this involves simply recording in one's mind what is observed in the moment. At a later stage analysis is also involved, but undertaken too soon this runs the risk of stopping observation by engrossing us in questions of "Why?" We first have to accumulate data and develop a record, not by thinking but through our attention to what is transpiring in the moment. As the Stoic Epictetus put it: "Watchfulness therefore is the vital need..."

What do we watch? We begin by observing and collecting information on our basic physical, affective, and cognitive functions: What bodily postures and movements do we typically manifest? How do we react emotionally in situations? What are our habits of thinking? In my understanding, these functions closely approximate the three types of man: the fakir who apprehends primarily with his bodily instincts, the monk who registers impressions primarily through feelings, and the yogi who does so mainly by thinking. The Gurdjieff system refers to these functions respectively as moving center, emotional center, and intellectual center. (There are additional functions or centers posited, but I'll skip those in order not to complicate an already challenging summarization.) These three centers are the fundamental categories by which the self's phenomena, its actions and feelings and thoughts, are observed.

It takes long and serious practice to determine, much less apply, these divisions correctly. The difficulty is increased tremendously in two ways. First, because we differ so much personally in our perceptions by virtue of the prevailing center by which each of us primarily experiences things, we have a terrible time even communicating what we observe to those who function through other centers. What I call a thought or an emotion or a sensation or an impulse may have little in common with what you're experiencing. Honestly, who among us has not been frustrated by misunderstandings with people who have different personalities and temperaments from ours? Second, accurate self-observation is challenging because the centers interact and are interdependent. For example: I walk down the sidewalk, careful, as is my habit, to keep to the right. Call that moving center. Two people, talking animatedly, walk towards me taking up both sides of the sidewalk. I imagine them forcing me off the sidewalk (although that hasn't happened yet and, in fact, might not happen, but that's a possibility I don't entertain). Call that intellectual center. Thoughtless idiots, I scream to myself, angry that they are surely about to disregard common rules of courtesy and responsible pedestrian behavior. Call that emotional center. Such examples are endless, even within a matter of minutes on any given day for any one of us. These automatic, habitual, function-driven reactions lead us around by the nose. We are slaves to them and don't even see how they hold us captive.

Such seeing requires that our eyes be open, that we be awake. But wakefulness does not come naturally. It takes a certain vital energy to struggle against the inertia of habit that keeps us in comfortable slumber. The development of such energy requires the efficient and harmonious participation of all our functions, all our centers. Work on one center isn't enough; the malfunctions in all of them have to be corrected or the energy required for change, for transformation, will be squandered by the deficiencies of one or another center's daydreaming, useless talking, negative thinking, muscular tension, indulging in memories, holding grudges, fantasizing, and the like. The work of educating and harmonizing the centers to do their jobs properly begins by concentrated *conscious* efforts to observe how we actually function in the moment. Doing this—really seeing—involves the capacity to be present and awake as we struggle against our habits. This requires that we exercise a certain quality of divided attention. Typically, and habitually, most if not all of our attention is taken up by whatever we are experiencing at a very basic level: eating, driving, walking, and the like. But now we have a moment of what the Work calls self-remembering, where two levels of awareness are operating simultaneously. Within the first level, the basic level which we ordinarily inhabit, we are totally identified with, attached to, and captured by whatever it is we are seeing or doing or feeling or thinking. We are on automatic pilot, unaware, outside the moment. At the second level, we are present. We are awake. We have a sense of being something more than our temporary actions, emotions, and thoughts. In such moments we remember our aim to be free. This is a beginning: first, the desire to be free; second, remembering the desire while developing the abilities that can lead to freedom; and third, actually being free.

Gurdjieff's cosmological scheme is too extensive and complex for me to summarize with any confidence. Instead, I'll limit my observations to five ideas (closely related, in my view) which I feel a bit more able to discuss by virtue of having had a taste of them in my own experiences.

The first is the idea of *the microcosm and the macrocosm*, which is another way of characterizing the relationship between Fourth Way psychology and cosmology. In this sense, man is the microcosm, and the universe is the macrocosm. Smaller and larger are different levels of the transcendent, unified reality. Various religious and esoteric traditions have represented this in the phrase "as above, so below": although the two levels manifest differently and are different in scale, they reflect each other; their origin and direction are the same; they are subject to the same forces and laws. As the Fourth Way teacher Jacob Needleman explains the microcosm-macrocosm relationship in *Lost Christianity: A Journey of Rediscovery to the Center of Christian Experience*:

> Man is a microcosmic being; he lives and moves within a field of forces and influences spanning the entire ontological range of forces in the universe. These forces have a direction—a vertical direction toward or away from unity with God. And the transactions of these forces take place within the mind and heart, within the 'soul,' as well as in the external universe.

The second idea, *the transformation of energy*, is suggested in the preceding mentions of "forces" and "substances." The possibility of transforming ourselves from sleeping, habit-controlled automatons to fully realized human beings requires intense effort. In turn, such effort—the Work—requires a certain kind and quality of energy. This higher-order, more refined and subtle energy is normally not part of us or available to us, but it is possible to develop and access it in the right conditions and with conscious, attentive efforts. "First," as Ouspensky writes in *The Fourth Way*, "we have to stop waste of energy; second, collect it by self-remembering; then, adjust things. We cannot begin in any other way.... We can only hope to become conscious beings if we use in the right way the energy that is now used in the wrong way..." Stopping the leakage of energy by not expressing negative emotions is an example of this at the psychological, microcosmic level. At the cosmological level, according to Gurdjieff, as "an apparatus for the transfer of energy" man has a role to play in maintaining the universe one way or the other: i.e., whether he produces energy voluntarily in the cause of self-perfection or involuntarily through leakage.

This brings us to the third idea I want to introduce, what Bennett has referred to, in *Gurdjieff: Making a New World*, as the doctrine of *Reciprocal Maintenance*. This "connotes that the universe has a built-in structure or pattern whereby every class of existing things produces energies or substances that are required for maintaining the existence of other classes." The transformation of energies, Bennett continues, "depends on the relationship of entities, whereby each maintains the existence of others in a kind of universal mutual support system. Each order of beings is endowed with a form of energy that enables it to play its part in the cosmic process." Man, of course, is one such order of being, and he plays his inevitable part either voluntarily by working and striving, or by involuntary default in the course of merely existing, leaking, and expiring.

The fourth and fifth ideas I want to mention are two universal laws that are central to Gurdjieff's system and philosophy, namely, *the Law of Three* and *the Law of Seven*—what Gurdjieff referred to as "the laws of world maintenance and world creation." An editorial note accompanying Jeanne de Salzmann's posthumously published *The Reality of Being: The Fourth Way of Gurdjieff*, describes the Law of Three, or the Law of Three Forces.

> In Gurdjieff's teaching every phenomenon, on whatever scale, from molecular to cosmic in whatever world, results from the combination of three opposing forces—the positive (affirming), the negative (denying), and the neutralizing (reconciling) force. The possibility of unity depends on a connection between the 'yes' and the 'no,' and the appearance of a third reconciling force that can relate the two....

For example, I resolve to be nicer to people, more sympathetic. This active, positive affirmation constitutes first force. But then my initiative encounters my habitual tendencies to be critical and judgmental, and these kick in as a negative, denying second force. The two forces keep fighting each other—affirm, deny; deny, affirm—with one or another in the ascendency, but only temporarily. Neither wins. A third, reconciling force needs to come in to strengthen my initial, first-force resolve and defeat my second-force inertia. I would liken this third force to something akin to Grace—a stream of help that enters the energy equation in response to my active, positive, conscious efforts to change.

In *The Gurdjieff Work*, Kathleen Speeth describes the relationship between the Law of Three and the second great law, the Law of Seven.

> When the three forces do meet and an act of creation takes place, a chain of manifestations may develop in which third [reconciling] force in one event becomes active [first] force in the next event—for the three forces change sign with respect to one another as they go about spinning or braiding the thread of occurrences. Now the second fundamental law, the Law of Seven, begins to operate.

As I understand it, the Law of Seven, also called the Law of Octaves, relates to the nonlinear succession of events and the ebb and flow of energy—"periodic accelerations and retardations at definite intervals" akin, as de Salzmann characterizes it, to the intervals *mi-fa* and *si-do* in the musical scale. For example, I start a project to plant a tree. With a burst of enthusiasm, I begin digging a hole. But the earth is rocky, and the summer sun is hot. After a while, I run out of steam. Then I take a break, drink some water, and give it another try. But my fatigue deepens, and I stop again. Even after I take another break, this time I'm feeling too bushed to continue. I despair that this hole will never get dug. But somehow, I summon the will to stand, take up my shovel, and resume digging. By making this special effort, as Ouspensky describes the process in *The Fourth Way*, "...the line changes its direction. There is a small but real change in inner strength. Then after some time there is again a slackening, and again, if there is no special effort, the direction changes." Ouspensky suggests that we can learn to anticipate these intervals and create ways to get past them, in effect avoiding breaks in the octave. "Everything goes by octaves" and the effects of the Law of Seven, Ouspensky claims. "With a certain kind of effort we can...change the work of our machine."

In my view, Ouspensky's statement is at the crux of the Work. "The Work," Gurdjieff said, "is against life," a struggle against habit and sleep. Over time, it is life that has conditioned us and created the legion of "I's" that comprise our personality. We react mechanically to everything from this personality, which is not our real self, our essence, our "Original Face," as Zen Buddhists might put it. The aim of the Work, to quote Gurdjieff again, is to learn how to "make things new." The starting point is self-observation in order to realize the mechanicalness of our inner states: we turn our attention inwards to notice our reactions to the external world so that, eventually, we might develop the capacity to liberate the energies required for self-transformation, or self-development of our inner states away from negative reactions. The realization of our mechanicalness provides one kind of shock. As Maurice Nicoll describes it in *Psychological Commentaries on the Teachings of Gurdjieff & Ouspensky*, your many 'I's will be babbling along in internal conversations when, "quite suddenly, a more conscious 'I', a Work 'I', may say to you: 'Why, aren't you in the Work?' And then everything changes completely, the talking stops completely, and the 'I's that were doing it all run away and hide themselves." This is the First Conscious Shock in the context of the Law of Seven. We are shocked into remembering ourselves: we realize our mechanicalness, and at the same time we see there is something in us that is separate from the machine. It is not "I" who does but "It" that does. We realize that we are not the personality, the machine, and that we can be free from It. But freedom requires change, and change requires the Second Conscious Shock—a shock that moves us to redirect negative emotional energy. We must see in order to do.

I've summarized only a few of the ideas in the Gurdjieff work. There are many more, but those I have commented on are ones I feel I have some sense of, largely because they were part of my actual experience during and since my time at Claymont and not just philosophical abstractions. So much has already been written about the Work at searchingly deep and well-integrated levels of understanding; this summary isn't meant to be other than my decidedly "Non-Adept's" effort to put my experience into a very basic conceptual frame of reference.

Arnold Kirinski's Efforts at a Different Kind of Writing

WHEN I RETIRED AND moved into Nate's rooms in Belmar, at first I was at a loss of how to spend my time after decades of laboring away on history projects. Then I read Nate's memoirs and observations and was inspired to record some of my own experiences, present and past, in forms of expression I hadn't tried before—more personal, reflective, poetic.

Hierarchies of Need

We flocked to Maslow's theory like pigeons to bread. He had come to conceive of human beings as purposeful, and we, all earnest graduate students of the late 1960s, were intent on being relevant, on seeing our lives as meaningful. So we liked Maslow, whose system nurtured our needs.

The system took a Pharaonic approach, layering the psyche into a pyramid of motives. Our biological and physiological needs are at the pyramid's base. Once we can breathe, eat, sleep, stay warm, and have sex, we climb, floor-by-floor, up the stairs. The second level satisfies our safety needs, the assurance that we are protected from the elements and can rely on law and order. On the third floor, our families, friends, and work groups offer society, belongingness, love. Self-esteem, status, pride of achievement, and independence reside on the fourth floor. Increasing knowledge and a sense of meaning dwell on the fifth. On the sixth, we seek and appreciate beauty, balance, forms that please. By the time we reach level seven, we are ready to fulfill our potential, to self-actualize, to experience the peaks of human existence. On level eight, the top floor, we have, in effect, transcended our personal needs and are now in a position to help others achieve theirs.

Maslow used an approach called biographical analysis to develop his theory, and he was criticized for his methodology. Using his subjective definition of what it means to be self-actualized, he identified 18 individuals who seemed to fit the bill. They were white, educated, prominent, and, but for one, males—people like Jefferson, Lincoln, Einstein, and Eleanor Roosevelt. So much for generalizability to the rest of us. There is also a problem with the idea that you can't fulfill higher-order needs until you've met lower-order ones. Starving artists and swamis might disagree.

I moved away from Maslow's system for reasons other than his methodological inadequacies. As my own life has unfolded, with its ups and downs, advances and retreats, I've concluded that his framework is too linear, too progressive, too positive and exalted. In direct contrast to his fundamentally optimistic attitude, my hope is to live without so much despair. Thus my hierarchy would include, as the third story after food and safety, the need not to dislike myself; not to react negatively to almost every person I see, finding fault with the way they walk, talk, look; not to treat virtually every situation—and life in general, for that matter—as inconveniences; not to blame myself and jump to take responsibility for whatever goes wrong in the world.

Instead of Maslow's bright-eyed model of fulfilling one positive purpose after the next on the way to sublimity, I'm more taken with the idea of negative need: the need to say no to hopes and expectations for any outcome at all, especially so-called good ones. In my experience, failing to meet expectations causes suffering. So why indulge the need to be purposeful? Why set things up only to make matters worse, when all I really want, in my very personal hierarchy of needs, is to be less sad?

Ian

Ian, an archivist at the Holocaust Museum, was one of the most broadly learned and ecumenical people I have ever known.

During my time as scholar-in-residence at the museum, Ian would regularly loan and tell me about books he thought would be useful for me to read. He would appear in my office bearing works or citations on all manner of topics—the Middle Ages, India, meditation, flamenco, the liberal arts, the autobiography of Malcolm Muggeridge, a 1923 work on the life of Christ by Giovanni Papini, an advertisement for a performance in New York City of García Lorca's *Yerma*. This array would have been chaotic and bewildering but for one cohering principle: their relevance to discussions we were engaged in *at that time*. We called it, only half- jokingly, The Principle of Immediate Relevance.

Whenever we could, we would have these conversations over a meal, either Ian cooking up something exotic at his home in Adams Morgan or at a restaurant we liked near the museum. When we were at his place, by the end of the meal the table would be littered with the books that factored into our discussion. I once counted 22 volumes by the time he served dessert. And it was fortunate that the restaurant we frequented was a short walk from the museum, since each of us had to carry an armload of books that Ian had selected for the occasion from his office shelves.

Ian and I once considered teaching a course together at one of the local universities—George Washington, Howard, Georgetown, American—founded on this Principle of Immediate Relevance, and I regret that we never did. As we envisioned it, the course would have begun with our taking a group of students into the school's library stacks and instructing them each to explore the shelves until they emerged with a topic of compelling personal interest. This topic would be their individual focus for the term. The Principle's corollary might have been called the "follow your nose to see where it leads you" approach to learning. The single criterion for the course was to be that the student would act as if this semester were to be the last four months of his or her life; thus one would settle only on a topic so burning and meaningful that it would justify commitment to the end.

I was reminded of the extraordinary scope, and also depth, of Ian's knowledge when a fellow named Alan, a friend in Columbia's literature department, visited me in Washington. Alan has devoted his scholarly work to the life and works of Lafcadio Hearn, a late 19th - early 20th century Irish-American writer. Although not obscure, neither is Hearn a household name, even for some who study literature. Anyway, I was showing Alan and his wife around the Holocaust Museum when we ran into Ian. I introduced them and mentioned that Alan specialized in Hearn. While I spoke with Alan's wife, Ian and Alan were off to the side, engrossed in their own conversation—in part about Hearn, I gathered from the little I overheard. We parted after 20 minutes or so. Later, Alan told me he was astounded by what Ian knew of Hearn's work. "Not only generalities," according to Alan, "but details!"

Another memory of Ian: I stopped by his office to collect him and the usual armload of book en route to our restaurant. He met me at the door, excited.

"There's a dead squirrel in the grass outside my window. It's beautiful! Do you want to see it?"

"No way," I answered, sounding more abrupt than I should have, I guess. But my squeamishness was genuine, especially before lunch. Ian looked at me in what I could only interpret as disappointment, sadness, and concern that I came up short in my capacity for wonder.

But then Ian's own capacity for wonder—at art, the mind, nature, the divine, life, relationships, and death—was entirely unparalleled in my experience. And his capacity for sharing, his generosity to all comers, was no less, even right up until the time of his death. Our mutual friend Rowan, a retired professor of history at Georgetown who predeceased Ian, had requested Ian to spread his ashes on a mountaintop in Maryland's Catoctin Range. Ian agreed. He apparently fulfilled his promise following a strenuous climb to the summit. Then he walked part way down the mountain, where another hiker found him dead from what the coroner later said was a massive heart attack. The hiker, who also happened to be a medical doctor, was quoted in the *Washington Post* as saying that he had found Ian sitting with his back against a tree. At first, given Ian's calm demeanor and until he checked for a pulse, the hiker thought Ian was meditating.

Responsibility

I walk through a wealthy area of the city. Some distance ahead I see a woman, well dressed, walking a dog—a King Charles Spaniel, purebred I guess. A high-end pooch, the type you'd expect to see in this neighborhood. The dog appears to be pooping on the sidewalk, but it's hard to be sure. The woman, in any event, does not stoop to pick anything up.

The woman and dog move on, walking towards me. After they pass I arrive at the suspected spot. And there it is—a turd on the sidewalk. I turn and call out, not yelling exactly, but in a loud voice: "I'm picking it up with my bag." I hold up a plastic bag for the woman to see. She looks startled. Is she embarrassed? Taken aback at having been caught out? Contrite? Affronted by my proprietary attitude on what is likely, judging from her attire and slow gait, her block?

I collect the little pile, then turn and walk away, at first pleased with myself for striking a blow on behalf of the law and civic sanitation, confident that the woman will think twice before being so negligent again. Then I begin to question myself. It's not my street, or even my neighborhood. What right do I have to police anyone anyway?

For whatever reasons, my anger in recent months has been growing and free-floating, in search of any target. When I find one, I feel a special satisfaction if there's no ambiguity about it, if the offending behavior clearly justifies my rage.

Long before I reach home my anger is spent. I feel sorry for the woman. Maybe she simply forgot to carry a bag on this particular walk. Maybe she's grateful that I had one to spare. Maybe, just maybe, she wishes she had picked a different time to walk her dog.

The Propensity to Be Bothered (Part 1)

I came across the phrase "the propensity to be bothered" in a book on Nathan's shelves by the Buddhist teacher Pema Chödrön. The phrase has been useful to me, though what it suggests about my attitude and behavior is not flattering. It hits the proverbial nail on my particular head.

The phrase is constantly, mercilessly, and inescapably accurate. I can't get away from it. Anyone and anything are likely to trigger my irritation. This person is walking too quickly, or too slowly. Why don't they walk on the right? It's the convention in this country, after all. And why do they, especially the young ones, it seems, insist on barging into an elevator before the occupants have exited? Traffic is the worst. A stop sign means "Stop!" damn it, not slow down. It's the law. How dare you treat it lightly or think it doesn't apply to you as well as me? And why don't you even pretend to slow down in one of those useless, striped pedestrian crossings? And what is wrong with the so-called transportation planners anyway? Do they actually think drivers will heed a toothless "yield to pedestrians in the cross-walk" sign? And you, the lady with big hair: It's not raining, or barely. Why is your umbrella open? Cell phone etiquette? Forget it. Don't get me started. Has he no regard for the boundaries of privacy, no sense that his loud "You know, like" conversation with some similarly mindless crony is a gross intrusion on my space? And I'm so sick and tired of people who litter, don't pick up after their dog, or put their trash in my recycling bin. I'm sure they're the same people who never collect their delivered newspapers or mow their lawn or shovel their sidewalk. The general inconsiderateness of people is unbearable.

Since coming across "the propensity to be bothered" phrase I've tried to notice whether anyone ever gets a pass from my prevailing negativity. Lo and behold, I have discovered an exemption: People who smile at me, especially those who do so before I've done anything to merit their friendliness. I've come to see that such proactive gestures, rare though they may be, typically come from younger women. I haven't tried to figure out why that is—a defensive tactic in a world ridden with street crime? Or perhaps simply a character trait so laudable in contrast to my own reactions to other people? Whatever.

But here's the rub: Ten seconds after I give someone a pass for their friendly smile, the old irritation erupts, this time because they were too damned nice, a trait that further irks my propensity to be bothered. I guess I shouldn't be surprised. As Nate suggested somewhere in his notebook, there's a vast distance between the intention and actual ability to change.

The Propensity to be Bothered (Part 2)

I've been working on this propensity to be bothered theme for several weeks now. I've noticed some things about myself, like what types of events and behaviors irritate me, my typical reactions to them, and my utter inability to change those reactions. Here's what I've thought about, observed, and concluded in the process.

I started with the unabridged dictionary. In sum, a propensity is a tendency, an inclination, a readiness— "*propendere*" from the Latin, "to hang forward, to lean." Being bothered is a state of anxiety, annoyance, fluster, vexation—a condition that arises from having troubled or concerned oneself. But we are not all inclined the same way or troubled by the same things. Having propensities is a general human attribute, but we each have different leanings. In other words, our triggers are individualized.

So the three questions I'm left with are what, specifically, troubles me, why does it trouble me, and how can I stop being concerned about it?

I get most annoyed by people who break the rules: biking on the sidewalk, double parking, not signaling turns, running lights and stop signs, walking too slowly, getting too close, not using designated cross-walks, smoking in public space, panhandling, using leaf blowers, talking too loudly. All of these are examples at the physical level. Some are formal or legal violations, others are violations of convention and accepted social practice.

More subtle examples of rule-breaking are defined by my emotional biases: this person's outfit is too physically revealing; that person's expression is too dour or grumpy; another is too impatient at the check-out counter.

Certain irksome examples of rule-breaking are clearly my projections, behaviors that I don't like in myself so jump to punish in others: the guy loading up on free cheese samples at Whole Foods really pisses me off, as does the woman with 17 items who's taking up space illicitly in the 15-item limit express lane.

And then there are the most aggravating violations of all, a deeper kind of projection, the transgressions, always personalized, that are fantasized rather than actual—what the Gurdjieff system calls internal considering: thinking what others think of me, always keeping an inner account about how they treat me, how they don't appreciate me. For example, just today I was remembering a conversation I had years ago with a colleague, during which he gave me uninvited feedback on an article I recently published. His comments, objectively assessed, were constructive and likely well-intentioned. But the content and quality of the feedback was not what I remembered. In fact, there was nothing about the actual conversation that I recalled. Rather, I began to imagine that this colleague was slighting *me*. Worse, in my mind he was representing the collective negative opinion of a cabal of history department faculty who did not value my work, or me for that matter. They were petty and jealous. Soon my memory of this very old occurrence turned into a crescendo of fantasies in which I confronted every one of the conniving shitheads. It took me some minutes to stop stewing about their imagined slights and recognize that this had nothing at all to do with them or anything they had actually done.

The available examples of my particular propensity to be bothered are endless. Which begs the question: Why does rule-breaking so bother me? Getting to the why of it forces one to look underneath the propensity and find whatever personal thread of experience caused it. The thread I've begun to see for myself is resentment. I go back to the unabridged dictionary. Resentment: a feeling of displeasure, indignation, anger, wrath, ire. Literally, "to feel again." Feel what? Feel again some early injury or offense, the sense of having been wronged. How was I wronged? How far back did it happen? And how do those early instances connect with on-going and current instances—any and all of which can trigger the propensity to feel, again and again, resentment?

I trace my resentment back to encroachment, both on my external and internal space. We always lived in duplexes or apartments or the house shared with a doctor's office. In his notebook, Nate described those circumstances, where there was little privacy even to use the toilet. And there was the matter of obligatory parental and societal expectations: kiss the relatives, whether or not you liked or even knew them; use your school vacation time to visit neighbors, even if they were not your personal friends; spend any "free" time working at the diner, even if it cuts into your friendships and normal youthful pleasures. Always play by the rules: don't jay walk, use the cross-walk; stay in line and stop where indicated; be nice, mannerly, neatly dressed—a consistent source of parental pride.

On the face of it, these certainly seem like virtues. But what is virtuous in the eyes of adults may well feel like deprivations in the experience of the child. Nate rebelled, but I, the ever-dutiful son, went along with it, even though I hated having my physical and emotional spaces invaded as much as he did. Now, 71 years old, I daily feel it all again and cannot figure out, try as I might, how to get free from the negativity that accompanies my propensity to be bothered.

I turn repeatedly to Nate's books for insight and help. Jean Vaysse describes my condition well in *Toward Awakening*: "Everything he dislikes appears to him as an affront and seems unjust, illegitimate, or wrong. Everybody's wrong, even the weather is at fault—only he is right." And Nicoll gives explicit suggestions for dealing with the condition in his *Commentaries*. Don't fight the negative emotions, he advises, much as the meditation masters advise against suppressing thoughts. That will only generate more of the same. Better just to watch the emotions that arise without indulging them. Recognize that these emotions come and go: they're not "I". Separate from them. Don't waste energy on them. Don't give them any control by allowing them to trigger habitual vexations.

But honestly, I find this tactic of dis-identification too hard to implement. It requires a capacity for self-observation that will take years of effort to develop. This doesn't mean I won't try. But at my age, I'd better be realistic about possible results.

Other books, mostly authored by Buddhists such as Pema Chödrön and Thich Nhat Hahn, encourage a kind and proactively positive approach. It begins with not judging oneself for the traits that naturally come with being human, especially our deficits, and accepting ourselves. Then apply that positivity to others. For example, on the bus I look for some positive feature in each person: hair, posture, demeanor, clothing, gait, behaviors. In other words, try to spot those first and pre-empt the propensity to be bothered. Try instead to supplant it with the propensity to be generous, kind, and accepting. This applies to everyone, including the glaring, ferocious looking guy wearing combat boots and a camouflage jacket. "He has a strong character," I say. Or the bus driver who beeps at cars before the light changes and mutters curses at double-parked construction vehicles. "She's being deliberate in doing her job as she understands it," I say. Looking for the good in everyone and appreciating them, myself included, strikes me as a worthy approach to try. If everything and everybody is part of the One, we should take joy in the "living quality" of it all, of us all—brushing our teeth, saying good morning, listening to the wind, walking in the rain. First see the positive quality in oneself, accept it, be happy for it, then turn the same attitude to others. Instead of "the way that guy walks annoys me," flip the thought to "his posture is straight as he walks" and so on. Change, in short, the habitual pattern of reacting with judgment and distaste toward oneself and others. Instead, this worthy approach urges, react with compassion, kindness, and love.

Worthy perhaps, but still too hard for me. For example, I see a lady with fat legs. I'm immediately critical, but then recall times I felt bad about my body. Does compassion arise? No. And soon I'm doubly damned: first, for not being able to stop being critical; second, for hating these thoughts I have but can't help harboring.

I try another approach: smiling. Paramahansa Yogananda, among others, proposes this. Who wants to be bitter and irritable? he rightly asks. Better to cut the mood with "the sword of wisdom," as the *Bhagavad-Gita* advises. Cut the negative thought as it arises, along with the negative emotion that comes along with that thought. Instead, look up, smile, and send out a positive thought to whoever was nearly the recipient of the negative thought.

But I have to say that this exhortation feels contrived, grudging. Yogananda was a saint, after all. I'm not used to it. After trying it a few times, my face begins to hurt from the unaccustomed effort, and I also suspect that I look strange and forced and unnatural. In addition, I realize that I expect reciprocation. If I smile at you, I expect you to smile back. I can't seem to do it for itself, or settle for not getting something back. If you don't smile at me, the whole judgment-resentment cycle repeats itself. I'm so inept at this. But I'll keep trying.

And just now, literally minutes ago, I came across a piece of advice I'm actually optimistic about. It's from the Zen teacher Dae Gak, who proposes what he calls bowing meditation. When you're bothered, or catch yourself about to be bothered by walkers, drivers, or whatever, incline your head. Dae Gak claims that a sense of respect, patience, and tolerance will ensue. Okay. I'll give it a try. I definitely want to find something that works.

Phenomenology

> Whatever happens. Whatever
> *what is* is is what
> I want. Only that. But that.
> > –Galway Kinnell, "Prayer"

Just. My friend hates the word.
It diminishes. Reduces. Dismisses,
she complains. I press her. *It just...*
She doesn't explain further.

I have a different take. I quite
like the word. It cuts to the
chase. Makes you think simply,
speak bluntly. Keeps you from
wandering. Brings you back.

I come across a Japanese word:
Shikantaza—just sitting. It is
a Zen meditation practice, I learn:
"nothing but precisely sitting,"
with no supportive techniques,
such as counting breaths. The mind
of someone facing death, I learn.

I research further and find a recording
titled "The Five Justs" which outlines
the practice of *shikantaza* in simple detail:
1. Just settle.
2. Just wait.
3. Just watch.
4. Just enjoy.
5. Just sit.

Now I really like the word: *Just*—
The sound of it, the feeling of it,
the stark understandability and do-ability
of it.

I tell this to my friend. She is dismissive.
Just hear me out, I say.

Appendix IV
Arnold Kirinski's Interest in Meditation

I WORK MY WAY through the books on Nathan's shelves. Many of his books concern meditation, and I begin to realize how often religious and wisdom traditions emphasize meditation, under one name or another, as an essential way forward. Soon, stimulated by my readings I begin to practice meditation and do so for increasing amounts of time every day.

I read *Bonpo Dzogchen Teachings* by Lopon Tenzin Namdak. Intellectually, he says, in the abstract we know that life is impermanent and death will come, although we don't know when, or what might happen next, or what we can do. He goes on to say that karmic causes, what we have done in the past, good and bad, "bring about future happiness or sorrow," and that there are meditation practices that can make the knowledge of impermanence concrete and also affect the future. "Yet most do not know how to realize this."

So I ask the authors on Nathan's shelves: how specifically? "Make a habit of practicing meditation," Krishna advises Arjuna in the *Bhagavad-Gita*, "and do not let your mind be distracted. In this way you will come finally to the Lord, who is the light-giver, the highest of the high...Indrawn utterly, held fast between the eyebrows, He goes forth to find his Lord, That light-giver, who is greatest."

Again: How?

"Practice," Paramahansa Yogananda emphasizes. "Now."

One last time, all you gurus: HOW?

Two ancient Buddhists, Buddhaghosa and Tilopa, provide some of the most practical and concrete advice I have found. In Buddhaghosa's *The Path of Purification*, the 5th century A. D. sage recommends reflecting on one's death from eight perspectives: first, think of it as an executioner about to murder you; second, as the great neutralizer, "the ruin of all success" you have gained in life; third, as everyone's inevitable end, regardless of status or station; fourth, as the result of countless mortal, bodily causes; fifth, as close by and potentially imminent; sixth, as never predictable; seventh, as the inevitable end of a limited lifespan; and eighth, as a reality that is constantly in progress. In the process of reflecting on these eight points, Philip Kapleau encourages us to remind ourselves repeatedly that we have "the rare privilege—the good karma—of being a human being in this lifetime" and the attendant opportunity "to awaken to the meaning of life and death."

Finally, there are the Six Words of Advice, so valued by Nate as I read in his notebook, and now me, from the 11th century A. D. Tantric Buddhist, Tilopa: 1. *Don't recall*, let go of what has passed. 2. *Don't imagine,* let go of what may come. 3. *Don't think*, let go of what is happening now. 4. *Don't examine*, don't try to figure anything out. 5. *Don't control*, don't try to make anything happen. 6. *Rest*, relax right now.

Something interesting happens. I had left the volumes on Judaism for last, figuring that their content, at least, would not be new to me or particularly revealing. Instead, I not only discover that the meditative and mystical aspects of Judaism are largely unfamiliar to me *as Judaism* per se, but that they have much in common with other wisdom traditions, such as Sufism and various streams of Buddhism, Taoism, and Yoga. Examples of this abound in sayings and practices, particularly in Hasidism. The first one I find is in Louis Newman's 1934 *Hasidic Anthology: Tales and Teachings of the Hasidim*, which gets at the idea of separation from and control of one's emotions. "Long ago," said the Koretzer Reb, "I conquered my anger and placed it in my pocket. When I have need of it, I take it out." Another example from the same source identifies, similar to every tradition, self-centeredness and egotism as primary obstacles to transformation. "Sadness is the worst quality in a man," the Lubliner Reb tells a Hasid who is bemoaning melancholy. "It is the attribute of an incurable egotist. He is always thinking: Something should rightfully come to me; something is wrongfully lacking to me...it is always 'I.'"

And many anecdotes describe encounters with Judaism's Prophet Elijah, with whom there are close parallels to Islam's al-Khidr, the lesson being that one must be awake and vigilant in behavior towards others at all times, since anyone you meet might be the prophet in disguise. One must, in other words, develop the capacity to be attentive, a capacity which is nurtured by meditation.

The affinities among the various traditions' specific meditative methods seem equally close, which makes sense to me historically given the flow of inter-religious influences over many centuries. But I never knew the depth of these influences and affinities. By extension, I hadn't begun to realize the depth of the meditative tradition within Judaism, which I admit shouldn't be a surprise since, unlike my brother, I never had an interest in such matters until I began these readings and explorations in my Las Palmas retirement.

I first recognized these common methods when I read Perle Epstein's *Kabbalah: The Way of the Jewish Mystic*, in which she discusses breath, spine, chakras, the relative and the Absolute, sound and light, concentration, energy, union—the same aspects of cosmology and spiritual practice found in the esoteric dimension of religions and wisdom traditions ranging across Christianity, Islam, Hinduism, Buddhism, Taoism, Yoga, the Fourth Way and more. This recognition is reinforced when I read (or rather re-read, this time seriously; my first reading years before had been cursory and unenthusiastic because of my disinterest in the subject matter) Gershom Scholem's *Major Trends in Jewish Mysticism*. In his comments on the 13th century Spaniard Abraham ben Samuel Abulafia ("an eminently practical

Kabbalist"), Scholem references the close connections between Yoga and both Jewish and non-Jewish "magical traditions and disciplines," including Kabbalism, Hasidism, and Moslem mysticism, which had been influenced by Abulafia's teachings as well. He specifically mentions the importance of breathing in Abulafia's system, which also "lays down certain rules of body posture, certain corresponding combinations of consonants and vowels, and certain forms of recitation..." Scholem points out that the similarity to Yoga "even extends to some aspects of the doctrine of ecstatic vision, as preceded and brought about by these practices" and suggests that some of Abulafia's passages "give the impression of a Judaized treatise on Yoga."

So I keep reading, exploring more deeply, and with growing excitement, a Jewish tradition of meditation, a tradition with Biblical origins and with practices that include mantra, contemplation, visualization, self-isolation (*hitbodedut* in Hebrew), self-understanding (*hitbonenut*), unification (*yichudim*), and more—methods more popularly associated with Buddhism, Hinduism, Sufism, and the East than with Judaism, particularly in the writings of such Jewish mystics as Yitzhak Luria, Yosef Caro, Yonah of Gerona, Yaakov ben Asher, the Baal Shem Tov, Alter of Teplik, Nachman of Breslov, and, in our modern day, the Lubavitch Hasids and Rabbi Aryeh Kaplan.

My excitement peaks when I discover Nehemia Polen's *The Holy Fire: The Teachings of Rabbi Kalonymous Kalman Shapira, the Rebbe of the Warsaw Ghetto*. The details of Shapira's meditative method reflect almost exactly aspects of Theravada insight meditation, Tibetan Buddhism, Sufism, contemplative Christianity, certain Yogas, and Zen. In *The Zookeeper's Wife: A War Story*, Diane Ackerman summarizes the key features of Shapira's approach as channeling one's emotions towards mystical visions, dispassionately observing and examining one's thoughts, stilling the mind, discovering one's inner holiness, and being mindful of, and taking pleasure in, the moments of everyday life. Shapira's Hasidism resonates for me as well with the Zen exhortation to appreciate your life and Gurdjieff's emphasis on the centrality of attention.

Early on, as I was beginning to make my way through Nate's library, I would ridicule myself: What could I know of Yogis, Sufis, Buddhists, Taoists, or any of the rest? These traditions aren't mine. But I kept searching for meaning in those traditions, because the Jewish world—as defined by *religious* doctrine and ritual—was not my world either. And now that I'm engrossed in all this reading and practice, it's the meditative aspects of the various traditions that captivate me, especially those aspects within Judaism, a *spiritual* tradition I newly appreciate for its sense of wonder and worship and promise.

Appendix V
Arnold Kirinski's Typology of Death And Dying Theories

IN ADDITION TO THE tracts on meditation and spiritual development, a number of the books on Nathan's shelves got me thinking about death and how one might go about preparing for it. As I read through these volumes and began to feel overwhelmed by the different perspectives I encountered, my historiographer's training took over, and I devised the following categories for organizing the various ideas.

▶ *Aunt Sadie's Theory: You live, you die*

I have vivid and fond memories of my father's sister Sadie, née Sarah. She was an ornery old girl, feared by most of the family. But for whatever reason, she and I hit it off and were always close. Sadie's daughter, my cousin Martha, complained about her mother to me soon after my father died.

"I phoned my mother to commiserate," said Martha. "I was worried about how she was doing after the death of Mort, her last remaining sibling. "How are you doing, Mom?" I asked.

"'Fine,' she answered. Period. I pushed her, knowing how she was inclined to hide any expression of sentimentality.

"I mean, he was the last, except for you. How does that make you feel? You must be so sad. And maybe anxious about yourself?"

"'Look, Martha. You live, you die,' Sadie replied, as matter-of-factly as she might have commented on the weather—that, like it or not, some days it rains."

Martha, a touchy-feely social worker, couldn't understand and was upset by her mother's lack of emotion. My reaction was quite different. I'm partial to Sadie's perspective, its cleanliness and simplicity, its unwillingness to speculate beyond what we actually know, its refusal to offer unwarranted reassurances. We live and we die. The rest, if there is anything else, is guesswork.

I think Sadie would have appreciated this quote I came upon several years ago in a letter from the author Marjorie Rawlings to Maxwell Perkins, her editor:

> If by chance I do not come out of it [upcoming surgery], I do wish I could make it clear to you and to everyone else interested in me for whatever reason, that it would be the sort of death that would not matter....I have lived so rich and full a life, with so much more than my share of everything, that I feel indebted to life, instead of life's still being indebted to me.

▶ *The Joe Paterno Theory: You're never in the clear*

Joe Paterno was the revered Penn State football coach brought down by a scandal involving Jerry Sandusky, Paterno's long-time assistant and friend who was prosecuted when his years of sexually abusing young boys, sometimes in the team's shower room on campus, were made public. Paterno said he never knew about it until a graduate student assistant reported an assault to him, and Paterno further claimed he reported it in turn to the university hierarchy, leaving them to address it. But the incidents happened under his watch, and Paterno was accused, at a minimum, of not following up on reported incidents or doing anything to prevent further abuses. Some accounts claim that Paterno knew about Sandusky's predations for years but chose not to intervene. In any event, Sandusky was jailed, and Paterno, the university's athletic department director, and Penn State's president all lost their jobs.

The point is that even a personage as lionized and seemingly immune from reproach as Joe Paterno, the winningest coach in major college football history and age 86 at the time, lost everything—position, reputation, and legacy—before he died. Innumerable fallen figures throughout history have experienced this: that you are never home free; you might only think you are. But in the end—and for Paterno it literally was in the end—you can't count on the past, in this case an entirely successful past, as a certain criterion for defining your life. So you have to ask: What, if anything, is certain?

I remember how Nate, Debbie, and I used to ridicule our mother Fay for the platitudes she was so fond of masquerading as wisdom. But in retrospect I think Mom was on to something with at least one of her clichés: "Life turns on a dime." Joe Paterno sure found this to be true. And it's worth keeping it in mind, I believe, because the message seems to apply universally.

▶ *The Little Big Man Theory: "Today is a good day to die"*

There's a memorable scene, at once humorous and serious, in the 1970 movie *Little Big Man*, in which Dustin Hoffman's character Jack Crabb, a Native American also known as Little Big Man, invokes his culture's traditional wisdom one morning and concludes that this would be a good day to die. He builds a funeral pyre, sets a fire beneath it, and lies on the elevated pallet to immolate himself. But as he lies there, the fire burning, it begins to rain. The rain puts out the flames and Little Big Man reluctantly trudges off. Dying must wait.

Four things impress me about this scene. First, that Little Big Man believes the manner and moment of his dying are matters of his choosing. Second, that this belief is disabused: the timing and manner of death are not up to Little Big Man, at least in the traditional form he chooses to do away with himself. Third, that it clearly is not a good day to die; it's just not his time.

And fourth, this might be a sign that he still has more to do before there will be a good day for him to die.

I remember leaving the movie theater thinking, "Do better now or it will never be a good day to die."

▶ **The Philo Theory: "Be kind, for everyone you meet is fighting a great battle"**

This quote by the Hellenistic-Jewish philosopher Philo of Alexandria back in the time of Christ basically says that whatever the superficial differences between human beings, we must all grapple with death. We're all in the same boat. Death is the ultimate leveler, the victor in the battle none of us can avoid. Another old philosopher, the 5th century B.C. Chinese sage Yang Chu, says pretty much the same thing in this sentence I found underlined in one of Nate's books: "That in which all things differ is life, that in which they are all alike is death."

If we could truly recognize this fundamental sameness, compassion and genuine fellow-feeling would reign. We would earnestly try to live out the exhortation to do unto others as we would have them do unto us.

▶ **The Spots of Time Theory: Be kind, even as you lay dying**

In my mind, this relates to the Philo Theory. In *Twelve Steps to a Compassionate Life*, the historian of religion Karen Armstrong suggests that "...one small act of kindness can turn a life around." She calls these acts "spots of time," a phrase taken from Wordsworth's poem *The Prelude*:

> There are in existence spots of time,
> That with distinct pre-eminence retain
> A renovating virtue, whence...our minds
> Are nourished and invisibly repaired.

Armstrong relates how a friend said something kind to her, something that made an important positive difference in Armstrong's life. That this kindness was bestowed as the friend lay dying led Armstrong to remark that "we can all create 'spots of time' for others" in the spirit of the Golden Rule. Whether the Rule is worded in its positive version (Do unto others...) or its negative formulation (Don't do unto others...), the effect is a "renovating virtue," in Wordsworth's phrase, for the giver and the recipient of the kindness alike.

I'm struck by the fundamentally social nature of this. By exercising kindness, one can create spots of time for others even as one is dying. One's death, in other words, will have some portion of its meaning in relation to others.

Ultimately, though, I consider this theory to be too idealistic. It expects too much. In my own case, the possibility of feeling genuine compassion seems remote. I haven't developed the capacity for it. I'm more with the Theravada than the Mahayana Buddhist perspective on this: concentrate on my own freedom, and someday I might reach a stage where I can save others.

▶ *The Pascal Theory: We live and die alone; no one can help us.*

The 17th century polymath's notion of dying is quite different from Armstrong's spots of time, and it strikes me as truer. It's a defiant yet somehow freeing credo. I like its emphatic individualism.

I recently read *Black Spring* by the estimable Henry Miller. To my way of thinking, the author, religious in his own way and no opponent to the possibility of God, exemplifies Pascal's idea. "...I think of myself standing out on a high hill in resplendent whiteness. It is no sacred heart that inspires me, no Christ I am thinking of. Something better than a Christ, something bigger than a heart, something beyond God Almighty I think of—MYSELF. I am a man. That seems to me sufficient."

The moral of this is clear: be prepared to go it alone, courageously and, in accord with another of Miller's maxims, "Always merry and bright."

▶ *The Ozymandias Theory: "Look on my works, ye mighty, and despair. Nothing beside remains."*

Shelley's poem, regardless that it was written by a 19th century English Christian, strikes me as essentially Buddhistic. Time will inevitably win out. Nothing is permanent, no matter the earthly status of the sculptor or his creation, the emperor or his kingdom.

The full poem, with its images of ruins and desolate sands stretching into oblivion, should be depressing. But when I first read the poem in high school, I remember experiencing a deep sense of reassurance, the same reassurance I felt later when I came across the phrase "This, too, shall pass" in some Sufi text. It isn't reassurance in the obvious sense that "Today's a bad day; tomorrow will be better." It's more a sense of inevitability, the intuition that I myself will someday be gone along with everyone and everything else no matter what material or biomedical or other measures are attempted to force a different outcome. Being resigned, contentedly resigned, to the inevitable consequence of being human—that's it; that's the reassurance: that we must all pass on, I as well: I needn't keep deluding myself into believing otherwise. Better that I should live my life, this life that is neither more nor less than anyone else's, doomed royalty included—even Ozymandias, king of kings.

► *The Existential Theory: We need to believe that we're living, and dying, for something*

The philosopher Corliss Lamont, in an article I just finished titled "Mistaken Attitudes Towards Death," writes that "[The mature man is] not preoccupied with death; nor does he permit it, on account of the heartache and crisis it causes, to overshadow the other phases of human existence....No, the wise man looks at death with honesty, dignity and calm, recognizing that the tragedy it brings is inherent in the great gift of life."

In *Death and Its Mysteries*, another of my recent reads, the Estonian-French depth psychologist Ignace Lepp elaborates on Lamont's quote in discussing several existentialist thinkers' views of death, including Heidegger, Camus, Sartre, and Malraux. All recognize "the sad reality of our nothingness" and the undeserved fate and "cruel irony" of our suffering and death. But we don't have to accept this fate stoically, they insist. Through dignity, courage, authenticity, and defiance, we can give beauty and meaning to our lives and deaths. Take all pains, they exhort us, despite destiny's odds against us, to live and die well, without illusions or regrets.

There is a poignant paradox in this view that we must force ourselves to exercise agency even knowing that the effort is futile. In other words, precisely because oblivion might well be our fate, how we make our way towards oblivion becomes all the more important. Perhaps it—the "how"—is the only consideration in all of our existence that actually is important.

► *The Morton Kirinski Theory: We must be dutiful*

I haven't figured out whether this theory contradicts the existentialists or, at a deeper level, affirms them. Mort Kirinski, I know better than anyone, was a hard-nosed taskmaster. I'm sure Nate would agree with this assessment and guess my brother might amend this to "hard-nosed SOB," although I'm not prepared to go that far myself. But I'm also sure Nate and I would both acknowledge that Mort drove himself much more than he drove his sons. Family meant everything to him, and he was devoted to all of the Kirinskis' well-being, at least at the material level. So how does this relate to conceptions of death?

Ignace Lepp, the psychologist just referred to, tells a story about one of his patients, a down-to-earth farmer named Bernard.

> One day, I introduced him to the ideas of Sartre and Camus about the absurdity of life. He was quite surprised but in no way disturbed. 'Are these men sane?' he asked me with some hesitation. 'Don't people make fun of them for talking such nonsense?' Bernard works his land, sows and

harvests, and cares for his live-stock. He tries to raise his children the best way he knows how and lends assistance to his elderly parents. He also makes an effort to contribute to the common good. The sum of his occupations and responsibilities fills his life materially and gives it adequate meaning. To be sure, Bernard loves life and hopes to live as long as possible. But, he says, 'we can die in peace when we have done our duty.'

If I substitute the Carousel Diner for the farm, I see right away that Bernard could be Morton. And if I skip "the absurdity of life" bit and instead emphasize living courageously, defiantly, and with no illusions, I see how Morton could be Camus or Sartre.

▶ The Castaneda–Ambrose Theory: From material to spirit, and back again

I found the parts in Nathan's notebook relating his experiences at Claymont, the Fourth Way school in West Virginia, very interesting. I'm particularly intrigued by a phrase Nathan reported from one of his conversations with Laurent Ambrose, Claymont's director, when Laurent spoke of a kind of two-directional relationship in the flow of energies between matter, a coarser energy, and spirit, a more refined vibration. "The materialization of spirit and the spiritualization of matter," according to Nate, is the phrase Laurent used. This reminds me of an episode at the end of Carlos Castaneda's *The Active Side of Infinity*, in which Carlos leaps off a mountain into the abyss, knowing that his identity as "Carlos" would be dissolved and his constituent parts would return to the Whole, the formless universe.

I recognize this idea in a number of the books on Nate's shelves. One example is in *Toward Awakening*, by Jean Vaysse: "In the universe we live in, it is obvious that nothing is lost. Everything comes from somewhere and, having been changed or transformed to some degree, returns somewhere. Nothing which has taken form or is alive remains immutable, and each of these changes serves life in some fashion. A human being cannot be an exception to this universal principle."

As a second example, in *The Master Game* Robert de Ropp distinguishes between *personal* survival after death and "a reblending of the separate consciousness with a larger, more generalized state that may be thought of as all-pervading." As a third example, this time from the Jewish tradition, in *Nine Gates to the Chassidic Mysteries* Jiri Langer writes that "The most beautiful Chassidic doctrine is undoubtedly that of the *spiritual nature* of all matter. According to Chassidism, all matter is *full of supernatural 'sparks' of the holiness of God...*"

These statements, it seems to me, track with science's explanation: according to the Law of the Conservation of Matter and Energy, energy is never lost, only transformed. Nate mentioned this in his Useful Ideas essay for Esther. As I understand this, and to put it in my own words, each of us is configured into our temporary individuality from many disparate parts. When we die, these parts, themselves having each been transformed in some measure, melt back into the universe and reconfigure into some new individuality. This, too, eventually dissolves. The parts and what they combine to make are differentiated matter, temporary forms. But their source is the undifferentiated void, formless and fine and eternal. I see the connection again to Lepp, who writes, "Due to the great mutation effected by death, the material body will simply be replaced by a 'spiritual' body—or better still, a *spiritualized* body."

▶ *The Karmic Theory: In the unending stream of cause and effect, every action is a referendum on what comes next*

In the long section of Nate's notebook titled "Almost Heaven: A Diary," Laurent Ambrose's caution to be patient with Holly because there was a process at work that Nate couldn't see the end of really caught my attention. I wasn't part of that conversation, obviously, but what I take from Laurent's statement is the idea that Nate needed to be patient because he couldn't see the full picture, that there were underlying, unseen patterns of longer-term causes and effects that could not all be known in the immediate situation. Nate should wait and see what would unfold.

In researching my preparing-to-die project, I've discovered that the pivot of this idea of cause and effect, known in some Eastern traditions as karma, is a reported observation by Shakyamuni Buddha. As quoted in Philip Kapleau's *The Wheel of Life and Death*:

> If you want to know your past [cause]
> look at yourself now [effect].
> If you want to know your future [effect]
> look at your present [cause].

Every action affects the actor sooner or later, Kapleau explains, and our karma is "determined by the sum total of our actions, good and bad, and by the larger karmic flux of which we are a part. These actions in turn create a pattern, a predisposition, as a result of which we respond to events in a certain way. That is, our karma creates a pathway, or perhaps a rut, which we tend habitually to follow."

As I understand the idea of karma, this doesn't mean that one's future is set or pre-ordained. If everything is temporary and subject to change, as the Buddha proposed, so is each of us. But we're also free to work on ourselves and, depending on our individual efforts, have the possibility to influence our future. In fact, each of us has two alternative potentialities: to be the passive victim of cause and effect, or the active determiner of our unfolding life in the present and our future life. Each alternative has its pros and cons. In the first, we're doomed to repeat the past, but at least this won't require any effort; we can just drift off into oblivion. In the second lies the promise of self-realization and liberation from the karmic cycle. But the struggle will be enormous, and with long odds against success.

I readily admit to not understanding many of the complexities of the karmic worldview. But I've gone this far, so I may as well be brazen and try to boil it all down to a maxim, by which I mean a subjective principle of action that goes as follows: *behave decently at every moment.* Doing willful harm in action or thought spawns negative karma, which in turn creates retributive conditions for one's future. Conversely, benevolent actions and thoughts create the conditions, moment by moment, for what will come next, both in this life and (there's always the possibility) the next.

Repenting for what one has done or not done also fosters positive conditions for the future. According to Kapleau, we need to reflect on past wrongs which have caused hurt to others and "make a searching and fearless moral inventory." I find this aspect of the karma idea especially meaningful, perhaps because I'm an historian, a profession that by definition makes its primary sense in terms of the past. Or it could be because I'm a Jew and appreciate that Kapleau relates repentance to the old Jewish saying that "You have only to repent the last day of your life, and since you don't know what day that is, you must repent every day." Or maybe it's because my brother told me how much he benefited from the 12-step program of Alcoholics Anonymous, particularly the steps aimed at repentance: Make a list of all the persons we've harmed, Step 8 says, and be willing to make amends to them all. Then, in Step 9, make direct amends to such people wherever possible, except when doing so would hurt them or others.

Behave decently at every moment. Behave impeccably in all realms of conduct— *brahmacarya* in the yogic tradition—to reduce the horrible costs of misdeeds in the constant cycle of suffering. Well...a too-tall order. But if I can remember to try, that in itself would be extraordinary.

▶ *The "Who Knows?" Theory: All of the above? Some of the above? One of the above? None of the above?*

In *After Buddhism,* Stephen Batchelor relates a story that sums up my state of mind as I complete my research on various ideas of death and dying. "[When] the Chinese Chan (Zen) patriarch Yunmen (c. 860–949) was asked 'What are the teachings of an entire lifetime?' Yunmen replied: 'An appropriate statement...' For Yunmen, what counts is whether your words and deeds are an appropriate response to the situation at hand, not whether they accord with an abstract truth."

After all these theories, the nagging question for me is: How? How can I die well, without fear, regret, sadness, or grievance? How can I let go of this life and accept death with awareness, intention, and a whole heart?

Reprising Plato, who thought of life as an apprenticeship for death, Hugh Fausset suggests that we should be rehearsing this death from the first breath we take and learning "how to die willingly and fruitfully." Such a death, "the lesson of all lessons that the Eastern sages taught," must involve release: "a loosening and eventual severance of our attachment to the unreal....To achieve this they taught that we should practice an inner detachment from all that is contingent in life as a means to realizing fully That Which is not contingent." Faithfulness in this practice will lead to the experience of "Union."

Ever the methodologist, I have to persist: how to do it? How, specifically, should I practice inner detachment and prepare to die? Contemplative traditions, Eastern and otherwise, all seem to point to similar methods. Breathe. Follow and count your breaths. Become still. Observe your thoughts and feelings, and then let them go. Let go, too, of memory (what has happened) and the imagined future (what hasn't happened). With an undistracted mind, stay awake and present. At the same time, these traditions don't minimize the effort required for such methods to be fruitful in the sense that one "is able with full awareness and without artificial aids," as Robert de Ropp puts it, "to *let the life process come to a halt* so far as this particular body is concerned" and come to "a reblending of the separate consciousness with a larger, more generalized state that may be thought of as all-pervading"—what Tantric Buddhism calls the *dharma-kaya*, the Clear Light.

The end of this particular body. Reblending the separate into the all-pervading. Finding the Clear Light. Nathan passed this way, and so shall I. Brothers until the end.

Acknowledgments

Ginnah Howard and Forrest Bachner commented on multiple drafts of *Kirinski's Life & Times*. I am deeply grateful to both of these novelists for their appraisals, suggestions, and encouragement.

My utmost thanks go to Robert Bensen, founder of Woodland Arts Editions, who designed the novel's cover and provided advice throughout the publication process. Many writers have benefited from Bob's guidance, generosity, and supportiveness. I feel fortunate to be one of them.

Works Cited

Ackerman, Diane. (2017). *The Zookeeper's Wife: A War Story*. New York: W.W. Norton

Angyal, Andras. (1941). *Foundations for a Science of Personality*. New York: The Commonwealth Fund

Aristotle. (1961). *Aristotle's Metaphysics*, IV, 3-6, on the Law of Non-Contradiction. John Warrington, ed. and tr. New York: Dutton

Armstrong, Karen. (2011). *Twelve Steps to a Compassionate Life*. New York: Anchor Books

Ashbery, John, "Someone You Have Seen Before" from APRIL GALLE-ONS by John Ashbery. Copyright © 1984, 1987 by John Ashbery. Reprinted by permission of Georges Borchardt, Inc., for the author.

Back, Kurt W. (1963). "The Game and the Myth as Two Languages of Science," *Behavioral Science*, Vol. 8(1), pp. 66-71

Batchelor, Stephen. (1997). *Buddhism Without Beliefs: A Contemporary Guide to Awakening*. New York: Riverhead Books

Batchelor, Stephen. (2015). *After Buddhism: Rethinking the Dharma for a Secular Age*. New Haven, CT: Yale University Press

Begley, Louis. (1991). *Wartime Lies*. New York: Knopf

Begley, Louis. (1998). *Mistler's Exit*. New York: Knopf

Bellow, Saul. (1976). *To Jerusalem and Back: A Personal Account*. New York: Viking Press

Ben-Gurion, David. (1919). Quoted in Roger Cohen's "An Israel of Pride and Shame," *New York Times*, December 29, 2017

Bennett, John G. (1973). *Gurdjieff: Making a New World*. New York: Harper & Row

Bennett, John G. (1974). *A Call for a New Society*. Sherborne, England: Sherborne House

Berlin, Isaiah. (2013). *The Power of Ideas*. Princeton, NJ: Princeton University Press

Bernard of Cluny. (1867). "Jerusalem the Golden". Tr. by J.M. Neale, London, England: Joseph Masters

Bertalanffy, Karl Ludwig von. (2009). *General Systems Theory: Foundations, Development, Applications*. New York: George Braziller

The Song of God: Bhagavad-Gita. (1954). Tr. by Prabhavananda and Christopher Isherwood, New York: Mentor Books

Brother Lawrence of the Resurrection (Nicolas Herman). (1996). *The Practice of the Presence of God*. London, England: Hodder & Stoughton

Bruyn, Severin. (2000). *A Civil Economy: Transforming the Marketplace in the Twenty-First Century*. Ann Arbor, MI: University of Michigan Press

Buddhaghosa. (2010). *The Path of Purification.* Tr. by Nyanamoli Himi, Kandy: Buddhist Publication Society

Buddhaghosa. (1989). As quoted in Philip Kapleau's *The Wheel of Life* and *Death: A Practical and Spiritual Guide.* Tr. by Philip Kapleau, New York: Doubleday

Bunyan, John. (1960). *The Pilgrim's Progress from This World to That Which is to Come.* Oxford, England: Clarendon Press

Camus, Albert. (1989). *The Stranger.* Tr. by Matthew Ward, New York: Vintage International

Castaneda, Carlos. (1972). *Journey to Ixtlan: The Lessons of Don Juan.* New York: Simon and Schuster

Castaneda, Carlos. (2000). *The Active Side of Infinity.* London, England: Harper Perennial

Chödrön, Pema. (2013). *How to Meditate: A Practical Guide to Making Friends with Your Mind.* Boulder, CO: Sounds True

Chödrön, Pema. (2019). *Living Beautifully with Uncertainty and Change.* Boulder, CO: Shambhala Publications, Inc.

Chögyam Trungpa. (2005). *The Myth of Freedom and the Way of Meditation.* Boston, MA: Shambhala Publications, Inc.

Coleridge, Samuel Taylor. (2009). *Biographia Literaria.* Auckland, NZ: The Floating Press

Dae Gak. (1997). *Going Beyond Buddha: The Awakening Practice of Listening.* Boston, MA: Charles E. Tuttle

de Ropp, Robert S. (1968). *The Master Game: Pathways to Higher Consciousness Beyond the Drug Experience.* New York: Dell Publishing

de Ropp, Robert S. (1979). *Warrior's Way.* London, England: George Allen & Unwin

de Salzmann, Jeanne. (2010). *The Reality of Being: The Fourth Way of Gurdjieff.* Boston, MA: Shambhala Publications, Inc.

Deuteronomy 22:12

Dewey, John. (1971). *The Essential Writings.* New York: Harper & Row

Dhammapada. (1950). *The Dhammapada: With Introductory Essays.* S. Radhakrishnan, ed., London, England: Oxford University Press

Dharmachari Subhuti. (2010). "Just Sitting in the System of Meditation." Free Buddhist Audio (freebuddhistaudio.com)

Einstein, Albert. (1986). For discussions of relativity and Einstein's search for a Unified Field Theory, see, e.g., Barry Parker's *Einstein's Dream: The Search for a Unified Theory of the Universe.* New York: Plenum Press

Epictetus. (1979). *Epictetus: The Discourses as Reported by Arrian, the Manual, and Fragments.* Cambridge, MA: Harvard University Press

Epstein, Perle. (1978). *Kabbalah: The Way of the Jewish Mystic.* Garden City, NY: Doubleday & Co., Inc.

Fausset, Hugh. (1969). *The Flame and the Light: Meanings in Vedanta and Buddhism.* New York: Greenwood Press

Fehrenbach, T. R. (1963). *This Kind of War: A Study in Unpreparedness.* New York: Macmillan

Galatians 6:7

Genesis 32:28

Gurdjieff, George I. (1973). *Beelzebub's Tales to His Grandson: An Objectively Impartial Criticism of the Life of Man.* New York: E.P. Dutton

Hartranft, Chip. (2003). *The Yoga-Sūtra of Patañjali.* Boston, MA: Shambhala Publications

Heat Moon, William Least. (1982). *Blue Highways.* Boston: Little, Brown

Josephus, Flavius. (1928). *The Wars of the Jews.* New York: E.P. Dutton

Jamgön Kongtrül. (1987). *The Great Path of Awakening.* Tr. by Ken McLeod, Boston, MA: Shambhala Publications, Inc.

Kapleau, Philip. (1989). *The Wheel of Life* and *Death: A Practical and Spiritual Guide.* New York: Doubleday

Kazin, Alfred. (1951). *A Walker in the City.* New York: Harcourt, Brace

Kermode, Frank. (1967). *The Sense of an Ending: Studies in the Theory of Fiction.* New York: Oxford University Press

Kierkegaard, Søren. (1959). *Either/or.* Tr. by David F. Swenson and Lillian Marvin Swenson, Garden City, NY: Doubleday

Kinnell, Galway. (1985). Excerpt from "Prayer" from THE PAST by Galway Kinnell. Copyright © 1985 by Galway Kinnell. Reprinted by permission of Houghton Mifflin Harcourt. All rights reserved.

Koestler, Arthur. (1967). *The Ghost in the Machine.* London, England: Hutchinson

Koestler, Arthur. (1978). *Janus: A Summing Up.* New York: Random House

Kushner, Kenneth. (1988). *One Arrow, One Life: Zen, Archery, and Daily Life.* New York: Arkana

Lamont, Corliss. (1965). "Mistaken Attitudes Towards Death," *The Journal of Philosophy*, 01-21, Vol. 62(2), pp. 29-36

Langer, Jiri. (1961). *Nine Gates to the Chassidic Mysteries.* Tr. by Stephen Jolly, New York: David McKay Company, Inc.

Lao-tzu. (1934). In *The Way and Its Power: A Study of the Tao Te Ching and Its Place in Chinese Thought*, by Arthur Waley. London, England: Allen and Unwin

Lawrence, Paul R., and Jay W. Lorsch. (1967). "Differentiation and Integration in Complex Organizations." *Administrative Science Quarterly*, pp. 1-47

Lepp, Ignace. (1976). *Death and Its Mysteries.* New York: Macmillan

Lewin, Kurt. (1951). *Field Theory in Social Science: Selected Theoretical Papers.* New York: Harper & Brothers

Lieh-tzu. (1995). Excerpt from *Lieh-tzu: A Taoist Guide to Practical Living* by Eva Wong. Copyright © 1995 by Eva Wong. Used by permission of Shambhala Publications, Inc. All rights reserved.

Little Big Man. (1970). Cinema Center Films, Paramount Home Entertainment

Maimonides, Moses. (ND). "Rules of Repentance," in his *Mishneh Torah, Teshuvah* Chapter Two

Malamud, Bernard. (1979). *Dubin's Lives.* New York: Farrar Straus Giroux

Maslow, Abraham. (1943). "A Theory of Human Motivation," *Psychological Review*, 50 (4): pp. 370-96

Miller, James Grier. (1965). "Living Systems: Cross-Level Hypotheses," *Behavioral Science*, Volume 10, Issue 4: pp. 380-411

Miller, Henry. (1944). *Sunday After the War.* Norfolk, CT: New Directions

Miller, Henry. (1963). *Black Spring.* New York: Grove Press

Miller, Henry. (1978). In *Always Merry and Bright: The Life of Henry Miller*, by Jay Martin. Santa Barbara, CA: Capra Press

Nāgārjuna. (2005). *Letter to a Friend.* Ithaca, NY: Snow Lion Publications

Namdak, Lopon Tenzin. (1992). *Bonpo Dzogchen Teachings.* Tr. by Vajranatha, ed., Freehold: Bonpo Translation Project

Needleman, Jacob. (1980). *Lost Christianity: A Journey of Rediscovery to the Center of Christian Experience.* Garden City, NY: Doubleday & Co., Inc.

Newman, Louis. (1934). *The Hasidic Anthology: Tales and Teachings of the Hasidim.* New York: Bloch Pub. Co.

Nicoll, Maurice. (1984). *Psychological Commentaries on the Teachings of Gurdjieff & Ouspensky.* Boulder, CO: Shambhala Publications, Inc.

Nietzsche, Friedrich. (1956). *The Birth of Tragedy & the Genealogy of Morals.* New York: Doubleday

Ouspensky, P. D. (1949). *In Search of the Miraculous: Fragments of an Unknown Teaching.* New York: Harcourt Brace Jovanovich

Ouspensky, P. D. (1971). *The Fourth Way.* New York: Vintage Books

Merriam-Webster's Encyclopedia of Literature. (1995). Springfield, MA: Merriam-Webster

Pascal, Blaise. (1954). *Pascal's Pensées.* New York: Dutton

Paul the Apostle, *1 Corinthians 12:1-11*

Philo of Alexandria. (1995). *The Works of Philo: Complete and Unabridged.* Peabody, MA: Hendrickson

Polanyi, Michael. (1964). *Personal Knowledge: Towards a Post-Critical Philosophy.* New York: Harper & Row

Polanyi, Michael. (1976). *The Study of Man.* Chicago, IL: University of Chicago Press

Polen, Nehemia. (1994). *The Holy Fire: The Teachings of Rabbi Kalonymous Kalman Shapira, the Rebbe of the Warsaw Ghetto.* Northvale, NJ: J. Aronson

Ponticus, Evagrius. (1978). *The Praktikos: Chapters on Prayer.* Tr. by John Eudes Bamberger, Kalamazoo, MI: Cistercian Publications

Prokosch, Frederic. (1935). *The Asiatics.* New York: Harper & Bros.

Rawlings, Marjorie. (1999). 1938 letter to Maxwell Perkins in *Max and Marjorie*, Roger Tarr, ed. Gainesville, FL: University Press of Florida

Reich, Wilhelm. (1972). *Character Analysis.* New York: Farrar, Straus and Giroux

Reiken, Frederick. (2000). Excerpt from THE LOST LEGENDS OF NEW JERSEY by Frederick Reiken. Copyright © 2000 by Frederick Reiken. Used by permission of Houghton Mifflin Harcourt. All rights reserved.

Rilke, Rainer Maria. (1983). *The Notebooks of Malte Laurids Brigge.* Tr. by Stephen Mitchell, New York: Random House

Ruiz, Don Miguel. (2012). *The Four Agreements: A Practical Guide to Personal Freedom.* San Rafael, CA: Amber-Allen Publishing

Sanai, Hakim. (1964). Passage from *The Walled Garden of Truth* quoted in Idries Shah's *The Sufis.* Garden City, NY: Doubleday & Co., Inc.

Scholem, Gershom. (1963). *Zohar: The Book of Splendor.* New York: Schocken Books

Scholem, Gershom. (1961). *Major Trends in Jewish Mysticism.* New York: Schocken Books

Schwarz-Bart, André. (1960). *The Last of the Just.* Tr. by Stephen Becker, New York: Atheneum Publishers

Segal, William. (2003). *A Voice at the Borders of Silence.* Woodstock, NY: The Overlook Press

Segev, Tom. (2017). Quoted in Roger Cohen's "An Israel of Pride and Shame," *New York Times*, December 29

Shakespeare, William. (1975). *As You Like It.* London, England: Methuen

Shelley, Percy Bysshe. (1975). "Ozymandias", in *The Complete Poetical Works of Percy Bysshe Shelley.* Oxford, England: Clarendon Press

Sherif, Muzafer. (1958). "Superordinate Goals in the Reduction of Intergroup Conflict," *American Journal of Sociology*, Vol. 63, No. 4, Jan. 1958, pp. 349-356

Shikantaza. (2002). See, e.g., *The Art of Just Sitting*, John Daido Loori, ed. Boston, MA: Wisdom Publications

Shulman, David. (2014). Afterword to S. Yizhar's *Khirbet Khizeh.* New York: Farrar, Straus and Giroux

Sigal, Clancy. (1984). *Going Away.* New York: Carroll & Graf Publishers, Inc.

Singh, Kirpal. (1973). *The Crown of Life: A Study in Yoga.* Delhi, India: Ruhani Satsang

Snow, C. P. (1960). *The Two Cultures and the Scientific Revolution.* Cambridge, England: Cambridge University Press

Socrates. (1961). In Plato's *Crito.* Cambridge, England: Cambridge University Press

Speeth, Kathleen. (1976). *The Gurdjieff Work*. Berkeley, CA: And/Or Press

Sri Yukteswar Giri. (2014). Quoted in *Autobiography of a Yogi*, by Parama-hansa Yogananda. Los Angeles, CA: Self-Realization Fellowship

Suzuki, Shunryu. (2011). *Zen Mind, Beginner's Mind*. Boston, MA: Shambhala Publications

Takahashi, Shinkichi. (1986). From *Triumph of the Sparrow: Zen Poems of Shinkichi Takahashi* copyright © 1986 by Lucien Stryk. Used by permission of Grove/Atlantic, Inc. Any third party use of this material, outside of this publication, is prohibited.

Talmud, source and date uncertain.

Tilopa. (2006). "Six Words of Advice," in *Pointing Out the Great Way: The Stages of Meditation in the Mahamudra Tradition*, by Daniel Brown. Boston, MA: Wisdom Publications

Upanishads. (1937). "Mundaka-Upanishad, Book II," in *The Ten Principal Upanishads*. Tr. by Shree Purohit Swami and W.B. Yeats, London, England: Faber & Faber

Uris, Leon. (1958). *Exodus*. Garden City, NY: Doubleday

Vaihinger, Hans. (1935). *The Philosophy of 'As If': A System of the Theoretical, Practical and Religious Fictions of Mankind*. Tr. by C.K. Ogden, London, England: Routledge and K. Paul

Vaysse, Jean. (1988). *Toward Awakening: An Approach to the Teaching Left by Gurdjieff*. New York: Arkana

Vivekananda. (2010). *Karma-Yoga*, in *The Complete Works of Swami Vivekananda*, Vol. I. Kolkata, India: Advaita Ashrama

Weingreen, Jacob. (1963). *A Practical Grammar for Classical Hebrew*. Oxford, England: Clarendon Press

Whorf, Benjamin. (1963). *Language, Thought, and Reality*. Cambridge, MA: M.I.T. Press

Wong, Eva. (1997). *Taoism: An Essential Guide*. Boston, MA: Shambhala Publications, Inc.

Wong, Eva. (2004). *Seven Taoist Masters: A Folk Novel of China*. Tr. by Eva Wong, Boston: Shambhala Publications, Inc.

Wong, Eva. (1995). Excerpt from *Lieh-tzu: A Taoist Guide to Practical Living* by Eva Wong. Used by permission of Shambhala Publications, Inc. All rights reserved.

Wordsworth, William. (1965). *The Prelude*. London, England: Oxford University Press

World Authors, 1900-1950. (1996). Entry on Frederic Prokosch, Martin Seymour-Smith and Andrew C. Kimmens, eds. New York: H.W. Wilson.

Yang Chu. (1912). *Garden of Pleasure*. Tr. by Anton Forke, New York: Dutton

Yerushalmi, Yosef Hayim. (1996). *Zakhor: Jewish History and Jewish Memory*. Seattle, WA: University of Washington Press

Yizhar, S. (2014). *Khirbet Khizeh*, see David Shulman above. New York: Farrar, Straus and Giroux

Yogananda, Paramahansa. (2000). *The Divine Romance*. Los Angeles, CA: Self-Realization Fellowship

Yogananda, Paramahansa. (2007). *The Yoga of Jesus: Understanding the Hidden Teachings of the Gospels*. Los Angeles, CA: Self-Realization Fellowship

Yogananda, Paramahansa. (2014). *Autobiography of a Yogi*. See Sri Yukteswar Giri reference above. Los Angeles, CA: Self-Realization Fellowship

Yoon, Paul. (2009). Excerpt from *Once the Shore: Stories*, by Paul Yoon. Louisville, KY: Sarabande Books, Inc. Used by permission of Sarabande Books, Inc. All rights reserved.

About the Author

David Bachner is a retired college dean and professor, most recently at American University's School of International Service, where he was scholar-in-residence and director of the Intercultural Management Institute. His research, teaching, and program administration focused on international education and intercultural relations, fields in which he has authored three books and a number of articles. His poems have appeared in several journals, the anthology *Seeing Things*, and the chapbook *Capital Ironies*. David lives in Washington, DC.

www.ingramcontent.com/pod-product-compliance
Lightning Source LLC
Chambersburg PA
CBHW051521250626
47156CB00001B/182